WHAT THE CRITICS ARE SAYING
ABOUT *THE CLAN OF THE CAVE BEAR*

"Real ROOTS...the author of this tale of pre-history, Jean Auel, has performed a minor miracle in bringing to life the story of a lost girl adopted into a tribe of hunter-gatherers...it is thoughtful, sensitive and intelligently made."
—*San Francisco Chronicle Examiner*

"These are real people in every sense, mirroring both our virtues and flaws in heightened color."
—*Newsday*

"Imaginative, exciting."
—*The New York Times Book Review*

"A page-turner...Jean Auel has used a remarkable setting...The conflict between past and future, the clash between the dying race and the new race that wonders and invents things... Amazingly, Ms. Auel not only makes us see, feel and smell what life was like then, but actually creates dimensional characters we can understand and sympathize with...She has a thorough understanding of human nature, a gift for story-telling." —*Kansas City Star*

"Our nomination for the year's great escape."
—*Playboy*

"A double achievement, doubly remarkable. Jean M. Auel gives us a powerful impression of a world alien in its ways of being and, at the same time, conveys that shock of recognition: these people are ourselves, they are what we were."
—*Lloyd Alexander*

"A good old-fashioned tale with a spunky Stone-Age tomboy named Ayla." —*New West*

THE CLAN OF THE CAVE BEAR

Ayla—Alone in a world of strangers, she is tall, blonde, slender and smarter than the rest. She must use her wit to survive when she breaks the Clan's most forbidden taboo.

Brun—Chinless, bearded, bow-legged and barrel-chested, he is the leader of the Clan and must decide the fate of the foreign girl.

Iza—Chief Medicine woman of the Clan, Iza sees the strange ugly girl and realizes that she is human and must be saved from starvation.

Creb—The Clan's Mog-ur, or magician, he is the most revered holy man of all the clans. But his position doesn't stop him from learning what Ayla knows.

Broud—The son of Brun, he is brutal, proud and resentful of the attention paid to the strange girl. He vows to get revenge on her in the most physically satisfying way he can.

Durc—born of a violent rape, belonging to neither one nor the other tribe, he is the future of the human race.

the Clan of the Cave Bear

a novel by
Jean M. Auel

Earth's Children

Bantam Books
Toronto • New York • London • Sydney

*This low-priced Bantam Book
has been completely reset in a type face
designed for easy reading, and was printed
from new plates. It contains the complete
text of the original hard-cover edition.*
NOT ONE WORD HAS BEEN OMITTED.

THE CLAN OF THE CAVE BEAR

*A Bantam Book / published by arrangement with
Crown Publishers, Inc.*

PRINTING HISTORY

*Crown edition published September 1980
4 printings through October 1980*
A Literary Guild Featured Alternate Selection October 1980
A Main Selection of Preferred Choice Bookplan January 1981
Earth's Children is a trademark of Jean M. Auel.
Bantam edition / August 1981

ISBN 0-553-14800-1

Published simultaneously in the United States and Canada

PRINTED IN THE UNITED STATES OF AMERICA

for RAY
My worst critic
—and best friend

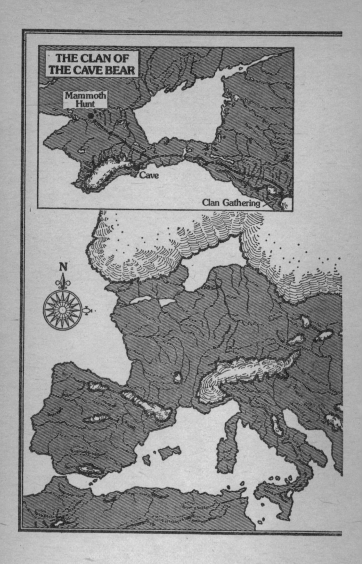

THE CLAN OF
THE CAVE BEAR

Mammoth
Hunt

Cave

Clan Gathering

N

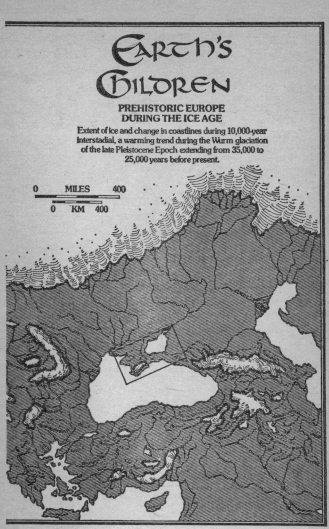

Earth's Children

PREHISTORIC EUROPE
DURING THE ICE AGE

Extent of ice and change in coastlines during 10,000-year
interstadial, a warming trend during the Würm glaciation
of the late Pleistocene Epoch extending from 35,000 to
25,000 years before present.

0   MILES   400

0   KM   400

Acknowledgments —————

No book published is ever solely the work of the author. Assistance comes from a variety of sources in as many different ways. But some contributions to my work came from people I have never met and probably never will. I am grateful, nonetheless, to the citizens of the city of Portland, and the country of Multnomah, Oregon, whose taxes support the Multnomah County Library, without whose reference materials this book would not have been written. I am also grateful to the archaeologists, anthropologists, and other specialists who wrote the books from which I gathered most of the information for the setting and background of this novel.

There were many who helped more directly. Among them, I want especially to thank:

Gin DeCamp, the first to hear my story idea, who was a friend when I needed one, who read a fat manuscript with enthusiasm and a meticulous eye for errors, and who sculpted a symbol for the series. John DeCamp, friend and fellow writer, who knew the agonies and the ecstasies, and had the uncanny knack of calling exactly when I *had* to talk to someone who did. Karen Auel, who encouraged her mother more than she ever knew because she laughed where she was supposed to laugh and cried where she was supposed to cry, though it was a first draft.

Cathy Humble, of whom I asked the greatest favor one can ask of a friend—honest criticism—because I valued her sense of words. She did the impossible; her critique was both acutely perceptive and gentle. Deanna Sterett, for getting caught up in the story, and who knew enough about hunting to point out some oversights. Lana Elmer, who listened with unflagging attention to hours of dissertation and still liked the story. Anna Bacus, who offered her unique insights and her sharp eye for spelling.

Not all my research was done in libraries. My husband and I made many field trips to learn firsthand various aspects of living close to nature. In the line of direct experience, special thanks are due to Frank Heyl, Arctic Survival Expert with the Oregon Museum of Science and Industry, who showed me how to make my bed in a snow cave and then expected me to lie in it! I survived that cold January night on the slopes of Mount Hood and learned much more about survival from Mr. Heyl, who has my vote as the one I'd most like to be around during the next Ice Age.

I am indebted to Andy Van't Hul for sharing with me his special knowledge of living in the natural environment. He showed me firemaking without matches, axes made of stone, cord twining and basket weaving, sinew and rawhide, and how to knap my own stone blade that cuts through leather as though it were butter.

Gratitude beyond measure goes to Jean Naggar, a literary agent so good she turned my wildest fantasy into reality and then bettered it. And to Carole Baron, my shrewd, sharp, and sensitive editor, who believed in the reality, then took my very best effort and made it better.

Finally, there are two individuals who had no idea they were helping me, yet whose assistance was invaluable. I have since met one of them, but the first time I heard writer and teacher Don James talk about the writing of fiction, he didn't know he was talking directly to me. He thought he was addressing a whole group. The words he said were exactly those I needed to hear. Don James didn't know it, but I might never have finished this book if it wasn't for him.

The other is a man I know only through his book, Ralph S. Solecki, author of *Shanidar* (Alfred A. Knopf, New York). The story of his excavation of Shanidar Cave and discovery of several Neanderthal skeletons profoundly moved me. He gave me a perspective of prehistoric cave man I might not otherwise have had and a better understanding of the meaning of humanity. But I must do more than thank Professor Solecki— I must apologize for one instance of literary license I took with his facts for the sake of my fiction. In real life, it was a Neanderthal who put flowers in the grave.

1

The naked child ran out of the hide-covered lean-to toward the rocky beach at the bend in the small river. It didn't occur to her to look back. Nothing in her experience ever gave her reason to doubt the shelter and those within it would be there when she returned.

She splashed into the river and felt rocks and sand shift under her feet as the shore fell off sharply. She dived into the cold water and came up sputtering, then reached out with sure strokes for the steep opposite bank. She had learned to swim before she learned to walk and, at five, was at ease in the water. Swimming was often the only way a river could be crossed.

The girl played for a while, swimming back and forth, then let the current float her downstream. Where the river widened and bubbled over rocks, she stood up and waded to shore, then walked back to the beach and began sorting pebbles. She had just put a stone on top of a pile of especially pretty ones when the earth began to tremble.

The child looked with surprise as the stone rolled down of its own accord, and stared in wonder at the small pyramid of pebbles shaking and leveling themselves. Only then did she become aware she was shaking too, but she was still more confused than apprehensive. She glanced around, trying to understand why her universe had altered in some inexplicable way. The earth was not supposed to move.

The small river, which moments before had flowed smoothly, was roiling with choppy waves that splashed over its banks as the rocking streambed moved at cross purposes to the current, dredging mud up from the bottom. Brush close by the upstream banks quivered, animated by unseen movement at the roots, and downstream, boulders bobbed in unaccustomed agitation. Beyond them, stately conifers of the forest into which the stream flowed lurched grotesquely. A giant pine near the bank, its roots exposed and their hold weakened by the spring runoff, leaned toward the opposite shore. With a crack, it gave way and crashed to the ground, bridging the turbid watercourse, and lay shaking on the unsteady earth.

The girl started at the sound of the falling tree. Her stomach churned and tightened into a knot as fear brushed the edge of her mind. She tried to stand but fell back, unbalanced by the sickening swaying. She tried again, managed to pull herself up, and stood unsteadily, afraid to take a step.

As she started toward the hide-covered shelter set back from the stream, she felt a low rumble rise to a terrifying roar. A sour stench of wetness and rot issued from a crack opening in the ground, like the reek of morning breath from a yawning earth. She stared uncomprehendingly at dirt and rocks and small trees falling into the widening gap as the cooled shell of the molten planet cracked in the convulsion.

The lean-to, perched on the far edge of the abyss, tilted, as half the solid ground beneath it pulled away. The slender ridgepole teetered undecidedly, then collapsed and disappeared into the deep hole, taking its hide cover and all it contained with it. The girl trembled in wide-eyed horror as the foul-breathed gaping maw swallowed everything that had given meaning and security to the five short years of her life.

"Mother! *Motherrr!*" she cried as comprehension overwhelmed her. She didn't know if the scream ringing in her ears was her own in the thunderous roar of rending rock. She clambered toward the deep crack, but the earth rose up and threw her down. She clawed at the ground, trying to find a secure hold on the heaving, shifting land.

Then the gap closed, the roar ceased, and the shaking earth stilled, but not the child. Lying face down on the soft damp soil churned loose by the paroxysm that convulsed the land, she shook with fear. She had reason to fear.

The child was alone in a wilderness of grassy steppes and scattered forests. Glaciers spanned the continent on the north, pushing their cold before them. Untold numbers of grazing animals, and the carnivores that preyed on them, roamed the vast prairies, but people were few. She had nowhere to go and she had no one who would come and look for her. She was alone.

The ground quivered again, settling itself, and the girl heard a rumbling from the depths, as though the earth were digesting a meal gulped in a single bite. She jumped up in panic, terrified that it would split again. She looked at the place where the lean-to had been. Raw earth and uprooted shrubs were all that remained. Bursting into tears, she ran back to the stream and crumpled into a sobbing heap near the muddy water.

But the damp banks of the stream offered no refuge from the restless planet. Another aftershock, this time more severe, shuddered the ground. She gasped with surprise at the splash of cold water on her naked body. Panic returned; she sprang to her feet. She had to get away from this terrifying place of shaking, devouring earth, but where could she go?

There was no place for seeds to sprout on the rocky beach and it was clear of brush, but the upstream banks were choked with shrubs just sending forth new leaves. Some deep instinct told her to stay near water, but the tangled brambles looked impenetrable. Through wet eyes that blurred her vision, she looked the other way at the forest of tall conifers.

Thin beams of sunlight filtered through the overlapping branches of dense evergreens crowding close to the stream. The shaded forest was nearly devoid of undergrowth, but many of the trees were no longer upright. A few had fallen to the ground; more leaned at awkward angles, supported by neighbors still firmly anchored. Beyond the jumble of trees, the boreal forest was dark and no more inviting than the brush upstream. She didn't know which way to go, and glanced first one way, then the other with indecision.

A tremble beneath her feet while she was looking downstream set her in motion. Casting one last yearning look at the vacant landscape, childishly hopeful that somehow the lean-to would still be there, she ran into the woods.

Urged on by occasional grumbling as the earth settled, the child followed the flowing water, stopping only to drink in her hurry to get far away. Conifers that had succumbed to the quaking earth lay prostrate on the ground and she skirted craters left by the circular tangle of shallow roots—moist soil and rocks still clinging to their exposed undersides.

She saw less evidence of disturbance toward evening, fewer uprooted trees and dislodged boulders, and the water cleared. She stopped when she could no longer see her way and sank down on the forest floor, exhausted. Exercise had kept her warm while she was moving, but she shivered in the chill night air, burrowed into the thick carpet of fallen needles and curled up in a tight little ball, throwing handfuls over herself for a cover.

But as tired as she was, sleep did not come easily to the frightened little girl. While busy making her way around obstacles near the stream, she was able to push her fear to the back of her mind. Now, it overwhelméd her. She lay perfectly still, eyes wide open, watching the darkness thicken and congeal around her. She was afraid to move, almost afraid to breathe.

She had never been alone at night before, and there had always been a fire to hold the black unknown at bay. Finally, she could hold back no longer. With a convulsive sob, she cried out her anguish. Her small body shook with sobs and hiccups, and with the release she eased into sleep. A small nocturnal animal nosed her in gentle curiosity, but she wasn't aware of it.

She woke up screaming!

The planet was still restless, and distant rumbling from deep within brought back her terror in a horrifying nightmare. She jerked up, wanted to run, but her eyes could see no more wide-open than they could behind closed lids. She couldn't remember where she was at first. Her heart pounded; why couldn't she see? Where were the loving arms that had always been there to comfort her when she woke in the night? Slowly the conscious realization of her plight seeped back into her mind and, shivering with fear and cold, she huddled down and burrowed into the needle-carpeted ground again. The first faint streaks of dawn found her asleep.

Daylight came slowly to the depths of the forest. When the child awoke it was well into the morning, but in the thick shade it was difficult to tell. She had wandered away from the stream as daylight faded the previous evening, and an edge of panic threatened as she looked around her at nothing but trees.

Thirst made her aware of the sound of gurgling water. She followed the sound and felt relieved when she saw the small river again. She was no less lost near the stream than she was in the forest, but it made her feel better to have something to follow, and she could quench her thirst as long as she stayed near it. She had been glad enough for the flowing water the day before, but it did little for her hunger.

She knew greens and roots could be eaten, but she didn't

know what was edible. The first leaf she tasted was bitter and stung her mouth. She spit it out and rinsed her mouth to remove the taste, but it made her hesitant to try another. She drank more water for the temporary feeling of fullness and started downstream again. The deep woods frightened her now and she stayed close to the stream where the sun was bright. When night fell, she dug a place out of the needled ground and curled up in it again.

Her second night alone was no better than her first. Cold terror lay in the pit of her stomach along with her hunger. She had never been so terrified, she had never been so hungry, she had never been so alone. Her sense of loss was so painful, she began to block out the memory of the earthquake and her life before it; and thoughts of the future brought her so close to panic, she fought to push those fears from her mind as well. She didn't want to think about what might happen to her, who would take care of her.

She lived only for the moment, getting past the next obstacle, crossing the next tributary, scrambling over the next log. Following the stream became an end in itself, not because it would take her anywhere, but because it was the only thing that gave her any direction, any purpose, any course of action. It was better than doing nothing.

After a time, the emptiness in her stomach became a numb ache that deadened her mind. She cried now and then as she plodded on, her tears painting white streaks down her grubby face. Her small naked body was caked with dirt; and hair that had once been nearly white, and as fine and soft as silk, was plastered to her head in a tangle of pine needles, twigs, and mud.

Traveling became more difficult when the evergreen forest changed to more open vegetation and the needle-covered forest floor gave way to obstructing brush, herbs, and grasses, the characteristic ground cover beneath small-leafed deciduous trees. When it rained, she huddled in the lee of a fallen log or large boulder or overhanging outcrop, or simply slogged through the mud letting the rain wash over her. At night, she piled dry brittle leaves left over from the previous season's growth into mounds and crawled into them to sleep.

The plentiful supply of drinking water kept dehydration from making its dangerous contribution to hypothermia, the lowering of body temperature that brought death from exposure, but she was getting weak. She was beyond hunger;

there was only a constant dull pain and an occasional feeling of light-headedness. She tried not to think about it, or about anything except the stream, just following the stream.

Sunlight penetrating her nest of leaves woke her. She got up from the snug pocket warmed by her body heat and went to the river for a morning drink, damp leaves still clinging to her. The blue sky and sunshine were welcome after the rain of the day before. Shortly after she started out, the bank on her side of the river gradually began to rise. By the time she decided to stop for another drink, a steep slope separated her from the water. She started down carefully but lost her footing and tumbled all the way to the bottom.

She lay in a scraped and bruised heap in the mud near the water, too tired, too weak, too miserable to move. Large tears welled up and streamed down her face, and plaintive wails rent the air. No one heard. Her cries became whimpers begging someone to come and help her. No one came. Her shoulders heaved with sobs as she cried her desperation. She didn't want to get up, she didn't want to go on, but what else could she do? Just stay there crying in the mud?

After she stopped crying, she lay near the water's edge. When she noticed a root beneath her jabbing uncomfortably in her side and the taste of dirt in her mouth, she sat up. Then, wearily, she stood up and went to the stream for a drink. She started walking again, doggedly pushing aside branches, crawling over moss-covered logs, splashing in and out of the edge of the river.

The stream, already high from earlier spring floods, had swelled to more than double from tributaries. The child heard a roar in the distance long before she saw the waterfall cascading down the high bank at the confluence of a large stream with the small river, a river about to double again. Beyond the waterfall, the swift currents of the combined watercourse bubbled over rocks as it flowed into the grassy plains of the steppes.

The thundering cataract rushed over the lip of the high bank in a broad sheet of white water. It splashed into a foaming pool worn out of the rock at the base, creating a constant spray of mist and whirlpools of countercurrents where the rivers met. At some time in the distant past, the river had carved deeper into the hard stone cliff behind the waterfall. The ledge over which the water poured jutted out beyond the wall behind the falling stream, forming a passageway between.

The girl edged in close and looked carefully into the damp tunnel, then started behind the moving curtain of water. She clutched at the wet rock to steady herself as the continuous falling, falling, falling of the flowing stream made her dizzy. The roar was deafening, rebounding from the stone wall in back of the tumultuous flow. She looked up fearfully, anxiously aware that the stream was above the dripping rocks over her head, and crept forward slowly.

She was nearly to the other side when the passageway ended, gradually narrowing until it was a steep wall again. The undercut in the cliff did not go all the way; she had to turn around and go back. When she reached her starting place, she looked at the torrent surging over the edge and shook her head. There was no other way.

The water was cold as she waded into the river, and the currents strong. She swam out to the middle and let the flow of the water carry her around the falls, then angled back to the bank of the widened river beyond. The swimming tired her, but she was cleaner than she had been for some time, except for her matted and tangled hair. She started out again feeling refreshed, but not for long.

The day was unseasonably warm for late spring, and when the trees and brush first gave way to the open prairie, the hot sun felt good. But as the fiery ball rose higher, its burning rays took their toll of the small girl's meager reserves. By afternoon, she was staggering along a narrow strip of sand between the river and a steep cliff. The sparkling water reflected the bright sun up at her, while the almost-white sandstone bounced light and heat down, adding to the intense glare.

Across the river and ahead, small herbaceous flowers of white, yellow, and purple, blending into the half-grown grass bright green with new life, extended to the horizon. But the child had no eyes for the fleeting spring beauty of the steppes. Weakness and hunger were making her delirious. She started hallucinating.

"I said I'd be careful, mother. I only swam a little ways, but where did you go?" she muttered. "Mother, when are we going to eat? I'm so hungry, and it's hot. Why didn't you come when I called you? I called and called, but you never came. Where have you been? Mother? Mother! Don't go away again! Stay here! Mother, wait for me! Don't leave me!"

She ran in the direction of the mirage as the vision faded, following the base of the cliff, but the cliff was pulling back from the water's edge, veering away from the river. She was leaving her source of water. Running blindly, she stubbed her toe on a rock and fell hard. It jarred her back to reality—almost. She sat rubbing her toe, trying to collect her thoughts.

The jagged sandstone wall was pockmarked with dark holes of caves and streaked with narrow cracks and crevices. Expansion and contraction from extremes of searing heat and subzero cold had crumbled the soft rock. The child looked into a small hole near the ground in the wall beside her, but the tiny cave made little impression.

Far more impressive was the herd of aurochs grazing peacefully on the lush new grass between the cliff and the river. In her blind rush to follow a mirage, she hadn't noticed the huge reddish brown wild cattle, six feet high at the withers with immense curving horns. When she did, sudden fear cleared the last cobwebs from her brain. She backed closer to the rock wall, keeping her eye on a burly bull that had stopped grazing to watch her, then she turned and started running.

She glanced back over her shoulder and caught her breath at a swift blur of movement, and stopped in her tracks. An enormous lioness, twice as large as any feline who would populate savannas far to the south in a much later age, had been stalking the herd. The girl stifled a scream as the monstrous cat vaulted for a wild cow.

In a flurry of snarling fangs and savage claws, the giant lioness wrestled the massive aurochs to the ground. With a crunch of powerful jaws, the terrified bawl of the bovine was cut short as the huge carnivore tore out its throat. Spurting blood stained the muzzle of the four-legged hunter and sprayed her tawny fur with crimson. The aurochs's legs jerked spasmodically even as the lioness ripped open its stomach and tore out a chunk of warm, red meat.

Stark terror charged through the girl. She fled in wild panic, carefully watched by another of the great cats. The child had stumbled into the territory of cave lions. Normally the large felines would have disdained so small a creature as a five-year-old human as prey, preferring a robust aurochs, oversize bison, or giant deer to satisfy the needs of a pride of hungry cave lions. But the fleeing child was approaching much too near to the cave that housed a pair of mewling newborn cubs.

Left to guard the young while the lioness hunted, the shaggy-maned lion roared in warning. The girl jerked her head up and gasped at the gigantic cat crouched on a ledge, ready to spring. She screamed, slid to a stop, falling and scraping her leg in the loose gravel near the wall, and scrambled to turn around. Spurred on by even greater fear, she ran back the way she had come.

The cave lion leaped with languid ease, confident of his ability to catch the small interloper who dared to broach the sanctity of the cave nursery. He was in no hurry—she moved slowly compared with his fluid speed—and he was in the mood for a game of cat and mouse.

In her panic, it was only instinct that led her to the small hole near the ground in the face of the cliff. Her side aching, and gasping for breath, she squeezed through an opening barely big enough for her. It was a tiny, shallow cave, not much more than a crack. She twisted around in the cramped space until she was kneeling with her back to the wall, trying to melt into the solid rock behind her.

The cave lion roared his frustration when he reached the hole and found his chase thwarted. The child trembled at the sound and stared in hypnotized horror as the cat snaked his paw, sharp curved claws outstretched, into the small hole. Unable to get away, she watched the claw come at her and shrieked in pain as it sunk into her left thigh, raking it with four deep parallel gashes.

The girl squirmed to get out of his reach and found a small depression in the dark wall to her left. She pulled her legs in, scrunched up as tight as she could, and held her breath. The claw slowly entered the small opening again, nearly blocking the scant light that penetrated the niche, but this time found nothing. The cave lion roared and roared as he paced back and forth in front of the hole.

The child remained in the small cramped cave through the day, that night, and most of the following day. The leg swelled and the festering wound was a constant pain, and the small space inside the rough-walled cave had little room to turn or stretch out. She was delirious most of the time from hunger and pain and dreamed terrifying nightmares of earthquakes, and sharp claws, and lonely aching fear. But it wasn't her wound or her hunger or even her painful sunburn that finally drove her from her refuge. It was thirst.

She looked fearfully out of the small opening. Sparse stands of wind-stunted willow and pine near the river cast long shadows of early evening. The child stared at the grass-covered stretch of land and the sparkling water beyond for a long time before gathering up enough courage to move beyond the entrance. She licked cracked lips with a parched tongue as she scanned the terrain. Only the windswept grass moved. The lion pride was gone. The lioness, anxious for her young and uneasy about the unfamiliar scent of the strange creature so near their cave, decided to find a new nursery.

The child crept out of the hole and stood up. Her head throbbed and spots danced dizzily before her eyes. Waves of pain engulfed her with every step and her wounds began to ooze a sickly yellow green down her swollen leg.

She wasn't sure if she could reach the water, but her thirst was overpowering. She fell to her knees and crawled the last few feet, then stretched out flat on her stomach and gulped greedy mouthfuls of cold water. When her thirst was finally slaked, she tried to stand again, but she had reached the limit of her endurance. Spots swam before her eyes, her head whirled, and everything went dark as she slumped to the ground.

A carrion bird circling lazily overhead spied the unmoving form and swooped lower for a closer look.

2

The band of travelers crossed the river just beyond the waterfall where it widened and foamed around rocks jutting up through the shallow water. They were twenty in number, young and old. The clan had totaled twenty-six before the earthquake that destroyed their cave. Two men led the way, far in front of a knot of women and children flanked by a couple of older men. Younger men trailed behind.

They followed the broad stream as it began its braided,

meandering course across the flat steppes, and watched the carrion birds circling. Flying scavengers usually meant that whatever had attracted their attention was still alive. The men in the lead hurried to investigate. A wounded animal was easy prey for hunters, providing no four-legged predators had similar ideas.

A woman, midway along in her first pregnancy, walked in front of the rest of the women. She saw the two men in the lead glance at the ground and move on. It must be a meat eater, she thought. The clan seldom ate carnivorous animals.

She was just over four and a half feet tall, large boned, stocky, and bow-legged, but walked upright on strong muscular legs and flat bare feet. Her arms, long in proportion to her body, were bowed like her legs. She had a large beaky nose, a prognathous jaw jutting out like a muzzle, and no chin. Her low forehead sloped back into a long, large head, resting on a short, thick neck. At the back of her head was a boney knob, an occipital bun, that emphasized its length.

A soft down of short brown hair, tending to curl, covered her legs and shoulders and ran along the upper spine of her back. It thickened into a head of heavy, long, rather bushy hair. She was already losing her winter pallor to a summer tan. Big, round, intelligent, dark brown eyes were deep set below overhanging brow ridges, and they were filled with curiosity as she quickened her pace to see what the men had passed by.

The woman was old for a first pregnancy, nearly twenty, and the clan thought she was barren until the life stirring within her started to show. The load she carried had not been lightened because she was pregnant, however. She had a large basket strapped to her back, with bundles tied behind, hanging below, and piled on top of it. Several drawstring bags dangled from a thong, which was wrapped around the pliable hide she wore in such a way as to produce folds and pouches for carrying things. One bag was particularly distinctive. It was made from an otter hide, obviously so because it had been cured with its waterproof fur, feet, tail, and head left intact.

Rather than a slit in the skin of the animal's belly, only the throat had been cut to provide an opening to remove the innards, flesh, and bones, leaving a pouchlike bag. The head, attached by a strip of skin at the back, was the cover flap, and a red-dyed cord of sinew was threaded through holes punched around the neck opening, drawn tight, and tied to the thong at her waist.

When the woman first saw the creature the men had left behind, she was puzzled by what appeared to be an animal without fur. But when she drew closer, she gasped and stepped back a pace, clutching the small leather pouch around her neck in an unconscious gesture to ward off unknown spirits. She fingered the small objects inside her amulet through the leather, invoking protection, and leaned forward to look closer, hesitant to take a step, but not quite able to believe she saw what she thought she was seeing.

Her eyes had not deceived her. It was not an animal that had drawn the voracious birds. It was a child, a gaunt, strange-looking child!

The woman looked around, wondering what other fearful enigmas might be nearby, and started to skirt the unconscious child, but she heard a moan. The woman stopped and, forgetting her fears, knelt beside the child and shook her gently. The medicine woman reached to untie the cord that held the otter-skin bag closed as soon as she saw the festering claw marks and swollen leg when the girl rolled over.

The man in the lead glanced back and saw the woman kneeling beside the child. He walked back to them.

"Iza! Come!" he commanded. "Cave lion tracks and scat ahead."

"It's a child, Brun. Hurt but not dead," she replied.

Brun looked at the thin young girl with the high forehead, small nose, and strangely flat face. "Not Clan," the leader gestured abruptly and turned to walk away.

"Brun, she's a child. She's hurt. She'll die if we leave her here." Iza's eyes pleaded as she made the hand signals.

The leader of the small clan stared down at the imploring woman. He was much bigger than she, over five feet tall, heavily muscled and powerful, with a deep barrel chest and thick bowed legs. The cast of his features was similar, though more pronounced—heavier supraorbital ridges, larger nose. His legs, stomach, chest, and upper back were covered with a coarse brown hair that was not enough to be called a pelt, but not far from it. A bushy beard hid his chinless jutting jaw. His wrap was similar, too, but not as full, cut shorter, and tied differently, with fewer folds and pouches for holding things.

He carried no burdens, only his outer fur wrap, suspended on his back by a wide band of leather wrapped around his sloping forehead, and his weapons. On his right thigh was a scar, blackened like a tattoo, shaped roughly like a **U** with the tops flaring outward, the mark of his totem, the bison. He needed no mark or ornament to identify his leadership. His bearing and the deference of the others made his position clear.

He shifted his club, the long foreleg of a horse, from his shoulder to the ground, supporting the handle with his thigh, and Iza knew he was giving her plea serious consideration. She waited quietly, hiding her agitation, to give him time to think. He set his heavy wooden spear down and leaned the shaft against his shoulder with the sharpened, fire-hardened point up, and adjusted the bola he wore around his neck along with his amulet so the three stone balls were more evenly balanced. Then he pulled a strip of pliable deerskin, tapered at the ends with a bulge in the middle to hold stones for slinging, out of his waist thong, and pulled the soft leather through his hand, thinking.

Brun didn't like making quick decisions about anything unusual that might affect his clan, especially now when they were homeless, and he resisted the impulse to refuse at once. I should have known Iza would want to help her, he thought; she's even used her healing magic on animals sometimes, especially young ones. She'll be upset if I don't let her help this child. Clan or Others, it makes no difference, all she can see is a child who is hurt. Well, maybe that's what makes her a good medicine woman.

But medicine woman or not, she is just a woman. What difference will it make if she's upset? Iza knows better than to show it, and we have enough problems without a wounded stranger. But her totem will know, all the spirits will. Would it make them more angry if she's upset? If we find a cave . . . no, when we find a new cave, Iza will have to make her drink for the cave ceremony. What if she's so upset she makes a mistake? Angry spirits could make it go wrong, and they're angry enough already. Nothing must go wrong with the ceremony for the new cave.

Let her take the child, he thought. She'll soon get tired of carrying the extra load, and the girl is so far gone, not even my sibling's magic may be strong enough to save her. Brun tucked his sling back in his waist thong, picked up his weapons, and shrugged noncommittally. It was up to her; Iza could take the girl with them or not as she pleased. He turned and strode off.

Iza reached into her basket and pulled out a leather cloak. She wrapped it around the girl, hoisted her up, and secured the unconscious child to her hip with the aid of the supple hide, surprised at how little she weighed for her height. The girl moaned as she was lifted and Iza patted her reassuringly, then fell into place behind the two men.

The other women had stopped, holding back from the encounter between Iza and Brun. When they saw the medicine woman pick something up and take it with her, their hands flew in rapid motions punctuated by a few guttural sounds, discussing it with excited curiosity. Except for the otter-skin pouch, they were dressed the same as Iza, and as heavily burdened. Among them they carried all the clan's worldly possessions, those that had been salvaged from the rubble after the quake.

Two of the seven women carried babies in a fold of their wraps next to their skin, convenient for nursing. While they were waiting, one felt a drop of warm wetness, whipped her naked infant out of the fold, and held it in front of her until it was through wetting. When they weren't traveling, babies were often wrapped in soft swaddling skins. To absorb moisture and soft milky stools, any of several materials were packed around them: fleece from wild sheep gathered from thorny shrubs when the mouflon were shedding, down from birds' breasts, or fuzz from fibrous plants. But while they traveled, it was easier and simpler to carry babies naked and, without missing a step, let them mess on the ground.

When they started out again, a third woman picked up a young boy, supporting him on her hip with a leather carrying cloak. After a few moments, he squirmed to get down and run by himself. She let him go, knowing he would be back when he got tired again. An older girl, not yet a woman but carrying a woman's load, walked behind the woman who followed Iza, glancing back now and then at a boy, very nearly a man, trailing the women. He tried to allow enough distance between himself and them so it would seem he was one of the three hunters bringing up the rear and not one of the children. He wished he had game to carry, too, and even envied the old man, one of the two flanking the women, who carried a large hare over his shoulder, felled by a stone from his sling.

The hunters were not the only source of food for the clan. The women often contributed the greater share, and their sources were more reliable. Despite their burdens, they foraged as they traveled, and so efficiently it hardly slowed them down. A patch of day lilies was quickly stripped of buds and flowers, and tender new roots exposed with a few strokes of the digging sticks. Cattail roots, pulled loose from beneath the surface of marshy backwaters, were even easier to gather.

If they hadn't been on the move, the women would have made a point of remembering the location of the tall stalky plants, to return later in the season to pick the tender tails at the top for a vegetable. Later still, yellow pollen mixed with starch pounded from the fibers of old roots would make doughy unleavened biscuits. When the tops dried, fuzz would be collected; and several of the baskets were made from the tough leaves and stalks. Now they gathered only what they found, but little was overlooked.

New shoots and tender young leaves of clover, alfalfa, dandelion; thistles stripped of prickles before they were cut down; a few early berries and fruits. The pointed digging sticks were in constant use; nothing was safe from them in the women's deft hands. They were used as a lever to overturn logs for newts and delectable fat grubs; freshwater molluscs were fished out of streams and pushed closer to shore for easy reach; and a variety of bulbs, tubers, and roots were dug out of the ground.

It all found its way to the convenient folds of the women's wraps or an empty corner of their baskets. Large green leaves were wrappers, some of them, such as burdock, cooked as greens. Dry wood, twigs, and grass, and dung from grazing animals, were collected too. Though the selection would be more varied later in the summer, food was plentiful —if one knew where to look.

Iza looked up when an old man, past thirty, hobbled up to her after they were on their way again. He carried neither burden nor weapon, only a long staff to help him walk. His right leg was crippled and smaller than the left, yet he managed to move with surprising agility.

His right shoulder and upper arm were atrophied and the shriveled arm had been amputated below the elbow. The powerful shoulder and arm and muscular leg of his fully developed left side made him appear lopsided. His huge cranium was even larger than those of the rest of the clan, and the difficulty of his birth had caused the defect that crippled him for life.

He was also a sibling of Iza and Brun, first-born, and would have been leader but for his affliction. He wore a leather wrap cut in the masculine style and carried his warm outer fur, which was also used as a sleeping fur, on his back as the other men did. But he had several pouches hanging from his waist thong and a cloak similar to the kind the women used which held a large bulging object to his back.

The left side of his face was hideously scarred and his left eye was missing, but his good right eye sparkled with intelligence, and something more. For all his hobbling, he moved with a grace that came from great wisdom and a sureness of his place within the clan. He was Mog-ur, the most powerful magician, most awesome and revered holy man of all the clans. He was convinced that his wasted body was given to him so that he could take his place as intermediary with the spirit world rather than at the head of his clan. In many ways he had more power than any leader, and he knew it. Only close relatives remembered his birth name and called him by it.

"Creb," Iza said in greeting and acknowledged his appearance with a motion that meant she was pleased he had joined her.

"Iza?" he questioned with a gesture toward the child she carried. The woman opened her cloak and Creb looked closely at the small flushed face. His eye traveled down to the swollen leg and suppurating wound, then back to the medicine woman and read meaning from her eyes. The girl moaned, and Creb's expression softened. He nodded his approval.

"Good," he said. The word was gruff, guttural. Then he made a sign that meant, "Enough have died."

Creb stayed beside Iza. He didn't have to conform to the understood rules that defined each person's position and status; he could walk with anyone, including the leader if he chose. Mog-ur was above and aside from the strict hierarchy of the clan.

Brun led them well beyond the spoor of cave lions before he stopped and studied the landscape. Across the river, as far as he could see, the prairie stretched out in low rolling hills into a flat green expanse in the distance. His view was unobstructed. The few stunted trees, distorted by the constant wind into caricatures of arrested motion, merely put the open country in perspective and emphasized the emptiness.

Near the horizon, a cloud of dust betrayed the presence of a large herd of hard-hoofed animals, and Brun sorely wished he could signal his hunters and take out after them. Behind him, only the tops of tall conifers could be seen beyond the smaller deciduous trees of the forest already dwarfed by the vastness of the steppes.

On his side of the river, the prairie ended abruptly, cut off by the cliff now some distance away and angling ever farther from the stream ahead. The rock face of the steep wall merged into the foothills of majestic glacier-topped mountains, looming near; their icy peaks vibrant with vivid pinks, magentas, violets, and purples reflecting the setting sun, gigantic sparkling jewels crowning the sovereign summits. Even the practical leader was moved by the pageant.

He turned away from the river and led his clan toward the cliff, which held out the possibility of caves. They needed a shelter; but almost more important, their protective totem spirits needed a home, if they hadn't already deserted the clan. They were angry, the earthquake proved that, angry enough to cause the death of six of the clan and destroy their home. If a permanent place for the totemic spirits was not found, they would leave the clan to the mercy of evil ones that caused illness and chased game away. No one knew why the spirits were angry, not even Mog-ur, though he conducted nightly rituals to appease their wrath and help relieve the clan's anxiety. They were all worried, but none more than Brun.

The clan was his responsibility and he felt the strain. Spirits, those unseen forces with unfathomable desires, baffled him. He was more comfortable in the physical world of hunting and leading his clan. None of the caves he had examined so far were suitable—they all lacked some condition that was essential—and he was getting desperate. Precious warm days when they should have been storing food for the next winter were being wasted in the search for a new home. Soon he might be forced to shelter his clan in a less than adequate cave and continue the search next year. That would be unsettling, physically and emotionally, and Brun fervently hoped it would not be necessary.

They walked along the base of the cliff as the shadows deepened. When they reached a narrow waterfall bouncing down the rock wall, its spray a shimmering rainbow in the long rays of the sun, Brun called a halt. Wearily, the women set down their burdens and fanned out along the pool at the bottom and its narrow outlet to find wood.

Iza spread out her fur wrap and put the child on it, then hurried to help the other women. She was worried about the girl. Her breathing was shallow and she hadn't roused; even her moans came less frequently. Iza had been thinking about how to help the child, considering the dried herbs she carried in her otter-skin pouch; and while she gathered wood, she looked over the plants growing in the vicinity. To her, whether it was familiar or not, everything had some value, medicinal or nutritional, but there was little she couldn't identify.

When she saw long stalks of iris ready to bloom on the marshy bank of the little creek, it settled one question and she dug up its roots. The three-lobed hop leaves twining around one of the trees gave her another idea, but she decided to use the powdered dry hops she had with her, since the conelike fruit would not mature until later. She peeled smooth grayish bark from an alder shrub growing near the pool and sniffed it. It was strongly aromatic and she nodded to herself as she put it in a fold of her wrap. Before she hurried back, she picked several handfuls of young clover leaves.

When the wood was gathered and the fireplace set, Grod, the man who walked in front with Brun, uncovered a glowing coal wrapped in moss and stuffed into the hollow end of an aurochs horn. They could make fire, but while traveling through unknown territory, it was easier to take a coal from one campfire and keep it alive to start the next one, than to try to start a new fire each evening with possibly inadequate materials.

Grod had nurtured the burning ember anxiously while they traveled. The hot coal from the fire of the night before had been started by a hot coal from the previous evening's fire and could be traced back to the fire they had rekindled on the remains of the fireplace at the mouth of the old cave. For the rites to make a new cave acceptable for residence, they needed to start the fire from a coal they could trace back to their old home.

Maintenance of the fire could only be entrusted to a male of high status. If the coal died out, it would be a sure sign that their protective spirits had deserted them, and Grod would be demoted from second-in-command to the lowest-ranked male position in the clan; a humiliation he did not care to suffer. His was a great honor and a heavy responsibility.

While Grod carefully placed the bit of burning charcoal on a bed of dry tinder and blew it into flame, the women turned to other tasks. With techniques passed down for generations, they quickly skinned the game. A few moments after the fire was blazing well, meat skewered with sharp green sticks set over forked branches was roasting. The high heat seared it to hold in juices, and when the fire died down to coals, little was lost to the licking flames.

With the same sharp stone knives they used to skin and cut the meat, the women scraped and sliced roots and tubers. Tightly woven waterproof baskets and wooden bowls were filled with water, and then hot stones were added. When cooled, the stones were put back in the fire and new ones were put in the water until it boiled and the vegetables cooked. Fat grubs were toasted crisp and small lizards roasted whole until their tough skins blackened and cracked, exposing tasty bits of well-cooked flesh.

Iza made her own preparations while helping with the meal. In a wooden bowl that she had chipped out of a section of log many years before, she started water boiling. She washed the iris roots, chewed them to a pulp, and spit them into the boiling water. In another bowl—the cup-shaped piece from the lower jaw of a large deer—she crushed clover leaves, measured out a quantity of powdered hops into her hand, tore the alder bark into shreds, and poured boiling water over it. Then she ground hard dry meat from their preserved emergency ration into a coarse meal between two stones and mixed the concentrated protein with water from cooked vegetables in a third bowl.

The woman who had walked behind Iza cast an occasional glance her way, hoping Iza would volunteer some comment. All the women, and the men, though they tried not to show it, were bursting with curiosity. They had seen Iza pick the girl up, and everyone had found a reason to walk near Iza's fur after they made camp. Speculation ran high about how the child happened to be there, where the rest of her people were, and mostly, why Brun had allowed Iza to take a girl along who was obviously born to the Others.

Ebra knew better than anyone the strain Brun was feeling. She was the one who tried to massage the tension out of his neck and shoulders, and she was the one who bore the brunt of his nervous temper, so rare in the man who was her mate. Brun was known for his stoic self-control, and she knew he regretted his outbursts, though he would not compound his transgression by admitting it. But even Ebra wondered why he had allowed the child to come with them, especially when any deviation from normal behavior might increase the anger of the spirits.

As curious as she was, Ebra asked no questions of Iza, and none of the other women had enough status to consider it. No one disturbed a medicine woman when she was obviously working her magic, and Iza was in no mood for idle gossip. Her concentration was directed at the child who needed her help. Creb was interested in the girl, too, but Iza welcomed his presence.

She watched with silent gratitude while the magician shuffled over to the unconscious child, looked at her thoughtfully for a while, then leaned his staff against a large boulder and made flowing one-handed motions over her, a request to benevolent spirits to assist in her recovery. Illness and accidents were mysterious manifestations of the war of the spirits, fought on the battleground of the body. Iza's magic came from protective spirits who acted through her, but no cure was complete without the holy man. A medicine woman was only an agent of the spirits; a magician interceded directly with them.

Iza didn't know why she felt such concern for a child so different from the clan, but she wanted her to live. When Mog-ur was through, Iza lifted the girl in her arms and carried her to the small pool at the foot of the waterfall. She submerged all but her head and washed away dirt and caked mud from the thin little body. The cool water revived the youngster, but she was delirious. She tossed and writhed, calling out and mumbling sounds like none the woman had ever heard before. Iza held the girl close as she walked back with her, making soothing murmurs that sounded like soft growls.

Gently, but with experienced thoroughness, Iza washed the wounds with an absorbent piece of rabbit skin dipped in the hot liquid in which the iris root had boiled. Then she scooped out the root pulp, put it directly on the wounds, covered it with the rabbit skin, and wrapped the child's leg in strips of soft deerskin to hold the poultice in place. She removed the mashed clover, the shredded alder bark, and stones from the bone bowl with a forked twig, and set it to cool beside the bowl of hot broth.

Creb gestured inquiringly toward the bowls. It was not a direct query—not even Mog-ur would question a medicine woman directly about her magic—it only indicated interest. Iza didn't mind her sibling's interest; he more than anyone appreciated her knowledge. He used some of the same herbs she did for different purposes. Except for Clan Gatherings where there were other medicine women, talking to Creb was the closest she could come to a discussion with a professional colleague.

"This destroys the evil spirits that make infection," Iza motioned, pointing to the antiseptic iris-root solution. "A poultice of the root draws out poisons and helps the wound heal." She picked up the bone bowl and dipped in a finger to check the temperature. "Clover makes the heart strong to fight evil spirits—stimulates it." Iza used a few spoken words when she talked, but primarily for emphasis. The people of the Clan could not articulate well enough for a complete verbal language, they communicated more with gestures and motions, but their sign language was fully comprehensive and rich with nuance.

"Clover is food. We had it last night," Creb signed.

"Yes," Iza nodded, "and we will tonight. The magic is in the way it's prepared. A large bunch boiled in little water extracts what is needed, the leaves are thrown out." Creb nodded with understanding and she went on. "Alder bark cleans the blood, purifies it, drives out the spirits that poison it."

"You used something from your medicine bag, too."

"Powdered hops, the mature cones with the fine hairs, to calm her and make her sleep restfully. While the spirits battle, she needs rest."

Creb nodded again; he was familiar with the soporific qualities of hops that induced a mild state of euphoria in a different use. Though he was always interested in Iza's treatments, he seldom volunteered information about the ways he used herbal magic. Such esoteric knowledge was for mog-urs and their acolytes, not women, not even medicine women. Iza knew more about the properties of plants than he did, and he was afraid she would deduce too much. It would be most unpropitious if she guessed much about his magic.

"And the other bowl?" he asked.

"That's just broth. The poor thing is half starved. What do you suppose happened to her? Where did she come from? Where are her people? She must have been wandering alone for days."

"Only the spirits know," Mog-ur replied. "Are you sure your healing magic will work on her? She's not Clan."

"It should; the Others are human, too. You remember mother telling about the man with the broken arm, the one her mother helped? Clan magic worked on him, although mother did say it took him longer to wake up from the sleeping medicine than expected."

"It's a shame you never knew her, our mother's mother. She was such a good medicine woman, people came from other clans to see her. It's too bad she left to walk the spirit world so soon after you were born, Iza. She told me about that man herself, so did Mog-ur-before-me. He stayed for a while after he recovered and hunted with the clan. He must have been a good hunter, he was allowed to join a hunting ceremony. It's true, they are human, but different, too." Mog-ur stopped. Iza was too astute, he couldn't afford to say too much or she might begin to draw some conclusions about the men's secret rituals.

Iza checked her bowls again, then cradling the child's head on her lap, she fed her the contents of the bone bowl in small sips. It was easier to feed her the broth. The girl mumbled incoherently and tried to fight off the bitter-tasting medicine, but even in her delirium her starving body craved food. Iza held her until she lapsed into a quiet sleep, then checked her heartbeat and breathing. She had done what she could. If the girl wasn't too far gone, she had a chance. It was up to the spirits now, and the inner strength of the child.

Iza saw Brun walking toward her, eyeing her with displeasure. She got up quickly and ran to help serve the meal. He had dismissed the strange child from his mind after his initial consideration, but now he was having second thoughts. Though it was customary to avert the eyes to avoid seeing other people in conversation, he couldn't help noticing what his clan was saying. Their wondering at his allowing the girl to come with them made him begin to wonder, too. He began to fear the spirits' anger might be aroused more by the stranger in their midst. He veered to intercept the medicine woman, but Creb saw him and headed him off.

"What's wrong, Brun? You look worried."

"Iza must leave that child here, Mog-ur. She is not Clan; the spirits won't like it if she is with us while we're looking for a new cave. I never should have let Iza take her."

"No, Brun," Mog-ur countered. "Protective spirits are not angered by kindness. You know Iza, she can't bear to see anything hurting without trying to help. Don't you think the spirits know her too? If they didn't want Iza to help her, the child would not have been put in her path. There must be a reason for it. The girl may die anyway, Brun, but if Ursus wants to call her to the spirit world, let the decision be his. Don't interfere now. She will surely die if she is left behind."

Brun didn't like it—something about the girl bothered him—but deferring to Mog-ur's greater knowledge of the spirit world, he acquiesced.

Creb sat in contemplative silence after the meal, waiting for everyone to finish eating so he could begin the nightly ceremony, while Iza arranged his sleeping place and made preparations for the morning. Mog-ur had put a ban on men and women sleeping together until a new cave was found so the men could concentrate their energies on the rituals and so everyone would feel they were making an effort that would bring them closer to a new home.

It didn't matter to Iza; her mate had been one of those killed in the cave-in. She had mourned him with proper grief at his burial—it would have been unlucky to do otherwise—but she was not unhappy he was gone. It was no secret he had been cruel and demanding. There had never been any warmth between them. She didn't know what Brun would decide to do with her now that she was alone. Someone would have to provide for her and the child she carried; she only hoped she could still cook for Creb.

He had shared their fire from the beginning. Iza sensed he hadn't liked her mate any more than she had, though he never interfered with the internal problems of her relationship. She had always felt it was an honor to cook for Mog-ur, but more, she had developed a bond of affection for her sibling like many women grew to feel for their mates.

Iza felt sorry for Creb sometimes; he could have had a mate of his own had he wanted one. But she knew for all his great magic and exalted position, no woman ever looked at his deformed body and scarred face without revulsion, and she was sure he knew it. He never took a mate, maintained a reserve. It added to his stature. Everyone, men included, with the possible exception of Brun, feared Mog-ur or regarded him with awe. Everyone but Iza, who had known his gentleness and sensitivity since her birth. It was a side of his nature he seldom showed openly.

And it was that side of his nature that was occupying the mind of the great Mog-ur just then. Rather than meditating on that evening's ceremony, he was thinking about the little girl. He had often been curious about her kind, but people of the Clan avoided the Others as much as possible, and he had never seen one of their young before. He suspected the earthquake had something to do with her being alone, though it surprised him that any of her people were so close. They usually stayed much farther north.

He noticed a few men start to leave the campsite and hauled himself up with his staff so he could supervise the preparations. The ritual was a masculine prerogative and duty. Only rarely were women allowed to participate in the religious life of the clan, and they were banned from this ceremony entirely. No disaster could be so great as that of a woman seeing the men's secret rites. It would not just bring bad luck, it would drive the protective spirits away. The whole clan would die.

But there was little danger of that. It would never occur to a woman to venture anywhere near such an important ritual. They looked forward to it as a time to relax, relieved of the constant demands of the men and the need to behave with proper decorum and respect. It was hard on the women having the men around all the time, especially when the men were so nervous and took it out on their mates. Usually they would be gone for periods of time hunting. The women were just as anxious to find a new home, but there was little they could do. Brun chose the direction they traveled and no advice was solicited from them, nor could they have given it.

The women relied on their men to lead, to assume responsibility, to make important decisions. The Clan had changed so little in nearly a hundred thousand years, they were now incapable of change, and ways that had once been adaptations for convenience had become genetically set. Both men and women accepted their roles without struggle; they were inflexibly unable to assume any other.

They would no more try to change their relationship than they would try to grow an extra arm or change the shape of their brain.

After the men left, the women gathered around Ebra and hoped Iza would join them so they could satisfy their curiosity, but Iza was exhausted and didn't want to leave the girl. She lay down beside her as soon as Creb left and wrapped her fur around both of them. She watched the sleeping girl for a while by the dim light of the cooled fire.

Peculiar-looking little thing, she thought. Rather ugly in a way. Her face is so flat with that high bulging forehead and little stub of a nose, and what a strange boney knob beneath her mouth. I wonder how old she is? Younger than I thought at first; she's so tall it's misleading. And so thin, I can feel her bones. Poor baby, I wonder how long it's been since she had anything to eat, wandering all alone. Iza put her arm around the girl protectively. The woman who had even helped young animals on occasion could not do less for the wretched skinny little girl. The warm heart of the medicine woman went out to the vulnerable child.

Mog-ur stood back as each man arrived and found his place behind one of the stones that had been arranged in a small circle within a larger circle of torches. They were on the open steppes away from the camp. The magician waited until all the men were seated, and a little longer, then stepped into the middle of the circle carrying a burning brand of aromatic wood. He set the small torch into the ground in front of the vacant place that had his staff behind it.

He stood up straight on his good leg in the middle of the circle and stared over the heads of the seated men into the dark distance with a dreamy unfocused look, as though he were seeing with his one eye a world to which the others were blind. Wrapped in his heavy cave bear–skin cloak that covered the lopsided bulges of his unsymmetrical frame, he was an imposing yet strangely unreal presence. A man, yet with his distorted shape, not quite a man; not more or less, but other than. His very deformities imbued him with a supernatural quality that was never more awesome than when Mog-ur conducted a ceremony.

Suddenly, with a magician's flourish, he produced a skull. He held it high over his head with his strong left arm and turned slowly around in a complete circle so each man could see the large, distinctive, high-domed shape. The men stared at the cave bear's skull glowing whitely in the flickering light of the torches. He placed it in front of the small torch in the ground and lowered himself down behind it, completing the circle.

A young man sitting beside him got up and picked up a wooden bowl. He was past his eleventh year and his manhood ceremony had been held shortly before the earthquake. Goov had been chosen as acolyte when he was a small boy and he had often assisted Mog-ur in preparations, but acolytes were not allowed at an actual ceremony until they were men. The first time Goov functioned in his new role was after they had begun their search, and he was still nervous.

For Goov, finding a new cave had a special meaning. It was his chance to learn the details of the seldom-performed and difficult-to-describe ceremony that made a cave acceptable for residence, from the great Mog-ur himself. As a child he had feared the magician, though he understood the honor of being chosen. The young man had since learned the cripple was not only the most skilled mog-ur of all the clans, but that he had a kind and gentle heart beneath his austere visage. Goov respected his mentor and loved him.

The acolyte had begun preparing the drink that was in the bowl as soon as Brun had called the halt. He started by pounding whole datura plants between two stones. The difficult part was estimating the quantity and proportion of leaves, stems, and flowers to use. Boiling water was poured over the crushed plants, and the mixture left to steep until the ceremony.

Goov had poured the strong datura tea into the special ceremonial bowl, straining it between his fingers, just before Mog-ur stepped into the circle, and hoped anxiously to get the holy man's nod of acceptance. While Goov held it, Mog-ur took a sip, nodded his approval, then drank, and Goov breathed an inaudible sigh of relief. Then he took the bowl to each of the men according to rank, beginning with Brun. He held it while they drank, controlling the portion each one consumed, and took his drink last.

Mog-ur waited for him to sit down, then gave a signal. The men began pounding the butt ends of their spears rhythmically on the ground. The dull thudding of the spears seemed to get louder until no other sound was heard.

They got caught up in the steady beat, then stood up and began moving in time to the rhythm. The holy man stared at the skull, and his intense gaze drew the men's attention to the sacred relic as though he willed it. Timing was important, and he was a master of timing. He waited just long enough for the anticipation to build to a peak—any longer and the keen edge would have been gone—then looked up at his sibling, the man who led the clan. Brun squatted down in front of the skull.

"Spirit of Bison, Totem of Brun," Mog-ur began. He actually spoke only one word, "Brun." The rest was said with his one-handed gestures, and he vocalized no other words. Formalized movements, the ancient unspoken language used to communicate with spirits and with other clans whose few guttural words and common hand signals were different, were all that followed. With silent symbols, Mog-ur implored the Spirit of the Bison to forgive them for any wrongs they might have done that offended him and begged for his help.

"This man has always honored the Spirits, Great Bison, always kept the traditions of the Clan. This man is a strong leader, a wise leader, a fair leader, a good hunter, a good provider, a self-controlled man, worthy of the Mighty Bison. Do not desert this man; guide this leader to a new home, a place where the Spirit of the Bison will be content. This clan begs for the help of the totem of this man," the holy man concluded. Then he looked at the second-in-command. As Brun moved back, Grod squatted in front of the cave bear skull.

No woman could be allowed to see the ceremony, to know that their men, who led with such stoic strength, begged and pleaded with unseen spirits just as the women begged and pleaded with the men.

"Spirit of Brown Bear, Totem of Grod," Mog-ur began once more and went through a similar formal pleading with Grod's totem; then all the rest of the men in turn. He continued to stare at the skull when he was through, while the men pounded their spears, letting the anticipation build again.

They all knew what came next, the ceremony never changed; it was the same night after night, but still they anticipated. They were waiting for Mog-ur to call upon the Spirit of Ursus, the Great Cave Bear, his own personal totem and most revered of all the spirits.

Ursus was more than Mog-ur's totem; he was everyone's totem, and more than totem. It was Ursus that made them Clan. He was the supreme spirit, supreme protector. Reverence for the Cave Bear was the common factor that united them, the force that welded all the separate autonomous clans into one people, the Clan of the Cave Bear.

When the one-eyed magician judged the time was right, he signaled. The men stopped pounding and sat behind their stones, but the heavy thudding rhythm coursed through their bloodstreams and still pounded inside their heads.

Mog-ur reached into a small pouch and withdrew a pinch of dried club-moss spores. Holding his hand over the small torch, he leaned forward and blew, at the same time he let them drop over the flame. The spores caught fire and cascaded dramatically around the skull in a magnesium brilliance of light, in stark contrast to the dark night.

The skull glowed, seemed to come alive, did, to the men whose perceptions were heightened by the effects of datura. An owl in a nearby tree hooted, seemingly on command, adding his haunting sound to the eerie splendor.

"Great Ursus, Protector of the Clan," the magician said with formal signs, "show this clan to a new home as once the Cave Bear showed the Clan to live in caves and wear fur. Protect your Clan from Ice Mountain, and the Spirit of Granular Snow who begot him, and the Spirit of Blizzards, her mate. This clan would beg the Great Cave Bear to let no evil come while they are homeless. Most honored of all Spirits, your Clan, your people, ask the Spirit of Mighty Ursus to join with them as they make the journey to the beginning."

And then, Mog-ur used the power of his great brain.

All those primitive people, with almost no frontal lobes, and speech limited by undeveloped vocal organs, but with huge brains—larger than any race of man then living or future generations yet unborn—were unique. They were the culmination of a branch of mankind whose brain was developed in the back of their heads, in the occipital and the parietal regions that control vision and bodily sensation and store memory.

And their memory made them extraordinary. In them, the unconscious knowledge of ancestral behavior called instinct had evolved. Stored in the back of their large brains were not just their own memories, but the memories of their forebears. They could recall knowledge learned by their ancestors and, under special circumstances, they could go a step beyond. They could recall their racial memory, their own evolution. And when they reached back far enough, they could merge that memory that was identical for all and join their minds, telepathically.

But only in the tremendous brain of the scarred, malformed cripple was the gift fully developed. Creb, gentle shy Creb, whose massive brain caused his deformity, had, as Mog-ur, learned to use the power of that brain to fuse the separate entities seated around him into one mind, and direct it. He could take them to any part of their racial heritage, to become in their minds any of their progenitors. He was The Mog-ur. His was a true power, not limited to tricks of lighting or drug-induced euphoria. That only set the stage and enabled them to accept his direction.

In that still, dark night, lit by ancient stars, a few men experienced visions impossible to describe. They did not see them, they were them. They felt the sensations, saw with the eyes, and remembered the unfathomable beginnings. From the depths of their minds they found the undeveloped brains of creatures of the sea floating in their warm, saline environment. They survived the pain of their first breath of air and became amphibians sharing both elements.

Because they venerated the cave bear, Mog-ur evoked a primordial mammal—the ancestor who spawned both species and a host of others—and merged the unity of their minds with the bear's beginning. Then down through the ages they became in succession each of their progenitors, and sensed those that diverged to other forms. It made them aware of their relationship with all life on the earth, and the reverence it fostered even for the animals they killed and consumed formed the basis of the spiritual kinship with their totems.

All their minds moved as one, and only as they neared the present did they separate into their immediate forebears and finally themselves. It seemed to take forever. In a sense it did, but little actual time elapsed. As each man reached himself again, he quietly got up and left to find his sleeping place and a deep dreamless sleep, his dreams already spent.

Mog-ur was the last. In solitude he meditated on the experience and after a time felt a familiar uneasiness. They could know the past with the depth and grandeur that exalted the soul, but Creb sensed a limitation that never occurred to the others. They could not see ahead. They could not even think ahead. He alone had a bare inkling of the possibility.

The Clan could not conceive a future any different from the past, could not devise innovative alternatives for tomorrow. All their knowledge, everything they did, was a repetition of something that had been done before. Even storing food for seasonal changes was the result of past experience.

There had been a time, long before, when innovation came easier, when a broken sharp-edged stone gave someone the idea to break a stone on purpose to make a sharp edge, when the warm end of a twirled stick made someone twirl it harder and longer just to see how warm it could get. But as more memories built up, crowding and enlarging the storage capacity of their brain, changes came harder. There was no more room for new ideas that would be added to their memory bank, their heads were already too large. Women had difficulty giving birth; they couldn't afford new knowledge that would enlarge their heads even more.

The Clan lived by unchanging tradition. Every facet of their lives from the time they were born until they were called to the world of the spirits was circumscribed by the past. It was an attempt at survival, unconscious and unplanned except by nature in a last-ditch effort to save the race from extinction, and doomed to failure. They could not stop change, and resistance to it was self-defeating, antisurvival.

They were slow to adapt. Inventions were accidental and often not utilized. If something new happened to them, it could be added to their backlog of information; but change was accomplished only with great effort, and once it was forced on them, they were adamant in following the new course. It came too hard to alter it again. But a race with no room for learning, no room for growth, was no longer equipped for an inherently changing environment, and they had passed beyond the point of developing in a different way. That would be left for a newer form, a different experiment of nature.

As Mog-ur sat alone on the open plain watching the last of the torches sputter and die, he thought of the strange girl Iza had found, and his uneasiness grew until it became a physical discomfort. Her kind had been met before, but only recently in his concept of reckoning, and not many of the chance meetings had been pleasant. Where they had come from was a mystery—her people were newcomers to their land—but since they arrived things had been changing. They seemed to bring change with them.

Creb shrugged off his uneasiness, carefully wrapped the cave bear's skull in his cloak, reached for his staff, and hobbled to bed.

3

The child turned over and began to thrash.

"Mother," she moaned. Flailing her arms wildly, she called out again, louder, "Mother!"

Iza held her, murmuring a soft rumbling undertone. The warm closeness of the woman's body and her soothing sounds penetrated the girl's feverish brain and quieted her. She had slept fitfully through the night, awakening the woman often with her tossing and moaning and delirious mutterings. The sounds were strange, different from the words spoken by Clan people. They flowed easily, fluently, one sound blending into another. Iza could not begin to reproduce many of them; her ear was not even conditioned to hearing the finer variations. But that particular set of sounds was repeated so often, Iza guessed it was a name for someone close to the child, and when she saw that her presence comforted the girl, she sensed who the someone was.

She can't be very old, Iza thought, she didn't even know how to find food. I wonder how long she's been alone? What could have happened to her people? Could it have been the earthquake? Has she been wandering by herself that long? And how did she escape from a cave lion with only a few scratches? Iza had treated enough maulings to know the girl's wounds were inflicted by the huge cat. Powerful spirits must protect her, Iza decided.

It was still dark, though dawn was approaching, when the child's fever finally broke in a drenching sweat. Iza cuddled her close, adding her warmth and making sure she was well covered. The girl woke shortly afterward and wondered where she was, but it was too dark to see. She felt the reassurance of the woman's body next to her and closed her eyes again, drifting into a more restful sleep.

As the sky lightened, silhouetting the trees against its faint glow, Iza crept quietly out of the warm fur. She stoked the fire, added more wood, then went to the small creek to fill her bowl and peel bark off a willow tree. She paused for a moment, clutched her amulet, and thanked the spirits for willow. She always thanked the spirits for willow, for its ubiquitous presence as well as for its painkilling bark. She couldn't remember how many times she had peeled willow bark for a tea to relieve aches and pains. She knew of stronger painkillers, but they also dulled the senses. The analgesic properties of willow just dulled the pain and reduced fever.

A few other people were beginning to stir as Iza sat hunched over the fire adding small hot stones to the bowl of water and willow bark. When it was ready, she carried it back to the fur, carefully rested the bowl in a small depression scooped out of the ground, then slid in beside the child. Iza watched the sleeping girl, noting that her breathing was normal, intrigued by her unusual face. The sunburn had faded to tan except for a little peeling skin across the bridge of her small nose.

Iza had seen her kind once, but only from a distance. Women of the Clan always ran and hid from them. Unpleasant incidents had been told at Clan Gatherings of chance encounters between the Clan and the Others, and Clan people avoided them. Women, especially, were allowed little contact. But the experience of their clan had not been bad. Iza remembered talking with Creb about the man who had stumbled into their cave long before, nearly out of his head with pain, his arm badly broken.

He had learned a little of their language, but his ways were strange. He liked to talk to women as well as men and treated the medicine woman with great respect, almost reverence. It hadn't kept him from gaining the respect of the men. Iza wondered about the Others, lying awake watching the child as the sky grew lighter.

While Iza was looking at her, a shaft of sunlight fell on the child's face from the bright ball of flame just edging over the horizon. The girl's eyelids fluttered. She opened her eyes and looked into a pair of large brown eyes, deep

set below heavy brow ridges in a face that protruded somewhat, like a muzzle.

The girl screamed and squeezed her eyes shut again. Iza
drew the child close to her, feeling her scrawny body
shaking with fear, and murmured soothing sounds. The
sounds were somehow familiar to the child, but more familiar was the warm comforting body. Slowly, her shaking
stilled. She opened her eyes a tiny crack and looked at Iza
again. This time she didn't scream. Then she opened her
eyes wide and stared at the frightening, totally unfamiliar
face of the woman.

Iza stared too, in wonder. She had never seen eyes the
color of the sky before. For a moment she wondered if the
child was blind. Eyes of older Clan people sometimes grew
a film over them, and as the film clouded the eyes to a
lighter shade, sight grew dimmer. But the pupils of the
child's eyes dilated normally and there could be no doubt
she had seen Iza. That light blue-gray color must be normal
for her, Iza thought.

The little girl lay perfectly still, afraid to move a muscle,
her eyes wide open. When the child sat up with Iza's help,
she winced in pain from the movement, and her memories
came flooding back. She recalled the monstrous lion with a
shudder, visualizing the sharp claw raking her leg. She
remembered struggling to the stream, thirst overcoming her
fear and the pain in her leg, but she remembered nothing
before. Her mind had blocked out all memory of her ordeal
wandering alone, hungry and afraid, the terrifying earthquake, and the loved ones she had lost.

Iza held the cup of liquid to the child's mouth. She was
thirsty and took a drink, and made a face at the bitter taste.
But when the woman put the cup back to her lips, she
swallowed again, too frightened to resist. Iza nodded approval, then left to help the women prepare the morning
meal. The little girl's eyes followed Iza, and she opened
them wider when she saw for the first time a camp full of
people who looked like the woman.

The smell of cooking food brought pangs of hunger, and
when the woman returned with a small bowl of meaty
broth thickened with grain into a gruel, the child gulped it
down ravenously. The medicine woman didn't think she
was ready for solid food yet. It didn't take much to fill her
shrunken stomach, and Iza put the remainder in a water

skin for the child to drink while they traveled. When the girl was through, Iza laid her down and removed the poultice. The wounds were draining and the swelling was down.

"Good," Iza said aloud.

The child jumped at the harsh guttural sound of the word, the first she had heard the woman speak. It didn't sound like a word at all, more like a growl or grunt of some animal to the girl's untutored ears. But Iza's actions were not animallike, they were very human, very humane. The medicine woman had another mashed root ready and while she was applying the new dressing, a misshapen, lopsided man hobbled toward them.

He was the most fearsomely repulsive man the girl had ever seen. One side of his face was scarred and a flap of skin covered the place where one of his eyes should have been. But all of these people were so alien and ugly to her, his forbidding disfiguration was only a matter of degree. She didn't know who they were or how she happened to be among them, but she knew the woman was taking care of her. She had been given food, the dressing cooled and soothed her leg, and most of all, from the depths of her unconscious mind, she felt a relief from the anxiety that had filled her with aching fear. Strange as these people were, with them she was, at least, no longer alone.

The crippled man eased himself down and observed the child. She returned his look with a frank curiosity that surprised him. The children of his clan were always a little afraid of him. They learned quickly that even their elders held him in awe, and his aloof manner didn't encourage familiarity. The gulf widened when mothers threatened to call Mog-ur if they misbehaved. By the time children were nearly adults, most of them, especially girls, really feared him. It wasn't until they gained the maturity of middle years that members of the clan came to temper their fear with respect. Creb's good right eye sparkled with interest at this strange child's fearless appraisal of him.

"The child is better, Iza," he indicated. His voice was lower pitched than the woman's, but the sounds he made were more like grunts than words to the girl. She didn't notice the accompanying hand signals. The language was totally alien to her; she only knew the man had communicated something to the woman.

"She is still weak from hunger," Iza said, "but the wound is better. The gashes were deep, but not enough to seriously damage her leg, and the infection is draining. She was clawed by a cave lion, Creb. Have you ever known a cave lion to stop with a few scratches once it decided to attack? I'm surprised she's alive. She must have a strong spirit protecting her. But," Iza added, "what do I know of spirits?"

It was certainly not a woman's place, not even his sibling's, to tell Mog-ur about spirits. She made a deprecating gesture that also begged his forgiveness for her presumption. He didn't acknowledge her—she hadn't expected him to—but he looked at the child with greater interest as a result of her comment about a strong protecting spirit. He had been thinking much the same thing himself, and though he would never admit it, his sibling's opinion carried weight with him, and confirmed his own thoughts.

They broke camp quickly. Iza, loaded with her basket and bundles, reached down to hoist the girl up to her hip and fell in behind Brun and Grod. Riding on the woman's hip, the little girl looked around her with curiosity while they traveled, watching everything Iza and the other women did. She was particularly interested whenever they stopped to gather food. Iza often gave her a bite of a fresh bud or tender young shoot, and it brought a vague recollection of another woman who had done the same thing. But now, the girl paid closer attention to the plants and began to notice identifying characteristics. Her days of hunger aroused in the young child a keen desire to learn how to find food. She pointed to a plant and was pleased when the woman stopped and dug up its root. Iza was pleased, too. The child is quick, she thought. She couldn't have known it before or she would have eaten it.

They stopped for a rest near midday while Brun looked over a possible cave site, and after giving the youngster the last of the broth from the water skin, Iza handed her a strip of hard dry meat to chew. The cave was not adequate for their needs. Later in the afternoon, the girl's leg began to throb as the effects of the willow bark wore off. She squirmed restlessly. Iza patted her and shifted her weight to a more comfortable position. The girl gave herself over completely to the woman's care. With total trust and confidence, she wrapped skinny arms around Iza's neck and rested her head on the woman's broad shoulder. The medicine woman, childless for so long, felt a surge of inner warmth for the orphaned girl. She was still weak and tired, and lulled by the rhythmic motion as the woman walked, she fell asleep.

By the time evening approached, Iza was feeling the strain of the additional burden she carried and was grateful to let the child down when Brun called a halt for the day. The girl was feverish, her cheeks flushed and hot, her eyes glazed, and while the woman looked for wood, she also looked for plants to treat the child again. Iza didn't know what caused infection, but she did know how to treat it, and many other ailments as well.

Though healing was magic and couched in terms of spirits, it didn't make Iza's medicine less effective. The ancient Clan had always lived by hunting and gathering, and generations of using wild plantlife had, by experiment or accident, built up a store of information about it. Animals were skinned and butchered and their organs observed and compared. The women dissected while preparing dinner and applied the knowledge to themselves.

Her mother had shown Iza the various internal parts and explained their functions as part of her training, but it was only to remind her of something she already knew. Iza was born to a highly respected line of medicine women and, through a means more mysterious than training, knowledge of healing was passed on to a medicine woman's daughters. A fledgling medicine woman of an illustrious line had a higher rank than an experienced one of mediocre antecedents—with good reason.

Stored in her brain at birth was the knowledge acquired by her ancestors, the ancient line of medicine women of which Iza was a direct descendant. She could remember what they knew. It was not much different from recalling her own experience; and once stimulated, the process was automatic. She knew her own memories primarily because she could also remember the circumstances associated with them—she never forgot anything—and she could only recall the knowledge in her memory bank, not how it was learned. And although Iza and her siblings had the same parents, neither Creb nor Brun had her medical knowledge.

Memories in Clan people were sex differentiated. Women had no more need of hunting lore than men had of more than rudimentary knowledge of plants. The difference in the brains of men and women was imposed by nature, and only cemented by culture. It was another of nature's attempts to limit the size of their brains in an effort to prolong the race. Any child with knowledge rightfully belonging to the opposite gender at birth lost it through lack of stimulation by the time adult status was reached.

But nature's attempt to save the race from extinction carried with it the elements to defeat its own purpose. Not only were both sexes essential for procreation, but for day to day living; one could not survive for long without the other. And they could not learn each other's skills, they hadn't the memories for it.

But the eyes and brain of people of the Clan had also endowed both genders with acute and perceptive vision, though it was used in different ways. The terrain had been changing gradually as they traveled, and, unconsciously, Iza recorded each detail of the landscape they passed through, noting especially the vegetation. She could discern minor variations in the shape of a leaf or the height of a stalk from a great distance, and though there were some plants, a few flowers, an occasional tree or shrub she had never seen before, they were not unfamiliar. From a recess deep in the back of her large brain she found a memory of them, a memory not her own. But even with that tremendous reservoir of information at her disposal, she had recently seen some vegetation that was completely unfamiliar, as unfamiliar as the countryside. She would have liked to examine it more closely. All women were curious about unknown plantlife. Though it meant acquiring new knowledge, it was essential to immediate survival.

Part of every woman's heredity was the knowledge of how to test unfamiliar vegetation, and like the rest, Iza experimented on herself. Similarities to known plants placed new ones in relative categories, but she knew the dangers of assuming similar characteristics meant identical properties. The procedure for testing was simple. She took a small bite. If the taste was unpleasant, she spit it out immediately. If it was agreeable, she held the tiny portion in her mouth, carefully noting any tingling or burning sensations or any changes in taste. If there were none, she swallowed it and waited to see if she could detect any effects. The following day, she took a larger bite and went through the same procedure. If no ill effects were noticed after a third trial, the new food was considered edible, in small portions at first.

But Iza was often more interested when there were noticeable effects, for that indicated a possibility of a medicinal use. The other women brought anything unusual to her when they applied the same test for edibility or anything that had characteristics similar to plants known to be poisonous or toxic. Proceeding with caution, she experimented with these too, using her own methods. But such experimentation took time, and she stayed with plants she knew while they traveled.

Near this campsite, Iza found several tall, wandlike, slim-stemmed hollyhocks with large bright flowers. The roots of the multicolored flowering plants could be made into a poultice similar to iris roots to promote healing and reduce swelling and inflammation. An infusion of the flowers would both numb the child's pain and make her sleepy. She collected them along with her wood.

After the evening meal, the little girl sat propped up against a large rock watching the activities of the people around her. Food and a fresh dressing had refreshed her and she jabbered at Iza, though she could tell the woman didn't understand her. Other clan members glanced disapprovingly in her direction, but the child was unaware of the meaning of the looks. Their underdeveloped vocal organs made precise articulation impossible for people of the Clan. The few sounds they used as emphasis had evolved from cries of warning or a need to gain attention, and the importance attached to verbalizations was a part of their traditions. Their primary means of communication—hand signals, gestures, positions; and an intuition born of intimate contact, established customs, and perceptive discernment of expressions and postures—were expressive, but limited. Specific objects seen by one were difficult to describe to others, and abstract concepts even more so. The child's volubility perplexed the clan and made them distrustful.

They treasured children, reared them with gentle fond affection and discipline which grew more stern as they grew older. Babies were pampered by women and men alike, young children rebuked most often by simply being ignored. When children became aware of the higher status of older children and adults, they emulated their elders and resisted pampering as fit only for babies. Youngsters learned early to behave within the strict confines of established custom, and one custom was that superfluous sounds were inappropriate. Because of her height, the girl seemed older than her years, and the clan considered her undisciplined, not well brought up.

Iza, who had been in much closer contact with her, guessed she was younger than she seemed. She was coming to a close approximation of the girl's true age and she responded to her helplessness more leniently. She sensed, too, from her mutterings while she was delirious, that her kind verbalized more fluently and more frequently. Iza was drawn to the child whose life depended on her and who had wrapped scrawny little arms around her neck in complete trust. There will be time, Iza thought, to teach her better manners. She was already beginning to think of the child as hers.

Creb wandered over while Iza was pouring boiling water over the flowers of the hollyhocks, and sat down near the child. He was interested in the stranger, and since the preparations for the evening ceremony were not yet complete, he went to see how she was recovering. They stared at each other, the young girl and the crippled, scarred old man, studying each other with equal intensity. He had never been so close to one of her kind and had never seen a young one of the Others at all. She didn't even know of the existence of Clan people until she woke up to find herself among them, but more than their racial characteristics, she was curious about the puckered skin of his face. In her limited experience, she had never seen a face so horribly scarred. Impetuously, with the uninhibited reactions of a child, she reached out to touch his face, to see if the scar felt different.

Creb was taken aback as she lightly stroked his face. None of the children of the clan had ever reached out to him like that. No adults reached out to him either. They avoided contact with him, as though they might somehow catch his deformity by touching him. Only Iza, who nursed him through his sieges of arthritis which attacked with greater severity every winter, seemed to have no compunction about it. She was neither repulsed by his misshapen body and ugly scars nor in awe of his power and position. The little girl's gentle touch struck an inner chord in his lonely old heart. He wanted to communicate with her and thought for a moment about how to begin.

"Creb," he said, pointing to himself. Iza was watching quietly, waiting for the flowers to steep. She was glad Creb was taking an interest in the girl, and the use of his personal name was not lost on her.

"Creb," he repeated, tapping his chest.

The child cocked her head, trying to understand. There was something he wanted her to do. Creb said his name a third time. Suddenly she brightened, sat up straight, and smiled.

"Grub?" she responded, rolling the *r* to mimic his sound.

The old man nodded approval; her pronunciation was close. Then he pointed at her. She frowned slightly, not quite sure what he wanted now. He tapped his chest, repeated his name, then tapped hers. Her wide smile of understanding looked like a grimace to him, and the polysyllabic word that rolled out of her mouth was not only unpronounceable, it was almost incomprehensible. He went through the same motions, leaning close to hear better. She said her name.

"Aay-rr," he hesitated, shook his head, tried again. "Aay-lla, Ay-la?" It was the best approximation he could make. There were not many in the clan who could have come as close. She beamed and nodded her head up and down vigorously. It was not exactly what she had said, but she accepted it, sensing even in her young mind that he could not say the word for her name any better.

"Ayla," Creb repeated, getting used to the sound.

"Creb?" the girl said, tugging at his arm to get his attention, then pointed at the woman.

"Iza," Creb said, "Iza."

"Eeez-sa," she repeated. She was delighted with the word game. "Iza, Iza," she reiterated, looking at the woman.

Iza nodded solemnly; name sounds were very important. She leaned forward and tapped the child's chest the way Creb had, wanting her to say her name-word again. The girl repeated her full name, but Iza just shook her head. She couldn't begin to make that combination of sounds that the girl made so easily. The child was dismayed, then glancing at Creb, said her name the way he had.

"Eye-ghha?" the woman tried. The girl shook her head and said it again. "Eye-ya?" Iza tried again.

"Aay, Aay, not Eye," Creb said. "Aaay-lla," he repeated very slowly so Iza could hear the unfamiliar combination of sounds.

"Aay-lla," the woman said carefully, struggling to make the word the way Creb had.

The girl smiled. It didn't matter that the name wasn't exactly right; Iza had tried so hard to say the name Creb had given her, she accepted it as her own. She would be Ayla for them. Spontaneously, she reached out and hugged the woman.

Iza squeezed her gently, then pulled away. She would have to teach the child that displays of affection were unseemly in public, but she was pleased nonetheless.

Ayla was beside herself with joy. She had felt so lost, so isolated among these strange people. She had tried so hard to communicate with the woman who was caring for her, and she was so frustrated when all her attempts failed. It was only a beginning, but at least she had a name to call the woman and a name to be called. She turned back to the man who had initiated the communication. He didn't seem nearly so ugly to her anymore. Her joy bubbled over, she felt a warmth toward him, and as she had done many times to another man she remembered only vaguely, the little girl put her arms around the crippled man's neck, pulled his head down to her, and rested her cheek against his.

Her gesture of affection unsettled him. He resisted an urge to return the hug. It would be totally improper to be seen hugging this strange little creature outside the boundary of a family hearth. But he allowed her to press her smooth, firm little cheek to his bushy-bearded face a moment longer before he gently removed her arms from around his neck.

Creb picked up his staff and used it to pull himself up. As he limped away, he thought about the girl. I must teach her to speak, she should learn to communicate properly, he said to himself. After all, I can't entrust all her instruction to a woman. He knew, though, that he really wanted to spend more time with her. Without realizing it, he thought of her as a permanent part of the clan.

Brun had not considered the implications of allowing Iza to pick up a strange child along the way. It was not a failing of him as a leader, it was the failing of his race. He could not have anticipated finding a wounded child who was not Clan and he could not foresee the logical consequences of rescuing her. Her life had been saved; the only alternative to letting her stay with them was to turn her out to wander alone again. She could not survive alone—that did not take foresight, it was fact. After saving her life, to expose her to death again he would have to oppose Iza, who, although she had no power personally, did have a formidable array of spirits on her side—and now Creb, the Mog-ur who had the ability to call upon any and all spirits. Spirits were a potent force to Brun, he had no desire to find himself at odds with them. To give him full credit, it was just that eventuality that bothered him about the girl. He hadn't been able to express it to himself, but the thought had been hovering. He didn't know it yet, but Brun's clan had increased to twenty-one.

When the medicine woman examined Ayla's leg the next morning, she could see the improvement. Under her expert care, the infection was nearly gone and the four parallel gashes were closed and healing, though she would always carry the scars. Iza decided a poultice was no longer needed, but she made a willow-bark tea for the child. When she moved her off the sleeping fur, Ayla tried to stand. Iza helped her and supported her while the girl gingerly tried to put her weight on the leg. It hurt, but after a few careful steps, it felt better.

Standing up at her full height, the girl was even taller than Iza thought. Her legs were long, spindly with knobby knees, and straight. Iza wondered if they were deformed. The legs of Clan people were bowed in an outward curvature, but, except for a limp, the child had no problem moving around. Straight legs must be normal for her too, Iza decided—like blue eyes.

The medicine woman wrapped the cloak around her and lifted the child to her hip as the clan got under way; her leg wasn't healed enough yet for her to walk any great distance. At intervals during the day's march, Iza let her down to walk for a while. The girl had been eating ravenously, making up for her long hunger, and Iza thought she could notice a weight gain already. She was glad to be relieved of the extra burden occasionally, especially since traveling was becoming more difficult.

The clan left the broad flat steppes behind and for the next few days traversed rolling hills that grew progressively steeper. They were in the foothills of the mountains whose glistening ice caps drew closer every day. The hills were thickly forested, not with the evergreens of boreal forest, but with the rich green leaves and thick gnarled trunks of broad-leafed deciduous trees. The temperature had warmed much faster than the season usually progressed, which puzzled Brun. The men had replaced their wraps with a shorter leather hide that left the torso bare. The women didn't change to their summer wear; it was easier to carry their loads with a full wrap that eased chafing.

The terrain lost all resemblance to the cold prairie that had surrounded their old cave. Iza found herself depending more and more on knowledge of memories more ancient than her own as the clan passed through shaded glens and over grassy knolls of a full temperate forest. The heavy brown barks of oak, beech, walnut, apple, and maple were intermixed with supple, straight, thin-barked willow, birch, hornbeam, aspen, and the high brush of alder and hazelnut. There was a tang to the air Iza couldn't readily identify that seemed to ride on the warm soft breeze from the south. Catkins still clung to fully leafed birches. Delicate petals of pink and white drifted down, blown blossoms of fruit and nut trees, giving early promise of autumn's bounty.

They struggled through brush and vines of the dense forest and climbed exposed faces. As they mounted rocky outcrops, the hillsides around them were resplendent with greens of every hue. The deep shades of pine reappeared as they climbed, along with silver fir. Higher up, blue spruce made an occasional appearance. The deeper colors of conifers intermingled with the rich primary greens of the broad-leafed trees and the limes and pale-white greens of the small-leafed varieties. Mosses and grass added their shades to the verdant mosaic of lush growth and small plants, from oxalis, the cloverlike wood sorrel, to tiny succulents clinging to exposed rock faces. Wild flowers were scattered through the woods, white trilliums, yellow violets, rose pink hawthorn, while yellow jonquils and blue and yellow gentians dominated some of the higher meadows. In a few of the heavily shaded places, the last of the yellow and white and purple crocus, off to a later start, still bravely showed their heads.

The clan stopped for a rest after reaching the top of a steep incline. Below, the panorama of wooded hillsides ended abruptly at the steppes expanding to the horizon. From their vantage point, several herds could be seen in the distance grazing on the tall grass already fading to summer gold. Fast-moving hunters, traveling light and unencumbered by heavily burdened women, could pick and choose among the several varieties of game and reach the steppes easily in far less than half a morning. The sky to the east, over the broad prairie, was clear, but scudding up fast from the south, thunderheads were brewing. If they continued to develop, the high mountain range to the north would cause the clouds to dump their load of moisture on the clan.

Brun and the men were having a meeting just out of range of the women and children, but the worried scowls and hand gestures left no doubt about the reason for the discussion. They were trying to decide if they should turn back. The countryside was unfamiliar, but more important, they were moving too far away from the steppes. Though they had caught glimpses of many animals in the wooded foothills, it was nothing like the tremendous herds supported by the plentiful fodder of the grassy plains below. Animals were easier to hunt out in the open, easier to see without the cover of forest to hide them, cover that hid their four-legged hunters as well. Plains animals were more social, tended to form in herds, not as isolated individuals or small family groups like the forest prey.

Iza guessed they would probably turn back, making their struggle to climb the steep hills all in vain. The gathering clouds and threatening rain cast a dreary pall over the dispirited travelers. While they were waiting, Iza let Ayla down and eased off her heavy load. The child, enjoying the freedom of movement her healing leg allowed after being confined to the woman's hip, wandered off. Iza saw her as she moved out of sight beyond the nose of a jutting ridge just ahead. She didn't want the girl to stray too far. The meeting might end at any time, and Brun would not look with favor on the girl if she held up their departure. She went after her, and rounding the ridge, Iza saw the child, but what she saw beyond the girl made her heart race.

She hurried back, casting quick glances over her shoulder. She didn't dare interrupt Brun and the men, and waited impatiently for the meeting to break up. Brun saw her, and though he gave no indication of it, he knew something was bothering her. As soon as the men separated, Iza ran to Brun, sat down in front of him, and looked at the ground—the position which meant she wanted to talk to him. He could grant an audience or not; the choice was his. If he ignored her, she would not be allowed to tell him what was on her mind.

Brun wondered what she wanted. He had noticed the girl exploring ahead—there was little about his clan that escaped his attention—but he had had more pressing problems. It must be about that girl, he thought scowling, and was tempted to disregard Iza's petition. No matter what Mog-ur said, he didn't like the child traveling with them. Glancing up, Brun saw the magician watching him and tried to discern what the one-eyed man was thinking, but he could not read the impassive face.

The leader looked back at the woman sitting at his feet; her posture gave away her tense agitation. She is really disturbed, he thought. Brun was not an unfeeling man, and he held his sibling in high regard. Despite the problems she had had with her mate, she had always conducted herself well. She was an example to the other women and seldom bothered him with insignificant requests. Perhaps he should let her speak; he did not have to act upon her request. He reached down and tapped her shoulder.

Iza's breath exploded at the touch; she hadn't realized she had been holding it. He would let her speak! He had taken so long to decide, she was sure he was going to ignore her. Iza stood up and, pointing in the direction of the ridge, she said one word, "Cave!"

4

Brun turned on his heel and strode toward the ridge. As he rounded the jutting nose, he stopped, held by the sight beyond. Excitement surged through his veins. A cave! And what a cave! From the first instant he saw it, he knew it was the cave he was looking for, but he fought to control his emotions, to keep his growing hopes in check. With conscious effort, he focused on the details of the cave and its setting. His concentration was so intense, he hardly noticed the little girl.

Even from his vantage of a few hundred yards, the roughly triangular mouth, hewn out of the grayish brown rock of the mountain, was large enough to promise a space inside more than adequate to accommodate his clan. The opening faced south, exposed to sunlight most of the day. As though confirming the fact, a beam of light, finding a chink in the clouds overhead, highlighted the reddish soil of the cave's broad front terrace. Brun scanned the area, making a quick survey. A large bluff to the north and a matching one to the southeast offered protection from winds. Water was close by, he thought, adding another positive feature to his growing mental list as he noticed the flowing stream at the foot of a gentle slope west of the cave. It was, by far, the most promising site he had seen. He signaled to Grod and Creb, repressing his enthusiasm while he waited for them to join him to examine the cave more closely.

The two men hurried toward their leader, followed by Iza who went to fetch Ayla. She, too, took a more searching look at the cave and nodded her head with satisfaction before returning with the child to the knot of people gesturing excitedly. Brun's repressed emotion communicated itself. They knew a cave had been found and they knew Brun thought it had good possibilities. Piercing the somber gloom of the overcast sky, bright rays of sun seemed to charge the atmosphere with hope, matched by the mood of the anxiously waiting clan.

Brun and Grod gripped their spears as the three men approached the cave. They saw no signs of human habitation, but that was no guarantee the cave was uninhabited. Birds darted in and out of the large opening, twittering and chirping as they swooped and circled. Birds are a good omen, Mog-ur thought. As they neared, they walked cautiously, skirting the mouth while Brun and Grod searched carefully for fresh tracks and droppings. The most recent were a few days old. The spoor and large toothmarks on heavy leg bones cracked by powerful jaws told their own story: a pack of hyenas had used the cave for temporary shelter. The carnivorous scavengers had attacked an aging fallow deer and dragged the carcass to the cave to finish their meal at leisure and in relative security.

Off to one side, near the west end of the opening nested in a tangle of vines and brush, was a spring-fed pool; its outlet a small rivulet trickling down the slope to the stream. While the others waited, Brun followed the spring to its source rising out of the rock a short way up the steep, rugged, overgrown side of the cave. The sparkling water just outside the mouth was fresh and pure. Brun added the pool to the benefits of the location and rejoined the others. The site was good, but the cave itself would contain the decision. The two hunters and the crippled magician prepared to enter the large dark opening.

Returning to the east end, the men looked up at the apex of the triangular entrance high overhead as they passed into the hole in the mountain. All senses alert, they proceeded warily into the cave, keeping close to the wall. When their eyes grew accustomed to the dim interior, they gazed around in wonder. A high-vaulted ceiling domed an enormous room, large enough for many times their number. They inched along the rough rock wall watching for openings that might lead to deeper recesses. Near the back, a second spring oozed out of the wall, forming a small dark pool that melted into the dry dirt floor a short distance beyond. Just past the pool, the cave wall turned sharply toward the entrance. Following the west wall back to the mouth, they saw in the gradually increasing light a dark crack outlined by the dim gray wall. At Brun's signal, Creb stopped his shuffling walk while Grod and the leader approached the fissure and looked inside. They saw absolute blackness.

"Grod!" Brun commanded, adding a gesture that signified his need.

The second-in-command dashed outside while Brun and Creb waited tensely. Grod scanned the vegetation growing nearby, then headed toward a small stand of silver fir. Clumps of hard resinous pitch, exuded through the bark, made shiny patches on the trunks. Grod pried the bark loose; fresh sticky sap beaded up in the white scar left on the tree. He broke off dead dry branches still clinging below the living, green-needled boughs, then withdrew a stone hand-axe from a fold of his wrap, hacked off a green branch, and quickly stripped it. He wrapped the pitchy bark and dry twigs with tough grass to the end of the green branch, and carefully removing the live coal from the aurochs horn at his waist, he held it to the pitch and began to blow. Soon, he ran back into the cave with a blazing torch.

With Grod holding the light high over his head and Brun in the lead gripping his club in readiness, the two men entered the dark crack. They crept silently along a narrow passage that turned abruptly after a few steps, doubling back toward the rear of the cave, and just beyond the turn, opened into a second cave. The room, much smaller than the main cave, was nearly circular, and piled against the far wall, a heap of bones glowed whitely in the flickering torchlight. Brun moved in closer to get a better look, and his eyes flew open. He struggled to maintain control of himself, signaled Grod, and both of them quickly retreated.

Mog-ur waited anxiously, leaning heavily on his staff. As Brun and Grod stepped out of the dark opening, the magician was surprised. It was not usual for Brun to be so agitated. At a gesture, Mog-ur followed the two men back into the dark passage. When they reached the small room, Grod held up the torch. Mog-ur's eyes narrowed as he saw the pile of bones. He rushed forward, his staff clattering to the floor as he dropped to his knees. Scrambling through the pile, he saw a large oblong object, and pushing the other bones aside, he picked up a skull.

There was no doubt. The high-domed frontal arch of the skull matched the one Mog-ur carried in his cloak. He sat back, held the huge cranium up to eye level, and looked into the dark eye holes with disbelief, and reverence. Ursus had used this cave. From the quantity of bones, cave bears had hibernated here for many winters. Now, Mog-ur understood Brun's excitement. It was the best of all possible signs. This cave had been the dwelling place of the Great Cave Bear. The essence of the massive creature whom the Clan revered above all others, honored above all others, permeated the very rock of the cave walls. Luck and good fortune were assured to the clan that lived there. From the age of the bones, it was clear the cave had been uninhabited for years, just waiting for them to find it.

It was a perfect cave, well-situated, spacious, with an annex for secret rituals that could be used winter and summer; an annex that breathed with the supernatural mystery of the Clan's spiritual life. Mog-ur was already envisioning ceremonies. This small cave would be his domain. Their search was over, the clan had found a home—providing the first hunt was successful.

As the three men left the cave the sun was shining, the clouds in rapid retreat, blown away by a sharp wind that came from the east. Brun took it as a good sign. It wouldn't have mattered if the clouds had split asunder in a deluge of rain complete with lightning and thunder; he would have taken it as a good sign. Nothing could have dampened his elation or dispelled his feeling of satisfaction. He stood on the terrace in front of the cave and looked out at the view from the mouth. Ahead, between a cleft formed by two hills, he could see a broad shimmering expanse of open water. He hadn't realized they were so close, and it triggered a memory that solved the puzzle of the rapidly warming temperature and unusual vegetation.

The cave was in the foothills of a chain of mountains at the southern tip of a peninsula that jutted halfway into a midcontinent inland sea. The peninsula was connected in two places to the mainland. The primary connection was a broad neck to the north, but a narrow strip of salt marsh formed a tie to the high mountainous land to the east. The salt marsh was also a swampy outlet channel for a smaller inland sea on the northeastern edge of the peninsula.

The mountains at their back protected the coastal strip from the frigid winter cold and fierce winds generated by the continental glacier to the north. Maritime winds, moderated by unfreezing waters of the sea, created a narrow temperate belt at the protected southern tip and provided enough moisture and warmth for the dense hardwood forest of broad-leafed deciduous trees common to cold temperate regions.

The cave was in an ideal location; they had the best of both worlds. Temperatures were warmer than any that prevailed in the surrounding area and there was an abundance of wood to supply fuel for warmth during the freezing winter months. A large sea was close at hand, filled with fish and seafood, and cliffs along the shore were home to a nesting colony of seabirds and their eggs. The temperate forest was a forager's paradise of fruits, nuts, berries, seeds, vegetables, and greens. They had easy access to fresh water from springs and streams. But most important, they were within easy reach of the open steppes, whose extensive grasslands sustained the massive herds of large grazing animals that supplied not only meat but clothing and implements. The small clan of hunter-gatherers lived off the land, and this land held an overwhelming abundance.

Brun hardly noticed the ground beneath his feet as he walked back to the waiting clan. He couldn't imagine a more perfect cave. The spirits have returned, he thought. Maybe they never left us, maybe they just wanted us to move to this larger, finer cave. Of course! That must be it! They were tired of the old cave, they wanted a new home, so they made an earthquake to make us leave it. Maybe the people who were killed were needed in the spirit world; and to make up for it, they led us to this new cave. They must have been testing me, testing my leadership. That's why I couldn't decide if we should turn back. Brun was glad his leadership had not been found wanting. If it hadn't been entirely improper, he would have run back to tell the others.

As the three men came into view, there was no need to tell anyone they were through traveling. They knew. Of those waiting, only Iza and Ayla had seen the cave, and only Iza could appreciate it; she had been sure Brun would claim it. He can't make Ayla leave now, Iza thought. If it hadn't been for her, Brun would have turned back before we found it. Her totem must be powerful, and lucky, too. She's even lucky for us. Iza looked at the little girl beside her, oblivious to the excitement she had caused. But if she's so lucky, why did she lose her people? Iza shook her head. I'll never understand the ways of the spirits.

Brun was looking at the child, too. As soon as he saw Iza and the girl, he remembered it was Iza who told him about the cave, and she would never have seen it if she hadn't gone after Ayla. The leader had been annoyed when he saw the child wander off by herself; he had told everyone to wait. But if she hadn't been so undisciplined, he would have missed the cave. Why would the spirits lead her to it first? Mog-ur was right, he's always right, the spirits weren't angered by Iza's compassion, weren't upset that Ayla was with them. If anything, they favored her.

Brun glanced at the deformed man who should have been leader in his place. We're lucky that my brother is our mog-ur. Strange, he thought, I haven't thought of him as my brother for a long time, not since we were children. Brun always used to think of Creb as his brother when he was young and fighting for the self-control necessary to males of the clan, especially to one destined to be leader. His older sibling had fought his own battle, against pain and ridicule because he couldn't hunt, and he seemed to know when Brun was close to tears. The crippled man's gentle look had a calming effect even then, and Brun always felt better when Creb sat next to him offering the solace of silent understanding.

All children born to the same woman were siblings, but only children of the same sex referred to each other with the more intimate term of brother or sister, and then only when they were young or in rare moments of special closeness. Males did not have sisters, as females did not have brothers; Creb was Brun's sibling and his brother; Iza was only sibling, and she had no sisters.

There was a time when Brun felt sorry for Creb, but he had long since forgotten the man's affliction in respect for his knowledge and his power. He had almost ceased seeing him as a man at all, only as the great magician whose sage counsel he often sought. Brun didn't think his brother ever regretted not being leader, but sometimes he wondered if the cripple ever regretted not having a mate and her children. Women could be trying at times, but they often brought warmth and pleasure to a man's fire. Creb never had a mate, never learned to hunt, never knew the joys or the responsibilities of normal manhood, but he was Mog-ur, The Mog-ur.

Brun knew nothing about magic and little about spirits, but he was leader, and his mate had given birth to a fine son. He glowed with pleasure, thinking of Broud, the boy he was training to take his place someday. I will take him on the next hunt, Brun suddenly decided, the hunt for the cave feast. That can be his manhood hunt. If he makes his first kill, we can include his manhood rites in the cave ceremony. Wouldn't that make Ebra proud. Broud is old enough and he's strong and brave. A little too headstrong sometimes, but he is learning to control his temper. Brun needed another hunter. Now that the clan had a cave, they had work ahead of them to prepare for the next winter. The boy was nearly twelve, more than old enough for manhood. Broud can share the memories for the first time in the new cave, Brun thought. They will be especially good; Iza will make the drink.

Iza! What am I going to do about Iza? And that girl? Iza's already attached to her, strange as she is. It must be because she has been childless for so long. But she will have one of her own soon, and she has no mate to provide for her now. With the girl, there will be two children to worry about. Iza isn't young anymore, but she is pregnant, and she has her magic and her status, which would bring honor to a man. Maybe one of the hunters would take her as a second woman, if it weren't for that strange one. The strange one that the spirits favor. I might really make them angry if I turn her away now. They might make the earth shake again. Brun shuddered.

I know Iza wants to keep her, and she did tell me about the cave. She deserves to be honored for it, but it must not be obvious. If I let her keep the girl, that would show her honor, but the girl isn't Clan. Would the clan spirits want her? She doesn't even have a totem; how can she be allowed to stay with us if she has no totem? Spirits! I don't understand spirits!

"Creb," Brun called. The magician turned at the sound, surprised to hear Brun address him by his personal name, and limped toward the leader when he signaled that he wanted to talk privately.

"That girl, the one Iza picked up, you know she is not Clan, Mog-ur," Brun started, a little unsure of how to begin. Creb waited. "You were the one who said I should allow Ursus to decide if she should live. Well, it looks like he has, but what do we do with her now? She is not Clan. She has no totem. Our totems won't even allow someone from another clan at the ceremony to make a cave ready for them; only those whose spirits will live in it are permitted. She's so young, she'd never survive alone, and you know Iza wants to keep her, but what about the cave ceremony?"

Creb had been hoping for just such an opening, he was prepared. "The child has a totem, Brun, a strong totem. We just don't know what it is. She was attacked by a cave lion, yet all she has to show for it are a few scratches."

"A cave lion! Few hunters would get away that easy."

"Yes, and she wandered alone for a long time, she was near starvation, yet she didn't die, she was put in our path for Iza to find. And don't forget, you didn't prevent it, Brun. She is young for such an ordeal," Mog-ur continued, "but I think she was being tested by her totem to see if she is worthy. Her totem is not only strong, it's lucky. We could all share her luck, maybe we already are."

"You mean the cave?"

"It *was* shown to her first. We were ready to turn back; you led us so close, Brun . . ."

"The spirits led me, Mog-ur. They wanted a new home."

"Yes, of course they led you, but still, they showed the cave to the girl first. I've been thinking, Brun. There are two babies who don't know what their totems are. I haven't had time; finding a new cave was more important. I think we should include a totem ceremony for those babies when we sanctify the cave. It would bring them luck and please their mothers."

"What does that have to do with the girl?"

"When I meditate for the totems of the two babies, I will ask for hers, too. If her totem reveals himself to me, she can be included in the ceremony. It wouldn't require much of her, and we can accept her into the clan at the same time. Then there won't be any problem with her staying."

"Accept her into the clan! She's not Clan, she was born to the Others. Who said anything about accepting her into the clan? It wouldn't be allowed, Ursus wouldn't like it. It's never been done before!" Brun objected. "I wasn't thinking of making her one of us, I only wondered if the spirits would allow her to live with us until she gets older."

"Iza saved her life, Brun, she carries part of the girl's spirit now, that makes her part Clan. She came close to walking in the next world, but she's alive now. That's almost the same as being born again, born to the Clan." Creb could see the leader setting his jaw against the idea and he hurried on before Brun could say anything.

"People of one clan join other clans, Brun. There's nothing unusual about that. There was a time when the young of many clans joined together to make new clans. Remember at the last Clan Gathering, didn't two small clans decide to join to make one? Both kept dwindling, not enough children were born, and of those who were, not enough lived past their birth year. Taking someone into a clan isn't new," Creb reasoned.

"It's true, sometimes people of one clan join another, but the girl isn't Clan. You don't even know if her totem's spirit will talk to you, Mog-ur; and if it does, how do you know you'll understand it? I can't even understand her! Do you really think you can do it? Discover her totem?"

"I can only try. I will ask Ursus to help me. Spirits have a language of their own, Brun. If she is meant to join us, the totem that protects her will make himself understood."

Brun considered for a moment. "But even if you can discover her totem, what hunter will want her? Iza and her baby will be burden enough, and we don't have as many hunters. We lost more than Iza's mate in the earthquake. The son of Grod's mate was killed, and he was a young, strong hunter. Aga's mate is gone and she has two children, and her mother was sharing that fire." A hint of pain touched the leader's eyes at the thought of the deaths in his clan.

"And Oga," Brun continued. "First her mother's mate was gored, and right afterward her mother died in the cave-in. I told Ebra to keep the girl with us. Oga is nearly a woman. When she's old enough I think I will give her to Broud, that should please him," Brun mused, distracted for a moment by thoughts of his other responsibilities. "There are burdens enough for the men who are left without adding the girl, Mog-ur. If I accept her into the clan, who can I give Iza to?"

"Who were you going to give her to until the girl would be old enough to leave us, Brun?" the one-eyed man asked. Brun looked uncomfortable, but Creb continued before Brun could respond. "There is no need to burden a hunter with Iza or the child, Brun. I will provide for them."

"You!"

"Why not? They are female. There are no boys to train, at least not yet. Am I not entitled to the mog-ur's portion of every hunt? I never claimed it all, I never needed it, but I can. Wouldn't it be easier if all the hunters gave me the full share allotted to Mog-ur so I can provide for Iza and the girl, rather than have one hunter burdened with them? I planned to talk to you about setting up my own hearth when we found a new cave anyway, to provide for Iza, unless another man wants her. I've shared a fire with my sibling for many years; it would be difficult for me to change after so long. Besides, Iza helps my arthritis. If her child is a girl, I will take her too. If it is a boy, well . . . we can worry about it then."

Brun mulled the idea over in his mind. Yes, why not? It would make it easier on everyone. But why does Creb want to do it? Iza would take care of his arthritis no matter whose fire she shared. Why does a man his age suddenly want to be bothered with small children? Why would he want to take on the responsibility of training and disciplining a strange girl? Maybe that's it, he feels responsible. Brun didn't like the idea of taking the girl into his clan—he wished the problem had never come up at all—but he liked even less the idea of having someone live with them who was an outsider, and outside of his control. Perhaps it was best to accept her and train her properly, as a woman should be. It might be easier for the rest of the clan to live with, too. And if Creb was willing to take them, Brun couldn't think of any reason not to allow it.

Brun made a gesture of acquiescence. "All right, if you can discover her totem, we'll take her into the clan, Mog-ur, and they can live at your hearth, at least until Iza has her child." For the first time in his life, Brun found himself hoping that an expected child would be a girl rather than a boy.

Once the decision was made, Brun felt a sense of relief. The problem of what to do with Iza had been bothering him, but he had put it aside. He had more important problems to worry about. Creb's suggestion not only offered a solution to a knotty decision he had to make as leader of the clan, but it solved a much more personal problem as well. Try as he might, ever since the earthquake that killed her mate, he could think of no other alternative than to take Iza and her expected baby, and probably Creb as well, to his own hearth. He was already responsible for Broud and Ebra, and now Oga. The addition of more people would create frictions in the one place he could relax and let down his guard a little. His mate might not have been too happy about it, either.

Ebra got along well enough with his sibling, but at the same fire? Though nothing had ever been said openly, Brun knew Ebra was jealous of Iza's status. Ebra was mated to the leader; in most clans, she would have been the highest-ranked woman. But Iza was a medicine woman who could trace her lineage back in an unbroken line of the most respected, prestigious medicine women of the Clan. She had status in her own right, not through her mate. When Iza picked up the girl, Brun thought he'd have to take her in, too. It hadn't occurred to him that Mog-ur might take responsibility not only for himself, but for Iza and her children too. Creb could not hunt, but Mog-ur had other resources.

With the problem solved, Brun hurried toward his clan, who were eagerly awaiting word from their leader to confirm what they had already guessed. He gave the signal: "We travel no more, a cave has been found."

"Iza," Creb said as she was preparing a tea of willow bark for Ayla. "I will not be eating tonight."

Iza bowed her head in acknowledgment. She knew he was

going to meditate in preparation for the ceremony. He never ate before meditating.

The clan was camped beside the stream at the foot of the gentle slope leading to the cave. Not until it had been consecrated by the proper rituals would they move in. Though it would be unpropitious to seem too anxious, each member of the clan found some pretext to get close enough to look inside. Foraging women made a point of searching near the mouth, and men followed the women, ostensibly to watch them. The clan was keyed-up but in a happy mood. The anxiety they had felt ever since the earthquake had vanished. They liked the look of the large new cave. Though it was difficult to see very far inside the dim, unlighted cavern, they could see enough to know it was spacious, much roomier than their former cave. The women pointed with delight at the still pond of spring water just outside. They wouldn't even have to go as far as the stream for water. They looked forward to the cave ceremony, one of the few rituals in which women had their own part, and everyone was anxious to move in.

Mog-ur headed away from the busy campsite. He wanted to find a quiet place where he could think, undisturbed. As he walked alongside the swiftly running stream rushing to its meeting with the inland sea, a warm breeze blew from the south again, ruffling his beard. Only a few distant clouds marred the crystal clarity of the late afternoon sky. The undergrowth was thick and lush; he had to pick his way around obstructions, but he hardly noticed, his mind deep in concentration. A noise from the brush nearby brought him up short. This was strange country and his only defense was his stout walking stick, but in his one powerful hand it could be a formidable weapon of defense. He held it in readiness, listening to the snorting and grunting coming from the dense underbrush and the sounds of snapping branches from the direction of moving bushes.

Suddenly, an animal burst through the screen of thick growth, its large powerful body supported by short stocky legs. Wickedly sharp lower canines protruded like tusks along both sides of its snout. The animal's name came to him though he had not seen one before. A boar. The wild pig glared belligerently at him, shuffled indecisively, then ignored him, and burrowing his snout into the soft earth, headed back into the brush. Creb breathed a sigh of relief, then continued downstream. He stopped at a narrow sandy bank, spread out his cloak, put the skull of the cave bear on it, and sat down facing it. He made formalized gestures asking Ursus for assistance, then cleared his mind of all thoughts except for the babies who needed to know their totems.

Children had always intrigued Creb. Often, when he sat in the midst of the clan, apparently lost in thought, he was observing the children without anyone being aware of it. One of the youngsters was a robust, strapping boy about halfway into his first year, who had howled belligerently at his birth and many times since, especially when he wanted to be fed. From the very first, Borg was always nuzzling his mother, burrowing into her soft breast until he found the nipple, and making little grunting noises of pleasure as he nursed. It reminded him, Creb thought with humor, of the boar he had just seen grunting as he burrowed into the soft earth. The boar was an animal worthy of respect. It was intelligent, the vicious canines could inflict serious damage when the beast was aroused, and the short legs could move with amazing speed when it decided to charge. No hunter would disdain such a totem. And it will be suitable for this new place; its spirit will rest easy in the new cave. A boar it is, he decided, convinced the boy's totem had shown himself so the magician would be reminded of him.

Mog-ur felt satisfied with the choice and turned his attention to the other baby. Ona, whose mother had lost her mate in the earthquake, had been born not long before the cataclysm. Vorn, her four-year-old sibling, was the only male around that fire now. Aga will need another mate soon, the magician mused, one who will take Aba, her old mother, too. But that's Brun's worry; it's Ona I need to think about, not her mother.

Girls needed gentler totems; they could not be stronger than a male totem or they would fight off the impregnating essence and the woman would bear no children. He thought about Iza. Her saiga antelope had been too much for her mate's totem to overcome for many years—or had it? Mog-ur often wondered about that. Iza knew more magic than many people realized, and she was not happy with the man to whom she had been given. Not that he blamed her, in many ways. She had always conducted herself properly, but the strain between them was apparent. Well, the man is gone now, Creb thought. Mog-ur will be her provider, if not her mate.

As her sibling, Creb could never mate Iza, it would be against all tradition, but he had long since lost his desire for a mate. Iza was a good companion, she had cooked for him and cared for him for many years, and it might be more pleasant around the hearth now without the constant undertone of animosity. Ayla might make it more so. Creb felt a flush of gentle warmth remembering her little arms reaching out to hug him. Later, he said to himself, first Ona.

She was a quiet contented baby who often stared at him solemnly with her large round eyes. She watched everything with silent interest, missing nothing, or so it seemed. The picture of an owl flashed in his mind. Too strong? The owl is a hunting bird, he thought, but it only hunts small animals. When a woman had a strong totem, her mate's needed to be much stronger. No man with weak protection could mate a woman with an owl totem, but perhaps she will have need of a man with strong protection. An owl, then, he decided. All women need mates with strong totems. Is that why I never took a mate? Creb thought. How much protection can a roe deer give? Iza's birth totem is stronger. Creb hadn't thought of the gentle, shy roe deer as his totem for many years. It, too, inhabited these thick forests, like the boar, he suddenly remembered. The magician was one of the few who had two totems—Creb's was the roe deer, Mog-ur's was Ursus.

Ursus Spelaeus, the cave bear, massive vegetarian towering over his omnivorous cousins by nearly twice their standing height, with a gigantic shaggy bulk of three times their weight, the largest bear ever known, was normally slow to anger. But one nervous she-bear attacked a defenseless, crippled boy who wandered, lost in thought, too close to a young cub. It was the lad's mother who found him, torn and bleeding, his eye ripped away with half his face, and she who nursed him back to health. She amputated his useless, paralyzed arm below the elbow, crushed by the huge creature's enormous strength. Not long afterward, Mog-ur-before-him selected the deformed and scarred child as acolyte and told the boy Ursus had chosen him, tested him and found him worthy, and took his eye as a sign that Creb was under his protection. His scars should be worn with pride, he was told, they were the mark of his new totem.

Ursus never allowed his spirit to be swallowed by a woman to produce a child; the Cave Bear offered his protection only after testing. Few were chosen; fewer survived. His eye was a great price to pay, but Creb was not sorry. He was The Mog-ur. No magician ever had his power, and that power, Creb was sure, was given to him by Ursus. And now, Mog-ur asked for his totem's help.

Clutching his amulet, he implored the spirit of the Great Bear to bring forth the spirit of the totem that protected the girl born to the Others. This was a true test of his ability, and he wasn't at all sure the message would come through to him. He concentrated on the child and what little he knew of her. She is fearless, he thought. She had been openly affectionate to him, showing fear neither of him nor of the censure of the clan. Rare for a girl; girls usually hid behind their mothers when he was around. She was curious and learned quickly. A picture started to form in his mind, but he pushed it aside. No, that's not right, she's female, that's not a female totem. He cleared his mind and tried again, but the picture returned. He decided to let it play out; perhaps it was leading to something else.

He envisioned a pride of cave lions lazily warming themselves in the hot summer sun of the open steppes. There were two cubs. One was leaping playfully in the tall sere grass, poking her nose curiously into the holes of small rodents and growling in mock attack. It was a she-cub; it was she who would grow into a lioness, the primary hunter of the pride; it was she who would bring her kill to her mate. The cub bounded up to a shaggy-maned male and tried to entice him to play. Fearlessly, she reached up with a paw and batted the adult cat's massive muzzle. It was a gentle touch, almost a caress. The huge lion pushed her down and held her with a heavy paw, then began washing the cub with his long, rough tongue. Cave lions rear their young with affection and discipline, too, he thought, wondering why this scene of feline domestic felicity came to him.

Mog-ur tried to clear his mind of the picture, tried once more to concentrate on the girl, but the scene would not shift.

"Ursus," he motioned, "a Cave Lion? It can't be. A female cannot have so powerful a totem. What man could she ever mate with?"

No man in his clan had a Cave Lion totem, not many men in all the clans did. He visualized the tall, skinny child, straight arms and legs, flat face with a large, bulging forehead, pale and washed out; even her eyes were too light. She will be an ugly woman, Mog-ur thought honestly. What man is likely to want her anyway? The thought of his own repulsiveness crossed his mind, and the way women had avoided him, especially when he was younger. Perhaps she will never mate, she would need the protection of a strong totem if she had to live out her life with no man to protect her. But, a Cave Lion? He tried to remember if there had ever been a woman of the Clan with the huge cat for a totem.

She is not really Clan, he reminded himself, and there was no doubt her protection was strong or she wouldn't be alive. She would have been killed by that cave lion. The thought crystallized in his mind. The cave lion! It attacked her, but it did not kill ... or did it attack? Was it testing her? Then another thought burst through and a chill of recognition crept up his spine. All doubt was swept out of his mind. He was sure. Not even Brun can doubt it, he thought. The cave lion had marked her with four parallel grooves in her left thigh, scars she would carry for the rest of her life. At a manhood ceremony, when Mog-ur carved the mark of a young man's totem on his body, *the mark for a Cave Lion was four parallel lines carved into the thigh!*

On a male, they are marked on the right thigh; but she is female, and the marks are the same. Of course! Why hadn't he realized it before? The lion knew it would be difficult for the clan to accept, so he marked her himself, but so clearly, no one could mistake it. And he marked her with Clan totem marks. The Cave Lion wanted the Clan to know. He wants her to live with us. He took her people so she would have to live with us. Why? The magician was jarred by a feeling of uneasiness, the same feeling he had experienced after the ceremony the day she was found. If he'd had a concept for it, he would have called it a sense of foreboding, yet tinged with a strange unnerving hope.

Mog-ur shook it off. Never had a totem come so strongly to him before; that was what unnerved him, he thought. The Cave Lion is her totem. He chose her, just as Ursus chose me. Mog-ur looked into the dark empty eye sockets of the skull in front of him. With profound acceptance, he marveled at the ways of the spirits, once they were understood. It was all so clear now. He was relieved—and overwhelmed. Why should this small girl have need of such powerful protection?

5

Black-leafed trees waved and fluttered in the twilight breeze, dancing silhouettes against a darkening sky. The camp was quiet, settling down for the night. By the dim glow of hot coals, Iza checked the contents of several small pouches spread out in orderly rows on her cloak, glancing up now and then in the direction she had seen Creb leave. She was concerned about him off by himself in unfamiliar woods without weapons to defend himself. The child was already asleep, and the woman grew more worried as the daylight waned.

Earlier, she had inspected the vegetation growing around the cave, wanting to know the availability of plants to replenish and enlarge her pharmacopoeia. She always carried certain things with her in the otter-skin bag, but to her, the small pouches of dried leaves, flowers, roots, seeds, and barks in her medicine bag were only first aid. In the new cave she would have room for greater quantity and variety. She never went far without her medicine bag, though. It was as much a part of her as her wrap. More. She would have felt naked without her medicines, not without her wrap.

Iza finally saw the old magician hobbling back, and relieved, she jumped up to put the food saved for him on the fire to warm and started water boiling for his favorite herb tea. He shuffled up, then eased himself down by her side as she was putting her small pouches into the larger one.

"How is the child tonight?" he motioned.

"Resting easier. Her pain is nearly gone. She asked for you," Iza replied.

Creb grunted, inwardly pleased. "Make an amulet for her in the morning, Iza."

The woman bowed her head in acknowledgment, then she jumped up again to check the food and water. She had to move. She was so happy, she couldn't sit still. Ayla is going to stay. Creb must have talked to her totem, Iza

61

thought, her heart beating with excitement. The mothers of the two babies had made amulets that day. They were very obvious about it so everyone would know their children would learn their totems at the cave ceremony. It presaged good luck for them and the two women were almost strutting with pride. Was that why Creb was gone so long? It must have been difficult for him. Iza wondered what Ayla's totem was but repressed an urge to ask. He wouldn't tell her anyway and she would find out soon enough.

She brought her sibling his food, and tea for both of them. They sat quietly together, a comfortable, affectionate warmth between them. When Creb finished, they were the only ones still awake.

"The hunters will go out in the morning," Creb said. "If they make a good kill, the ceremony will be the next day. You will be prepared?"

"I checked the bag, there are enough roots. I will be ready," Iza motioned, holding up a small pouch. It was different from the others. The leather had been dyed a deep brownish red, with fine-powdered red ochre mixed into the bear fat that had been used to cure the cave bear skin it was made from. No other woman had anything colored the sacred red, although everyone in the clan carried a piece of red ochre in their amulets. It was the holiest relic Iza possessed. "I will purify myself in the morning."

Again Creb grunted. It was the usual noncommittal comment used by men when responding to a woman. It carried only enough meaning to indicate the woman had been understood, without acknowledging too much significance in what she said. They remained quiet for a while, then Creb put his small tea bowl down and looked at his sibling.

"Mog-ur will provide for you and the girl, and your child if it is a girl. You will share my fire in the new cave, Iza," he said, then reached for his staff to help himself up and hobbled to his sleeping place.

Iza had started to get up but sat back down, thunderstruck by his announcement. It was the last thing she expected. With her mate gone, she knew some other man would have to provide for her. She had tried to put thoughts of her fate out of her mind—it made no difference how she felt, Brun would not consult her—but she couldn't help thinking about it sometimes. Of the possible options, some didn't appeal to her and the rest she thought were unlikely.

There was Droog; since Goov's mother had been killed in the earthquake, he was alone now. Iza respected Droog. He was the best maker of tools in the clan. Any of them could chip flakes from a flint boulder to make a rough hand-axe or scraper, but Droog had a real talent for it. He could preshape the stone so that the flakes he knapped off would have the size and shape he wanted. His knives, scrapers, all his tools, were highly prized. If the choice were hers, of all the men in the clan, Iza would choose Droog. He had been good to the acolyte's mother. There had been a genuine fondness in their relationship.

It was more likely, though, Iza knew, that Aga would be given to him. Aga was younger, and already the mother of two children. Her son, Vorn, would soon need a hunter to be responsible for his training, and the baby, Ona, needed a man to provide for her until she grew up and mated herself. The toolmaker would probably be willing to take her mother, Aba, too. The old woman needed a place as well as her daughter. Taking on all those responsibilities would make quite a change in the life of the quiet, orderly toolmaker. Aga could be a little difficult at times, and she didn't have the understanding Goov's mother had had, but Goov would be setting up his own hearth soon, and Droog needed a woman.

Goov as a mate for her was entirely out of the question. He was too young, just barely a man, and hadn't even mated for the first time. Brun would never give him an old woman, and Iza would feel more like his mother than his mate.

Iza had thought about living with Grod and Uka, and the man who had been mated to Grod's mother, Zoug. Grod was a stiff, laconic man, but never cruel, and his loyalty to Brun was beyond question. She wouldn't have minded living with Grod, even though she'd be second woman. But Uka was Ebra's sister and had never quite forgiven Iza her status that had usurped her sibling's place. And since the death of her son—when he had not yet even moved to his own hearth—Uka was grieving and withdrawn. Not even Ovra, her daughter, was able to soften the woman's pain. There is too much unhappiness at that hearth, Iza had thought.

She had hardly considered Crug's fire. Ika, his mate and the mother of Borg, was an open, friendly young woman. That was just the trouble, they were both so young, and Iza had never gotten along very well with Dorv, the old man who had been the mate of Ika's mother, who shared their fire.

That left Brun, and she could not even be second woman at his hearth; he was her sibling. Not that it mattered, she had her own status. At least she wasn't like the poor old woman who had finally found her way to the world of the spirits during the earthquake. She had come from another clan, her mate had died long before, she never had any children, and had been traded off from fire to fire, always a burden; a woman with no status, no value.

But the possibility of sharing a hearth with Creb, of his providing for her hadn't even entered her mind. There was no one in the clan of whom she was fonder, man or woman. He even likes Ayla, she thought, I'm sure of it. It's a perfect arrangement—unless I have a boy. A boy needs to live with a man who can train him to be a hunter, and Creb can't hunt.

I could take the medicine to make me lose it, she thought for a moment. Then I could be sure I wouldn't have a boy. She patted her stomach and shook her head. No, it's too late, there could be problems. She realized she wanted the baby, and despite her age, her pregnancy had progressed without difficulty. The chances were good that the child would be normal and healthy, and children were too precious to give up lightly. I will ask my totem again to make the baby a girl. He knows I've wanted a girl all along. I promised I'd take care of myself so the baby he allowed to start would be healthy, if only he'd make it a girl.

Iza knew women of her years could have problems, and she ate foods and medicines that were helpful to pregnant women. Though never a mother, the medicine woman knew more about pregnancy, delivery, and nursing than most women. She had helped deliver all the youngsters in the clan and she dispensed her knowledge with her medication freely to the women. But there was some magic, passed down from mother to daughter, that was so secret, Iza would have died before revealing it, especially to a man. Any man who found out about it would never permit its use.

The secret had been kept only because no one, man or

woman, asked a medicine woman about her magic. The custom of avoiding direct queries was so long-standing, it had become tradition, almost law. She could share her knowledge if someone indicated an interest, but Iza never discussed her special magic because if a man had thought to ask, she could not have refused to answer—no woman could refuse to answer a man—and it was impossible for people of the Clan to lie. Their form of communication, dependent for subtle nuance on barely perceptible changes in expressions, gestures, and postures, made any attempt immediately detectable. They didn't even have a concept for it; the closest they could come to untruth was to refrain from speaking, and that was usually discerned, though often allowed.

Iza never mentioned the magic she had learned from her mother, but she had been using it. The magic prevented conception, prevented the spirit of a man's totem from entering her mouth to start a child. It never occurred to the man who had been her mate to ask her why she had not conceived a child. He assumed her totem was too strong for a woman. He often told her so and bemoaned the fact to the other men as the reason his totem's essence was not able to overcome hers. Iza used the plants to prevent conception because she wanted to shame her mate. She wanted the clan, and him, to think the impregnating element of his totem was too weak to break down the defenses of hers, even though he beat her.

The beatings were given, supposedly, to force her totem into submission, but Iza knew he enjoyed it. At first, she hoped her mate would give her to some other man if she produced no children. She hated the strutting braggart even before she was given to him, and when she found out who her mate was to be, she could do nothing but cling to her mother in desperation. Her mother could offer only consolation; she had no more say in the matter than her daughter. But her mate did not give her away. Iza was medicine woman, the highest-ranked woman in the Clan, and it gave him a feeling of manliness to have control over her. When the strength of his totem, and his manhood, was in question because his mate produced no offspring, the physical power he had over her compensated for it.

Though the beatings were allowed in the hope that they would result in a child, Iza sensed that Brun disapproved. She was sure if Brun had been leader at the time, she would not have been given to that particular man. A man did not prove his manhood, in Brun's opinion, by overcoming women. Women had no alternative but to submit. It was unworthy of a man to pit himself against a lesser adversary or to allow his emotions to be provoked by a woman. It was a man's duty to command women, to maintain discipline, to hunt and provide, to control his emotions, and to show no sign of pain when he was suffering. A woman might be cuffed if she was lazy or disrespectful, but not in anger and not with joy, only to discipline. Though some men struck women more often than others, few men made a habit of it. Only Iza's mate had made it a regular practice.

After Creb joined their fire, her mate was even more reluctant to give her away. Iza was not only medicine woman, she was the woman who cooked for Mog-ur. If Iza left his fire, Mog-ur would too. Her mate had imagined that the rest of the clan thought he was learning secrets from the great magician. In truth, Creb was never more than properly polite in all the time they shared the same hearth and hardly deigned to notice the man on many occasions. Especially, Iza was sure, when Creb noticed a particularly colorful bruise.

For all the beatings, Iza continued to make use of her herbal magic. Yet, when she found herself pregnant, she resigned herself to her fate. Some spirit had finally overcome both her totem and her magic. Perhaps it was his; but, Iza thought, if the vital principle of his totem had finally prevailed, why had the spirit deserted him when the cave collapsed? She held out one last hope. She wished for a daughter, a girl to detract from his newly gained esteem, and a girl to carry on her line of medicine women, though she had been ready to end the line with herself rather than have a child while she lived with her mate. If she gave birth to a son, her mate would have been fully vindicated; a girl would still leave something to be desired. Now Iza wanted a girl even more—not to deny her dead mate's posthumous prestige, but to allow her to live with Creb.

Iza put her medicine bag away and crawled into her fur beside the peacefully sleeping child. Ayla must be lucky, Iza thought. There's the new cave, and she is going to be allowed to stay with me, and we are going to share Creb's fire. Maybe her luck will bring me a daughter, too. Iza put her arm around Ayla and snuggled close to her warm little body.

After breakfast the next morning, Iza beckoned to the child and headed upstream. As they walked beside the water, the medicine woman looked for certain plants. After a few moments, Iza saw a clearing on the other side and crossed over. Growing on the open ground were several plants, about a foot high with dull green leaves attached to long stalks tipped with spikes of small, densely packed, green flowers. Iza dug up the red-rooted pigweed and headed for a marshy area beside sluggish backwater and found scouring-rush horsetail ferns and, farther upstream, soaproot. Ayla, following her, watched with interest, wishing she could communicate with the woman. Her head was full of questions she couldn't ask.

They went back to the campsite and Ayla watched her fill a tightly woven basket with water and add the stalky ferns and hot rocks from the fire. Ayla squatted beside the woman while Iza cut a circular piece with a sharp flake of stone out of the cloak she had used to carry the girl. Though soft and pliable, the fat-cured leather was tough, but the stone knife cut it with ease. With another stone tool, chipped to a point, Iza pierced several holes around the edge of the circle. Then she twisted tough stringy bark from a low-growing shrub into a cord and threaded it through the holes and pulled it tight to make a pouch. With a quick flick of her knife, one made by Droog and a tool Iza treasured, she cut off a piece of the long thong that held her wrap closed, first measuring it around Ayla's neck. The entire process took only a few moments.

When the water in the cooking basket was bubbling, Iza gathered up the other plants she had collected, along with the watertight wicker bowl, and went back to the stream. They walked along the bank until they came to a place where it eased into the water in a gradual slope. Finding a round stone she could hold easily in her hand, Iza pounded the soaproot with water in a saucerlike depression of a large flattish rock near the stream. The root sudsed into a rich, saponin-filled lather. Taking stone tools and other small items from the folds, Iza unwound the thong and removed her wrap. She slipped her amulet over her head and carefully placed it on top.

Ayla was delighted when Iza took her hand and led her into the stream. She loved the water. But after a thorough wetting, the woman picked her up, sat her on the rock, and lathered her from head to foot, including her stringy, matted hair. After dunking her in the cool water, the woman made a motion and squeezed her eyes shut. Ayla didn't understand the motion, but when she mimicked the woman, Iza nodded, and she understood the woman wanted her to close her eyes. The child felt her head being bent forward, then the warm liquid from the bowl of ferns poured over her. Her head had been itching and Iza had noticed tiny crawling vermin. The woman massaged in the lice-killing liquid extracted from the horsetail fern. After a second rinsing in the cold stream, Iza crushed the pigweed root together with its leaves and lathered it into her hair. A final dunking followed, then Iza performed the same ablutions on herself while the child played in the water.

While they were sitting on the bank letting the sun dry them, Iza peeled the bark off a twig with her teeth and used it to pull snarls out of their hair as it dried. She was astonished at the fine, silky softness of Ayla's near-white hair. Certainly unusual, Iza thought, but rather nice. It's really her best feature. She looked at the child without making it obvious. Though suntanned, the child was still lighter than she, and Iza thought the skinny, pale little girl with her light eyes was amazingly unattractive. Unusual looking people; there's no doubt they are human, but so ugly. Poor child. How will she ever find a mate?

If she doesn't mate, how will she ever have any status? She could be like the old woman who died in the earthquake, Iza thought. If she were my real daughter, then she'd have her own status too. I wonder if I could teach her some healing magic? That would give her some value. If I have a girl, I could train them both; and if I have a boy, there won't be another woman to carry on my line. The clan will need a new medicine woman someday. If Ayla knew the magic, they might accept her—some man might even be willing to mate her. She's going to be accepted into the clan; why can't she be my daughter? Iza already thought of the girl as hers, and her musings planted the germ of an idea.

She looked up, noticed the sun was much higher, and realized it was getting late. I must finish her amulet and then prepare to make the drink from the root, Iza said to herself, suddenly remembering her responsibilities.

"Ayla," she called to the child who had wandered toward the stream again. The girl came running. Looking at her leg, Iza saw the water had softened the scabs, but it was healing well. Hurrying back into her wrap, Iza led the child toward the ridge, stopping first to get her digging stick and the small pouch she had made. She had noticed a ditch of red soil just on the other side of it, near the place they had stopped before Ayla showed them the cave. When they reached it, she poked with her stick until several small chunks of red ochre broke loose. Picking up a few small pieces, she held them out to Ayla. The girl looked at them, not sure what was expected, then tentatively touched one. Iza took the small lump, put it in the pouch, and tucked the pouch in a fold. Before turning to go back, Iza looked out over the view and saw small figures moving across the plains below. The hunters had left early in the morning.

Many ages before, men and women, far more primitive than Brun and his five hunters, learned to compete for game with four-legged predators by watching and copying their methods. They saw, for example, how wolves, working together, could bring down prey many times larger and more powerful than themselves. Over time, using tools and weapons rather than claws and fangs, they learned that by cooperating, they, too, could hunt the large beasts that shared their environment. It prodded them along their evolutionary journey.

With a need for silence so as not to warn the game they were stalking, they developed hunting signals that evolved into the more elaborate hand signals and gestures used to communicate other needs and desires. Warning cries changed in pitch and tone to include greater informational content. Though the branch of the tree of man that led to the people of the Clan did not include sufficiently developed vocal mechanisms to evolve a full verbal language, it did not impair their ability to hunt.

The six men started out at first light. From their vantage point near the ridge, they watched the sun, sending its beams ahead as scouts, creep tentatively over the edge of the earth, then blazon forth in full command of the day. Toward the northeast, a vast cloud of soft loess dust shrouded an undulating mass of shaggy brown movement accented by curving black spikes; a broad trail of trampled earth, entirely devoid of vegetation, followed the slowly moving herd of bison defacing the golden green plains. No longer slowed by women and children, the hunters covered the distance to the steppes quickly.

Leaving the foothills behind, they fell into a ground-eating dogtrot, approaching the herd downwind. As they drew close, they crouched low in the tall grass watching the huge beasts. Gigantic humpbacked shoulders, tapering to narrow flanks behind, supported massive woolly heads bearing enormous black horns that spanned well over a yard in mature animals. The rangy, sweaty smell of the close-packed multitude assaulted their nostrils and the earth vibrated with the movement of thousands of hooves.

Brun, holding up a hand to shade his eyes, studied each individual creature that passed, waiting for the right animal in the right circumstances. To look at the man, it was impossible to tell the unbearable tension the leader kept under tight control. Only his pulsing temples above locked jaws betrayed his nervously pounding heart and raw-edged nerves. This was the most important hunt of his life. Not even his first kill that had elevated him to the status of manhood matched this one, for on it rested the final condition for residence in the new cave. A successful hunt would not only bring meat for the feast that would be part of the cave ceremony, but would assure the clan that their totems did, indeed, favor their new home. If the hunters returned empty-handed from their first hunt, the clan would be required to search further for a cave more acceptable to their protective spirits. It was their totems' way of warning them that the cave was unlucky. When Brun saw the huge herd of bison, he was encouraged. They were the embodiment of his own totem.

Brun glanced at his hunters waiting anxiously for his signal. Waiting was always the hardest part, but a premature move could have disastrous results, and if it was humanly possible, Brun was going to make sure nothing went wrong with the hunt. He caught the worried expression on Broud's face and almost regretted, for a fleeting moment, his decision to let the son of his mate make the kill. Then he remembered the boy's shining eyes filled with pride when the leader told him to prepare himself for his manhood hunt. It's normal for the boy to be nervous, Brun thought. It's not only his manhood hunt, the clan's new home may depend on his strong right arm.

Broud noticed Brun's glance and quickly controlled the expression that gave away his inner turmoil. He hadn't realized how huge a living bison was—standing up straight, the hump at the shoulders of the lumbering beast was a foot or more above his head—or how overpowering a full herd of them could be. He would have to make at least the first telling wound to be credited with the kill. What if I miss? What if I strike wrong and he gets away? Broud's thoughts were in turmoil.

Gone was the lad's feeling of superiority strutting in front of Oga making practice thrusts while she looked on with adoration. He pretended not to notice; she was only a child, a girl child at that. But it would not be long before she was a woman. Oga might not be a bad mate when she grows up, Broud thought. She will need a strong hunter to protect her now that both her mother and her mother's mate are gone. Broud liked the way she took special pains to wait on him since she had come to live with them, eagerly running to obey his every wish even though he wasn't even a man yet. But what will she think of me if I don't make the kill? What if I can't become a man at the cave ceremony? What would Brun think? What would the whole clan think? What if we have to leave the beautiful new cave already blessed by Ursus? Broud clutched his spear tighter and reached for his amulet in a pleading gesture to the Woolly Rhinoceros to give him courage and a strong arm.

There was little chance of the animal getting away if Brun could help it. He let the lad think the fate of the clan's new cave rested on him. If he was going to be leader someday, he might as well learn the weight of responsibility of the position now. He would give the boy his chance, but Brun planned to be nearby to make the kill himself, if necessary. He hoped, for the boy's sake, he wouldn't have to. The lad was proud, his humiliation would be great, but the leader had no intention of sacrificing the cave to Broud's pride.

Brun turned back to watching the herd. Shortly, he sighted a young bull straggling away from the throng. The animal was nearly full grown, but still young and inexperienced. Brun waited until the bison drifted farther away from the rest, for a moment when he was a solitary creature away from the security of the herd. Then he signaled.

The men darted off instantly, fanning out, Broud leading off. Brun watched as they spaced themselves at regular intervals, anxiously keeping an eye on the straying young bison. He signaled again and the men sprang toward the herd, yelping and shouting and waving their arms. Startled animals near the edge began to run into the main body of the herd, closing the gaps and nudging the ones near the edge toward the center. At the same time, Brun dashed between them and the young bull, veering him away.

While the frightened beasts at the periphery plowed into the milling multitude, Brun pounded after the one he had singled out. He poured every ounce of energy into the chase, driving the bull as fast as his thick muscular legs could move. The dry earth of the steppes filled the air with fine silty soil, churned up by the hoard of hard-hooved bison as the movement at the edge rippled through the throng. Brun squinted and coughed, blinded by the swirling dust that clogged his nostrils and choked his breath. Gasping, nearly spent, he saw Grod pick up the chase.

The bull veered again at Grod's fresh spurt. The men were moving in, forming a large circle that would bring the beast back to Brun as he jogged, still panting, to close the circle. The vast herd was in full stampede, charging across the prairie—their unreasoned fear multiplied by the movement itself. Only the young bull was left, running in panic from a creature with a fraction of his strength, but with more than enough intelligence and determination to compensate for the difference. Grod pummeled after him, refusing to give in though his pounding heart threatened to burst. Sweat made rivulets in the film of dust that covered his body and gave his beard a dun cast. Grod finally stumbled to a halt just as Droog took his place.

The hunters' endurance was great, but the strong young bison pushed ahead with untiring energy. Droog was the tallest man in the clan, his legs a shade longer. Urging the beast forward, Droog bore down on him with a fresh burst of speed, heading him off when he tried to follow the trail of the departing herd. By the time Crug took over from the exhausted Droog, the young animal was visibly winded. Crug was fresh and he pushed the beast on, forcing a new spurt of energy from the flagging bison with a touch of his sharp spear on the flank.

When Goov jumped into the relay, the huge shaggy creature was slowing. The bull ran blindly, doggedly, followed closely by Goov, constantly prodding him to drain the last drop of strength remaining to the young animal. Broud saw Brun moving in as he let out a yelp and took his turn racing after the massive beast. His sprint was short-lived. The bison had had enough. He slowed, then stopped altogether and refused to move, his hide lathered, his head drooping, his mouth foaming. With his spear held ready, the boy approached the exhausted bull.

With a judgment born of experience, Brun made a quick appraisal. Was the lad unusually nervous for a first kill, or overanxious? Was the beast completely drained? Some wily old bison stopped short of total exhaustion, and a last-minute charge could kill or seriously injure a hunter, especially an inexperienced one. Should he use his bola to trip the animal and knock him down? The brute's head nearly dragged the ground, his heaving sides left no doubt, the bison was spent. If he used his bola, the boy's first kill would have less distinction. Brun decided to allow Broud the full honor.

Quickly, before the bison regained his wind, Broud stepped up to the enormous shaggy animal and lifted his spear. With a last-minute thought of his totem, he pulled back and lunged. The long heavy spear bit deep into the young bull's side; its fire-hardened point pierced the tough hide and cracked a rib in the swift, fatal thrust. The bison bellowed with pain, turning to gore his attacker even as his legs buckled. Brun saw the motion and jumped to the young man's side, and with the full force of his powerful muscles, crashed his club down on the great head. His blow added impetus to the creature's fall. The bison fell over on his side, his sharp hooves pawed the air in final death throes, then he lay still.

Broud was stunned at first and a little overwhelmed, then his sharp cry burst into the air as the young man screamed his triumph. He did it! He made his first kill! He was a man!

Broud was exultant. He reached for his deeply embedded spear sticking upright out of the animal's side. Yanking it free, he felt a warm spurt of blood on his face and tasted its salty flavor. Brun clapped Broud on the shoulder, pride in his eyes.

"Well done," the gesture eloquently said. Brun was glad to add another strong hunter to his ranks, a strong hunter who was his pride and joy, the son of his mate, the son of his heart.

The cave was theirs. The ritual ceremony would cement it, but Broud's kill had assured it. The totems were pleased. Broud held up the bloody point of his spear as the rest of the hunters ran toward them, joy in their steps at the sight of the downed beast. Brun's knife was out, ready to slit open the belly and gut the bison before they carried it back to the cave. He removed the liver, cut it into slices, and gave a piece to each hunter. It was the choicest part, reserved for men alone, imparting strength to muscle and eye needed for hunting. Brun cut out the heart of the great shaggy creature, too, and buried it in the ground near the animal, a gift he had promised his totem.

Broud chewed the warm raw liver, his first taste of manhood, and thought his heart would burst with happiness. He would become a man at the ceremony to sanctify the new cave, he would lead the hunt dance, he would join the men in the secret rituals to be held in the small cave, and he would gladly have given his life just to see that look of pride on Brun's face. This was Broud's supreme moment. He anticipated the attention that would be his after his manhood rites at the cave ceremony. He would have all the clan's admiration, all their respect. All their talk would be of him and his great hunting prowess. It would be his night, and Oga's eyes would shine with unspoken devotion and worshipful homage.

The men tied the legs of the bison together well above the knee joints. Grod and Droog bound their spears together, Crug and Goov did the same, making two reinforced poles of the four spears. One was passed between the forelegs, the other between the hind legs, horizontally across the great beast. Brun and Broud stepped to either side of the shaggy head and gripped a horn, leaving one hand free to hold their spears. Grod and Droog each grabbed one end of the pole on each side of the forelegs, while Crug went to the left and Goov to the right of the hind legs. At a signal from their leader, all six men heaved forward, half dragging and half lifting the huge animal along the grassy plains. The journey back to the cave took much longer than the trip out. The men, for all their strength, strained under the load as they skidded the bison across the steppes and up the foothills.

Oga was watching for them and saw the returning hunters far down on the plains below. When they neared the ridge, the clan was waiting for them and trouped out to accompany the hunters the last part of the way back to the cave, walking beside them in silent acclaim. Broud's position in front of the victorious men announced his kill. Even Ayla, who couldn't understand what was going on, was caught up in the excitement that hung palpably in the air.

6

"The son of your mate did well, Brun. It was a good clean kill," Zoug said as the hunters eased the great beast down in front of the cave. "You have a new hunter to be proud of."

"He showed courage and a strong arm," Brun gestured. He laid his hand on the young man's shoulder, his eyes glowing with pride. Broud basked in the warm praise.

Zoug and Dorv examined the mighty young bull with admiration, tinged with nostalgia for the excitement of the chase and the thrill of success, forgetting the dangers and disappointments that were part of the arduous adventure of hunting big game. No longer able to hunt with the younger men, but not wanting to be left out, the two old men had spent the morning scouting the wooded hillsides for smaller prey.

"I see you and Dorv put your slings to good use. I could smell the meat cooking halfway up the hill," Brun continued. "When we get settled in the new cave, we'll have to find a place to practice. The clan would benefit if all the hunters had your skill with the sling, Zoug. And it won't be long before Vorn will need to be trained."

The leader was aware of the contribution the older men still made to the sustenance of the clan and wanted them to know it. The hunters were not always successful. More than once meat was supplied by the efforts of the older men, and during the heavy snows of winter, occasional fresh meat was often more easily brought down with a sling. It provided a welcome change from their winter diet of dried preserved meat, especially later in the season when the frozen supplies from late fall hunts ran out.

"Nothing like the young bison there, but we got a few rabbits and a fat beaver. The food is ready, we've just been waiting for you," Zoug motioned. "I did notice a level clearing not far away that might make a good practice field."

Zoug, who had lived with Grod since the death of his mate, had worked to improve his skill with the sling after he retired from the ranks of Brun's hunters. It, and the bola, were the most difficult weapons for the men of the clan to master. Though their muscular, heavy-boned, and slightly bowed arms were tremendously powerful, they could perform functions as delicate and precise as knapping flint. The development of their arm joints, particularly the way muscles and tendons were attached to bones, gave them precise manual dexterity coupled with unbelievable strength. But there was a penalty. That same joint development restricted arm movement. They could not make a full, free-swinging arc, which limited their ability to hurl objects. Not fine control but leverage was the price they paid for strength.

Their spear was not a javelin, thrown across a distance, but rather a lance thrust at close range with great force. Training with spear or club was little more than developing powerful muscles, but learning to use a sling or a bola took years of practice and concentration. The sling, a strip of flexible leather held together at both ends and whirled around the head to gain momentum before flinging the round pebble held in the bulging cup at the middle, took great effort, and Zoug was proud of his ability to sling a stone accurately. He was equally proud that Brun called upon him to train young hunters in the use of that weapon.

While Zoug and Dorv ranged the hillsides hunting with slings, the women had foraged over the same terrain, and the tantalizing aroma of cooking food whetted the appetites of the hunters. It made them realize that hunting was hungry work. They did not have long to wait.

The men relaxed after the meal, replete with satisfaction, retelling the incidents of the exciting hunt for their own pleasure and the benefit of Zoug and Dorv. Broud, glowing with his new status and the hearty congratulations of his new peers, noticed Vorn looking at him with unabashed admiration. Until that morning, Broud and Vorn had been equals, and Vorn had been his only male companion among the children of the clan since Goov had become a man.

Broud remembered hanging around hunters just returned from the hunt as Vorn was doing. No more would he have to stand on the fringes ignored by the men as he eagerly watched them tell their stories; no more would he be subject to the commands of his mother and the other women calling him away to help with the chores. He was a hunter now, a man. His manhood status lacked only the final ceremony, and that would be part of the cave ceremony, which would make it especially memorable and lucky.

When that happened, he would be the lowest-ranked male, but it mattered little to him. It would change, his place was foreordained. He was the son of the mate of the leader; someday the mantle of leadership would fall to him. Vorn had been a pest sometimes, but now Broud could afford to be magnanimous. He walked over to the four-year-old boy, not unaware that Vorn's eyes lit up with eager anticipation when he saw the new hunter approaching.

"Vorn, I think you're old enough," Broud motioned a little pompously, trying to seem more manly. "I will make a spear for you. It's time you began training to be a hunter."

Vorn squirmed with delight, pure adulation shining out of his eyes as he looked up at the young man who had so recently gained the coveted status of hunter.

"Yes," he nodded in vigorous agreement. "I'm old enough, Broud," the youngster motioned shyly. He gestured toward the stout shaft with the dark bloodstained point. "Could I touch it?"

Broud laid the point of his spear on the ground in front of the boy. Vorn reached out a tentative finger and touched the dried blood of the huge bison that now lay on the ground in front of the cave. "Were you scared, Broud?" he asked.

"Brun says all hunters are nervous on their first hunt," Broud replied, not wanting to admit his fears.

"Vorn! There you are! I should have guessed. You're supposed to be helping Oga collect wood," Aga said, seeing her son who had slipped away from the women and children. Vorn straggled after his mother, glancing back over his shoulder at his new idol. Brun had been watching the son of his mate with approval. It is the sign of a good leader, he thought, not to forget the boy just because he is still a child. Someday Vorn will be a hunter, and when Broud is leader, Vorn will remember a kindness shown to him as a child.

Broud watched Vorn trail behind his mother dragging his feet. Just the day before, Ebra had come for him to help with the chores, he remembered. He glanced at the women digging a pit and had an urge to sneak away so his mother wouldn't see him, but then he noticed Oga looking in his direction. My mother can't tell me what to do anymore. I'm not a child, I'm a man. She has to obey me now, Broud thought, puffing up his chest a little. She does, doesn't she . . . and Oga is watching.

"Ebra! Bring me a drink of water!" he commanded imperiously, swaggering toward the women. He half expected his mother to tell him to get wood. Technically he wouldn't be a man until after his manhood ceremony.

Ebra looked up at him, and her eyes filled with pride. That was her baby boy who had discharged his mission so effectively, her son who had reached the exalted status of manhood. She jumped up, went to the pool near the cave, and returned quickly with water, glancing haughtily at the other women as if to say, "Look at my son! Isn't he a fine man? Isn't he a brave hunter?"

His mother's alacrity and her look of pride eased his defensiveness and disposed him to favor her with a grunt of acknowledgment. Ebra's response pleased him almost as much as the demurely bowed head of Oga and the look of adoration he noticed as her eyes followed him when he turned to leave.

Oga had been grief-stricken over the death of her mother, following so soon after the death of her mother's mate. As the only child of the pair, even though she was a girl she had been dearly loved by both. Brun's mate was kind to her when she went to live with the leader's family, sitting with them when she ate and walking behind Ebra while they were searching for a cave. But Brun frightened her. He was more stern than her mother's mate had been; his responsibility lay heavily on his shoulders. Ebra's main concern was for Brun and no one had much time for the orphaned girl while they were traveling. But Broud had seen her sitting alone staring dejectedly into the fire one evening. Oga was overwhelmed with gratitude when the proud boy, almost a man, who had seldom paid attention to her before, sat down beside her and put an arm around her shoulder as she softly keened her grief. From that moment on, Oga lived with one desire: when she became a woman, she wanted to be given to Broud as his mate.

The late afternoon sun was warm in the motionless air. Not the hint of a breeze stirred the least leaf. The expectant hush was disturbed only by the drone of flies taking their turn at the remains of the repast and the sounds of the women digging a roasting pit. Ayla was sitting beside Iza as the medicine woman searched in her otter-skin pouch for the red bag. The child had been tagging behind her all day, but now there were certain rituals Iza had to perform with Mog-ur in preparation for the important role she had to play in the cave ceremony the next day, now that they were certain there would be one. She led the towheaded girl toward the group of women excavating a deep hole not far from the cave mouth. It would be lined with rocks, with a large fire built inside that would burn all night. In the morning, the skinned and quartered bison, wrapped in leaves, would be lowered into the pit, covered with more leaves and a layer of soil, and left to cook in the stone oven until late afternoon.

The excavation was a slow and tedious process. Pointed digging sticks were used to break up the soil that was scooped out by throwing handfuls on a leather cloak, which was hauled up out of the pit and dumped. But once the pit was dug, it could be used many times, only requiring an occasional cleaning out of ashes. While the women dug, Oga and Vorn, under the watchful eye of Uka's unmated daughter, Ovra, were collecting wood and bringing stones up from the stream.

As Iza approached holding the child's hand, the women stopped. "I must see Mog-ur," Iza said with a gesture. Then she gave Ayla a little shove toward the group. Ayla started to follow Iza as she turned to go, but the woman shook her head and pushed her back toward the women, then hurriedly left.

It was Ayla's first contact with anyone in the clan besides Iza and Creb, and she felt lost and shy without Iza's comforting presence. She stood rooted to the spot, nervously staring at her feet, glancing up apprehensively now and then. Against all propriety, everyone stared at the thin, long-legged girl with the peculiar flat face and bulging forehead. They had all been curious about the child, but this was their first opportunity to get a close look at her.

Ebra finally broke the spell. "She can gather wood," the leader's mate indicated with an unspoken motion to Ovra, then started digging again. The young woman walked toward a patch of trees and fallen logs. Oga and Vorn could hardly tear themselves away. Ovra beckoned to the two children impatiently, then beckoned to Ayla as well. The girl thought she understood the gesture, but she wasn't sure what was expected of her. Ovra motioned again, then turned and headed for the trees. The two clan members who were closest to Ayla's age reluctantly trailed after Ovra. The girl watched them go, then took a few hesitant steps after them.

When she reached the trees, Ayla stood around for a while watching Oga and Vorn pick up dried branches while Ovra hacked away at a good-sized fallen log with her stone hand-axe. Oga, returning from depositing a load of wood near the pit, started dragging toward the woodpile a section of the log Ovra had detached. Ayla saw her struggling and walked over to help. She bent over to pick up the opposite end of the log, and as they both stood up, she looked into Oga's dark eyes. They stopped and stared at each other for a moment.

The two girls were so different, yet so provocatively similar. Sprung from the same ancient seed, the progeny of their common ancestor took alternate routes, both leading to a richly developed, if dissimilar, intelligence. Both sapient, for a time both dominant, the gulf that separated them was not great. But the subtle differences created a vastly different destiny.

With each holding an end of the log, Ayla and Oga carried it to the pile of wood. As they walked back, side by side, the women stopped their work again and watched them go. The two girls were near the same height, though the taller was nearly twice the age of the other. One was slender, straight-limbed, fair-haired; the other stocky, bow-legged, darker. The women compared them, but the young girls, as with children everywhere, soon forgot their differences. Sharing made the task easier, and before the day was through they found ways to communicate and to add an element of play into the chore.

That evening they sought each other out and sat together while they ate, enjoying the pleasure of company closer to their own size. Iza was happy to see that Oga was accepting Ayla and waited until dark before she went to get the child for bed. They stared after each other as they parted, then Oga turned away and walked to her fur beside Ebra. The women and men still slept separately. Mog-ur's prohibition would not be lifted until they moved into the cave.

Iza's eyes were open with the first glimmer of early light. She lay still, listening to the melodious cacophony of birds chirping, warbling, twittering, and trilling in greeting to the new day. Soon, she was thinking, she would open her eyes to stone walls. She didn't mind sleeping outside as long as the weather was pleasant, but she looked forward to the security of walls. Her thoughts made her remember everything she had to do that day, and thinking about the cave ceremony with growing excitement, she quietly got up.

Creb was already awake. She wondered if he had slept at all; he was still sitting in the same place she left him the night before, staring in contemplative silence at the fire. She started heating water, and by the time she brought him his morning tea of mint, alfalfa, and nettle leaves, Ayla was up and sitting beside the crippled man. Iza brought the child a breakfast of leftovers from the previous evening's meal. The men and women would not eat that day until the ritual feast.

By late afternoon, delicious smells were drifting away from the several fires where food was cooking, and pervading the area near the cave. Utensils and other cooking paraphernalia that had been salvaged from their former cave and carried in the bundles by the women had been unpacked. Finely made, tightly woven waterproof baskets of subtle texture and design, created by slight alterations in weaving, were used to dip water from the pool and as cooking pots and containers. Wooden bowls were used in similar ways. Rib bones were stirrers, large flat pelvic bones were plates and platters along with thin sections of logs. Jaw and head bones were ladles, cups, and bowls. Birchbark glued together with balsam gum, some reinforced with a well-placed knot of sinew, were folded into shapes for many uses.

In an animal hide, hung from a thong-lashed frame set over a fire, a savory broth bubbled. Careful watch was kept to make sure the liquid didn't boil down too far. As long as the level of boiling broth was above the level reached by the flames, it kept the temperature of the skin pot too low to burn. Ayla watched Uka stir up chunks of the meat and bone from the neck of the bison that were cooking with wild onion, salty coltsfoot, and other herbs. Uka tasted it, then added peeled thistle stalks, mushrooms, lily buds and roots, watercress, milkweed buds, small immature yams, cranberries carried from the other cave, and wilted flowers from the previous day's growth of day lilies for thickening.

The hard fibrous old roots of cattails had been crushed and the fibers separated and removed. Dried blueberries they had carried with them and parched ground grains were added to the resulting starch that settled in the bottom of the baskets of cold water. Lumps of the flat, dark, unleavened bread were cooking on hot stones near the fire. Pigweed greens, lamb's-quarter, young clover, and dandelion leaves seasoned with coltsfoot were cooking in another pot, and a sauce of dried, tart apples mixed with wild rose petals and a lucky find of honey steamed near another fire.

Iza had been especially pleased when she saw Zoug returning from a trip to the steppes with a clutch of ptarmigan. The low-flying, heavy birds, easily brought down with stones from the marksman's sling, were Creb's favorite. Stuffed with herbs and edible greens that nested their own whole eggs, and wrapped in wild grape leaves, the savory fowl were cooking in a smaller stone-lined pit. Hares and giant hamsters, skinned and skewered, were roasting over hot coals, and mounds of tiny, fresh wild strawberries glistened bright red in the sun.

It was a feast worthy of the occasion.

Ayla wasn't sure she could wait. She had been wandering aimlessly around the fringes of the cooking area all day. Both Iza and Creb were off somewhere most of the time, and when Iza was around she was busy. Oga, too, was busily working with the women preparing the feast and no one had time or inclination to bother with the girl. After a few gruff words and not-so-gentle nudges from the harried women, she tried to stay out of the way.

As the long shadows of the late afternoon sun lay across the red soil that fronted the cave, a hush of anticipation descended on the clan. Everyone gathered around the large pit in which the haunches of bison were cooking. Ebra and Uka began removing the warm soil from the top. They pulled back limp, scorched leaves and exposed the sacrificial beast in a cloud of mouth-watering steam. So tender it almost fell from the bones, the meat was carefully raised. To Ebra, as the leader's mate, fell the duty of carving and serving, and her pride was obvious when she gave the first piece to her son.

Broud evidenced no false modesty as he stepped forward to receive his due. After all the men were served, the women received their share and then the children. Ayla was last, but there was more than enough for everyone, with leftovers to spare. The next hush that descended was the result of the hungry clan busily devouring the meal.

It was a leisurely feast, with one person or another going back to pick at a bit more bison or a second helping of a favorite dish. The women had worked hard, but their reward was not only the comments from the satisfied clan; they would not have to cook again for a few days. They all rested afterward, getting ready for a long evening.

When the lengthening shadows merged into the dull gray half-light of approaching darkness, the mood of the lazy afternoon subtly altered, became charged with expectation. At a glance from Brun, the women quickly cleared away the remains of the feast and took up places around an unlit fireplace at the mouth of the cave. The random look of the group belied the formality of their positions. The women stood in relation to each other according to their status. The men who gathered on the other side fell into a pattern according to their hierarchical place within the clan, but Mog-ur was not in sight.

Brun, closest to the front, signaled Grod, who stepped forward with slow dignity and from his aurochs horn produced a glowing coal. It was the most important in the long line of coals that began with the fire lighted in the debris of the old cave. A continuation of that fire symbolized the continuation of the life of the clan. Lighting this fire at the entrance would lay claim to the cave, establish it as their place of residence.

Controlled fire was a device of man, essential to life in a cold climate. Even smoke had beneficial properties; the smell alone evoked a feeling of safety and home. The smoke from the cave fire, filtering up through the cavern to the high-vaulted ceiling, would find its way out through cracks and on drafts through the opening. It would take away with it any unseen forces that might be inimical to them, purge the cave, and permeate it with their essence, the essence of human.

Lighting the fire was sufficient ritual to purify and lay claim to the cave, but certain other rituals were performed so often along with it, they were almost considered a part of the cave ceremony. One was familiarizing the spirits of their protective totems with their new home, usually done in private by Mog-ur with an audience of men only. Women were allowed their own celebration, which gave Iza reason to make a special drink for the men.

The successful hunt had already shown that their totems approved of the site, and the feast confirmed their intention to make it a permanent home, though the clan might be gone for extended periods at certain times. Totemic spirits traveled too, but as long as members of the clan had their amulets, their totems could track them from the cave and come when they were needed.

Since the spirits would be present at the cave ceremony anyway, other ceremonies could be included, and often were. Any ceremony was enhanced by association with the establishment of a new home and, in turn, added to the clan's territorial bond. Though each kind of ceremony had its own traditional ritual which never changed, ceremonial occasions had different characters depending upon which rituals were conducted.

Mog-ur, usually in consultation with Brun, decided how the various parts would be put together to form the total celebration, but it was an organic thing that depended on how they felt. This one would include Broud's manhood ceremony and one to name the totems of certain youngsters, since that needed to be done and they had a desire to please the spirits. Time was not an important factor—it would take as long as it took—but had they been harassed or in danger, simply lighting a fire would have made the cave theirs.

With gravity befitting the importance of the task, Grod kneeled down, put the glowing ember on the dry tinder, and began to blow. The clan leaned forward anxiously and expelled their breath in one communal sigh as flaming tongues licked the dry sticks in their first fatal taste. The fire took hold and, suddenly, appearing from nowhere, a frightful figure was seen standing so close to the bonfire, its roaring flames seemed to envelop him in their midst. It had a bright red face surmounted by an eerie white skull that appeared to hang within the fire itself unscathed by the leaping tendrils of lambent energy.

Ayla didn't see the fiery apparition at first and gasped when she caught sight of it. She felt Iza squeeze her hand in reassurance. The child felt the vibrations of the dull thud of spear butts pounding the ground and jumped back when the newest hunter leaped to the area in front of the flames just as Dorv beat a sharp tattoo in rhythmic counterpoint on a large wooden bowl-shaped instrument, turned face down against a log.

Broud crouched down and looked far into the distance, his hand shading his eyes from a nonexistent sun, as other hunters leaped up to join him in a reenactment of the bison hunt. So evocative was their skill at pantomime, polished by generations of communicating by gesture and signal, the intense emotion of the hunt was re-created. Even the five-year-old stranger was captivated by the impact of the drama. The women of the clan, perceptive of the fine nuances, were transported to the hot dusty plains. They could feel the thundering hooves vibrating the earth, taste the choking dust, share the exultation of the kill. It was a rare privilege for them to be allowed this glimpse into the sacrosanct life of the hunters.

From the first, Broud took command of the dance. It had been his kill, and it was his night. He could sense the empathetic emotions, feel the women quivering with fear, and he responded with more passionately intense dramatics. Broud was a consummate actor and never more in his element than when he was the center of attention. He played on the emotions of his audience, and the ecstatic shudder that passed through the women as he replayed his final thrust had an erotic quality. Mog-ur, watching from behind the fire, was no less impressed: he often saw the men talk of hunting, but only during these infrequent ceremonies was he able to share the experience in anything close to its full range of excitement. The lad did well, the magician thought, moving around to the front of the fire; he earned his totem mark. Perhaps he deserves to swagger a little.

The young man's final lunge brought him directly in front of the powerful man of magic as the dull thudding rhythm and the excited staccato counterpoint ended with a flourish. The old magician and the young hunter stood facing each other. Mog-ur knew how to play his role, too. The master of timing waited, letting the excitement of the hunt dance subside and a sense of expectancy rise. His hulking, lopsided figure, cloaked in a heavy bearskin, was silhouetted against the blazing fire. His ochre-reddened face was shadowed by his own frame, masking his features to an indefinable blur with the baleful, asymmetrical eye of a supernatural daemon.

The stillness of the night was disturbed only by the

crackling fire, a soft wind soughing through the trees, and the whooping cackle of a hyena in the distance. Broud was panting and his eyes glittered, partly from the exertion of the dance, partly from the excitement and his pride, but more from a growing, disquieting fear.

He knew what came next, and the longer it took, the more he fought to control a chill that wanted to be a tremble. It was time for Mog-ur to carve his totem mark into his flesh. He hadn't let himself think about it, but now that the time had come, Broud found himself dreading more than the pain. The magician projected an aura that filled the young man with a much greater fear.

He was treading on the threshold of the spirit world; the place that encompassed beings far more terrifying than gigantic bison. For all their size and strength, bison were at least solid, substantial creatures of the physical world, creatures that a man could come to grips with. But the invisible yet far more powerful forces that could make the very earth shake were another matter entirely. Broud was not the only one present who stifled a shudder as thoughts of the recently experienced earthquake suddenly imploded on their minds. Only holy men, mog-urs, dared to face that insubstantial plane, and the superstitious young man wished this greatest of all mog-urs would hurry and get it over with.

As though in answer to Broud's silent plea, the magician lifted his arm and stared up at the crescent moon. Then with smooth-flowing motions, he began an impassioned appeal. But his audience was not the mesmerized watching clan. His eloquence was directed to the ethereal, though no less real, world of the spirits—and his motions were eloquent. Using every subtle trick of posture, every nuance of gesture, the one-armed man had overcome his handicap to his own language. He was more expressive with his single arm than most men were with two. By the time he was through, the clan knew they were surrounded by the essence of their protective totems and a host of other unknown spirits, and Broud's chill became a shiver.

Then quickly, with a suddenness that brought a gasp to a few lips, the magician whipped out a sharp stone knife from a fold of his wrap and held it high over his head. He brought the sharp tool down swiftly, plunging it toward Broud's chest. In a movement that was under absolute control, Mog-ur stopped short of fatal penetration. Instead, with quick strokes, he carved two lines into the young man's flesh, both curved in the same direction and joined in a point like the great curved horn of a rhinoceros.

Broud closed his eyes but didn't flinch as the knife pierced his skin. Blood welled to the surface and overflowed, spilling down his chest in red rivulets. Goov appeared at the magician's side holding a bowl of salve made from the rendered fat of the bison mixed with antiseptic ashes from the wood of an ash tree. Mog-ur smeared the black grease into the wound, stopping the flowing blood and assuring that a black scar would form. The mark announced to all who saw him that Broud was a man; a man forever under the protection of the Spirit of the formidable, unpredictable Woolly Rhinoceros.

The young man returned to his place, acutely conscious of the attention focused on him and thoroughly enjoying it, now that the worst was over. He was sure his bravery and hunting skill, his evocative performance during the dance, his unflinching acceptance of his totem mark, would be the subject of animated talk of both men and women for a long time. He thought it might become a legend, a story repeated many times during the long cold winters that confined the clan to the cave, and retold at Clan Gatherings. If it wasn't for me this cave wouldn't be ours, he said to himself. If I hadn't killed the bison, we wouldn't be having a ceremony, we'd still be looking for a cave. Broud had begun to feel the new cave and the whole eventful occasion were entirely due to him.

Ayla watched the ritual with fear and fascination, unable to suppress a shudder as the fearsome, hulking man stabbed Broud and drew blood. She hung back as Iza led her toward the frightening, bear-cloaked magician, wondering what he would do to her. Aga with Ona in her arms and Ika carrying Borg were also approaching Mog-ur. Ayla was glad when both women lined up in front of Iza and herself.

Goov now held a tightly woven basket dyed red from the many times it had been used to hold the sacred red ochre, ground to a fine powder and heated together with animal fat to make a richly colored paste. Mog-ur looked over the heads of the women standing in front of him at the sliver of moon overhead. He made gestures in the unspoken formal language, asking the spirits to gather close and observe the youngsters whose protective totems were to be revealed.

Then, dipping a finger into the red paste, he drew a spiral on the hip of the male child, like the corkscrew tail of the wild pig. A low, gruff murmur rose from the clan as they made gestures commenting on the appropriateness of the totem.

"Spirit of Boar, the boy, Borg, is delivered into your protection," the magician's hand signals stated as he slipped a small pouch attached to a thong over the baby's head.

Ika bowed her head in acquiescence and the motion carried overtones that she was pleased. It was a strong, respectable spirit and she felt the inherent rightness of the totem for her son. Then she stepped aside.

The magician called upon the spirits again and, reaching into the red basket held by Goov, he drew a circle on Ona's arm with the paste.

"Spirit of Owl," his gestures proclaimed, "the girl, Ona, is delivered into your protection." Then Mog-ur put the amulet her mother had made around the infant's neck. Once more there was an undercurrent of grunts as hands flashed in comment on the strong totem that protected the girl. Aga was happy. Her daughter was well protected and it meant the man she mated could not have a weak totem. She only hoped it wouldn't make it too difficult for her to have children.

The group strained forward with interest as Aga moved aside and Iza reached down to lift Ayla in her arms. The girl was no longer frightened. She realized, now that she was closer, that the imposing figure with the red-stained face was none other than Creb. There was a glow of warmth in his eye when he looked at her.

To the clan's surprise, the magician's gestures were different when he called upon the spirits to attend this ritual. They were the gestures he used when he named a newborn child seven days after its birth. The strange girl was not only going to have her totem revealed, she was going to be adopted by the clan! Dipping his finger into the paste, Mog-ur drew a line from the middle of her forehead, the place on people of the Clán where the boney ridges overhanging their eyes met, to the tip of her small nose.

"The child's name is Ayla," he said, pronouncing her name slowly and carefully so both the clan and the spirits would understand.

Iza turned to face the watching people. Ayla's adoption was as much a surprise to her as it was to the rest, and the girl could feel her rapidly beating heart. This must mean she is my daughter, my first child, she thought. Only a mother holds the infant when it is named and recognized as a member of the clan. Has it been seven days since I found her? I'm not sure, I'll have to ask Creb, but I think it has. She must be my daughter; who else can be her mother now?

Each person filed past Iza holding the five-year-old girl in her arms like a baby, and each repeated her name with varying degrees of accuracy. Then Iza turned back to face the magician. He looked up and called upon the spirits to gather once more. The clan waited expectantly. Mog-ur was aware of their eager attention and used it to his advantage. With slow deliberate movements, drawing out the moment to sustain the suspense, he scooped out a bit of the oily red paste and then painted one line directly over one of the healing claw marks on Ayla's leg.

What can that mean? What totem is that? The watching clan was mystified. The holy man dipped into the red basket again and painted a second line over the next mark. The girl felt Iza begin to shake. None of the others moved, not a breath could be heard. With the third line, Brun, with an angry scowl, tried to catch Mog-ur's eye, but the magician evaded the look. When the fourth line was drawn, the clan knew, but they did not want to believe. It was, after all, the wrong leg. Mog-ur turned his head and looked straight at Brun as he made the final gesture.

"Spirit of Cave Lion, the girl, Ayla, is delivered into your protection."

The formalized movement removed the last shred of doubt. As Mog-ur put the amulet around her neck, hands flew in shocked surprise. Could it really be true? Could a girl's totem be one of the strongest of male totems? The Cave Lion?

Creb's stare into the angry eyes of his brother was firm and uncompromising. For a moment, they were locked in a silent battle of wills. But Mog-ur knew that the logic of a Cave Lion totem for the girl was implacable no matter how illogical it seemed for a female to have the protection of so powerful a spirit. Mog-ur had only emphasized what the Cave Lion himself had done. Brun had never questioned the revelations of his crippled brother before, but for some reason he felt tricked by the magician. He didn't like it, but he had to admit he had never seen a totem so obviously corroborated. He was the first to look away, but he wasn't happy.

The idea of taking the strange child into the clan had been difficult enough, but this totem of hers was too much. It was irregular, unconventional; Brun didn't like anomalies in his well-ordered clan. He clamped his jaw shut with determination. There would be no further deviations. If the girl was to be a member of his clan, she would conform, Cave Lion or no Cave Lion.

Iza was stunned. Still holding the child in her arms, she lowered her head in acceptance. If Mog-ur decreed it, it must be so. She knew Ayla's totem was strong, but a Cave Lion? The thought made her apprehensive; a female with the mightiest of cats for a totem? Now Iza was sure the girl would never mate. It reinforced her decision to teach Ayla healing magic so she would have some status of her own. Creb had named her, recognized her, and revealed her totem while the medicine woman held her. If that didn't make the girl her daughter, what did? Birth itself was no guarantee of acceptance. Iza suddenly remembered that if everything continued to go well, she would find herself standing in front of the magician again, before long, with a baby in her arms. She, who had been childless for so long, would soon have two.

The clan was in an uproar, amazement in their gestures and voices. Self-consciously, Iza returned to her place amid the astonished glances of both women and men. They tried not to stare at her and the girl—it was discourteous to stare—but one man was more than staring.

The look of hatred in Broud's eyes as he glowered at the small girl frightened Iza. She tried to place herself between the two, to shield Ayla from the proud young man's malevolent glare. Broud could see he wasn't the center of attention; no one was talking about him anymore. Forgotten was his mighty deed that assured the cave was an acceptable home, forgotten was his marvelous dance and his stoic courage when Mog-ur carved his totem mark into his chest. The astringent, antiseptic ointment hurt worse than the cut—it still stung—but was anyone noticing how bravely he bore the pain?

No one was noticing him at all. The rites of passage for boys becoming men occurred with ordinary regularity, even for those destined to be leader. They didn't compare with the wonder and unexpectedness of Mog-ur's unprecedented revelation about the strange girl. Broud saw people recalling that she had been led to the cave first. They were saying that the ugly girl found their new home! So what if her totem is the Cave Lion, Broud thought petulantly. Did she kill the bison? This was supposed to be his night, he was supposed to be the center of attention, he was supposed to be the object of the clan's admiration and awe, but Ayla had stolen his thunder.

He glowered at the strange girl, but when he noticed Iza running toward the camp beside the stream, his attention was drawn back to Mog-ur. Soon, very soon, he would be allowed to participate in the secret rituals with the men. He didn't know what to expect; all he'd ever been told was that he would learn for the first time what memories really were. It was the final step that would make him a man.

Beside the fireplace near the stream, Iza quickly removed her wrap and picked up a wooden bowl and red bag of dried roots she had set out. Stopping first to fill the bowl with water, she returned to the huge bonfire, soaring to brighter heights with the additional wood Grod added.

Iza's wrap had covered up part of the reason for her long absences earlier in the day. When the medicine woman stepped in front of the magician again, she was completely naked except for her amulet and the streaks of red painted on her body. A large circle accented the fullness of her stomach. Both breasts were circled, too, with a streak drawn from the top of each over her shoulders and joining in a V at the small of her back. Red circles enclosed both cheeks of her buttocks. The enigmatic symbols, whose meaning was known only to Mog-ur, were for her protection as well as the men's. It was dangerous to have a woman involved in religious rituals but for this she was necessary.

Iza was standing close to Mog-ur, close enough to see beads of perspiration on his face from standing in front of the hot fire in his heavy bearskin. At an imperceptible signal from him, she held the bowl up and turned to face the clan. It was an ancient bowl, preserved for generations for use only during these special occasions. Some ancestral medicine woman had long and carefully chipped out the center and shaped the outside of a section of the trunk of a tree, then even longer lovingly rubbed the bowl smooth with gritty sand and a round stone. A final smoothing with the abrasive stalks of the scouring-rush fern gave it a silky polished finish. The bowl was coated on the inside with a whitish patina from repeated use as the container for the ceremonial drink.

Iza put the dried roots in her mouth and chewed them slowly, careful not to swallow any saliva as her large teeth and strong jaws began to break down the tough fibers. Finally she spat the masticated pulp into the bowl of water and stirred the fluid until it turned a milky white. Only the medicine women of Iza's line knew the secret of the potent root. The plant was relatively rare though not unknown, but the fresh root showed little evidence of its narcotic qualities. The root had been dried, aged for at least two years; and when hanging to dry, it had been suspended root-down rather than top-down as was customary for most herbs. Though only a medicine woman was allowed to make the drink, by long-standing tradition only men were allowed to drink it.

There was an ancient legend, passed down from mother to daughter along with the esoteric instructions for concentrating the effective component of the plant into the root, that at one time, long ago, only women used the potent drug. The ceremony and rituals associated with its use were stolen by the men, and women were forbidden to use it, but the men could not steal the secret of its preparation. The medicine women who knew it were so reluctant to share the secret with anyone except their own offspring that it had been lost to all but the woman who could claim a direct, unbroken line of descent into the depths of antiquity. Even now, the drink was never given without receiving something of like kind and value in return.

When the drink was ready, Iza nodded her head and Goov stepped forward with a bowl of datura tea prepared the way he usually did for the men, but this time for the women. With dignified formality, the bowls were exchanged, then Mog-ur led the way as the men retreated into the small cave.

After they left, Iza took the datura around to each of the women. The medicine woman often used the same drug as an anesthetic, painkiller, or soporific, and she had a different preparation of the datura plant ready as a sedative for the children. The women could relax completely only if they knew their youngsters would not come seeking attention and yet would be safe. On the rare occasions when women allowed themselves the luxury of a ceremony, Iza made sure the children would be safe in the arms of sleep.

Before long, the women began putting their drowsy children to bed, then returned to the fire. After tucking Ayla into her fur, Iza went to the overturned bowl Dorv had used during the hunt dance and began beating out a slow, steady rhythm, altering the tone by beating on the top with the stick, then closer to the rim.

At first, the women sat unmoving. They were too accustomed to guarding their actions in the presence of men. But gradually, as the effects of the drug began to be felt, and with the knowledge that the men were out of sight, some of the women began to move to the stately rhythm. Ebra was the first to jump up. She danced with intricate steps in a circle around Iza, and as the medicine woman increased the tempo, it stirred the senses of more of the women. Soon they all joined the leader's mate.

As the rhythm became faster and more complex, the normally docile women threw off their wraps and danced with movements that were unrestrained and frankly erotic. They didn't notice when Iza stopped and joined them herself; they were too involved with dancing to their own internal rhythms. Their pent-up emotions, so repressed in everyday life, were released in the uninhibited motion. Tensions drained in a catharsis of freedom, a catharsis that allowed them to accept their restricted existence. In a whirling, jumping, stomping frenzy, the women danced until, near dawn, they dropped, exhausted, and slept where they fell.

With the first light of the new day, the men started leaving the cave. Stepping over the bodies of prostrate women, they found their sleeping places and soon drifted into dreamless slumber. The men's catharsis came from the emotional tension of the hunt. Their ceremony had a different dimension—more restrained, turned inward, much older, but no less exciting.

As the sun broke over the ridge to the east, Creb hobbled out of the cave and surveyed the scene littered with bodies. He had, on one rare occasion, watched the women's celebration out of curiosity. With a deep inner sense, the wise old magician understood their need for release. He knew the men always wondered what they did that left them in such a state of exhaustion, but Mog-ur never enlightened them. The men would have been as shocked by the women's unrestrained abandon as the women would by their stoic mates' fervent supplications to the invisible spirits that shared their existence.

Mog-ur had wondered, occasionally, if he could direct the minds of women back to the beginnings. Their memories were different, but they had the same ability to recall ancient knowledge. Did they have racial memories? Could they join a ceremony with the men? Mog-ur wondered, but he would never chance the ire of the spirits by attempting to find out. It would destroy the clan if a woman were included in such sacred ceremonies.

Creb shuffled to the campsite and eased himself down on his sleeping fur. He saw the disarray of fine blonde hair on Iza's fur, and it set him to thinking about the events that had occurred since he had barely stumbled out in time before the old cave collapsed. How had the strange child charmed her way into his heart so quickly? He was disturbed by the undercurrent of bad feeling from Brun about her, and he hadn't missed Broud's evil looks in her direction. The dissension in the close-knit group marred the ceremony and left him a bit uneasy.

Broud will not let it rest, Creb thought. The Woolly Rhinoceros is a suitable totem for our future leader. Broud can be brave, but he's headstrong and too full of pride. One moment he's calm and rational, even gentle and kind. Then the next, for some insignificant reason, he can charge with fury in a blind rage. I hope he doesn't turn on the girl.

Don't be stupid, he chided himself. The son of Brun's mate isn't going to let himself get upset over a girl. He's going to be leader; and besides, Brun would disapprove. Broud is a man now, he will learn to control his temper.

The crippled old man lay down and realized how tired he was. Tension had gripped him since the earthquake, but he could relax now. The cave was theirs, their totems were firmly established in their new home, and the clan could move in when they woke up. The tired magician yawned and stretched out, then he closed his eye.

7

A hushed feeling of awe at the cathedral spaciousness of the cave overcame the clan when they first walked into their new quarters, but they soon grew accustomed to it. Thoughts of the old cave and their anxious search receded quickly, and the more they learned about the environment of their new home, the more pleased they became with it. They settled into the usual routine of the short hot summers: hunting, gathering, and storing food to carry them through the long freezing cold which they knew from past experience lay ahead. They had a bountiful variety from which to choose.

Silver trout flashed through the white spray of the riotous stream, tickled out of the water by hand with infinite patience as the unwary fish rested under overhanging roots and rocks. Giant sturgeon and salmon, often filled with a bonus of fresh black caviar or bright pink roe, hovered near the stream's mouth, while monstrous catfish and black cod swept the bottom of the inland sea. Seine nets, made from the long hair of animals, hand-twisted into cord, strained the large fish from the water as they darted away from waders herding them toward the barrier of knotted strands. They often hiked the ten easy miles to the seacoast and soon had a supply of salty fish dried over smoky fires stored away. Molluscs and crustaceans were collected for ladles, spoons, bowls, and cups, as well as for their succulent morsels. Craggy cliffs were scaled to collect eggs from the multitude of seabirds nesting on the rocky promontories facing the water, and an occasional well-aimed stone brought an added treat of gannet, gull, or great auk.

Roots, fleshy stems, and leaves, squashes, legumes, berries, fruits, nuts, and grains were each collected in their season as the summer ripened. Leaves and flowers and herbs were dried for teas and flavorings, and sandy chunks of salt, left high and dry when the great northern glacier robbed moisture and caused coastlines to recede, were carried back to the cave to season winter fare.

The hunters went out often. The nearby steppes, rich in grasses and herbs and bereft of all but an occasional stand of stunted trees, abounded in herds of grazing animals. Giant deer ranged the grassy plains, their huge palmate antlers spreading as much as eleven feet in the larger animals, along with oversize bison with horn spreads of similar dimensions. Steppe horses seldom traveled so far south, but asses and onagers—the half-ass intermediate between horses and asses—roamed the open plains of the peninsula, while their massive robust cousin, the forest horse, lived singly or in small family groups nearer the cave. The steppes also hosted infrequent smaller bands of the lowland-dwelling relative of the goat, the saiga antelope.

The parkland between prairie and foothills was home to aurochs, the dark brown or black wild cattle that were the ancestors of gentler domestic breeds. The forest rhinoceros —related to brush-browsing later tropical species, but adapted to cool temperate forests—overlapped only slightly the territory of another variety of rhinos that preferred the grass of the parkland. Both, with their shorter, upright snout horns and horizontal head carriage, differed from the woolly rhino which, along with the woolly mammoths, were only seasonal visitors. They had a long anterior horn set at a forward-sloping angle and a downward head carriage useful for sweeping snow away from winter pastures. Their thick layer of subcutaneous fat and their deep red, long-haired overcoat and soft woolly undercoat were adaptations that confined them to cold climates. Their natural habitat was the northern freeze-dried steppes, the loess steppes.

Only when glaciers were on the land could there be loess steppes. The constant low pressure over the vast sheets of ice sucked moisture from the air, allowing little snow to fall in periglacial regions and creating a constant wind. Fine calcareous dust, loess, was picked up from the crushed rock at the edges of the glaciers and deposited for hundreds of miles. A short spring melted the scant snow and the top layer of permafrost enough for fast-rooting grasses and herbs to sprout. They grew quickly and dried into standing hay, thousands upon thousands of acres of fodder for the millions of animals that had adapted to the freezing cold of the continent.

The continental steppes of the peninsula only beckoned

the woolly beasts in late fall. The summers were too hot and the heavy snows of winter were too deep to brush away. Many other animals were driven north in winter to the borders of the colder but dryer loess. Most of them migrated back in summer. The forest animals who could browse on brush or bark or lichen stayed on the wooded slopes that offered seclusion and precluded large herds.

Besides forest horses and forest rhinos, wild pigs and several varieties of deer found a home in the tree-filled landscape: red deer, later called elk in other lands, in small herds; individuals and small groups of shy roe-deer with simple three-pointed antlers; the slightly larger, fawn-and-white dappled fallow deer; and a few elk, referred to as moose by those who call the red deer elk; all shared the wooded environment.

Higher up the mountain, large-horned sheep, mouflon, clung to crags and outcrops, feeding on alpine pastures; and higher still, ibex, the wild mountain goat, and chamois gamboled from precipice to precipice. Darting swift-winged birds lent color and song to the forest, if not often a meal. Their place on the menu was more easily satisfied by the fat, low-flying ptarmigan and willow grouse of the steppes brought down by swift stones, and the autumn visitations of geese and eider ducks snared by nets as they landed on marshy mountain ponds. Birds of prey and carrion-eaters floated lazily on thermal updrafts, scanning the bountiful plains and woodlands below.

A host of smaller animals filled the mountains and steppes near the cave, providing food and fur: hunters—minks, otters, wolverines, ermines, martens, foxes, sables, raccoons, badgers, and the small wild cats that later gave rise to legions of domestic mouse chasers; and hunted—tree squirrels, porcupines, hares, rabbits, moles, muskrats, coypu, beavers, skunks, mice, voles, lemmings, ground squirrels, great jerboas, giant hamsters, pikas, and a few never named and lost to extinction.

Larger carnivores were essential to thin the ranks of the abundant prey. There were wolves and their more ferocious relatives, the doglike dholes. And there were cats: lynxes, cheetahs, tigers, leopards, mountain-dwelling snow leopards, and, twice as large as any, cave lions. Omnivorous brown bears hunted near the cave, but their overgrown cousins, the vegetarian cave bears, were now absent. The ubiquitous cave hyena filled out the complement of wildlife.

The land was unbelievably rich, and man only an insignificant fraction of the multifarious life that lived and died in that cold, ancient Eden. Born too raw, without superior natural endowments for it—save one, his oversize brain—he was the weakest of the hunters. But for all his apparent vulnerability, lacking fang or claw or swift leg or leaping strength, the two-legged hunter had gained the respect of his four-legged competitors. His scent alone was enough to veer a far more powerful creature from a chosen path wherever the two lived in close proximity for very long. The capable, experienced hunters of the clan were as skilled in defense as they were in offense, and when the safety or security of the clan was threatened, or if they wanted a warm winter coat decorated by nature, they stalked the unsuspecting stalker.

It was a bright sunlit day, warm with the beginning fullness of summer. The trees were leafed out but still a shade lighter than they would be later. Lazy flies buzzed around scattered bones from previous meals. A fresh breeze from the sea carried a hint of the life within it, and the moving foliage sent shadows chasing across the sunny slope in front of the cave.

With the crisis of finding a new home over, Mog-ur's duties were light. All that was required of him was an occasional hunting ceremony or ritual to drive away evil spirits or, if someone was hurt or ill, to ask the assistance of beneficent ones to aid Iza's healing magic. The hunters were gone and several of the women with them. They would not be back for many days. The women went along to preserve the meat after it was killed; game was easier to bring home already dried for winter storage. The warm sun and ever-present wind on the steppes quickly desiccated meat cut into thin strips. Smoky fires of dried grass and dung were more for keeping away blowflies that laid eggs in fresh meat, making it rot. The women would also carry most of the load on the way back.

Creb had spent time with Ayla nearly every day since they moved into the cave, trying to teach her their language. The rudimentary words, usually the more difficult part for Clan youngsters, she picked up with ease, but their intricate system of gestures and signals was beyond her. He had tried to make her understand the meaning of gestures, but neither had a basis in each other's method of communicating, and there was no one to interpret or explain. The old man had racked his brain, but he had not been able to think of a way to get the meanings across. Ayla was equally frustrated.

She knew there was something she was missing and she ached to be able to communicate beyond the few words she knew. It was obvious to her that the people of the clan understood more than the simple words, but she just didn't know how. The problem was that she didn't *see* the hand signals. They were random movements to her, not purposeful motions. She simply hadn't been able to grasp the concept of talking with movement. That it was even possible had never occurred to her; it was totally beyond her realm of experience.

Creb had begun to get an inkling of her problem, though he found it hard to believe. It has to be that she doesn't know the motions have meaning, he thought. "Ayla!" Creb called, beckoning to the girl. That must be the trouble, he thought as they walked along a path beside the glinting stream. Either that, or she just isn't intelligent enough to comprehend a language. From his observations, he couldn't believe she lacked intelligence, for all that she was different. But she does understand simple gestures. He had assumed it would only be a matter of enlarging on them.

Many feet starting out to hunt, forage, or fish in their direction had already beaten down grass and brush forming a path along the line of least resistance. They came to a spot the old man favored, an open stretch near a large, leafy oak whose high exposed roots offered a shaded, raised seat easier for him to rest on than lowering himself to the ground. Starting the lesson, he pointed to the tree with his staff.

"Oak," Ayla quickly responded. Creb nodded approval, then he aimed his staff at the stream.

"Water," the girl said.

The old man nodded again, then made a motion with his hand and repeated the word. "Flowing water, river," the combined gesture and word stated.

"Water?" the girl said hesitantly, puzzled that he had indicated her word was correct but asked her again. She was getting a feeling of panic deep in her stomach. It was the same as before, she knew there was something more he wanted, but she didn't understand.

Creb shook his head no. He had gone over the same kind of exercises with the child many times. He tried again, pointing to her feet.

"Feet," Ayla said.

"Yes," the magician nodded. Somehow I must make her see as well as hear, he thought. Getting up, he took her hand and walked a few steps with her, leaving his staff behind. He made a motion and said the word "feet." "Moving feet, walking," was the sense he was trying to communicate. She strained to listen, trying to hear if there was something she missed in his tone.

"Feet?" the child said tremulously, sure it was not the answer he wanted.

"No, no, no! Walking! Feet moving!" he repeated again, looking directly at her, exaggerating the gesture. He moved her forward again, pointing at her feet, despairing that she would ever learn.

Ayla could feel tears begin to well up in her eyes. Feet! Feet! She knew it was the right word, why did he shake his head no? I wish he'd stop moving his hand around in front of my face like that. What am I doing wrong?

The old man walked her forward again, pointed at her feet, made the motion with his hand, said the word. She stopped and watched him. He made the gesture again, exaggerating it so much it almost meant something else, said the word again. He was bent over, looking her squarely in the face, making the motion directly in front of her eyes. Gesture, word. Gesture, word.

What does he want? What am I supposed to do? She wanted to understand him. She knew he was trying to tell her something. Why does he keep moving his hand? she thought.

Then the barest glimmer of an idea came to her. His hand! He keeps moving his hand. She lifted her hand hesitantly.

"Yes, yes! That's it!" Creb's vigorous affirmative nodding almost shouted. "Make the signal! Moving! Moving feet!" he repeated.

With dawning comprehension, she watched his motion, then tried to copy it. Creb was saying yes! That's what he wants! The movement! He wants me to make the movement.

She made the gesture again saying the word, not understanding what it meant, but at least understanding that it was the gesture he wanted her to make when she said the word. Creb turned her around and headed back to the oak, limping heavily. Pointing to her feet again as she moved, he repeated the gesture-word combination once again.

Suddenly, like an explosion in her brain, she made the connection. Moving on feet! Walking! That's what he means! Not just feet. The hand movement with the word "feet" means walking! Her mind raced. She remembered always seeing the people of the clan moving their hands. She could see Iza and Creb in her mind's eye, standing, looking at each other, moving their hands, saying few words, but moving their hands. Were they talking? Is that how they talk to each other? Is that why they say so little? Do they talk with their hands?

Creb seated himself. Ayla stood in front of him, trying to calm her excitement.

"Feet," she said, pointing down to hers.

"Yes," he nodded, wondering.

She turned and walked away, and as she approached him again, she made the gesture and said the word "feet."

"Yes, yes! That's it! That's the idea!" he said. She has it! I think she understands!

The girl paused for a moment, then turned and ran away from him. After running back across the small clearing, she waited expectantly in front of him again, a little out of breath.

"Running," he motioned as she watched carefully. It was a different movement; like the first, but different.

"Running," her hesitant motion mimicked.

She does have it!

Creb was excited. The movement was gross, it lacked the finesse of even the young children of the clan, but she had the idea. He nodded vigorously and was almost knocked off his seat as Ayla threw herself at him, hugging him in joyful understanding.

The old magician looked around. It was almost instinctive. Gestures of affection were confined to the boundaries of the fire. But he knew they were alone. The crippled man responded with a gentle hug and felt a glow of warmth and satisfaction he had never felt before.

A whole new world of comprehension opened up for Ayla. She had an innate dramatic flair and a talent for mimicry which she put to use with deadly earnest copying

Creb's motions. But Creb's one-handed speaking gestures were necessarily adaptations of normal hand signals, and it was Iza who taught her the finer details. She learned as a baby would, starting with expressions of simple needs, but she learned much faster. Too long had she been frustrated in her attempts to communicate; she was determined to make up for the lack as quickly as possible.

As she began to understand more, the life of the clan sprang into vivid relief. She watched the people around her as they communicated, staring in rapt attention, trying to grasp what they were saying to each other. At first the clan was tolerant of her visual intrusion, treating her like a baby. But as time went on, disapproving glances cast in her direction made it obvious that such ill-mannered behavior would not be accepted much longer. Staring, like eavesdropping, was discourteous; custom dictated that the eyes should be averted when other people were in private discussion. The problem came to a head one evening in midsummer.

The clan was inside the cave, gathered around their family fires after the evening meal. The sun had sunk below the horizon and the last dim afterglow outlined the leafy silhouettes of dark foliage rustling in the gentle night breeze. The fire at the mouth of the cave, lit to fend off evil spirits, curious predators, and the damp night air, sent up wisps of smoke and shimmering heat waves, making the shadowed black trees and brush beyond undulate to the silent rhythm of the flickering flames. Its light danced with shadows on the rough rock wall of the cave.

Ayla sat within the stones that outlined Creb's territory staring across at Brun's household. Broud was upset and taking it out on his mother and Oga by exercising his prerogatives as an adult male. The day had started out badly for Broud and got worse. Long hours spent tracking and stalking were wasted when he missed his shot, and the red fox, whose pelt he had grandly promised to Oga, melted into the dense brush only warned by the swiftly slung stone. Oga's looks of understanding forgiveness just hurt his wounded pride more; he was the one who should be forgiving of her inadequacies, not the other way around.

The women, tired from a busy day, were trying to finish their last chores, and Ebra, exasperated by his constant interruptions, made a slight signal to Brun. The leader had been more than aware of the young man's imperious, demanding behavior. It was Broud's right, but Brun felt he should be more sensitive to them. It wasn't necessary to make them run for everything when they were already so busy and tired.

"Broud, let the women alone. They have enough to do," Brun signaled in silent reprimand. The rebuke was too much, especially in front of Oga, and from Brun. Broud stomped off to the far edge of the territory of Brun's hearth near the boundary stones to sulk and caught sight of Ayla staring directly at him. It didn't matter that Ayla had barely caught the drift of the subtle domestic squabble within the confines of the adjacent household; as far as Broud was concerned, the ugly little interloper had seen him scolded just like a child. It was the final crushing blow to his tender ego. She doesn't even have the courtesy to look away, he thought. Well, she's not the only one who can ignore simple politeness. All the day's frustrations overflowed, and flaunting conventions on purpose, Broud directed a malevolent glare across the boundaries at the girl he detested.

Creb was conscious of the mild spat at Brun's hearth, just as he was aware of all the people in the cave. Most of the time, like background noise, it was filtered out of his consciousness, but anything that involved Ayla sharpened his attention. He knew it had taken deliberate effort and supremely malignant intent for Broud to overcome the conditioning of his entire life and stare directly into the confines of another man's hearth. Broud feels too much animosity toward the child, Creb thought. For her sake, it is time to teach her some manners.

"Ayla!" Creb commanded sharply. She jumped at the tone in his voice. "Not look other people!" he signaled. She was puzzled.

"Why not look?" she queried.

"Not look, not stare; people not like," he tried to explain, aware that Broud was watching out of the corner of his eye, not even bothering to hide his gloating pleasure at the strong scolding the girl was receiving from Mog-ur. She is favored too much by the magician anyway, Broud thought. If she lived here, I'd show her soon enough how a female is supposed to behave.

"Want learn talk," Ayla motioned, still puzzled and a little hurt.

Creb knew full well why she had been watching, but she

had to learn sometime. Perhaps it would ease Broud's hatred of her if he saw she was being rebuked for staring at them.

"Ayla not stare," Creb motioned with a severe look. "Bad. Ayla not talk back when man talks. Bad. Ayla not look at people at their hearths. Bad. Bad. Understand?"

Creb was harsh. He wanted to make his point. He noticed Broud get up and return to the fireplace at Brun's call, obviously in a better mood.

Ayla was crushed. Creb had never been harsh with her. She thought he was pleased that she was learning their language; now he told her she was bad for watching people and trying to learn more. Confused and hurt, tears welled up, filled her eyes, and overflowed down her cheeks.

"Iza!" Creb called, concerned. "Come here! There's something wrong with Ayla's eyes." The eyes of Clan people watered only when something got in them or if they had colds or suffered from eye disease. He had never seen eyes overflowing with tears of unhappiness. Iza came running up.

"Look at that! Her eyes are watering. Maybe a spark got into one. You'd better take a look at them," he insisted.

Iza was worried, too. Lifting Ayla's eyelids, she peered closely into the child's eyes. "Eye hurt?" she asked. The medicine woman could see no sign of inflammation. Nothing appeared to be wrong with her eyes, they were just watering.

"No, not hurt," Ayla sniffled. She couldn't understand their concern about her eyes, but it made her realize they cared about her even if Creb did say she was bad. "Why Creb mad, Iza?" she sobbed.

"Must learn, Ayla," Iza explained, looking at the girl seriously. "Not polite to stare. Not polite to look at other man's fire, see what other people say at fire. Ayla must learn, when man talk, woman look down, like this," Iza demonstrated. "When man talk, woman do. No ask. Only little ones stare. Babies. Ayla big. Make people angry at Ayla."

"Creb angry? Not care for me?" she asked, bursting out in fresh tears.

Iza was still mystified by the child's watering eyes, but she sensed the girl's confusion. "Creb care for Ayla. Iza, too. Creb teach Ayla. More to learn than talk. Must learn Clan ways," the woman said, taking the girl in her arms. She held her gently while Ayla cried her hurt, then wiped the girl's wet swollen eyes with a soft skin and looked into them again to satisfy herself they were all right.

"What's wrong with her eyes?" Creb asked. "Is she sick?"

"She thought you didn't like her. She thought you were mad at her. It must have given her a sickness. Maybe light eyes like hers are weak, but I can't find anything wrong and she says they don't hurt. I think her eyes watered with sadness, Creb," Iza explained.

"Sadness? She was so sad because she thought I didn't like her, it made her sick? Made her eyes water?"

The astounded man could hardly believe it, and it filled him with mixed emotions. Was she sickly? She seemed healthy, but no one ever got sick because they thought he didn't like them. No one, except Iza, had ever cared for him in that way. People feared him, held him in awe, respected him, but no one had ever wanted him to like them so much their eyes watered. Maybe Iza is right, maybe her eyes are weak, but her sight is fine. Somehow I must let her know it is for her own good that she learns to behave properly. If she doesn't learn the ways of the Clan, Brun will turn her out. It is still within his power. But it doesn't mean I don't like her. I do like her, he admitted to himself; strange as she is, I like her very much.

Ayla shuffled slowly toward the crippled old man, nervously looking down at her feet. She stood in front of him, then looked up with sad round eyes, still wet with tears.

"I not stare anymore," she gestured. "Creb not mad?"

"No," he signaled, "I'm not mad, Ayla. But you belong to the clan now, you belong to me. You must learn the language, but you must learn Clan ways, too. Understand?"

"I belong Creb? Creb care for me?" she asked.

"Yes, I like you, Ayla."

The girl broke into a smile, reached out and hugged him, then crawled into the lap of the disfigured, misshapen man and snuggled close.

Creb had always had an interest in children. In his function as Mog-ur, he seldom revealed a child's totem that wasn't immediately understood by the child's mother as appropriate. The clan attributed Mog-ur's skill to his magical powers, but his real skill lay in his powers of perceptive observation. He was aware of children from the day they were born and often saw women and men alike cuddling and comforting them. But the old cripple never knew the joy of cradling a child in his own arms.

The little girl, worn out by her emotions, had fallen asleep. She felt secure with the fearsome magician. He had replaced in her heart a man she no longer remembered except in some unconscious corner. As Creb looked at the peaceful, trusting face of the strange girl in his lap, he felt a deep love flowering in his soul for her. He couldn't have loved her more if she were his own.

"Iza," the man called out softly. The woman took the sleeping child from Creb, but not before he hugged her to him for a moment.

"Her illness has made her tired," he said after the woman laid her down. "Make sure she rests tomorrow and you'd better examine her eyes again in the morning."

"Yes, Creb," she nodded. Iza loved her crippled sibling; she knew more than anyone the gentle soul that lived beneath the grim exterior. It made her happy that he had found someone to love, someone who loved him, too, and it made her feelings for the girl stronger.

Not since she was a little girl herself could Iza remember being so happy. Only her nagging fear that the child she was carrying would be male marred her joy. A son born to her would have to be raised by a hunter. She was Brun's sibling; their mother had been the mate of the leader before him. If something happened to Broud, or if the woman he mated produced no male offspring, the leadership of the clan would fall to her son, if she had one. Brun would be forced to give her and the baby to one of the hunters, or take her in himself. Every day she asked her totem to make her unborn baby a girl, but she couldn't rid herself of her worry.

As the summer progressed, with Creb's gentle patience and Ayla's eager willingness, the girl began to understand not only the language but the customs of her adopted people. Learning to avert her eyes to allow the people of the Clan the only privacy possible to them was only the first of many hard lessons. Much more difficult was learning to curb her natural curiosity and impetuous enthusiasm to conform to the customary docility of females.

Creb and Iza were learning, too. They discovered that when Ayla made a certain grimace, pulling back her lips

and showing her teeth, often accompanied by peculiar aspi-
rating sounds, it meant she was happy, not hostile. They
never completely overcame their anxiety at the strange
weakness of her eyes that made them water when she was
sad. Iza decided the weakness was peculiar to light-colored
eyes and wondered if the trait was normal for the Others or
if only Ayla's eyes watered. To be safe, Iza flushed her eyes
with the clear fluid from the bluish white plant that grew
deep in shaded woods. The corpselike plant derived nourishment from decaying wood and vegetable matter since it
lacked chlorophyll, and its waxy-looking surface turned
black when touched. But Iza knew of no better remedy for
sore or inflamed eyes than the cool liquid that oozed from
its broken stem and applied the treatment whenever the
child cried.

She didn't cry often. Though tears quickly brought her
attention, Ayla tried hard to control them. Not only were
they disturbing to the two people she loved, but to the rest
of the clan it was a sign of her differentness, and she wanted
to fit in and be accepted. The clan was learning to accept
her, but they were still wary and suspicious of her peculiarities.

Ayla was getting to know the clan and accept them, too.
Though the men were curious about her, it was beneath
their dignity to show too much interest in a female child no
matter how unusual, and she ignored them as much as they
ignored her. Brun showed more interest than the rest, but
he frightened her. He was stern and not open to advances
the way Creb was. She couldn't know that to the rest of the
clan, Mog-ur appeared far more aloof and forbidding than
Brun, and they were amazed at the closeness that developed
between the awesome magician and the strange little girl.
The one she especially disliked was the young man who
shared Brun's fire. Broud always looked mean when he
looked at her.

It was the women she became familiar with first. She
spent more time with them. Except when she was within the
boundaries of Creb's hearthstones, or when the medicine
woman took her along when she went to gather the plants
unique to her own uses, she and Iza were usually with the
female members of the clan. In the beginning, Ayla just
followed Iza around and watched while they skinned animals, cured hides, stretched thongs cut in one spiral piece
from a single hide, wove baskets, mats, or nets, gouged

bowls out of logs, gathered wild foods, prepared meals, preserved meat and plant food for winter, and responded to the wishes of any man who called upon them to perform a service. But as they saw the girl's willingness to learn, they not only helped her with the language, they began to teach her those useful skills.

She was not as strong as Clan women or children—her thinner frame couldn't support the powerful musculature of the heavy-boned clan—but she was surprisingly dexterous and limber. The heavy tasks were difficult for her, but for a child, she did well weaving baskets or cutting out thongs of uniform widths. She quickly developed a warm relationship with Ika, whose friendly nature made her easy to like. The woman let Ayla carry Borg around when she saw the girl's interest in the baby. Ovra was reserved, but she and Uka were especially kind to her. Their own grief at the loss of the young man in the cave-in made both sibling and mother sensitive to the child's loss of her family. But Ayla had no playmates.

Her first flush of friendship with Oga cooled after the ceremony. Oga was torn between Ayla and Broud. The newcomer, although younger, was someone with whom she could have shared her girlish thoughts, and she felt empathetic toward the young orphan since she shared the same fate, but Broud's feelings about her were obvious. Oga reluctantly chose to avoid Ayla in deference to the man she hoped to mate. Except when they worked together, they seldom associated, and after Ayla's attempts at friendship were rebuffed several times, the girl withdrew and made no further efforts to socialize.

Ayla didn't like playing with Vorn. Though a year her junior, his idea of playing usually involved ordering her around in conscious imitation of adult male behavior toward adult females, which Ayla still found hard to accept. When she rebelled, it brought down the wrath of both men and women upon her, especially from Aga, Vorn's mother. She was proud that her son was learning to behave "just like a man," and she was no less aware of Broud's resentment of Ayla than the rest. Someday Broud would be leader, and if her son remained in his favor, he might be selected as second-in-command. Aga used every opportunity to increase her son's stature, to the point of picking on the girl when Broud was near. If she noticed Ayla and

Vorn together when Broud was around, she quickly called her son away.

Ayla's ability to communicate improved rapidly, especially with the help of the women. But it was by her own observation that she learned one particular symbol. She still watched people—she hadn't learned to close her mind to those around her—though she was less obvious about it.

One afternoon she watched Ika playing with Borg. Ika made a gesture to her son and repeated it several times. When the baby's random hand movements seemed to imitate the gesture, she called the other women's attention to it and praised her son. Later, Ayla saw Vorn run up to Aga and greet her with the same gesture. Even Ovra made the motion when beginning a conversation with Uka.

That evening she shyly approached Iza, and when the woman looked up, Ayla made the hand signal. Iza's eyes flew open.

"Creb," she said. "When did you teach her to call me mother?"

"I didn't teach her that, Iza," Creb responded. "She must have learned it herself."

Iza turned back to the girl. "Did you learn that yourself?" she asked.

"Yes, mother," Ayla gestured, making the symbol again. She wasn't exactly sure what the hand signal meant, but she had an idea. She knew it was used by children to the women who cared for them. Though her mind had blocked out memories of her own mother, her heart had not forgotten. Iza had replaced that woman whom Ayla had loved and lost.

The woman who had been childless for so long felt a surge of emotion. "My daughter," Iza said with a rare spontaneous hug. "My child. I knew she was my daughter from the first, Creb. Didn't I tell you? She was given to me; the spirits meant for her to be mine, I'm sure of it."

Creb didn't argue with her. Perhaps she was right.

After that evening, the child's nightmares decreased, though she still had them occasionally. Two dreams recurred most frequently. One was of hiding in a small cramped cave trying to get out of the way of a huge, sharp claw. The other was more vague and more disturbing. There was a sensation of the earth moving, a deep rolling rumble, and an infinitely painful sense of loss. She cried out in her strange language, used less and less, when she awoke and clung to Iza. When she first came to them, she lapsed into her own tongue sometimes without realizing it, but as she learned to communicate more in the way of the Clan, it only came out in her dreams. After a time, it even left her dreams, but she never woke from the haunting nightmare of crumbling earth without a feeling of desolation.

The short hot summer passed and the light morning frosts of autumn brought a nip to the air and a brilliant splash of scarlet and amber to the verdant forest. A few early snows, sluiced away by heavy seasonal rains that stripped branches of their colorful cloaks, hinted at the coming cold. Later, when only a few tenacious leaves still clung to the bare branches of trees and shrubs, a brief interlude of bright sunshine brought a last reminder of summer heat before the harsh winds and bitter cold closed down most outside activities.

The clan was out, savoring the sun. On the broad front exposure of the cave the women were winnowing grain harvested from the grassy steppes below. A brisk wind kicked up an extravagance of dry leaves, lending a semblance of life to the whirling vestiges of summer's fullness. Taking advantage of the gusty air, the women tossed up the grain from wide shallow baskets, letting the wind carry away the chaff before they caught the heavier seeds.

Iza was leaning over behind Ayla, her hands over the girl's as she held the basket, showing her how to fling the grain high in the air without throwing it out with the husks and bits of straw.

Ayla was conscious of Iza's hard, protruding stomach against her back and felt the strong contraction that made the woman stop suddenly. Shortly afterward, Iza left the group and went into the cave, followed by Ebra and Uka. The girl shot an apprehensive glance at the knot of men who had stopped their conversation and followed the women with their eyes, expecting them to reprimand the three women for leaving while there was still work to be done. But the men were inexplicably permissive. Ayla decided to chance their displeasure and followed after the women.

In the cave, Iza was resting on her sleeping fur with Ebra and Uka on either side of her. Why is Iza lying down in the middle of the day? Ayla thought. Is she sick? Iza saw the girl's worried look and made a gesture of reassurance, but it didn't ease Ayla's concern. It grew when she saw her adopted mother's strained expression at the next contraction.

Ebra and Uka talked with Iza about ordinary things, all the food that was stored, the change in the weather. But Ayla had learned enough to pick up their concern from the expressions and posture of the women. Something was wrong, she was sure. Ayla decided nothing would make her leave Iza until she found out what it was, and she sat down near her feet to wait.

Toward evening, Ika walked over with Borg on her hip, then Aga brought her daughter, Ona, and both women sat and visited while they nursed, adding their moral support. Ovra and Oga were full of concern, and curiosity, when they crowded around Iza's bed. Though Uka's daughter was not mated yet, she was a woman, and Ovra knew she could bring forth life now. Oga would soon become a woman, and they were both intensely interested in the process Iza was going through.

When Vorn saw Aba go over and sit beside her daughter, he wanted to know why all the women were at Mog-ur's fire. He wandered over and crawled on Aga's lap beside his sibling to see what was going on, but Ona was still nursing, so the old woman picked up the boy and held him on her lap. He couldn't see anything of great interest, just the medicine woman resting, so he wandered off again.

The women started leaving not long afterward, to begin preparing evening meals. Uka stayed with Iza, though Ebra and Oga kept glancing over inconspicuously while they cooked. Ebra served Creb as well as Brun, then brought food for Uka, Iza, and Ayla. Ovra cooked for her mother's mate, but she and Oga returned quickly when Grod went over to Brun's hearth to join the leader and Creb. They didn't want to miss anything and sat down beside Ayla who hadn't stirred from her place.

Iza only sipped a little tea and Ayla wasn't very hungry either. She picked at her food, unable to eat with the tight knot constricting her stomach. What's wrong with Iza? Why isn't she getting up to make Creb's evening meal? Why isn't Creb here asking the spirits to make her well? Why is he staying with all the rest of the men at Brun's hearth?

Iza was straining harder. Every few moments she took several quick breaths, then pushed hard holding the hands of the two women. Every member of the clan kept vigil as the night wore on. The men were clustered around the leader's fire, apparently involved in some deep discussion. But the occasional surreptitious glances betrayed their real interest. The women visited periodically, checking on Iza's progress, sometimes staying for a while. They all waited, united in their encouragement and anticipation while their medicine woman labored to give birth.

It was well after dark. Suddenly there was a flurry of activity. Ebra spread out a hide while Uka helped Iza up into a squatting position. She was breathing hard, straining hard, crying out in pain. Ayla was trembling, sitting between Ovra and Oga who groaned and strained in sympathy with Iza. The woman took a deep breath, and with a long, teeth-gritting, muscle-straining push, the round crown of the baby's head appeared in a gush of water. Another tremendous effort eased out the baby's head. The rest was easier as Iza delivered the wet, squirming body of a tiny infant.

A final push brought forth a mass of bloody tissue. Iza lay down again, exhausted from her labor, while Ebra picked up the baby, extracted a gob of mucus from its mouth with her finger, and laid the newborn on Iza's stomach. As she thumped the baby's feet, the infant's mouth opened and a loud squall announced the first breath of life of Iza's first child. Ebra tied a piece of red-dyed sinew around the umbilical cord and bit off the part still attached to the placental mass, then lifted the baby for Iza to see. She got up and went back to her own hearth to report the medicine woman's successful delivery and the gender of the child to her mate. She sat in front of Brun, bowed her head, and looked up at a tap on her shoulder.

8

"I am grieved to report," Ebra said, making the customary gesture of sorrow, "Iza's baby is a girl."

But the news was not received with sorrow. Brun was

relieved, though he would never admit it. The arrangement of the magician providing for his sibling, especially with the addition of Ayla to the clan, was working out well and the leader was reluctant to change it. Mog-ur was doing a creditable job of training the newcomer, much better than he expected. Ayla was learning to communicate and to behave within Clan customs. Creb was not only relieved, he was overjoyed. In his old age, for the first time in his life, he had come to know the pleasures of a warm and loving family, and the birth of a girl to Iza assured it would remain together.

And for the first time since they moved into the new cave, Iza could draw a breath free of anxiety. She was glad the birth had gone so well, as old as she was. She had attended many women who had far more difficulty than she. Several came close to dying, a few did, and more than a few babies as well. It seemed to her that babies' heads were just too large for the women's birth passages. Her worry over the actual delivery had not been nearly as great as her concern over the sex of the child. Such insecurity about the future was almost unbearable for Clan people.

Iza lay back on her fur, relaxing. Uka wrapped the infant in a swaddling of soft rabbit fur and laid the babe in her mother's arms. Ayla hadn't moved. She was looking with longing curiosity at Iza; the woman saw her and beckoned.

"Come here, Ayla. Would you like to see the baby?"

Ayla approached shyly. "Yes," she nodded. Iza pulled back the covering so the girl could see the infant.

The tiny replica of Iza had a light down of brown fuzz on her head, and the boney occipital knob at the back was more noticeable without the thick head of hair she would soon have. The baby's head was somewhat rounder than in adults, but still long, and her forehead sloped back sharply from her not quite fully developed brow ridges. Ayla reached out to touch the newborn's soft cheek and the baby instinctively turned toward the touch, making small sucking noises.

"She's beautiful," Ayla motioned, her eyes full of soft wonder at the miracle she had seen. "Is she trying to talk, Iza?" the girl asked as the infant waved small clenched fists in the air.

"Not yet, but she will soon and you will have to help teach her," Iza replied.

"Oh, I will. I'll teach her to talk. Just like you and Creb taught me."

"I know you will, Ayla," the new mother said, covering her baby again.

The girl stayed protectively close by while Iza rested. Ebra had wrapped the afterbirth tissue in the hide that had been put down just before the delivery and hid it in an inconspicuous corner until Iza could take it outside to bury it in a place only she would know. If the baby had been stillborn, it would have been buried at the same time, and no one would ever mention the birth; nor would the mother show her grief openly, but a subtle gentleness and sympathy would be extended.

If the baby had been born alive but deformed, or if the leader of the clan decided the newborn was unacceptable for some other reason, the mother's task would have been more onerous. Then she would be required to take the baby away and bury it or leave it exposed to the elements and carnivores. Rarely was a deformed child allowed to live; if it was female, almost never. If a baby was male, especially first-born, and if the woman's mate wanted the child, he could at the discretion of the leader be allowed to remain with his mother for the first seven days of his life as a test of his ability to survive. Any child still alive after seven days, by Clan tradition which had the force of law, had to be named and accepted into the clan.

The first days of Creb's life had hung in just such a balance. His mother had barely survived his birth. Her mate was also the leader and the decision of whether the newborn male would be allowed to live rested solely with him. But his decision was made more for the woman's sake than for the baby's, whose malformed head and unmoving limbs gave early indication of the damage the difficult birth had inflicted. She was too weak, she had lost too much blood, she hovered on the edge of death herself. Her mate could not require that she dispose of the child; she was too weak to do it. If the mother couldn't do it, or if she died, the task fell to the medicine woman, but Creb's mother was the medicine woman of the clan. So he was left with his mother, though no one expected him to survive.

His mother's milk was slow to start. When he clung to life against all odds, another nursing woman took pity on the poor infant and fed Creb his first life-sustaining nourishment. In such tenuous circumstances, life began for Mog-ur, the holiest of holy men, the most skilled and powerful magician of the entire Clan.

Now the crippled man and his brother approached Iza and the baby. At a peremptory signal from Brun, Ayla quickly got up and moved away but watched from a distance out of the corner of her eye. Iza sat up, unwrapped her baby, and held her up to Brun, careful not to look at either man. Both men examined the infant, wailing loudly at being taken from her mother's warm side and exposed to the cold air of the cave. They were just as careful not to look at Iza.

"The child is normal," Brun's gesture announced gravely. "She may stay with her mother. If she lives until the naming day, she will be accepted."

Iza really didn't have any fear that Brun would reject her child, but she was relieved nonetheless at the formal statement from the leader. Only one last twinge of worry remained. She hoped her daughter would not be unlucky because its mother had no mate. He had been alive, after all, at the time she became certain she was expecting, Iza reasoned, and Creb was like a mate, at least he provided for them. Iza put the thought out of her mind.

For the next seven days Iza would be isolated, confined to the boundaries of Creb's fire, except for necessary trips to relieve herself and to bury the placenta. None of the clan officially recognized the existence of Iza's baby while she was in isolation except those who shared the same hearth, but other women brought food for them so Iza could rest. It allowed a brief visit and an unofficial peek at the new baby. Beyond the seven days until she stopped bleeding, she would be under a modified woman's curse. Her contacts would be restricted to women, the same as during her menses.

Iza spent her time nursing and caring for her child and, when she felt rested, reorganizing food areas, cooking areas, sleeping areas, and her medicine storage area within the boundary stones that defined Creb's hearth, his territory inside the cave now shared by three females.

Because of Mog-ur's unique position in the clan hierarchy, his location was in a very favorable spot: close enough to the mouth of the cave to benefit from daylight and summer sun, but not so close that it was subject to the worst of the winter drafts. His hearth had an additional feature, for which Iza was particularly grateful for Creb's sake. An outcrop of stone extending from the side wall gave extra protection from winds. Even with the wind barrier and a constant fire near the opening, cold winds often blasted more exposed sites. The old man's rheumatism and arthritis were always much worse in winter, aggravated by the cold dampness of the cave. Iza had made sure that Creb's sleeping furs, resting on a soft layer of straw and grass packed into a shallow trench, were in the protected corner.

One of the few tasks that had been required of the men, aside from hunting, was the construction of the wind barrier—hides stretched across the entrance supported by posts sunk into the ground. Another was paving the area around the mouth with smooth rocks brought up from the stream to keep rains and melting snows from turning the cave entrance into a quagmire of mud. The floor of the individual hearths was bare earth, with woven mats scattered around for sitting or serving food.

Two other shallow trenches filled with straw and covered with fur were near Creb's, and the top fur of each was the one also used as a warm outer cloak by the person who slept there. Besides Creb's bearskin, there was Iza's saiga antelope hide and a new white fur from a snow leopard. The animal had been lurking near the cave, well below its usual haunts in the higher elevations of the mountain. Goov was credited with the kill and he gave the pelt to Creb.

Many of the clan wore skins or kept a piece of horn or tooth from the animal that symbolized their protective totem. Creb thought the snow leopard fur would be appropriate for Ayla. Although it was not her totem, it was a similar creature and he knew it was unlikely that hunters would stalk a cave lion. The huge feline seldom strayed far from the steppes and posed little threat to the clan in their cave on the wooded slopes. They were not disposed to hunt the massive carnivore without good reason. Iza had just finished curing the hide and making new footwear for the girl before she started into labor. The child was delighted with it and looked for any excuse to go outside so she could wear it.

Iza was making herself a wormseed tea to encourage the flow of milk and to relieve the painful cramps of her uterus contracting back to its normal shape. She had collected and dried the long narrow leaves and small greenish flowers earlier in the year in anticipation of the birth of her child. She glanced toward the cave entrance looking for Ayla. The woman had just changed the absorbent leather strap she wore during her menstrual cycles and since her delivery, and she had wanted to go into the nearby woods to bury the soiled one. She was looking for the girl to keep an eye on the sleeping infant for the few moments she would be gone.

But Ayla was nowhere near the cave. She was looking for small round stones along the stream. Iza had commented that she wanted more cooking stones before the stream iced over, and Ayla thought it would please her if she got some. The girl was on her knees on a rocky strand near the water's edge searching for rocks of just the right size. She glanced up and noticed a small lump of white fur beneath a bush. Moving the leafless brush aside, she saw a half-grown rabbit lying on its side. Its leg was broken and crusted with dried blood.

The wounded animal, panting with thirst, was unable to move. It looked at the girl with nervous eyes as she reached out and felt its warm soft fur. A young wolf pup, just learning his hunting skills, had caught the rabbit, but it had managed to break free. Before the young carnivore could make another dash for his prey, his mother issued a yelping summons. The pup, who was not really hungry, turned in mid-stride in answer to the urgent call. The rabbit had dived for the thicket and froze, hoping not to be seen. By the time it felt safe enough to hop away, it couldn't, and had been lying beside the running water dying of thirst. Its life was nearly drained.

Ayla lifted the warm furry animal and cuddled it in her arms. She had held Iza's new baby, wrapped in soft rabbit fur, and the bunny felt like the baby to her. She sat on the ground rocking it, then noticed the blood and the leg bent at an odd angle. Poor baby, your leg is hurt, the child thought. Maybe Iza can fix it; she fixed mine once. Forgetting her plan to find cooking stones, she got up and carried the wounded animal back to the cave.

Iza was napping when Ayla walked in, but she woke at the sound of her step. The child held the rabbit out to the medicine woman, showing her its wounds. Iza had sometimes taken pity on small animals and applied a little first aid, but she had never brought one back to the cave.

"Ayla, animals don't belong in the cave," Iza motioned.

Ayla's hopeful expectations dashed, she cuddled the rabbit to her, bowed her head sadly, and started to leave, tears starting to fill her eyes.

Iza saw the little girl's disappointment. "Well, since you brought it, I might as well take a look at it," she said. Ayla brightened and handed the wounded animal to Iza.

"This animal is thirsty, get some water for it," Iza gestured. Ayla quickly poured clear liquid from a large waterbag and brought a cup, full to the brim. Iza was slivering wood for a splint. Freshly cut strips of leather were on the ground to tie on the splint.

"Take the waterbag and bring in more water, Ayla, we're nearly out; then we'll start some heating. I'll need to clean the wound," the woman directed as she stirred up the fire and put some stones in it. Ayla snatched the bag and ran to the pool. The water had revived the small creature and it was nibbling on seeds and grain Iza had given it when the child came back.

Creb was astonished when he returned later and saw Ayla cuddling the rabbit while Iza was nursing her baby. He saw the splint on its leg and caught a look from Iza that said, "What else could I do?" While the girl was engrossed with her live doll, Iza and Creb spoke in silent signals.

"What made her bring a rabbit into the cave?" Creb asked.

"It was hurt. She brought it to me to heal it. She didn't know we don't bring animals into our home. But her feelings were not wrong, Creb, I think she has the instincts of a medicine woman. Creb," Iza paused—"I wanted to talk to you about her. She is not an attractive child, you know."

Creb glanced in Ayla's direction. "She's appealing, but you're right, she's not attractive," he admitted. "But what does that have to do with the rabbit?"

"What chance will she ever have to mate? Any man with a totem strong enough for her would never want her. He could have his pick of women. What will happen to her when she becomes a woman? If she doesn't mate, she will have no status."

"I've thought about it, but what's to be done?"

"If she were a medicine woman, she would have her own status," Iza suggested, "and she's like a daughter to me."

"But she's not of your line, Iza. She was not born to you. Your daughter will carry on your line."

"I know, I have a daughter now, but why can't I train Ayla, too? Didn't you name her as I held her in my arms? Didn't you announce her totem at the same time? That makes her my daughter, doesn't it? She was accepted, she's Clan now, isn't she?" Iza asked fervently, then rushed on, afraid Creb would answer unfavorably. "I think she has a natural talent for it, Creb. She shows an interest, she is always asking me questions when I work the healing magic."

"She asks more questions than anyone I've ever met," Creb interjected, "about everything. She must learn it is discourteous to ask so many questions," he added.

"But look at her, Creb. She sees a wounded animal and wants to heal it. That's the sign of a medicine woman if I ever saw one."

Creb was silent, thoughtful. "Acceptance into the Clan doesn't change who she is, Iza. She was born to the Others, how can she learn all the knowledge you have? You know she doesn't have the memories."

"But she learns quickly. You've seen that. Look how fast she learned to talk. You'd be surprised how much she has learned already. And she has good hands for it, a gentle touch. She held the rabbit while I put on the splint. It seemed to trust her." Iza leaned forward. "Neither of us is young anymore, Creb. What will happen to her when we're gone to the world of the spirits? Do you want her to be traded from fire to fire, always a burden, always the lowest-ranked woman?"

Creb had worried about the same thing himself, but unable to come up with a solution, he put the thought out of his mind. "Do you really think you can train her, Iza?" he asked, still doubtful.

"I can start with that rabbit. I can let her take care of it, show her how. I'm sure she can learn, Creb, even without the memories. I can teach her. There are not so many different illnesses and injuries, she's young enough, she can learn them, she doesn't need to have a memory of them."

"I will have to think about it, Iza," Creb said.

The child was rocking and crooning to the rabbit. She saw Iza and Creb talking and remembered that she had often seen Creb make gestures calling on the spirits to help Iza's healing magic work. She brought the small furry animal to the magician.

"Creb, will you ask the spirits to make the rabbit well?" she motioned after putting it down at his feet.

Mog-ur looked into her earnest face. He had never asked

for help from spirits to heal an animal, and he felt a little foolish about it, but he didn't have the heart to refuse her. He glanced around, then made a few quick gestures.

"Now it's sure to get well," Ayla gestured decisively, then seeing that Iza was through nursing, she asked, "Can I hold the baby, mother?" The rabbit was a warm and cuddly substitute, but not when she could hold the real thing.

"All right," Iza said. "Be careful with her, the way I showed you."

Ayla rocked and crooned to the tiny girl as she had done with the rabbit. "What will you name her, Creb?" she asked.

Iza was curious, too, but she would never have asked him. They lived at Creb's fire, were supported by him, and it was his right to name the children born to his hearth.

"I haven't decided, yet. And you must learn not to ask so many questions, Ayla," Creb chided, but he was pleased at her trust in his magical skill, even with a rabbit. He turned to Iza and added, "I suppose it wouldn't hurt if the animal stayed here until its leg is mended, it's a harmless creature."

Iza made a gesture of acquiescence and felt a warm flush of pleasure. She was sure Creb wouldn't object if she began training Ayla, even if he never gave his explicit consent. All Iza really needed to know was that he wouldn't stop her.

"How does she make that sound in her throat, I wonder?" Iza asked, to change the subject, listening to Ayla's humming. "It's not unpleasant, but it is unusual."

"It's another difference between Clan and Others," Creb motioned with an air of imparting a fact of great wisdom to an admiring student, "like not having the memories, or the strange sounds she used to make. She doesn't make them much anymore since she has learned to talk properly."

Ovra arrived at Creb's hearth with their evening meal. Her amazement was no less than Creb's at seeing the rabbit. It increased when Iza let the young woman hold her baby and she saw Ayla pick up the rabbit and rock it as if it were a baby, too. Ovra gave Creb a sidewise glance to check his reaction, but he seemed not to have noticed it. She could hardly wait to tell her mother. Imagine, mothering an animal. Maybe the girl wasn't right in the head. Did she think the animal was human?

Not long afterward, Brun strolled over and signaled Creb that he wanted to talk to him. Creb was expecting it.

They walked together toward the entrance fire, away from both hearths.

"Mog-ur," the leader started hesitantly.

"Yes."

"I've been thinking, Mog-ur. It's time to have a mating ceremony. I've decided to give Ovra to Goov, and Droog has agreed to take Aga and her children and will allow Aba to live with him, too," Brun said, not quite knowing how to bring up the subject of the rabbit at Creb's fire.

"I was wondering when you were going to decide to mate them," Creb answered, not offering any comment on the subject he knew Brun wanted to discuss.

"I wanted to wait. I couldn't afford to have two hunters restricted while hunting was good. When do you think will be the best time?" Brun was having difficulty trying not to stare into Creb's rock-outlined territory, and Creb was rather enjoying the leader's discomfiture.

"I will be naming Iza's child soon; we could have the matings then," Creb offered.

"I'll tell them," Brun said. He stood on one foot, then the other, looking up at the high-vaulted ceiling and down at the ground, toward the rear of the cave, and then outside, anyplace except directly at Ayla holding the rabbit. Courtesy demanded that he refrain from looking into another man's hearth, yet for him to know about the rabbit, he obviously had to see it. He was trying to think of an acceptable way to broach the subject. Creb waited.

"Why is there a rabbit at your fire?" Brun motioned quickly. He was at a disadvantage and he knew it. Creb deliberately turned and looked at the people within the limits of his domain. Iza knew full well what was going on. She busied herself with the baby, hoping not to be drawn in. Ayla, the cause of the problem, was oblivious to the whole situation.

"It's a harmless animal, Brun," Creb evaded.

"But why is there an animal in the cave?" the leader retorted.

"Ayla brought it in. Its leg is broken and she wanted Iza to fix it," Creb said as though there was nothing unusual about it.

"No one has ever brought an animal into the cave before," Brun said, frustrated that he couldn't find a stronger objection.

"But what's the harm? It won't be around for long, just until its leg is healed," Creb returned, calmly reasonable.

Brun couldn't think of a good reason to insist that Creb get rid of the animal as long as he was willing to keep it. It was within his hearth. There were no customs forbidding animals in caves; it just hadn't been done before. But that wasn't the real source of his distress. He realized the real problem was Ayla. Ever since Iza had picked up the girl, there had been too many unusual incidents associated with her. Everything about her was unprecedented, and she was still a child. What would he have to face when she got older? Brun had no experience, no set of rules to deal with her. But he didn't know how to tell Creb about his doubts either. Creb sensed his brother's uneasiness and tried to give him another reason to let the rabbit stay at his hearth.

"Brun, the clan that hosts the Gathering keeps a cave bear cub in their cave," the magician reminded him.

"But that's different, that's Ursus. That's for the Bear Festival. Cave bears lived in caves even before people, but rabbits don't live in caves."

"The cub is an animal that is brought into a cave, though."

Brun didn't have an answer, and Creb's rationale seemed to offer some guidelines, but why did the girl have to bring the rabbit into the cave in the first place? If it wasn't for her, the problem would never have come up. Brun felt the firm basis of his objections sinking under him like quicksand and he let the matter rest.

The day before the naming ceremony was cold but sunny. There had been a few flurries and Creb's bones had been aching of late. He was sure a storm was on the way. He wanted to enjoy the last few days of clear weather before the snows began in earnest and was walking along the path beside the stream. Ayla was with him, trying out her new footwear. Iza had made them by cutting out roughly circular pieces of aurochs hide, cured with the soft underlayer of hair left on and rubbed with extra fat for waterproofing. She pierced holes around the edge in the manner of a pouch and drew them up around the girl's ankles with the fur side in for warmth.

Ayla was pleased with them and lifted her feet high as she strutted beside the man. Her snow leopard fur covered her inner wrap, and a soft furry rabbit skin was draped over her head, fur side in, covering her ears and tied under her chin with the parts that had once served to cover the animal's legs. She scampered ahead, then ran back and walked beside the old man, slowing her exuberant pace to match his shuffle. They were comfortably silent for a while, each involved with their own thoughts.

I wonder what I should name Iza's baby, Creb was thinking. He loved his sibling and wanted to pick a name she would like. Not one from her mate's side, he thought. Thinking about the man who had been Iza's mate left a bad taste in his mouth. The cruel punishment her mate had inflicted on her made Creb angry, but his feelings went much further back. He remembered how the man had taunted him when he was a boy, calling him *woman* because he could never hunt. Creb guessed it was only his fear of Mog-ur's power that stopped the ridicule. I'm glad Iza had a girl, he thought. A boy would have given him too much honor.

With the man no longer a thorn in his side, Creb enjoyed the pleasures of his hearth more than he ever thought possible. Being the patriarch of his own little family, being responsible for them, providing for them, gave him a sense of manhood he had never experienced. He detected a different kind of respect from the other men and found he had a greater interest in their hunting now that a portion of each fell to him. Before, he was more concerned about the hunt ceremonies; now he had other mouths to feed.

I'm sure Iza's happier, too, he said to himself, thinking about the attention and affection she lavished on him, cooking for him, caring for him, anticipating his needs. In all ways but one, she was his mate, the closest he had ever come to having one. Ayla was a constant joy. The inherent differences he discovered kept him interested; training her was a challenge like that which any natural teacher felt with a bright and willing but unusual pupil. The new baby intrigued him too. After the first few times, he got over his nervousness when Iza laid the infant in his lap, and watched her random hand movements and unfocused eyes in rapt attention, contemplating in wonder how something so tiny and undeveloped could grow into an adult woman.

She assures the continuation of Iza's line, he thought, and it is a line worthy of its rank. Their mother had been one of the most renowned medicine women of the Clan. People from other clans had sometimes come to her, bringing their sick if possible or taking back medicine. Iza, herself, was of equal stature, and her daughter had every possibility of attaining the same eminence. She deserved a name in keeping with her ancient and distinguished heritage.

Creb thought about Iza's line and remembered the woman who had been their mother's mother. She had always been kind and gentle with him, took care of him more than his mother after Brun was born. She, too, was famous for her healing skill, she had even healed that man born to the Others, just as Iza healed Ayla. It's a shame Iza never knew her, Creb mused. Then he stopped.

That's it! I'll give the baby her name, he thought, pleased with his inspiration.

With a name for the infant decided, he turned his attention to the mating ceremonies. He thought about the young man who was his devoted acolyte. Goov was quiet, serious, and Creb liked him. His Aurochs totem should be strong enough for Ovra's Beaver totem. Ovra worked hard and seldom needed to be reprimanded. She would make him a good mate. There's no reason that she shouldn't produce children for him; and Goov is a good hunter, he will provide for her well. When he becomes Mog-ur, his share will compensate when his duties don't allow him to hunt.

Will he ever be a powerful mog-ur? Creb wondered. He shook his head. Much as he liked his acolyte, he realized Goov would never have the skill Creb knew he himself possessed. The crippled body that prevented normal activities like hunting and mating had allowed him time to concentrate all his awesome mental endowment into developing his renowned power. That was why he was The Mog-ur. He was the one that directed the minds of all the other mog-urs at the Clan Gathering in the ceremony that was the holiest of the holy. Although he achieved a symbiosis of minds with the men of his clan, it did not compare with the blending of souls that happened with the trained minds of the other magicians. He thought about the next Clan Gathering, even though it was many years away. Clan Gatherings were held once every seven years, and the last one was the summer before the cave-in. If I live to the next, it will be my last, he suddenly realized.

Creb brought his attention back to the mating ceremony, which would mate Droog and Aga, too. Droog was an experienced hunter who had long since proven his skill. His skill at toolmaking was even greater. He was as quiet and serious as his dead mate's son, and he and Goov shared the same totem. They were much alike in other ways, and Creb was sure it was the spirit of Droog's totem that created Goov. It's a pity Droog's mate was called to the next world, he thought. There had been a fondness between the couple that would probably never develop with Aga. But both needed new mates, and Aga had already proven more prolific than Droog's first mate. It was a logical match.

Creb and Ayla were startled out of their thoughts by a rabbit that dashed across their path. It made the girl think about the rabbit in the cave and turned her mind back to what she had been thinking about all along, Iza's baby.

"Creb, how did the baby get inside Iza?" the girl asked.

"A woman swallows the spirit of a man's totem," Creb motioned casually, still lost in his own thoughts. "It fights with the spirit of her totem. If the man's overcomes the woman's, it leaves a part of itself to start a new life."

Ayla looked around her, wondering at the omnipresence of spirits. She could not see any, but if Creb said they were there, she believed it.

"Can any man's spirit get inside the woman?" she asked next.

"Yes, but only a stronger spirit can defeat hers. Often the totem of a woman's mate asks another spirit to help. Then the other spirit may be allowed to leave its essence. It's usually the spirit of a woman's mate that tries most; it's the closest one, but it often needs help. If a boy has the same totem as his mother's mate, it means he will be lucky," Creb explained carefully.

"Can only women have babies?" she asked, warming to her subject.

"Yes," he nodded.

"Does a woman have to be mated to have a baby?"

"No, sometimes she swallows a spirit before she is mated. But if she doesn't have a mate by the time the baby is born, the baby may be unlucky."

"Could I have a baby?" was her next hopeful query.

Creb thought about her powerful totem. Its vital principal was too strong. Even with the help of another spirit, it was not likely it would ever be defeated. But she will find that out soon enough, he thought.

"You're not old enough, yet," he evaded.

"When will I be old enough?"

"When you are a woman."

"When will I be a woman?"

Creb was beginning to think she would never run out of questions. "The first time your totem's spirit battles with another spirit, you will bleed. That is the sign that it was wounded. Some of the essence of the spirit that fought with it is left behind to make your body ready. Your breasts will grow, and there will be some other changes. After that, your totem's spirit will fight with other spirits regularly. When the time for blood to flow comes and there is none, it means the spirit you swallowed has defeated yours and a new life has started."

"But *when* will I be a woman?"

"Perhaps when you have lived through the cycle of all the seasons eight or nine times. That's when most girls become women, some as early as seven years," he replied.

"But how long will that be?" she insisted.

The patient old magician heaved a sigh. "Come here, I'll see if I can explain," he said, picking up a stick and taking a flint knife from his pouch. He doubted that she would understand, but it might still her questions.

Numbers were a difficult abstraction for people of the Clan to comprehend. Most could not think beyond three: you, me, and another. It was not a matter of intelligence; for example, Brun knew immediately when one of the twenty-two members of his clan was missing. He had only to think of each individual, and he could do it quickly without being conscious of it. But to transfer that individual into a concept called "one" took effort few could master. "How can this person be *one* and another time that person also be *one*—they are different people?" was the first question usually asked.

The Clan's inability to synthesize and abstract extended into other areas of their lives. They had a name for everything. They knew oak, willow, pine, but they had no generic concept for all of them; they had no word for tree. Every kind of soil, each kind of rock, even the different kinds of snow had a name. The Clan depended on their rich memory and their ability to add to that memory—they forgot almost nothing. Their language was replete with color and description but almost totally devoid of abstractions. The idea was foreign to their nature, their customs, the way they had developed. They depended on Mog-ur to keep track of those few things that needed to be counted: the time between Clan Gatherings, the ages of the members of the clan, the length of isolation after a mating ceremony, and the first seven days of a child's life. That he could do so was one of his most magical of powers.

Sitting down, Creb held the stick firmly wedged between his foot and a rock. "Iza says she thinks you are a little older than Vorn," Creb began. "Vorn has lived through his birth year, his walking year, his nursing year, and his weaning year," he explained, cutting a slash in the stick for each year as he said it. "I will make one more mark for you. This is how old you are now. If I take my hand and fit it in each mark, I will cover all of them with one hand, see?"

Ayla looked with concentration at the slash marks, holding out the fingers of her hand. Then she brightened. "I am as many years as this!" she said, showing him her hand with all the fingers extended. "But, how long before I can have a baby?" she asked, far more interested in reproduction than reckoning.

Creb was thunderstruck. How had the girl been able to grasp the idea so quickly? She hadn't even asked what slash marks had to do with fingers or what either had to do with years. It had taken many repetitions before Goov had understood. Creb made three more slash marks and put three fingers over them. With only one hand, it had been especially difficult for him when he was learning. Ayla looked at her other hand and immediately held up three fingers, folding down her thumb and forefinger.

"When I am this many?" she asked, holding out her eight fingers again. Creb nodded affirmatively. Her next action caught him completely by surprise; it was a concept he had spent years mastering himself. She put down the first hand and held up only the three fingers.

"I will be old enough to have a baby in this many years," she gestured with assurance, positive of her deduction. The old magician was rocked to his core. It was unthinkable that a child, a girl child at that, could reason her way to that conclusion so easily. He was almost too overwhelmed to remember to qualify the prediction.

"That is probably the earliest time. It might not be for this many, or possibly this many," he said, making two more slashes on the stick. "Or, perhaps even more. There is no way of knowing for sure."

Ayla frowned slightly, held up her index finger, then her thumb. "How do I know more years?" she asked.

Creb eyed her suspiciously. They were getting into a

realm with which even he had difficulty. He was beginning to be sorry he had begun. Brun would not like it if he knew this girl was capable of such potent magic, magic reserved only for mog-urs. But his curiosity was piqued too. Could she comprehend such advanced knowledge?

"Take both your hands and cover all the marks," he instructed. After she had carefully fitted her fingers over all the slash marks, Creb made one more and put his little finger on it. "The next mark is covered by the small finger of my hand. After the first set, you must think of the first finger of the other person's hand, then the next finger of the other person's hand. Do you understand?" he motioned, watching her closely.

The child hardly blinked. She looked at her hands, then at his hand, then made the grimace that Creb had come to understand meant she was happy. She nodded her head vigorously to indicate that she did understand. Then she made a quantum leap, a jump almost beyond Creb's powers of comprehension.

"And, after that, another person's hands, and then another person's, isn't that right?" she asked.

The impact was too much. His mind reeled. With difficulty, Creb could count to twenty. Numbers beyond twenty blurred into some indistinct infinity called *many*. He had, on a few rare occasions after deep meditation, caught a bare glimpse of the concept Ayla comprehended with such ease. His nod was almost an afterthought. He had a sudden understanding of the gulf between the mind of this girl and his own, and it shook him. He struggled to compose himself.

"Tell me, what is the name of this?" he asked to change the subject, holding up the stick he had been using to mark. Ayla stared at it, trying to remember.

"Willow," she said, "I think."

"That's right," Creb answered. He put his hand on her shoulder and looked directly into her eyes. "Ayla, it would be best if you refrain from mentioning anything about these to anyone," he said, touching the marks on the stick.

"Yes, Creb," she replied, sensing how important it was to him. She had learned to understand his actions and expressions more than anyone's, except Iza's.

"It's time to go back now," he said. He wanted to be alone to think.

"Do we have to?" she pleaded. "It's still nice out."

"Yes, we do," he said, pulling himself up with the help of his staff. "And it's not proper to question a man when he has made a decision, Ayla," he chided gently.

"Yes, Creb," she responded, bowing her head in acquiescence as she had learned. She walked silently beside him as they headed back to the cave, but soon her youthful exuberance took over, and she was running ahead again. She ran back holding out sticks and rocks, telling Creb the names, or asking him if she couldn't remember. He answered absentmindedly, finding it hard to pay attention for the tumult in his mind.

The first light of dawn scattered the enveloping darkness of the cave, and the fresh crispness in the air smelled of snow on its way. Iza was lying in her bed watching the familiar contours of the cave overhead take shape and definition in the gradually increasing light. This was the day her daughter would be named and accepted as a full member of the clan, the day she would be recognized as a living, viable human. She looked forward to the relaxation of her mandatory confinement, though her association with other members of the clan would still be limited to the women until she stopped bleeding.

At the onset of menarche, girls were required to spend the duration of their first period away from the clan. If it occurred during the winter, the young woman stayed alone in an area set aside at the rear of the cave but was still required to spend one menstrual period alone in spring. Living alone was both frightening and dangerous for a young, unarmed woman used to the protection and company of the whole clan. It was a trial that marked the passage of girls into womanhood, similar to the male's trial of making his first kill, but no ceremony marked her return to the fold. And, though the young woman had fire for protection from carnivorous beasts, it was not totally unknown for a woman never to return—her remains usually found later by some hunting or foraging party. The girl's mother was allowed to visit her once a day to bring her food and reassurance. But if the girl disappeared or was killed, her mother was forbidden to mention it until a minimum number of days had elapsed.

The battles waged by spirits within the bodies of women in the elemental struggle to produce life were deep mysteries to the men. While a woman bled, her totem's essence was powerful: it was winning, defeating some male essential principle, casting out his impregnating essence. If a woman looked at a man during that time, his spirit might be drawn into the losing battle. That was the reason female totems had to be less powerful than male totems, for even a weak totem gained strength from the life force that resided in females. Women drew on the life force; it was they who produced new life.

In the physical world, a man was bigger, stronger, far more powerful than a woman, but in the fearful world of unseen forces, the woman was endowed with potentially more power. Men believed that a woman's smaller, weaker physical form that allowed them to dominate her was a compensating balance and that no woman must ever be allowed to realize her full potential, or the balance would be upset. She was kept from full participation in the spiritual life of the clan to keep her ignorant of the strength the life force gave her.

Young men were warned at their first manhood ceremony of the dire consequences that could result if a woman even glimpsed the esoteric rites of the men, and legends were told of the time when women were the ones who controlled the magic to intercede with the spirit world. The men had taken their magic from them but not their potential. Many young men looked at women in a new light once they became aware of these possibilities. They assumed their male responsibilities with great seriousness. A woman had to be protected, provided for, and totally dominated, or the delicate balance of physical and spiritual forces would be disrupted and the continuing existence of the life of the Clan destroyed.

Because her spiritual forces were so much more powerful during menses, a woman was isolated. She had to stay with the women, was not allowed to touch any food that might be consumed by a man, and spent her time doing unimportant tasks like collecting wood or curing hides that could only be worn by women. The men did not acknowledge her existence, completely ignored her, did not even reprimand her. If a man's eye chanced to fall on her, it was as though she were invisible; he looked through her.

It seemed a cruel penalty. The woman's curse resembled a death curse, the supreme punishment that was inflicted upon members of the Clan if they committed a serious crime. Only the leader could command a mog-ur to call down the evil spirits and lay a curse of death. A mog-ur could not refuse, though it was dangerous for the magician and the clan. Once cursed, the criminal was neither spoken to nor seen by any member of the clan. He was ignored, ostracized; he no longer existed, just as though he were dead. Mate and family grieved his death, no food was shared. A few left the clan and were never seen again. Most simply stopped eating, stopped drinking, and fulfilled the malediction they, too, believed.

Occasionally a death curse might be imposed for a limited period of time, but even that was often fatal since a criminal gave up living for the duration of the curse. But if he lived through a limited death curse, he was admitted back into the clan as a full member, even to his previous status. He had paid his debt to society and his crime was forgotten. Crimes were rare, though, and such punishment was rarely dealt. Though the woman's curse ostracized her partially and temporarily, most women welcomed the periodic respite from the unceasing demands and watchful eyes of the men.

Iza was looking forward to the greater contact she would have after the naming ceremony. She was bored with staying within the stone boundary of Creb's fire and looked with longing at the bright sunshine that streamed in through the mouth of the cave during the last few days before winter snows. She waited anxiously for Creb's signal that announced he was ready and the clan all gathered. Namings were often held before breakfast, shortly after the sun rose while the totems were still close by after protecting the clan during the night. When he beckoned, she hurried to join them and stood in front of Mog-ur, looking down at the ground while she uncovered her child. She held the babe up while the magician looked over her head making the gestures that called the spirits to attend the ceremony. Then, with a flourish, he began.

Dipping into the bowl Goov held, he drew a stripe from the point where the baby's brow ridges joined to the tip of her nose with the red-ochre paste.

"Uba, the girl's name is Uba," Mog-ur said. The naked infant, assailed by the cold wind that whipped past the sunny front porch of the cave, voiced a healthy howl which drowned out the approving murmur of the clan.

"Uba," Iza repeated, cuddling her shivering baby in her arms. It's a perfect name, she thought, wishing she had known the Uba her daughter was named for. The members of the clan filed past, each repeating the name to familiarize themselves and their totems with this newest addition. Iza was careful to keep her head down so she would not inadvertently look upon any of the men who came forward to acknowledge her daughter. Afterward, she wrapped the infant in warm rabbit skins and put her inside her wrap next to her skin. The baby's cries abruptly ceased as she began nursing. Iza stepped back to her place among the women to make way for the mating rituals.

For this ceremony, and this one alone, yellow ochre was used in the sacred ointment. Goov handed the bowl of yellow salve to Mog-ur who held it firmly between the stump of his arm and his waist. Goov could not serve as acolyte at his own mating. He took his position in front of the holy man and waited for Grod to bring forth the daughter of his mate. Uka looked on with mixed emotions—pride that her daughter had made a good match and sorrow to see her leave the hearth. Ovra, dressed in a new wrap, watched her feet as she walked forward closely behind Grod, but a radiance emanated from her demurely lowered face. It was obvious she was not unhappy with the choice that had been made for her. She sat down cross-legged in front of Goov, keeping her eyes down.

With silent formal gestures, Mog-ur again addressed the spirits, then he dipped his middle finger into the bowl of dun-yellow paste and drew the sign of Ovra's totem over the scar of Goov's totem mark, symbolizing the union of their spirits. Dipping again into the ointment, he painted Goov's mark over hers, following the outline of the scar and blurring her mark, showing his dominance.

"Spirit of Aurochs, Totem of Goov, your sign has overcome Spirit of Beaver, Totem of Ovra," Mog-ur gestured. "May Ursus allow that it will always be so. Goov, do you accept this woman?"

Goov answered by tapping Ovra on the shoulder and motioning to her to follow him into the cave to the place newly outlined with small boulders that was now Goov's hearth. Ovra jumped up and followed behind her new mate. She had no choice nor was she asked if she accepted him. The couple would remain isolated, confined to the hearth for fourteen days, during which time they would sleep separately. At the end of the isolation, a ceremony would be held in the small cave by the men to cement the union.

In the Clan, the mating of two people was entirely a spiritual affair, begun with a declaration to the whole clan but consummated by the secret ritual that included only the men. In this primitive society, sex was as natural and unrestrained as sleeping or eating. Children learned, as they learned other skills and customs, by observing adults, and they played at intercourse as they mimicked other activities from a young age. Often a boy who reached puberty, but had not yet made his first kill and existed in a limbo between child and adult, penetrated a girl child even before she reached her menarche. Hymens were pierced young, though males were a little fearful if blood was spilled and quickly ignored the girl if it happened.

Any man could take any woman whenever he wished to relieve himself, with the exception, through long tradition, of his female sibling. Usually, once a pair were mated, they remained more or less faithful out of courtesy for another man's property, but it was counted worse for a man to restrain himself than to take the nearest woman. And a woman was not averse to making subtle, coy gestures that were understood as suggestive if a man appealed to her, inviting his advances. To the Clan, a new life was formed by the ubiquitous essences of the totems, and any relationship between sexual activity and childbirth was beyond conception.

A second ceremony was performed uniting Droog and Aga. Though the couple would be isolated from the clan, except for the other members of the hearth, the rest of those who now shared Droog's fire were free to come and go as they liked. After the second pair entered the cave, the women clustered around Iza and her baby.

"Iza, she is just perfect," Ebra raved. "I must admit I was a little worried when I learned you were pregnant after all this time."

"The spirits watched over me," Iza motioned. "A strong totem helps to make a healthy child, once it succumbs."

"I was afraid the girl's totem might have a bad effect. She looks so different, and her totem is so powerful, it might have deformed the baby," Aba commented.

"Ayla's lucky, she brought me luck," Iza quickly countered, looking to see if Ayla had noticed. The child was watching Oga holding the baby, and hovering close and beaming with pride as though Uba were her own. She hadn't been aware of Aba's comment, but Iza didn't like such thoughts aired openly. "Hasn't she brought us all luck?"

"But you weren't lucky enough to have a boy," Aba pressed her point.

"I wished for a girl, Aba," Iza said.

"Iza! How can you say such a thing!" The women were shocked. They seldom admitted to preferring a girl.

"I don't blame her," Uka jumped to Iza's defense. "You have a son, take care of him, nurse him, raise him, then as soon as he's grown, he's gone. If he isn't killed hunting, he's killed some other way. Half of them are killed while they're still young men. At least Ovra may live for a few more years yet."

They all felt sorry for the mother who had lost her son in the cave-in. They all knew how she had grieved. Ebra tactfully changed the subject.

"I wonder how winters will be at this new cave."

"Hunting has been good, and we've gathered so much and put it away, there's plenty of food stored. The hunters are going out today, probably for their last time. I hope there'll be room enough in the cache so we can freeze it all," Ika said. "And it looks like they're getting impatient. We'd better go make them something to eat."

The women reluctantly left Iza and her baby and went to prepare the morning meals. Ayla sat down beside Iza and the woman put her arm around the girl, holding the baby in the other. Iza was feeling good—glad to be outside on this brisk, cold, sunny, early winter day; glad her child was born, and healthy, and a girl; glad for the cave and that Creb had decided to provide for her; and glad for the thin, blonde, strange girl beside her. She looked at Uba and then Ayla. My daughters, the woman thought, and they *are* both my daughters. Everyone knows Uba will be a medicine woman, but Ayla will be one, too. I'll make sure of that. Who knows, maybe someday she will be a great medicine woman.

9

"The Spirit of Light Dry Snow took the Spirit of Granular Snow as his mate and after a time she gave birth to a Mountain of Ice far to the north. The Sun Spirit hated the glittering child spreading across the land as he grew, keeping away his warmth so no grass could grow. The Sun decided to destroy Ice Mountain, but Storm Cloud Spirit, the sibling of Granular Snow, found out the Sun wanted to kill her child. In the summer when the Sun was most powerful, Storm Cloud Spirit fought with him to save Ice Mountain's life."

Ayla was sitting with Uba in her lap watching Dorv tell the familiar legend. She was captivated, though she knew the story by heart. It was her favorite, she never got tired of it. But the restless year-and-a-half-old toddler in her arms was far more interested in Ayla's long blonde hair and grabbed chubby handfuls of it. Ayla untangled her hair from Uba's clenched fists without taking her eyes off the old man who stood near the fire, retelling the tale in dramatic pantomime as the clan eagerly watched.

"On some days the Sun won the battle and beat down on the hard, cold ice, turning it to water, draining Ice Mountain's life away. But many days Storm Cloud won, covering the face of the Sun, keeping his heat from melting the Ice Mountain too much. Though Ice Mountain starved and shrunk in summer, in winter his mother took the nourishment her mate brought and nursed her son back to health. Every summer the Sun struggled to destroy Ice Mountain, but Storm Cloud kept the Sun from melting all that the mother had fed her child the winter before. At the beginning of each new winter, Ice Mountain was always a little bigger than he had been the winter before; he grew larger, spread farther, covered more land every year.

"And as he grew, a great cold went before him. The winds howled, the snow swirled, and Ice Mountain spread, creeping closer to the place where the People lived. The

Clan shivered, huddling close to the fire while the snow fell on them."

The wind whistling through the bare-limbed trees outside the cave added sound effects to the story, sending a sympathetic shiver of excitement down Ayla's spine.

"The Clan didn't know what to do. 'Why are the spirits of our totems no longer protecting us? What have we done to make them angry with us?' The mog-ur decided to go off by himself to find the spirits and talk to them. He was gone a long time. Many people became restless waiting for the mog-ur to return, especially the younger ones.

"But Durc was more impatient than anyone. 'The mog-ur will never come back,' he said. 'Our totems don't like the cold, they have gone away. We should leave, too.'

"'We cannot leave our home,' the leader said. 'This is where the Clan has always lived. It is the home of our ancestors. It is the home of the spirits of our totems. They have not gone away. They are unhappy with us, but they would be more unhappy without a place, away from the home they know. We cannot leave and take them away. Where would we go?'

"'Our totems have already left,' Durc argued. 'If we find a better home, they may come back. We can go to the south, following the birds that flee from the cold in autumn, and to the east to the land of the Sun. We can go where Ice Mountain cannot reach us. Ice Mountain moves slowly; we can run like the wind. He would never catch us. If we stay here, we will freeze.'

"'No. We must wait for mog-ur. He will return and tell us what to do,' the leader commanded. But Durc would not listen to his sound advice. He pleaded and argued with the People and a few were swayed. They decided to leave with Durc.

"'Stay,' the others begged. 'Stay until the mog-ur returns.'

"Durc would not pay attention. 'The mog-ur will not find the spirits. He will never return. We are leaving now. Come with us to find a new place where Ice Mountain cannot live.'

"'No,' they replied. 'We will wait.'

"Mothers and their mates grieved for the young men and women who left, sure they were doomed. They waited for the mog-ur, but after many days had passed and the mog-ur still hadn't returned, they began to doubt. They began to wonder if they should have left with Durc.

"Then, one day, the Clan saw a strange animal approaching, an animal who was not afraid of the fire. The People were frightened and stared in wonder. They had never seen such an animal before. But when it came closer, they saw it wasn't an animal at all, it was the mog-ur! He was covered with the fur of a cave bear. He had finally come back. He told the Clan what he had learned from Ursus, the Spirit of the Great Cave Bear.

"Ursus taught the People to live in caves, to wear the fur of animals, to hunt and gather in the summer and save food for winter. The People of the Clan always remembered what Ursus taught them, and though Ice Mountain tried, he could not drive the People from their home. No matter how much cold and snow Ice Mountain sent before him, the People would not move, they would not get out of his way.

"Finally, Ice Mountain gave up. He sulked and wouldn't fight the Sun anymore. Storm Cloud became angry because Ice Mountain would not fight and refused to help him anymore. Ice Mountain left the land and went back to his home in the north, and the great cold left with him. The Sun exulted at his victory and chased him all the way to his northern home. There was no place he could hide from the great heat and he was defeated. For many, many years there was no winter, only long days of summer.

"But Granular Snow grieved for her lost child, and the grief made her weak. Light Dry Snow wanted her to have another son and asked Storm Cloud Spirit for help. Storm Cloud felt pity for his sibling and he helped Light Dry Snow to bring her nourishment to make her strong. He covered the face of the Sun again while Light Dry Snow hovered near, sprinkling his spirit for Granular Snow to swallow. She gave birth again to another Ice Mountain, but the People remembered what Ursus taught them. Ice Mountain will never drive the Clan from their home.

"And what happened to Durc and those who left with him? It is said by some that they were eaten by wolves and lions, and by some they were drowned in the great waters. Others say that when they reached the land of the Sun, he became angry because Durc and his people wanted his land. He sent a ball of fire down from the sky to devour them. They disappeared and no one ever saw them again."

"You see, Vorn," Ayla noticed Aga telling her son as she always did after the legend of Durc was told. "You must always pay attention to your mother and to Droog and Brun and Mog-ur. You must never disobey and never leave the clan or you may disappear, too."

"Creb," Ayla said to the man seated beside her. "Do you think Durc and his people might have found a new place to live? He disappeared, but no one ever saw him die, did they? He could have lived, couldn't he?"

"No one ever saw him disappear, Ayla, but hunting is difficult when there are only two or three men. Maybe during the summer they could kill enough small animals, but the big animals they would need to store up enough to carry them through the winter would be much harder and very dangerous. And they would have had to live through many winters before they ever reached the land of the Sun. Totems want a place to live. They would probably desert people who wandered homeless. You wouldn't want your totem to desert you, would you?"

Ayla unconsciously reached for her amulet. "But my totem didn't desert me, even though I was alone and had no home."

"That was because he was testing you. He found you a home, didn't he? The Cave Lion is a strong totem, Ayla. He chose you, he may decide to protect you always because he chose you, but all totems are happier with a home. If you pay attention to him, he will help you. He will tell you what is best."

"How will I know, Creb?" Ayla asked. "I have never seen a Cave Lion Spirit. How do you know when a totem is telling you something?"

"You cannot see the spirit of your totem because he is part of you, inside you. Yet, he will tell you. Only you must learn to understand. If you have a decision to make, he will help you. He will give you a sign if you make the right choice."

"What kind of sign?"

"It's hard to say. Usually it will be something special or unusual. It may be a stone you have never seen before or a root with a special shape that has meaning for you. You must learn to understand with your heart and mind, not your eyes and ears, then you will know. Only you can understand your own totem, no one can tell you how. But when the time comes and you find a sign your totem has left you, put it in your amulet. It will bring you luck."

"Do you have signs from your totem in your amulet, Creb?" the girl motioned, staring at the lumpy leather pouch that hung around the magician's neck. She let the squirming baby get up and go to Iza.

"Yes," he nodded. "One is a tooth from a cave bear given to me when I was chosen to be an acolyte. It wasn't stuck in a jawbone; it was lying on some stones at my feet. I didn't see it when I sat down. It is a perfect tooth, with no decay and no wear. It was a sign from Ursus that I had made the right decision."

"Will my totem give me signs, too?"

"No one can tell. Perhaps, when you have important decisions to make. You will know when the time comes, as long as you have your amulet so your totem can find you. Take care that you never lose your amulet, Ayla. It was given to you when your totem was revealed. It holds the part of your spirit he recognizes. Without it, your totem's spirit will not find his way back when he travels. He will get lost and look for his home in the spirit world. If you lose your amulet and do not find it quickly, you will die."

Ayla shuddered, felt the small pouch hanging from a sturdy thong around her neck, and wondered when she would get a sign from her totem. "Do you think Durc's totem gave him a sign when he decided to leave to find the land of the Sun?"

"No one knows, Ayla. It is not a part of the legend."

"I think Durc was brave to try to find a new home."

"He may have been brave, but he was foolish," Creb answered. "He left his clan and the home of his ancestors and took a great risk. For what? To find something different. He wasn't content to stay. Some young men think Durc was brave, but when they get older and wiser, they learn."

"I think I like him because he was different," Ayla said. "It's my favorite legend."

Ayla saw the women getting up to start the evening meal and jumped to follow them. Creb shook his head after the girl. Every time he thought Ayla was really learning to accept and understand the ways of the Clan, she said or did something that made him wonder. It wasn't that she did anything wrong or bad, just not Clan. The legend was supposed to show the fallacy of trying to change the old ways, but Ayla admired the foolhardiness of the young man in the story who wanted something new. Will she ever get over her unClanlike ideas? he wondered. She has learned quickly, though, Creb admitted.

Girls of the Clan were expected to be well-versed in the skills of adult women by the time they were seven or eight. Many came of age then and were mated soon after. In the nearly two years since they found her—alone, near starvation, unable to find food for herself—she had learned not only how to find food, but how to prepare and preserve it. She was capable of many other important skills as well, and if not as proficient at them as the older, more experienced women, she was at least as adept as some of the younger ones.

She could skin and dress a hide and make wraps, cloaks, and pouches used in various ways. She could cut thongs of even widths in one long spiral from a single hide. Her cords made of long animal hair, sinew, or fibrous bark and roots were strong and heavy or thin and fine depending on their use. Her baskets, mats, and nets woven from tough grasses, roots, and barks were exceptional. She could make a rough hand-axe from a nodule of flint or flake off a sharp-edged piece to use as a knife or scraper so well even Droog was impressed. She could gouge bowls out of sections of logs and smooth them to a fine finish. She could make fire by twirling a sharpened stick between her palms against another piece of wood until a smoldering hot coal developed that fired dry tinder; easier to do if two people alternated the tedious, difficult chore of keeping the sharpened stick moving under a constant firm pressure. But more surprising, she was picking up Iza's medical lore with what seemed to be a natural instinct. Iza was right, Creb thought, she's learning even without the memories.

Ayla was slicing pieces of yam to put into a skin pot that was boiling over a cooking fire. After cutting away the parts that had spoiled, there wasn't much left of each one. The back of the cave, where they were stored, was cool and dry, but vegetables started to soften and rot so late in the winter. Her daydreaming about the coming season had begun a few days before when she had noticed a trickle of water in the ice-locked stream, one of the first signs that it would soon be breaking free. She could hardly wait for spring with its first greens, new buds, and the sweet maple sap that rose and oozed out of notches cut into the bark. It was collected and boiled long in large skin pots until it became a thick, viscous syrup or crystallized into sugar, and stored in birchbark containers. Birch had a sweet sap, too, but not as sweet as maple.

She was not alone in being restless and bored with the long winter, and the inside of the cave. Earlier that day the wind had shifted to the south for a few hours, bringing warmer air from the sea. The melting water ran down the long icicles hanging from the apex of the cave's triangular mouth. They froze again when the temperature dropped, lengthening and thickening the glistening, pointed shafts that had been growing all winter, when the wind veered and brought the chilling blasts from the east again. But the breath of warm air turned the thoughts of everyone to the end of winter.

The women were talking and working, moving their hands rapidly in quick conversational gestures while preparing the food. Toward the end of winter, when food supplies ran low, they combined resources and cooked communally, though still eating separately, except for special occasions. There were always more feasts in winter—it helped to break up the monotony of their confinement—though as the season drew to a close, their feasts were often meager fare. But they had enough food. Fresh meat from small game or an aging deer that the hunters managed to bring in between blizzards was welcomed, though not essential. They still had an adequate supply of dried food on hand. The women were still caught up in the storytelling mood and Aba was telling a woman's story.

"...but the child was deformed. His mother took him out as she was told by the leader, but she could not bear to leave him to die. She climbed high up in a tree with him and tied him to the topmost branches that even cats could not reach. He cried when she left him, and by night he was so hungry he howled like a wolf. No one could sleep. He cried day and night, and the leader was angry with the mother, but as long as he cried and howled, his mother knew he was still alive.

"On the naming day, the mother climbed the tree again early in the morning. Her son was not only still alive, but his deformity was gone! He was normal and healthy. The leader hadn't wanted her son in his clan, but since the baby was still alive, he had to be named and accepted. The boy became a leader himself when he grew up and was always grateful to his mother for putting him where nothing could harm him. Even after he mated, he always brought her part of every hunt. He never cuffed her, never scolded her, always treated her with honor and respect," Aba finished.

"What baby could live through his first days without being fed?" Oga asked, looking at Brac, her own healthy son who had just fallen asleep. "And how could her son become a leader if his mother was not mated to a leader or to a man who would someday become a leader?"

Oga was proud of her new son, and Broud even more proud that his mate had given birth to a son so soon after their mating. Even Brun relaxed his stoic dignity around the baby, his eyes softening as he held the infant who assured the continuity of the leadership of the clan.

"Who would be the next leader if you did not have Brac, Oga?" Ovra asked. "What if you had no sons, only daughters? Maybe the mother was mated to the second-in-command and something happened to the leader." She was a little envious of the younger woman. Ovra didn't have a child yet, though she had become a woman and had been mated to Goov before Oga and Broud were mated.

"Well, anyway, how could a baby that was born deformed suddenly become normal and healthy?" Oga countered.

"I suspect the story was made up by a woman who had a deformed son and wished he were normal," Iza said.

"But it's an ancient legend, Iza. It has been told for generations. Maybe long ago things happened that are no longer possible. How do we know for sure?" Aba said, defending her tale.

"Some things may have been different long ago, Aba, but I think Oga is right. A baby that is born deformed isn't suddenly going to become normal, and it's not likely he could live until his naming day without nursing. But it is an old story. Who knows, there may be some truth in it," Iza conceded.

When the food was ready, Iza carried it back to Creb's hearth as Ayla picked up the husky toddler and followed behind. Iza was thinner, not as strong as she once was, and it was Ayla who carried Uba most of the time. There was a special attachment between the two. Uba followed the girl everywhere and Ayla never seemed to tire of the youngster.

After they ate, Uba went to her mother to nurse, but

soon started fussing. Iza began to cough, making the baby more restless. Finally, Iza pushed the fussing, whining baby toward Ayla.

"Take this child. See if Oga or Aga will nurse her," Iza motioned with irritation, breaking into a hacking cough.

"Are you all right, Iza?" Ayla motioned with a worried look.

"I'm just an old woman, too old to have such a young baby. My milk is drying up, that's all. Uba's hungry; last time Aga fed her, but I think she has already nursed Ona and may not have much milk left. Oga says she has more than enough milk; bring this baby to her tonight." Iza noticed Creb eyeing her closely and looked the other way as Ayla carried the baby to Oga.

She was very careful of the way she walked, keeping her head down with the proper attitude as she neared Broud's hearth. She knew the least infraction would bring down the young man's wrath. She was sure he looked for reasons to scold or hit her, and she did not want him to tell her to take Uba away because of something she did. Oga was happy to nurse Iza's daughter, but with Broud watching, there was no conversation. When Uba had her fill, Ayla carried her back, then sat rocking back and forth, crooning softly under her breath, which always seemed to soothe the baby, until she fell asleep. Ayla had long since forgotten the language she spoke when she first came, but she still crooned when she held the baby.

"I'm just an old woman who gets irritable, Ayla," Iza said as the girl laid Uba down. "I was too old when I gave birth, my milk is drying up already, and Uba shouldn't have to be weaned yet. She's not even through her walking year, but it can't be helped. Tomorrow I'll show you how to make special food for babies. I don't want to give Uba to another woman if I can help it."

"Give Uba to another woman! How can you give Uba to someone else, she belongs with us!"

"Ayla, I don't want to give her up either, but she must get enough to eat and she's not getting it from me. We can't just keep bringing her to one woman or another to nurse when my milk isn't enough. Oga's baby is young yet, that's why she has so much milk. But as Brac grows older, her milk will adjust to his needs. Like Aga, she won't have much extra unless she has another baby always nursing," Iza explained.

"I wish I could nurse her!"

"Ayla, you may be almost as tall as one, but you're not a woman yet. And you're not showing any signs of becoming one soon. Only women can be mothers and only mothers can make milk. We'll start giving Uba regular food and see how she does, but I wanted you to know what to expect. Food for babies must be prepared a special way. Everything must be soft for her; her milk teeth can't chew very well. Grains must be ground very fine before they are cooked, dried meat has to be crushed to a meal and cooked with a little water into a paste, fresh meat must be scraped away from the tough fibers, vegetables mashed. Are there any acorns left?"

"There was a pile of them last time I looked, but the mice and squirrels steal them and many are rotten," Ayla said.

"Find what you can. We'll leach out the bitterness and grind them up to add to the meat. Yams will be good for her, too. Do you know where those small clamshells are? They should be small enough for her mouth; she'll have to learn to eat from them. I'm glad winter is almost over, spring will bring more variety—for all of us."

Iza saw the worried concentration on the girl's earnest face. More than once, especially this past winter, she had been grateful for Ayla's willing help. She wondered if Ayla had been given to her while she was pregnant so she could be a second mother to the baby she had so late in life. It was more than just old age that drained Iza. Though she brushed off references to her failing health, and never mentioned the pain in her chest or the blood she sometimes spit up after a particularly bad coughing spell, she knew Creb was aware that she was far more sick than she let on. He's aging, too, Iza thought. This winter has been hard on him, too. He sits too much in that little cave of his with only a torch to keep him warm.

The old magician's shaggy mane was shot with silver. His arthritis, coupled with his lame leg, made walking an agonizing trial. His teeth, worn down from years of using them to hold things, in place of his missing hand, had begun to ache. But Creb had long ago learned to live with suffering and pain. His mind was as powerful and perceptive as ever, and he worried about Iza. He watched the woman and the girl discussing how to make baby food, noticing how Iza's robust body had shrunk. Her face was gaunt, and her eyes were sunk into deep hollows that emphasized her overhanging brow ridges. Her arms were thin, her hair was turning gray, but it was her persistent cough that bothered him most. I'll be glad when this winter is over, he thought. She needs some warmth and sun.

The winter finally released its frozen grip on the land, and the warming days of spring brought torrents of rain. Ice floes from farther up the mountain careened down the flooding stream long after the snow and ice were gone at the elevation of the cave. The runoff from the melted accumulation turned the saturated soil that fronted the cave into a soggy, slippery sink of oozing mud. Only the stones that paved the entrance kept the cave reasonably dry as the groundwater seeped inside.

But the sucking quagmire couldn't keep the clan in the cave. After their long winter confinement, they spilled out to greet the first warm rays of sun and softer sea breezes. Before the snows were entirely melted, they were squishing barefoot through the cold ooze or slogging in soaked boots that not even the extra layer of rubbed-in fat could keep dry. Iza was busier treating colds in the warming days of spring than she had been in the freezing winter.

As the season waxed and the sun soaked up the moisture, the pace of the clan's life increased. The slow quiet winter spent telling stories, gossiping, making implements and weapons, and in other sedentary activities to pass the time, gave way to the busy active bustle of spring. Women went foraging to collect the first green shoots and buds, and men exercised and practiced to prepare for the first major hunt of the new season.

Uba thrived on her new diet, only nursing out of habit or for the warmth and security. Iza coughed less, though she was weak and had little energy to range too far afield, and Creb began to take his shambling walks along the stream with Ayla again. She loved the springtime better than any other season.

Since Iza had to stay close to the cave most of the time, Ayla fell into the habit of roaming the hillsides looking for plants to replenish Iza's pharmacopoeia. Iza was concerned about her going off alone, but the other women were busy foraging for food, and medicinal plants didn't always grow in the same places as food plants. Iza went with Ayla occasionally, mostly to show her new plants and to identify familiar ones at an earlier stage so she would know where to look for them later. Though Ayla carried Uba, Iza's few trips were tiring for her. Reluctantly, she allowed the girl to go alone more and more.

Ayla found that she enjoyed the solitude of ranging the area by herself. It gave her a sense of freedom to be away from the ever-watchful clan. She often went along with the women when they gathered, too; but whenever she could, she hurried through the tasks that were expected of her so she could have time to search the woods alone. She brought back not only plants she knew, but anything unfamiliar so Iza could tell her about it.

Brun made no open objections; he understood the need for someone to find the plants for Iza to work her healing magic. Iza's illness had not escaped his notice either. But Ayla's eagerness to go off by herself disturbed him. Women of the Clan did not relish being alone. Whenever Iza had gone to look for her special materials, she did it with reservations and a little fear, always returning as quickly as possible if she went alone. Ayla never shirked her duties, always behaved properly, there was nothing she did that Brun could identify as wrong. It was more a feeling, a sense that her attitude, her approach, her thoughts were, not wrong, but different, that kept Brun on edge about her. Whenever the girl went out, she always returned with the folds of her wrap and her collecting basket full, and as long as her forays were so necessary, Brun could not object.

Occasionally, Ayla brought back more than plants. Her idiosyncrasy, that had so amazed the clan, had become a habit. Though they had become accustomed to it, the clan was still a little surprised when she returned with a wounded or ailing animal to nurse back to health. The rabbit she had found shortly after Uba's birth was only the first of many to come. She had a way with animals; they seemed to sense she wanted to help them. And once the precedent had been set, Brun felt disinclined to change it. The only time she was refused was when she brought in a wolf cub. The line was drawn at carnivorous animals that were competition for the hunters. More than once an animal that had been tracked, perhaps wounded, and finally within reach, was snatched at the last moment by a quicker carnivore. Brun would not allow the girl to help an animal that might someday steal a kill from his clan.

Once, when Ayla was down on her knees digging up a root, a rabbit with a slightly crooked hind leg bounded out of the brush and sniffed at her feet. She remained very still, then, making no sudden moves, she slowly extended her hand to pet the animal. Are you my Uba-rabbit? she thought. You've grown into a big, healthy man-rabbit. Did that close call teach you to be more wary? You should be wary of people, too, you know. You might end up over a fire, she continued to herself as she stroked the rabbit's soft fur. Something startled the animal and he sprang away, dashing headlong in one direction, then making an about-face in one bound to charge back the way he had come.

"You move so fast, I don't understand how anyone can catch you. How do you turn around like that?" she motioned after the rapidly retreating rabbit and laughed. Suddenly, she realized it was the first time she had laughed aloud in a long time. She seldom laughed when she was around the clan anymore; it always drew disapproving looks. She found many things humorous that day.

"Ayla, this wild cherry bark is old. It's just not any good anymore," Iza gestured early one morning. "When you go out today, why don't you get some fresh? There's a grove of cherry trees near that clearing to the west, across the stream. Do you know where I mean? Get the inner bark, it's best this time of year."

"Yes, mother, I know where they are," she replied.

It was a beautiful spring morning. The last of the crocus nestled white and purple beside the tall graceful stems of the first bright yellow jonquils. A sparse carpet of new green grass, just beginning to shoot its tiny leaves through the moist soil, painted a thin watercolor wash of verdancy on the rich brown earth of clearings and knolls. Flecks of green dotted the bare branches of bushes and trees with the first buds straining to begin life anew, and pussy willows white-tipped others with their fake fur. A benign sun beamed encouragement to the earth's new beginnings.

Once she was out of sight of the clan, Ayla's carefully controlled walk and demure posture relaxed into a free-swinging gait. She skipped down a gradual slope and ran up the other side, smiling unconsciously with her freedom to move naturally. She scanned the vegetation she passed with an apparent casualness that belied her actively working mind as she categorized and filed away for future reference the growing plants.

There's the new pokeweed coming up, she thought as she

passed the marshy hollow where she had gathered its purple berries the previous autumn. I'll dig some roots on the way back. Iza says the roots are good for Creb's rheumatism, too. I hope the fresh cherry bark will help Iza's cough. She's getting better, I think, but she's so skinny. Uba's getting so big and heavy, Iza shouldn't lift her at all. Maybe I'll bring Uba with me next time, if I can. I'm so glad we didn't have to give her to Oga. She's really starting to talk now. It'll be fun when she gets a little bigger and we can go out together. Look at those pussy willows. Funny how they feel like real fur when they're small like that, but they grow out green. The sky is so blue today. I can smell the sea in the wind. I wonder when we'll be going fishing. The water should be warm enough to swim in soon. I wonder why no one else likes to swim? The sea tastes salty, not like the stream, but I feel so light in it. I can hardly wait until we go fishing. I think I love sea fish best of all, but I like eggs, too. And I like climbing the cliff to get the eggs. The wind feels so good way up high on the cliff. There's a squirrel! Look at him run up that tree! I wish I could run up a tree.

Ayla wandered over the wooded slopes until midmorning. Then, suddenly realizing how late it was getting, she headed purposefully toward the clearing to get the cherry bark Iza wanted. As she neared, she heard activity and an occasional voice, and caught a glimpse of the men within the clearing. She started to leave, but remembered the cherry bark and stood undecided for a moment. The men won't like it if they see me around here, she thought. Brun might get angry and not let me go out alone anymore, but Iza needs the cherry bark. Maybe they won't stay long. I wonder what they're doing, anyway? Quietly, she crept in closer and hid behind a large tree, peeking out through the tangled bare brush.

The men were practicing with their weapons in preparation for a hunt. She remembered watching them make new spears. They had chopped down slim, supple, straight young trees, stripped them of branches and sharpened one end by charring it in a fire, and scraping the burnt end to a point with a sturdy flint scraper. The heat also hardened the point so it would resist splintering and fraying. She still cringed when she remembered the commotion she had caused by touching one of the wooden shafts.

Females did not touch weapons, she was told, or even any

tools that were used to make weapons, though Ayla could see no difference between a knife used to cut the leather to make a sling and a knife used to cut the leather to make a cloak. The newly made spear, offended by her touch, had been burned, much to the irritation of the hunter who made it, and Creb and Iza had both subjected her to long, gestured lectures in an effort to instill in her a sense of the abomination of her act. The women were aghast that she would consider such a thing, and Brun's glower left no doubt of his opinion. But, most of all, she hated the look of malicious pleasure on Broud's face as the recriminations rained down upon her. He was positively gloating.

The girl stared uneasily from behind the brushy screen at the men on the practice field. Besides their spears, the men had their other weapons. Except for a discussion at the far end between Dorv, Grod, and Crug about the relative merits of spear versus club, most of the men were practicing with slings and bolas. Vorn was with them. Brun had decided it was time to begin teaching the boy the rudiments of the sling, and Zoug was explaining them to the youngster.

The men had been taking Vorn along with them to the practice field occasionally since he was five, but most of the time he practiced with his miniature spear, jabbing it into the soft earth or a rotten tree stump to get the feel of handling the weapon. He was always pleased to be included, but this was the first attempt to teach the youngster the more difficult art of using a sling. A post had been pounded into the ground, and not far away was a heap of smooth round stones picked up from streams along the way.

Zoug was showing Vorn how to hold the two ends of the strip of leather together and how to place a pebble into the slight bulge in the middle of a well-worn sling. It was an old one that Zoug had planned to throw away until Brun asked him to start the boy's training. The old man thought it would still be serviceable if he cut it shorter to match Vorn's smaller size.

Ayla watched and found herself caught up in the lesson. She concentrated on Zoug's explanations and demonstrations with as much attention as the lad. On Vorn's first attempt, the sling got tangled and the stone dropped. It was difficult for him to get the knack of whirling the weapon around to build up the momentum of centrifugal force necessary to hurl the stone. The pebble kept dropping before he could get up enough speed to keep it in the cup of the leather strip.

Broud was standing off to the side watching. Vorn was his protégé, and it kept Broud the object of Vorn's adoration. It was Broud who had made the small spear the boy carried with him everywhere, even to his bed, and it was the young hunter who showed Vorn how to hold the spear, discussing the balance and thrust with him as though the boy were an equal. But now, Vorn was directing his admiring attention to the older hunter and Broud felt displaced. He had wanted to be the one to teach the boy everything and was angry when Brun told Zoug to instruct him in the use of the sling. After Vorn made several more unsuccessful tries, Broud interrupted the lesson.

"Here, let me show you how to do it, Vorn," Broud motioned, brushing the old man aside.

Zoug stepped back and shot a piercing look at the arrogant young man. Everyone stopped and stared, and Brun was glaring. He did not like Broud's cavalier treatment of the clan's best marksman. He had told Zoug to train the boy, not Broud. It's one thing to show an interest in the youngster, Brun thought, but he's carrying it too far. Vorn should learn from the best and Broud knows the sling is not his best weapon. He needs to learn that a good leader must utilize the skills of every man. Zoug is the most skilled and he will have time to teach the boy when the rest of us are hunting. Broud is becoming overbearing; he's too proud. How can I give him a higher rank if he doesn't show better judgment? He needs to learn he's not so important just because he will be leader, just *because* he will be leader.

Broud took the sling from the lad and picked up a stone. He inserted it in the pocket of the sling and hurled it toward the post. It landed short of the mark. That was the most common problem men of the clan had with the sling. They had to learn to compensate for the limitation of their arm joints that prevented a full-swinging arc. Broud was angry at missing and felt a little foolish. He reached for another stone, flung it hurriedly, wanting to show he could do it. He was aware that he was being watched by everyone. The sling was shorter than he was accustomed to, and the stone went far to the left, still short of the post.

"Are you trying to teach Vorn or do you want a few

lessons yourself, Broud?" Zoug gestured derisively. "I could move the post closer."

Broud fought to restrain his temper—he didn't like being the object of Zoug's ridicule and he was angry that he kept missing after he'd made such an issue of it. He cast another stone, this time overcompensating and sending it far beyond the post.

"If you'll wait until I'm through with the boy's lesson, I'll be glad to give you one," Zoug motioned, heavy sarcasm showing in his stance. "It looks like you could use it." The proud old man was feeling vindicated.

"How can Vorn learn on a rotten old sling like this?" Broud flared defensively, throwing the leather strap down with disgust. "No one could throw a stone with that worn-out old thing. Vorn, I'll make you a new sling. You can't be expected to learn on an old man's used-up sling. He can't even hunt anymore."

Now Zoug was angry. Retirement from the ranks of the active hunters was always a blow to a man's pride, and Zoug had worked hard to perfect his skill with the difficult weapon to retain a measure of it. Zoug had once been second-in-command like the son of his mate, and his pride was especially tender.

"It's better to be an old *man*, than a boy who thinks he's a man," Zoug countered, reaching for the sling at Broud's feet.

The slur on his manhood was more than Broud could bear, it was the last straw. He could contain himself no longer and gave the old man a shove. Zoug was unbalanced, caught off guard, and fell down heavily. He sat where he landed, his legs stretched out in front of him, looking up with wide-eyed surprise. It was the last thing he'd expected.

Hunters of the Clan never attacked each other physically; such punishment was reserved for women who couldn't understand more subtle reproaches. Exuberant energies of young men were drained off with supervised wrestling bouts, or running-and-spear-thrusting competitions, or sling and bola meets that also served to increase hunting skills. Skill in hunting and self-discipline were the measure of manhood in the Clan that depended on cooperation for survival. Broud was almost as surprised as Zoug at his own rashness, and as soon as he realized what he had done, his face turned red with embarrassment.

"*Broud!*" The word came out of the leader's mouth in a

restrained roar. Broud looked up and cringed. He had never seen Brun so angry. The leader approached him, planting his feet firmly with each step, his gestures clipped and tightly controlled.

"This childish display of temper is inexcusable! If you were not already the lowest-ranked hunter, I would put you there. Who told you to interfere with the boy's lesson in the first place? Did I tell you, or Zoug, to train Vorn?" Anger flashed from the leader's eyes. "You call yourself a hunter? You cannot even call yourself a man! Vorn controls himself better than you. A woman has more self-discipline. You are the future leader; is this how you will lead men? You expect to control a clan when you can't even control yourself? Don't be so sure of your future, Broud. Zoug is right. You are a child who thinks he's a man."

Broud was mortified. He had never been shamed so severely, and in front of the hunters, and Vorn. He wanted to run and hide, he'd never be able to live it down. He would rather have faced a charging cave lion than Brun's anger—Brun, who seldom showed his anger, who seldom had to. One penetrating look from the leader, who commanded with stoic dignity, capable leadership, and unswerving self-discipline, was enough to make any member of his clan, man or woman, jump to obey him. Broud hung his head submissively.

Brun glanced toward the sun, then made a signal to leave. The other hunters, uncomfortably watching the scathing reprimand Brun had delivered, were relieved to get away. They fell in behind the leader who set a fast pace back to the cave. Broud brought up the rear, his face still crimson.

Ayla crouched unmoving, rooted to the spot, hardly daring to breathe. She was petrified for fear they would see her. She knew she had witnessed a scene no woman would ever be allowed to see. Broud would never have been castigated like that in front of a woman. The men, no matter what the provocation, maintained a brotherhood of solidarity around women. But the episode had opened the girl's eyes to a side of the men she never realized existed. They were not the all-powerful, free agents who reigned with impunity, as she had thought. They too had to follow orders and they too could be reprimanded. Brun alone seemed to be the one omnipotent figure who ruled supreme. She didn't understand that Brun was under constraints far more binding than any of the others: the traditions and customs of the Clan, the unfathomable, unpredictable spirits that controlled the forces of nature, and his own sense of responsibility.

Ayla remained hidden long after the men left the practice field, afraid they might return. She was still apprehensive when she finally dared to step out from behind the tree. Though she didn't fully comprehend the implications of her new insight into the nature of the men of the clan, one thing she did understand; she had seen Broud as submissive as any woman, and that pleased her. She had learned to hate the arrogant young man who picked on her unmercifully, scolding her for the least infraction whether she knew it was wrong or not, and she often wore the bruises of his quick temper. She couldn't seem to please him, no matter how hard she tried.

Ayla walked across the clearing thinking about the incident. As she neared the post, she saw the sling still on the ground where Broud had flung it in anger. No one had remembered to retrieve it before they left. She stared at it, afraid to touch it. It was a weapon, and fear of Brun made her tremble at the thought of doing anything that might make him as angry at her as he had been at Broud. Her mind wandered back over the whole series of incidents she had just witnessed, and looking at the limp strap of leather reminded her of Zoug's instructions to Vorn, and Vorn's difficulty. Is it really so hard? If Zoug showed me, could I do it?

She was appalled at the temerity of her own thought and glanced around to make sure she was alone, fearful that even her thoughts would be known if someone saw her. Broud couldn't even do it, she recalled. She thought about Broud trying to hit the post and Zoug's disparaging gestures at his failure, and a fleeting smile crossed her face.

Wouldn't he be mad if I could do it when he couldn't? She liked the thought of bettering Broud at anything. Looking around once more, she glanced down at the sling apprehensively, then stooped down and picked it up. She felt the supple leather of the worn weapon and suddenly thought about the punishment that would descend on her if anyone saw her with a sling in her hand. She nearly dropped it again, looking quickly across the clearing in the direction the men had gone. Her eye fell on the small pile of stones.

I wonder, could I do it? Oh, Brun would be so mad at me, I don't know what he'd do. And Creb would say I was bad. I'm already bad, just for touching this sling. What can be so bad about touching a piece of leather? Just because it's used to throw stones. Would Brun beat me? Broud would. He'd be glad I touched it, it would give him an excuse to beat me. Wouldn't he be mad if he knew what I saw. They'd be so angry, could they be any madder if I tried it? Bad is bad, isn't it? I wonder, could I hit that post with a stone?

The girl was torn between wanting to try out the sling and the knowledge that she was forbidden to do it. It was wrong. She knew it was wrong. But she wanted to try it. What difference will one more bad thing make? No one will ever know, there's no one here but me. She glanced around guiltily once more, then walked toward the stones.

Ayla picked one up and tried to remember Zoug's instructions. Carefully, she put the two ends together and gripped them firmly. The loop of leather hung limp. She felt clumsy, unsure of how to put the stone in the well-worn cup. Several times the stone dropped as soon as she began to move it. She concentrated, trying to visualize Zoug's demonstrations. She tried again, almost got it started, but the sling became hung up and the stone dropped to the ground again.

The next time, she managed to get some momentum going and flung the round pebble a few paces. Elated, she reached for another stone. After a few more false starts, she lobbed a second stone. The next few tries were unsuccessful, then one stone flew, wide of the mark, but closer to the post. She was beginning to get the knack.

When the pile of stones was gone, she gathered them up again, and then a third time. By the fourth round, she was able to fling most of the stones without dropping them very often. Ayla looked down and saw three stones left on the ground. She picked one up, placed it in the sling, whirled it over her head and launched the missile. She heard a *thunk* as it hit the post squarely and bounced back, and she jumped into the air filled with the thrill of success.

I did it! I hit the post! It was pure chance, a lucky fluke, but that didn't diminish her joy. The next stone flew wide, but far beyond the post, and the last fell to the ground only a few feet ahead. But she had done it once, and she was sure she could do it again.

She started to collect the stones again and noticed the sun was nearing the horizon in the western sky. Suddenly, she remembered she was supposed to be getting wild cherry bark for Iza. How did it get so late? she thought. Have I been here all afternoon? Iza will be worried; Creb will be, too. Quickly, she stuffed the sling into a fold of her wrap, raced to the cherry trees, cut away the outer bark with her flint knife, and scraped off long thin pieces of the inner cambium layer. Then she ran back to the cave as fast as she could, slowing only as she neared the stream to assume the careful posture proper for females. She was afraid she would be in enough trouble for being gone so long; she didn't want to give anyone more reason to be angry.

"Ayla! Where have you been? I've been worried sick. I was sure you had been attacked by some animal. I was ready to ask Creb to have Brun look for you." Iza scolded the moment she saw her.

"I was looking around to see what was starting to grow, and down by the clearing," Ayla said, feeling guilty. "I didn't realize how late it was." It was the truth, but not the whole truth. "Here's your cherry bark. The pokeweeds are coming up where they grew last year. Didn't you tell me the roots were good for Creb's rheumatism, too?"

"Yes, but you steep the root and apply it as a wash to relieve the pain. The berries are made into a tea. Juice from squeezed berries is good for growths and lumps, too," the medicine woman started, answering her question automatically, then stopped. "Ayla, you're trying to distract me with healing questions. You know you shouldn't have been gone so long, making me worry like that," Iza motioned. Her anger, now that she knew the child was safe, was gone, but she wanted to make sure Ayla would not go off by herself so long again. Iza worried whenever Ayla went out.

"I won't do it again without telling you, Iza. It just got late before I knew it."

As they walked into the cave, Uba, who had been looking for Ayla all day, spied her. She ran toward the girl on her chubby, bowed legs, and stumbled just as she reached her. But Ayla scooped the baby up before she fell and swung her around in the air. "Could I take Uba with me sometime, Iza? I wouldn't be gone too long. I could start to show her some things."

"She's too young to understand, yet. She's just learning to talk," Iza said, but seeing how happy the two were together, she added, "I suppose you could take her along for company once in a while, if you don't go too far."

"Oh, good!" Ayla said, giving Iza a hug with the baby in her arms. She held the small girl up in the air and laughed out loud, while Uba gazed at her with twinkling eyes full of adoration. "Won't that be fun, Uba?" she said after she put the child down. "Mother is going to let you come with me."

What's gotten into that child? Iza thought. I haven't seen her so excited for a long time. There must be strange spirits in the air today. First, the men come back early; and they don't sit around talking as usual, they each go to their own fires and hardly pay any attention to the women. I don't think I've seen one of them scold anyone. Even Broud was almost nice to me. Then, Ayla stays out all day and comes back full of energy, hugging everyone. I don't understand it.

10

"Yes? What do you want?" Zoug gestured impatiently. It was unusually warm for so early in the summer. Zoug was thirsty and uncomfortable, sweating in the hot sun working a large deer hide with a blunt scraper as it was drying. He was not in the mood for interruptions, especially from the flat-faced, ugly girl who had just sat down near him with her head bowed waiting for him to acknowledge her.

"Would Zoug like a drink of water?" Ayla motioned, looking up demurely at his tap on her shoulder. "This girl was at the spring and saw the hunter working in the hot sun. This girl thought the hunter might be thirsty, she did not mean to interrupt," she said with the formality proper to addressing a hunter. She offered a birchbark cup and held out the cool, dripping waterbag made from the stomach of a mountain goat.

Zoug grunted affirmatively, hiding his surprise at the girl's thoughtfulness while she poured the cold water into the cup for him. He hadn't been able to catch the eye of a woman to tell her he wanted a drink, and he didn't want to get up himself just then. The hide was nearly dry. It was critical to keep working it for the finished product to be as supple and flexible as he wanted. His glance followed the girl as she put the waterbag in a shady spot nearby, then brought out a bundle of tough grasses and water-soaked woody roots to prepare to weave a basket.

Although Uka was always respectful and responded to his requests without hesitation since he had moved in with the son of his mate, she seldom tried to anticipate his needs the way his own mate had done before she died. Uka's primary attention was directed at Grod, and Zoug had missed the special little accommodations of a devoted mate. Zoug occasionally glanced at the girl sitting near him. She was silent, intent on her work. Mog-ur has trained her well, he thought. He didn't notice her watching him out of the corner of her eye as he pulled and stretched and scraped the damp skin.

Later that evening, the old man was sitting alone in front of the cave, staring off into the distance. The hunters were gone. Uka and two other women had gone with them, and Zoug had eaten at Goov's hearth with Ovra. Seeing the young woman, fully adult now and mated, when it seemed not so long ago she was just an infant in Uka's arms, made Zoug feel the passage of time that had robbed him of the strength to hunt with the men. He had left the hearth shortly after eating. He was in the midst of his thoughts when he noticed the girl coming toward him with a wicker bowl in her hands.

"This girl picked more raspberries than we can eat," she said after he acknowledged her. "Can the hunter find room to eat them so they are not wasted?"

Zoug accepted the proffered bowl with a pleasure he couldn't quite hide. Ayla sat quietly at a respectful distance while Zoug savored the sweet, juicy berries. When he was through, he returned the bowl and she left quickly. I don't know why Broud says she is disrespectful, he thought, watching her go. I can't see anything so wrong with her, except that she is remarkably ugly.

The next day, Ayla again brought water from the cool

spring while Zoug worked, and set out the materials for the collecting basket she was making nearby. Later, as Zoug was just finishing rubbing fat into the soft deerskin, Mog-ur hobbled over to the old man.

"It's hot work to cure a hide in the sun," he motioned.

"I'm making new slings for the men, and I promised Vorn a new one, too. The leather must be very flexible for slings; it must be worked constantly while it's drying and the fat must be completely absorbed. It's best to do it in the sun."

"I'm sure the hunters will be pleased to have them," Mog-ur remarked. "It's well known you're the expert when it comes to slings. I've watched you with Vorn. He's fortunate to have you teaching him. It's a difficult skill to master. There must be an art to making them, too."

Zoug beamed under the magician's praise. "Tomorrow I will cut them out. I know the sizes for the men, but I'll have to fit Vorn to his. A sling must suit the arm for best accuracy and power."

"Iza and Ayla are preparing the ptarmigan you brought the other day as Mog-ur's share. Iza is teaching the girl to cook them the way I like. Would you take your meal at Mog-ur's hearth tonight? Ayla wanted me to ask and I would be happy for your company. Sometimes a man likes to talk to another man, and I have only females at my hearth."

"Zoug will eat with Mog-ur," the old man replied, obviously pleased.

Though communal feasts were frequent, and often two families shared a meal, especially if they were related, Mog-ur seldom invited others to his fire. Having a place of his own was still rather new to him, and he enjoyed relaxing in the company of his females. But he had known Zoug since boyhood, had always liked and respected him. The pleasure on the old man's face made Mog-ur think he should have asked him before. He was glad Ayla mentioned it. Zoug had, after all, given him the ptarmigan.

Iza was not used to company. She worried and fretted and outdid herself. Her knowledge of herbs extended to seasonings as well as medicines. She knew how to use a subtle touch and compatible combinations that enhanced the flavor of foods. The meal was delicious, Ayla especially attentive in unobtrusive ways, and Mog-ur was pleased with them both. After the men had stuffed themselves, Ayla served them a delicate herb tea of chamomile and mint that Iza knew would aid digestion. With two females ready to anticipate their every wish, and a chubby contented baby, who crawled in both their laps tugging happily on beards, making them feel young again, the two old men relaxed and talked about times past. Zoug was appreciative and just a little envious of the happy hearth the old magician could call his own, and Mog-ur felt his life couldn't be sweeter.

The next day, Ayla watched Zoug measure a leather strip to Vorn and paid close attention while the old man explained why the ends had to be tapered just so, why it should be neither too long nor too short, and saw him put a round stone that had been soaking in water in the middle of the loop to stretch the leather enough to form the cup. He was gathering up the scraps after cutting out several more slings when she brought him a drink of water.

"Does Zoug have other uses for the pieces left? The leather looks so soft," she motioned.

Zoug felt expansive toward the attentive, admiring girl. "I have no further use for the scraps. Would you like them?"

"This girl would be grateful. I think some of the pieces are large enough to use," she gestured with her head bowed.

The next day Zoug rather missed Ayla working beside him and bringing him water. But his task was finished, the weapons were made. He noticed her heading for the woods with her new collecting basket strapped to her back and her digging stick in her hand. She must be going to gather plants for Iza, he thought. I don't understand Broud at all. Zoug didn't care much for the young man; he hadn't forgotten the attack on him earlier in the season. Why does he always keep after her? The girl is hardworking, respectful, a credit to Mog-ur. He's fortunate to have her and Iza. Zoug was remembering the pleasant evening he had spent with the great magician, and though he never mentioned it, he recalled it was Ayla who had asked Mog-ur to invite him to share a meal with them. He watched the tall, straight-legged girl walking away. It's a shame she's so ugly, he thought, she'd make some man a good mate someday.

After Ayla made herself a new sling out of Zoug's scraps to replace the old one that had finally worn out, she decided to look for a place to practice away from the cave. She was always afraid someone would catch her. She started upstream along the watercourse that flowed near the cave, then began ascending the mountain along a tributary creek, forcing her way through heavy underbrush.

She was stopped by a steep rock wall over which the creek spilled in a cascading spray. Jutting rocks, whose jagged outlines were softened by a deep cushion of lush green moss, separated the falling water bouncing from rock to rock into long thin streams that splashed up, creating veils of mist, and fell again. The water collected itself in a foaming pool that filled a shallow rocky basin at the foot of the waterfall before it continued down to meet the larger waterway. The wall presented a barrier that ran parallel to the stream, but as Ayla hiked along its base back toward the cave, the sheer drop angled up in a steep but climbable grade. At the top the gound leveled out, and as she continued she came to the upper course of the creek and began to follow it upstream again.

Moist, gray green lichen draped the pine and spruce that dominated the higher elevation. Squirrels darted up the tall trees and across the underlying turf of variegated moss, carpeting earth and stones and fallen logs alike in a continuous cover that shaded from light yellow to deep green. Ahead she could see bright sunshine filtering through the evergreen woods. As she followed the creek, the trees thinned out, intermixed with a few deciduous trees dwarfed to brush, then opened out to a clearing. She emerged from the woods into a small field whose far end terminated in the gray brown rock of the mountain, sparsely covered with clinging growth as it soared to higher reaches.

The creek, which meandered across one side of the meadow, found its source in a large spring gushing out of the side of a rock wall near a large hazelnut clump growing flush against the rock. The mountain range was honeycombed with underground fissures and chutes that filtered the glacial runoff, which appeared again as clear, sparkling springs.

Ayla crossed the high mountain meadow and drank deeply of the cold water, then stopped to examine the still unripe double and triple clusters of nuts encased in their green, prickly coverings. She picked a clump, peeled away the casing, and cracked the soft shell with her teeth, exposing a shiny white half-grown nut. She always liked unripe hazelnuts better than fully mature ones that had dropped to the ground. The taste aroused her appetite and she began to pick several clusters and put them into her basket. While reaching, she noticed a dark space behind the heavy foliage.

Cautiously, she pushed aside the branches and saw a small cave hidden by the heavy hazelnut shrubs. She forced aside the brush, looked carefully inside, then stepped in, letting the branches swing back. Sunlight dappled one wall with a pattern of light and shadows and dimly lit the interior. The small cave was about twelve feet deep and half as wide. If she reached up, she could almost touch the top of the entrance. The roof sloped down gently for about half the depth, angling more sharply down to the dry dirt floor toward the rear.

It was just a small hole in the mountain wall, but large enough for a girl to move around in comfortably. She saw a cache of rotted nuts and a few squirrel droppings near the entrance and knew the cave had not been used by anything larger. Ayla danced around in a full circle, delighted with her find. The cave seemed to be made just for her.

She went back out and looked across the glade, then climbed a short way up the bare rock and inched out on a narrow ledge that snaked around the outcrop. Far ahead, between the cleft of two hills, was the sparkling water of the inland sea. Below, she could make out a tiny figure near a thin silver ribbon of a stream. She was almost directly above the cave of the clan. Climbing back down, she walked around the perimeter of the clearing.

It's just perfect, she thought. I can practice in the field, there's water to drink nearby, and if it rains I can go into the cave. I can hide my sling in there, too. Then I won't have to be afraid Creb or Iza will find it. There are even hazelnuts, and later I can bring some back for winter. The men almost never climb up this high to hunt. This will be my own place. She ran across the clearing to the creek and began looking for smooth, round pebbles to try out her new sling.

Ayla climbed to her retreat to practice every chance she could. She found a more direct, if steeper, route to her small mountain meadow and often surprised wild sheep, chamois, or shy deer from their grazing. But the animals that frequented the high pasture soon grew accustomed to her and only moved to the opposite end of the grassy clearing when she came.

When hitting the post with a stone lost its challenge as

she gained skill with the sling, she set more difficult targets for herself. She watched Zoug give instructions to Vorn, then applied the advice and techniques when she practiced alone. It was a game to her, something fun to do; and to add interest, she compared her progress with Vorn's. The sling was not his favorite weapon, it smacked of an old man's device. He was more interested in the spear, the weapon of the primary hunters, and had managed to make a few small kills of slower-moving creatures, snakes and porcupines. He didn't apply himself the way Ayla did and it was more difficult for him. It gave her a sense of pride and accomplishment when she knew she was better than the boy, and a subtle shift in attitude—a change that was not lost on Broud.

Females were supposed to be docile, subservient, unpretentious, and humble. The domineering young man took it as a personal affront that she didn't cower a little when he came near. It threatened his masculinity. He watched her, trying to see what was different about her, and was quick to cuff just to see a fleeting look of fear in her eyes or to make her cringe.

Ayla tried to respond properly, did everything he commanded as quickly as she could. She didn't know there was freedom in her step, an unconscious carry-over from roaming the forests and fields; pride in her bearing, from learning a difficult skill and doing it better than someone else; and a growing self-confidence in her mien. She didn't know why he picked on her more than anyone else. Broud didn't know himself why she annoyed him so much. It was indefinable, and she could no more have changed it than she could change the color of her eyes.

Part of it was his memory of the attention she had usurped from him at his manhood rites, but the real problem was she was not Clan. She had not had subservience bred into her for untold generations. She was one of the Others; a newer, younger breed, more vital, more dynamic, not controlled by hidebound traditions from a brain that was nearly all memory. Her brain followed different paths, her full, high forehead that housed forward-thinking frontal lobes gave her an understanding from a different view. She could accept the new, shape it to her will, forge it into ideas undreamed of by the Clan, and, in nature's way, her kind was destined to supplant the ancient, dying race.

At a deep, unconscious level, Broud sensed the opposing

destinies of the two. Ayla was more than a threat to his masculinity, she was a threat to his existence. His hatred of her was the hatred of the old for the new, of the traditional for the innovative, of the dying for the living. Broud's race was too static, too unchanging. They had reached the peak of their development; there was no more room to grow. Ayla was part of nature's new experiment, and though she tried to model herself after the women of the clan, it was only an overlay, a façade only culture-deep, assumed for the sake of survival. She was already finding ways around it in answer to a deep need that sought an avenue of expression. And though she tried in every way she could to please the overbearing young man, inwardly she began to rebel.

One particularly trying morning, Ayla went to the pool for a drink. The men were gathered together at the opposite side of the cave opening planning their next hunt. She was glad, for it meant Broud would be gone for a while. She was sitting with a cup in her hands beside the still water, lost in thought. Why is he always so mean to me? Why does he always pick on me? I work as hard as anyone else. I do everything he wants. What good does it do to try so hard? None of the other men keep after me the way he does. I just wish he'd leave me alone.

"Ouch!" she cried involuntarily as Broud's hard blow caught her by surprise.

Everyone stopped and looked at her, then quickly looked away. A girl so close to womanhood didn't cry out like that just because a man cuffed her. She turned toward her tormentor, her face red with embarrassment

"You were just staring at nothing, sitting there doing nothing, lazy girl!" Broud gesticulated. "I told you to bring us some tea and you ignored me. Why should I have to tell you more than once?"

A rising surge of anger flushed her cheeks even more. She felt humiliated by her outcry, shamed in front of the whole clan, and furious at Broud for causing it. She got up, but not with the usual quick jump to obey his command. Slowly, insolently, she got to her feet, shot Broud a look of cold hatred before she moved away to get the tea, and heard a gasp from the watching clan. How did she dare to behave with such brazenness?

Broud exploded in a rage. He sprang after her, spun her around, and plowed his fist into her face. It knocked her to the ground at his feet and he followed with another smashing blow. She cowered, trying to protect herself with her arms as he pounded her again and again. She fought to voice no sound, though silence was not expected under such abuse. Broud's fury mounted with his violence; he wanted to hear her cry out and rained down one crashing blow after another in his uncontrolled rage. She gritted her teeth, steeling herself to the pain, stubbornly refusing to give him the satisfaction he wanted. After a time, she was beyond crying out.

Dimly, through a red foggy haze, she realized the beating had stopped. She felt Iza help her up and leaned heavily on the woman as she stumbled into the cave, nearly unconscious. Surges of pain washed over her as she wavered in and out of numbed insensibility. She was only vaguely aware of cool, soothing poultices and Iza supporting her head so that she could drink a bitter-tasting brew before she slipped into a drugged sleep.

When she awoke, the faint light of predawn barely outlined the familiar objects within the cave, feebly assisted by the dull glow of dying coals in the fireplace. She tried to rise. Every muscle and bone in her body rebelled at the movement. A moan escaped her lips, and a moment later Iza was beside her. The woman's eyes spoke eloquently; they were filled with pain and concern for the girl. Never had she seen anyone beaten so brutally. Not even her mate at his worst had ever beaten Iza so hard. She was sure Broud would have killed her if he hadn't been forced to stop. It was a scene Iza never thought she would see and never wanted to see again.

As her memory of the incident returned, Ayla was filled with fear and hatred. She knew she should not have been so insolent, but she had no reason to expect such a violent reaction. Why was it that she drove him to such raging outbursts?

Brun was angry, the quiet cold anger that made the whole clan walk softly and avoid him as much as possible. He had disapproved of Ayla's impudence, but Broud's reaction shocked him. He was right to punish the girl, but Broud had overdone the punishment by far. He didn't even respond to the leader's command to stop; Brun had to drag him away. Worse, his loss of control was over a female. He had allowed a girl to prod him into the emasculating display of uncontrolled rage.

After Broud's fit of temper at the practice field, Brun had been sure the young man would never allow himself to lose control again, but now he had just thrown a tantrum that was worse than childish, worse because Broud had the powerful body of a grown man. For the first time, Brun began to seriously doubt the wisdom of Broud becoming the next leader, and it hurt the stoic man more than he cared to admit. Broud was more than the child of his mate, more than the son of his heart. Brun was sure it was his own spirit that had created him and he loved him more than life itself. He felt the young man's failure with a stab of guilt. The fault must be his. Somewhere he had failed, he had not raised him properly, trained him properly, had shown him too much favor.

Brun waited several days before talking to Broud. He wanted to give himself time to think everything through carefully. Broud spent the time in a state of nervous agitation, hardly leaving his hearth, and it was almost a relief when Brun finally signaled him, though his heart beat with trepidation as he followed behind Brun. There was nothing in the world he feared so much as Brun's anger, but it was Brun's very lack of anger that brought his message home.

In simple gestures and quiet tones, Brun told Broud exactly what he had been thinking. He took the blame for Broud's failures, and the young man felt more shame than he ever had in his life. He was made to understand Brun's love, and his anguish, in a way he had not known before. Here was not the proud leader Broud had always respected and feared, here was a man who loved him and was deeply disappointed in him. Broud was filled with remorse.

Then Broud saw a hard look of resolution in Brun's eyes. It nearly broke Brun's heart, but the interests of the clan must come first.

"One more outburst, Broud. Just one more hint of such a display, and you are no longer the son of my mate. It is your place to follow me as leader, but before I will entrust the clan to a man with no self-control, I will disown you and have you cursed with death." No emotion showed on the leader's face as he continued. "Until I see some sign that you are a man, there is no hope that you are capable of leadership. I will be watching you, but I will be watching the other hunters, too. I will have to see more than just no outward displays of temper, I will have to know you are a man, Broud. If I have to choose someone else as leader, your status will be set at the lowest rank, permanently. Have I made myself clear?"

Broud couldn't believe it. Disowned? Death cursed? Someone else chosen as leader? Always the lowest-ranked male? He can't mean it. But Brun's set jaw and hard look of determination left no doubt.

"Yes, Brun," Broud nodded. His face was ashen.

"We will say nothing of this to the others. Such a change will be difficult for them to accept and I don't want to cause unnecessary concern. But have no doubt I will do as I say. A leader must always put the clan's interests before his own; it is the first thing you must learn. That is why self-control is so essential to a leader. The clan's survival is his responsibility. A leader has less freedom than a woman, Broud. He must do many things he may not want to. If necessary, he must even disown the son of his mate. Do you understand?"

"I understand, Brun," Broud replied. He wasn't really sure that he did. How could a leader have less freedom than a woman? A leader could do anything, command everyone, women and men alike.

"Go now, Broud. I want to be alone."

It was several days before Ayla was able to get up, and much longer before the purplish discolorations that covered her body turned to a sickly yellow and finally faded away. At first, she was so apprehensive that she was afraid to go near Broud, and jumped at the sight of him. But as the last ache left her, she began to notice the change in him. He no longer picked on her, no longer badgered her, positively avoided her. Once she forgot the pain, she began to feel the beating was almost worth it. Ever since then, she realized, Broud had let her entirely alone.

Life was easier for Ayla without his constant harassment. She hadn't realized the pressure she was under until it stopped. She felt free by comparison, though her life was still as limited as the rest of the women's. She walked with enthusiasm, sometimes breaking into an excited run or happy skip, held her head high, swung her arms freely, even laughed out loud. Her feeling of freedom translated itself into her movements. Iza knew she was happy, but her actions were uncommon and brought disapproving looks. She was just too exuberant; it wasn't proper.

Broud's avoidance of her was obvious to the clan, too, and the subject of speculation and wonder. From casual notice of gestured conversations, Ayla began to piece together a notion that Brun had threatened Broud with dire consequences if he hit her again, and she became convinced when the young man ignored her even when she provoked him. She was just a little careless at first, allowing her natural inclinations a freer rein, but then she began a purposeful campaign of subtle insolence. Not the brazen disrespect that had caused the beating, but small things, petty tricks calculated to annoy him. She hated him, wanted to get back at him, and felt protected by Brun.

It was a small clan, and as much as he tried to avoid her, in the course of the clan's normal interactions, there were occasions when Broud had to tell her what to do. She made a point of being slower to respond to him. If she thought no one was watching, she'd raise her eyes and stare at him with the peculiar grimace of which only she was capable while she watched him struggle for control. She was careful when others were around, especially Brun. She had no desire to feel the leader's wrath, but she became scornful of Broud's anger and pitted her will against his more openly as the summer progressed.

Only when she accidentally happened to catch a glance of venomous hatred did she wonder at the wisdom of her actions. His look of hostility was so malevolently intense, it came almost as a physical blow. Broud blamed her entirely for his untenable position. If she had not been so insolent, he would not have gotten so angry. If it wasn't for her, he wouldn't have a death curse hanging over his head. Her happy exuberance irritated him no matter how he tried to control it. It was patently obvious her behavior was shockingly indecent. Why couldn't the other men see it? Why did they let her get away with it? He hated her more deeply than before, but he was careful not to show it when Brun was around.

The battle between them had gone below the surface, but it was played out with fiercer intensity, and the girl was not as subtle as she thought. The whole clan was aware of the tension between them and wondered why Brun allowed it. The men, taking their cue from the leader, refrained from interference and even permitted the girl more freedom than they normally would have, but it made the clan uncomfortable, men and women both.

Brun disapproved of Ayla's behavior; he hadn't missed any of what she thought were subtle ploys, nor did he like seeing Broud let her get away with it. Insolence and rebellion were unacceptable from anyone, especially females. It shocked him to see the girl pitting her will against a male. No woman of the Clan would consider it. They were content with their place; their position was not a veneer of culture, it was their natural state. They understood with a deep instinct their importance to the existence of the Clan. The men could no more learn their skills than the women could learn to hunt; they hadn't the memories for it. Why should a woman struggle and fight to change a natural state—would she struggle to stop eating, to stop breathing? If Brun hadn't been absolutely certain she was female, he would have thought from her actions she was male. Yet she had learned the women's skills and was even showing an aptitude for Iza's magic.

As much as it disturbed him, Brun refrained from interfering because he could see Broud struggling for self-control. Ayla's defiance was helping Broud master his temper, a mastery so essential to a future leader. For all that he had seriously considered finding a new successor, Brun was sympathetic where the son of his mate was concerned. Broud was a fearless hunter, and Brun was proud of his bravery. If he could learn to control his one obvious fault, Brun thought Broud would make a good leader.

Ayla was not fully aware of the tensions surrounding her. She was happier that summer than she could ever remember. She took advantage of her increased freedom to wander by herself more, collecting herbs and practicing with her sling. She didn't shirk any chores that were required of her—she wasn't allowed to—but one of her tasks was to bring Iza the plants she needed and it gave her an excuse to be away from the hearth. Iza never did regain her full strength, though her cough subsided with the warmth of summer. Both Creb and Iza worried about Ayla. Iza was sure things could not go on the way they were and decided to go out with the girl on a foraging trip and use the opportunity to talk to her.

"Uba, come here, mother's ready," Ayla said, picking up the toddler and securing her firmly to her hip with the cloak. They walked down the slope and crossed the stream to the west and continued through woods along an animal trail that had been enlarged slightly by occasional use as a path. When they came to an open meadow, Iza stopped and looked around, then headed for a stand of tall, showy, yellow flowers that resembled asters.

"This is elecampane, Ayla," Iza said. "It usually grows in fields and open places. The leaves are large ovals with pointed ends, dark green on top and downy underneath, see?" Iza was down on her knees holding a leaf as she explained. "The rib in the middle is thick and fleshy." Iza broke it to show her.

"Yes, mother, I see."

"It's the root that's used. The plant grows from the same root every year, but it's best to collect it the second year, late in summer or fall, then the root is smooth and solid. Cut it into small pieces and take about as much as will fit in your palm, boil it down in the small bone cup to more than half full. It should cool before it's drunk, about two cups a day. It brings up phlegm and is especially good for the lung disease of spitting blood. It also helps to bring on sweating and to pass water." Iza had used her digging stick to expose a root and was sitting on the ground, her hands moving rapidly as she explained. "The root can be dried and ground to a powder, too." She dug up several roots and put them in her basket.

They moved across a small knoll, then Iza stopped again. Uba had fallen asleep, secure in her comfortable closeness. "See that little plant with the funnel-shaped yellowish flowers, purple in the middle?" Iza pointed to another plant.

Ayla touched a foot-high plant. "These?"

"Yes. That's henbane. Very useful to a medicine woman but should never be eaten; it can be dangerously poisonous if used as food."

"What part is used? The root?"

"Many parts. Roots, leaves, seeds. The leaves are larger than the flowers, grow one after the other on alternate sides of the stem. Pay close attention, Ayla. The leaves are a dull, pale green with spiky edges, and see the long hairs growing along the middle?" Iza touched the fine hairs while Ayla looked closely. Then the medicine woman picked a leaf and bruised it. "Smell," she instructed. Ayla sniffed; the leaf had a strong narcotic odor.

"The smell goes away after it's dried. Later there will be many small brown seeds." Iza dug down and pulled out a thick, yam-shaped, corrugated root with a brown skin. The white inner color showed where it had broken. "The different parts are used for different things, but all of them are good for pain. It can be made into a tea and drunk—it's very strong, doesn't take much—or into a wash and applied on the skin. It stops muscle spasms, calms and relaxes, brings sleep."

Iza gathered several plants, then walked to a nearby stand of brilliant hollyhocks and picked several of the rose, purple, white, and yellow blossoms from the tall simple stems. "Hollyhocks are good for soothing irritations, sore throats, scrapes, scratches. The flowers make a drink that can ease pain, but it makes a person sleepy. The root is good for wounds. I used hollyhock roots on your leg, Ayla." The girl reached down and felt the four parallel scars on her thigh and thought suddenly about where she'd be now if it weren't for Iza.

They walked along together for a while, enjoying the warm sun and the warmth of each other's company without talking. But Iza's eye was constantly scanning the area. The chest-high grass of the open field was golden and gone to seed. The woman looked across the field of grain, tops bent with their heavy load of mature seeds, undulating gently in the warm breeze. Then she saw something and walked purposefully through the tall stalks and stopped at a section of the rye grass whose seeds had a violet black discoloration.

"Ayla," she said, pointing to one of the stalks. "This is not the way rye grass normally grows, it is a sickness of the seeds, but we are lucky to find it. It's called ergot. Smell it."

"It smells awful, like old fish!"

"But there's magic in those sick seeds that's especially helpful for pregnant women. If a woman is a long time in labor, it can help bring the baby faster. It causes contractions. It can start labor, too. It can make a woman lose her baby early, and that's important, especially if she's had problems with earlier deliveries or is still nursing. A woman shouldn't have babies too close together, it's hard on her, and if she loses her milk, who will feed the baby she has? Too many babies die at birth or in their first year; a mother has to take care of the one that's already living and has a chance to grow up. There are other plants that can help her lose the baby early if she needs to, ergot is only one. It's good after delivery, too. It helps push out the old blood and shrink her organs back to normal. It tastes bad, not as bad as it smells, but it's useful if used wisely. Too much can cause severe cramps, vomiting, even death."

"It's like henbane, it can be harmful or helpful," Ayla commented.

"That's often true. Many times the most poisonous plants make the best and strongest medicines, if you know how to use them."

On the way back toward the stream, Ayla stopped and pointed to an herb with bluish purple flowers, about a foot high. "There's some hyssop. The tea is good for coughs when you have a cold, right?"

"Yes, and it adds a nice spicy flavor to any tea. Why don't you pick some?"

Ayla pulled out several plants by the roots and plucked off the long thin leaves as she walked. "Ayla," the woman said. "Those roots send up new plants every year. If you pull the roots there will be no plants here next summer. It's best just to pick off the leaves if you have no use for the roots."

"I didn't think about that," Ayla said contritely. "I won't do it again."

"Even if you use the roots, it's best not to dig them all up from one place. Always leave some to grow more."

They doubled back toward the stream, and when they came to a marshy spot, Iza pointed out another plant. "This is sweet rush. It looks something like iris, but it's not the same. The boiled root made into a wash soothes burns, and chewing the roots sometimes helps toothaches, but you must be careful when giving it to a pregnant woman. Some women have lost their babies from drinking the juice, though I've never had much luck with it when I gave it to a woman for that purpose. It can help an upset stomach, especially constipation. You can tell the difference by this growth here," Iza pointed. "It's called a corm, and the plant smells stronger, too."

They stopped and rested in the shade of a broad-leafed maple near the stream. Ayla took a leaf, curled it into the shape of a cornucopia, folded up the bottom and tucked it under her thumb, then dipped up a cool drink from the stream. She brought a drink for Iza in the makeshift cup before throwing it away.

"Ayla," the woman began after finishing the drink. "You should do as Broud tells you, you know. He is a man, it's his right to command you."

"I do everything he tells me," she countered defensively.

Iza shook her head. "But you don't do it the way you should. You defy him, you provoke him. Someday you may regret it, Ayla. Broud will be leader one day. You must do what the men say, all the men. You are a woman, you have no choice."

"Why should men have the right to command women? What makes them better? They can't even have babies!" she gestured bitterly, feeling rebellious.

"That's the way it is. That's the way it has always been in the Clan. You are Clan now, Ayla. You are my daughter. You must behave as a girl of the Clan should."

Ayla hung her head, feeling guilty. Iza was right, she did provoke Broud. What would have happened to her if Iza had not found her? If Brun had not let her stay? If Creb had not made her Clan? She looked at the woman, the only mother she could remember. Iza had aged. She was thin and drawn. The flesh of her once-muscular arms hung from her bones and her brown hair was almost gray. Creb had seemed so old to her at first, but he had hardly changed at all. It was Iza who looked old now, older than Creb. Ayla worried about Iza, but whenever she said anything, the woman put her off.

"You're right, Iza," the child said. "I haven't behaved the way I should to Broud. I'll try harder to please him."

The toddler Ayla was carrying began to squirm. She looked up, suddenly bright-eyed. "Uba hungry," she motioned, then stuffed a chubby fist into her mouth.

Iza glanced at the sky. "It's getting late, and Uba's hungry. We'd better start back," she gestured.

I wish Iza were strong enough to go out with me more often, Ayla said to herself as they hurried back to the cave. Then we could spend more time with each other, and I always learn so much more when she's with me.

Though Ayla tried to live up to her decision to please Broud, she found her resolution hard to keep. She had fallen into the habit of not paying attention to him, knowing he would turn to someone else or do it himself if she didn't move quickly. His dark looks held no fear for her, she felt secure from his wrath. She did stop trying to provoke him on purpose, but her impertinence had become a habit, too. For too long had she looked up at him instead of bowing her head, ignoring him instead of scurrying to do his bidding; it was automatic. Her unconscious disdain grated on him worse than her attempts to annoy him. He felt she had no respect for him. It wasn't respect for him she had lost, it was fear.

The time when cold winds and heavy snows would force the clan into the cave again was drawing near. Ayla hated to see the leaves starting to turn, though autumn's brilliant display always captivated her and its rich harvest of fruits and nuts kept the women busy. Ayla had little time to climb to her secret retreat during the last rush to lay in a supply of fall's harvest, but the time passed so quickly she hardly noticed until near the end of the season.

The pace finally slowed and one day she strapped on her basket, took her digging stick, and climbed to her hidden clearing once more, planning to collect hazelnuts. The moment she arrived, she shrugged her basket off her back and went inside the cave for her sling. She had furnished her playhouse with a few implements she had made and an old sleeping fur. She took a birchbark cup from a flattish piece of wood stretched across two large rocks that also held a few shell dishes, a flint knife, and some rocks she used to crack nuts. Then she got her sling from the covered wicker basket where she kept it. After getting a drink from the spring, she ran along the creek looking for pebbles.

She made a few practice shots. Vorn doesn't hit his targets as often as I do, she thought, pleased with herself when her stones landed where she aimed them. After a while, she grew tired of the sport, put her sling and the last few pebbles away, and began to pick up the nuts scattered on the ground beneath the thick, gnarled old bushes. She was thinking how wonderful life was. Uba was growing and thriving and Iza seemed much better. Creb's aches and pains were always less severe in the warm summers and she loved the slow shambling walks with him beside the stream. Playing with the sling was a game she loved and she had become quite skillful with it. It was almost too easy to hit the post or the rocks and branches she sighted as targets, but there was still an excitement about playing with the forbidden weapon. And best of all, Broud didn't bother her at all anymore. She didn't think anything could ever spoil her happiness as she filled her gathering basket with nuts.

Brown, dry leaves were caught by the brisk winds as they fell from the trees, whirled around by their unseen partner, and dropped gently to the ground. They covered the nuts still scattered beneath those trees that had brought them to maturity. Fruit not picked for winter storage hung ripe and heavy on branches bereft of foliage. The eastern steppes were a golden sea of grain, rippled by wind in imitation of the foam-bedecked waves of gray water to the south; and the last of the sweet clusters of plump, round grapes, bursting with juice, beckoned to be picked.

The men were in their usual knot planning one of the last hunting trips of the season. They had been discussing the proposed trek since early morning, and Broud had been sent to tell a woman to bring them water to drink. He saw Ayla sitting near the mouth of the cave with sticks and pieces of thong spread out around her. She was constructing frames from which bunches of grapes would be hung until they dried to raisins.

"Ayla! Bring water!" Broud signaled and started back.

The girl was lashing a critical corner, supporting the unfinished frame against her body. If she moved just then, it would collapse and she'd have to start over again. She hesitated, looked to see if another woman was nearby, then heaving a sigh of reluctance, got up slowly, and went to find a large waterbag.

The young man fought to quell the anger that quickly rose at her obvious reluctance to obey him, and struggling with his fury, he looked for another woman who would respond to his request with proper alacrity. Suddenly, he changed his mind. He looked back at Ayla just getting up and narrowed his eyes. What gave her the right to be so insolent? Am I not a man? Isn't it her place to obey me? Brun never told me to allow such disrespect, he thought. He can't put a death curse on me just for making her do what she's supposed to do. What kind of leader would let a female defy him? Something snapped inside Broud. Her impudence has gone on too long! I won't let her get away with it. She *will* obey me!

The thoughts came to him in the split second it took to make the three strides covering the distance between them. Just as she stood up, his hard fist caught her by surprise and knocked her flat. Her startled look quickly changed to anger. She glanced around and saw Brun watching, but there was a quality about his expressionless face that warned her to expect no assistance from him. The rage in Broud's eyes changed her anger to fear. He had seen her flash of anger and it aroused his passionate hatred of her. How dare she defy him!

Quickly, Ayla scrambled out of the way of the next blow. She ran toward the cave to find the waterbag. Broud stared after her, his fists clenched, fighting to keep his fury within manageable bounds. He glanced toward the men and saw Brun's impassive face. There was no encouragement in his expression, but no denial either. Broud watched as Ayla hurried to the pool to fill the bag, then hoist the heavy bladder on her back. He had not missed her quick response nor her look of fear when she saw that he meant to hit her again. It made his anger a little easier to control. I've been too easy on her, he thought.

As Ayla passed close to Broud, bent over with the weight of the heavy water-filled bag, he gave her a shove that nearly knocked her down again. Anger flushed her cheeks. She straightened up, shot him a quick hate-filled glance, and slowed her step. He went after her again. She ducked, taking the blow on her shoulder. The clan was watching now. The girl looked toward the men. Brun's hard stare hurried her more than Broud's fists had. She ran the short distance, knelt down, and began pouring water into a cup, keeping her head bowed. Broud followed slowly behind, fearful of Brun's reaction.

"Crug was saying he saw the herd traveling north, Broud," Brun motioned casually as Broud rejoined the group.

It was all right! Brun was not angry at him! Of course, why should he be angry? I did the right thing. Why should he make any reference to a man disciplining a female who deserved it? Broud's sigh of relief was almost audible.

When the men were through drinking, Ayla returned to the cave. Most of the people had gone back to what they were doing, but Creb still stood at the entrance watching her.

"Creb! Broud almost beat me again," she gestured, running up to him. She looked up at the old man she loved, but the smile on her face faded as she saw a look on his she had never seen before.

"You only got what you deserved," he motioned with a grim scowl. His eye was hard. He turned his back on her and limped back to his hearth. Why is Creb mad at me? she thought.

Later that evening, Ayla shyly approached the old magician and reached out to put her arms around his neck, a gesture that had never failed to melt his heart before. He made no response, didn't even bother to shrug her away. He just stared into the distance, cold and aloof. She shrunk back.

"Don't bother me. Go find worthwhile work to do, girl. Mog-ur is meditating, he has no time for insolent females," he motioned with an abrupt, impatient gesture.

Tears filled her eyes. She was hurt and suddenly a little frightened of the old magician. He wasn't the Creb she knew and loved anymore. He was Mog-ur. For the first time since she came to live with the clan, she understood why everyone else kept their distance and stood in awe and fear of the great Mog-ur. He had withdrawn from her. With a look and a few gestures, he conveyed disapproval and a sense of rejection stronger than she had ever felt. He didn't love her anymore. She wanted to hug him, to tell him she loved him, but she was afraid. She shuffled over to Iza.

"Why is Creb so angry with me?" she motioned.

"I told you before, Ayla, you should do as Broud says. He is a man, he has the right to command you," Iza said gently.

"But, I *do* everything he says. I've never disobeyed him."

"You resist him, Ayla. You defy him. You know you are insolent. You do not behave as a well brought-up girl should. It's a reflection on Creb—and on me. Creb feels he has not trained you properly, has allowed you too much freedom, has let you have your own way with him so you think you can have your own way with everyone. Brun is not happy with you either, and Creb knows it. You run all the time. Children run, Ayla, not girls the size of women. You make those sounds in your throat. You do not move quickly when you are told to do something. Everyone disapproves of you, Ayla. You have shamed Creb."

"I didn't know I was so bad, Iza," Ayla gestured. "I did not want to be bad, I just didn't think about it."

"But you should think about it. You're too big to behave like a child."

"It's just that Broud has always been so mean to me, and he beat me so hard that time."

"It makes no difference if he is mean or not, Ayla. He can be as mean as he wants; it's his right, he's a man. He can beat you anytime he wants, as hard as he wants. He will be leader someday, Ayla, you must obey him, you must do just as he says, when he says it. You have no choice," Iza explained. She looked at the stricken face of the child. Why is it so hard for her? she wondered. Iza felt a sadness and sympathy for the girl who had such difficulty accepting the facts of life. "It's late, Ayla, go to bed."

Ayla went to her sleeping place, but it was a long time before she went to sleep. She tossed and turned and slept badly when sleep did finally overcome her. She was awake early, took her basket and digging stick, and was gone before breakfast. She wanted to be alone, to think. She climbed to her secret meadow and got her sling, but she didn't feel much like practicing.

It's all Broud's fault, she thought. Why does he always pick on me? What did I ever do to him? He never has liked me. So what if he's a man, what makes men better? I don't care if he is going to be leader, he's not so great. He's not even as good as Zoug with the sling. I could be as good as he is, I'm already better than Vorn. He misses a lot more than I do; Broud probably does, too. He missed when he was showing off for Vorn.

Angrily, she started slinging stones. One bounced into a copse of bushes and flushed a sleepy porcupine from his hole. The small nocturnal animals were seldom hunted. Everyone made a big thing about Vorn killing a porcupine, she thought. I could, too, if I wanted to. The animal was ambling up a sandy hill near the creek, quills extended. Ayla fitted a stone into the bulge of her leather sling, took aim, and fired the stone. The slow-moving porcupine was an easy target; it dropped to the ground.

Ayla ran toward the creature, pleased with herself. But when she touched it, she realized the porcupine wasn't dead, only stunned. She felt his beating heart and saw the blood trickling from the wound on his head and had a sudden impulse to bring the small animal back to the cave to heal him as she had done with so many wounded creatures. She wasn't pleased anymore; she felt terrible. Why did I hurt him? I didn't want to hurt him, she thought. I can't bring him back to the cave. Iza would know right away he was hit with a stone; she's seen too many animals killed with a sling.

The child stared at the wounded animal. I can't ever hunt, she realized. Even if I killed an animal, I could never bring it back to the cave. What good is all this practicing with a sling? If Creb is mad at me now, what would he do if he knew? What would Brun do? I'm not even supposed to touch a weapon, much less use one. Would Brun make me go away? Ayla was overcome with guilt and fear. Where would I go? I can't leave Iza and Creb and Uba. Who would take care of me? I don't want to leave, she thought, bursting into tears.

I've been bad. I've been so bad, and Creb is so mad at me. I love him, I don't want him to hate me. Oh, why is he so mad at me? Tears streamed down the unhappy girl's face. She lay down on the ground, sobbing her misery. When she had cried herself out, she sat up and wiped her nose with the back of her hand, her shoulders shaking with renewed sobs every now and then. I won't be bad anymore, ever. Oh, I'll be so good. I'll do whatever Broud wants, no matter what. And I won't ever touch a sling again. To emphasize her conviction, she threw the sling under a bush, raced to get her basket, and started down to the cave. Iza had been looking for her and saw her returning.

"Where have you been? You've been gone all morning and your basket is empty."

"I've been thinking, mother," Ayla motioned, looking at Iza with earnest seriousness. "You were right, I've been bad. I won't be bad anymore. I will do everything Broud wants me to. And I will behave the way I should, I won't run or anything. Do you think Creb will ever love me again, if I'm very, very good?"

"I'm sure he will, Ayla," Iza replied, patting her gently. She's had that sickness again, the one that makes her eyes water when she thinks Creb doesn't love her, the woman thought, looking at Ayla's tear-streaked face and red swollen eyes. Her heart ached for the girl. It's just harder for her, her kind are different. But perhaps it will be better now.

11

The change in Ayla was unbelievable. She was a different person. She was contrite, she was docile, she raced to do Broud's bidding. The men were convinced it was brought about by his tightened discipline. They nodded their heads knowingly. She was living proof of what they had always maintained: if men were too lenient, women became lazy and insolent. Women needed the firm guidance of a strong hand. They were weak, willful creatures, unable to exert the self-control of men. They wanted men to command them, to keep them under control, so they would be productive members of the clan and contribute to its survival.

It didn't matter that Ayla was only a girl or that she was not truly Clan. She was nearly old enough to be a woman, already taller than most, and she was female. The women felt the effects as the men took their own ideas to heart. The men of the clan didn't want to be guilty of leniency.

But Broud took the male philosophy to heart with a vengeance. Though he clamped down harder on Oga, it was nothing to the assault he launched on Ayla. If he had been hard on her before, he was doubly hard on her now. He kept after her constantly, hounded her, harassed her, sought her out with every kind of insignificant task to make her jump to his demands, cuffed her at the least infraction, or at no infraction—and he enjoyed it. She had threatened his manhood and now she was going to pay. Too often had she resisted him; too often had she defied him; too often had he fought to keep from hitting her. Now it was his turn. He had bent her to his will and he was going to keep her there.

Ayla did everything she could to please him. She even tried to anticipate his wants, but that backfired when he reprimanded her for assuming she could know what he wanted. The moment she stepped outside the boundaries of Creb's hearth, he was ready, and she could not stay within the stones that marked off the magician's private domain without reason. It was the last busy time of the season, with the final preparations for winter; there were just too many things that needed to be done to secure the clan from the fast-approaching cold. Iza's stock of medicine was essentially complete, so there was little excuse for Ayla to leave the environs of the cave. Broud ran her ragged all day, and at night she collapsed in bed exhausted.

Iza was sure Ayla's change of heart had less to do with Broud than he imagined. It was her love for Creb more than her fear of Broud. Iza told the old man Ayla had suffered from her unique sickness again when she thought he didn't love her.

"You know she went too far, Iza. I had to do something. If Broud hadn't begun disciplining her again, Brun would have. That could have been worse. Broud can only make her life miserable; Brun can make her leave," he replied, but it gave the magician cause to wonder about the power of love having more force than the power of fear, and the theme occupied his thoughts during his meditations for days. Creb softened toward her almost immediately. It had been all he could do to maintain his indifferent aloofness from the beginning.

The first light siftings of snow were washed away by frigid downpours that changed to sleet or freezing rain with the cooling temperatures of evening. Morning found puddles crusted with thin shattery ice, portending a deeper cold, only to melt again when the capricious wind blew from the south and an irresolute sun decided to press its authority. All during the indecisive transition from late fall to early winter, Ayla never faltered in her proper feminine obedience. She acquiesced to Broud's every whim, jumped at his every demand, bowed her head submissively, controlled the way she walked, never laughed or even smiled, and was totally unresisting—but it wasn't easy. And though she struggled against it, tried to convince herself she was wrong, forced herself to be even more docile, she began to chafe under the yoke.

She lost weight, lost her appetite, was quiet and subdued even within Creb's hearth. Not even Uba could make her smile, though she often picked the baby up the moment she returned to the hearth at night and held her until they both fell asleep. Iza worried about her, and when a day of bright sunshine followed one of freezing rain, she decided it was time to give Ayla a little respite before the winter closed in on them completely.

"Ayla," Iza said loudly as they stepped outside the cave before Broud could make his first demand. "I was checking my medicines and I don't have any snowberry stems for stomachaches. It's easy to identify. It's a bush covered with white berries that stay on after the leaves have fallen."

Iza neglected to mention that she had many other remedies in stock for stomachaches. Broud frowned as Ayla raced into the cave for her collecting basket. But he knew that gathering Iza's magic plants was more important than getting him a drink of water, or tea, or a piece of meat, or the fur skins he purposely forgot to wrap around his legs as leggings, or his hood, or an apple, or two stones from the stream to crack nuts because he didn't like the stones near the cave, or any of the other inconsequential tasks he might think of for her to do. He stalked away when Ayla emerged from the cave with her basket and digging stick.

Ayla ran into the forest grateful to Iza for the chance to be alone. She glanced around her as she walked, but her mind wasn't on snowberry bushes. She didn't pay any attention to her direction and didn't notice when her feet began to take her along a small creek to a mist-veiled mossy falls. Without thinking, she headed up the steep incline and found herself at her high mountain meadow above the cave. She had not been back since wounding the porcupine.

She sat on the bank near the creek, throwing stones into the water absentmindedly. It was cold. The previous day's rain had been snow at the higher elevation. A thick blanket of white covered the open ground and patches between the snow-dusted trees. The still air glowed with a clarity that matched the sparkling snow reflecting, with untold millions of tiny crystals, the brilliant sun in a sky so blue it was almost purple. But Ayla couldn't see the serene beauty of the early winter landscape. It only reminded her that soon the cold would force the clan into the cave and she would not be able to get away from Broud again until spring. As the sun rose higher in the sky, sudden showers of snow fell from branches and plopped to the ground beneath.

The long cold winter loomed bleakly ahead with Broud hounding her day in and day out. I just can't satisfy him, she thought. It doesn't matter what I do, how hard I try, nothing helps. What else can I do? She happened to glance at a patch of bare ground and saw a partially rotted pelt and a few scattered quills, all that remained of the porcupine. A hyena probably found him, she thought—or a wolverine. With a twinge of guilt, she thought about the day she hit it. I should never have taught myself to use a sling, it was wrong. Creb would be angry, and Broud...Broud wouldn't be angry, he'd be glad if he ever found out. It would really give him an excuse to beat me. Wouldn't he just love to know. Well, he doesn't and he won't. It gave her a feeling of pleasure to know she had done something he didn't know about that would give him a reason to get after her. She felt like doing something, like slinging a stone to work out her frustrated rebellion.

She remembered throwing her sling under a bush and looked for it. She spied the piece of leather under a nearby bush and picked it up. It was damp, but exposure to the weather hadn't damaged it yet. She pulled the smooth supple deerskin through her hands, liking the way it felt. She recalled the first time she picked up a sling, and a smile crossed her face when she thought about Broud quailing before Brun's anger for knocking Zoug down. She wasn't the only one who had ever provoked Broud's rage.

Only with me, he can get away with it, Ayla thought bitterly. Just because I'm female. Brun was really angry when he hit Zoug, but he can hit me anytime he feels like it and Brun wouldn't care. No, that's not really true, she admitted to herself. Iza said Brun dragged Broud away to make him stop beating me, and Broud doesn't hit me as much when Brun's around. I wouldn't even care if he just hit me, if he would just leave me alone sometimes.

She had been picking up pebbles and throwing them into the creek and found she had fitted one into the sling without thinking. She smiled, sighted a last withered leaf dangling from the end of a small branch, aimed, and hurled. A warm feeling of satisfaction came over her as she saw the stone tear the leaf off the tree. She picked up a few more pebbles, got up and walked to the middle of the field, and hurled them. I can still hit what I want to, she thought, then frowned. What good does that do? I never even tried to hit anything that was moving; the porcupine doesn't count, it had almost stopped. I don't even know if I could, and if I did learn to hunt, really hunt, what good would it do? I couldn't bring anything back; all I'd do is make it easy for some wolf or hyena or wolverine, and they steal enough from us as it is

Hunting and the animals that were killed were so important to the clan they had to be constantly on their guard against competing predators. Not only did large cats or wolf packs or hyenas sometimes snatch an animal from the hunters, but skulking hyenas or sneaky wolverines were always around when meat was drying, or they were trying to break into caches. Ayla rejected the idea of helping the competitors to survive.

Brun wouldn't even let me bring a wolf cub into the cave when it was hurt, and lots of times hunters kill them even if we don't need their pelts. The meat eaters are always giving us trouble. That thought stayed in her mind. Then another idea began to take shape. Meat eaters, she thought, meat eaters can be killed with a sling, except for the biggest ones. I remember Zoug telling Vorn. He said sometimes it's better to use a sling, then you don't have to get so close.

Ayla recalled the day Zoug was extolling the virtues of the weapon with which he was most proficient. It was true that with a sling a hunter didn't have to get as close to sharp fangs or claws; but he didn't mention that if the hunter missed, he could be subject to attack from a wolf or lynx without another weapon to back him up, though he did stress it would be unwise to attempt it on anything larger.

What if I hunted only meat eaters? We never eat them, so it wouldn't be wasting, she thought, even if they would be left for carrion eaters to finish off. The hunters do it.

What am I thinking? Ayla shook her head to banish the shameful thought from her mind. I'm female, I'm not supposed to hunt, I'm not even supposed to touch a weapon. But I do know how to use a sling! Even if I'm not supposed to, she thought defiantly. It would help. If I killed a wolverine or a fox or anything, it couldn't steal our meat anymore. And those ugly hyenas. I might even get one of those someday, think what a help that would be. Ayla imagined herself stalking the wily predators.

She had been practicing with the sling all summer, and though it was only a game, she understood and respected any weapon enough to know its real purpose was game—not target practice, but hunting. She sensed that the excitement of hitting posts or marks on rocks or branches would soon pall without further challenge. And even if it were possible, the challenge of competition for the sake of competition was a concept that would not take hold until the earth was tamed by civilizations that no longer needed to hunt for survival. Competition within the Clan was for the purpose of sharpening survival skills.

Though she couldn't define it as such, part of her bitterness was caused by giving up the skill she had developed and was ready to expand. She had enjoyed stretching her capacities, training her coordination of hand and eye, and she was proud that she had taught herself. She was ready for the bigger challenge, the challenge of the hunt, but she needed a rationalization.

From the beginning, while she was just playing, she visualized herself hunting and the pleased and surprised looks of the clan when she brought home the meat she had killed. The porcupine made her realize how impossible such a daydream was. She could never bring back a kill and have her prowess recognized. She was female, and females of the Clan did not hunt. The idea of killing the clan's competitors gave her a vague feeling that her skill would be appreciated, if not acknowledged. And it gave her a reason to hunt.

The more she thought about it, the more she convinced herself that hunting carnivores, even if secretly, was the answer, though she couldn't quite overcome her feelings of guilt.

She struggled with her conscience. Creb and Iza had both told her how wrong it was for females to touch weapons. But I've already done more than touch a weapon, she thought. Can it be so much worse to hunt with it? She looked at the sling in her hand and suddenly made up her mind, fighting down her sense of wrongdoing.

"I will! I will do it! I will learn to hunt! But I will only kill meat eaters." She said it emphatically, making the gestures to add finality to her decision. Flushed with excitement, she ran to the creek to look for more stones.

While searching for smooth round pebbles of just the right size, her eye was caught by a peculiar object. It looked like a stone, but it looked like the shell of a mollusc that might be found at the seashore, too. She picked it up and examined it carefully. It was a stone, a stone shaped like a shell.

What a strange stone, she thought. I've never seen a stone like this before. Then she remembered something Creb had told her and had a flash of insight so overwhelming, she felt her blood drain and a chill crawl down her spine. Her knees were so weak and she was shaking so hard, she had to sit down. Cupping the fossil cast of a gastropod in her hands, she stared at it intently.

Creb said, she remembered, when you have a decision to make your totem will help you. If it's the right decision, he will give you a sign. Creb said it would be something very unusual, and no one else can tell you if it's a sign. You have to learn to listen with your heart and your mind, and the spirit of your totem inside you will tell you.

"Great Cave Lion, is this a sign from you?" She used the formal silent language for addressing her totem. "Are you telling me I made the right decision? Are you telling me it's all right for me to hunt, even if I am a girl?"

She sat quietly, staring at the shell-shaped stone in her hand, and tried to meditate as she had seen Creb do. She knew she was considered unusual because she had a Cave Lion totem, but she never thought much about it before. She reached under her wrap and felt the scars of the four parallel lines on her leg. Why would a Cave Lion choose me, anyway? He's a powerful totem, a male totem, why would he pick a girl? There must be some reason. She thought about the sling and learning to use it. Why did I pick up that old sling that Broud threw away? None of the women would have touched it. What would make me do it? Did my totem want me to? Does he want me to learn to hunt? Only men hunt, but my totem is a male totem. Of course! That must be it! I have a strong totem and he wants me to hunt.

"O Great Cave Lion, the ways of the spirits are strange to me. I don't know why you want me to hunt, but I am happy you gave me this sign." Ayla turned the stone over in her hand again, then she took the amulet from around her neck, pried loose the knot that held the small pouch closed, and put the fossil cast into the leather bag beside the piece of red ochre. Tying it tightly again, she slipped it back over her head and noticed the difference in weight. It seemed to add weight to her totem's sanction of her decision.

Her guilt was gone. She was supposed to hunt; her totem wanted her to. It didn't matter if she was female. I'm like Durc, she thought. He left his clan even though everyone said it was wrong. I think he did find a better place where Ice Mountain couldn't reach him. I think he started a whole new clan. He must have had a strong totem, too. Creb says strong totems are hard to live with. He says they test you to make sure you are worthy before they give you something.

He says that's why I almost died before Iza found me. I wonder if Durc's totem tested him. Will my Cave Lion test me again?

A test can be hard, though. What if I'm not worthy? How will I know if I'm being tested? What hard thing will my totem make me do? Ayla thought about what was hard in her life and it suddenly came to her.

"Broud! Broud is my test!" she gestured to herself. What could be harder than having to face a whole winter with Broud? But if I'm worthy, if I can do it, my totem will let me hunt.

There was a difference in the way Ayla walked when she returned to the cave, and Iza noticed it, though she couldn't quite say what was different about it. It wasn't less proper, it just seemed easier, not as tense, and there was a look of acceptance on the girl's face when she saw Broud approaching. Not resignation, just acceptance. But it was Creb who noticed the extra bulge in her amulet.

As the winter closed in, they were both glad to see her return to normal, despite Broud's demands. Though she was often tired, when she played with Uba her smiles were back, if not her laughter. Creb guessed she had come to some decision and found a sign from her totem, and her easier acceptance of her place in the clan gave him a feeling of relief. He was aware of her inward struggle, but he knew it was not only necessary to bend to Broud's will, she had to stop fighting it. She had to learn self-control, too.

During the winter that began her eighth year, Ayla became a woman. Not physically; her body still had the straight, undeveloped lines of a girl, without the least hint of the changes to come. But it was during that long cold season that Ayla put her childhood aside.

At times her life was so unbearable, she wasn't sure if she wanted it to continue. Some mornings, when she opened her eyes to the familiar rough texture of the bare rock wall above her, she wished she could go back to sleep and never wake up. But when she thought she couldn't stand it any longer, she clutched her amulet, and the feel of the extra stone somehow gave her the patience to endure another day. And each day lived through brought her just that much closer to the time when the deep snows and icy blasts would change to green grass and sea breezes, and she could roam the fields and forests in freedom again.

Like the woolly rhinoceros, whose spirit he called his totem, Broud could be as stubborn as he could be unpredictably vicious. Characteristic of the Clan, once he settled on a particular course of action, he persisted with unswerving dedication, and Broud dedicated himself to keeping Ayla in line. Her daily ordeal of clouts and curses and constant harassment was obvious to the rest of the clan. Many felt she did deserve some discipline and punishment, but few approved of the lengths to which Broud went.

Brun was still concerned that Broud was letting the girl provoke him too much, but since the young man controlled his fury, the leader felt it was a definite improvement. But Brun hoped to see the son of his mate pursue a more moderate approach on his own and decided to let the situation run its course. As the winter wore on, he began to develop a certain grudging respect for the strange girl, the same kind of respect he had felt for his sibling when she had endured the beatings of her mate.

Like Iza, Ayla was setting an example of womanly behavior. She endured, without complaint, as a woman should. When she paused momentarily to clutch her amulet, Brun, and many of the others, took it as an indication of her reverence for the spiritual forces so fearfully important to the Clan. It added to her feminine stature.

The amulet did give her something to believe in; she did revere the spiritual forces, as she understood them. Her totem was testing her. If she proved worthy, she could learn to hunt. The more Broud badgered her, the more determined she became that she would begin to teach herself when spring came. She was going to be better than Broud, better even than Zoug. She was going to be the best sling-hunter in the clan, though no one would know it but her. That was the thought she clung to. It solidified in her mind, like the long tapering shafts of ice that formed at the top of the entrance to the cave where warm air from the fires rose to meet the freezing temperatures outside, and grew, like the heavy translucent curtains of ice, all through the winter.

Though it wasn't intentional, she was already training herself. Despite the fact that it brought her into closer contact with Broud, she found herself interested and drawn to the men when they sat together spending long days rehashing earlier hunts or discussing strategy for future ones. She found ways to work near them and especially liked it when Dorv or Zoug told tales of hunting with the sling. She revived her interest in Zoug and her feminine response to his wishes, and developed a genuine affection for the old hunter. He was like Creb in a way, proud and stern, and glad for a little attention and warmth, if only from a strange, ugly girl.

Zoug was not blind to her interest as he recounted past glories when he was second-in-command as Grod was now. She was an appreciative, if silent, audience and always demurely respectful. Zoug began to seek Vorn out to explain some technique of tracking or bit of hunting lore knowing the girl would find a way to sit nearby if she could, though he affected not to notice. If she enjoyed his tales, what harm could there be in that?

If I were younger, Zoug thought, and still a provider, I might take her as a mate, when she becomes a woman. She'll need a mate someday, and ugly as she is, she's going to have some trouble finding one. But she is young, and strong, and respectful. I have kin in other clans. If I'm strong enough to go to the next Clan Gathering, I'll speak for her. She may not want to stay here after Broud becomes leader, not that it matters what she wants, but I wouldn't blame her. I hope I will be gone to the next world before that happens. Zoug never forgot Broud's attack on him and didn't like the son of Brun's mate. He thought the future leader was unreasonably hard on the girl for whom he had developed an affection. She did deserve to be disciplined, but there were limits and Broud went beyond them. She was never disrespectful to him; it took an older, wiser man to know how to handle women. Yes, I will speak for her. If I can't go, I'll send a message. If only she weren't so ugly, he mused.

As difficult as it was for Ayla, it wasn't all bad. Activities were at a slower pace and there were fewer chores to do. Even Broud could find only so many tasks before there were none left. As time went along, he got a little bored; there wasn't any fight in her anymore, and the intensity of his harassment slackened. And there was another reason that Ayla began to find the winter more bearable.

At first, in an effort to find valid reasons for her to stay within the boundaries of Creb's fire, Iza decided to begin training her in the preparation and application of the herbs and plants Ayla had been gathering. Ayla found herself fascinated with the art of healing. The girl's avid interest soon involved Iza in a regular program and made the medicine woman think she should have begun sooner, as she became fully aware of just how differently her adopted daughter's mind worked.

If Ayla had been her true child, Iza would only have had to remind her of what was already stored in her brain, to get her accustomed to using it. But Ayla struggled to memorize knowledge Uba was born with, and Ayla's conscious memory wasn't as good. Iza had to drill her, go over the same material many times, and constantly test her to make sure she had it right. Iza pulled information from her memories as well as her own experience and was surprised, herself, at the wealth of knowledge she had. She'd never had to think about it before; it was just there when she needed it. Sometimes Iza despaired of ever teaching Ayla what she knew, or even enough to make her an adequate medicine woman. But Ayla's interest never flagged and Iza was determined to give her adopted daughter an assured status in the clan. The lessons went on daily.

"What is good for burns, Ayla?"

"Let me think. Hyssop flowers mixed with goldenrod flowers and cone flowers, dried and powdered together in equal parts. Wet it and make it into a poultice, cover with a bandage. When it dries, wet it again with cold water poured on the bandage," she finished in a rush, then paused to think. "And dried horsemint flowers and leaves are good for scalds; wet them in the hand and put them on the burn. Boiled roots of sweet rush make a wash for burns."

"Good, anything else?"

The girl searched her mind. "Giant hyssop, too. Chew the fresh leaves and stalk for a poultice, or wet the dried leaves. And ... oh, yes, boiled yellow-spined thistle blossoms. Put on as a wash after it's cooled."

"That's good for skin sores, too, Ayla. And don't forget that horsetail-fern ashes mixed with fat make a good burn ointment."

Ayla began to do more of the cooking, too, under Iza's direction. She soon took over the chore of preparing most of Creb's meals, except, for her, it wasn't a chore. She took pains to grind his grains especially fine before they were cooked to make it easier for him to chew with his worn teeth. Nuts, too, were chopped fine before she served them to the old man. Iza taught her to prepare the painkilling drinks and poultices that eased his rheumatism, and Ayla made a specialty of the remedies for that affliction of the older members of the clan, whose suffering invariably worsened with their confinement to the cold stone cave. That winter was the first time Ayla assisted the medicine woman, and their first patient was Creb.

It was midwinter. The heavy snowfalls had blocked the mouth of the cave several feet up. The insulating blanket of snow helped to keep the warmth from fires inside the large cavern, but the wind still whistled in through the large opening above the snow. Creb was unusually moody, vacillating from silence to grouchiness to apologetic repentance to silence again. His behavior confused Ayla, but Iza guessed the reason. Creb had a toothache, a particularly painful toothache.

"Creb, won't you just let me look at the tooth?" Iza pleaded.

"It's nothing. Just a toothache. Just a little pain. Don't you think I can stand a little pain? Don't you think I've had pain before, woman? What's a little toothache?" Creb snapped.

"Yes, Creb," Iza replied, head bowed. He was immediately contrite.

"Iza, I know you're only trying to help."

"If you'd let me look at it, I might be able to give you something for it. How can I know what to give you if you won't let me see it?"

"What's to see?" he motioned. "One bad tooth is the same as another. Just make me some willow-bark tea," Creb grumbled, then sat on his sleeping fur gazing into space.

Iza shook her head and went to make the tea.

"Woman!" Creb shouted shortly afterward. "Where's that willow bark? What's taking you so long? How can I meditate? I can't concentrate," he gestured impatiently.

Iza hurried over with a bone cup, signaling Ayla to follow. "I was just bringing it, but I don't think willow bark is going to be much help, Creb. Just let me look at it."

"All right. All right, Iza. Look." He opened his mouth and pointed at the offending tooth.

"See how deep the black hole goes, Ayla? The gum is swelling, it's decayed through. I'm afraid it will have to come out, Creb."

"Come out! You told me you just wanted to look so you could give me something for it. You didn't say anything about taking it out. Well, give me something for it, woman!"

"Yes, Creb," Iza said. "Here's your willow-bark tea."
Ayla watched the exchange with amazement.

"I thought you said willow bark wouldn't help much?"

"Nothing will help much. You can try a piece of sweet-rush root to chew, it might do some good. But I doubt it."

"Some medicine woman! Can't even cure a toothache," Creb grumbled.

"I could try burning out the pain," Iza motioned matter-of-factly.

Creb flinched. "I'll take the root," he replied.

The next morning Creb's face was swollen and puffy, making his one-eyed scarred face more fearsome. His eyes were red from lack of sleep. "Iza," he moaned. "Can't you do something for this toothache?"

"If you had let me take it out yesterday, the pain would be gone by now," Iza motioned and went back to stirring a bowl of parched, ground grain, watching bubbles slowly rising with a gentle *pukkah, pukkah, pukkah.*

"Woman! Have you no feelings? I haven't slept all night!"

"I know. You kept me awake."

"Well, do something!" he exploded.

"Yes, Creb," Iza said. "But, I can't take it out now until the swelling goes down."

"Is that all you can think of? Taking it out?"

"I can try one more thing, Creb, but I don't think I can save the tooth," she gestured sympathetically. "Ayla, bring me that packet with the splinters of charred wood from the tree that was struck by lightning last summer. We'll have to lance the gum to reduce the swelling now, before we can get the tooth out anyway. We might as well see if we can burn out the pain."

Creb shuddered at the instructions the medicine woman gave the girl, then he shrugged. It can't be much worse than the toothache, he thought.

Iza sorted through the packet of splinters and withdrew two. "Ayla, I want you to get the tip of this one red hot. The end should be like a coal, but still strong enough so it won't break off. Rake a coal out of the fire and hold the tip next to it until it smolders. But first, I want you to watch how to lance the gum. Hold his lips back for me."

Ayla did as she was instructed and looked into Creb's huge open mouth and at the two rows of large worn teeth.

"We puncture the gum with a hard sharp splinter beneath the tooth until the blood flows," Iza gestured, then demonstrated.

Creb's hand was clenched into a fist, but he made no sound. "Now, while this is draining, get the other splinter hot."

Ayla quickly ran to the fire and soon returned with a smoldering ember on the end of the charred splinter. Iza took it, looked at it critically, nodded her head, and motioned to Ayla to hold back his lips again. She inserted the hot point into the cavity. Ayla felt Creb jerk as she heard a sizzle and watched a thin wisp of steam rise out of the large hole in Creb's tooth.

"There, it's done. Now we wait to see if that will kill the pain. If not, the tooth will have to come out," Iza said after she swabbed the wound on Creb's gum with a mixture of geranium and spikenard-root powders on the tip of her finger.

"It's too bad I don't have any of the fungus that is so good for toothaches. Sometimes it will deaden the nerve, often draw it out. Then I might not have to take the tooth. It's best to use when it's fresh, but dried works, and it should be collected at the end of summer. If I find some next year, I'll show you, Ayla."

"Does your tooth still ache?" Iza asked the next day.

"It's better, Iza," Creb answered hopefully.

"But does it still hurt? If the pain isn't completely gone, it will just swell up again, Creb," Iza insisted.

"Well . . . yes, it still aches," he admitted, "but not as much. Really, not as much. Why not wait another day or so? I have cast a powerful spell. I have asked Ursus to destroy the bad spirit that is causing the pain."

"Haven't you already asked Ursus many times to rid you of that pain? I think Ursus wants you to sacrifice your tooth before he will make the pain stop, Mog-ur," Iza said.

"What do you know of the Great Ursus, woman?" Creb demanded irritably.

"This woman was presumptuous. This woman knows nothing of the ways of the spirits," Iza replied with bowed head. Then, looking up at her sibling: "But a medicine woman knows about toothaches. The pain will not stop until the tooth comes out," she motioned firmly.

Creb turned his back and limped away. He sat on his sleeping fur with his eye closed.

"Iza?" he called out after a while.

"Yes, Creb?"

"You are right. Ursus wants me to give up the tooth. Go ahead. Get it over with."

Iza walked over to him. "Here, Creb, drink this. It will make the pain less. Ayla, there is a small peg near the packet of splinters and a long piece of sinew. Bring them here."

"How did you know to have the drink ready?" Creb asked.

"I know Mog-ur. It is hard to give up a tooth, but if Ursus wants it, Mog-ur will give it. It is not the hardest sacrifice he has made to Ursus. A powerful totem is difficult to live with, but Ursus would not have chosen you if you were not worthy."

Creb nodded and swallowed the drink. It's from the same plant I use to help men with the memories, he thought. But I think I saw Iza boil it; she makes a decoction rather than an infusion. It's stronger than when it's steeped. It has many uses. Datura must be a gift from Ursus. He was beginning to feel the narcotic effects.

Iza told Ayla to hold open the old magician's mouth again while she carefully placed the wooden spike at the base of the aching tooth. She gave the peg a sharp blow with a stone held in her hand to loosen it. Creb jumped, but it was not as painful as he thought it would be. Then Iza tied the piece of sinew around the loosened tooth and told Ayla to secure the other end around one of the posts set firmly into the ground that was part of the frame from which the herbs were hanging to dry.

"Now, move his head back until the cord is taut, Ayla," Iza told the girl. With a quick jerk, Iza yanked on the sinew. "Here it is," she said, and held up the cord with the heavy molar dangling from it. She sprinkled dried geranium root on the bleeding hole and dipped a small piece of absorbent rabbit skin in an antiseptic solution of balsam-gum bark and a few of the dried leaves, and packed his jaw with the damp leather.

"Take your tooth, Mog-ur," Iza said, putting the decayed molar into the hand of the still-dazed magician. "It's all over."

He clenched it in his hand, then let it drop as he lay down. "Must give Ursus," he fumbled groggily.

The clan watched to see how well Creb recovered after Ayla assisted the medicine woman with her dental surgery. When his mouth healed quickly without any complications, they felt more assured that the girl's presence didn't alienate the spirits. It made them more willing to allow her to assist when Iza helped them. As the winter progressed, Ayla learned to treat burns, cuts, bruises, colds, sore throats, stomachaches, earaches, and many of the minor injuries and ailments they fell heir to in the normal course of living.

In time, members of the clan went as easily to Ayla as to Iza for treatment of minor problems. They knew Ayla had been collecting herbs for Iza and saw the medicine woman training her. They knew, too, that Iza was getting old and wasn't well and Uba was too young. The clan was getting used to the strange girl in their midst and was beginning to accept the idea that a girl born to the Others might someday be the medicine woman of their clan.

It was during the coldest time of the year, after the winter solstice and before the first breakup of spring, that Ovra went into labor.

"It's too early," Iza told Ayla. "She should not deliver until spring, and she hasn't felt movement recently. I'm afraid the birth will not go well. I think her baby will be stillborn."

"Ovra wanted this baby so much, Iza. She was so happy when she found out she was pregnant. Can't you do anything?" Ayla asked.

"We'll do what we can, but there are some things that are beyond help, Ayla," the medicine woman replied.

The whole clan was concerned about the early labor of Goov's mate. The women tried to offer moral support while the men waited anxiously nearby. They had lost several members during the earthquake and looked forward to any increases in their number. New babies meant more mouths for Brun's hunters and the foraging women to feed, but, in time, the babies would grow and provide for them when they grew old. The continuation and survival of the clan was essential to individual survival. They needed each other and were saddened that Ovra would probably not give birth to a living baby.

Goov was more worried for his mate than for the child, and wished there was something he could do. He didn't like to see Ovra suffering, especially when the outcome had so little hope of being anything but unhappy. She wanted the baby; she had felt inadequate to be the only woman in the clan without children. Even the medicine woman had given birth, as old as she was. Ovra had been elated when she finally became pregnant, and now Goov wished he could think of some way to ease her loss.

Droog seemed to understand the younger man better than anyone. He'd had occasion to have similar feelings about Goov's mother, though he was glad she had given birth to Goov, and Droog had to admit he was enjoying his new family, once he had gotten used to them. He even had hopes that Vorn might yet develop an interest in toolmaking, and Ona was sheer delight, especially now that she was weaned and was beginning to imitate grown women in her own little-girl way. Droog had never had a girl around his fire before, and she was so young when he had mated Aga, it felt as though Ona had been born to his hearth.

Ebra and Uka were sitting beside Ovra, sympathizing, while Iza prepared medication. Uka had been looking forward to her daughter's expected child, too, and held Ovra's hand while she strained. Oga had gone to prepare an evening meal for Brun and Grod along with Broud, and had asked Goov as well. Ika offered to help, but when Goov declined, Oga said she didn't need help. Goov didn't feel much like eating and went to visit Droog's hearth and was finally coaxed by Aba to try a few bites.

Oga was distracted, worried about Ovra, and was beginning to wish she hadn't turned down Ika's offer. She didn't know how it happened, but as she was serving bowls of hot soup to the men, she stumbled. Boiling-hot soup spilled on Brun's shoulder and arm.

"Aarghhh!" Brun cried as the scalding liquid poured over him. He was dancing around, gritting his teeth at the pain. Every head turned and every breath was held. The silence was broken by Broud.

"Oga! You stupid, clumsy woman!" he gesticulated to cover up his embarrassment that it was his mate who had done such a thing.

"Ayla, go help him, I can't leave now," Iza signaled.

Broud advanced toward his mate with his fists doubled, ready to punish her.

"No, Broud," Brun gestured, putting out his hand to stop the young man. The hot grease from the soup still clung to him and he struggled not to show the pain he felt. "She couldn't help it. Beating her will do no good." Oga was crumpled in a heap at Broud's feet, shaking with humiliation and fear.

Ayla was apprehensive. She had never treated the leader of the clan, and regarded him with inordinate fear. She raced toward Creb's hearth, grabbed a wooden bowl, then raced to the mouth of the cave. She scooped up a mound of snow and went to the hearth of the leader, dropping to the ground in front of him.

"Iza sent me, she cannot leave Ovra now. Will the leader allow this girl to help him?" she asked when Brun acknowledged her.

Brun nodded. He harbored doubts about Ayla becoming the clan's medicine woman, but under the circumstances he had little choice but to allow her to treat him. Nervously, she applied the cooling snow to the angry red burn, feeling Brun's hard muscles relax as the snow eased the pain. She ran back, found the dried horsemint, and added hot water to the leaves. After they softened, she put snow in the bowl to cool it quickly and returned to her patient. With her hand she applied the soothing medication, feeling more tension leave the leader's rock-hard muscular body as she worked. Brun breathed a little easier. The burn still hurt, but it was far more bearable. He nodded his approval, and the girl relaxed a little.

She does seem to be learning Iza's magic, Brun thought. And she's learning to behave well, as a woman should; perhaps all she needed was a little maturity. If anything happens to Iza before Uba grows up, we will be without a medicine woman. Perhaps Iza is wise to train her.

Not long afterward, Ebra came and told her mate that Ovra's son was stillborn. Brun nodded and glanced in her direction, shaking his head. And a boy, too, he thought. She must be heartbroken, everyone knows how much she wanted this baby. I hope she'll have an easier time getting pregnant again. Who would think a Beaver totem could fight so hard? Though the leader felt a great pity for the young woman, he said nothing, for no one would mention the tragedy. But Ovra understood Brun's reason for coming to Goov's hearth a few days later to tell her she should take as long as she wanted to recuperate from her "illness." Though the men often congregated at Brun's fire, the leader seldom visited the other men's hearths, and very rarely talked to the women if he did. Ovra was grateful for his concern, but nothing could ease her pain.

Iza insisted that Ayla continue to treat Brun, and as the scald healed, the clan accepted her even more. Ayla felt easier around the leader afterward. He was, after all, only human.

12

As the long winter ended, the tempo of the clan's life increased to match the pace of life quickening within the rich earth. The cold season enforced not a true hibernation, but an alteration in metabolic rates brought about by reduced activities. In winter they were more sluggish, slept more, ate more, causing an insulating layer of subcutaneous fat to develop as protection against the cold. With a rise in temperature, the trend was reversed, making the clan restless and eager to be out and moving.

The process was assisted by Iza's spring tonic, compounded of triticum roots, collected early in spring from the coarse grass that resembled rye, dried woodruff leaves, and iron-rich yellow dock root powder, administered universally to young and old alike by the clan's medicine woman. With new vigor, the clan burst out of the cave ready to begin a new cycle of seasons.

The third winter in the cave had not been too hard on them. The only death was Ovra's stillborn child, and that didn't count because it had never been named and accepted. Iza, no longer drained by the demands of nursing a hungry baby, had weathered it well. Creb had suffered no more than usual. Both Aga and Ika were pregnant again, and since both women had given birth successfully before, the clan looked forward to its increase. The first greens, shoots, and buds were gathered and an early hunt planned to provide fresh meat for a spring feast to honor the spirits that awakened new life and to give thanks to the spirits of the clan's protective totems for seeing them through another winter.

Ayla felt she had special reason to give thanks to her totem. The winter had been both trying and exciting. She grew to hate Broud even more intensely, but she learned she could cope with him. He had thrown his worst at her and she learned to take it in stride. There was a limit beyond which even Broud could not go. Learning more of Iza's healing magic helped; she loved it. The more she learned, the more she wanted to learn. She found she was as eager to search out the medicinal plants for their own uses—now that she understood them better—as to use plant gathering as a means of escape. As long as the bitter winds and icy blizzards blew, she waited patiently. But with the first hints of change, restless anticipation set in. She looked forward to this spring more than any spring she could remember. It was time to learn to hunt.

As soon as the weather allowed, Ayla took to the woods and fields. She stopped hiding her sling in the small cave near her practice meadow. She kept it with her, tucked into a fold of her wrap or beneath a layer of leaves in her collecting basket. Teaching herself to hunt was not easy. Animals were quick and elusive, and moving targets far more difficult to hit than stationary ones. The women always made noise when they were out gathering, to scare off any lurking animals, and it was a hard habit to break. Many times she became angry with herself for warning an animal of her approach when she caught a glimpse of one darting for cover. But she was determined, and with practice she learned.

Through trial and error she learned to track and began to understand and apply the bits of hunting lore gleaned from the men. Her eye was already trained to pick up small details that differentiated plants, and it took only an extension to learn to define the meaning in the telltale droppings of an animal, a faint print in the dust, a bent blade of grass or a broken twig. She learned to distinguish the spoor of different animals, became familiar with their habits and habitats. Though she didn't overlook the herbivorous species, she concentrated on the carnivores, her chosen prey.

She watched to see which way the men went when they left to go hunting. But it was not Brun and his hunters that gave her the most concern. More often than not they chose the steppes as their hunting ground, and she didn't dare try to hunt the open plains with no cover. It was the two older men she worried about most. She had seen Zoug and Dorv occasionally when she was foraging for Iza in the past. They were the ones she was most likely to find hunting the same terrain as herself. She had to be constantly on her guard to avoid them. Even starting out in the opposite direction was no guarantee they wouldn't double back and catch her with a sling in her hands.

But as she learned to move silently, she sometimes followed them to watch and learn. She was especially careful then. It was more dangerous for her to track the trackers than the objects of their pursuit. It was good training, however. She learned to move noiselessly as much from following the men as from trailing an animal, and could melt into a shadow if one happened to glance her way.

As Ayla gained skill tracking, learned to move with stealth, trained her eye to discern a shape within its camouflaged cover, there were times when she was sure she could have hit a small animal. Though she was tempted, if it was not carnivorous she passed it by without trying. She had made her decision to hunt only predators, and her totem sanctioned only those. Spring buds became blossoms and leafed out the trees, blossoms fell and fruits swelled from their hearts, hanging half-grown and green, and still Ayla had not killed her first animal.

"Get out! Shoo! Scat!"

Ayla started out of the cave to see what the commotion was about. Several women were waving their arms and chasing after a short, squat, shaggy animal. The wolverine headed toward the cave but veered aside with a snarl when it saw Ayla. It dodged between the women's legs and escaped with a strip of meat in its jaws.

"That sneaky glutton! I just put that meat out to dry," Oga gesticulated in angry frustration. "I hardly turned my back. He's been hanging around here all summer, getting braver every day. I wish Zoug would get him! It's a good thing you were just coming out, Ayla. He almost ran into the cave. Think what a stink he would have left if he'd gotten cornered in there!"

"I think your *he* is a *she*, Oga, and probably has a nest somewhere nearby. I'd guess she has several hungry babies that must be getting pretty big by now."

"That's all we need! A bunch of them." Angry words punctuated her gestures. "Zoug and Dorv took Vorn with them early this morning. I wish they'd gone hunting for that wolverine instead of hamsters and ptarmigan down below. Gluttons are good for nothing!"

"They're good for something, Oga. Their fur doesn't frost up from your breath in winter. Their pelts make good hats and hoods."

"I wish that one were a pelt!"

Ayla started back to the hearth. There was really nothing she had to do then, and Iza did say she was running low on a few things. Ayla decided to go out and find the wolverine's nest. She smiled to herself and quickened her step, and shortly afterward left the cave with her basket, heading into the forest not far from the place where the animal had gone.

Scanning the ground, she spied the print of a claw with long sharp nails in the dust; a little farther on, a bent stem. Ayla started trailing the creature. In a few moments, she heard scuttling sounds, surprisingly close to the cave. She moved ahead softly, hardly disturbing a leaf, and caught sight of the wolverine with four half-grown young, snarling and bickering over the strip of stolen meat. Carefully, she withdrew her sling from a fold of her wrap and fitted a stone into the bulging pocket.

She waited, watching for a chance at a clean shot. A stray shift in the wind brought a strange scent to the wily glutton. She looked up, sniffing the air, alerted to possible danger. It was the moment Ayla was waiting for. Quickly, even as the animal caught the movement, she hurled the stone. The wolverine slumped to the ground as the four young bounded off, startled by the bouncing rock.

She stepped out of the concealing brush and stooped to examine the scavenger. The bearlike weasel was about three feet long from its nose to the tip of its bushy tail, with coarse, long, blackish brown fur. Wolverines were intrepid, scrappy scavengers, fierce enough to drive away predators larger than themselves from their kills, fearless enough to steal drying meat or anything portable they could carry off, and wily enough to break into storage caches. They had musk glands that left behind a skunklike odor and were a bane to the clan even worse than the hyena, who was as much predator as scavenger and didn't depend for his survival on the kills of others.

The stone from Ayla's sling had landed above the eye, just where she aimed. This is one wolverine that won't steal from us anymore, Ayla thought, filled with a glow of satisfaction that verged on exultation. It was her first kill. I think I'll give the pelt to Oga, she thought, reaching for her knife to skin the animal. Won't she be glad to know it won't bother us anymore. The girl stopped.

What am I thinking of? I can't give Oga this pelt. I can't give it to anyone, I can't even keep it. I'm not supposed to hunt. If anyone found out I killed this wolverine, I don't know what they'd do. Ayla sat down beside the dead glutton, pulling her fingers through its long coarse coat. Her elation was gone.

She had made her first kill. Maybe it wasn't a great bison killed with a heavy sharp spear, but it was more than Vorn's porcupine. There would be no celebration marking her entrance into the ranks of the hunters, no feast held in her honor, not even the looks of praise and congratulations Vorn received when he proudly showed off his small game. If she returned to the cave with the wolverine, all she could expect would be shocked looks and severe punishment. It mattered little that she wanted to help the clan or that she was able to hunt and showed promise of doing well. Women did not hunt, women did not kill animals. Men did.

She heaved a sigh. I knew it, I knew it all along, she said to herself. Even before I started to hunt, before I ever picked up that sling, I knew I wasn't supposed to. The bravest of the young gluttons came out of its hiding place, tentatively sniffing at the dead animal. Those young ones are going to give us as much trouble as their mother, Ayla thought. They're close enough to full grown that a couple of them will survive. I'd better get rid of this carcass. If I drag it far away, the young will probably follow her scent. Ayla got up and began to haul the dead wolverine by its tail deeper into the woods. Then she started looking for plants to gather.

The wolverine was only the first of the smaller predators and scavengers to fall to her sling. Martens, minks, ferrets, otters, weasels, badgers, ermines, foxes, and the small, gray-and-black tabby-striped wildcats became fair game for her swift stones. She didn't realize it, but Ayla's decision to hunt predators had one important effect. It speeded up her learning process and honed her skill far more than hunting the gentler herbivorous animals would have. Carnivores were faster, more crafty, more intelligent, and more dangerous.

She quickly surpassed Vorn with her chosen weapon. It wasn't only that he tended to look upon the sling as an old man's weapon and lacked the determination to master it, it was more difficult for him. He didn't have her physical build with its free-swinging arm movement better adapted to throwing. Her full leverage and practiced hand-and-eye coordination gave her speed, force, and accuracy. She no longer compared herself with Vorn; in her mind it was Zoug whose ability she challenged, and the girl was fast approaching the old hunter's skill. Too fast. She was getting overconfident.

Summer was nearing its end with its full charge of crackling heat and a bumper crop of lightning-singed thunderstorms. The day was hot, unbearably hot. Not the hint of a breeze stirred the still air. The previous evening's storm, with its fantastic displays of arcing flashes illuminating the mountain crests and with hail the size of small stones, had sent the clan scurrying into the cave. The damp forest, normally cool from the shade of the trees, was humid and stifling. Flies and mosquitoes droned interminably around the slimy ooze of the drying creek's backwater, trapped by lowered water levels into stagnant ponds and algae-coated puddles.

Ayla was following the spoor of a red fox, moving silently through the woods near the edge of a small glade. She was hot and sweaty, not especially interested in the fox, and thinking about giving it up and going back to the cave to take a swim in the stream. Walking across the seldom-exposed rocky bed, she stopped for a drink where the creek still ran freely between two large boulders that forced the meandering trickle into an ankle-deep pool.

She stood up and, as she looked straight ahead, caught her breath in her throat. Ayla stared apprehensively at the distinctive head and tufted ears of a lynx crouched on the rock just in front of her. He was eyeing her warily, his short tail whipping back and forth.

Smaller than most large felines, the long-bodied, short-legged Pardel lynx, like his northern cousin of later years, was capable of fifteen-foot standing leaps. He subsisted mainly on hares, rabbits, large squirrels, and other rodents, but could bring down a small deer if he felt so inclined; and an eight-year-old girl was easily within his range. But it was hot, and humans were not his normal prey. He would probably have let the girl go on her way.

Ayla's first tingle of fear was replaced by a chill of excitement as she watched the unmoving cat watching her.

Didn't Zoug tell Vorn a lynx could be killed with a sling? He said not to try for anything larger, but he did say a stone from a sling could kill a wolf or hyena or lynx. I remember him saying *lynx*, she thought. She had not hunted the medium-sized predators, but she wanted to be the best sling-hunter in the clan. If Zoug could kill a lynx, she could kill a lynx, and here, right in front of her, was the perfect target. On impulse, she decided the time had come for larger game.

She reached slowly into the fold of her short summer wrap, never taking her eyes off the cat, and felt for her largest stone. Her palms were sweaty, but she gripped the two ends of the leather strap together tighter while she put the stone in the pocket. Then, quickly, before she lost her nerve, she aimed for a spot just between his eyes and flung the stone. But the lynx caught the motion as she raised her arm. He turned his head as she hurled. The rock grazed the side of his head, causing a sharp pain at the point-blank range, but little more.

Before Ayla could think of reaching for another stone, she saw the cat's muscles bunch under him. It was with sheer reflex that she threw herself to the side as the annoyed lynx leaped for his attacker. She landed in the mud near the creek and her hand fell on a stout driftwood branch, churned clean of leaves and twigs by its journey downstream, water-logged and heavy. Ayla clutched it and rolled over just as the angry lynx with fangs bared pounced again. Swinging wildly, with all the strength fear poured into her, she struck a solid blow, knocking his head aside. The stunned lynx rolled over, crouched for a moment shaking his head, then moved silently into the forest. He'd had enough hurting blows to his head.

Ayla was shaking as she sat up, breathing hard. Her knees felt like water when she went to retrieve her sling and she had to sit down again. Zoug had never imagined that anyone would attempt to hunt a dangerous predator with just a sling, with no other hunter or even another weapon as backup. But Ayla hardly ever missed her targets anymore, she had become too sure of her skill, she didn't think about what might happen if she missed. She was in such a state of shock as she walked back to the cave, she almost forgot to get her collecting basket from the place she had hidden it before deciding to track the fox.

"Ayla! What happened to you? You're all muddy!" Iza motioned when she saw her. The girl's face was ashen, something must have scared her.

Ayla didn't answer, she just shook her head and went into the cave. Iza knew there was something the girl didn't want to tell her. She thought of pressing her further, then changed her mind, hoping the child would tell her voluntarily. And Iza wasn't so sure she wanted to know.

It bothered the woman when Ayla went off by herself, but someone needed to gather her medicinal plants; they were necessary. She couldn't go, Uba was too young, and none of the other women knew what to look for or had any inclination to learn. She had to let Ayla go, but if the girl told her of some frightening incident, it would worry her all the more. She just wished Ayla wouldn't stay out so long.

Ayla was subdued that evening and went to bed early, but she couldn't sleep. She lay awake thinking about the incident with the lynx, and in her imagination it became even more frightening. It was early morning before she finally dozed off.

She woke up screaming!

"Ayla! Ayla!" She heard Iza call her name as the woman shook her gently to bring her back to reality. "What's wrong?"

"I dreamed I was in a little cave and a cave lion was after me. I'm all right now, Iza."

"You haven't had bad dreams for a long time, Ayla. Why should you have them now? Did something frighten you today?"

Ayla nodded and bowed her head but didn't explain. The dark of the cave lit only by the dim glow of red coals hid her guilty expression. She hadn't felt guilty about hunting since she found the sign from her totem. Now, she wondered if it really was a sign. Maybe she just thought it was. Maybe she wasn't supposed to hunt after all. Especially such dangerous animals. What ever made her think a girl should be trying to hunt lynxes?

"I never have liked the idea of your going out alone, Ayla. You're always gone so long. I know you like to get off by yourself sometimes, but it worries me. It's not natural for girls to want to be alone so much. The forest can be dangerous."

"You're right, Iza. The forest can be dangerous," Ayla

motioned. "Maybe next time I can take Uba with me, or maybe Ika would like to go."

Iza was relieved to see that Ayla seemed to be taking her advice to heart. She hung around the cave, and when she did go out after medicinal plants, she returned quickly. When she couldn't get someone to go with her, she was nervous. She kept expecting to see a crouching animal ready to spring. She began to understand why women of the clan didn't like to go out alone to gather food, and why her eagerness to be off by herself always surprised them. When she was younger, she was just too innocent of the dangers. But it took only one attack, and most of the women had felt threatened at least once, to make her look upon her environment with more respect. Even a nonpredator could be dangerous. Boars with sharp canines, horses with hard hooves, stags with heavy antlers, mountain goats and sheep with lethal horns, all of them could inflict serious damage if aroused. Ayla wondered how she ever dared to think about hunting. She was afraid to go again.

There was no one Ayla could talk to about it, no one to tell her a little fear sharpened the senses, especially when stalking dangerous game, no one to encourage her to go out again before the fear inhibited her. The men understood fear. They didn't talk about it, but every one of them had known it many times in their lives, beginning with their first major hunt that elevated them to men. Small animals were for practice, to gain skill with their weapons, but manhood status was not granted until they had known and overcome fear.

For a woman, her days spent alone away from the safety of the clan were no less a test of bravery, though more subtle. In some ways, it required more courage to face those days and nights alone, knowing that no matter what happened, she was on her own. From the time she was born, a girl always had other people around her, protecting her. But she had no weapons to bring to her own defense, and no weapon-bearing protective male to save her during her rites of passage. Girls, as well as boys, did not become adults until they had faced and overcome fear.

For the first few days, Ayla had no desire to wander far from the cave, but after a while she became restless. In winter she had no choice and accepted her confinement to the cave with the rest, but she had grown accustomed to roaming freely when the weather was warm. Ambivalence tormented her. When she was alone in the forest away from the security of the clan, she was uneasy and apprehensive; when she was with the clan near the cave, she longed for the privacy and freedom of the forest.

One foraging expedition when she was out alone brought her close to her private retreat, and she climbed the rest of the way to the high meadow. The place had a soothing effect on her. It was her private world, her cave, her meadow, she felt possessive about the small herd of roe deer that frequently grazed there. They had become so tame, she could get close enough to almost touch one before it pranced out of range. The open field gave her a sense of security, lacking now in the dangerous woods that hid lurking beasts. She hadn't visited the place at all this season and memories came flooding back. This was where she first taught herself to use the sling, where she hit the porcupine, and where she had found the sign from her totem.

She had her sling with her—she didn't dare leave it in the cave for Iza to find—and after a while she picked up a few pebbles and made a few practice shots. But that was far too tame a sport to interest her for long now. Her mind went back to the incident with the lynx.

If only I'd had another stone in the sling, she thought. If I could have hit him right away, right after the stone that missed, I might have gotten him before he had a chance to jump. She had two pebbles in her hand and looked at them both. If there was only a way to throw one right after the other. Had Zoug ever said anything like that to Vorn? She racked her brain trying to remember. If he had, it must have been when I wasn't around, she decided. She pondered the idea. If I could get a second stone in the pocket on the downstroke after the first hurl, without stopping it, I could throw it on the next upstroke. I wonder if that would work?

She began making a few tries and felt as clumsy as she had the first time she tried to use a sling. Then she began to develop a rhythm: throw the first stone; catch the sling as it comes down, with the second stone ready; get it in the pocket while it is still moving; throw the second stone. The pebbles dropped often, and even after she began to lob them her accuracy on both shots suffered. But she was satisfied that it could be done. She returned every day after that to practice. She still felt uneasy about hunting, but the challenge of working out the new technique renewed her interest in the weapon.

By the time the forested hillsides were ablaze with the turning season, she was as accurate with two stones as she had been with one. Standing in the middle of the field hurling stones at a new post she had pounded into the ground, she felt a warm sense of accomplishment when a satisfactory *thwack, thwack* told her both stones had hit the mark. No one told her it was impossible to rapid-fire two stones from a sling, because it had never been done before, and since no one told her she couldn't, she taught herself to do it.

Early one warm day in late fall, nearly a year from the time she first made her decision to hunt, Ayla decided to climb to the high pasture to collect the mature hazelnuts that had fallen to the ground. As she drew near the top, she heard the whooping and cackling and snuffling of a hyena, and when she reached the meadow, she saw one of the ugly beasts half buried in the bloody entrails of an old roe deer.

It made her mad. How dare that noisome creature defile *her* meadow, attack *her* deer? She started to run toward the hyena to scare him off, then thought better of it. Hyenas were predators, too, with jaws strong enough to crack the large leg bones of grazing ungulates, and not easily chased from their own prey. She quickly shrugged off her basket and reached to the bottom of it for her sling. She scanned the ground for stones as she edged toward an outcrop near the rock wall. The old stag was half devoured, but her movement caught the attention of the scraggly spotted animal, nearly as large as the lynx. The hyena looked up, found her scent, and turned in her direction.

She was ready. Stepping out from behind the outcrop, she hurled a missile, followed quickly by a second. She didn't know the second was unnecessary—the first had done the job—but it was good insurance. Ayla had learned her lesson. She had a third stone in her sling and a fourth in hand, prepared for a second series if it proved necessary. The cave hyena had crumpled on the spot and didn't move. She looked around to make sure there were no more nearby, then cautiously moved toward the beast, her sling ready. On her way, she picked up a leg bone, a few shreds of red meat still clinging to it and not yet broken. With a skull-cracking blow, Ayla made sure the hyena would not rise again.

She looked at the dead animal at her feet and let the club fall from her hand. Awareness of the implications of her deed came slowly. I killed a hyena, she said to herself as the impact hit her. I killed a hyena with my sling. Not a small animal, a hyena, an animal that could kill me. Does that mean I'm a hunter now? Really a hunter? It wasn't exultation she felt, not the excitement of a first kill or even the satisfaction of overcoming a powerful beast. It was something deeper, more humbling. It was the knowledge that she had overcome herself. It came as a spiritual revelation, a mystical insight; and with a reverence deeply felt, she spoke to the spirit of her totem in the ancient formal language of the Clan.

"I am only a girl, Great Cave Lion, and the ways of the spirits are strange to me. But I think I understand a little more now. The lynx was a test even more than Broud. Creb always said powerful totems are not easy to live with, but he never told me the greatest gifts they give are inside. He never told me how it feels when you finally understand. The test is not just something hard to do, the test is knowing you can do it. I am grateful you chose me, Great Cave Lion. I hope I will always be worthy of you."

As the brilliant polychrome autumn lost its luster and skeletal branches dropped withered leaves, Ayla returned to the forest. She tracked and studied the habits of the animals she chose to hunt, but she treated them with more respect, both as creatures and as dangerous adversaries. Many times, though she crept close enough to hurl a stone, she refrained and merely watched. She developed a stronger feeling that it was a waste to kill an animal who did not threaten the clan and whose pelt she could not use. But she was still determined to be the best sling-hunter in the clan; she didn't realize she already was. The only way she could continue to increase her skill was to hunt. And hunt she did.

The results were beginning to be noticed, and it made the men uneasy.

"I found another wolverine, or what was left of it, not far from the practice field," Crug motioned.

"And there were pieces of fur, looked like a wolf, over the ridge halfway down the hill," Goov added.

"It's always the meat eaters, the stronger animals, not female totems," Broud said. "Grod says we should talk to Mog-ur."

"Small and middle-sized ones, but not the big cats. Deer and horses, sheep and mountain goats, even boars are always hunted by the big cats and wolves and hyenas, but what's hunting the smaller hunters? I've never seen so many of them killed," Crug remarked.

"That's what I'd like to know, what's killing them? It's not that I mind a few less hyenas or wolves around, but if it's not us...Is Grod going to talk to Mog-ur? Do you think it could be a spirit?" The young man quelled a shudder.

"And if it is a spirit, is it a good spirit who is helping us or an evil spirit who is angry at our totems?" Goov asked.

"Leave it to you, Goov, to come up with a question like that. You're Mog-ur's acolyte, what do you think?" Crug returned.

"I think it will take deep meditation and consultation with the spirits to answer that question."

"You already sound like a mog-ur, Goov. Never give a direct answer," Broud quipped.

"Well, what's your answer, Broud?" the acolyte countered. "Can you give one any more direct? What's killing the animals?"

"I'm not a mog-ur, or even training to be one. Don't ask me."

Ayla was working nearby and repressed a desire to smile. So now I'm a spirit, but they can't figure out if I'm a good one or a bad one.

Mog-ur approached unnoticed, but he had seen the discussion. "I don't have an answer yet, Broud," the magician motioned. "It will take meditation. But I will say this, it is not the normal way of spirits."

Spirits, Mog-ur thought to himself, might make it too hot or too cold, or bring too much rain or snow, or drive herds away, or bring disease, or make thunder or lightning or earthquakes, but they don't usually cause the death of individual animals. This mystery has the feel of a human hand. Ayla got up and walked to the cave and the magician watched her go. There's something different about her, she has changed, Creb mused. He noticed Broud's eyes had followed her, too, and they were filled with frustrated malice. Broud's noticed the difference, too. Maybe it's just that she's not really Clan and walks differently, she is growing up. Something nagged at the edge of his mind that made Creb feel that wasn't the answer.

Ayla had changed. As her hunting skill grew, she developed an assurance and sinewy grace unknown to Clan women. She had the silent walk of an experienced hunter, a tight muscular control of her young body, a confidence in her own reflexes, and a far-seeing look in her eye that clouded over imperceptibly whenever Broud began to harass her, as though she wasn't really seeing him. She jumped just as quickly to his commands, but her response lacked the edge of fear no matter how he cuffed her.

Her composure, her confidence, was far more intangible, but no less apparent to Broud, than the near-open rebellion of earlier times. It was as though she was condescending to obey him, as though she knew something he didn't. He watched her, trying to discern the subtle shift, trying to find something to punish her for, but it eluded him.

Broud didn't know how she did it, but every time he tried to assert his superiority, she made him feel below her, inferior to her. It frustrated him, infuriated him, but the more he kept after her, the less control he felt over her, and he hated her for it. But gradually, he found himself harassing her less, even staying away from her, only occasionally remembering to demonstrate his prerogatives. As the season came to an end, his hatred intensified. Someday he would break her, he vowed to himself. Someday he would make her pay for the wounds she inflicted on his self-esteem. Oh, yes, someday she would be sorry.

13

Winter came, and with it the diminished activity they shared with all living things that followed the cycle of the seasons. Life still pulsed, but at a slower pace. For the first time, Ayla looked forward to the cold season. The rushed and active warm seasons allowed little time for Iza to continue training her. With the first snows, the medicine woman began her lessons again. The pattern of the clan's life repeated itself with only minor variations, and winter again drew to a close.

Spring was late, and wet. The melt from the highlands, abetted by heavy rains, swelled the stream to a surging turbulence overflowing its banks and sweeping along whole trees and brush in its headlong flight to the sea. A logjam downstream diverted its course, taking over part of the path the clan had made. A brief reprieve of warmth, just long enough to unfold tentative blossoms on fruit trees, was reversed by late spring hailstorms that ravaged the delicate blooms, dashing hopes of the promised harvest. Then, as though nature had a change of heart and wanted to make up for the offer of fruits withheld, the early summer crop produced vegetables, roots, squashes, and legumes in bountiful profusion.

The clan missed their accustomed spring visit to the seacoast for salmon, and everyone was pleased when Brun announced they would make the trip to fish for sturgeon and cod. Though members of the clan often walked the ten miles to the inland sea to gather molluscs and eggs from the multitude of birds that nested on the cliffs, catching the huge fish was one of the few clan activities that was a community effort of both men and women.

Droog had his own reason for wanting to go. The heavy spring runoff had washed down fresh nodules of flint from the chalk deposits of higher elevations and left them stranded on the floodplain. He had scouted the coast earlier and seen several alluvial deposits. The fishing trip would be a good opportunity to replenish their supply of tools with new ones of high-quality stone. It was easier to knap the flint at the site than to carry the heavy rocks back to the cave. Droog hadn't made tools for the clan for some time. They'd had to make do with their own rougher implements when the brittle stone of their favorite ones broke. They could all make usable tools, but few compared with Droog's.

A lighthearted spirit of holiday accompanied their preparations. It wasn't often that the entire clan left the cave at one time, and the novelty of camping on the beach was exciting, especially for the children. Brun planned for one or two of the men to make daily excursions back to make sure nothing was disturbed in their absence. Even Creb looked forward to the change of scene. He seldom wandered very far from the cave.

The women worked on the net, repairing weakened strands and making a new section from cords of fibrous vines, stringy barks, tough grasses, and long animal hairs to lengthen it. Although it was a strong, tough material, sinew was not used. As with leather, water made it hard and stiff and it didn't absorb the softening fat well.

The massive sturgeon, often upward of twelve feet in length and weighing over a ton, migrated from the sea, where it spent most of the year, into freshwater streams and rivers to spawn in early summer. The fleshy feelers on the underside of its toothless mouth gave the ancient, sharklike fish a fearsome appearance, but its diet consisted of invertebrates and small fish foraged from the bottom. The smaller cod, usually no more than twenty-five pounds, but ranging up to two hundred pounds and more, migrated seasonally northward into shallower water in summer. Although mostly a bottom feeder, it sometimes swam near the surface and into freshwater outlets when migrating or chasing food.

For the fourteen days of the sturgeon's summer spawning, the mouths of the streams and rivers were full. Though the fish that chose the smaller waterways did not reach the size of the giants that churned their way up the great rivers, the sturgeon that found their way into the clan's net would be more than enough for them to beach. As the time for the migrations neared, Brun sent someone to the seacoast every day. The first of the mighty beluga sturgeon had just broached the stream when he gave the word. They would leave the next morning.

Ayla woke up full of excitement. She had her sleeping fur tied into a bundle, food and cooking gear packed in her collecting basket, and the large hide that would be used as a shelter loaded on top even before breakfast. Iza never left the cave without her medicine bag, and she was still packing it when Ayla ran outside the cave to see if they were ready to leave.

"Hurry, Iza," she encouraged, running back in. "We're almost ready to go."

"Settle down, child. The sea isn't going anywhere," Iza replied after she pulled the drawstring tight.

Ayla lifted the collecting basket to her back and picked up Uba. Iza followed, then turned to look back, trying to remember if she had forgotten anything. She always felt as though she was forgetting something when she left the cave. Well, Ayla can come back for it, if it's important, she thought. Most of the clan were outside and shortly after Iza fell into her proper place, Brun gave the signal to start.

They had barely gotten under way when Uba squirmed to get down.

"Uba not baby! Want to walk myself," she motioned with childish dignity. At three and a half, Uba had begun to emulate the adults and older children and to reject the pampering that infants and babies received. She was growing up. In something close to four years, she would likely be a woman. She had much to learn in four short years, and through an inner sense of her rapid maturation she was beginning to prepare herself for the added responsibilities that would be hers so soon.

"All right, Uba," Ayla motioned as she let her down. "But stay close behind me."

They followed the stream down the side of the mountain, working around its altered course along a new path that had already been formed near the logjam. It was an easy hike—though the trip back would take more exertion—and before noon they reached a broad stretch of beach. They set up temporary shelters well back from encroaching tides using driftwood and brush for supports. Fires were started and the net rechecked. They would begin fishing the next morning. After camp was set up, Ayla wandered toward the sea.

"I'm going in the water, mother," she motioned.

"Why do you always want to go in the water, Ayla? It's dangerous, and you always go out so far."

"It's wonderful, Iza. I'll be careful."

It was always the same, when Ayla went swimming, Iza worried. Ayla was the only one who liked to swim; she was the only one who could. The large heavy bones of Clan people made swimming difficult. They didn't float easily and had a great fear of deep water. They waded into the water to catch fish, but they never liked to go in deeper than waist level. It made them uneasy. Ayla's predilection for swimming was considered one of her peculiarities. It was not the only one.

By the time Ayla reached her ninth year, she was taller than any of the women and as big as some of the men, but she still showed no signs of approaching womanhood. Iza sometimes wondered if she would ever stop growing. Her height and lateness in blooming led to speculation in some quarters that her strong male totem would prevent her from blossoming altogether. They wondered if she would live out her life as a sort of neutered female, neither a man nor fully a woman.

Creb limped up to Iza as she was watching Ayla walk toward the shore. Her tough lean body, flat wiry muscles, and long coltish legs made her seem awkward and clumsy, but her supple movement belied her ungainly-seeming gawkiness. Though she tried to mimic the Clan women's subservient scramble, she lacked their short, bowed legs. No matter how she minced her steps, her longer legs took longer, almost masculine strides.

But it wasn't only her long legs that made her different. Ayla radiated a self-confidence that no Clan woman ever felt. She was a hunter. No man of the clan was better than she with her weapon, and by now she knew it. She could not feign a submission to greater male superiority she did not feel. She lacked the commitment of genuine belief that was part of a Clan woman's appeal. In the eyes of the men, her tall, lanky body, devoid of any womanly attributes, and her unconscious attitude of assurance detracted from her already dubious beauty—Ayla was not only ugly, she was unfeminine.

"Creb," Iza gestured. "Aba and Aga say she will never become a woman. They say her totem is too strong."

"Of course she will become a woman, Iza. Don't you think the Others have young? Just because she was accepted into the clan doesn't change who she is. It's probably normal for their women to mature later. Even some Clan girls don't become women until their tenth year. You'd think people would give her at least that long before they start imagining some abnormality. It's ridiculous!" he snorted in annoyance.

Iza was pacified but still wished her adopted daughter would start to show some signs of womanliness. She saw Ayla wade into the water up to her waist, then kick off and head out to sea with long clean strokes.

The girl loved the freedom and buoyancy of the salty water. She never remembered learning how to swim, it just seemed she always knew. The underwater shelf of the coastline dropped off abruptly after a few more feet; she knew when she passed the place by the deeper hue and colder water. She flipped over on her back and floated lazily for a while rocked by the motion of the waves. Sputtering from a briny mouthful splashed on her face, she rolled over and turned back to the beach. The tide was going out and she had drifted into the outflowing stream. The force of the combined currents made swimming back harder. She exerted herself and soon regained her footing, then waded back to shore. Rinsing off in the fresh water of the stream, she could feel the swift current pushing against her legs and the unstable sandy bottom crumble beneath her feet. She flopped down near the fire outside their shelter, tired but feeling refreshed.

After they ate, Ayla stared dreamily into the distance wondering what lay beyond the water. Squawking, squealing seabirds swooped and wheeled and dived above the booming surf. White, weathered old bones of once-living trees, sculpted into twisted contours, relieved the flat sands, and the wide expanse of blue gray water glinted in the long rays of the setting sun. The scene had a vacant, surreal, otherworld feeling to it. The contorted driftwood became grotesque silhouettes, then faded into the darkness of the moonless night.

Iza put Uba down in the shelter, then returned to sit beside Ayla and Creb near the small fire that sent wisps of smoke to the star-splattered sky.

"What are they, Creb?" Ayla signaled quietly, motioning upward.

"Fires in the sky. Each one is the hearth of someone's spirit in the otherworld."

"Are there so many people?"

"They are the fires of all the people who have gone to the world of the spirits, and all the people not yet born. They are the fires of totems' spirits, too, but most totems have more than one. See those over there?" Creb pointed. "That is the home of Great Ursus himself. And see those?" he pointed in another direction. "They are the fires of your totem, Ayla, the Cave Lion."

"I like sleeping out where you can see the little fires in the sky," Ayla said.

"But it's not so nice when the wind is blowing and the snow is falling," Iza interjected.

"Uba like little fires, too," the child motioned, appearing out of the darkness into the circle of light from the fire.

"I thought you were asleep, Uba," Creb said.

"No. Uba watch little fires like Ayla and Creb."

"It's time we all went to sleep," Iza motioned. "Tomorrow will be a busy day."

Early the next morning, the clan stretched their net across the stream. Swim bladders from previous catches of sturgeon, carefully washed and air-dried to hard, clear, isinglass balloons, served as floats for the net, and stones tied to the bottom were weights. Brun and Droog took one end to the far shore, then the leader signaled. Adults and older children began to wade into the stream. Uba started to follow.

"No, Uba," Iza gestured, "you stay, you're not old enough."

"But Ona is helping," the child pleaded.

"Ona is older than you, Uba. You can help later, after we bring the fish in. It's too dangerous for you. Even Creb is staying close to shore. You stay here."

"Yes, mother," Uba motioned, her disappointment obvious.

They moved slowly, creating as little disturbance as possible as they fanned out to form a large semicircle, then waited until the sand stirred up by their movement settled back down again. Ayla stood with her feet apart braced against the strong current surging around her legs, her eye on Brun waiting for his signal. She was in midchannel, equally distant from both shores and closest to the sea. She watched a large dark shape glide past a few feet away. The sturgeon were on the move.

Brun raised his arm, everyone held their breath. Abruptly, as he brought his arm down, the clan began to shout and beat on the water, raising foamy splashes. What appeared to be a disorderly chaos of noise and spray was soon revealed as a purposeful drive. The clan was herding the fish toward the net drawing their circle in tighter. Brun and Droog moved in from the far shore, bringing the net around while the churning confusion created by the clan kept the fish from heading back to sea. The net closed in, crowding the silvery mass of struggling fish into less and less space. A few of the monsters strained against the knotted cords, threatening to break through. More hands reached for the net, pushing it toward the bank while those on the shore pulled, as the clan fought to beach the flopping convulsive horde.

Ayla glanced up and saw Uba knee-deep in squirming fish trying to reach her from the other side of the net.

"Uba! Go back!" she signaled.

"Ayla! Ayla!" the child cried, then pointed out toward the sea. "Ona!" she screamed.

Ayla turned to look and barely caught sight of a dark head bobbing up once before it disappeared under the water. The child, little more than a year older than Uba, had lost her footing and was being swept out to sea. In the confusion of hauling in the catch, she had been overlooked. Only Uba, watching her older playmate with admiration from the shore, had noticed Ona's desperate plight and tried frantically to get someone's attention to tell them.

Ayla dived back into the muddy, churning stream and plowed through the water toward the sea. She swam faster than she ever had before. The outflowing current helped her along, but the same current was dragging the little girl toward the drop-off with equal force. Ayla saw her head bob up once more and pulled harder. She was gaining on her, but she was afraid not enough. If Ona reached the drop-off before Ayla reached her, she'd be pulled into the deep water by the strong undertow.

The water was changing to salt, Ayla could taste it. The small dark head bobbed up one more time a few feet ahead, then sunk out of sight. Ayla felt the drop of water temperature as she made a desperate lunge, diving underwater to reach for the disappearing head. She felt streaming tendrils and clenched her fist around the long flowing hair of the young girl.

Ayla thought her lungs would burst—she hadn't had time for a deep breath before diving under—and a growing dizziness threatened her just as she broke the surface, dragging her precious load with her. She lifted Ona's head above water, but the child was unconscious. Ayla had never tried to swim supporting another person, but she had to get Ona back to shore as quickly as possible keeping her head above water. Ayla struck out with one arm finding the right stroke, holding on to the child with the other.

By the time she regained her footing, she saw the whole clan had waded out to meet her. Ayla lifted Ona's limp body out of the water and gave her to Droog, not realizing how exhausted she was until that moment. Creb was beside her, and she looked up with surprise to see Brun on the other side helping her to shore. Droog pushed on ahead, and by the time Ayla collapsed on the beach, Iza had the small child stretched out on the sand pumping water out of her lungs.

It was not the first time a member of the clan had come near drowning; Iza knew what to do. A few people had been lost to the cold depths before, but this time the sea was cheated of its victim. Ona began to cough and sputter as water drained from her mouth, and her eyelids flickered.

"My baby! My baby!" Aga cried, throwing herself down. The distraught mother picked up the girl and held her. "I thought she was dead. I was sure she was gone. Oh, my baby, my only girl."

Droog lifted the girl from her mother's lap, and holding her close to him, carried her back to the camp. Contrary to custom, Aga walked by his side, patting and caressing the daughter she thought she had lost.

People stared, pointedly stared, at Ayla as she walked by. No one had ever been saved before, once they had been swept away. It was a miracle that Ona had been rescued. Never again would a member of Brun's clan look at her with deriding gestures when she indulged in her particular idiosyncrasy. It's her luck, they said. She always was lucky. Didn't she find the cave?

The fish were still flopping spasmodically on the beach. A few had managed to find their way back into the stream after the clan realized what happened and raced to meet Ayla returning with the half-drowned girl, but most of the fish were still tangled under the net. The clan went back to the task of hauling them in, then the men clubbed them into stillness and the women began to clean them.

"A female!" Ebra shouted as she slit open the belly of a huge beluga sturgeon. They all raced toward the big fish.

"Look at it all!" Vorn motioned and reached for a handful of the tiny black eggs. Fresh caviar was a treat they all relished. Usually, everyone grabbed handfuls from the first female sturgeon caught and gorged themselves. Later catches would be salted and preserved for future use, but it was never quite as good as it was fresh from the sea. Ebra stopped the boy and motioned to Ayla.

"Ayla, you take first," Ebra gestured.

She looked around, embarrassed to be the center of attention.

"Yes, Ayla take first," others joined in.

The girl looked at Brun. He nodded. She walked forward shyly and reached for a handful of shiny black caviar, then stood up and took a taste. Ebra signaled and everyone dived in and grabbed a share, crowding around the fish happily. They had been spared a tragedy, and in their relief, it felt like a holiday.

Ayla walked slowly back to their shelter. She knew she had been honored. Taking small bites, she savored the rich caviar and savored the warm glow of their acceptance. It was a feeling she would never forget.

After the fish had been landed and clubbed, the men stood aside in their inevitable knot leaving cleaning and preserving to the women. Besides the sharp flint knives used to open the fish and filet the large ones, they had a special tool for scraping off scales. It was a knife that was not only blunted along the back so it could be held easily in the hand, but a notch had been knocked off the pointed tip where the index finger was placed to control pressure so the scales could be scraped away without tearing the skin of the fish.

The clan's net brought in more than sturgeon. Cod, freshwater carp, a few large trout, even some crustaceans were part of the haul. Birds drawn by the fish gathered to gorge on the entrails, stealing a few filets when they could get close enough. After the fish were set out to dry in the air or over smoky fires, the net was strung out over them. It allowed the net to dry and showed where repairs were needed, and it kept the birds from snatching the clan's hard-won catch.

Before they were through fishing, they would all be tired of the taste, and smell, of fish, but on the first night it was a welcome treat and they always feasted together. The fish saved for the celebration, mostly cod whose delicate white flesh was a particular favorite when fresh, were wrapped in a bed of fresh grass and large green leaves and set over hot coals. Although nothing was said explicitly, Ayla knew this feast was in her honor. She was the recipient of many choice morsels urged on her by the women and a whole filet prepared with special care by Aga.

The sun had disappeared in the west and most people had straggled off to their own shelters. Iza and Aba were talking on one side of the large bonfire, died down to embers, while Ayla and Aga sat silently watching Ona and Uba play. Aga's year-old son, Groob, was sleeping peacefully in her arms, contentedly full of warm milk.

"Ayla," the woman began, a little hesitantly. "I want you to know something. I have not always been nice to you."

"Aga, you have always been courteous," Ayla interrupted.

"That is not the same as nice," Aga said. "I talked to

Droog. He has grown fond of my daughter, even though she was born to the hearth of my first mate. He never had a girl at his fire before. Droog says you will always carry a part of Ona's spirit with you. I don't really understand the ways of the spirits, but Droog says whenever a hunter saves the life of another hunter, he keeps a piece of the spirit of the man he saved. They become something like siblings, like brothers. I'm glad you share Ona's spirit, Ayla. I'm glad she is still here to share it with you. If I am ever fortunate enough to have another child, and if it is a girl, Droog has promised to name her Ayla."

Ayla was stunned. She didn't know how to respond. "Aga, that is too great an honor. Ayla is not a Clan name."

"It is now," Aga said.

The woman rose, motioned to Ona, and started toward her shelter. She turned back for a moment. "I am going now," she said.

It was the closest gesture people of the Clan had for "good-bye." Most often that was omitted; they simply left. The Clan had no term for "thank you" either. They understood gratitude, but that carried a different connotation, generally a sense of obligation, usually from a person of lesser status. They helped each other because it was their way of life, their duty, necessary for survival, and no thanks were expected or received. Special gifts or favors carried the onus of obligation to return them with something of like value; this was understood and no thanks were necessary. As long as Ona lived, unless an occasion arose where she, or, until she came of age, her mother, could return the favor in kind and secure a piece of Ayla's spirit, she would be in Ayla's debt. Aga's offer was not the return of an obligation, it was more, it was her way of saying thank you.

Aba got up to leave shortly after her daughter had gone. "Iza always said you were lucky," the old woman gestured as she passed the girl. "I believe it now."

Ayla walked over and sat beside Iza after Aba left. "Iza, Aga told me I will always carry a piece of Ona's spirit with me, but I only brought her back, you were the one who made her breathe again. You saved her life as much as I did. Don't you carry a part of her spirit, too?" the girl asked. "You must carry pieces of many spirits, you have saved many lives."

"Why do you suppose a medicine woman has status of her own, Ayla? It's because she carries part of the spirits of all her clan, both men and women. Of the whole Clan for that matter, through her own clan. She helps bring them into this world and cares for them all through their lives. When a woman becomes a medicine woman, she is given that piece of the spirit from everyone, even those whose life she hasn't saved, because she never knows when she will.

"When a person dies and goes to the world of the spirits," Iza continued, "the medicine woman loses a part of her spirit. Some believe it makes a medicine woman try harder, but most of them would try just as hard anyway. Not every woman can be a medicine woman, not even every daughter of one. There must be something inside that makes her want to help people. You have it, Ayla, that's why I've been training you. I saw it from the first when you wanted to help the rabbit after Uba was born. And you didn't stop to think of the danger to yourself when you went after Ona, you just wanted to save her life. The medicine women of my line have the highest status. When you become a medicine woman, Ayla, you will be of my line."

"But I'm not really your daughter, Iza. You're the only mother I remember, but I wasn't born to you. How can I be of your line? I don't have your memories. I don't really understand what memories are."

"My line has the highest status because they have always been the best. My mother, and her mother, and hers before for as long as I can remember have always been the best. Each one passed on what they knew and learned. You are Clan, Ayla, my daughter, trained by me. You will have all the knowledge I can give you. It may not be all I know—I don't know myself how much I know—but it will be enough because there is something else. You have a gift, Ayla, I think you must come from your own line of medicine women. You are going to be very good someday.

"You don't have the memories, child, but you have a way of thinking, a way of understanding what is hurting someone. If you know what's hurting, then you can help, and you have a way of knowing how to help. I never told you to put snow on Brun's arm when Oga burned it. I might have done the same thing, but I never told you. Your gift, your talent, may be as good as memories, maybe better, I don't know. But a good medicine woman is a good medi-

cine woman. That's what is important. You will be of my
line because you are going to be a good medicine woman,
Ayla. You will be worthy of the status, you will be one of
the best."

The clan fell into a regular routine. They made only one
catch a day, but it was enough to keep the women busy
until late afternoon. There were no further mishaps, though
Ona did not help the beaters herd fish anymore. Droog
decided she was still too young, next year would be soon
enough. Toward the end of the sturgeon run, the catches
got smaller and the women had more time to relax in the
afternoons. It was just as well. It took a few days for the
fish to dry and the row of racks stretching across the beach
grew longer every day.

Droog had scoured the floodplain of the stream for the
nodules of flint that had washed down the mountain, and
dragged several back to the campsite. On several afternoons
he could be seen knapping new tools. One afternoon not
long before they planned to leave, Ayla saw Droog take a
bundle from his shelter to a driftwood log nearby where he
usually made his tools. She loved to watch him work the
flint and followed him, then sat in front of him with her
head bowed.

"This girl would like to watch, if the toolmaker does not
object," she motioned when Droog acknowledged her.

"Hhmmmf," he nodded in agreement. She found herself a
place on the log to sit quietly and observe.

The girl had watched him before. Droog knew she was
genuinely interested and would not interfere with his concentration. If only Vorn showed as much interest, he
thought. None of the youngsters in the clan had shown a
real aptitude for toolmaking, and like any really skilled
technician, he wanted to share his knowledge and pass it
on.

Maybe Groob will have the interest, he thought. He was
pleased that his new mate had given birth to a boy so soon
after Ona was weaned. Droog had never had such a full
hearth, but he was glad he had decided to take Aga and her
two children. Even the old woman wasn't so bad to have
around—Aba often took care of his needs when Aga was
busy with the baby. Aga didn't have the quiet understanding
depth of Goov's mother, and Droog had to exert himself in
the beginning to let her know her place. But she was young

and healthy and had produced a son, a boy Droog had high hopes he could train to be a toolmaker. He had learned the stone knapper's art from the mate of his mother's mother, and understood, now, the old man's pleasure when, as a young boy, he had become interested in developing the skill.

But Ayla had watched him often since she came to live with the clan, and he had seen the tools she made. She was adept with her hands, applied the techniques well. Women were free to make tools so long as they did not make any implements whose ultimate purpose was as a weapon or to make weapons. There just wasn't much value in training a girl, and she would never be a real expert; but she had some skill, made very serviceable tools, and a female apprentice was better than none at all. He had explained something of his craft to her before.

The toolmaker opened the bundle and spread out the leather hide that held the tools of his trade. He looked at Ayla and decided to give her the benefit of some useful knowledge about stone. He picked up a piece he had discarded the day before. Through long years of trial and error, Droog's forebears had learned that flint had the right combination of properties to make the best tools.

Ayla watched with rapt attention while he explained. First a stone had to be hard enough to cut, scrape, or split a variety of animal and vegetable materials. Many of the siliceous minerals of the quartz family had the necessary hardness, but flint had another quality that most of them, and many stones made of softer minerals, did not have. Flint was brittle; it would break under pressure or percussion. Ayla jumped back with a start when Droog demonstrated by bashing the flawed stone against another, breaking it in two and exposing material of a different nature in the heart of the shiny dark gray flint.

Droog didn't quite know how to explain the third quality, though he understood it at the deep gut level that came from working with the stone for so long. The quality that made his craft possible was the way the stone broke, and the homogeneity of flint made the difference.

Most minerals break along plane surfaces parallel to their crystal structure, which means they would only fracture in certain directions, and a flint worker could not shape them for specific uses. When he could find it, Droog sometimes used obsidian, the black glass of volcanic eruptions, even though it was much softer than many minerals. It did not have a well-defined crystal structure, and he could break it easily in any direction, homogeneously.

The crystal structure of flint, though well-defined, was so small it was homogeneous too, the only limitation to shaping it being the skill of the knapper, and that was Droog's special talent. Yet flint was hard enough to cut through thick hides or tough stringy plants, and brittle enough to break with an edge as sharp as a broken piece of glass. To show her, Droog picked up one of the pieces of the flawed stone and pointed to an edge. She didn't need to touch it to know how sharp it was; she had used knives equally as sharp many times.

Droog thought of his years of experience that had honed the knowledge passed on to him as he dropped the broken piece and spread the leather hide across his lap. A good knapper's ability began with selection. It took a practiced eye to distinguish minor color variations in the chalky outer covering that pointed to high-quality, fine-grained flint. It took time to develop a sense that nodules in one location were better, fresher, less subject to inclusions of foreign materials, than stones from a different location. Perhaps someday he'd have a real apprentice who would have his appreciation for those finer details.

Ayla thought he had forgotten her as he set out his implements, carefully examined the stones, then sat quietly holding his amulet with his eyes closed. It surprised her when he began to talk with unspoken gestures.

"The tools I am going to make are very important. Brun has decided we will hunt mammoth. In the fall, after the leaves have turned, we will travel far to the north to find the mammoth. We must be very lucky for the hunt to be successful; the spirits must favor it. The knives I am going to make will be used as weapons and the other tools to make weapons especially for the hunt. Mog-ur will make a powerful charm to bring luck to them, but first the tools must be made. If the making goes well, it will be a good sign."

Ayla wasn't sure if Droog was talking to her or just stating the facts so he would have them clearly in his mind before he began. It made her even more conscious that she must remain very still and do nothing to disturb Droog while he worked. She half expected him to tell her to go, now that she knew the importance of the tools he was about to make.

What he didn't know was that from the time she had shown Brun the cave, Droog thought she carried luck with her, and saving Ona's life confirmed his conviction. He thought of the strange girl as an unusual stone or tooth that one received from his totem and carried in his amulet for good luck. He wasn't sure if she herself was lucky, only that she brought luck, and her asking to watch at this particular time he considered propitious. He noticed out of the corner of his eye that she reached for her amulet as he picked up the first nodule. Though he didn't define it to himself in precisely that way, he felt she was bringing the luck of her powerful totem to bear on his endeavor, and he welcomed it.

Droog was sitting on the ground, a leather hide draped across his lap, holding a nodule of flint in his left hand. He reached for an oval-shaped stone and hefted it until it felt comfortable in his hand. He had searched long for a hammerstone with just the right feel and resiliency and had had this one for many years. The many nicks on it attested to its long use. With the hammerstone, Droog broke off the chalky gray outer covering exposing the dark gray flint underneath. He stopped and examined the flint critically. The grain was right, the color was good, there were no inclusions. Then he began roughing out the basic shape of a hand-axe. The thick flakes that fell off had sharp edges; many would be used as cutting implements just as they fell from the stone. The end of each flake where the striker hit the flint had a heavy bulge that tapered to a thinner cross section at the opposite end, and each piece that fell off left a deep rippled scar on the flint core.

Droog put the hammerstone down and picked up a section of bone. Taking careful aim, he struck the flint core very close to the sharp rippled edge. The softer, more elastic bone hammer caused longer, thinner flakes, with a flatter bulb of percussion and straighter edges, to fall away from the flint core, and it did not crush the sharp thin edge as the harder stone striker would have.

In a few moments, Droog held up the finished product. The tool was about five inches long, pointed at one end, with straight cutting edges, a relatively thin cross section, and faces that were smooth with only shallow facets showing where the flakes had been chipped away. It could be held in the hand and used to chop wood like an axe, or to hollow out a wooden bowl from a section of log like an adze, or to chop off a piece of mammoth ivory, or to break the bones of animals when butchering, or for any of the many uses to which a sharp hitting instrument could be put.

It was an ancient tool, and Droog's ancestors had been producing similar hand-axes for millennia. A simpler form was one of the earliest tools ever devised, and it was still useful. He rummaged through the pile of flakes, picking out several with wide straight cutting edges and setting them aside to be used for cleavers useful in butchering and cutting through tough hides. The hand-axe was only a warm-up exercise. Droog turned his attention next to another nodule of flint, one he had selected for its particularly fine grain. He would apply a more advanced and difficult technique to this one.

The toolmaker was loosened up now, not as nervous, and he was ready for the next task. He moved the foot bone of a mammoth between his legs to use as an anvil, and grasping the nodule, he set it on the platform and held it firmly. Then he picked up his hammerstone. This time as he chipped off the chalky outer covering, he carefully shaped the stone so that the nucleus of flint remaining was a roughly flattened egg-shape. He turned it on its side and, switching to the bone hammer, trimmed flakes from the top, working from the edge toward the center all the way around. When he was through, the egg-shaped stone had a flat oval top.

Then Droog stopped, wrapped his hand around his amulet, and closed his eyes. An element of luck as well as skill was necessary for the next crucial steps. He stretched his arms, flexed his fingers, and reached for the bone hammer. Ayla held her breath. He wanted to make a striking platform, to remove a small chip from one end of the oval-shaped flat top that would leave a dent with a surface perpendicular to the flake he wanted to remove. The striking platform was necessary for the flake to fall away cleanly with sharp edges. He examined both ends of the oval surface, decided on one, took careful aim, and struck a sharp blow, then let out his breath as the small piece chipped away. Droog held the discoidal nucleus firmly on the anvil, and gauging the distance and point of impact with precision, he struck the small dent he had made, with the bone hammer. A perfect flake fell away from the prefabricated core. It had a long oval shape, sharp edges, was roughly flattened on the outside with a smooth inner bulbar face, and was slightly thicker at the end that was struck, diminishing to a thin section at the other.

Droog looked at the core again, turned it, and struck off another small chip to form a platform, opposite to the end of the previous striking platform, then removed a second preformed flake. Within a few moments, Droog had cleaved six flakes and discarded the butt of the flint core. They all had a long oval shape and tended to narrow at the thinner end to a point. He looked over the flakes carefully and arranged them in a row ready for the finishing touches that would turn them into the tools he wanted. From a stone of almost the same size as the one used to make a single hand-axe, he had gotten six times the cutting edge with the newer technique, a cutting edge he could shape to a variety of useful tools.

With a small, slightly flattened round stone, Droog gently knicked off the sharp edge on one side of the first flake to define the point, but more importantly, to blunt the back so the handheld knife could be used without cutting the user; retouching, not to sharpen the already thin sharp edge, but to dull the back for safe handling. He gave the knife a critical evaluation, removed a few more tiny chips, then, satisfied, he put it down and reached for the next flake. Going through the same process, he made a second knife.

The next flake Droog selected was a larger one from nearer the center of the egg-shaped core. One edge was nearly straight. Holding the flake against the anvil, Droog applied pressure with a small bone and detached a small piece from the blade edge, then several more, leaving a series of V-shaped notches. He blunted the back of the denticulated tool and reexamined the small-toothed saw he had just made, then nodded and put it down.

Using the same piece of bone, the toolmaker retouched the entire blade edge of a smaller, rounder flake into a steep convex form, creating a sturdy, slightly blunt-edged tool that would not break easily from the pressure of scraping wood or animal hides, and would not tear the skins. On another flake, he made one deep V notch on the cutting edge, especially useful for shaping the points of wooden spears, and on the last flake—which came to a sharp point on the thin end but had rather wavy blade edges—he blunted both sides, leaving the point. The tool could be used as an awl to pierce holes in leather or as a borer to make holes in wood or bone. All of Droog's tools were made to be held in the hand.

Droog looked once more over the kit of tools he had manufactured, then motioned to Ayla who had been watching in rapt attention, hardly daring to breathe. He handed her the scraper and one of the wide sharp flakes that were removed in the process of making the hand-axe.

"You can have these. You may find them useful if you come with us on the mammoth hunt," he gestured.

Ayla's eyes were glowing. She handled the tools as if they were the most precious of gifts. They were. Is it possible I might be chosen to go along with the hunters on the mammoth hunt? she wondered. Ayla wasn't a woman yet, and usually only women and any small children they happened to be nursing went with the hunters. But she was woman-size, and she had gone on a few short hunts already that summer. Maybe I will be picked. I hope so, I really hope so, she thought.

"This girl will save the tools until the time of the mammoth hunt. If she is chosen to accompany the hunters, she will use them for the first time on the mammoth the hunters will kill," she told him.

Droog grunted, then he shook out the leather that was spread across his lap to remove the small chips and splinters of stone, placed the mammoth-foot anvil, hammerstone, bone hammer, and the bone and stone retouchers in the middle of it, and wrapped them up and tied them securely with a cord. Then he gathered up the new implements and walked to the shelter he shared with the other members of his hearth. He was through for the day though it was still afternoon. In a very short time he had produced some very fine tools and he did not want to push his luck.

"Iza! Iza! Look! Droog gave these to me. He even let me watch while he made them," Ayla motioned with Creb's one-handed symbols, holding the tools carefully in the other as she ran toward the medicine woman. "He said the hunters were going on a mammoth hunt in the fall and he was making the tools for the men to make new weapons especially for it. He said I might find these useful if I go along with them. Do you think I might get to go with them?"

"You might, Ayla. But I don't know why you're so excited about it. It will be hard work. All the fat must be rendered and most of the meat dried, and you can't believe how much meat and fat is on a mammoth. You'll have to travel far and carry it all back."

"Oh, I don't care if it's hard work. I've never seen a mammoth, except once far in the distance from the ridge. I want to go. Oh, Iza, I hope I can go."

"Mammoth don't often come this far south. They like it cold and the summers are too hot here. There's too much snow in winter for them to graze. But I haven't had mammoth meat in a long time. There's nothing better than good, tender mammoth, and they have so much fat that can be used for so many things."

"Do you think they'll take me, mother?" Ayla gestured excitedly.

"Brun doesn't tell me his plans, Ayla. I didn't even know they were going; you know more about it than I do," Iza said. "But I don't think Droog would have said anything if it wasn't a possibility. I think he was grateful that you saved Ona from drowning and the tools and news about the hunt are his way of telling you. Droog is a fine man, Ayla. You are fortunate he finds you worthy of his gifts."

"I'm going to save them until the mammoth hunt. I told him if I go, I'll use them for the first time then."

"That's a good idea, Ayla, and it was the proper thing to say."

14

The mammoth hunt, planned for early fall when the huge woolly beasts migrated south, was a chancy undertaking at best, and it had the whole clan excited. Every able-bodied person would be included in the expedition to the northern end of the peninsula, close to where it joined the mainland. During the time it would take to travel, butcher and preserve the meat, render the fat, and return to the cave, all other hunting activities would be precluded. And there was no assurance they would find mammoth once they got there, or, if they did, that the hunters would be successful. Only the fact that if they were successful, one gigantic beast would provide enough meat to sustain the clan for many months, along with a large supply of fat so essential to their existence, made it worthwhile to even consider.

The hunters crammed many more than the usual amount of regular hunts into the early summer season to lay in enough meat to see them through the coming winter—if they were careful. They couldn't afford the luxury of gambling on a mammoth hunt without making some provision for the next cold season. But the next Clan Gathering would be held in two years, and during that summer, there would be almost no hunting. The entire season would be spent traveling to the cave of the clan hosting the significant event, participating in the great festival, and returning again. The long history of such meetings made Brun aware that the clan had to begin stockpiling food and supplies well in advance to tide them over the winter following the Gathering. That was the reason he decided to hunt mammoth. Adequate stores for the coming winter, plus a successful mammoth hunt, would give them a good head start. Dried meat, vegetables, fruits, and grains would easily last two years if properly stored.

There was not only an aura of excitement about the forthcoming hunt, there was a palpable undercurrent of superstition. The success of the hunt depended so much on luck, omens were seen in the most insignificant occurrences. Everyone was careful of their every action and especially circumspect with anything remotely related to spirits. No one wanted to be the cause of an angered spirit that might bring bad luck. The women were even more careful when they cooked; a burned meal might be a bad omen.

The men held ceremonies over every phase of the planning, offering fervent supplication to propitiate the invisible forces around them, and Mog-ur was busy casting good-luck spells and making powerful charms, usually from the bones in the small cave. Everything that went well was seen as a favorable indication, and every hitch was cause for worry. The whole clan was edgy, and Brun hardly had one good night's rest from the time he made the decision to hunt mammoth and sometimes wished he had never thought of it.

Brun called a meeting of the men to discuss who would go and who would stay behind. Protecting the home cave was the important issue.

"I have been considering leaving one of the hunters behind," the leader began. "We will be gone at least a whole moon, perhaps as much as two. That is a long time to leave the cave unprotected."

The hunters avoided looking at Brun. None of them wanted to be excluded from the hunt. Each one was afraid if the leader caught his eye, he might be the one selected to remain behind.

"Brun, you will need all your hunters," Zoug motioned. "My legs may not be fast enough to hunt mammoth, but my arm is still strong enough to wield a spear. The sling is not the only weapon I can use. Dorv's sight is failing, but his muscles are not weak and he's not blind yet. He can still use a club or a spear, at least well enough to protect the cave. As long as we keep the fire going, no animal is going to come too close. You don't need to worry about the cave, we can protect it. You will have enough to worry about hunting mammoth. The decision is not mine, of course, but I think you should take all the hunters."

"I agree, Brun," Dorv added, leaning forward and squinting a little. "Zoug and I can protect the cave while you are gone."

Brun looked from Zoug to Dorv and back to Zoug. He didn't want to leave any of his hunters behind. He didn't want to do anything that might jeopardize his chances for success.

"You're right, Zoug," Brun finally gestured. "Just because you and Dorv can't hunt mammoth doesn't mean you are not strong enough to protect the cave. The clan is fortunate you are both still so able, and I am fortunate that the second-in-command to the leader-before-me is still with us to give me the benefit of his wisdom, Zoug." It never hurt to let the old man know he was appreciated.

The rest of the hunters relaxed. None of them would be left behind. They felt sorry for the old men who could not share in the great hunt, but grateful it was they who would be left to guard the cave. It was understood that Mog-ur would not make the trek, either; he was no hunter. But Brun had, on occasion, seen the old cripple brandish his stout walking stick with some force in self-protection, and mentally added the magician to the cave protectors. Certainly the three of them could do as well as a single hunter.

"Now, which of the women will we take with us?" Brun asked. "Ebra will come."

"Uka, too," Grod added. "She is strong and experienced and has no small children."

"Yes, Uka is a good choice," Brun approved, "and Ovra," he said, looking at Goov. The acolyte nodded in agreement.

"What about Oga?" Broud asked. "Brac is walking now and he'll soon reach his weaning year; he doesn't take much of her time."

Brun thought a moment. "I don't see why not. The other women can help watch him, and Oga is a good worker. We can use her."

Broud looked pleased. He liked to know his mate was well thought of by the leader; it was a compliment to his good training.

"Some women must stay to watch the children," Brun motioned. "What about Aga and Ika; Groob and Igra are still young to travel so far."

"Aba and Iza could watch them," Crug volunteered. "Igra is not much trouble for Ika." Most men liked to have their own mates along on an extended hunt, then they didn't have to depend on another man's mate to serve them.

"I don't know about Ika," Droog commented, "but I think Aga would rather stay this time. Three of the children are hers, and even if she takes Groob, I know Ona would miss her. Vorn would like to come with us, though."

"I think both Aga and Ika should stay," Brun decided, "and Vorn, too. There will be nothing for him to do, he's not old enough to hunt, and he wouldn't be very eager to help the women, especially without his mother to keep after him. There will be other mammoth hunts for him."

Mog-ur hadn't volunteered any comment up till then, but felt the time was right. "Iza is too weak to go, and she needs to stay and take care of Uba, but there's no reason Ayla can't go."

"She's not even a woman," Broud interjected, "and, besides, the spirits might not like it if the strange one is with us."

"She's bigger than a woman, and as strong," Droog contended, "a hard worker, good with her hands, and the spirits favor her. What about the cave? And Ona? I think she will bring luck."

"Droog is right. She's a fast worker and as strong as a woman. She doesn't have any children to worry about, and she's had some training as a medicine woman. That could be useful, though if Iza were stronger, I'd rather take her. Ayla comes with us," Brun gestured with finality.

Ayla was so excited when she found out she was going along on the mammoth hunt, she couldn't sit still. She pestered Iza with questions of what to take with her and had her basket packed and repacked several times in the final days before they planned to leave.

"You don't want to take too much, Ayla. Your load is going to be much heavier on the way back, if the hunt is successful. But I do have something for you that I think you should take. I just finished making it."

Tears of happiness came to Ayla's eyes as she saw the pouch Iza held out. It was made from the whole skin of an otter, cured with the fur, head, tail, and feet left intact. Iza had asked Zoug to get one for her and she had kept it hidden at Droog's hearth, including Aga and Aba in on her surprise.

"Iza! My own medicine bag!" Ayla cried, and hugged the woman. She immediately sat down and removed all the small pouches and packets, setting them out in rows as she had seen Iza do so many times. She opened each one and sniffed at the contents, then tied them all back up with exactly the same knots with which they had been tied originally.

It was difficult to distinguish between many dried herbs and roots by smell alone, though particularly dangerous ones were often mixed with an innocuous but strong-smelling herb to prevent accidental misuse. The real system of classification was the type of cord or thong that held the pouches closed and an intricate combination of knots. Certain classes of herbal remedies were tied with cord made of horsehair, others with the hair of bison or some other animal whose hair had a distinctive color and texture, still others were tied with sinew or the cords made of stringy barks or vines, and some with leather thongs. Part of memorizing the uses of a particular plant was knowing the type of cord and the system of knots used to close the pouch or packet that held it.

Ayla put the pouches back into her medicine bag, then tied it to the cord at her waist, admiring it. She took it off and put it near her collecting basket along with the large bags that would be used to hold the mammoth meat they hoped to bring back. Everything was ready. The only problem that gave Ayla any cause for concern was what to do with her sling. She would have no use for it, but she was afraid to leave it behind for Iza or Creb to find. She thought of hiding it in the woods, but thought some animal might dig it up or the exposure might ruin it. Finally, she decided to take it with her, but keep it well hidden in a fold of her wrap.

It was still dark when the clan got up on the day of the hunters' departure, and the multihued leaves were just starting to show their true colors as the sky lightened when they started out. But as they passed beyond the ridge east of the cave, the radiant gleam of the rising sun broached the horizon, illuminating the broad plain of standing hay below with an intense golden glow. They trooped down the wooded flanks of the foothills and reached the steppes while the sun was still low. Brun set a fast pace, nearly as rapid as when the men went out alone. The women's burdens were light, but unused to the rigors of rapid travel, they had to push to keep up.

They traveled from sunup to sundown, covering a much greater distance in a day than when the entire clan was looking for a new cave. They did no cooking except to boil water for tea, and little was required of the women. No game was hunted along the way; they all ate the traveling food the men usually took hunting: dried meat ground to a coarse meal, mixed with clean rendered fat and dried fruit, formed into small cakes. The highly concentrated traveling food supplied their nutritional needs more than adequately.

It was cold on the open windy prairie and got colder rapidly as they traveled north. Even so, shortly after they started out in the mornings, they removed layers of their clothing. Their pace warmed them quickly and only when they stopped for short rests did they notice the frigid temperature. The aching muscles of the first few days, especially the women's, soon disappeared as they hit a stride and developed traveling legs.

The terrain of the northern part of the peninsula was rougher. Broad flat plateaus suddenly disappeared into steep ravines or abutted sheer cliffs—the result of rumbling up-heavals in the violent earth of earlier times shaking free the constraints of limestone bonds. Narrow canyons were walled with jagged rocky faces, some dead-ending where the walls conjoined and some strewn with the rubble of sharp-edged fallen boulders cleaved from the surrounding bulwarks. Others channeled occasional waterways ranging from small seasonal streams to rushing rivers. Only near watercourses did a few wind-twisted pines, larches, and firs, crowded by birches and willows stunted to little more than brush, relieve the monotony of the grassy steppes. In rare instances where a ravine opened into a watered valley, sheltered from the incessant, driving wind and supplied with sufficient moisture, the coniferous and small-leafed decidu-ous trees more closely approached their true proportions.

The journey was uneventful. They traveled at the steady, fast pace for ten days before Brun began sending out men to scout the surrounding area, slowing their progress for the next few days. They were close to the broad neck of the peninsula. If they were going to find mammoth, they should begin to see them soon.

The hunting party had stopped at a small river. Brun had sent Broud and Goov out earlier in the afternoon, and he was a short distance off from the rest looking in the direc-tion they had gone. He would have to make a decision soon whether they would camp beside this river or continue farther before they stopped for the night. The late after-noon shadows were lengthening into evening, and if the two young men did not return soon, the decision would be made for him. He squinted his eyes as he faced directly into the sharp east wind that whipped his long fur wrap around his legs and flattened his bushy beard against his face.

Far in the distance he thought he saw movement, and as he waited, the running figures of two men became more distinct. He felt a sudden twinge of excitement. Perhaps it was intuition, or perhaps it was his sensitive attunement to the way their bodies moved. They saw the solitary figure and put on a fresh burst of speed, waving their arms. Brun knew long before their voices could be heard.

"Mammoth! Mammoth!" the men shouted, out of breath as they raced toward the group. Everyone crowded around the exultant men.

"A large herd, to the east," Broud gestured excitedly.

"How far?" Brun asked.

Goov pointed straight up, then moved his arm down in a short arc. "A few hours," the signal indicated.

"Show the way," Brun motioned and signaled the rest to follow. There were still enough hours of daylight left to move closer to the herd.

The sun was crowding the horizon before the hunting party saw the dark blur of movement in the distance. It is a large herd, Brun thought, as he called a halt. They would have to make do with the water they carried from the previous stop; it was too dark to look for a stream. In the morning they could find a better campsite. The important thing was that they had found mammoth. Now it was up to the hunters.

After the troupe moved to a new encampment beside a meandering creek defined by a double row of scraggly brush along each bank, Brun took his hunters to reconnoiter the possibilities. A mammoth could not be run down like a bison, or tripped with bolas. A different tactic had to be devised to hunt the woolly pachyderms. Brun and his men scouted the ravines and canyons in the vicinity. He was looking for a particular formation, a blind canyon that narrowed to a close defile with boulders lining the sides and piled up at the closed end, not too far from the slowly moving herd.

Early in the morning of the second day, Oga nervously sat down in front of Brun, head bowed, while Ovra and Ayla waited anxiously behind her.

"What do you want, Oga?" Brun motioned as he tapped her shoulder.

"This woman would make a request," she began hesitantly.

"Yes?"

"This woman has never seen a mammoth. Neither have Ovra or Ayla. Would the leader allow us to go closer so we can get a better look?"

"What about Ebra and Uka, do they want to see a mammoth, too?"

"They say they will see enough mammoth before we are through to satisfy them. They have no wish to go," Oga replied.

"They are wise women, but then, they have seen mammoth before. We are downwind; it should not disturb the herd if you do not go too close and do not try to circle around."

"We will not go too close," Oga promised.

"No, I think when you see them, you will not want to go too close. Yes, you may go," he decided.

It won't hurt to let the young women make a small excursion, he thought. They have little to do now, and they will be busy enough later—if the spirits favor us.

The three were excited about their proposed adventure. It was Ayla who finally convinced Oga to ask, though they had all talked about it. The hunting trip had thrown them into a closer association than they normally had at the cave, and it gave them an opportunity to get to know each other better. Ovra, who was quiet and reserved by nature, had always considered Ayla one of the children and did not seek her out for companionship. Oga did not encourage too much social contact, knowing how Broud felt about her, and neither of the young women felt they had much in common with the girl. They were mated women, adults, mistresses of their men's hearths; Ayla was still a child who did not have the same responsibilities.

It was only that summer, when Ayla assumed a quasi-adult status and began going on hunting trips, that the women began to think of her as more than a child, and especially during the trek to hunt for mammoth. Ayla was taller than any of the women, which gave her the appearance of an adult, and she was treated in most ways as though she were a woman by the hunters. Crug and Droog in particular called upon her. Their mates were back at the cave, and Ayla was unmated. They didn't have to make their requests through another man, or with his permission, however informally it was asked or granted. With the common interest of the hunt, a friendlier relationship developed among the three younger females. Ayla's closest associations before were with Iza, Creb, and Uba, and she enjoyed the newfound warmth of friendship with the women.

Shortly after the men left in the morning, Oga left Brac with Ebra and Uka and the three started out. It was a pleasant hike. They soon fell into animated conversation with rapidly moving hands and emphatic words. As they drew closer to the animals, their conversation fell off and soon ceased altogether. They stopped and gawked at the massive creatures.

The woolly mammoths were well adapted to the harsh periglacial climate of their cold environment. Their thick hides were covered with an undercoat of dense soft fur and an overlayer of shaggy, long, reddish brown hair up to twenty inches in length. They were further insulated by a three-inch layer of subcutaneous fat. The cold had caused modifications in their body structure, too. They were compact for their species, averaging ten feet high at the withers. Their massive heads, large in proportion to their overall height and more than half the length of their trunks, rose high above their shoulders in a peaked dome. They had small ears, short tails, and relatively short trunks with two fingers at the end, an upper and a lower one. In profile, they had a deep depression at the nape of the neck between their domed heads and a high hump of stored fat on the withers. Their backs sloped down sharply to the pelvis and somewhat shorter hind legs. But most impressive were their long, curved tusks.

"Look at that one!" Oga gestured and pointed to an old bull. His ivory tusks originated close together, pointed steeply downward, curved sharply outward, upward, then inward, crossing over in front of him and continuing on for a full sixteen feet.

The mammoth was tearing out swaths of grass, herbs, and sedge with his trunk and stuffing the tough, dry fodder into his mouth to break it down with efficient rasplike grinders. A younger animal, one whose tusks were not so long and still useful, uprooted a larch and began to strip it of twigs and bark.

"They're so big!" Ovra motioned with a shudder. "I didn't think any animal could be so big. How are they ever going to kill one? They can't even reach one with a spear."

"I don't know," Oga said, just as apprehensive.

"I almost wish we hadn't come," Ovra said. "It will be a dangerous hunt. Someone could get hurt. What will I do if something happens to Goov?"

"Brun must have a plan," Ayla said. "I don't think he'd even try to hunt them if he didn't think the men could. I wish I could watch," she added wistfully.

"I don't," Oga said. "I don't want to be anywhere near. I'll just be glad when it's over." Oga remembered her mother's mate had been killed in a hunting accident just before the earthquake that took her mother. She was well aware of the dangers in spite of the best of plans.

"I think we should go back now," Ovra said. "Brun

didn't want us to get too close. This is closer than I want to be."

The three of them turned to go. Ayla looked back a few times as they hurried away. They were more quiet on the return trip, each lost in her own thoughts and not in the mood for much talk.

When the men returned, Brun directed the women to break camp and move after the hunters left the next morning. He had found a suitable location, they would hunt tomorrow, and he wanted the women well out of the way. He had seen the canyon early the day before. It was an ideal site but too far from the mammoths. He considered it a particularly good omen that the herd, moving slowly in a southwesterly direction, had wandered close enough by the end of the second day to make the site feasible.

A light, dry, powdery snow whipped up by gusting east winds greeted the hunting party as they unrolled from their warm furs and poked their noses out of low tents. The dismal gray sky, hiding the glowing sun that lighted the planet, could not dampen the keen anticipation. On this day they would hunt mammoth. The women scurried to make tea; like athletes finely tuned for the game, the hunters would take nothing else. They stamped around, making practice lunges into the air with their spears to stretch and loosen taut muscles. The tension they projected charged the air with excitement.

Grod took a glowing coal from the fire and put it in the aurochs horn attached to his waist. Goov took another. They wrapped furs securely around themselves. Not the usual heavy outer wraps, but lighter garments that would not restrict them. None of them felt the cold; they were too keyed up. Brun went over the plan quickly, one last time.

Each man closed his eyes and clutched his amulet, picked up an unlit torch they had made the evening before, and set out. Ayla watched them go, wishing she dared to follow them. Then she joined the women who had begun to collect dried grass, dung, brush, and wood for fires before they broke camp.

The men reached the herd quickly. The mammoths had already begun to move again after resting for the night. The hunters squatted down in the tall grass to wait while Brun appraised the animals that moved past. He saw the old bull with the massive curving tusks. What a prize he would be, he said to himself, but rejected the beast. They had a long distance to travel back to the cave and the huge tusks would weigh them down unnecessarily. The tusks of a younger animal would be easier to carry and the meat more tender, besides. That was more important than the glory of displaying massive tusks.

Younger bulls were more dangerous, though. Their shorter tusks were not only useful for uprooting trees, they were very effective weapons. Brun waited patiently. He had not made all the preparations and the long trip in order to rush now. He knew the circumstances he was looking for and would rather return the next day than risk their chance for success. The rest of the hunters waited, too, not all of them as patiently.

The rising run had warmed the dull overcast sky and scattered the clouds. The snow stopped and bright rays broke through open spaces.

"When is he going to give the signal?" Broud motioned silently to Goov. "Look how high the sun is already. Why start out early and just sit here? What is he waiting for?"

Grod caught Broud's gestures. "Brun is waiting for the right time. Would you rather go back empty-handed or wait awhile? Be patient, Broud, and learn. Someday it will be you who must decide when the time is right. Brun is a good leader, a good hunter. You are fortunate to have him to teach you. It takes more than bravery to be a leader."

Broud wasn't too pleased with Grod's lecture. He will not be my second-in-command when I am leader, he thought. He's getting too old, anyway. The young man shifted his position, shivered a little from a strong gust of wind, and settled down to wait.

The sun was high in the sky when Brun finally gave a "get ready" signal. Every hunter felt a sharp stab of excitement. A female, heavy with young, was near the periphery of the herd, and edging farther out. She was fairly young, but by the length of her tusks, the pregnancy was probably not her first. She was far enough along in it to make her ponderous. She wouldn't be as fast or agile, and fetal meat would be a succulent bonus.

The mammoth spied a stand of grass not yet encountered by the rest and moved toward it. For a moment, she stood alone, a solitary animal away from the protection of the herd. It was the moment Brun was waiting for. He gave the signal.

Grod had the hot coal out and a torch held in readiness. The moment Brun signaled, he held the torch to the ember and blew until it caught and leaped into flames. Droog lit two others from the first and gave one to Brun. The three younger hunters had dashed toward the canyon the moment they saw the signal. Their part would come later. As soon as the torches were lit, Brun and Grod ran behind the mammoth and laid the fiery brands to the dry grass of the prairie.

Full-grown mammoths had no natural enemies; only the very young and very old ever fell prey to any predator—except man. But they feared fire. Prairie fires from natural causes sometimes raged unchecked for days, destroying everything in their path. A man-caused fire was no less devastating. The moment they sensed danger, the herd instinctively closed in. The fire had to take hold quickly to prevent the female from rejoining the rest, and Brun and Grod were between the she-mammoth and the herd. They could be charged from either direction or caught in a stampede of behemoths.

The scent of smoke turned the peacefully grazing animals into a bedlam of trumpeting confusion. The female turned toward the herd, but it was too late. A wall of fire separated her. She sirened for help, but the flames, fanned by the brisk east wind, had converged on the milling animals. They were already stampeding to the west, trying to outdistance the fast-encroaching blaze. The prairie fire was out of control, but that was of little concern to the men. The wind would carry the destruction away from the place they wanted to go.

The she-mammoth, screaming her fright, lurched in panic toward the east. Droog waited until he saw the flames take hold, then raced away. When he saw the mammoth begin her charge, he ran toward the confused and frightened beast, shouting and waving his torch, veering her to the southeast.

Crug, Broud, and Goov, the youngest and fastest of the hunters, were pelting away at top speed in front of her. They were afraid the frantic mammoth would outpace them even with their head start. Brun, Grod, and Droog raced behind her, trying to keep up and hoping she wouldn't alter her course. But once started, the behemoth charged blindly straight ahead.

The three young hunters reached the box canyon and

Crug turned into it. Broud and Goov stopped at the south wall. Nervous and out of breath, Goov reached for the aurochs horn, sending an unspoken plea to his totem that the coal had not died. It was live, but neither of them had much breath to blow flame to the torch. The brisk wind provided an assist. They both lit two torches, holding one in each hand, and moved out from the wall, trying to anticipate where the mammoth would approach. The wait was not long. With a silent prayer to their totems as the frightened, trumpeting, gigantic animal stampeded toward them, the brave young men raced into the face of the charging mammoth waving smoky torches in front of them. They had the difficult and dangerous job of turning the petrified animal into the canyon.

The panic-stricken pachyderm, already running in fear from the fire and confronted with the smell of smoke ahead, looked for an escape. She swerved and pounded into the canyon, with Broud and Goov right behind her. The bellowing behemoth plowed through the canyon, reached the narrow defile, and found her way blocked. Unable to move ahead or to turn in the tight space, she screamed her frustration.

Broud and Goov sprinted up breathlessly. Broud had a knife in his hand, one carefully shaped by Droog and charmed by Mog-ur. In a swift, reckless dash, Broud ran for her left hind leg and with the sharp blade slashed her tendons. Her strident cry of pain split the air. She could not move forward, she could not turn sideward, and now she could not move backward. Goov followed Broud and hamstrung her right foot. The great beast fell to her knees.

Then Crug jumped up from behind the boulder in front of the faltering mammoth trumpeting in agony, and plunged his long, pointed spear straight into her open mouth. Instinctively she tried to attack and spewed blood over the weaponless man. But he was not weaponless for long. Other spears had been stashed behind the rocks. As Crug reached for another spear, Brun, Grod, and Droog reached the canyon and raced to the blind end, leaping up on the rocks at either side of the huge, pregnant mammoth. They lunged their spears into the wounded creature almost simultaneously. Brun's penetrated one small eye, spurting him with warm scarlet. The animal lurched. With her last burst of life, the mammoth trumpeted a defiant scream, and slumped to the ground.

Realization came slowly to the exhausted men. In the sudden silence, the hunters looked at each other. Their hearts beat faster with a new kind of excitement. A formless, primal urge from deep within rose and exploded from their mouths in a cry of victory. They did it! They killed the mighty mammoth!

Six men, pitifully weak by comparison, using skill and intelligence and cooperation and daring, had killed the gigantic creature no other predator could. No matter how fast or how strong or how cunning, no four-legged hunter could match their feat. Broud leaped up on the rock beside Brun, then jumped onto the fallen animal. In a moment, Brun was beside him, clapped him warmly on the shoulder, then pulled his spear from the mammoth's eye and held it aloft. The other four quickly joined them and, moving to the rhythm of their own heartbeats, they jumped and danced their elation on the back of the massive beast.

Then Brun leaped down and circled the mammoth nearly filling the narrow space. Not one man was wounded, he thought. Not one man has so much as a scratch. This was a very lucky hunt. Our totems must be pleased with us.

"We must let the spirits know we are grateful," he announced to the men. "When we return, Mog-ur will hold a very special ceremony. For now, we will take the liver—each man will have his piece and we will bring back a piece for Zoug and Dorv and Mog-ur. The rest will be given to the Spirit of the Mammoth, it is what Mog-ur told me to do. We will bury it here where she fell, and the liver of the young mammoth inside her, too. And Mog-ur said we are not to touch the brain, that must be left where it is for the Spirit to keep. Who struck the first blow, Broud or Goov?"

"Broud did," Goov responded.

"Then Broud will get the first piece of liver, but the kill is credited to all."

Broud and Goov were sent to bring the women. In one burst of energy, the men's job was completed. Now it was up to the women. To them fell the tedious task of butchering and preserving. The men remaining behind eviscerated the huge mammoth while they waited for them and removed the nearly full-term fetus. After the women arrived, the men helped them skin the animal. It was so large, it took the effort of all. Selected favorite parts were cut out and stored in stone caches, to freeze. Fires were built around the rest, partly to keep it from freezing and partly to keep away the inevitable scavengers drawn to the smell of blood and raw meat.

The tired but happy hunting party sank gratefully into their beds of warm furs after their first meal of fresh meat since leaving the cave. In the morning, while the men gathered together to relive the exciting hunt and admire each other's bravery, the women went to work. There was a stream close by but enough of a distance from the canyon that it presented a minor inconvenience. Once they had the carcass divided into large haunches, they moved closer to the stream, leaving most of the bones with bits of meat still clinging to them to the prowling and flying scavengers, but little else.

The clan used nearly every part of the animal. The tough mammoth hide could be made into foot coverings—sturdier and longer lasting than the skin of other animals—windbreaks for the mouth of the cave, cooking pots, sturdy thongs for lashings, outdoor shelters. The soft undercoat of downy hair could be beaten into a kind of felt material, used for stuffing pillows or pallets for beds, even as absorbent filling for babies' swaddling. The long hair was twisted into sturdy cord, the tendons into strands of sinew; bladders, stomach, intestines could be used as water containers, soup pots, food storage, even waterproof rainwear. Little was wasted.

Not only were meat and other parts used, the fat was particularly essential. It made up the balance of necessary calories to fuel their energy requirements, which included metabolic warmth in winter as well as vigorous activity during warmer seasons; it was used as a dressing to cure hides, since many of the animals they killed—deer, horses, range-grazing aurochs and bison, rabbits, and birds—were essentially lean; it supplied fuel for stone lamps that added an element of warmth as well as light; it was used for waterproofing and as a medium for salves, unguents, and emollients; it could be used to help start fires in wet wood, for long-burning torches, even as fuel to cook with in the absence of other fuels. The uses for fat were many.

Every day, while the women worked, they watched the sky. If the weather was clear, the meat would dry in about seven days aided by the winds which blew continually. There was no need for smoky fires—it was too cold for blowflies to spoil the meat—and it was just as well. Fuel was far more scarce on the steppes than on the wooded hillsides of their cave or even the warmer southern steppes which supported more trees. With intermittent clouds, overcast sky, or precipitation, it might take up to three times as long for the thin strips of meat to dry. The light powdery snow whipped about by the gusting winds was not a major problem; only if the weather turned unseasonably warm and wet would the work be halted. They hoped for dry, clear, cold weather. The only way the mountains of flesh could be hauled back to the cave was if it was dried before they left.

The heavy, shaggy skin with its thick layer of fat and connective blood vessels, nerves, and follicles was scraped clean. Thick slabs of the cold-hardened fat were placed in a large skin pot set over a fire and the rendered fat poured into sections of the cleaned intestines and tied off like large fat sausages. The hide, with the hair left on, was cut into manageable sections and tightly rolled, then allowed to freeze hard for the return trip. Later in the winter, back at the cave, it would be dehaired and cured. The tusks were broken off and proudly displayed at the campsite. They, too, would be carried back.

During the days while the women worked, the men hunted smaller game or kept watch in a desultory fashion. Moving closer to the stream had eliminated one inconvenience, but there was another, harder to remedy. The scavengers drawn to the fresh kill followed the hunting party to their new location. The strips of meat draped over lines of cords and thongs had to be constantly watched. One huge spotted hyena was more than persistent. It had been driven off many times, but it continued to lurk on the fringes of the camp, eluding the halfhearted efforts of the men to kill it. The fierce-looking creature was just crafty enough to snatch a mouthful of drying mammoth meat several times a day. It was a nuisance.

Ebra and Oga were hurrying to finish slicing the last of the huge chunks of meat into thin strips to start them drying. Uka and Ovra were pouring fat into a section of intestine, and Ayla was at the stream flushing out another section. A crust of ice had formed at the edges, but the water was still flowing. The men were standing near the tusks trying to decide if they wanted to hunt jerboas with their slings.

Brac had been sitting near his mother and Ebra playing with pebbles. He became bored with the stones and got up to find something more interesting to do. The women were concentrating on their task and didn't notice him wandering off toward the open plains, but another pair of eyes watched him.

Every head in the camp turned at the sound of his terrified, high-pitched scream.

"My baby!" Oga cried. "The hyena has my baby!"

The loathsome scavenger, which was also a predator and always ready to attack the unwary young or enfeebled old, had seized the child by his arm with powerful jaws and was quickly retreating, dragging the small boy with him.

"Brac! Brac!" Broud was shouting as he ran after them, followed by the rest of the men. He reached for his sling—he was too far away for a spear—and stooped to pick up a stone, hurrying before the beast got out of his range.

"No! Oh, no!" he cried in despair as the stone fell short and the hyena kept going. "Brac! Braaac!"

Suddenly, from another direction came the *thwack, thwack* of two stones fired in quick succession. They landed squarely on the animal's head and the hyena dropped in his tracks.

Broud stood in open-mouthed amazement that turned to stunned astonishment when he saw Ayla running toward the wailing child with her sling still in her hand and two more stones held ready. The hyena was her prey. She had studied these animals, knew their habits and their weak spots, trained herself until hunting such quarry was second nature. When she heard Brac scream, she didn't think of the consequences, she just reached for her sling, quickly grabbed two pebbles, and hurled them. Her only thought was to stop the hyena that was dragging Brac away.

It was only after she reached the child, extracted him from the dead hyena's grip, and turned to face the staring eyes of the others that the full impact hit her. Her secret was out. She had given herself away. They knew she could hunt. A wave of cold fear washed over her. What will they do to me? she thought.

Ayla cuddled the baby, avoiding the unbelieving stares as she walked back to the campsite. Oga came out of her shock first. She ran toward them, holding out her arms, and gratefully accepted her baby boy from the girl who had saved his life. As soon as they reached the camp, Ayla began examining the child, as much to keep from looking at anyone else as to determine the extent of his injuries. Brac's arm and shoulder were mangled, and his upper arm bone was broken, but it looked like a clean break.

She had never set an arm, but she had watched Iza do it, and the medicine woman had talked to her about what to do if an emergency came up. Iza's concern had been for the hunters; it didn't occur to her that something might happen to the baby. Ayla stirred up the fire, started water boiling, and got her medicine bag.

The men were silent, still stunned, not quite able, or willing, to accept what they had just seen. For the first time in his life, Broud felt grateful to Ayla. His thoughts didn't go much beyond relief that the son of his mate had been saved from a certain and ugly death. But Brun's did.

The leader was quick to grasp the implications and knew he was suddenly faced with an impossible decision. By Clan tradition, in effect, Clan law, the punishment for any woman who used a weapon was no less than death. It was clear-cut. There were no provisions for unusual circumstances. The custom was so ancient and so well understood, it hadn't even been invoked for generations beyond count. The legends surrounding it were closely linked with the legends about a time when women controlled the access to the world of the spirits before the men took them over.

That custom was one of the forces that had caused the marked differentiation between Clan men and Clan women, since no woman with an unfeminine desire to hunt was allowed to survive. Over countless ages, only those with properly female attitudes and actions were left. As a result the adaptability of the race—the very trait upon which survival depends—was curtailed. But it was the Clan way, Clan law, even though there were no longer deviant Clan women. But Ayla was not born to the Clan.

Brun loved the son of Broud's mate. Only with Brac did the leader's stoic reserve soften. The baby could do anything to him: pull his beard, poke curious fingers in his eyes, spit up all over him. It didn't matter. Brun was never so gentle, so pliable, as when the small boy fell asleep with the peaceful assurance of security in the proud and stiff leader's arms. He had no doubt Brac would not be alive if Ayla had not killed the hyena. How could he condemn to death the girl who had saved Brac's life? She had saved him with the weapon she must die for using.

How had she done it? he wondered. The beast was out of range and she was farther away from it than the men. Brun walked over to where the slain hyena still lay and touched the drying blood that oozed from the fatal wounds. Wounds? Two wounds? His eyes hadn't been deceived. He thought he had seen two stones. How had the girl learned to use a sling with such skill? Not Zoug, or anyone he ever heard of, could fire two stones from a sling so rapidly, so accurately, and with such force. Force enough to kill a hyena from that distance.

No one ever used a sling to kill a hyena, anyway. He had been sure from the start that Broud's attempt would be a futile gesture. Zoug always said it could be done, but privately Brun wasn't sure. He had never contradicted the man; Zoug was still too valuable an asset to the clan, there was no point in belittling him. Well, Zoug had been proved right. Could a sling be used to kill a wolf or a lynx, too, as Zoug so stoutly maintained? Brun mused. Suddenly his eyes opened wide, then narrowed. A wolf or a lynx? Or a wolverine, or wildcat, or badger, or ferret, or a hyena! Brun's mind raced. Or all the other predators that have been found dead lately?

"Of course!" Brun's motion emphasized his thought. She did it! Ayla's been hunting for a long time. How else could she have gained such skill? But she's female, she learned the women's skills easily, how could she learn to hunt? And why predators? And why such dangerous ones? And why at all?

If she were a man, she'd be the envy of every hunter. But she's not a man. Ayla is female and she used a weapon and she must die for it or the spirits will be very angry. Angry? She's been hunting for a long time, why aren't they angry? They're anything but angry. We just killed a mammoth in a hunt so lucky not one man was even injured. The spirits are pleased with us, not angry.

The confused leader shook his head. Spirits! I don't understand spirits. I wish Mog-ur were here. Droog says she carries luck; I half think he's right, things have never gone so well since we found her. If they favor her so much, would it make them unhappy if she was killed? But it's the Clan way, he agonized. Why did she have to be found by my clan? She may be lucky, but she's given me more headaches than I ever thought possible. I can't make a decision without talking to Mog-ur. I'll just have to let it wait until we get back to the cave.

Brun strode back to the camp. Ayla had given the boy painkilling medicine that put him to sleep, then cleaned his wounds with an antiseptic solution, set the arm, and put on a cast of dampened birch bark. It would dry stiff and hard and hold the bones in place. She'd have to watch it, though, in case it swelled too much. She watched Brun coming back from examining the hyena and trembled as he approached. But he walked past her without a sign, ignoring her completely, and she realized she would not learn her fate until they got back to the cave.

15

The seasons changed in reverse as the hunting party traveled south, from winter to fall. Threatening clouds and the smell of snow hurried their departure; they had no desire to be caught by the first real blizzard of the peninsula's northern winter. The warmer weather at the southern end gave a false feeling of approaching spring, with an unsettling twist. Rather than new shoots and budding wild flowers, tall grass swayed in golden waves on the steppes, and the bloom of the temperate trees at the protected tip was in shades of crimson and amber patchworked with evergreen. But the view from the distance was deceiving. Most deciduous trees had dropped their leaves and the onslaught of winter was close behind.

It took longer to return than to reach the site of the mammoth herd. The fast, distance-devouring pace was impossible with their heavy loads. But Ayla was weighed down with more than mammoth. Guilt, anxiety, and depression were far heavier burdens. No one spoke of the incident, but it wasn't forgotten. Often, her casual glance caught someone staring at her before they turned aside, quickly, and few spoke to her unless it was necessary. She felt isolated, lonely, and more than a little frightened. As little conversation as she had, it was enough for her to learn the penalty for her crime.

The people left behind at the cave had been watching for the return of the hunters. From the time of their earliest expected arrival, someone was posted near the ridge where there was a good view of the steppes, most often one of the children.

When Vorn first took his turn early in the day, he stared out at the distant panorama conscientiously, but then he got bored. He didn't like being off by himself without even Borg to play with. He devised imaginary hunts and jabbed his not quite full-sized spear into the ground so often that the point became frayed despite fire hardening. It was only by accident that he happened to glance down the hill as the hunting party came into view.

"Tusks! Tusks!" Vorn shouted, racing back to the cave.

"Tusks?" Aga asked. "What do you mean, 'tusks'?"

"They're back!" Vorn gesticulated excitedly. "Brun and Droog and the rest, and I saw them carrying tusks!"

Everyone ran halfway to the steppes to greet the victorious hunters. But when they reached them, it was apparent something was wrong. The hunt was successful, the hunters should have been jubilant. Instead their step was heavy and their manner subdued. Brun was grim, and Iza needed only one look at Ayla to know something terrible had happened that involved her daughter.

While the hunting party unloaded some of their burden on those who had remained behind, the reason for the somber silence unfolded. Ayla trudged up the slope with bowed head, oblivious to the surreptitious glances cast in her direction. Iza was dumbfounded. If she had ever worried over the unorthodox actions of her adopted daughter before, it was nothing to the icy shaft of fear she felt for her now.

When they reached the cave, Oga and Ebra brought the child to Iza. She cut away the birchbark cast and examined the boy.

"His arm should be as good as new before long," she pronounced. "He'll be scarred, but the wounds are healing and the arm is set well. I'd better put another cast on it, though."

The women breathed easier. They knew Ayla was inexperienced, and though they had little choice but to allow the girl to treat Brac, they were concerned. A hunter needed two good strong arms. If Brac lost the use of one, he would never become a leader as he was destined. If he was unable to hunt, he would not even become a man, but would live out his life in the ambiguous limbo in which older boys, who had reached physical maturity but had not made their first kill, existed.

Brun and Broud were relieved, too. But for Brun, at least, the news was received with mixed emotions. It made his decision more difficult. Ayla had not only saved Brac's life, she had assured his useful existence. The matter had been put off long enough. He signaled Mog-ur and they walked off together.

The story, as Brun explained it, left Creb deeply troubled. Ayla was his responsibility to raise and train and he had obviously failed. But there was something else that troubled him even more. When he first learned of the animals the men kept finding, he felt it had nothing to do with spirits. He even wondered if Zoug or one of the other men was playing some kind of elaborate joke on the rest. It seemed unlikely, but his intuition told him the deaths were caused by a human agent. He had also been aware of changes in Ayla, changes he should have recognized now that he thought about it. Women did not walk with the quiet stealth of a hunter, they made noise and with good reason. More than once, Ayla had startled him by approaching so silently he didn't hear her coming. There were other things, too, small things that should have made him suspicious.

But he was blinded by his love for her. He didn't allow himself to imagine she could be hunting, he was far too aware of the consequences. It caused the old magician to question his own integrity, his ability to perform his function. He had let his feeling for the girl come before the spiritual safekeeping of the clan. Did he still merit their trust? Was he still worthy of Ursus? Could he still justifiably continue as Mog-ur?

Creb took the blame for her actions on himself. He should have questioned her; he should not have let her roam so freely; he should have disciplined her more severely. But all his anguish over what he should have done didn't change in the least what he still had to do. The decision was Brun's, but it was his function to carry it out, his duty to kill the child he loved.

"It's only a guess that she's the one who has been killing

the animals," Brun said. "We need to question her, but she did kill the hyena and she had a sling. She had to practice on something, there's no other way she could have gained such skill. She's better than Zoug with that weapon, Mog-ur, and she's female! How did she ever learn? I've won-dered before if there isn't some male in her, and I'm not the only one. She's as tall as a man and not even a woman yet. Do you think there's any truth in the idea that she may never become one?"

"Ayla's a girl, Brun, and someday she'll become a woman, just like any other girl—or she would have. She's a female who used a weapon." The magician's jaw was set; he would not allow himself to grasp at false illusions.

"Well, I still want to know how long she's been hunting. But it can wait until morning. We're all tired now; it was a long journey. Tell Ayla we'll question her tomorrow."

Creb limped back to the cave, but stopped at his hearth only long enough to signal Iza to tell the girl she would be questioned in the morning, before continuing on to his small annex. He did not return to his hearth all night.

The women stared silently after the men who were walk-ing into the woods with Ayla trailing behind. They were at a loss, filled with mixed emotions. Ayla was confused her-self. She had always known it was wrong to hunt, if not how serious the crime was. I wonder if it would have made any difference if I had known? she asked herself. No. I wanted to hunt. I would have hunted anyway. But I don't want the evil ones to chase me all the way to the spirit world. She shuddered at the thought.

The girl feared the invisible, malign entities as much as she believed in the power of protective totems. Not even the Spirit of the Cave Lion could protect her from them, could he? I must have been wrong, she thought. My totem wouldn't have given me a sign to let me hunt knowing I'd die for it. He probably left me the first time I picked up a sling. She didn't like thinking about it.

The men came to a clearing and arranged themselves on logs and boulders on either side of Brun, while Ayla slumped to the ground at his feet. Brun tapped her shoulder to allow her to look up at him and began without prelimi-naries.

"Were you the one who killed the meat eaters the hunters kept finding, Ayla?"

"Yes," she nodded. There was no point in trying to hide anything now. Her secret was out and they would have known if she tried to evade their questions. She could no more lie than any other member of the clan could.

"How did you learn to use a sling?"

"I learned from Zoug," she replied.

"Zoug!" Brun echoed. All heads turned accusingly toward the old man.

"I never taught the girl to use a sling," he gestured defensively.

"Zoug didn't know I was learning from him." Ayla motioned quickly, springing to the old sling-hunter's defense. "I watched him when he was teaching Vorn."

"How long have you been hunting?" Brun asked next.

"Two summers, now. And the summer before that I just practiced, but I didn't hunt."

"That's as long as Vorn has been training," Zoug commented.

"I know," Ayla said. "I started the same day he did."

"How do you know exactly when Vorn started, Ayla?" Brun asked, curious how she could be so sure.

"I was there, I watched him."

"What do you mean, you were there? Where?"

"At the practice field. Iza sent me to get some wild cherry bark, but when I got there, you were all there," she explained. "Iza needed the cherry bark, and I didn't know how long you were going to stay, so I waited and watched. Zoug was giving Vorn his first lesson."

"You watched Zoug give Vorn his first lesson?" Broud cut in. "Are you sure it was his first?" Broud remembered that day only too well. It still brought a blush of shame to his face.

"Yes, Broud. I'm sure," she replied.

"What else did you see?" Broud's eyes were narrowed and his gestures clipped. Brun, too, suddenly remembered what had happened in the practice field the day Zoug began Vorn's training, and he wasn't happy at the thought of a female witnessing the incident.

Ayla hesitated. "I saw the other men practicing, too," she answered, trying to evade the issue, then she saw Brun's eyes become stern. "And I saw Broud push Zoug down, and you got very mad at him, Brun."

"You saw that! You saw the whole thing?" Broud demanded. He was livid with anger and embarrassment. Of all people, of all the people in the clan, why was she the one who had to see it? The more he thought about it, the more mortified he became, and the more furious. She was witness to Brun's harshest denunciation of him. Broud even remembered how badly he missed his shots and suddenly recalled that he had missed the hyena, too. The hyena she killed. A female, *that* female, had shown him up.

Every kind thought, every bit of gratitude he had so recently felt toward her vanished. I'll be so glad when she's dead, he thought. She deserves it. He couldn't bear the idea of her continuing to live with her knowledge of his supreme moment of shame.

Brun watched the son of his mate and could almost read his thoughts from the expressions on his face. Too bad, he thought, just when there was some chance of ending the animosity between them, not that it matters anymore. He continued the questioning.

"You said you began to practice the same day as Vorn, tell me about it."

"After you left, I walked across the field and saw the sling Broud threw on the ground. Everyone forgot about it after you got mad at Broud. I don't know why, but I just wondered if I could do it. I remembered Zoug's lesson and tried. It wasn't easy, but I kept trying all afternoon. I forgot how late it was getting. I hit the post once, I think it was just an accident, but it made me think I could do it again if I worked at it, so I kept the sling."

"I suppose you learned how to make one from Zoug, too."

"Yes."

"And you practiced that summer?"

"Yes."

"Then you decided to hunt with it, but why did you hunt meat eaters? They're more difficult, more dangerous, too. We've found dead wolves, even dead lynxes. Zoug always said they could be killed with a sling, you proved he was right, but why those?"

"I knew I could never bring anything back for the clan, I knew I wasn't supposed to touch a weapon, but I wanted to hunt, I wanted to try, anyway. Meat eaters are always stealing food from us; I thought if I killed them, I would be helping. And it wouldn't be such a waste, we don't eat them. So I decided to hunt them."

It satisfied Brun's curiosity about why she chose predators, but not why she wanted to hunt in the first place. She was female; no woman ever wanted to hunt.

"You know it was dangerous to try for the hyena from so far away; you might have hit Brac instead." Brun was probing. He had been ready to try his bola, though the chance of killing the boy with one of the large stones was more than a possibility. But instant death from a cracked skull was preferable to the one the child faced, and at least they would have had the boy's body to bury, so he could be sent on his way to the spirit world with proper rituals. They would have been lucky to find scattered bones if the hyena had had his way.

"I knew I could hit it," Ayla answered simply.

"How could you be sure? The hyena was out of range."

"He wasn't out of my range. I've hit animals before from that distance. I don't miss often."

"I thought I saw the marks of two stones," Brun motioned.

"I threw two stones," Ayla confirmed. "I taught myself after the lynx attacked me."

"You were attacked by a lynx?" Brun pressed.

"Yes," Ayla nodded, and told of her close call with the large cat.

"What is your range?" Brun asked. "No, don't tell me, show me. Do you have your sling?"

Ayla nodded and got up. They all moved to the far end of the clearing where a small brook trickled over a rocky bed. She selected a few pebbles of the right size and shape. Round ones were best for accuracy and distance, but jagged, sharp-edged broken pieces would work.

"The small white rock beside the large boulder at the other end," she motioned.

Brun nodded. It was easily half again as far as any of them could hurl a stone. She sighted carefully, inserted a stone in her sling, and had a second one in the sling and on its way the next instant. Zoug jogged over to confirm her accuracy.

"There are two fresh chips knocked out of the white stone. She hit the mark both times," he announced on his return, with a trace of wonder and the barest hint of pride.

She was female, she should never have touched the sling—Clan tradition was absolutely clear on that—but she was good. She gave him credit for teaching her, whether he knew it or not. That double-stone technique, he thought, that's a trick I'd like to learn. Zoug's pride was the pride of a true teacher for a pupil who excelled; a student who paid attention, learned well, and then did the master one better. And she had proved him right.

Brun's eye caught a movement in the clearing.

"Ayla!" he cried. "That rabbit. Get him!"

She glanced in the direction he was pointing, saw the small animal bounding across the field, and dropped him. There was no need to check her accuracy. Brun looked at the girl appreciatively. She's quick, he thought. The idea of a woman hunting offended the leader's sense of propriety, but with Brun, the clan always came first; their safety, their security, their prosperity were foremost. In a corner of his mind, he knew what an asset she could be to the clan. No, it's impossible, he said to himself. It's against the traditions, it's not the Clan way.

Creb didn't have the same appreciation for her skill. If he had any doubts left, her exhibition convinced him. Ayla had been hunting.

"Why did you ever pick up a sling in the first place?" Mog-ur gestured with a bleak, dark look.

"I don't know," she shook her head and looked down. More than anything, she hated the thought of the magician's displeasure.

"You did more than touch it. You hunted with it, killed with it, when you knew it was wrong."

"My totem gave me a sign, Creb. At least I thought it was a sign." She was undoing the knots in her amulet. "After I decided to hunt, I found this." She handed the fossil cast to Mog-ur.

A sign? Her totem gave her a sign? There was consternation among the men. Ayla's revelation put a new twist on the situation, but why did she decide to hunt?

The magician examined it closely. It was a very unusual stone, shaped like a sea animal, but definitely a stone. It could have been a sign, but that didn't prove anything. Signs were between a person and his totem; no one could understand another person's signs. Mog-ur gave it back to the girl.

"Creb," she said pleadingly. "I thought my totem was testing me. I thought the way Broud treated me was the test. I thought if I could learn to accept it, my totem would let me hunt." Quizzical glances were cast in the young man's direction to see his reaction. Did she really think Broud was used by her totem to test her? Broud looked uncomfortable. "I thought when the lynx attacked me, it was a test, too. I almost stopped hunting after that, I was too afraid. Then I got the idea to try two stones, so I would have something to try again if I missed the first time. I even thought my totem gave me the idea."

"I see," the holy man said. "I'd like some time to meditate on this, Brun."

"Maybe we should all think about it. We'll meet again tomorrow morning," he announced, "without the girl."

"What is there to think about?" Broud objected. "We all know the punishment she deserves."

"Her punishment could be dangerous to the whole clan, Broud. I need to be absolutely sure there isn't something we've overlooked before I condemn her. We will meet again tomorrow."

As the men returned to the cave, they talked among themselves.

"I never knew of a woman who wanted to hunt," Droog said. "Could it have something to do with her totem? It's a male totem."

"I didn't want to question Mog-ur's judgment at the time," Zoug said, "but I always did wonder about her Cave Lion, even with the marks on her leg. I don't doubt it anymore. He was right, he always is."

"Could she be part male?" Crug commented. "There's been some talk."

"That would account for her unwomanly ways," Dorv added.

"She's female all right, there's no doubt of that," Broud said. "She must be killed, everyone knows it."

"You're probably right, Broud," Crug said.

"Even if she is part male, I don't like the idea of a woman hunting," Dorv commented dourly. "I don't even like her being part of the clan. She's too different."

"You know I've always felt that way, Dorv," Broud agreed. "I don't know why Brun wants to talk about it again. If I were leader, I'd just do it and be done with it."

"It's not a decision to make lightly, Broud," Grod said. "What's your hurry? One more day won't matter."

Broud hurried ahead without bothering to respond. That

old man is always lecturing, he thought, always sticking up for Brun. Why can't Brun make a decision? I've made up my mind. What good is all this talk? Maybe he's getting old, too old to lead anymore.

Ayla stumbled back after the men. She went straight to the cave to Creb's hearth and sat on her sleeping fur, staring into space. Iza tried to coax her to eat, but she just shook her head. Uba wasn't sure what was going on, but something was troubling the tall, wonderful girl, the special friend she loved and idolized. She went to Ayla and crawled into her lap. Ayla held the small girl, silently rocking her. Somehow Uba knew she was a comfort. She didn't squirm to get down, she just allowed herself to be held and rocked and finally fell asleep. Iza took the child from Ayla's arms and put her to bed, then retired to her own, but she didn't sleep. Her heart was too full of grief for the strange girl she called daughter who sat staring at the glowing coals of the cooling fire.

The morning dawned clear and cold. Ice was forming on the edges of the stream, and a thin film of solidified water covered the still, spring-fed pond near the mouth of the cave in the mornings, usually melted by the time the sun was high. Before very much longer, the clan would be confined to the cave for the winter.

Iza didn't know if Ayla had slept; she was still sitting on her fur when the woman awoke. The girl was silent, lost in a world of her own, hardly conscious of her own thoughts. She just waited. Creb did not return to his hearth for the second night. Iza saw him shuffle into the dark crevice that was the entrance to his inner sanctum. He didn't come out again until morning. After the men left, Iza brought the girl some tea, but Ayla didn't respond to the medicine woman's gentle questions. When she returned, the tea was still beside the girl, cold and untouched. It's as though she's already dead, Iza thought. Her breath caught in her throat as the icy claw of sorrow gripped her heart. It was almost more than Iza could bear.

Brun led the men to a place in the lee of a large boulder, sheltered from the brisk wind, and had a fire built before he opened the meeting. The discomfort of sitting in the cold might encourage the men to be hasty, and he wanted to know the full range of their feelings and opinions. When he began, it was in the completely silent symbols used to address spirits, and it told the men this was not a casual gathering, but a formal meeting.

"The girl, Ayla, a member of our clan, used a sling to kill the hyena that attacked Brac. For three years, she has used the weapon. Ayla is female; by Clan tradition, a female who uses a weapon must die. Does anyone have anything they want to say?"

"Droog would speak, Brun."

"Droog may speak."

"When the medicine woman found the girl, we were looking for a new cave. The spirits were angry with us and sent an earthquake to destroy our home. Maybe they weren't so angry, maybe they just wanted a better place, and maybe they wanted us to find the girl. She is strange, unusual, like a sign from a totem. We have been lucky since we found her. I think she brings luck and I think it comes from her totem.

"It's only part of her strangeness that she was chosen by the Great Cave Lion. We thought she was peculiar because she liked to go into the water of the sea, but if she had not been so peculiar, Ona would be walking the spirit world now. Ona is only a girl, and not even born to my hearth, but I have grown to love her. I would have missed her; I'm grateful she didn't drown.

"She is strange to us, but we know little of the Others. She is Clan now, but she was not born Clan. I don't know why she ever wanted to hunt; it's wrong for Clan women to hunt, but maybe their women do. It doesn't matter, it was still wrong, but if she hadn't taught herself to use a sling, Brac would be dead, too. It's not pleasant to think of the way he would have died. For a hunter to be killed by a meat eater is one thing, but Brac is a baby.

"His death would have been a loss to the whole clan, Brun, not just to Broud and you. If he had died, we wouldn't be sitting here trying to decide what to do about the girl who saved his life, we'd be grieving for the boy who will one day be leader. I think the girl should be punished, but how can she be condemned to die? I am finished."

"Zoug would speak, Brun."

"Zoug may speak."

"What Droog says is true; how can you condemn the girl when she saved Brac's life? She is different, she wasn't born Clan, and maybe she doesn't think like a woman should, but except for the matter of the sling, she behaves like a good Clan woman. She had been a model woman, obedient, respectful..."

"That's not true! She is rebellious, insolent," Broud interrupted.

"I am speaking now, Broud," Zoug returned angrily. Brun shot him a disapproving glance and Broud curbed his outburst.

"It's true," Zoug continued, "when the girl was younger, she was insolent to you, Broud. But you brought it on yourself, you're the one who let it bother you. If you act like a child, is it so strange that the girl does not treat you like a man? She has never been anything but dutiful and obedient to me. Nor has she ever been insolent to any other man."

Broud glowered at the old hunter but held himself in check.

"Even if it were not true," Zoug continued, "I have never seen anyone as good with the sling as she is. She says she learned from me. I never knew it, but I will say openly I wish I had so apt a pupil to teach, and I must admit, I could learn from her now. She wanted to hunt for the clan, and when she couldn't, she tried to find another way to help the clan. She may have been born to the Others, but in her heart she is Clan. She has always put the interests of the clan before herself. She didn't think of the danger when she went after Ona. She may be able to move on the water, but I saw how tired she was when she brought Ona back. The sea could have taken her, too. She knew it was wrong for her to hunt, kept her secret hidden for three years, but she didn't hesitate when Brac's life was in danger.

"She is skilled with that weapon, more skilled than anyone I've ever seen. It would be a shame to let that skill go to waste. I say let her be a benefit to the clan, let her hunt..."

"No! No! No!" Broud jumped up in anger. "She is female. Females cannot be allowed to hunt..."

"Broud," the proud old hunter said. "I am not through. You may ask to speak when I am done."

"Let Zoug finish, Broud!" the leader cautioned. "If you do not know how to conduct yourself at a formal meeting, you may leave!" Broud sat down again, struggling to control himself.

"The sling is not an important weapon. I only began to develop my skill after I got too old to hunt with a spear. It's the other weapons that are the real men's weapons. I say let her hunt, but only with the sling. Let the sling be the weapon of old men and women, or at least this one. I am finished now."

"Zoug, you know as well as I that it is more difficult to use a sling than a spear, and many times you have provided meat when the hunt was a failure. Don't belittle yourself for the girl's sake. With a spear, you only need a strong arm," Brun said.

"And strong legs and heart, and good lungs, and a great deal of courage," Zoug replied.

"I wonder how much courage it took to face another lynx after being attacked by one, alone, with only a sling?" Droog commented. "I wouldn't object to Zoug's suggestion, if she hunts only with a sling. The spirits don't seem to object; she is still bringing us luck. What about our mammoth hunt?"

"I'm not sure that's a decision we can make," Brun said. "I don't see any way we can even allow her to live, much less hunt. You know the traditions, Zoug. It's never been done before; would the spirits really approve? What made you think of it, anyway? Clan women don't hunt."

"Yes, Clan women don't hunt, but this one has. I probably wouldn't have thought of it if I didn't know she could, if I hadn't already seen her. All I'm saying is let her continue to do what she has already done."

"What do you say, Mog-ur?" Brun asked.

"What do you expect him to say, she lives at his hearth!" Broud interjected bitterly.

"Broud!" Brun stormed. "Are you accusing Mog-ur of putting his own feelings, his own interests, before those of the clan? Is he not Mog-ur? The Mog-ur? You think he will not say what is right, what is true?"

"No, Brun. Broud has made a good point. My feelings for Ayla are well known; it's not easy to forget I love her. I think you should all remember that, even though I've tried to put emotions aside. I can't be sure that I have. I have been fasting and meditating since you returned, Brun. Last night I found my way to memories I never knew, perhaps because I never looked.

"Long ago, long before we were Clan, women helped men to hunt." There was a gasp of disbelief. "It's true. We will have a ceremony, and I will take you there. When we were first learning to make tools and weapons, and we were born with a knowing that was like memories, but different, women and men both killed animals for food. Men did not always provide for women then. Like a mother bear, a woman hunted for herself and her children.

"It was later that men began to hunt for a woman and her young, and even later before women with children stayed behind. When men began to care about the young, when they began to provide, it was the beginnings of the Clan and helped it to grow. If a mother of a young child died while she was trying to get food, the baby died, too. But it wasn't until people stopped fighting each other and learned to cooperate, to hunt together, that the Clan really began. Even then, some women hunted, when they were the ones who talked to the spirits.

"Brun, you said it's never been done before. You are wrong; Clan women have hunted before. The spirits approved then, but they were different spirits, ancient spirits, not the spirits of totems. They were powerful spirits, but they have long since gone to rest. I'm not sure if they can rightfully be called Clan spirits. It wasn't that they were honored or venerated, more that they were feared; but they weren't evil, just powerful."

The men were stunned. He spoke of times so ancient and so little recalled, they were almost forgotten, almost new. Yet just his mentioning of them evoked a recollection of the fear, and more than one man shuddered.

"I doubt that women born to the Clan now would ever want to hunt," Mog-ur continued. "I'm not sure they could. It's been too long, women have changed since then, so have men. But Ayla is different, the Others are different, more different than we think. I don't think letting her hunt would make any difference as far as the other women are concerned. Her hunting, her wanting to hunt, surprises them as much as us. I have nothing more to say."

"Does anyone have anything more to say?" Brun asked. He wasn't sure, though, that he was ready for more. Too many new ideas had already been proposed for comfort.

"Goov would speak, Brun."

"Goov may speak."

"I am only an acolyte, I don't know as much as Mog-ur, but I think he overlooked something. Maybe it's because he has tried so hard to put aside his feeling for Ayla. He has concentrated on remembering, not on the girl herself, perhaps out of fear it would be his love speaking and not his mind. He hasn't thought about her totem.

"Has anyone considered why a powerful male totem would choose a girl?" He answered his own rhetorical question. "Except for Ursus, the Cave Lion is the most powerful totem. The cave lion is more powerful than the mammoth; he hunts mammoth, only the young and old, but he does hunt mammoth sometimes. The cave lion does not hunt mammoth."

"You're not making sense, Goov. You say the cave lion hunts mammoth, then you say he doesn't," Brun gestured.

"He doesn't, *she* does. We overlook that when we speak of protective totems; even the male cave lion is the protector. But who is the hunter? The largest meat eater of all, the strongest hunter is the lioness! The female! Is it not true she brings her kill to her mate? He can kill, but his job is to protect while she hunts.

"It's curious that a Cave Lion would choose a girl, isn't it? Has anyone ever thought that perhaps her totem is not the Cave Lion, but the Cave Lioness? The female? The hunter? Couldn't that explain why the girl *wanted* to hunt? Why she was given a sign? Maybe it was the Lioness who gave her the sign, maybe that's why she was marked on her left leg. Is it really more exceptional for her to hunt than it is for her to have such a totem? I don't know if it's true, but you must admit it's reasonable. Whether her totem is Cave Lion or Cave Lioness, if she was meant to hunt, can we deny it? Can we deny her powerful totem? And do we dare condemn her for doing what her totem wishes?" Goov concluded. "I am finished."

Brun's head was whirling. Ideas were coming at him too fast. He needed time to think, to work it out. Of course it's the lioness who hunts, but who ever heard of a female totem? The spirits, the essences of protective spirits are all male, aren't they? Only someone who spends long days dwelling on the ways of the spirits would come to the conclusion that the totem of the girl who had been hunting was the hunter of the species that embodied her totem. But Brun wished Goov hadn't brought up the idea of denying the wishes of so powerful a totem.

The whole concept of a woman hunting was so unique, so thought-provoking, that several of the men had been jarred into making the small incremental step that pushed the frontiers of their comfortable, secure, well-defined world. Each man spoke from his own viewpoint, from his own area of concern or interest, and each had pushed forward the frontier only in that one small area; but Brun had to embrace them all, and it was almost too much. He felt duty-bound to consider every aspect before he made a judgment, and he wished he had time to mull them over carefully. But a decision could not be held off much longer.

"Does anyone else have any more opinions?"

"Broud would speak, Brun."

"Broud may speak."

"All these ideas are interesting, and may give us something to think about on cold winter days, but the traditions of the Clan are clear. Born to the Others or not, the girl is Clan. Clan females may not hunt. They may not even touch a weapon, or any tool that is used to make a weapon. We all know the punishment. She must die. It makes no difference if long ago women once hunted. Because a she-bear hunts, or a lioness, doesn't mean a woman may. We are neither bears nor lions. It makes no difference if she has a powerful totem or if she brings luck to the clan. It makes no difference if she is good with a sling or even that she saved the life of the son of my mate. I am grateful for that, of course—everyone has noticed I said so many times on the way back, I'm sure—but it makes no difference. The traditions of the Clan make no allowances. A woman who uses a weapon must die. We cannot change that. It is the way of the Clan.

"This whole meeting is a waste of time. There is no other decision you can make, Brun. I am finished."

"Broud is right," Dorv said. "It is not our place to change the traditions of the Clan. One exception leads to another. Soon there would be nothing we can count on. The punishment is death; the girl must die."

There were a couple of nods of agreement. Brun did not respond immediately. Broud is right, he thought. What other decision can I make? She saved Brac's life, but she used a weapon to do it. Brun wasn't any closer to a resolution than he was the day Ayla pulled out her sling and killed the hyena.

"I will take all your thoughts into consideration before I make my decision. But now I want to ask each of you to give me a definite answer," the leader finally said. The men were sitting in a circle around the fire. They each clenched a fist and held it in front of their chests. A movement up and down would mean an affirmative answer, a lateral movement of the fist, no.

"Grod," Brun began with his second-in-command, "do you think the girl Ayla should die?"

Grod hesitated. He sympathized with the leader's dilemma. He had been Brun's second for many years, he could almost read the leader's thoughts, and his respect for him had grown with time. But he could see no alternative; he moved his fist up, then down.

"What other choice is there, Brun?" he added.

"Grod says yes. Droog?" Brun asked, turning to the toolmaker.

Droog did not hesitate. He moved his fist across his chest.

"Droog says no. Crug, how about you?"

Crug looked at Brun, then Mog-ur, and finally Broud. He moved his fist up.

"Crug says yes, the girl should die," Brun confirmed. "Goov?"

The young acolyte responded immediately by drawing his fist across his chest.

"Goov's opinion is no. Broud?"

Broud moved his fist up before Brun could say his name, and Brun moved on just as quickly. He knew Broud's answer.

"Yes. Zoug?"

The old sling-master sat up proudly and moved his fist back and forth across his chest with an emphasis that left no doubt.

"Zoug thinks the girl should not die, what do you think, Dorv?"

The hand of the other old man went up, and before he could bring it down, all eyes turned toward Mog-ur.

"Dorv says yes. Mog-ur, what is your opinion?" Brun asked. He had guessed what the others would say, but the leader wasn't sure about the old magician.

Creb agonized. He knew the Clan traditions. He blamed himself for Ayla's crime, for giving her too much freedom. He felt guilty about his love for her, afraid it would usurp his reason, afraid he would think of himself before his duty to his clan, and began to move his fist up. Logically he decided she must die. But before he could start the movement, his fist jerked to the side, as though someone had grabbed it and moved it for him. He could not bring himself to condemn her, though he would do what he must, once the decision was made. He had no choice. The choice was Brun's and only Brun's.

"The opinions are evenly divided," the leader announced. "The decision was never anything but mine anyway, I only wanted to know how you felt. I will need some time to think about what was said today. Mog-ur says we will have a ceremony tonight. That's good. I will need the help of the spirits, and we all may need their protection. You will know my decision in the morning. She will know then, too. Go now and prepare for the ceremony."

Brun remained by the fire alone after the men left. Clouds scudded across the sky, driven by brisk winds, and dropped intermittent icy showers as they passed, but Brun was as oblivious to the rain as he was to the last dying embers sputtering in the fireplace. It was nearing dark when he finally hauled himself up and plodded slowly back to the cave. He saw Ayla still sitting where he had seen her when they left in the morning. She expects the worst, he said to himself. What else can she expect?

16

The clan gathered outside the cave early. A chill east wind was blowing, hinting of icier blasts, but the sky was clear and the morning sun just above the ridge, bright, in contrast to the somber mood. They avoided each other's eyes; arms hung limp with the absence of conversation as they shuffled to their places to learn the fate of the strange girl who was no stranger to them.

Uba could feel her mother shaking and her hand gripped so hard it hurt. The child knew it was more than the wind that made her mother shiver so hard. Creb was standing at the mouth of the cave. Never had the great magician seemed more forbidding, his ravaged face set in chiseled granite, his single eye opaque as stone. At a signal from Brun, he limped into the cave, slowly, wearily, weighted by an overwhelming burden. He walked into his hearth and looked at the girl sitting on her fur, and with a supreme effort of will, forced himself to approach her.

"Ayla. Ayla," he said gently. The girl looked up. "It's time. You must come now." Her eyes were dull, uncomprehending. "You must come now, Ayla. Brun is ready," Creb repeated.

Ayla nodded and dragged herself up. Her legs were stiff from sitting so long. She hardly noticed. She followed dumbly behind the old man, staring at the trampled dust still bearing traces of those who had walked that way before —a heelmark, the imprint of toes, the blurred outline of a foot encased in a loose leather pouch, the round butt of Creb's staff and the furrow of his dragging lame leg. She stopped when she saw Brun's feet, wrapped in their dusty coverings, and dropped to the ground. At a light tap on her shoulder, she forced herself to look up into the clan leader's face.

The impact jolted her to awareness and awakened an undefinable fear. It was familiar—low, swept-back forehead, heavy brows, large beaky nose, grizzled beard—but the proud, stern, hard look in the leader's eyes was gone, replaced by sincere compassion and luminous sorrow.

"Ayla," he said aloud, then continued with the formal gestures reserved for serious occasions, "girl of the Clan, the traditions are ancient. We have lived by them for generations, almost as long as the Clan has existed. You were not born to us, but you are one of us, and you must live, or die, by those same customs. While we were north, hunting mammoth, you were seen using a sling and you have hunted with a sling before. Clan females may not use weapons, that is one of our traditions. The punishment, too, is part of the traditions. It is the Clan way, it may not be changed." Brun leaned forward and looked into the frightened blue eyes of the girl.

"I know why you used the sling, Ayla, though I still can't understand why you ever started. Brac would not be alive if it hadn't been for you." He straightened and with the most formal of gestures, made so everyone could see, he added, "The leader of this clan is grateful to the girl for saving the life of the son of the mate of the son of my mate."

A few glances passed among the watching clan. It was a rare concession for a man to make publicly, and more rare for a leader to admit gratitude to a mere girl.

"But the traditions make no allowances," he continued. He made a signal to Mog-ur, and the magician entered the cave. "I have no choice, Ayla. Mog-ur is now setting the bones and speaking aloud the names of those who are unmentionable, names known only to mog-urs. When he is through, you will die. Ayla, girl of the Clan, you are Cursed, Cursed with Death."

Ayla felt the blood drain from her face. Iza screamed and sustained it in a high-pitched wail, keening for her lost child. The sound was abruptly cut off as Brun held up his hand.

"I am not finished," he motioned. In the sudden silence, glances of expectant curiosity passed quickly among the clan. What else could Brun have to say?

"The traditions of the Clan are clear, and as leader, I must follow the customs. A female who uses a weapon must be cursed with death, but there are no customs that say for how long. Ayla, you are Cursed with Death for one whole moon. If, by the grace of the spirits, you are able to return from the otherworld after the moon has gone through its cycle once and is in the same phase as now, you may live with us again."

Commotion stirred the group; it was unexpected.

"That's true," Zoug motioned. "Nothing says the curse must be permanent."

"But what difference does it make? How can someone be dead for so long and live again? A few days, maybe, but a whole moon?" Droog questioned.

"If the curse was only for a few days, I'm not sure it would fulfill the punishment," Goov said. "Some mog-urs believe the spirit never goes to the next world if the curse is short. It just hovers around waiting for the time to pass so it can come back if it's able. If the spirit stays near, the evil ones will too. It's a limited death curse, but it's so long, it might as well be permanent. It satisfies the customs."

"Then why didn't he just curse her and be done?" Broud motioned angrily. "There's nothing in the traditions about temporary death curses for her crime. She's supposed to die for it, the death curse is supposed to be the end of her."

"You think it won't be, Broud? Do you really think she might come back?" Goov asked.

"I don't think anything. I just want to know why Brun didn't just curse her. Can't he make a simple decision anymore?"

Broud was flustered by the pointed question. It brought out in the open the idea everyone had privately wondered. Would Brun impose a temporary death curse if he didn't think there was some chance, no matter how remote, that she might return from the dead?

Brun had wrestled with his dilemma the whole night. Ayla had saved the baby's life; it wasn't right that she should die for it. He loved the child and he was sincerely grateful to her, but there was more to it than his personal feelings. The traditions demanded her death, but there were other customs, too: customs of obligation, customs that said a life for a life. She carried part of Brac's spirit; she deserved, she was owed, something of equal value—she was owed her life.

Only with the first faint light of dawn had he finally thought of a way. Some hardy souls had returned after a temporary death curse. It was a long chance, almost no chance at all, just the barest glimmer of hope. In return for the life of the child, he gave her the one slim chance he could. It wasn't enough, but he could offer no more, and it was better than nothing at all.

Suddenly a deadly silence fell. Mog-ur was standing at the mouth of the cave, and he looked like death himself, ancient and drawn. There was no need for him to signal. It was done. Mog-ur had fulfilled his duty. Ayla was dead.

Iza's wail pierced the air. Then Oga began and Ebra, then all the women joined Iza, keening in sympathy with her. Ayla saw the woman she loved overwrought with grief and ran to her to comfort her. But just as she was about to throw her arms around the only mother she could remember, Iza turned her back and moved away to avoid the embrace. It was as though she didn't see her. The girl was confused. She looked at Ebra questioningly; Ebra looked through her. She went to Aga, then Ovra. No one saw her. When she approached, they turned away or moved aside. Not deliberately to let her pass, but as though they had planned to move away before she came. She ran to Oga.

"It's me. It's Ayla. I'm standing right here. Don't you see me?" she motioned.

Oga's eyes glazed over. She turned around and walked away, making no response, no sign of recognition, as though Ayla were invisible.

Ayla saw Creb walking toward Iza. She ran to him.

"Creb! It's Ayla. I'm here," she gestured frantically. The

old magician kept walking, barely turning aside to avoid the girl who crumpled at his feet, as he would an inanimate boulder in his path. "Creb," she wailed. "Why can't you see me?" She got up and ran back to Iza.

"Mother! Motherrr! Look at me! LOOK AT ME!" she gesticulated in front of the woman's eyes. Iza began a high-pitched wail again. She flailed her arms and pounded her chest.

"My child. My Ayla. My daughter is dead. She is gone. My poor, poor Ayla. She lives no more."

Ayla spied Uba hugging her mother's legs in fear and confusion. She knelt down in front of the little girl.

"You see me, don't you, Uba? I'm right here." Ayla saw recognition register in the child's eyes, but the next moment Ebra swooped down and carried the little girl away.

"I want Ayla," Uba motioned, struggling to get down.

"Ayla is dead, Uba. She's gone. That's not Ayla, it's only her spirit. It must find its way to the next world. If you try to talk to it, if you see it, the spirit will try to take you with it. It will bring you bad luck if you see it. Don't look at it. You don't want bad luck, do you, Uba?" Ayla slumped to the ground. She hadn't really known what a death curse meant and had imagined all kinds of horrors, but the reality was far worse.

Ayla had ceased to exist for the clan. It was no sham, no act put on to frighten her, she did not exist. She was a spirit who happened to be visible, who still gave a semblance of life to her body, but Ayla was dead. Death was a change of state to the people of the Clan, a journey to another plane of existence. The life force was an invisible spirit, it was obvious. A person could be alive one moment and dead the next, with no apparent change, except that that which caused movement and breath and life was gone. The essence that was the real Ayla was no longer a part of their world; it had been forced to move on to the next. It mattered not at all if the physical part that remained behind was cold and unmoving or warm and animated.

It was only another step to believe the essence of life could be driven away. If her physical body didn't know it yet, it would soon enough. No one really believed she would ever return, not even Brun. Her body, the empty shell, could never remain viable until her spirit was allowed to return. Without the life spirit, the body couldn't eat, couldn't drink, and would soon deteriorate. If such a concept was firmly believed, and if loved ones no longer acknowledged existence, there was no existence, no reason to eat or drink or live.

But as long as the spirit stayed near the cave, animating the body though no longer a part of it, the forces that drove it away hovered nearby, too. They might harm those still living, might try to take another life with them. It was not unknown for the mate or another close loved one of someone who had been cursed to die soon afterward themselves. The clan didn't care if the spirit took the body with it, or left the unmoving shell behind, but they wanted the spirit of Ayla to go, and go quickly.

Ayla watched the familiar people around her. They moved away, began doing routine tasks, but there was a strain. Creb and Iza went into the cave. Ayla got up and followed. No one tried to stop her, only Uba was kept away. Children were thought to have extra protection, but no one wanted to push it too far. Iza gathered all of Ayla's belongings, including her sleeping furs and the stuffing of dried grass that lined the scooped-out hollow in the ground, and carried them outside the cave. Creb went with her, stopping to get a burning brand from the cave fire. The woman dumped everything beside an unlit fireplace Ayla hadn't noticed before and hurried back into the cave while Creb started a fire. He made silent gestures over her things and the fire, most of them unfamiliar to the girl.

With growing dismay, Ayla watched Creb start to feed each of her things to the hot flames. There would be no burial ceremony for her; that was part of the punishment, part of the curse. But all traces of her had to be destroyed, there must be nothing left that might hold her back. She watched her digging stick catch fire, then her collecting basket, the padding of dried grass, clothing, everything went into the fire. She saw Creb's hand tremble as he reached for her fur wrap. He clutched it to his breast for a moment, then threw it on the fire. Ayla's eyes overflowed.

"Creb, I love you," she gestured. He didn't seem to see. With a sinking feeling of horror, she watched him pick up her medicine bag, the one Iza had made for her just before the ill-fated mammoth hunt, and add it to the smoking flames.

"No. Creb, no! Not my medicine bag," she pleaded. It was too late, it was already burning.

Ayla could stand no more. She tore blindly down the

slope and into the forest, sobbing her heartache and desolation. She didn't see where she was going and she didn't care. Branches reached out to block her way, but she plowed through them, tearing gashes in her arms and legs. She splashed through icy cold water, but didn't notice her soaked feet or feel them getting numb until she stumbled over a log and sprawled on the ground. She lay on the cold damp earth wishing death would hurry and relieve her of her misery. She had nothing. No family, no clan, no reason to live. She was dead, they said she was dead.

The girl was close to having her wish granted. Lost in her private world of misery and fear, she hadn't eaten or drunk since her return more than two days before. She wore no warm clothing, her feet ached with cold. She was weak and dehydrated, an easy target for a quick death from exposure. But there was something inside her stronger than her death wish, the same thing that had kept her going before, when a devastating earthquake left the five-year-old girl bereft of love and family and security. An indomitable will to live, a stubborn survival instinct would not let her quit while she still drew breath, still had life to go on.

The stop had rested her. Bleeding from scratches and shivering with cold, she sat up. Her face had landed on damp leaves and she licked her lips, her tongue reaching for the moisture. She was thirsty. She couldn't remember ever being so thirsty in her life. The gurgle of water nearby brought her to her feet. After a long, satisfying drink of cold water, she pushed on. She was shivering so hard her teeth chattered and it hurt to walk on her cold, aching feet. She was light-headed and disconcerted. Her activity warmed her a little, but her lowered body temperature was having its effects.

She didn't know for sure where she was, she had no destination in mind, but her feet followed a route traveled many times before, etched in her brain by repetition. Time had no meaning for her, she didn't know how long she had been walking. She climbed up along the base of a steep wall beyond a misty waterfall and became conscious of a familiar feeling to the area. Walking out of a sparse coniferous forest intermixed with dwarfed birch and willow, she found herself at her high secluded meadow.

She wondered how long it had been since she visited the place. She had seldom gone there after she started hunting except for the time she taught herself the double-stone technique. It had always been a place for practicing, not hunting. Had she been there at all that summer? She couldn't recall. Pushing aside the thick, tangled branches that hid it even without foliage, Ayla went into her small cave.

It seemed smaller than she remembered. There's the old sleeping fur, she said to herself, thinking back to the time she had brought it up so long before. Some ground squirrels had made a nest in it, but when she took it outside and shook it out, she saw it was not too badly damaged—a little stiff with age, but the dry cave had preserved it. She wrapped it around herself, grateful for its warmth, and went back into the cave.

There was a leather hide, an old cloak she had brought to the cave to stuff grass under for a pad. I wonder if that knife is still here? she thought. The shelf is down, but it ought to be somewhere near it. There it is! Ayla picked the flint blade out of the dirt, brushed it off, and began to cut up the old leather cloak. She removed her wet foot coverings and threaded the thongs through holes cut into the circles she had cut, then wrapped her feet with dry ones, stuffing them with insulating sedge grass from under the cloak. She spread the wet ones out to dry and began to take stock.

I need a fire, she thought. The dry grass will make good tinder. She shoved it together and piled it next to a wall. The shelf is dry; I can shave it for kindling and use it as a base to start a fire, too. I need a stick to twirl against it. There's my birchbark drinking cup. I could use that for a fire, too. No, I'll save it for water. This basket is all chewed up, she thought, looking inside. What's this? My old sling. I didn't know I left it here. I guess I just made another one. She held the sling up. It's too small, and the mice got to it; I'll need a new one. She stopped and stared at the strip of leather in her hands.

I was cursed. Because of this, I was cursed. I'm dead. How can I be thinking about fires and slings? I'm dead. But I don't *feel* dead—I feel cold and hungry. Can a dead person feel cold and hungry? What does *dead* feel like? Is my spirit in the next world? I don't even know what my spirit is. I've never seen a spirit. Creb says no one can see spirits, but he can talk to them. Why couldn't Creb see me? Why couldn't anyone see me? I must be dead. Then why am I thinking about fires and slings? Because I'm hungry!

Should I use a sling to get something to eat? Why not? I've already been cursed, what more can they do to me? But this one's no good; what can I use to make a new one? The cloak? No, it's too stiff, it's been out here too long. I need soft pliable leather. She looked around the cave. I can't even kill anything to make a sling if I don't have one. Where can I find soft leather? She racked her brain, then sat down in despair.

She looked down at her hands in her lap, then suddenly noticed what her hands were resting on. My wrap! My wrap is soft and pliable. I can cut a piece out of it. She brightened and started looking around the cave with enthusiasm again. Here's an old digging stick; I don't remember leaving one here. And some dishes. That's right, I did bring some shells up. I am hungry, I wish there was something to eat around here. Wait! There is! I didn't collect the nuts this year, they should be all over the ground outside.

She hadn't realized it yet, but Ayla had begun to live again. She gathered the nuts, brought them into the cave, and ate as many as her stomach, shrunken from lack of food, could hold. Then she took off the old fur and her wrap and cut a piece from it for a sling. The strip didn't have the bulging pocket to hold the stones, but she thought it would work.

She had never hunted animals for food before, and the rabbit was quick, but not quick enough. She thought she remembered passing a beaver dam. She got the aquatic animal just as it was diving for the water. On her way back, she saw a small, gray, chalky boulder near the creek. That's flint! I know that's flint. She picked up the nodule and hauled it back with her, too. She took the rabbit and beaver inside the cave and went back out to gather wood and find a hammerstone.

I need a fire stick, she thought. It should be good and dry; this wood is a little damp. She noticed her old digging stick. That should work, she said to herself. It was a little difficult to start a fire by herself; she was used to alternating the downward-pressured twirling motion with another woman to keep it spinning. After intense effort and concentration, a smoldering chunk of the fire platform slipped onto the bed of dry tinder. She blew at it carefully and was rewarded with small, licking flames. She added the dry kindling piece by piece, then larger pieces of the old shelf. When the fire was firmly established, she laid on the larger chunks of wood she had collected, and a cheerful fire warmed the small cave.

I'm going to have to make a cooking pot, she thought as she spitted the skinned rabbit and laid the beaver tail on top to add its fatty richness to the lean meat. I'm going to need a new digging stick and a collecting basket. Creb burned my collecting basket. He burned everything, even my medicine bag. Why did he have to burn my medicine bag? Tears began to well up and soon spilled down her cheeks. Iza said I was dead. I begged her to look at me, but she just said I was dead. Why couldn't she see me? I was standing right there, right in front of her. The girl cried for a while, then sat up straight and wiped away her tears. If I'm going to make a new digging stick, I'll need a hand-axe, she said to herself firmly.

While the rabbit was cooking, she knapped herself a hand-axe the way she had learned by watching Droog, and with it chopped down a green branch to make a digging stick. Then she gathered more wood and stacked it inside the cave. She could hardly wait for the meat to cook—the smell made her mouth water and her empty stomach growl. She was sure nothing had ever tasted so good when she took her first bite.

It was dark by the time she was through, and Ayla was glad for the fire. She banked it to be sure it wouldn't die before morning and lay down wrapped in the old fur, but sleep eluded her. She stared at the flames while the dismal events of the day marched through her mind in woeful procession, not realizing when tears started to flow. She was afraid, but more, she was lonely. She hadn't spent a night alone since Iza found her. Finally exhaustion closed her eyes, but her sleep was disturbed by bad dreams. She called out for Iza, and she called out for another woman in a language all but forgotten. But there was no one to comfort the desperately, achingly lonely girl.

Ayla's days were busy, filled with activity to ensure her survival. She was no longer the inexperienced, unknowledgeable child she was at five. During the years with the clan, she had had to work hard, but she had learned in the process. She wove tight waterproof baskets to carry water and for cooking, and made herself a new collecting basket. She cured the skins of animals she hunted and made rabbit-fur linings for the insides of her foot coverings, leggings wrapped and tied with cord, and hand coverings made in the style of foot coverings—circular pieces that tied at the wrist in a pouch, but with slits cut in the palms for thumbs. She made tools from flint and collected grass to make her bed softer.

The meadow grasses supplied food, too. They were top-heavy with seeds and grains. In the immediate vicinity were also nuts, high-bush cranberries, bearberries, hard small apples, starchy potatolike roots, and edible ferns. She was pleased to find milk vetch, the nonpoisonous variety of the plant whose green pods held rows of small round legumes, and she even collected the tiny hard seeds from dried pigweed to grind and add to grains that she cooked into mush. Her environment supplied her needs.

She decided shortly after she arrived that she needed a new fur wrap. Winter held back the worst of its weather, but it was cold and she knew the snow would not be long in coming. She thought first of a lynx fur; the lynx held a special meaning for her. But its meat would be inedible, at least to her taste, and food was as important to her as fur. She had little trouble taking care of her immediate needs as long as she was able to hunt, but she needed to lay in a store for the time ahead when snow would keep her in the cave. Food was now her reason for hunting.

She hated the thought of killing one of the gentle shy creatures that had shared her retreat for so long, and she wasn't sure if a deer could be killed with a sling. She was surprised they still used the high pasture when she saw the small herd, but decided she had to take advantage of the opportunity before they moved to lower elevations. A stone hurled with force at close range felled a doe, and a hard blow with a wooden club finished it off.

The fur was thick and soft—nature had prepared the animal for the cold winter—and venison stew made a welcome supper. When the smell of fresh meat brought a bad-tempered wolverine, a swift stone killed it and reminded her the first animal she ever killed was a wolverine who had been stealing from the clan. Wolverines were good for something, she had told Oga. Frost from breathing did not build up on the fur of a wolverine; their pelts always made the best hoods. This time I will make a hood from his pelt, she thought, dragging the slain scavenger back to the cave.

She built fires in a circle around her lines of drying meat to keep other carnivores away and to hasten the process of drying, and she rather liked the taste the smoke gave to the meat. She dug a hole in the rear of her cave, shallow, since the layer of earth was not deep at the back of the small crack in the mountain, and lined it with stones from the stream. After her meat was stored, she covered her cache with heavy rocks.

Her new fur, cured while the meat was drying, had a smoky odor, too, but it was warm and, with the old one, made her bed comfortable. The deer provided a waterbag, too, from its well-washed, waterproof stomach, and sinew for cord, and fat from the lump above its tail where the animal stored its winter supply. She worried about snow every day while her meat was drying, and slept outside within her circle of fires to keep them fed during the night. She felt relieved and much more secure once it was safely stashed away.

When a heavily overcast sky hid the moon, she became concerned about the passage of time. She remembered exactly what Brun had said: "If, by the grace of the spirits, you are able to return from the otherworld after the moon has gone through its cycle once and is in the same phase as now, you may live with us again." She didn't know if she was in the "otherworld," but more than anything, she wanted to go back. She wasn't really sure if she could, didn't know if they would see her if she went back, but Brun said she could, and she clung to the leader's words. Only how would she know when she could return if the clouds covered the moon?

She remembered a time long before when Creb showed her how to make notches on a stick. She guessed that the collection of notched sticks he kept in a part of the hearth—off limits for the other members of his household—were tallies of the times between significant events. Once, out of curiosity, she decided to keep track of something like he did, and since the moon moved through repetitive cycles, she decided it would be fun to see how many notches it would take to complete one cycle. When Creb found out, he scolded her severely. The reprimand reinforced her memory of the occasion as well as warning her not to do it again. She worried a whole day how she would ever know when she could return to the cave before she remembered that time and decided to notch a stick every night. No matter how she tried to control them, tears came to her eyes every time she made a mark. .

Tears came to her eyes often. Small things triggered memories of love and warmth. A startled rabbit bounding across her path reminded her of long shambling walks with Creb. She loved his craggy, one-eyed, scarred old face. The thought of it filled her eyes to overflowing. Seeing a plant she had gathered for Iza, Ayla would burst into sobs remembering the woman explaining how it was used; and a freshet of new tears came when she recalled Creb burning her medicine bag. Nights were the worst.

She was accustomed to being alone during the day from her years of roaming the countryside gathering plants or hunting, but she had never been away from people at night. Sitting alone in her small cave staring at the fire and its glowing reflection dancing against the wall, she cried for the companionship of those she loved. In some ways, she missed Uba most of all. Often she hugged her fur to her chest and rocked back and forth, humming softly under her breath as she had done so often with Uba. Her environment supplied her physical needs but not her human needs.

The first snow sifted down silently during the night. Ayla exclaimed with delight when she stepped out of her cave in the morning. A pristine whiteness softened the contours of the familiar landscape creating a magical dreamland of fantastic shapes and mythical plants. Bushes had top hats of soft snow, conifers were dressed in new gowns of white finery, and bare exposed limbs were clothed in shining coats that outlined each twig against the deep blue sky. Ayla looked at her footprints, marring the perfect, smooth layer of glistening white, then ran across the snowy blanket, crossing and recrossing her own path to make a complex design whose original intent was lost in the execution. She started to follow the tracks of a small animal, then spontaneously changed her mind and climbed out on the narrow ledge of the rocky outcrop swept clean of snow by the wind.

The entire mountain range marching up behind her in a series of majestic peaks was covered with white, shadowed in blue. It sparkled in the sun like a gigantic, luminous jewel. The vista spread out before her showed the lowest reaches of the snowfall. The blue green sea, whipped to a frothy foam of waves, nestled between the cleft of snow-covered hills, but the steppes to the east were still bare. Ayla saw tiny figures scuttling across the white expanse directly below her. It had snowed at the cave of the clan, too. One of the figures seemed to shuffle with a slow limp. Suddenly the magic left the snowy landscape and she climbed back down.

The second snowfall had no magic at all. The temperature dropped sharply. Whenever she left the cave, fierce winds drove sharp needles into her bare face, leaving it raw. The blizzard lasted four days, piling snow so high against the wall, it nearly blocked the entrance to her cave. She tunneled out, using her hands and a flat hipbone of the deer she had killed, and spent the day gathering wood. Drying the meat had depleted the supply of fallen wood nearby, and floundering through deep snow left her exhausted. She was sure she had food enough to last her, but she hadn't been as careful about stockpiling wood. She wasn't sure she had enough, and if it snowed much more, her cave would be buried so deep she wouldn't be able to get out.

For the first time since she found herself at her small cave, she feared for her life. The elevation of her meadow was too high. If she got trapped in her cave, she'd never last through the winter. She hadn't had time to prepare for the entire cold season. Ayla returned to her cave in the afternoon and promised herself to get more wood the next day.

By morning, another blizzard was howling with full force, and the entrance to her cave was completely blocked. She felt closed in, trapped, and frightened. She wondered how deeply she was buried under the snow. She found a long branch and poked it up through the branches of the hazelnut bush, knocking snow into her cave. She felt a draft and looked up to see snow flying horizontally in the driving wind. She left the branch in the hole and went back to her fire.

It was fortunate she had decided to measure the height of the drift. The hole, kept open by the stick, brought fresh air into the tiny space she occupied. The fire needed oxygen, and so did she. Without the air hole, she could easily doze into a sleep from which she'd never wake up. She had been in more danger than she knew.

She found she didn't need much of a fire to keep the cave warm. The snow, trapping minuscule air pockets between its frozen crystals, was a good insulator. Her body heat alone could almost have kept the small space warm. But she needed water. The fire was more important to melt snow than to maintain heat.

Alone in the cave, lit only by the small fire, the only way she could tell the difference between day and night was by the dim light that filtered in through the air hole during the daytime. She was careful to mark a notch on her stick each evening when the light faded.

With nothing much to do except think, she stared long at the fire. It was warm and it moved and, enclosed in her tomblike world, it began to take on a life of its own. She watched it devour each stick of wood leaving only a residue of ash. Does fire have a spirit, too? she wondered. Where does the fire spirit go when it dies? Creb says when a person dies, the spirit goes to the next world. Am I in the next world? It doesn't feel any different; lonelier, that's all. Maybe my spirit is someplace else? How do I know? I don't feel like it, though. Well, maybe. I think my spirit is with Creb and Iza and Uba. But I'm cursed, I must be dead.

Why would my totem give me a sign, knowing I'd be cursed? Why would I think he gave me a sign if he didn't? I thought he tested me. Maybe this is another test. Or has he deserted me? But why would he choose me and then desert me? Maybe he didn't desert me. Maybe he went to the spirit world for me. Maybe he's the one who's fighting the evil spirits; he could do it better than I could. Maybe he sent me here to wait. Could it be that he's still protecting me? But if I'm not dead, what am I? I'm alone, that's what I am. I wish I weren't so alone.

The fire is hungry again, she wants something to eat. I think I'll have something to eat, too. Ayla got another piece of wood from her dwindling supply and fed it to the flames, and then went to check her air hole. It's getting dark, she thought, I'd better mark my stick. Is that blizzard going to blow all winter? She got her notched stick, made a mark, then fitted her fingers over the marks, first one hand, then the other hand, then the first hand again, continuing until she had covered all the marks. Yesterday was my last day. I can go back now, but how can I leave in this blizzard? She checked her air hole a second time. She could barely make out the snow still flying laterally in the growing dark. She shook her head and went back to the fire.

When she woke the next day, the first thing she did was check her air hole again, but the gale raged on. Will it never stop? It can't just go on like that, can it? I want to go back. What if Brun had made my curse permanent? What if I could never go back, even if it did stop blowing? If I'm not dead now, I would die for sure. There just wasn't enough time. I hardly had time to get enough to last a moon; I would never make it through the whole winter. I wonder why Brun made it a limited death curse? I wasn't expecting it. Could I really have come back if I went to the spirit world instead of my totem? How do I know my spirit didn't go? Maybe my totem has been protecting my body here while my spirit is away. I don't know. I just don't know. I only know if Brun hadn't made the curse temporary, I'd never have a chance.

A chance? Did Brun mean to give me a chance? With a flash of insight, everything came together with a new depth that revealed her growing maturity. I think Brun really meant it when he said he was grateful to me for saving Brac's life. He had to curse me, it's the Clan way, even if he didn't want to, but he wanted to give me a chance. I don't know if I'm dead. Do people eat or sleep or breathe when they're dead? She shivered with a chill not caused by the cold. I think most people just don't want to. And I know why.

Then what made me decide to live? It would have been so easy to die if I had just stayed where I fell when I ran away from the cave. If Brun hadn't told me I could come back, would I have gotten up again? If I didn't know there was some chance, would I have kept trying? Brun said, "by the grace of the spirits..." What spirits? Mine? My totem's? Does it matter? Something made me want to live. Maybe it was my totem protecting me, and maybe it was just knowing I had a chance. Maybe it was both. Yes, I think it was both.

It took a while for Ayla to comprehend that she was awake, and then she had to touch her eyes to know they were open. She stifled a scream in the thick suffocating blackness of the cave. I'm dead! Brun cursed me, and now I'm dead! I'll never get out of here, I'll never get back to the cave, it's too late. The evil spirits, they tricked me. They made me think I was alive, safe in my cave, but I'm dead. They were mad when I wouldn't go with them by the stream, so they punished me. They made me think I was alive when all the while I was really dead. The girl shook with fear, huddled in her fur, afraid to move.

The girl had not slept well. She kept waking and remembering eerie, frightening dreams of hideous evil spirits and earthquakes, and lynxes that attacked and turned into cave lions, and snow, endless snow. The cave had a dank, peculiar odor, but the smell was the first thing that made her realize her other senses were functioning, if not her sight. The next was when she panicked, bolted upright, and banged her head on the stone wall.

"Where's my stick?" she motioned in the darkness. "It's night and I have to mark my stick." She scrambled around in the dark looking for her stick as though it was the most important thing in her life. I'm supposed to mark it at night; how can I mark it if I can't find it? Did I mark it already? How will I know if I can go home if I can't find my stick? No, that's not right. She shook her head trying to clear it. I can go home, it's past the time. But I'm dead. And the snow won't stop. It's just going to snow and snow and snow. The stick The other stick. I've got to see the snow. How can I see the snow in the dark?

She crawled around in the cave at random, bumping into things, but when she reached the mouth, she saw a faint, dim glow high above. My stick, it must be up there. She climbed up the bush growing partway into the cave, felt the end of the long branch, and pushed it. Snow fell on her as the stick went through the snow and opened the air hole. She was greeted by a waft of fresh air and a bright blue patch of sky. The storm had finally blown itself out, and when the wind stopped blowing, the last of the snow sifting down had clogged the hole.

The fresh cold air cleared her head. It's over! It stopped snowing! It finally stopped snowing! I can go home. But how am I going to get out of here? She poked and prodded with the stick, trying to enlarge the hole. A large section loosened, fell through the opening, and plopped into the cave, covering her with the cold damp snow. I will bury myself if I'm not careful. I'd better think about this. She clambered down and smiled at the light streaming in through the enlarged opening. She was excited, eager to leave, but she forced herself to settle down and think everything through.

I wish the fire hadn't gone out, I'd like some tea. But I think there's some water in the waterbag. Yes, good, she thought and took a drink. I won't be able to cook anything to eat, but missing one meal won't hurt me. Anyway, I can eat some dried deer meat. It doesn't have to be cooked. She ran back to the mouth of the cave to make sure the sky was still blue. Now, what should I take with me? Don't have to worry about food, there's plenty stored, especially since the mammoth hunt.

Suddenly, everything came back to her in a rush—the mammoth hunt, killing the hyena, the death curse. Will they really take me back? Will they really *see* me again? What if they won't? Where will I go? But Brun said I could come back, he said so. Ayla hung on to that idea.

Well, I won't take my sling, that's for sure. What about my collecting basket; Creb burned my other one. No, I won't need it until next summer; I can make a new one then. My clothes, I'll take all my clothes, I'll wear them all, and maybe a few tools. Ayla got together all the things she wanted to take with her, then began to dress. She put on the rabbit-skin lining and both pairs of foot coverings, wrapped her legs with rabbit-fur leggings, put her tools in her wrap and then tied her fur around her securely. She put on her wolverine hood and her fur-lined hand coverings and started toward the hole. She turned and looked at the cave that had been her home for the past moon, then removed her hand coverings and walked back.

She didn't know why it was important to her to leave the small cave in order, but it gave her a sense of completion, like putting it away now that she was through with it. Ayla had an inherent sense of orderliness, reinforced by Iza who had to maintain a systematic arrangement of her store of medicines. Quickly, she arranged everything neatly, put her hand coverings back on, then turned purposefully toward the snow-blocked entrance. She was going to get out; she didn't know how yet, but she was going to get back to the cave of the clan.

I'd better go out the top through the hole, I'll never be able to tunnel through all that snow, she thought. She started climbing up the hazelnut bush and used the stick that had kept the air hole open to widen it. Standing on the highest branches, which sagged only a little in the deep snow under her weight, she poked her head out of the hole and caught her breath. Her mountain meadow was unrecognizable. From her perch, the snow sloped away in a gentle grade. She couldn't identify a single landmark; everything was covered with snow. How will I ever get through this? It's so deep. The girl was almost overwhelmed with dismay.

As she looked around, she began to get her bearings. That birch clump, next to the tall fir, it's not much bigger than I am. The snow can't be very deep over there. But how am I going to get there? She scrambled to get out of the hole she was standing in, tamping the snow down to a firmer base as she struggled. She crawled over the edge and sprawled on top of the snow. Her weight distributed over a larger area kept her from sinking through.

Carefully, she pulled herself to her knees and finally to her feet, standing only a foot or so below the level of the surrounding snow. She took a couple of short steps forward, stamping the snow down as she went. Her foot coverings were loose-fitting circles of leather gathered together at the ankle, and two pair made for somewhat clumsy walking, the second pair fitting even more loosely over the first in a ballooning effect. While not exactly snow-shoes, they did tend to spread her weight over a larger area, and they made it easier for her to keep from floundering too deeply into the light powder snow.

But the going was hard. Stamping down as she went, taking short steps, occasionally sinking in up to her hips, she worked her way toward the place where the creek had been. The snow covering the frozen water wasn't as deep. The wind had piled a huge drift against the wall that held her cave, but in other areas it had swept the ground almost bare. She stopped there, trying to make up her mind whether to follow the frozen creek to the stream and then to the cave in the long way around, or take the steeper, more direct way down to the cave. She was eager, she could hardly wait to get back, and she decided on the shorter way. She didn't know how much more dangerous it would be.

Ayla started out carefully, but it was slow and difficult to pick her way down. By the time the sun was high in the sky, she was barely halfway down the route that in summer she could clamber down in the time it took to go from early twilight to dark. It was cold, but the bright rays of the noon sun warmed the snow, and she was getting tired and a little careless.

She started over a bare, windswept ridge that led to a steep, smooth, snow-covered slope, and skidded on a patch of scree. The loose gravel kicked loose a few larger rocks, which jolted a few more from their place. The rocks slammed into a mound of snow, jarring it from its insecure footing at the same time that Ayla lost hers. In an instant, she found herself sliding and rolling down the slope, swimming through a cascade of falling snow, amid the thunderous rumbling of an avalanche.

Creb was lying awake when Iza silently appeared with a cup of hot tea.

"I knew you were awake, Creb. I thought you might like something hot before you got up. The storm broke last night."

"I know, I can see blue sky around the wall."

They sat together sipping tea. They often sat quietly together lately. The hearth felt empty without Ayla. It was hard to believe one girl could leave so large a void. Creb and Iza tried to fill it with closeness, deriving comfort from contact with each other, but it was small comfort. Uba moped and whined. No one could convince the child Ayla was dead; she kept asking for her. She would toy with her food, wasting half by spilling or dropping it. Then she'd get cranky and want more, driving Iza to distraction until she lost her temper and scolded, and was immediately sorry. The woman's cough had returned, keeping her awake half the night.

Creb had aged more than it seemed possible in so short a time. He had not gone near the small cave since the day he set the white bones of the cave bear in two parallel rows, the last one on the left poking into the base of a bear skull and out its left eye socket, and spoke aloud the names of the evil spirits in clipped, gruff syllables, giving them recognition and power. He could not bring himself to look upon those bones again and had no desire to use the beautiful flowing movements used to commune with more beneficent spirits. He had been giving serious consideration to stepping down and turning the function of mog-ur over to Goov. Brun tried to convince him to reconsider when the old magician brought it up.

"What will you do, Mog-ur?"

"What does any man do when he retires? I'm getting too old to sit for long times in that cold cave. My rheumatism is getting worse."

"Don't be hasty, Creb," the leader motioned gently. "Think about it for a while."

Creb thought about it and had just about decided to announce it that day.

"I think I'll let Goov become the mog-ur, Iza," Creb motioned to the woman sitting beside him.

"That can only be your decision, Creb," she replied. She didn't try to talk him out of it. She knew he had no heart for it anymore, since the day he laid the death curse on Ayla, though it had been his entire life.

"It's past the time, isn't it, Creb?" Iza asked.

"Yes, it's past the time, Iza."

"How would she know it's past the time? No one could see the moon with that storm."

Creb thought about the time he showed a small girl how to count the years until she could have a baby, and about the older one who counted the days of the moon's cycle herself. "If she were alive, she'd know, Iza."

"But the storm was so bad. No one could go out in it."

"Don't think about it. Ayla is dead."

"I know it, Creb," Iza said with hopeless gestures. Creb looked at his sibling, thought about her grief, and wanted to give her something, some gesture of understanding.

"I shouldn't say this, Iza, but it's past the time; her spirit has left this world and the evil ones, too. There's no harm anymore. Her spirit talked to me before it left, Iza. It said she loved me. It was so real, I almost gave in to it. But the spirit of a cursed one is the most dangerous. It always tries to trick you into believing it is real so it can take you with it. I almost wish I had gone."

"I know, Creb. When her spirit called me mother, I... I..." Iza flung up her hands, she couldn't go on.

"Her spirit pleaded with me not to burn the medicine bag, Iza. Water came to its eyes, just like when she was alive. That was the worst. I think if I hadn't already thrown it in the fire, I would have given it to her. It was the last trick, though. That's when it finally left."

Creb got up, wrapped himself in his fur, and reached for his staff. Iza watched him; he seldom left the hearth anymore. He walked to the cave entrance and stood for a long time, staring out at the glistening snow. He didn't return until Iza sent Uba to tell him to come and eat. He returned to his post shortly afterward. Iza joined him later.

"It's cold here, Creb. You shouldn't stand in the wind like that," she motioned.

"It's the first time there's been a clear sky for days. It's a relief to see something besides a howling blizzard."

"Yes, but come to the fire and get warm once in a while."

Creb hobbled back and forth from his hearth to the entrance several times, standing for long periods looking out at the winter scene. But as the day wore on, he went there less and less. At the evening meal, when twilight was fading into darkness, he motioned to Iza. "I'm going over to Brun's hearth after we finish eating. I'm going to tell him that Goov will be mog-ur from now on."

"Yes, Creb," she said with bowed head. It was hopeless. Now she was sure it was hopeless.

Creb stood up while Iza was putting the food away. Suddenly a frightened scream came from Brun's hearth. Iza looked up. A strange apparition stood at the entrance to the cave, completely covered with snow and stamping its feet.

"Creb," Iza cried. "What is it?"

Creb stared hard for a moment, on guard against strange spirits. Then his eye opened wide.

"It's Ayla!" he shouted and hobbled toward her; forgetting his staff, forgetting his dignity, and forgetting every custom against showing emotions outside one's hearth, he threw his arm around the girl and hugged her to his breast.

17

"Ayla? Is it really Ayla, Creb? It's not her spirit?" Iza motioned as the old man led the snow-covered girl back to his hearth. She was afraid to believe it, afraid the very real-looking girl would turn out to be a mirage.

"It's Ayla," Creb gestured. "It's past the time. She has overcome the evil spirits; she has returned to us."

"Ayla!" Iza ran to her, arms open wide, and enfolded the girl in a fierce loving embrace, wet snow and all. Not only snow made them wet. Ayla cried enough tears of joy for all of them. Uba tugged at the girl as she was clenched in Iza's arms.

"Ayla. Ayla come back. Uba know Ayla not dead!" the child asserted with the conviction of one who knew she was right all along. Ayla picked her up and held her so tight, Uba squirmed to get loose and catch her breath.

"You wet!" Uba motioned when she could get her arms free.

"Ayla, take off those wet clothes!" Iza said, and bustled around adding wood to the fire and finding something for the girl to wear, as much to cover the intensity of her emotions as to express maternal concern. "You'll catch your death of cold."

Iza glanced at the girl with embarrassment, suddenly realizing what she had said. The girl smiled.

"You're right, mother. I will catch cold," she gestured, and removed her wrap and hood. She sat down and began struggling to loosen the wet, swollen bindings of her footwear.

"I'm starved. Is there anything to eat? I haven't eaten all day," she said after she had put on one of Iza's old wraps. It was a little small and too short, but it was dry. "I would have been back earlier, but I got caught in an avalanche coming down the mountain. I was lucky I didn't get buried under too much snow, but it took a long time to dig my way out."

Iza's amazement lasted only a moment. Ayla could have said she walked through fire to return and Iza would have believed it. Her return itself was proof enough of her invincibility. What could one little avalanche do to her? The woman reached for Ayla's fur to hang it up to dry, but pulled her hand back suddenly, eyeing the unfamiliar deer hide suspiciously.

"Where did you get this wrap, Ayla?" she asked.

"I made it."

"Is it . . . is it of this world?" the woman inquired apprehensively. Ayla smiled again.

"Very much of this world. Did you forget? I know how to hunt."

"Don't say that, Ayla!" Iza said nervously. She turned her back so the clan she knew was watching wouldn't see, and gestured inconspicuously. "You don't have a sling, do you?"

"No, I left it behind. But that doesn't change anything. Everyone knows it, Iza. I had to do something after Creb burned everything. The only way to get a wrap is to hunt. Fur doesn't grow on willows, or fir, either."

Creb had been watching silently, hardly daring to believe she was really back. There were stories of people returning after a death curse, but he still didn't believe it was possible. There's something different about her; she's changed. She's more confident, more grown up. No wonder, after what she's been through. She remembers, too. She knows I burned her things. I wonder what else she remembers? What is it like in the world of the spirits?

"Spirits!" he motioned, suddenly remembering. The bones are still set! I must go break the curse.

Creb hurried away to break the pattern of cave bear bones still set in the form of a death curse. He snatched the torch burning outside the crack in the wall and went in, and gaped in surprise when he came to the small room beyond the short passage. The skull of the cave bear had moved, the long bone no longer protruded through the eye socket, the pattern was already broken.

Many small rodents shared the cave of the clan, drawn by the stored food and warmth. One of them had likely brushed past or jumped on the skull, tipping it over. Creb shuddered slightly, made a sign of protection, then moved the bones back to the pile at the far end. As he walked out, he saw Brun waiting for him.

"Brun," Mog-ur gestured when he saw the man. "I can't believe it. You know I haven't been in here since I laid the curse. No one has. I just went in to break it, but it was already broken." His expression held a look of wonder and awe.

"What do you think happened?"

"It must have been her totem. It's past the time; maybe he broke it so she could return," the magician answered.

"You must be right." The leader started to make another motion, then hesitated.

"Did you want to speak to me, Brun?"

"I want to talk to you alone." He hesitated again. "Excuse my intrusion. I looked into your hearth. The girl's return was a surprise."

Every member of the clan had broken the custom of averting eyes to avoid looking into another's hearth. They couldn't help it. They had never seen someone who had returned from the dead before.

"It's understandable, under the circumstances. You don't have to be concerned," Mog-ur replied and started to move on.

"That's not what I wanted to see you about," Brun said, putting out a hand to detain the old magician. "I want to ask you about ceremonies." Mog-ur waited expectantly, watching Brun grope for words. "A ceremony now that she's back."

"No ceremonies are necessary, the danger is over. The evil ones are gone, there's no need for protection."

"I don't mean that kind of ceremony."

"What kind do you mean?"

Brun hesitated again, then started in a new direction. "I watched her talking to you and Iza. Do you notice a difference in her, Mog-ur?"

"What do you mean, a difference?" Mog-ur signaled warily, unsure of Brun's intent.

"She has a strong totem; Droog always said she was lucky. He thinks her totem brings us luck, too. He might be right. She would never have come back without luck and strong protection. I think she knows it, now. That's what I meant by different."

"Yes, I think I noticed a difference like that. But I still don't understand what it has to do with ceremonies."

"Remember the meeting we had after the mammoth hunt?"

"You mean when you were questioning her?"

"No, the one after, without her. I've been thinking about that meeting ever since she left. I didn't think she would come back, but I knew if she did, it would mean her totem is very strong, even more powerful than we thought. I've been thinking about what we should do if she did come back."

"What we should do? There's nothing we have to do. The evil spirits are gone, Brun. She's back, but she's no different than she always was. She's just a girl, nothing has changed."

"But what if I want to change something? Is there a ceremony for that?"

Mog-ur was puzzled. "A ceremony for what? You don't need a ceremony to change the way you act toward her. What kind of change? I can't tell you about ceremonies if I don't know what they're for."

"Her totem is a clan totem, too, isn't it? Shouldn't we try to keep all the totems happy? I want you to hold a ceremony, Mog-ur, but you have to tell me if there is such a ceremony."

"Brun, you're not making sense."

Brun threw up his hands, abandoning his attempt to communicate. While Ayla was gone, he'd had the time to mull over the many new ideas some of the men had put forth. But the disconcerting result of his musings intruded uncomfortably into the clan leader's mind.

"The whole thing doesn't make sense, how can I make sense out of it? Whoever expected her to come back, anyway? I don't understand spirits, I never have. I don't know what they want, that's what you're here for. But you're not much help! The whole idea is ridiculous anyway. I'd better think about it again."

Brun turned on his heel and stalked off, leaving behind a very confused magician. He turned back after a few steps.

"Tell the girl I want to see her," he signaled and continued on to his hearth.

Creb shook his head as he returned to his own hearth. "Brun wants to see Ayla," he announced when he got back.

"Did he say he wanted to see her right away?" Iza asked, pushing more food in front of her. "He won't mind if she finishes eating, will he?"

"I'm through, mother. I can't eat another bite. I'll go now."

Ayla walked to the next hearth and sat at the feet of the leader of the clan with her head bowed. He had on the same foot coverings that were worn and creased in the same places. The last time she had looked at those feet, she was terrified. She was no longer terrified. To her surprise, she didn't fear Brun at all, but she respected him more. She waited. It seemed to be taking an extraordinarily long time for him to acknowledge her. Finally, she felt a tap on her shoulder and looked up.

"I see you're back, Ayla," he began lamely. He didn't quite know what to say.

"Yes, Brun."

"I'm surprised to see you. I didn't expect it."

"This girl did not expect to be back, either."

Brun was at a loss. He wanted to talk to her, but he didn't know what to say, and he didn't know how to end the audience he had requested. Ayla waited, then made a gesture of request.

"This girl would speak, Brun."

"You may speak."

She hesitated, trying to find the right expression to say what she wanted to say.

"This girl is glad to be back, Brun. More than once I was frightened, more than once I was sure I would never return."

Brun grunted. I'm sure of that, he thought.

"It was difficult, but I think my totem protected me. At first, there was so much work to do, I didn't have much time to think. But after I was trapped, I didn't have much else to do."

Work? Trapped? What kind of world is the spirit world? Brun almost asked her, then changed his mind. He didn't really want to know.

"I think I began to understand something then."

Ayla stopped, still groping. She wanted to express a feeling that was akin to gratitude, but not the way gratitude was normally felt, not gratitude that carried a sense of obligation or the kind a woman usually expressed to a man. She wanted to say something to him as a person, she wanted to tell him she understood. She wanted to say thank you, thank you for giving me a chance, but she didn't quite know how.

"Brun, this girl is . . . is grateful to you. You said that to me. You said you were grateful for Brac's life. I am grateful to you for my own."

Brun leaned back and studied the girl—tall, flat-faced, blue-eyed. The last thing he expected was her gratitude. He had cursed her. But she didn't say she was grateful for the death curse, he thought, she said she was grateful for her life. Did she understand he had no choice? Did she understand he had given her the only chance he could? Did this strange girl understand that more than his hunters, more even than Mog-ur? Yes, he decided, she does understand. For an instant, Brun had a feeling toward Ayla he'd never before had toward a woman. At that moment, he wished she were a man. He didn't have to think any more about what he wanted to ask Mog-ur. He knew.

"I don't know what they're planning, I don't think the rest of the hunters even know," Ebra was saying. "All I know is I've never seen Brun so nervous."

The women were sitting together preparing food for a feast. They didn't know the reason for the feast—Brun just told them to prepare a feast that night—and they plied Iza and Ebra with questions trying to get some hint.

"Mog-ur has been spending all day and half the night in the place of the spirits. It must be a ceremony. While Ayla was gone, he wouldn't go near it; now he hardly ever comes out," Iza commented. "When he does, he's so absentminded he forgets to eat. Sometimes he forgets to eat while he's eating."

"But if they're having a ceremony, why did Brun work half a day clearing out a space in back of the cave?" Ebra motioned. "When I offered to do it, he chased me away. They have their place for ceremonies; why would he work like a woman clearing out the back?"

"What else could it be?" Iza asked. "Seems like every time I look, Brun and Mog-ur have their heads together. And if they notice me, they stop talking and have guilty looks on their faces. What else could those two be planning? And why are we having a feast tonight? Mog-ur's been back in that space Brun cleared out all day. Sometimes he goes into the place of the spirits, but he comes right back out again. It looks like he's carrying something, but it's so dark back there I can't tell."

Ayla was just enjoying the companionship. After five days, it was still hard for her to believe she was back in the cave of the clan sitting with the women preparing food just as though she had never been away. It wasn't exactly the same. The women were not entirely comfortable around her. They thought she had been dead; her return to life was nothing less than miraculous. They didn't know what to say to someone who had gone to the world of the spirits and returned. Ayla didn't mind, she was just glad to be back. She watched Brac toddling up to his mother to nurse.

"How's Brac's arm, Oga?" she asked the young mother sitting beside her.

"See for yourself, Ayla." She opened his wrap and showed Ayla his arm and shoulder. "Iza took the cast off the day before you came back. His arm is just fine, except a little thinner than the other one. Iza says once he starts using it again, it will get stronger."

Ayla looked at the healed wounds and felt the bone gently while the sober, big-eyed boy stared at her. The women had been careful to steer away from subjects that were remotely connected with Ayla's curse. Often someone would begin a conversation, then drop her hands in mid-sentence seeing where it was leading. It tended to stifle the warm communication that was usual when the women gathered together to work.

"The scars are still red, but they should fade in time," Ayla said, then looked at the child. "Are you strong, Brac?" He nodded. "Show me how strong. Can you pull my arm down?" She held out her forearm. "No, not with that hand, the other one," she corrected when he reached up with the uninjured arm. Brac changed hands and pulled against her arm. Ayla resisted just enough to feel the strength of his pull, then let her arm be lowered. "You are a strong boy, Brac. Someday you will be a brave hunter, just like Broud."

She held out her arms to see if he would come to her. At first he turned away, then changed his mind and allowed Ayla to pick him up. She held him up in the air, then cuddled him in her lap. "Brac is a big boy. So heavy, so sturdy." He stayed there comfortably for a few moments, but when he discovered she had nothing to feed him with, he squirmed to get back to his mother, reached for her breast, and began to nurse, staring at Ayla with big, round eyes.

"You're so lucky, Oga. He's a wonderful baby."

"I wouldn't be so lucky if it wasn't for you, Ayla." Oga had finally broached the subject they had painstakingly avoided. "I never told you how grateful I am. First I was too worried about him, and I didn't know what to say. You didn't seem to want to talk much, either, and then you were gone. I still don't know what to say. I never expected to see you again; it's hard to believe you're back. It was wrong for you to touch a weapon, and I can't understand why you wanted to hunt, but I'm glad you did. I can't tell you how much. I felt so awful when you were ... when you had to go, but I'm happy you're back."

"I am too," Ebra added. The other women nodded in agreement.

Ayla was overwhelmed by their unconditional acceptance of her and struggled to control tears that wanted to flow much too easily. She was afraid the women would be uncomfortable if her eyes watered.

"I'm glad to be back," she motioned, and the tears escaped her control. Iza now knew her eyes watered when she felt strongly about something, not because she was sick. The women, too, had grown accustomed to that peculiarity of hers and had come to know the meaning of her tears. They only nodded with understanding.

"How was it, Ayla?" Oga asked, her eyes full of troubled compassion. Ayla thought for a moment.

"Lonely," she answered. "Very lonely. I missed everyone so much." The women's eyes held such pity, Ayla had to say something to change the mood. "I even missed Broud," she added.

"Hhmmf," Aga said. "That was pretty lonely." Then she glanced at Oga, a little embarrassed.

"I know he can be difficult," Oga admitted. "But Broud is my mate, and he's not so bad to me."

"No, don't apologize for him, Oga," Ayla said gently. "Everyone knows Broud cares for you. You should be proud to be his mate. He's going to be leader, and he's a brave hunter, he was even the first to wound the mammoth. You can't help it if he doesn't like me. Some of it is my fault; I haven't always behaved as I should to him. I don't know how it started and I don't know how to end it; I would if I could, but that's not anything you should worry about."

"He always did have a temper," Ebra commented. "He's not like Brun. I knew Mog-ur was right when he said Broud's totem was the Woolly Rhinoceros. I think in some ways you helped him to control his temper, Ayla. It will make him a better leader."

"I don't know," Ayla shook her head. "If I wasn't around, I don't think he'd lose it so much. I think I bring out the worst in him."

A strained silence followed. Women did not ordinarily discuss the real failings of their men so openly, but the discussion had cleared the air of tension around the girl. Iza wisely decided it was time to drop the subject.

"Does anyone know where the yams are?" she motioned.

"I think they were in the place Brun cleared out," Ebra answered. "We may not find them until next summer."

Broud noticed Ayla sitting with the women and frowned when he saw her examine Brac and hold him in her lap. It made him remember it was she who had saved the boy's life, and that reminded him that she had been witness to his humiliation. Broud had been as overwhelmed by her return as the rest of them. The first day he viewed her with awe, and some apprehension. But the change that Creb had interpreted as growing maturity, and Brun had seen as her sense of her own luck, Broud took as flagrant insolence. During her trial by snow, Ayla had gained not only the confidence that she could survive, but a serene acceptance of life's noisome trivialities. After her ordeal, with its life-and-death struggles, nothing as insignificant as a reprimand, whose effectiveness had long since worn thin from overuse, could ruffle her placid composure.

Ayla *had* missed Broud. In her utter isolation, even his harassment would have been preferable to the stark emptiness of total invisibility to people who loved her. The first few days, she positively relished his close, if abusive, attention. He not only saw her, he saw every move she made.

By the third day of her return, old patterns reestablished themselves but with a difference. Ayla didn't have to fight herself to bend to his will, her response didn't even have the undercurrent of subtle condescension. She was genuinely unmoved. He could do nothing to disturb her. He could cuff and curse and work himself up to the edge of explosive violence. It had absolutely no effect. She patiently acquiesced to his most unreasonable demands. Though it was unintentional, Ayla was giving Broud a small measure of the ostracism she had been dealt in such abundance. She excluded him from her responses. His most towering rage, controlled only by supreme expenditures of effort, was met with no more reaction than the bite of a flea; less, for a fleabite is at least scratched. It was the worst thing she could do; she infuriated him.

Broud craved attention, he thrived on it. For him, it was a necessity. Nothing drove him to greater heights of frustration than someone who failed to react to him. It mattered little, in the depths of his being, whether the reaction was positive or negative, but there had to be one. He was sure her indifference was because she had seen him belittled, witnessed his disgrace, had no respect for his authority. He was partly right. She knew the outer limits of his control over her, had tested the mettle of his inner strength, and found them both insufficient to gain her respect. But it wasn't only that she didn't respect him and didn't respond to him, she usurped the attention he wanted.

By her very appearance she drew attention to herself, and everything about her drew attenton: her powerful totem; sharing the hearth, and the love, of the formidable magician; training to become a medicine woman; saving Ona's life; her skill with the sling; killing the hyena that saved Brac's life; and now, returning from the world of the spirits. Every time Broud had exhibited great courage and rightfully deserved the admiration, respect, and attention of the clan, she upstaged him.

Broud glowered at the girl from a distance. Why did she have to come back? Everybody is talking about her; they're always talking about her. When I killed the bison and became a man, everybody talked about her stupid totem. Did she stand up to a charging mammoth? Did she almost get trampled to cut the tendons? No. All she did was throw a couple of stones with a sling, and all they could think about was her. Brun and his meetings, all about her. And then he couldn't do it right, and now she's back again and they're all talking about her. Why does she always have to spoil everything?

"Creb, why are you so fidgety? I can't ever remember seeing you so nervous. You act like a young man about to take his first mate. Do you want me to make a cup of tea to settle your nerves?" Iza asked, after the magician jumped up for the third time, started to leave the hearth, changed his mind, and went back and sat down again.

"What makes you think I'm nervous? I'm just trying to remember everything and meditate a little," he said sheepishly.

"What do you need to remember? You've been Mog-ur for years, Creb. There can't be a single ceremony you couldn't do in your sleep. And I've never seen you meditate by jumping up and down. Why don't you let me fix you a little tea?"

"No. No. I don't need any tea. Where's Ayla?"

"She's over there, just beyond the last hearth looking for yams. Why?"

"I just wanted to know," Creb replied as he settled back down. Not long afterward, Brun walked by and signaled Mog-ur. The magician got up again and both men walked to the rear of the cave. What can be wrong with those two? Iza shook her head in wonder.

"Isn't it nearly time?" the leader asked when they reached the place he had cleared out. "Is everything ready?"

"All the preparations are made, but the sun should be lower, I think."

"You think! Don't you know? I thought you said you knew what to do. I thought you said you meditated and found a ceremony. Everything must be absolutely right. How can you say 'you think'?" Brun snapped.

"I did meditate," Mog-ur countered defensively. "But it was long ago, a different place. There wasn't any snow. I don't think there was snow even in winter. It's not easy to get the time right. I just know the sun was low."

"You didn't tell me that! How can you be sure it will be right? Maybe we'd better forget it. It's a ridiculous idea anyway."

"I've already talked to the spirits; the stones are in place. They're expecting us."

"I don't like the idea of moving the stones, either. Maybe we should've decided to have it in the place of the spirits. Are you sure they won't be upset because we moved them from the small cave, Mog-ur?"

"We already discussed that, Brun. We decided it was better to move the stones than to bring the Ancient Ones to the Totems' place of the spirits. The old ones might not want to leave again if they see it."

"How do you know they'll go back once we wake them up? It's too dangerous, Mog-ur. We'd better call it off."

"They may stay for a while," Mog-ur conceded. "But after everything is put back and they see there is no place for them, they'll leave. The totems will tell them to go. But it's up to you. If you want to change your mind, I'll try to placate the spirits. Just because they're expecting a ceremony doesn't mean we have to have one."

"No. You're right. We'd better go ahead with it now. They're expecting something. The men may not be too happy about it, though."

"Who is leader, Brun? Besides, they'll get used to it once they understand it's all right."

"Is it, Mog-ur? Is it really? It's been so long. It's not the men I'm thinking about now. Will our totems accept it? We've been so lucky, almost too lucky. I keep thinking something terrible is going to happen. I don't want to do anything to upset them. I want to do what they want. I want to keep them happy."

"That's what we're doing, Brun," Mog-ur said gently, "trying to do what they want. All of them."

"But are you sure the others will understand? If we please one, won't the others feel slighted?"

"No, Brun, I'm not sure they will." The magician could

feel the leader's worry and tension. He knew how difficult it was for him. "No one can be absolutely sure. We are only human. Even a mog-ur is only human. We can only try. But you said it yourself, we've been lucky. That must mean the spirits of all the totems are happy. If they were fighting with each other, do you think we'd have been so lucky? How often does a clan kill a mammoth without anyone getting hurt? Anything could have gone wrong. You could have traveled all that way and not found a herd, and some of the best hunting time would have been wasted. You took a chance, but it worked. Even Brac is still alive, Brun."

The leader looked at the serious face of the magician. Then he stood up straighter, and firm resolution replaced the indecision in Brun's eyes.

"I'll go get the men," he gestured.

The women had been told to stay away from the back of the cave, not even to look in that direction. Iza noticed Brun get the men, but she ignored it. Whatever they were doing was their business. She wasn't sure what made her glance up just as two men, faces painted red with ochre, rushed toward Ayla. Iza felt herself tremble. What could they possibly want with Ayla?

The girl hadn't even noticed the men going with Brun. She was rummaging through baskets and stiff rawhide containers piled in disordered confusion behind the hearth farthest from the mouth of the cave, looking for yams. When she saw the red-painted face of the leader suddenly appear in front of her, she gasped with surprise.

"Do not resist. Do not make a sound," Brun signaled.

She didn't become frightened until she felt the blindfold, but she was petrified when they nearly lifted her off the ground as they dragged her away.

The men were apprehensive when they saw Brun and Goov bringing the girl. They knew no more than the women of the reason for the ceremony Brun and Mog-ur were planning, but unlike them, the men knew their curiosity would eventually be satisfied. Mog-ur had only warned them not to make a single gesture or sound after they seated themselves in a circle behind the stones brought out from the small cave, but the warning gained force when he passed out two long cave bear bones to each man to be held crossed like an **X** in front of him. The danger must be great indeed if they needed such extreme protection. They began to get an inkling of the danger when they saw Ayla.

Brun forced the female to sit in the open space in the circle directly opposite Mog-ur, and sat down behind the girl. At the magician's signal, Brun removed her blindfold. Ayla blinked to clear her vision. In the light from the torches, she could see Mog-ur seated behind a cave bear skull and the men holding the crossed bones, and she huddled down with fear, trying to sink lower into the ground.

What have I done? I haven't touched a sling, she thought, trying to remember if she had committed some terrible crime that would supply a reason for her being there. She couldn't think of a thing she had done wrong.

"Do not move. Do not make a sound," Mog-ur warned again.

She didn't think she could if she wanted to. Wide-eyed, she watched the magician pull himself up, lay his staff down, and begin the formal motions entreating Ursus and the totemic spirits to watch over them. Many of the gestures were unfamiliar to her, but she stared in rapt attention, not so much for the meaning of the symbols Mog-ur was making as for the old magician himself.

She knew Creb, knew him well, a crippled old man who hobbled awkwardly when he moved, leaning heavily on his staff. He was a lopsided caricature of a man, one side of his body stunted, muscles atrophied with disuse, the other side overdeveloped to make up for the paralysis that forced him to depend on it so heavily. In the past she had noticed his graceful motions when he used the formal language for public ceremonies—abbreviated by the absence of one arm, yet in some indefinable way fraught with subtleties and complexities, and fuller in meaning. But the motions of the man standing behind the skull showed a side of the magician she never knew existed.

Gone was the awkwardness. In its place were hypnotically powerful rhythms of motion flowing smoothly, compelling the eyes to look. The movement of hand and subtle posture was not a graceful dance, for all it appeared to be; Mog-ur was an orator speaking with a persuasive force Ayla had never seen; and the great holy man was never so expressive as he was when addressing the unseen audience more real to him, at times, than the humans seated before him. The Mog-ur of the Clan of the Cave Bear poured forth even greater efforts when he began to direct his attention to the incredibly venerable spirits he wished to call to this unique ceremony.

"Most Ancient Spirits, Spirits we have not invoked since the early mists of our beginnings, heed us now. We call upon you, we would pay homage to you, and we would ask for your assistance and your protection. Great Spirits, so venerable your names are but a whisper of memory, awake from your deep sleep and let us honor you. We have an offering, a sacrifice to placate your ancient hearts; we need your sanction. Heed us as we call your names.

"Spirit of Wind. Oooha!" Ayla felt a chill up her spine as Mog-ur spoke the name aloud. "Spirit of Rain. Zheena! Spirit of Mists. Eeesha! Attend us! Look upon us with favor. We have one of your own with us, one who has walked with your shades and returned, returned at the wish of the Great Cave Lion."

He's talking about me, Ayla suddenly realized. This is a ceremony. What am I doing at a ceremony? Who are those spirits? I never heard them mentioned before. The names are female names; I thought all protective spirits were male. Ayla was quaking with fear, yet intrigued. The men sitting like the stones in front of them had never heard of the ancient spirits, either, until Mog-ur called their names, yet they were not unfamiliar. Hearing the ancient names stirred an equally ancient memory stored in the deep recesses of their minds.

"Most Honored Ones of Old, the ways of the Spirits are a mystery to us, we are only human, we do not know why this female was chosen by one so powerful, we do not know why he has led her to your ancient ways, but we may not deny him. He fought for her in the shadowed land, defeated the evil ones, and returned her to us to make his wishes clear, to make it known we may not deny him. O Powerful Spirits of the Past, your ways are no longer the ways of the Clan, yet once they were and must be again for this one who sits with us. We entreat you, Ancient Spirits, sanctify her to your ways. Accept her. Protect her and give your protection to her clan." Mog-ur turned to Ayla. "Bring the female forward," he commanded.

Ayla felt herself lifted bodily from the ground by Brun's strong arms and moved forward until she stood in front of the old magician. She gasped as Brun grabbed a handful of her long blonde hair and yanked her head back. From the bottom of her eyes, she saw Mog-ur take a sharp knife from his pouch and lift it high above his head. Terrified, she watched the face of the one-eyed man loom closer, knife raised, and nearly fainted when she saw him bring the sharp edge down quickly to her bared throat.

She felt a sharp pain, yet was too frightened to cry out. But Mog-ur only made a small nick in the hollow at the base of her throat. The trickle of warm blood was quickly absorbed by a small square of soft rabbit skin. He waited until the square was soaked with her blood, then wiped the cut with a stinging liquid from a bowl held by Goov. Then Brun released her.

Fascinated, she watched Mog-ur put the blood-soaked square into a shallow stone bowl partially filled with oil. The magician was handed a small torch by his acolyte, and with it he set fire to the oil in the bowl and watched silently as the skin burned to a charred crisp with a sharp, acrid smell. When it was burned out, Brun moved aside her wrap and exposed her left thigh. Mog-ur dipped his finger in the residue left in the stone bowl and drew a black line over each of the four lines that scarred her leg. She stared at it in wonder. It looked like a totem mark, cut and stained black during the ceremony that marked a boy's passage into manhood. She felt herself being moved back, and watched Mog-ur address the spirits again.

"Accept this sacrifice of blood, Most Venerable Spirits, and know it is her totem, the Spirit of the Cave Lion, that chose her to follow your ancient ways. Know that we have shown you honor, know that we have paid you homage. Give us your favor and return to your deep rest, content that your ways are not forgotten."

It's over, Ayla thought, breathing a sigh of relief as Mog-ur sat down again. She still didn't know why she was made to participate in the unusual ceremony. But they weren't through with her yet. Brun moved around in front of her and motioned to her to stand. Quickly, she scrambled to her feet. He reached into a fold of his wrap and withdrew a small, red-stained oval of ivory sawed from near the tip of a mammoth tusk.

"Ayla, this one time alone, while we are under the protection of the Most Ancient Spirits, you stand as an equal with the men." She wasn't sure she understood the leader correctly. "Once you leave this place, you must never again think of yourself as an equal. You are female, you will always be female."

Ayla was nodding her head in agreement. Of course, she knew she was female, but she was puzzled.

"This ivory is from the tusk of the mammoth we killed. It was a very lucky hunt; no man was hurt, yet we brought down the great beast. This piece has been sanctified by Ursus, colored the sacred red by Mog-ur, and is a powerful hunting talisman. Every hunter of the clan carries one like it in his amulet, and every hunter must have one.

"Ayla, no boy becomes adult until he makes his first kill, but once he has, he cannot be a child. Long ago, during the time of the Spirits that still hover near, women of the Clan hunted. We don't know why your totem has led you to follow that ancient path, but we cannot deny the Spirit of the Cave Lion; it must be allowed. Ayla, you have made your first kill; you must now assume the responsibilities of an adult. But you are a woman, not a man, and you will be a woman always, in all ways but one. You may use only a sling, Ayla, but you are now the Woman Who Hunts."

Ayla felt a sudden rush of blood rise to her face. Could it be true? Had she really understood Brun? For using a sling, she had just been through an ordeal she didn't think she would survive; now she was going to be allowed to use it? Allowed to hunt? Openly? She could hardly believe it.

"This talisman is for you. Put it in your amulet." Ayla took the pouch from around her neck and fumbled to untie the knots. She took the red-stained oval of ivory from Brun and put it beside the chunk of red ochre and the fossil cast, then closed the leather bag and slipped it back over her neck.

"Do not tell anyone yet; I will announce it before the feast tonight. It is in your honor, Ayla, in honor of your first kill," Brun said. "I hope your next one will be more palatable than a hyena," he added with a twinkle of humor in his eyes. "Now, turn around."

She did as she was told, and felt the blindfold cover her eyes and the two men lead her back, then remove the blindfold. She watched Brun and Goov return to the circle of men. Was I dreaming? She felt her throat and the sting of the wound where Mog-ur had cut her, then slid her hand down and felt three objects inside her amulet. She moved her wrap aside and stared at the slightly smeared black lines that covered her scars. A hunter! I am a hunter! A hunter for the clan. They said it was my totem who wanted it and they couldn't deny him. She clutched her amulet, closed her eyes, and then began the formal gestures.

"Great Cave Lion, why did I ever doubt you? The death curse was a difficult test, the worst yet, but it had to be for so great a gift. I am so grateful you found me worthy. I know Creb was right—my life will never be easy with you as my totem, but it will always be worth it."

The ceremony had been effective enough to convince the men that Ayla should be allowed to hunt—all but one. Broud was furious. If he hadn't been so frightened by Mog-ur's warning, he would have left the ceremony. He wanted no part of anything that gave that female special privileges. He glowered at Mog-ur, but his special bitterness was directed at Brun, and he couldn't swallow his gall.

It's his doing, Broud thought. He's always protected her, always favored her. He threatened me with a death curse just for punishing her for her insolence. Me, the son of his mate, and she deserved it. He should have cursed her right, it should have been forever. Now he's letting her hunt, hunt, just like a man. How could he do it? Well, Brun's getting old. He won't be leader forever. Someday I'll be leader, then we'll see. Then she won't have him to protect her. Then we'll see what privileges she gets; just let her try to get away with her insolence then.

18

The Woman Who Hunts earned the full title during the winter that began her tenth year. Iza felt a private satisfaction and a small sense of relief when she noticed the changes in the girl that heralded the onset of menarche. Ayla's spreading hips and the two bumps swelling her chest, changing the contours of her straight, child's body, assured the woman that her unusual daughter was not doomed to perennial childhood after all. Swelling nipples and a light down of pubic and underarm hair were followed by Ayla's first menstrual flow; the first time the spirit of her totem battled with another.

Ayla understood now that it was unlikely she would ever give birth; her totem was too strong. She wanted a baby—ever since Uba was born she had wanted a baby of her own to love and care for—but she accepted the trials and restrictions imposed by the powerful Cave Lion. She always enjoyed caring for the infants and children of the growing clan when their mothers were busy, and she felt a pang of remorse when they went to someone else to nurse. But at least now she was a woman, no longer a child who was taller than a woman.

Ayla felt an empathetic sense of identity with Ovra who had miscarried several more times, though earlier in her pregnancies and not with as much difficulty. Ovra's Beaver totem was a little too ferocious, too. She seemed destined to be childless. Ever since the mammoth hunt, and especially after Ayla reached physical adulthood, the two young women often shared each other's company. The quiet woman didn't talk much—she was reticent by nature, the opposite of Ika's open and friendly disposition—but Ayla and Ovra developed an understanding that ripened slowly into a close friendship and extended to include Goov. The fondness between the young acolyte and his mate was apparent to everyone. It made Ovra the object of greater pity. Since her mate was so understanding and gentle about her inability to produce a child for him, they knew it made her want a baby even more.

Oga was expecting again, much to Broud's delight. She had gotten pregnant soon after weaning three-year-old Brac. It looked as though she was going to be as prolific as Aga and Ika. Droog was sure Aga's two-year-old son would be the toolmaker he wanted when he found the boy banging stones together one day. He found a hammerstone to fit Groob's pudgy little hand and allowed him to play nearby when he worked, hitting broken pieces of flint to mimic the knapper. Ika's two-year-old, Igra, promised to be as outgoing as her mother, a cheerful, chubby, friendly little girl that delighted everyone. Brun's clan was growing.

Ayla spent the few days in early spring away from the clan, her required woman's curse, in the small cave of her high retreat. After the far more traumatic death curse, it was almost a holiday. She used the time to work out the kinks and sharpen her throwing skills after the long winter, though she had to remind herself constantly that she no longer had to be secretive about it. Though she had little trouble securing food for herself, she looked forward to her daily visits with Iza at a prearranged place near the cave of the clan. Iza brought her more food than she could hope to eat, but more, she brought company. It was still difficult to spend her nights alone, though the knowledge that the ostracism was limited and of short duration made it easier.

They often visited until dark and Ayla had to use a torch to find her way back. Iza never got over her nervousness about the deerskin Ayla had made for herself while she was "dead," so the young woman decided to leave it in the small cave. Ayla learned the things a woman needed to know from her mother, just as all young women did. Iza gave her the straps of soft, absorbent leather that were worn tied to a waist thong, and explained the proper symbols to make when she buried the straps soiled with menstrual flow deep in the ground. She was told the proper position to assume if a man decided to relieve his needs with her, the movements to make, and how to clean herself afterward. Ayla was a woman now; she could be required to fulfill all the functions of a fully adult female member of the clan. They talked of many things of interest to women, though some were familiar to her from her medical training. They discussed childbirth, nursing, and medicine to relieve cramps. Iza explained the positions and motions considered seductive to men of the clan, the ways that a woman might encourage a man to develop a desire to relieve his needs. They talked of the responsibilities of a mated woman. Iza told Ayla all the things her mother had told her, but privately she wondered if the unattractive girl would ever have need for much of the knowledge.

There was one subject Iza never brought up. Most young women, by the time they became women, usually had their eye on a particular young man. Though neither a girl nor her mother had any direct say in the matter, the mother, if she was on good terms with her mate, could tell him of her daughter's wishes. The mate, if he chose, could make them known to the leader, with whom the decision rested. If there were no other considerations, and especially if the young man in question had shown an interest in the girl, the leader might let the young woman's wishes prevail.

Not always, certainly not in Iza's case, but the subject of mates never came up between Iza and Ayla, though it was usually one of great interest to a nubile young woman and her mother. There were no young unmated men in the clan, and Iza was sure if there had been, they would not have wanted Ayla any more than any man in the clan wanted her as a second woman. And Ayla herself had no interest in any of them. She hadn't even thought about a mate until Iza brought up the subject of a mated woman's responsibilities. But she thought about it later.

On a sunny spring morning not long after she returned, Ayla went to fill a waterbag at the spring-fed pool near the cave. No one else was out yet. She knelt down and bent over, ready to dip the bag in, then suddenly stopped. The morning sun slanting across the still water gave it a mirror-like surface. Ayla stared at the strange face looking at her out of the pool; she had not seen a reflection of herself before. Most water near the cave was in the form of running streams or creeks, and she didn't usually look in the pool until after she had dipped in the container she wanted to fill, disturbing the tranquil surface.

The young woman studied her own face. It was somewhat square with a well-defined jaw, modified by cheeks still rounded with youth, high cheekbones and a long, smooth neck. Her chin had the hint of a cleft, her lips were full, and her nose straight and finely chiseled. Clear, blue gray eyes were outlined with heavy lashes a shade or two darker than the golden hair that fell in thick soft waves to well below her shoulders, glimmering with highlights in the sun. Eyebrows, the same shade as her lashes, arched above her eyes on a smooth, straight, high forehead without the slightest hint of protruding brow ridges. Ayla backed stiffly away from the pool and ran into the cave.

"Ayla, what's wrong?" Iza motioned. It was obvious something was troubling her daughter.

"Mother! I just looked in the pool. I'm so ugly! Oh, mother, why am I so ugly?" was her impassioned response. She burst into tears in the woman's arms. For as long as she could remember, Ayla had never seen anyone except people of the clan. She had no other standard of measure. They had grown accustomed to her, but to herself, she looked different from everyone around her, abnormally different.

"Ayla, Ayla," Iza soothed, holding the sobbing young woman in her arms.

"I didn't know I was so ugly, mother. I didn't know.

What man will ever want me? I'll never have a mate. And I'll never have a baby. I'll never have anyone. Why do I have to be so ugly?"

"I don't know if you're really so ugly, Ayla. You're different."

"I'm ugly! I'm ugly!" Ayla shook her head, refusing to be comforted. "Look at me! I'm too big, I'm taller than Broud and Goov. I'm almost as tall as Brun! And I'm ugly. I'm big and ugly and I'll never have a mate," she gestured with fresh sobs.

"Ayla! Stop it!" Iza commanded, shaking her shoulders. "You can't help the way you look. You were not born to the Clan, Ayla, you were born to the Others, you look the way they look. You can't change that, you must accept it. It's true you may never have a mate. That can't be helped; you must accept that, too. But it's not certain, it's not hopeless. Soon you will be a medicine woman, a medicine woman of my line. Even without a mate, you will not be a woman without status, without value.

"Next summer is the Clan Gathering. There will be many clans there; this is not the only clan, you know. You may find a mate in one of the other clans. Maybe not a young man or one with high status, but a mate. Zoug thinks very well of you; you are fortunate that he holds you in such high regard. He has already given Creb a message to take with him. Zoug has kin in another clan; he told Creb to tell them of his regard for you. He thinks you will make some man a good mate and wants them to consider you. He even said he would take you if he were younger. Remember that, this is not the only clan, these are not the only men in the world."

"Zoug said that? Even though I'm so ugly?" Ayla gestured, a look of hope in her eyes.

"Yes, Zoug said that. With his recommendation and the status of my line, I'm sure there will be some man who will take you, even if you do look different."

Ayla's tremulous smile faded. "But won't that mean I'll have to go away? Live someplace else? I don't want to leave you and Creb and Uba."

"Ayla, I am old. Creb is no young man either, and in a few years Uba will be a woman and mated. What will you do then?" Iza motioned. "Someday Brun will pass the leadership on to Broud. I don't think you should live with this clan when Broud becomes leader. I think it might be best if you moved away, and the Clan Gathering may be your opportunity."

"I suppose you're right, mother. I don't think I want to live here when Broud is leader, but I hate the thought of leaving you," she said with a frown, then brightened. "But next summer is a whole year away. I don't have to worry about it until then."

A whole year, Iza thought. My Ayla, my child. Maybe you have to be my age to know how fast a year goes. You don't want to leave me? You don't know how I'll miss you. If only there were a man in this clan who would take you. If only Broud were not going to be leader.

But the woman gave no hint of her thoughts as Ayla wiped her eyes and went back to get water. This time she avoided looking in the still pool.

Later that afternoon, Ayla stood at the edge of the woods looking through the brush at the cave. Several people were outside working or talking. She shifted the two rabbits that were slung over her shoulder, looked down at the sling tucked in her waist thong, stuffed it in a fold of her wrap, then took it out and tucked it back at her waist in plain sight. She looked again at the cave, shuffling nervously.

Brun said I could, she thought. They had a ceremony so I could. I'm a hunter, I'm the Woman Who Hunts. Ayla lifted her chin and stepped out from behind the concealing screen of foliage.

For a long, frozen moment, everyone outside the cave stopped and stared at the young woman walking toward them with two rabbits slung over her shoulder. As soon as they got over the shock and realized their bad manners, they looked away. Ayla's face burned, but she walked straight ahead with dogged determination, ignoring the surreptitious glances. She was relieved to reach the cave after passing the gauntlet of shocked looks and glad for its cool, dim interior. It was easier to ignore the looks of the people inside.

Iza's eyes opened wide, too, when Ayla reached Creb's hearth, but recovering quickly, she looked away making no mention of the rabbits. She didn't know what to say. Creb was sitting on his bearskin apparently meditating and didn't seem to notice her. He had seen her come into the cave, and by the time she reached the hearth he had managed to mask his expression. No one said a thing as she put the animals down beside the fireplace. A moment later Uba came racing in, and she had no qualms at all about her reactions.

"Did you really hunt those yourself, Ayla?" she asked.

"Yes," Ayla nodded.

"They look like nice fat rabbits. Are we going to have them for dinner, mother?"

"Well, yes, I guess we are," Iza replied, still embarrassed and unsure.

"I'll skin them," Ayla said quickly, taking out her knife. Iza watched for a moment, then walked over and took the knife from her hand.

"No, Ayla. You hunted them, I'll skin them." Ayla stepped back while Iza skinned the rabbits, quickly spitted them, and put them over the fire. She was just as uncomfortable as Iza.

"That was a good meal, Iza," Creb said later, still avoiding direct comment about Ayla's hunting, but Uba felt no such compunction.

"Those were good rabbits, Ayla, but next time why don't you get some ptarmigan," she said. Uba shared Creb's predilection for the fat birds with the feathered feet.

The next time Ayla brought her kill to the cave it wasn't such a shock, and before long her hunting became almost commonplace. With a hunter at his own hearth, Creb reduced the share he took from the other hunters except for the large animals hunted only by the men.

It was a busy spring for Ayla. Her share of the women's work was not lessened because she hunted, and there were still Iza's herbs to be collected. But Ayla loved it, she was full of energy, happier than she could remember. She was happy she could hunt without secrecy, happy to be back with the clan, and happy she was finally a woman, and glad for the closer relationships she was developing with the other women.

Ebra and Uka accepted her, though the two older women never could quite forget she was different; Ika had always been friendly; and the attitudes of Aga and her mother had completely reversed since she saved Ona from drowning. Ovra had become a close confidante, and Oga warmed toward her despite Broud. The adolescent ardor Oga had felt for the man had moderated to an indifferent habit, cooled by the years of living with his unpredictable outbursts. But Broud's vindictive hatred of Ayla grew after her acceptance as a hunter. He kept trying to find ways to bedevil her, kept trying to get a reaction out of her. His harassment had become a way of life she had learned to live with; it left her unmoved. She had begun to think he would never be able to disturb her again.

Spring was in full flower the day she decided to hunt ptarmigan for Creb's favorite dish. She thought she would look over the new growths and begin restocking Iza's pharmacopoeia while she was at it. She spent the morning ranging the nearby countryside; then headed for a broad meadow near the steppes. She flushed a couple of low-flying fowl, brought down quickly by swifter stones, then searched through the tall grass looking for a nest and hopefully some eggs. Creb liked the birds stuffed with their own eggs in a nest of edible greens and herbs. She uttered an exclamation of joy when she spied it, and carefully wrapped the eggs in soft moss and tucked them into a deep fold of her wrap. She was delighted with herself. Out of sheer joyful exuberance, she sprinted across the meadow in a fast run, coming to a halt, out of breath, at the top of a knoll covered with new green grass.

Flopping to the ground, she checked her eggs to make sure they were undamaged and took out a piece of dried meat to lunch on. She watched a bright yellow-breasted meadowlark trill gloriously from an open perch, then take to wing and continue its song in flight. A pair of golden-crowned sparrows, warbling their woeful tune of descending pitch, flitted among the blackberry canes at the border of the open field. Another pair of black-capped, gray-coated birds named by the chick-a-dee-dee of their call, darted in and out of their nesting hole in a fir tree near a small creek winding its way through the dense vegetation at the foot of the knoll. Small, vivacious brown wrens scolded the others as they carried twigs and dried moss to a nest cavity in an ancient, gnarled apple tree, proving its youthful fecundity with its flock of pink blooms.

Ayla loved these moments of solitude. Basking in the sun, feeling relaxed and content, she thought about nothing in particular, except the beautiful day and how happy she was. She was completely unaware that anyone else was near until a shadow fell across the ground in front of her. Startled, she looked up into Broud's glowering face.

No hunting trips had been planned for that day and

Broud had decided to hunt alone. He hadn't been very diligent; his hunting foray was more an excuse to take a walk on the warm spring day than to provide meat he didn't especially need. He had seen Ayla relaxing on the knoll from a distance and couldn't pass up the opportunity to berate her for laziness, caught in the act of sitting still.

Ayla jumped up when she saw him, but that annoyed him. She was taller and he didn't like looking up at a woman. He motioned her down and prepared to give her a sound scolding. But as she lowered herself, the unresisting, unresponsive look that glazed her eyes irritated him even more. He wished he could think of some way to get a reaction out of her. At the cave, he could at least make her get something for him to see her jump to his command.

He looked around, then down at the woman sitting at his feet, waiting with unruffled composure for him to get on with his rebuke and be on his way. She's worse than ever since she became a woman, he thought. The Woman Who Hunts, how could Brun do it? He noticed her ptarmigan and thought of his own empty hand. Even the look on her ugly face is insolent; she's gloating because she got those birds and I don't have anything. What can I make her do? There's nothing out here I can tell her to get. Wait, she's a woman now, isn't she? There's something I can make her do.

Broud gave her a signal, and Ayla's eyes flew open. It was unexpected. Iza told her men only wanted that from women they considered attractive; she knew Broud thought she was ugly. Broud hadn't missed Ayla's shocked surprise, her reaction encouraged him. He signaled her again, imperiously, to assume the position so he could relieve his needs, the position for sexual intercourse.

Ayla knew what was expected. Not only had Iza explained, she had often seen adult members of the clan engage in the activity—all the children had; there were no artificial restraints in the clan. Children learned adult behavior by emulating their parents, and sexual behavior was just one of many activities they mimicked. It always puzzled Ayla, she wondered why it was done, but it didn't disturb her to see a young boy bounce harmlessly on a young girl in conscious imitation of adults.

Sometimes it wasn't imitation. Many young girls of the Clan were pierced by pubescent boys who lingered in the limbo of not-yet-men, before their first kill; and occasionally a man, beguiled by a young coquette, pleased himself with a not-quite-ripe female. Most young men, though, felt it beneath their dignity to play games with former playmates.

But Ayla had no male playmates near her age except Vorn, and since the earlier days when Aga actively discouraged their association, there had never developed any close contact between them. Ayla was not particularly fond of Vorn, who imitated Broud's actions toward her. Despite the incident on the practice field, the boy still idolized Broud, and Vorn was not about to play "mates" with Ayla. There was no one else who might have, so she had never even engaged in the imitation of the act. Within a society that indulged in sex as naturally as they breathed, Ayla was still a virgin.

The young woman felt awkward; she knew she must comply, but she was flustered and Broud was enjoying it. He was glad he had thought of it; he had finally broken down her defenses. It excited him to see her so confused and bewildered, and aroused him. He hovered close as she got up, then started to lower herself to her knees. Ayla wasn't accustomed to men of the clan being so near. Broud's heavy breathing frightened her. She hesitated.

Broud got impatient, pushed her down, and moved aside his wrap exposing his organ, thick and throbbing. What is she waiting for? She's so ugly, she should be honored, no other man would have her, he thought angrily, grabbing at her wrap to move it out of the way as his need grew.

But as Broud closed in on her, something snapped. She couldn't do it! She just couldn't. Her reason left her. It didn't matter that she was supposed to obey him. She scrambled to her feet and started to run. Broud was too quick for her. He grabbed her, pushed her down, and punched her in the face, cutting her lip with his hard fist. He was beginning to enjoy this. Too many times had he restrained himself when he wanted to beat her, but there was no one to stop him here. And he had justifiable reason—she was disobeying him, actively disobeying him.

Ayla was frantic. She tried to get up and he hit her again. He was getting a reaction from her he never expected, and it stirred him to greater lust. He would cow this insolent woman yet. He hit her again and again, and felt a great satisfaction to see her cringe as he made a move to hit her once more.

Her head was ringing, blood trickled out of her nose and the corner of her mouth. She tried to get up, but he held her down. She struggled against him, pummeling his chest with her fists. They had no effect on his hard muscular body, but her resistance aroused him to new heights. Never had he felt so stimulated—violence increased his passion and lust added force to his blows. He reveled in her resistance and clouted her again.

She was nearly unconscious when he threw her over on her face, feverishly ripped her wrap aside, and spread her legs. With one hard thrust, he penetrated deeply. She screamed with pain. It added to his pleasure. He lunged again, drawing forth another painful cry, then again, and again. The intensity of his excitement urged him on, rising quickly to unbearable peaks. With a last hard drive that extracted a final agonized scream, he ejected his built-up heat.

Broud collapsed on top of her for a moment, his energy spent. Then, still breathing heavily, he withdrew himself. Ayla sobbed incoherently. The salt from her tears stung the open wounds on her blood-smeared face. One eye was swollen nearly shut and turning dark. Her thighs were stained with blood and she hurt deep inside. Broud got up and looked down at her. He felt good; he had never enjoyed penetrating a woman so much. He picked up his weapons and headed back to the cave.

Ayla lay with her face in the dirt long after her sobbing stopped. Finally she pulled herself up. She touched her mouth, felt the swelling, and looked at the blood on her fingers. Her whole body ached, inside and out. She saw blood between her thighs and the stains on the grass. Is my totem fighting again? she wondered. No, I don't think so, it's not time. Broud must have wounded me. I didn't know he could beat me on the inside, too. But the other women don't hurt from it; why should Broud's organ wound me? Is there something wrong with me?

Slowly she got up and walked to the creek, hurting with every step. She washed herself, but it didn't help the throbbing, aching pain, or the turmoil in her mind. Why did Broud want me to do that? Iza says men want to relieve their needs with attractive women. I'm ugly. Why should a man want to hurt a woman he likes? But women like it, too; why else would they make the gestures to encourage men? How can they like it? Oga never minds it when

Broud does it to her, and he does it every day, more than once, sometimes.

Suddenly Ayla was horrified. Oh, no! What if Broud makes me do it again? I won't go back. I can't go back. Where can I go? My little cave? No, it's too close, and I can't stay there in winter. I have to go back, I can't live alone, where else can I go? And I can't leave Iza, and Creb, and Uba. What am I going to do? If Broud wants it, I can't refuse him. None of the other women would even try. What's wrong with me? He never wanted that when I was still a girl. Why did I have to become a woman? I was so happy about it, now I wouldn't care if I was a girl all my life. I'll never have a baby anyway. What good is being a woman if you can't have a baby? Especially if a man can make you do something like that? What good is it anyway? What's it for?

The sun was low when she plodded back up the knoll to look for her ptarmigan. The eggs, cushioned so carefully, were crushed, and stained the front of her wrap. She looked back at the creek and remembered how happy she was watching the birds. It seemed ages ago, another time, another place. She dragged herself back to the cave, dreading every step.

As Iza watched the sun disappear behind the trees in the west, she grew more anxious. She walked partway up all the paths in the nearby woods and to the ridge to scan the slope toward the steppes. A woman shouldn't be out alone; I never do like it when Ayla hunts, Iza thought. What if she was attacked by some animal? Maybe she's hurt? Creb was concerned, too, though he tried not to show it. Even Brun began to worry as it grew dark. Iza was the first to see her walking toward the cave from the ridge. She started to scold her for making her worry, but stopped before her first gesture.

"Ayla! You're hurt! What happened?"

"Broud beat me," she motioned, her expression dull.

"But why?"

"I disobeyed him," the young woman gestured as she walked into the cave and straight to the hearth.

What could have happened? Iza wondered. Ayla hasn't disobeyed Broud for years. Why would she rebel against him now? And why didn't he tell me he saw her? He knew I was worried. He's been back since noon, why is Ayla so late? Iza cast a quick glance in the direction of Broud's hearth and saw him staring across the boundary stones at Ayla, against all good manners, with a pleased smirk on his face.

Creb had taken in the whole scene: Ayla's bruised and swollen face and look of utter desolation, Broud watching her from the moment she returned with an arrogant sneer. He knew Broud's hatred had grown over the years—her placid obedience seemed to affect him worse than her girlish rebellion—but something had happened that gave Broud a sense of power over her. As perceptive as Creb was, he could not have guessed the cause.

Ayla was afraid to leave the hearth the next day, dawdling over her morning meal as long as she could. Broud was waiting for her. Thinking about his intense excitement of the day before had him stimulated and ready. When he gave her the signal, she almost bolted, but forced herself to assume the position. She tried to repress her cries, but the pain forced them from her lips, causing curious glances from those who happened to be nearby. They could no more understand why she was crying out in pain than they could understand Broud's sudden interest in her.

Broud reveled in his newfound dominance over Ayla and used her often, though many people wondered why he chose the ugly woman he hated over his own comely mate. After a time, it was no longer painful, but Ayla detested it. And it was her hatred that Broud enjoyed. He had put her in her place, gained superiority over her, and finally found a way to make her react to him. It didn't matter that her response was negative, he preferred it. He wanted to see her cower, to see her fear, to see her force herself to submit. Just thinking about it stimulated him. He had always had a strong drive; now he was more sexually active than ever. Every morning that he wasn't away hunting, he waited for her, usually forced her again in the evening and sometimes at midday as well. He even found himself aroused at night and used his mate to relieve himself. He was young and healthy, at the peak of his sexual prowess, and the more intensely she hated him, the more pleasure he derived.

Ayla lost her sparkle. She was dispirited, morose, unresponsive to anything else. The only emotion she felt was an all-consuming hatred of Broud and his daily penetration of her. Like a massive glacier that sucks all moisture from the surrounding land, her loathing and bitter frustration drained away all other feelings.

She had always kept herself clean, washing herself and her hair in the stream to keep it free of lice, even bringing in large bowls of snow to set beside the constantly burning fire to melt for fresh water in winter. Now her hair hung limp in greasy tangles and she wore the same wrap day in and day out, not bothering to clean the spots or let it air out. She dragged at her chores until men who had never before scolded were rebuking her. She lost interest in Iza's medicines, never talked except to answer direct questions, seldom hunted and often returned empty-handed when she did. Her despondency cast a pall on everyone else around Creb's hearth.

Iza was beside herself with worry; she couldn't understand the drastic change in Ayla. She knew it was because of Broud's inexplicable interest in her, but why it should have that effect was beyond the woman. She hovered over Ayla, watching her constantly, and when the young woman first began to get sick in the mornings, she was afraid that whatever evil spirit had gotten into her was gaining a greater hold.

But Iza was an experienced medicine woman. She was the first to notice when Ayla did not keep herself in the nominal isolation required of women when their totems battled, and watched her adopted daughter even closer. She could hardly believe what she suspected. But by the time another moon had passed and the summer was waxing into full heat, Iza was sure. Early one evening when Creb was away from the hearth, she beckoned to Ayla.

"I want to talk to you."

"Yes, Iza," Ayla replied, hauling herself up from her fur and slumping down in the dirt near the woman.

"When was the last time your totem battled, Ayla?"

"I don't know."

"Ayla, I want you to think about it. Have the spirits fought within you since the blossoms dropped?"

The young woman tried to think. "I'm not sure, maybe once."

"That's what I thought," Iza said. "You're getting sick in the mornings, aren't you?"

"Yes," she nodded. Ayla thought her sickness was because every morning that Broud wasn't gone hunting, he was there, waiting for her, and she hated it so much, she was losing her breakfast, and sometimes her evening meal, too.

"Have your breasts felt sore?"

"A little."

"And they've grown larger, too, haven't they?"

"I think so. Why are you asking? Why all these questions?"

The woman looked at her seriously. "Ayla, I don't know how it happened, I can hardly believe it, but I'm sure it's true."

"What's true?"

"Your totem has been defeated; you are going to have a baby."

"A baby? Me? I can't have a baby," Ayla protested. "My totem is too strong."

"I know, Ayla. I can't understand it, but you are going to have a baby," Iza repeated.

A look of wonder crept into Ayla's unresponsive eyes. "Can it be true! Can it really be true! Me, have a baby? Oh, mother, how wonderful!"

"Ayla, you're not mated. I don't think there's a man in the clan who will take you, even as second woman. You can't have a child without a mate, it might be unlucky," Iza motioned earnestly. "It would be best to take something to lose it. I think mistletoe would be best. You know, the plant with the small white berries that grows high in the oak. It's very effective and, if properly handled, not too dangerous. I'll make you a tea of the leaves with just a few berries. It will help your totem expel the new life. It will make you a little sick, but . . ."

"No! No!" Ayla was shaking her head vigorously. "Iza, no. I don't want to take mistletoe. I don't want to take anything to lose it. I want a baby, mother. I've wanted one ever since Uba was born. I never thought it would be possible."

"But Ayla, what if the baby is unlucky? It might even be deformed."

"It won't be unlucky, I won't let it. I promise, I'll take good care of myself so it will be healthy. Didn't you say a strong totem helps to make a healthy baby once it succumbs? And I'll take good care of it after it's born, I won't let anything happen. Iza, I've got to have this baby. Don't you see? My totem may never be defeated again. This may be my only chance."

Iza looked into the pleading eyes of the young woman. It was the first spark of life she had seen since the day Broud beat her while she was out hunting. She knew she should insist that Ayla take the medicine; it wasn't right for an unmated woman to give birth if it could be helped. But Ayla wanted the baby so desperately, she might go into a worse depression if she was made to give it up. And maybe she was right—it might be her only chance.

"All right, Ayla," she acquiesced. "If you want it so much. It would be best not to mention it to anyone yet; they'll know soon enough."

"Oh, Iza," she said, and gave the woman a hug. As the miracle of her impossible pregnancy filled her, a smile danced across her face. She jumped up, charged with energy. She couldn't sit still, she just had to do something.

"Mother, what are you cooking tonight? Let me help."

"Aurochs stew," the woman replied, amazed at the sudden transformation in the young woman. "You can cut up the meat if you want."

As the two women worked, Iza realized she had almost forgotten what a joy Ayla could be. Their hands flew, talking and working, and Ayla's interest in medicine suddenly returned.

"I didn't know about mistletoe, mother," Ayla remarked. "I know about ergot and sweet rush, but I didn't know mistletoe could make a woman lose a baby."

"There will always be some things I haven't told you about, Ayla, but you'll know enough. And you know how to test; you will always be able to keep learning. Tansy will work, too, but it can be more dangerous than mistletoe. You use the whole plant—flowers, leaves, roots—and boil it. If you fill the water up to here," Iza pointed to a mark on the side of one of her medicine bowls, "and boil it down to a cup this size," Iza held up a bone cup, "it should be about right. One cup is usually enough. Chrysanthemum flowers sometimes work. It's not as dangerous as mistletoe or tansy, but not always effective, either."

"That would be better for women who tend to lose babies easily. It's better to use something milder if it will work—less dangerous."

"That's right. And Ayla, there's something else you should know about." Iza looked around to make sure Creb was still gone. "No man must ever learn of this; it is a secret known only to medicine women, and not all of them know it. It's best not even to tell a woman. If her mate asked her, she'd have to tell him. No one will ask a medicine woman. If a man ever found out, he would forbid it. Do you understand?"

"Yes, mother," Ayla nodded, surprised at Iza's secrecy and very curious.

"I didn't think you'd ever need to know this for yourself, but you should know it as a medicine woman anyway. Sometimes, if a woman has a very difficult birth, it's best if she never has any more children. A medicine woman can give her the medicine without ever telling her what it is. There are other reasons that a woman might not want a child. Some plants have special magic, Ayla. They make a woman's totem very strong, strong enough to stop a new life from ever starting."

"You know magic to prevent pregnancy, Iza? Can a weak woman's totem become that strong? Any totem? Even if a mog-ur makes a charm to give strength to a man's totem?"

"Yes, Ayla. That's why a man must never find out. I used it myself after I was mated. I didn't like my mate; I wanted him to give me to another man. I thought if I never had children, he wouldn't want to keep me," Iza confessed.

"But you did have a child. You had Uba."

"Maybe after a long time the magic loses strength. Maybe my totem didn't want to fight anymore, maybe he wanted me to have a child. I don't know. Nothing works all the time. There are forces stronger than any magic, but it worked for many years. No one understands spirits completely, not even Mog-ur. Who would have thought your totem could be defeated, Ayla?" The medicine woman glanced around quickly. "Now, before Creb comes, you know the little yellow vine with tiny leaves and flowers?"

"Golden thread?"

"Yes, that's the one. Sometimes it's called strangle weed because it kills the plant it grows on. Let it dry, crush about this much in the palm of your hand, boil it in enough water to fill the bone cup until the decoction is the color of ripe hay. Drink two swallows every day that the spirit of your totem is not fighting."

"Doesn't it also make a good poultice for stings and bites?"

"Yes, and that gives you a good reason to have it around, but the poultice is used on the skin, outside the body. To give your totem strength, you drink it. There's something else you must take, while your totem is fighting. The root of antelope sage, dried or fresh. Boil it and drink the water, one bowl every day you are isolated," Iza continued.

"Isn't that the plant with the ragged leaf that's good for Creb's arthritis?"

"That's the one. I know of one other, but I've never used it. It's the magic of another medicine woman; we traded knowledge. There is a certain yam—it doesn't grow around here, but I'll show you how it is different from the ones that do. Cut it into chunks and boil it down and mash it into a thick paste, then let it dry and pound it into a powder. It takes a lot, half a bowl of the powder mixed with water to make it a paste again, every day you are not isolated, when the spirits are not fighting."

Creb entered the cave and saw the two women deeply engrossed in conversation. He could see the difference in Ayla immediately. She was animated, attentive, thoughtful, smiling. She must have snapped out of it, he thought, limping toward his hearth.

"Iza!" he announced loudly to get their attention. "Must a man starve around here?"

The woman jumped up looking a little guilty, but Creb didn't notice. He was so pleased to see Ayla busily working and talking, he didn't see Iza.

"It'll be ready soon, Creb," Ayla motioned, and smiling, ran up and gave him a hug. It made Creb feel better than he had for a long time. As he settled down on his mat, Uba came running into the cave.

"I'm hungry!" the little girl gestured.

"You're always hungry, Uba." Ayla laughed as she picked up the girl and swung her around. Uba was delighted. It was the first time Ayla felt like playing with her all summer.

Later, after they had eaten, Uba crawled into Creb's lap. Ayla was humming under her breath while she helped Iza clean up. Creb sighed contentedly; it felt much more like home. Boys are very important, he thought, but I think I like girls better. They don't have to be big and brave all the time and don't mind cuddling in a lap to go to sleep. I almost wish Ayla were still a little girl.

Ayla woke the next morning wrapped in a warm glow of anticipation. I'm going to have a baby, she thought. She hugged herself, lying in her furs. Suddenly she was eager to get up. I think I'll go down to the stream this morning, my hair needs a washing. She bounced out of bed, but a wave of nausea overcame her. Maybe I'd better eat something solid to see if it will stay down. I've got to eat if I want my baby to be healthy. It didn't stay down, but after she was up for a while, she ate again and felt better. She was still thinking about the miracle of her pregnancy when she left the cave and started for the stream.

"Ayla!" Broud sneered, as he swaggered up and made the signal.

Ayla was startled. She had forgotten all about Broud. She had more important things to think about, like warm cuddly nursing babies, her own warm cuddly nursing baby. Might as well get it over with, she thought, and patiently assumed the position for Broud to relieve his needs. I hope he hurries, I want to go down to the stream and wash my hair.

Broud felt deflated. Something was missing. There was no response in her at all. He missed the excitement of forcing her against her will. Her seething hatred and bitter frustration, which she had never quite succeeded in covering before, were gone. She wasn't fighting him anymore. She acted as though he wasn't even there, as though she didn't feel a thing. She didn't. Her mind was in another realm, she no more noticed his penetration than his rebukes or sharp blows. It was just one more thing she had to accept and she resigned herself to it. Her calm, self-possessed serenity had returned.

Broud's enjoyment was in dominating her, not in the pleasure of the sexual experience. He found he wasn't stimulated anymore; he had trouble maintaining an erection. After a few times of not reaching a climax at all, he backed off, and soon stopped altogether. It was too humiliating. She might as well be a stone, for all her response, he thought. She's so ugly anyway, I've given her enough of my time. She doesn't even appreciate the honor of the future leader's interest.

Oga welcomed him back, relieved that he seemed to be over his unfathomable attraction for Ayla. She hadn't been jealous; it wasn't something to be jealous about. Broud was her mate, and he gave no indication he was ready to give her up. Any man could relieve his needs with any woman he wanted, there was nothing extraordinary about that. She just couldn't understand why he paid so much attention to

Ayla when, for some strange reason, she obviously didn't enjoy it.

For all his rationalizing, Broud was galled at Ayla's sudden indifference. He thought he had finally found a way to dominate her, to break down her wall of reserve once and for all, and he had discovered the pleasure it gave him. It made him all the more determined to find a way to get to her again.

19

Ayla's pregnancy astounded the whole clan. It seemed impossible that a woman with as powerful a totem as hers could conceive life. Speculation was rampant about the spirit of which man's totem had succeeded in overpowering the Cave Lion, and every man in the clan would have liked to claim the credit—and the boost to his prestige. Some felt it must have been a combination of several totemic essences, perhaps the entire male population, but most opinions fell into one of two camps, divided almost entirely along the lines of age.

Proximity to the woman was the determining factor, which was why most men believed the children of their mates were the result of their own totem's spirit. A woman inevitably spent more time with the man whose hearth she shared; the opportunity for swallowing his totem's spirit was greater. Even though a man's totem might call upon the assistance of another man's totem during the ensuing battle, or any spirit that happened to be nearby, the vital force of the first totem had primary claim. A helping spirit might be honored with the privilege of beginning a new life, but it was at the discretion of the totem that asked for help. The two men who had been closest to Ayla since she had become a woman were Mog-ur and Broud.

"I say it's Mog-ur," Zoug asserted. "He's the only one with a totem stronger than the Cave Lion. And whose hearth does she share?"

"Ursus never allows a woman to swallow his essence," Crug countered. "The Cave Bear chooses those he will protect, as he did Mog-ur. Do you think a Roe Deer defeated a Cave Lion?"

"With the Cave Bear's help. Mog-ur has two totems. The Roe Deer wouldn't have to go far for help. No one says the Cave Bear left his spirit, I'm only saying he helped," Zoug contended hotly.

"Then why didn't she get pregnant last winter? She lived at his hearth then. It was only after Broud developed his attraction for her, though don't ask me what he ever saw in her. It was after he spent so much time near her that the new life started. A Woolly Rhinoceros is powerful, too. With help, it could have overcome the Cave Lion," Crug argued.

"I think it was everyone's totem," Dorv put in. "The question is, who wants to mate her? Everyone wants the credit, but who wants the woman? Brun asked if any man was willing. If she's not mated, the child will be unlucky. I'm too old, though I can't say I'm sorry."

"Well, I'd take her if I still had a hearth of my own," Zoug gestured. "She's ugly, but she's hardworking and respectful. She knows how to take care of a man. That's more important than good looks in the long run."

"Not me," Crug shook his head. "I don't want the Woman Who Hunts at my hearth. It's all right for Mog-ur, he can't hunt anyway and he doesn't care. But imagine coming back from a hunt empty-handed and eating the meat provided by my mate. Besides, my hearth is full enough with Ika and Borg and the baby, Igra. I'm just glad Dorv can still contribute. And Ika's still young enough to have more—who can tell?"

"I've thought about it," Droog said, "but my hearth is just too full. Aga and Aba, Vorn and Ona and Groob. What would I do with another woman and child? What about you, Grod?"

"No. Not unless Brun commands it," Grod replied tersely. The second-in-command had never quite gotten over a certain uneasiness around the woman who was not born to the Clan. She just made him uncomfortable.

"What about Brun, himself?" Crug queried. "He's the one who accepted her into the clan in the first place."

"Sometimes it's wise to consider the first woman before a man takes a second," Goov commented. "You know how

Ebra feels about the medicine woman's status. Iza's been training Ayla. If she becomes a medicine woman of Iza's line, do you think Ebra would like to share a hearth with a younger woman, a second mate, with more status than she? I would take Ayla. When I'm mog-ur, I won't be hunting as much; I wouldn't care if she brought a rabbit or a hamster to the hearth. They're just small animals anyway. I don't even think Ovra would mind a second woman with more status, they get along well. But Ovra wants a baby of her own. It would be difficult for her to share a hearth with a woman and a new baby. Especially when no one ever expected Ayla to have one. I think it was the spirit of Broud's totem who started it; it's too bad he feels the way he does, he's the one who should take her."

"I'm not so sure it was Broud's," Droog said. "What about you, Mog-ur? You could take her for a mate."

The old magician had been quietly watching the men's discussion as he often did. "I've considered it. I don't think it was Ursus or the Roe Deer that started Ayla's baby. I'm not sure if it was Broud's totem either. Her totem has always been an enigma; who knows what happened. But she needs a mate. It's not only that the baby may be unlucky, some man needs to be responsible for it, to provide for it. I'm too old, and if it should be a boy, I couldn't train him to hunt. And she can't do it, she only hunts with a sling. I couldn't mate her anyway. It would be like Grod mating Ovra, especially with Uka still his first mate. To me, she's like the daughter of one's mate, a child of one's hearth, not a woman to be mated."

"It's been done," Dorv said. "The only woman a man cannot mate is his sibling."

"It's not prohibited, but it's not looked upon with favor, either. And most men don't want to. Besides, I've never had a mate; I'm too old to start now. Iza takes care of me, that's good enough. I'm comfortable with her. Men are expected to relieve their needs with their mates once in a while. I haven't had those needs for a long time; I learned to control them long ago. I wouldn't be much of a mate for a young woman. But it may be she won't need one. Iza says she may have a difficult pregnancy, she's already having problems, she may not keep it full term. I know Ayla wants the baby, but it would be better for everyone if she lost it."

As reported to the men, Ayla's pregnancy was not going well. The medicine woman feared there was something wrong with the baby. Many miscarriages were of malformed fetuses, and Iza thought it was better to lose them than to give live birth and have to dispose of a deformed baby. Ayla's morning sickness lasted well beyond the first trimester, and even by late fall when her thickened waist had grown to a bulge, she had trouble keeping food down. When she started spotting and passing clots, Iza asked Brun's permission for Ayla to be excused from normal activities and she confined the young woman to her bed.

Iza's fears about Ayla's baby grew with the difficulties of her pregnancy. She felt strongly that Ayla should let the baby go. She was sure it wouldn't take much to dislodge it, for all that her stomach attested to the baby's growth. She feared more for Ayla. The baby was taking too much out of her. Her arms and legs grew thinner in contrast to her expanding middle. She had no appetite and forced herself to eat the special foods Iza prepared for her. Dark circles formed around her eyes and her thick lustrous hair became limp. She was always cold, just didn't have the physical reserves to keep warm, and spent most of the time huddled close to the fire, bundled in furs. But when Iza suggested that Ayla should take the medicine that would end the pregnancy, the young woman refused.

"Iza, I want my baby. Help me," Ayla pleaded. "You can help me, I know you can. I'll do whatever you say, just help me to have my baby."

Iza could not refuse. For some time she had depended on Ayla to bring her the plants she needed, seldom going out herself. Strenuous exercise brought on coughing spasms. Iza had been keeping herself heavily dosed with medicines to hide the consumptive lung disease that grew worse each winter. But for Ayla she would go out to look for a certain root that helped prevent miscarriage.

The medicine woman left the cave early one morning to search the upland forests and damp barrens for the special root. The sun was shining in a clear sky when she started out. Iza thought it was going to be one of those warm days in late fall and didn't want to burden herself with extra clothes. Besides, she planned to be back before the sun was high. She followed a path into the forest near the cave, then turned off along a creek and began climbing the steep slopes. She was weaker than she thought, her breath was short, and she had to rest often or wait for a racking spasm of coughing to pass. By midmorning the weather turned.

Clouds blew in from the east on a chill wind and when they reached the foothills, dropped their heavy load of moisture in a driving sleet. In the first few moments, Iza was soaked.

The rain had slackened by the time she found the kind of pine forest, and plants, she was looking for. Shivering in the cold drizzle, she dug the roots out of the muddy ground. Her cough was worse on the way back, convulsing her body every few moments and bringing bloody foam to her lips. She wasn't as familiar with the terrain around this cave as she had been with the environment of the clan's previous home. She became disoriented, followed the wrong creek down the slope, and had to backtrack before she found the right one. It was nearing dark when the thoroughly wet and chilled medicine woman found her way back to the cave.

"Mother, where have you been?" Ayla gestured. "You're soaked and shivering. Come to the fire. Let me get you some dry clothes."

"I found some rattlesnake root for you, Ayla. Wash it and chew..." Iza had to stop as another spasm overwhelmed her. Her eyes were feverish, her face flushed: "... chew it raw. It will help you keep the baby."

"You didn't go out in that rain just to find a root for me, did you? Don't you know I'd rather lose the baby than lose you? You're too sick to go out like that, you know you are."

Ayla knew Iza had not been well for years, but until then she didn't know just how sick the woman really was. The young woman forgot her pregnancy, ignored it when she bled occasionally, forgot to eat half the time, and refused to leave Iza's side. When she slept, it was on a fur beside the woman's bed. Uba, too, kept a constant watch.

It was the young girl's first experience with grave illness in one she loved, and the effect was traumatic. She watched everything Ayla did, helped her, and it opened up an understanding of her own heritage and destiny. Uba wasn't the only one who watched Ayla. The whole clan was concerned for the medicine woman and not entirely certain of the young woman's skill. She was oblivious to their apprehension; her complete attention was focused on the woman she called mother.

Ayla searched her brain for every remedy Iza had ever taught her, she questioned Uba for the information she knew was stored in the child's memory, and applied a certain logic of her own. The special talent Iza had noticed, an ability to discover and treat the real problem, was Ayla's forte. She was a diagnostician. From small clues, she could put together a picture like pieces of a puzzle and fill in the blanks with reasoning and intuition. It was an ability for which *her* brain alone, among all those who shared the cave, was uniquely suited. The crisis of Iza's illness was the stimulus that sharpened her talent.

Ayla applied the remedies she had learned from the medicine woman, then tried new techniques that suggested themselves from other uses, sometimes far removed. Whatever it was, the medication, or the loving care, or the medicine woman's own will to live—most likely it was all of them—by the time winter had piled high drifts against the wind barriers at the entrance, Iza was sufficiently recovered to take charge of Ayla's pregnancy again. It was none too soon.

The strain of nursing Iza back to health had its effect. Ayla spotted blood continuously the rest of the winter and lived with a constant backache. She woke in the middle of the night with cramps in her legs and still vomited frequently. Iza expected her to lose the baby anytime. She didn't know how Ayla hung on to it, and she didn't know how the baby could continue to develop with Ayla so weak. But develop it did. The young woman's stomach swelled to unbelievable proportions, and the baby kicked so vigorously and continuously she could hardly sleep. Iza had never seen a woman suffer through a more difficult pregnancy.

Ayla never complained. She was afraid Iza would think she was ready to give the baby up, though she was much too far along for the medicine woman to consider it. Nor did Ayla consider it. Her suffering only made her more convinced that if she lost this one, she would never have another baby.

From her bed, Ayla watched the spring rains wash away the snow, and the first crocus she saw was one Uba brought her. Iza wouldn't let her out of the cave. The pussy willows had blown and turned green, and the first buds hinted at verdant foliage on the soggy spring day early in her eleventh year when Ayla's labor began.

The beginning contractions were easy. Ayla sipped willow-bark tea, talking to Iza and Uba, excitedly pleased that the time had finally come. By the next day, she was sure, she would be holding her own baby in her arms. Iza had reservations but tried not to show them. The conversation turned, as it did so often lately with Iza and her two daughters, to medicine.

"Mother, what was that root you brought me the day you went out and got so sick?" Ayla motioned.

"It's called rattlesnake root. It's not commonly used because it should be chewed when it's fresh, and it must be collected in late fall. It's very good for preventing miscarriage, but how many women threaten to miscarry only in late fall? It loses its effectiveness when it's dried."

"What does it look like?" Uba asked. Iza's illness had sharpened Uba's interest in the healing herbs she would one day dispense, and both Iza and Ayla were training her. But training Uba was different from training Ayla. To gain the full value of her brain, Uba only needed to be reminded of what she knew and see how it was applied.

"It's really two plants, a male and a female. It has a long stalk growing out of a cluster of leaves near the ground, and small flowers clinging close to the top, partway down the stalk. The male flowers are white. The root is from the female plant; its flowers are smaller and green."

"Did you say it grows in pine forests?" Ayla motioned.

"Only damp ones. It likes moisture, bogs, wet places in meadows, often in upland woods."

"You should never have gone out that day, Iza. I was so worried. . . . Oh, wait, another one is starting!"

The medicine woman studied Ayla. She was trying to judge how long the pains were. It would be a long time yet, she decided.

"It wasn't raining when I started out," Iza said. "I thought it was going to be warm that day. I was wrong. Fall weather is always unpredictable. I've been wanting to ask you something, Ayla. I was delirious with fever part of the time, but I thought you made a chest plaster out of herbs used to relieve Creb's rheumatism."

"I did."

"I didn't teach you that."

"I know. You were coughing so hard, spitting so much blood, I wanted to give you something to calm the spasms, but I thought you should bring up the phlegm without so much effort, too. That medicine for Creb's rheumatism penetrates deep with warmth and stimulates the blood. I thought it might loosen the phlegm so you wouldn't have to cough so hard to bring it up, then I could still give you the decoction to calm the spasms. It seemed to work."

"Yes, I think it did." After Ayla explained her reasoning, it seemed logical, but Iza wondered if she would have considered it. I was right, Iza thought. She is a good medicine woman, and she's going to get better. She deserves the status of my line. I must talk to Creb. It may not be much longer before I leave this world. Ayla is a woman now, she should be medicine woman—if she survives this birth.

After the morning meal, Oga strolled over with Grev, her second son, and sat beside Ayla while she nursed. Ovra joined them soon after. The three young women chatted amiably between Ayla's contractions, though no mention was made of her forthcoming delivery. All through the morning while Ayla was in the first stage of labor, the women of the clan visited Creb's hearth. Some just stopped for a few moments to offer moral support with their presence, some sat with her almost continuously. There were always a few women seated around her bed, but Creb stayed away. He paced nervously in and out of the cave, stopping to exchange a few gestures with the men gathered at Brun's hearth, but not able to stay in one place too long. The hunt planned for that day was postponed. Brun's excuse was that it was still too wet, but everyone knew the real reason.

By late afternoon, Ayla's labor was stronger. Iza gave her a root decoction of a certain yam with special qualities that relieved the pain of childbirth. As the day dragged into evening, her contractions got stronger and closer together. Ayla lay in her bed, drenched with sweat, clutching Iza's hand. She tried to stifle her cries, but as the sun dropped below the horizon, Ayla was writhing in pain, screaming with every convulsion that racked her body. Most of the women couldn't bear to stay near anymore; everyone except Ebra went back to their own hearths. They found some chore to keep busy, glancing up when Ayla started into another agonized scream. Conversation had stopped around Brun's fire, too. The men sat listlessly, staring at the ground. Every attempt at small talk was cut short by Ayla's cries of pain.

"Her hips are too narrow, Ebra," Iza gestured. "They won't let her birth canal open wide enough."

"Would breaking the water sac help? It does sometimes," Ebra suggested.

"I've been thinking of that. I didn't want to do it too soon; she couldn't stand a dry birth. I was hoping it would break itself, but she's getting weaker and not making much progress. Perhaps I'd better do it now. Will you give me that slippery-elm stick? She's starting another contraction, I'll do it when this one is over."

Ayla arched her back and gripped the hands of the two women as a crescendo of convulsing agony was torn from her lips.

"Ayla, I'm going to try to help you," Iza motioned after the contraction passed. "Do you understand me?"

Ayla nodded mutely.

"I'm going to break the water, then I want you to get up into a squatting position. It helps if the baby is pushed downward. Can you do it?"

"I'll try," Ayla waved weakly.

Iza inserted the slippery-elm stick, and Ayla's birth waters gushed out, bringing on another contraction.

"Get up now, Ayla," the medicine woman motioned. She and Ebra pulled the weakened young woman up from her bed and supported her while she squatted on the leather hide, like the one placed under all women when they gave birth.

"Push now, Ayla. Push hard." She strained with the next pain.

"She's too weak," Ebra signaled. "She can't push hard enough."

"Ayla, you've got to push harder," Iza commanded.

"I can't," Ayla motioned.

"You must, Ayla. You must or your baby will die," Iza said. She didn't mention that Ayla, too, would die. Iza could see her muscles bunching for another contraction.

"Now, Ayla! Now! Push! Push as hard as you can," Iza urged.

I can't let my baby die, Ayla thought. I can't. I'll never have another baby if this one dies. From some unknown reserve, Ayla drew a last surge of strength. As the pain mounted, she took a deep breath and grabbed Iza's hand for support. She bore down with an effort that brought beads of sweat to her forehead. Her head swam dizzily. It felt as though her bones were cracking, as though she was trying to force her insides out.

"Good, Ayla, good," Iza encouraged. "The head is showing, one more like that."

Ayla gulped another breath of air and strained again. She felt skin and muscles tear, and still she pushed. With a gush of thick red blood, the baby's head was forced through the narrow birth canal. Iza took it and pulled, but the worst was over.

"Just a little more, Ayla, just enough for the afterbirth." Ayla strained once more, felt her head whirl and everything go dark, and collapsed, unconscious.

Iza tied a red-dyed piece of sinew around the newborn's umbilical cord and bit off the rest. She thumped the feet until a mewling cry became a loud squall. The baby's alive, Iza thought with relief as she began to clean the infant. Then her heart sank. After all her suffering, after all she's been through, why this? She wanted the baby so much. Iza wrapped the infant in the soft rabbit skin Ayla had made, then made a poultice of chewed roots for Ayla, held in place with an absorbent leather strap. Ayla groaned and opened her eyes.

"My baby, Iza. Is it a boy or a girl?" she asked.

"It's a boy, Ayla," the woman said, then quickly continued so her hopes would not be raised, "but he's deformed."

Ayla's first hint of a smile turned to a look of horror. "No! He can't be! Let me see him!"

Iza brought the infant to her. "I was afraid of this. It often happens when a woman's pregnancy is difficult. I'm sorry, Ayla."

The young woman opened the cover and looked at her tiny son. His arms and legs were thinner than Uba's when she was born, and longer, but he had the right number of fingers and toes in the right places. His tiny penis and testes gave mute evidence of his sex. But his head was definitely unnatural. It was abnormally large, the cause of Ayla's difficult delivery, and a little misshapen from his harrowing entrance into the world, but that in itself was no cause for alarm. Iza knew it was only the result of the pressures of birth and would quickly straighten out. It was the conformation of the head, the basic shape, that would never change, that was deformed, and the thin, scrawny neck that was unable to support the baby's huge head.

Ayla's baby had heavy brow ridges, like people of the Clan, but his forehead, rather than sloping back, rose high and straight above the brows, bulging, to Iza's eyes, into a high crown before it swept back in a long, full shape. But the back of his head was not quite as long as it should have been. It looked as though the baby's skull was pushed forward into the bulging forehead and crown, shortening and rounding the back. He had only a nominal occipital bun at the rear and his features were oddly altered. He had large round eyes, but his nose was much smaller than normal. His mouth was large, his jaws were not quite as large as Clan jaws; but below his mouth was a boney protrusion disfiguring his face, a well-developed, slightly receding chin, entirely lacking in Clan people. The baby's head flopped back when Iza first picked him up and she automatically put her hand behind it for support, shaking her own head on her short, thick neck. She doubted if the boy would ever be able to hold his head up.

The baby nuzzled toward the warmth of his mother as he lay in Ayla's arms, already looking to suck as though he hadn't had enough before his birth. She helped him to her breast.

"You shouldn't, Ayla," Iza said gently. "You should not add to his life when it must soon be taken away. It will only make it harder for you to get rid of him."

"Get rid of him?" Ayla looked stricken. "How can I get rid of him? He's my baby, my son."

"You have no choice, Ayla. It's the way. A mother must always dispose of a deformed child she has brought into the world. It's best to do it as soon as possible, before Brun commands it."

"But Creb was deformed. He was allowed to live," Ayla protested.

"His mother's mate was the leader of the clan; he allowed it. You have no mate, Ayla, no man to speak for your son. I told you in the beginning your child could be unlucky if you gave birth before you were mated. Doesn't his deformity prove it, Ayla? Why let a child live that will have nothing but bad luck all his life? It's better to get it over now," Iza reasoned.

Reluctantly, Ayla pulled her son away from her breast, tears overflowing her eyes. "Oh, Iza," she cried, "I wanted a baby so much, a baby of my own like other women. I never thought I'd have one. I was so happy. I didn't care if I was sick, I just wanted my own baby. It was so hard, I didn't think he'd ever come, but when you said he'd die, I had to push. If he has to die anyway, why was it so hard? Mother, I want my baby, don't make me get rid of him."

"I know it's not easy, Ayla, but it must be done." Iza's heart ached for her. The baby was searching for the breast so abruptly withheld, for the security and to satisfy his need to suck. She had no milk for him yet, that would take a day or so; there was only the thick, milky fluid that could impart to the infant her own immunity to diseases for the first few months of his life. He started whimpering and soon let go with a lusty howl, flailing his arms and kicking off the cover. His cry filled the cave with the demanding insistence of an angry, red-faced infant. Ayla couldn't stand it. She put him back to her breast.

"I just can't do it," she gestured. "I won't do it! My son is alive. He's breathing. He might be deformed, but he's strong. Did you hear him cry? Did you ever hear a baby cry like that? Did you see him kick? Look how he sucks! I want him, Iza, I want him and I'm going to keep him. I'll leave before I'll kill him. I can hunt. I can find food. I'll take care of him myself!"

Iza paled. "Ayla, you can't mean that. Where would you go? You're too weak, you've lost a lot of blood."

"I don't know, mother. Somewhere. Anywhere. But I won't give him up." Ayla was adamant, determined. Iza had no doubt the young mother meant what she said. But she was too weak to go anyplace; she'd die herself if she tried to save the baby. Iza was appalled to think Ayla would flaunt the customs of the Clan, but Iza was sure she would.

"Ayla, don't talk like that," Iza pleaded. "Give him to me. If you can't, I'll do it for you. I'll tell Brun you are too weak; that's reason enough." The woman reached for the infant. "Let me take him. Once he's gone, it will be easier to forget him."

"No! No, Iza," Ayla shook her head forcefully, clinging tighter to the bundle in her arms. She huddled over him, protecting him with her body, moving only one hand to speak with Creb's abbreviated symbols. "I'm going to keep him. Somehow, some way, even if I have to leave, I am going to keep my baby."

Uba was watching the two women, ignored by them both. She had seen Ayla's bone-wrenching delivery, as she had seen other women give birth before. No secrets of life or death were withheld from children; they shared the fate of the clan as much as their elders. Uba loved the golden-haired girl who was playmate and friend, mother and sister. The hard, painful birth had frightened the girl, but Ayla's talk of leaving frightened her even more. It reminded her of the time when she had gone before, when everyone said she would never come back. Uba was sure if Ayla left now, she would never see her again.

"Don't go, Ayla," the girl ran up gesturing frantically. "Mother, you can't let Ayla leave. Don't go away again."

"I don't want to go, Uba, but I can't let my baby die," Ayla said.

"Can't you put him high up in a tree like the mother in Aba's story? If he lives for seven days, Brun will have to let you keep him," Uba begged.

"Aba's story is a legend, Uba," Iza explained. "No baby can live outside in the cold with no food." Ayla wasn't paying attention to Iza's explanation; Uba's childish suggestion had given her an idea.

"Mother, part of that legend is true."

"What do you mean?"

"If my baby is still alive after seven days, Brun has to accept him, doesn't he?" Ayla asked earnestly.

"What are you thinking, Ayla? You can't leave him outside hoping he'll still be alive after seven days. You know it's impossible."

"Not leave him, take him. I know a place where I can hide, Iza. I can go there and take him with me and then come back on his naming day. Brun will have to let me keep him then. There's a small cave..."

"No! Ayla, don't tell me such things. That would be wrong. It would be disobedient. I can't approve; it's not the way of the Clan. Brun would be very angry. He'd search for you, he'd find you and bring you back. It's not right, Ayla," Iza admonished. She got up and walked toward the fire but turned back after a few steps. "And if you left, he'd ask me where you were."

Never in her life had Iza done anything contrary to Clan customs or Brun's wishes. The very idea was appalling. Even the secret contraceptive medicine had the sanction of past generations of medicine women, it was part of her heritage. Keeping the secret was not disobedient—there was no tradition or custom prohibiting its use—she just refrained from mentioning it. Ayla's plan was nothing short of rebellion, a rebellion Iza would never have dreamed of; she couldn't approve.

But she knew how much Ayla wanted the baby; her heart ached thinking how she had suffered through the long, difficult pregnancy and how only the fear of the baby's death had given her the strength that saved her own life. Ayla's right, Iza thought, looking at the newborn. He's deformed, but he's strong and healthy otherwise. Creb was deformed—now he's Mog-ur. This is her firstborn son, too. If she had a mate, he might allow the baby to live. No, he wouldn't, she thought again. She couldn't lie to herself any more than she could lie to anyone else. But she could refrain from speaking.

She thought about telling Creb or Brun, and she knew she should, but she couldn't bring herself to do it. Iza could not approve of Ayla's plan, but she could keep it to herself. It was the most willfully wrong thing she had ever done in her life.

She put some hot stones in a bowl of water to make an infusion of ergot for Ayla. The young woman was sleeping with the baby in her arms when Iza brought her the medicine. She shook her gently.

"Drink this, Ayla," she said. "I wrapped the afterbirth and put it in that corner. You can rest tonight, but it should be buried tomorrow. Brun already knows, Ebra told him. He'd rather not have to examine the baby and make it an official order. He will expect you to take care of it when you hide the evidence of birth." Iza was telling her daughter how long she had to make her plans.

Ayla lay awake after Iza left, thinking about what to take with her. I'll need my sleeping fur, rabbit skins for the baby, and bird down, and a couple of extra blankets for changes, too. Straps for myself, my sling, and knives. Oh, and food, I'd better bring some food, and a waterbag. If I wait until the sun is high before I go, I can get everything ready in the morning.

The next morning, Iza cooked well in excess of the amount of food needed to feed four people for a morning meal. Creb had come back to his hearth late to sleep; he wanted to avoid any communication with Ayla. He didn't know what to say to her. Her totem is just too strong, he thought. It was never completely overcome; that's why she bled so much during her pregnancy. That's what made the baby deformed. It's too bad, she wanted him so much.

"Iza, that's enough food for a whole clan," Creb remarked. "How can we eat so much?"

"It's for Ayla," Iza said, and quickly put her head down.

Iza should have had many children, the old man thought,

she dotes so much on the ones she has. But Ayla does need to regain her strength. It's going to take her a long time to get over this. I wonder if she'll ever have a normal child?

Ayla's head reeled when she got up, and she felt a rush of warm blood. It hurt to walk even a few steps and bending over was an ordeal. She was weaker than she realized, and almost panicked. How am I going to climb up to the cave? But I have to. If I don't, Iza will take my baby and get rid of him. What will I do if I lose my baby?

I won't lose him, she decided with firm determination, forcing the panic from her mind. I'll get up there somehow, if I have to crawl the whole way.

It was drizzling when Ayla left the cave. She packed some things in the bottom of her collecting basket and covered them with the smelly package of birth effluvium. The rest she hid under her outer fur wrap. The baby was held securely to her chest with a carrying cloak. The first wave of dizziness passed as she started to walk into the woods, but it left her nauseous. She turned off the path and worked her way deep into the forest before she stopped. It was difficult to dig a hole with her digging stick, she was so weak. She buried the package deep, as Iza had told her, and made the proper symbols. Then she looked at her son sleeping soundly, warm and comfortably secure. No one will put you in a hole like that, she said to herself. Then she began to climb the steep foothills, unaware that someone was watching her.

Shortly after Ayla left the cave, Uba slipped out after her. The winter of training after her mother's illness had made the girl much more conscious of the danger Ayla was in. She knew how weak the young woman was, and was afraid she might faint and become easy prey for a roaming carnivore drawn by the smell of blood on her. Uba almost ran back to the cave to tell Iza, but she didn't want Ayla to go alone, so she started to follow her. The girl lost sight of her after she turned off the path, but saw her again climbing up an open stretch of slope.

Ayla leaned heavily on her digging stick as she climbed, using it for a walking staff. She stopped often, swallowing hard to keep down her nausea and fighting not to give in to the dizziness that threatened to become darkness. She felt blood running down her legs but didn't stop to replace her absorbent strap. She remembered a time when she could run up the steep slope without even getting winded. Now, she couldn't believe how far it was to the high meadow. The distance between familiar landmarks was impossibly long. Ayla pushed herself until she was ready to collapse, then struggled to stay conscious until she was rested enough to go on.

By late afternoon, when the baby started crying, she heard him only through a dim fog. She didn't stop for him, she just forced herself to climb. Her mind clung to one thought—I've got to reach the meadow, I've got to get to the cave. She wasn't even sure why anymore.

Uba stayed far behind her, not wanting to let Ayla see her. She didn't know Ayla could hardly see beyond her next step. The young mother's head was swimming in a red haze when she finally reached the mountain pasture. A little more, she told herself, just a little more. She plodded across the field and hardly had the strength to push the branches aside as she stumbled into the small cave that had been her sanctuary so many times before. She collapsed on the deerskin fur, uncaring that her fur wrap was wet, and didn't remember putting her crying son to her breast before she finally allowed herself to succumb to her exhaustion.

It was fortunate that Uba reached the meadow just as Ayla disappeared into the cave, or she would have thought the woman had vanished into thin air. The thick, old hazelnut bushes with their confusion of branches completely camouflaged the hole in the mountain wall even without summer foliage. Uba ran back to the cave. She had been gone longer than she expected; it had taken Ayla much longer than the girl thought to reach the small cave. She was afraid Iza would be worried and scold her. But Iza ignored Uba's late return. She had seen her daughter slip out after Ayla and guessed her intention, but she didn't want to know for sure.

20

"Shouldn't she be back, Iza?" Creb asked. He had been anxiously pacing in and out of the cave all afternoon. Iza nodded nervously, not looking up from the cold, cooked venison haunch she was cutting into chunks.

"Ouch!" she cried suddenly as the sharp blade she was using opened a gash in her finger. Creb looked up, surprised as much by the fact that she cut herself as by her spontaneous outburst. Iza was so skilled with the stone knife, he couldn't remember the last time she did it. *Poor Iza,* Creb thought. *I've been so worried myself, I forgot how she must feel,* he berated himself. *No wonder she's nervous, she's worried, too.*

"I talked to Brun a while ago, Iza," Creb motioned. "He's reluctant to look for her yet. No one should know where a woman disposes . . . where she is at a time like this. You know how unlucky it would be for a man to see her. But she's so weak, she could be out there lying in the rain someplace. You could go look for her, Iza, you're a medicine woman. She can't have gone too far. Don't worry about cooking, I can wait. Why don't you go ahead, it'll be dark soon."

"I can't," Iza gestured and put her cut finger back in her mouth.

"What do you mean, you can't?" Creb was puzzled.

"I can't find her."

"How do you know you can't find her if you don't look?" The old magician was thoroughly confused. *Why doesn't Iza want to look for her? Come to think of it, why hasn't she been out looking long before this? I would have thought she'd be scouring the woods, turning over stones to find Ayla by now. She's so nervous, something is wrong.*

"Iza, why don't you want to look for Ayla?" he asked.

"It wouldn't help, I couldn't find her."

"Why?" he pressed.

The woman's eyes were filled with fearful anxiety. "She's hiding," Iza confessed.

"Hiding! What is she hiding from?"

"Everyone. Brun, you, me, the whole clan," she replied.

Creb was completely at a loss, and Iza's enigmatic answers only made it worse. "Iza, you'd better explain. Why is Ayla hiding from the clan, or me, or you? Especially you. She needs you now."

"She wants to keep the baby, Creb," Iza gestured, then rushed on, begging him with her eyes to understand. "I told her it was the mother's duty to dispose of a deformed baby, but she refused. You know how much she wanted it. She said she was going to take him and hide him until his naming day so Brun would have to accept him." Creb stared hard at the woman, quickly grasping the full implications of Ayla's willfulness.

"Yes, Brun will be forced to accept her son, Iza, and then he'll curse her for deliberate disobedience, this time forever. Don't you know if a woman forces a man against his will, he loses face? Brun can't afford that, the men wouldn't respect him anymore. Even if he curses her he'll lose face, and the Clan Gathering is this summer. Do you think he can face the other clans now? The whole clan will lose face because of Ayla," the magician gestured angrily. "What ever made her think of such a thing?"

"It was one of Aba's stories, about the mother who put her deformed baby up in a tree," Iza answered. The distraught woman was beside herself. Why hadn't she thought about it more?

"Old women's tales!" Creb motioned with disgust. "Aba should know better than to fill a young woman's head with such nonsense."

"It wasn't only Aba, Creb. It was you, too."

"Me! When did I ever tell her such stories?"

"You didn't have to tell her any stories. You were born deformed, but you were allowed to live. Now you're Mogur."

Iza's statement jolted the lopsided, one-armed magician. He knew the series of fortuitous events that led to his acceptance. Only luck had preserved the highest holy man of the Clan. His mother's mother once told him it was nothing short of a miracle. Was Ayla trying to make a miracle happen for her son because of him? It would never work. She'd never force Brun into accepting her son and live. It had to be his wish, his decision, entirely his.

"And you, Iza. Didn't you tell her it was wrong?"

"I begged her not to go. I told her I'd get rid of the baby if she couldn't. But she wouldn't let me near him after that. Oh, Creb, she suffered so much to have him."

"So you let her go, hoping her plan would work. Why didn't you tell me, or Brun?"

Iza just shook her head. Creb is right, I should have told him. Now Ayla will die, too, not just her baby, she thought.

"Where did she go, Iza?" Creb's eye had turned to stone.

"I don't know. She said something about a small cave,"

the woman replied with sinking heart. The magician turned abruptly and limped to the hearth of the leader.

The baby's cries finally woke Ayla from her exhausted sleep. It was dark and the little cave was damp and chilly without a fire. She went to the back to relieve herself and winced as the warm, ammoniacal fluid stung her raw, torn flesh. She fumbled in the dark through her collecting basket for a clean strap and a fresh wrap for the wet and soiled infant, drank some water; then wrapping her fur around them, she lay back down to nurse her son. The next time she woke up, the wall of the cave was dappled with sunlight streaming through the tangled hazelnut branches that hid the entrance. She ate her food cold while the baby suckled.

The food and rest revived her, and she sat up holding her baby, musing dreamily. I'll need to get some wood, she thought, and my food won't last too long, I should get some more. Alfalfa should be sprouting; it'll strengthen my blood, too. New clover and vetch shoots must be ready, and bulbs. The sap is up, the inner bark will be sweet now, especially maple. No, maple doesn't grow this high, but there's birch, and fir. Let's see, new burdock and coltsfoot and young dandelion leaves, and fern, most of it will still be curled. I remembered my sling—there's lots of ground squirrels around here, and beaver, and rabbits.

Ayla daydreamed about the pleasures of the warming season, but when she stood up she felt a gush of blood and a wave of dizziness. Her legs were caked with dried blood that stained her foot coverings and her wraps, jolting her into a more realistic awareness of her desperate situation.

When the dizziness passed, she decided to clean herself and then get some wood, but she didn't know what to do with the baby. She was torn between taking him with her or letting him sleep where he was. Women of the Clan never left babies untended, they were always within sight of some woman, and Ayla hated the thought of leaving him alone. But she had to clean herself and get more water, and she could carry more wood without him.

She peeked out through the bare-limbed bushes to make sure no one was near, then pushed the branches aside and left the cave. The ground was soggy; near the creek it was a slippery mire of mud. Patches of snow still lingered in shaded nooks. Shivering in the brisk wind that blew from the east pushing more rain clouds before it, Ayla stripped and stepped into the cold creek to rinse herself, then sponged her wraps. The clammy damp leather did little to warm her when she put them back on.

She walked to the woods that surrounded the high pasture and tugged at some of the lower dried branches of a fir tree. A whirling vertigo overwhelmed her, her knees buckled, and she reached for a tree to steady herself. Her head was pounding; she swallowed hard to keep from retching as her weakness engulfed her. All thoughts of hunting or gathering food left her. The depleting pregnancy, the ravaging delivery, and the grueling climb all had taken their toll—she had little strength left.

The baby was crying when she got back to the cave. It was cool and damp and he missed her warm closeness. She picked him up and held him, then remembered the waterbag she had left by the creek. She had to have water. She put her son down and dragged herself out of the cave again. It was starting to rain. When she returned, she sunk down, exhausted, and pulled the damp heavy fur over them. She was too tired to notice the sharp edges of fear nicking away at the corners of her mind as sleep overwhelmed her.

"Didn't I tell you she was insolent and willful?" Broud gestured self-righteously. "Did anyone believe me? No. They took her side, made excuses, let her have her way, even let her hunt. I don't care how strong her totem is, women are not supposed to hunt. The Cave Lion didn't lead her to it, it was just defiance. See what happens when you give a woman too much freedom? See what happens when you're too lenient? Now she thinks she can force her deformed son into the clan. No one can make excuses for her this time. She deliberately disobeyed the customs of the Clan. It's inexcusable."

At last Broud had been vindicated and he gloried in his chance to say "I told you so." He rubbed it in with a vengeance that made the leader wince. Brun didn't like losing face and the son of his mate didn't make it any easier.

"You've made your point, Broud," he signaled. "There's no need to keep on about it. I'll take care of her when she comes back. No woman has ever forced me to do anything against my will and gotten away with it, and no woman will start now.

"When we search again tomorrow morning," Brun said, going on to the reason he called the meeting, "I think we should look at places we seldom go. Iza said Ayla knew of a small cave. Has anyone ever seen a small cave nearby? It can't be too far, she was too weak to get very far. Let's forget about the steppes or the forest and search where caves are likely to be. With this rain her trail has been washed away, but there might be a footprint left. Whatever it takes, I want her found."

Iza waited anxiously for Brun's meeting to end. She had been trying to work up courage to speak to him and decided the time was now. When she saw the men leave, she walked to his hearth with bowed head and sat at his feet.

"What do you want, Iza?" Brun asked after tapping her shoulder.

"This unworthy woman would speak to the leader," Iza began.

"You may speak."

"This woman was wrong not to come to the leader when she learned what the young woman planned to do." Iza forgot to use the formal form of address as her emotions overcame her: "But Brun, she wanted a baby so much. No one thought she would ever conceive life, least of all her. How could the Spirit of the Cave Lion be overcome? She was so happy about it. Even though she suffered, she never complained. She almost died giving birth, Brun. Only the thought that her baby would die gave her strength at the end. She just couldn't bear to give him up, even if he was deformed. She was sure it was the only baby she would ever have. She was out of her head from the shock and the pain, she wasn't thinking straight. I know I have no right to ask, Brun, but I beg you to let her live."

"Why didn't you come to me before, Iza? If you thought begging for her life would do any good now, why didn't you come to me then? Have I been so unkind to her? I was not blind to her suffering. A man can avert his eyes to avoid looking into another man's hearth, but he cannot close his ears. There is not a person in this clan who does not know the pain Ayla suffered to give birth to her son. Do you think me so hardhearted, Iza? If you had come to me, told me how she felt, what she planned to do, don't you think I would have considered allowing her baby to live? I could have overlooked her threat to run and hide as the ravings of a woman out of her head. I would have examined the child. Even without a mate, if the deformity is not too gross, I might have allowed it. But you gave me no opportunity. You assumed to know what I would do. That's not like you, Iza.

"I have never known you to be derelict in your duty. You have always been an example for the other women. I can only blame your behavior on your illness. I know how sick you are, though you try to hide it. I respected your wishes and made no mention of it, but I was sure you were ready to walk in the world of the spirits last autumn. I was well aware Ayla believed this was her one chance to have a child. I suspect she is right. Yet, I saw her put all thoughts of herself aside when you were ill, Iza, and she pulled you through. I don't know how she did it. Maybe it was Mog-ur who placated the spirits that wanted you to join them and convinced them to allow you to stay, but it wasn't Mog-ur alone.

"I was ready to grant his request and allow her to become medicine woman. I had come to respect her as much as I once respected you. She has been an admirable woman, a model of dutiful obedience, in spite of the son of my mate. Yes, Iza, I am aware of Broud's harsh treatment of her. Even her one lapse early last summer was provoked by him in some way, though I don't fully understand how. It is unworthy of him to pit himself against a woman the way he does; Broud is a very brave and strong hunter and has no reason to feel his manhood is threatened by any female. But perhaps he did see something I overlooked. Perhaps he's right, I have been blind to her. Iza, if you had come to me before, I might have considered your request, I might have let her son live. It is too late now. When she returns on her child's naming day, both Ayla and her son will die."

The next day Ayla tried to make a fire. There were still a few sticks of dry wood left from her previous stay. She twirled a stick between her palms against another piece of wood, but she didn't have the endurance to maintain the sustained effort required to make it smolder, and it was fortunate for her that she couldn't. Droog and Crug found their way to the mountain meadow while she and the baby slept. They would have smelled a fire or the remains of one and found her. As it was, they walked so close to the cave that if the baby had whimpered in his sleep, they would have heard. But the entrance to the small hole in the rock wall was so well hidden by the thick old stand of hazelnut bushes, they didn't notice it.

But fortune smiled on her even more. The spring rains dripping sullenly from a leaden sky, turning the bank of the small creek into a sink of mud, and the ground of the meadow into a sodden marsh, and casting a pall over her spirits, washed away all traces of her. So expert were the hunters at tracking, they could identify the individual footprints of each member of the clan, and their sharp eyes would easily have seen broken-off shoots or disturbed earth from dug-up bulbs or roots if she had gathered any food. Her very weakness saved her from discovery.

When Ayla went out later and saw the men's footprints in the mud near the spring that gave rise to the creek, where they had stopped for a drink of water, her heart nearly stopped. It made her afraid to go outside. She started at every gust that shook the brush fronting her cave, and strained to hear imagined sounds.

The food she had brought with her was nearly gone. She searched through the baskets she had made to store food during the long, lonely stay of her temporary death curse. All she found were some dried nuts, rotten, and the droppings of small rodents, evidence that her store had been found and long since eaten. She found the rotten, dried remains of the surplus of food Iza had given her when she used the cave as shelter during her woman's curse—totally inedible.

Then she remembered the cache of dried deer meat in the stone pit at the back of the cave, from the deer she killed for a warm wrap. Ayla found the small mound of rocks and moved them. The preserved meat in the cache was undisturbed, but the easing of her tensions was short-lived. The branches at the mouth of the cave moved, and Ayla's heart raced.

"Uba!" she gestured with shocked surprise as the girl entered the cave. "How did you find me?"

"I followed you the day you left. I was so afraid something would happen to you. I brought you some food and some tea to make your milk flow. Mother made it."

"Does Iza know where I am?"

"No. She knows I do, though. I don't think she wants to

know or she'll have to tell Brun. Oh, Ayla, Brun is so mad at you. The men have been searching for you every day."

"I saw their footprints by the spring, but they didn't see the cave."

"Broud is bragging about how he knew all along how bad you were. I've hardly seen Creb at all since you left. He spends all day in the place of the spirits, and mother is so upset. She wants me to tell you not to come back," Uba said, her eyes wide with fear for the young woman.

"If she hasn't talked to you about me, how could Iza give you a message for me?" Ayla asked.

"She cooked extra last night and this morning, too. Not too much—I think she was afraid Creb would guess it was for you—but she didn't eat her share. Later she made the tea, then she started moaning and talking to herself like she was grieving for you, she's been grieving for you ever since you left, but she was looking right at me. She kept saying, 'If only someone could tell Ayla not to come back. My poor child, my poor daughter, she has no food, she's weak. She needs to make milk for her baby,' and things like that. Then she left the hearth. This waterbag was right next to the tea and the food was all wrapped.

"She must have seen me go when I followed you," Uba continued. "I wondered why she didn't scold me for being gone so long. Brun and Creb are both mad at her for not telling that you were going to hide. If they knew she had some idea how to find you and didn't tell them, I don't know what they'd do to her. But no one has asked me. No one pays much attention to children anyway, especially girls. Ayla, I know I should tell Creb where you are, but I don't want Brun to curse you, I don't want you to die."

Ayla could feel her heart beating in her ears. What have I done? She hadn't realized the extent of her weakness or how difficult it would be to survive alone with a small baby when she threatened to leave the clan. She had counted on going back on her baby's naming day. What am I going to do now? She picked up her baby and held him close. But I couldn't let you die, could I?

Uba looked sympathetically at the young mother who seemed to have forgotten she was there. "Ayla," she said tentatively. "Could I see him? I never did get a chance to see your baby.

"Oh, Uba, of course you can see him," she motioned, feeling bad that she had been ignoring the girl after she came all the way to bring Iza's message. She could get into trouble for it, too. If it was ever found out that Uba knew how to find Ayla and didn't tell, her punishment would be severe. It could ruin her life.

"Would you like to hold him?"

"Could I?"

Ayla put the baby in her lap. Uba started to move aside his swaddling, then looked up at Ayla for permission. The mother nodded.

"He doesn't look so bad, Ayla. He's not crippled like Creb. He's kind of skinny, but it's mostly his head that looks different. Not as different as you, though. You don't look like anyone else in the clan."

"That's because I wasn't born to the Clan. Iza found me when I was a little girl. She says I was born to the Others. I'm Clan now, though," Ayla said proudly, then her face dropped. "But not for long."

"Do you ever miss your mother? I mean your real mother, not Iza?" the girl asked.

"I don't remember any mother except Iza. I don't remember anything before I came to live with the clan." She suddenly blanched. "Uba, where will I go if I can't go back? Who will I live with? I'll never see Iza again, or Creb either. This is the last time I'll ever see you. But I didn't know what else to do. I couldn't let my baby die."

"I don't know, Ayla. Mother says Brun will lose face if you make him accept your son, that's why he's so mad. She says if a woman makes a man do something, the other men won't respect him anymore. Even if he curses you afterward, he'll lose face, just because you forced him to do something against his will. I don't want you to go away, Ayla, but you'll die if you come back."

The young woman looked at the stricken face of the girl, not realizing her own tear-streaked face held a similar expression. They both reached out to each other simultaneously.

"You'd better go, Uba, before you get in trouble," Ayla said. The girl gave the baby back to his mother and got up to leave. "Uba," Ayla called as the girl started to move the branches aside. "I'm glad you came to see me, just so I could talk to you once more. And tell Iza... tell my mother I love her." Tears were flowing again. "Tell Creb, too."

"I will, Ayla." The girl lingered for a moment longer. "I am going now," she said and quickly left the cave.

After Uba left, Ayla unwrapped the package of food she had brought. There wasn't much, but with the dried venison, it would last a few days, but what then? She couldn't think, her mind whirled in a maelstrom of confusion sucking her into a black hole of utter despair. Her plan had backfired. Not only her baby's life, but her own was in jeopardy. She ate, without tasting, and drank some tea, then lay down with her infant again, and slipped into the oblivion of sleep. Her body had its own needs, it demanded rest.

It was night when she woke again and drank the last of the cold tea. She decided to get more water while it was dark and there was no chance of being seen by searching men. She fumbled in the dark for the waterbag, and in a moment of panic lost her sense of direction in the stark blackness of the cave. The branches camouflaging the entrance, outlined eerily by a darkness not quite as black, reoriented her, and she quickly scrambled out.

A crescent moon, playing tag with racing clouds, shed little light, but her eyes, fully dilated by the black inside the cave, could see ghostly trees vaguely silhouetted in the dim glow. The whispering water of the spring, splashing over rocks in a miniature waterfall, reflected the shining sliver with a faint iridescence. Ayla was still weak, but she didn't get dizzy when she stood up anymore and walking was easier.

No men of the clan saw her as she bent near the spring under the concealing cover of darkness, but she was watched by other eyes more used to seeing by moonlight. Nocturnal prowlers and their night-feeding prey both drank from the same source as she. Ayla had never been so vulnerable since she wandered alone as a naked five-year-old child—not so much because of her weakness, but because she wasn't thinking in terms of survival. She wasn't on guard; her thoughts were turned inward. She would have been easy prey to any lurking predator drawn by the rich smells. But Ayla had made her presence felt before. Swift stones, not always lethal, but painful, had left their mark. Carnivores whose territory included the cave tended to shy away from it. It gave her an edge, a safety factor, a reserve of security from which she drew heavily now.

"There has to be some sign of her," Brun gestured angrily. "If she took food, it can't last forever; she's got to come out of hiding soon. I want every place that's been searched, searched again. If she's dead, I want to know it. Some scavenger would find her and there would be evidence of it. I want her found before the naming day. I will go to no Clan Gathering unless she's found."

"Now she's going to keep us from going to the Clan Gathering," Broud sneered. "Why was she ever accepted into the clan in the first place? She's not even Clan. If I were leader, I would never have accepted her. If I were leader, I wouldn't have let Iza keep her, I wouldn't even have let Iza pick her up. Why couldn't anyone else see her for what she is? This is not the first time she's been disobedient, you know. She has always flaunted the ways of the Clan, and gotten away with it. Did anyone stop her from bringing animals into the cave? Did anyone stop her from going off alone like no good Clan woman would think of doing? No wonder she spied on us when we were practicing. And what happened when she got caught using a sling? A *temporary* death curse, and when she got back, she was allowed to hunt! Imagine, a woman of the Clan hunting. Do you know what the other clans would think of that? It's not surprising we're not going to the Clan Gathering. Is it any wonder she'd think she could force her son on us?"

"Broud, we've all heard that before," Brun motioned wearily. "Her disobedience will not go unpunished, I promise you."

Broud's constant harping on the same theme was not only wearing on Brun's nerves, it was making an impression. The leader was beginning to question his own judgment, judgment that had to be based on adherence to long-standing traditions and customs that allowed little room for deviation. Yet, as Broud kept reminding him, Ayla had gotten away with a gradually worsening list of transgressions that did seem to lead to this unforgivable, deliberate act of defiance. He had been too generous with the outsider not born with an inherent sense of Clan rightness, too lenient with her. She took advantage of him. Broud was right, he should have been more strict, he should have made her conform, perhaps he never should have allowed the medicine woman to pick her up, but did the son of his mate have to keep on about it?

Broud's constant nagging made an impression on the rest of the hunters, too. Most were all but convinced Ayla had somehow blinded them with a smokescreen of deception and only Broud had seen her with clear eyes. When Brun was not around, the young man cast aspersions on the leader, hinting that he was too old to lead them effectively any longer. Brun's loss of face was a devastating blow to his confidence; he could sense the men's respect slipping away, and he could not bear to face a Gathering of the clans under such circumstances.

Ayla stayed in the cave, leaving only for water. Bundled in furs, she was warm enough even without a fire. The food Uba brought and the forgotten store of deer meat, dry as leather and tough to chew but highly concentrated nourishment, seasoned by hunger, made gathering or hunting unnecessary. It gave her time for the rest she needed. No longer drained by the demands of nurturing a not-quite-right fetus, her healthy young body, toughened by the years of strenuous physical exercise, was recuperating. She didn't need to sleep as much, but in some ways that was worse. Her troubled thoughts weighed on her constantly. At least when she was sleeping, she was free of anxiety.

Ayla was sitting near the mouth of the cave holding her sleeping son in her arms. White, watery fluid dribbling out of the corner of his mouth, and dripping from the other breast stimulated by his nursing, gave evidence that her milk had started to flow. The afternoon sun, hidden occasionally by fast-moving clouds, warmed the spot near the entrance with its dappled light. She was looking at her son, watching his regular breathing interrupted by twitching eye movements and little jerky spasms that started him making sucking motions with his mouth before relaxing again. She looked at him more closely, turning his head to see his profile.

Uba said you don't look so bad, Ayla thought; I don't think you do either. Just a little different. That's what Uba said, too. You just look different, but not as different as me. Ayla suddenly remembered the reflection of herself she had seen in the still pool. Not as different as me!

Ayla examined her son again, trying to remember the reflection of herself. My forehead bulges out like that, she thought, reaching up to touch her face. And that bone under his mouth, I've got one, too. But he's got brow ridges, and I haven't. Clan people have brow ridges. If I'm different, why shouldn't my baby be different? He should look like me, shouldn't he? He does, a little, but he looks a little like Clan babies, too. He looks like both. I wasn't born to the Clan, but my baby was, only he looks like me and them, like both mixed together.

I don't think you're deformed at all, my son. If you were born to me and born to the Clan, you should look like both. If the spirits were mixed together, shouldn't you look mixed together, too? That's the way you look, the way you should look. But whose totem started you? No matter whose it was, it must have had help. None of the men have a stronger totem than I have, except Creb. Did the Cave Bear start you, my baby? I live at Creb's hearth. No, it couldn't be. Creb says Ursus never allows his spirit to be swallowed by a woman, Ursus always chooses. Well, if it wasn't Creb, who else have I been close to?

Ayla got a sudden image of Broud hovering close to her. No! She shook her head, rejecting the thought. Not Broud. He didn't start *my* baby. She shuddered with revulsion thinking of the future leader and the way he had forced her to submit to his desires. I hate him! I hated it every time he came close to me. I'm so glad he doesn't bother me anymore. I hope he never, never wants to relieve his needs with me again. How does Oga stand it? How does any woman stand it? Why do men have needs like that? Why should a man want to put his organ in the place babies come from? That place should be just for babies, not for men's organs to make all sticky. Men's organs don't have anything to do with babies, she thought indignantly.

The incongruity of the meaningless act stayed in her mind, then a strange thought insinuated itself. Or do they? Could a man's organ have something to do with babies? Only women can have babies, but they have both girl and boy babies, she mused. I wonder, when a man puts his organ in the place babies come from, could he be getting it started? What if it's not the spirit of a man's totem, what if it's a man's organ that starts a baby? Wouldn't that mean the baby belongs to him, too? Maybe that's why men have that need, because they want to start a baby. Maybe that's why women like it, too. I've never seen a woman swallow a spirit, but I've seen men put their organs in women often. No one ever thought I'd have a baby, my totem is too strong, but I did anyway, and it started just about the time Broud was relieving his needs with me.

No! It's not true! That would mean my baby is Broud's baby, too, Ayla thought with horror. Creb is right. He's always right. I swallowed a spirit that fought with my totem and defeated him, maybe more than one, maybe all of them. She clutched her baby fiercely as though trying to keep him to herself. You're my baby, not Broud's! It wasn't even the spirit of Broud's totem. The infant was startled by the sudden movement and began to cry. She rocked him gently until he quieted.

Maybe my totem knew how much I wanted to have a baby and let himself be defeated. But why would my totem let me have a baby when he knew it would have to die? A baby that is part me and part Clan is always going to look different; they'll always say my babies are deformed. Even if I had a mate, my babies wouldn't look right. I'll never be able to keep one; they'll all have to die. What difference does it make, I'm going to die anyway. We're both going to die, my son.

Ayla held her baby close, rocking him and crooning while tears streamed down her face unnoticed. What am I going to do, my baby? What am I going to do? If I go back on your naming day, Brun will curse me. Iza said not to come back, but where can I go? I'm not strong enough to hunt yet, and even if I were, what would I do with you? I couldn't take you with me; I couldn't hunt with a baby. You might cry and warn the animals away, but I couldn't leave you alone. Maybe I wouldn't have to hunt, I can find food. But we need other things, too—wraps and furs and cloaks and foot coverings.

And where will I find a cave to live in? I can't stay here, there's too much snow in winter and it's too close; they'd find me sooner or later. I could go away, but I might not find a cave, and the men would track me and bring me back. Even if I did get away and found a cave and stored enough food to last through next winter, and even managed to hunt a little, we'd still be alone. You need more people than just me. Who would you play with? Who would teach you to hunt? And what if something happened to me? Who would take care of you then? You'd be all alone, just as I was before Iza found me.

I don't want you to be alone; I don't want to be alone, either. I want to go home, Ayla sobbed, burying her head in her infant's swaddling. I want to see Uba again, and Creb. I want my mother. But I can't go home. Brun's mad at me. I made him lose face and he's going to curse me. I didn't know it would make him lose face, I just didn't want you to die. Brun's not so bad; he let me hunt. What if I didn't try to force him to accept you? What if I just begged him to let you live? If I went back now, he wouldn't lose face; there's still time, there are two fingers left before your naming day. Maybe then he wouldn't be so angry.

What if he is? What if he says no? What if they take you away from me? I wouldn't want to live if they took you away now. If you have to die, I want to die too. If I go back and Brun says you have to die, I'll beg him to curse me. I'll die too. I won't let you go back to the world of the spirits alone, my baby; I promise if you have to go, I'll go with you. I'm going right now and beg Brun to let me keep you. What else can I do?

Ayla began throwing things into her collecting basket. She wrapped the baby in the carrying cloak and both of them in her fur wrap and pushed aside the branches that hid the small cave. As she was crawling out, her eyes fell on something glittering in the sun. A sparkling gray rock lay at her feet. She picked it up. It wasn't just one rock, but three small nodules of iron pyrite stuck together. She turned it over in her hand and watched the fool's gold glitter. As often as she had gone in and out of the small cave over the years, she had never seen the unusual stone before.

Ayla clutched it in her hand and closed her eyes. Can this be a sign? A sign from my totem?

"Great Cave Lion," she motioned. "Did I make the right decision? Are you telling me I should go back now? O Cave Lion, let this be a sign. Let this be a sign that you have found me worthy, that it was all another test. Let this be a sign that my baby will live."

Her fingers shook as she untied the knots of the small leather bag she wore around her neck. She added the oddly shaped glittering stone to the red-stained oval of mammoth tusk, the fossil cast of a gastropod, and the lump of red ochre. Her heart pounding with fear, and one desperate hope, Ayla started down to the cave of the clan.

21

Uba came running into the cave gesticulating wildly. "Mother! Mother! Ayla's back!"

Iza's face drained. "No! It can't be. Is the baby with her? Uba, did you go to see her? Did you tell her?"

"Yes, mother, I saw her. I told her how mad Brun was, I told her not to come back," the girl motioned.

Iza hurried to the entrance and saw Ayla walking slowly toward Brun. She crumpled to the ground at his feet, leaning forward over her infant protectively.

"She's early, she must have misjudged the time," Brun motioned to the magician hurriedly shuffling out of the cave.

"She didn't misjudge, Brun. She knows it's early, she came back on purpose," Mog-ur signaled.

The leader eyed the old man, wondering how he could be so positive. Then he glanced down at the young woman and back at Mog-ur a little apprehensively.

"Are you sure the charms you made to protect us will work? She should still be isolated, her female curse cannot be over yet, it's always much longer after giving birth."

"The charms are strong, Brun, made from the bones of Ursus. You are protected. You may 'see' her," the magician replied.

Brun turned back and stared at the young woman huddled over her infant, quaking with fear. I should curse her right now, he thought angrily. But it's not the child's naming day. If Mog-ur is right, why did she come back early? And with the baby? He must still be alive or she wouldn't have him with her. Her disobedience is unforgivable, but why did she come back early? His curiosity was too much for him; he tapped her on the shoulder.

"This unworthy woman has been disobedient," Ayla began with the silent, formal motions, not looking directly at him, and not sure he would respond. She knew she shouldn't be trying to talk to a man, she should be in isolation, but he had tapped her shoulder. "This woman would speak to the leader, if it were allowed."

"You don't deserve to speak, woman, but Mog-ur has invoked protection in your case. If I want you to speak, the spirits will allow it. You are right, you have been very disobedient, what do you have to say for yourself?"

"This woman is grateful. This woman knows the customs of the Clan; she should have disposed of the infant as the medicine woman told her, but she ran away. She was going to return on her son's naming day so the leader would have to accept him into the clan."

"You returned too soon," Brun gestured triumphantly. "It is not the naming day yet. I can command the medicine woman to take him from you now." The tension that had knotted Brun's back since Ayla left relaxed as he made the motions and the full realization hit him. Only if the child lived seven days would tradition force him to accept the baby. The full time had not elapsed, he did not have to take him, he had not lost face, he was in command again.

Ayla's arms clutched involuntarily at the baby held to her breast with the cloak, then she continued: "This woman knows it is not yet the naming day. This woman realized it was wrong for her to try to make the leader accept her son. It is not a woman's place to decide if her child should live or die. Only the leader can make that decision. That is why this woman returned."

Brun looked at Ayla's earnest face. At least she came to her senses in time, he thought. "If you know the customs of the Clan, why did you return with a child that is deformed? Iza said you were unable to perform your duty as a mother; are you ready to give him up now? Do you want the medicine woman to do it for you?"

Ayla hesitated, hovering over her son. "This woman will give him up if the leader commands it." She made the signs slowly, painfully, forcing herself, feeling as though a knife were twisting in her heart. "But this woman promised her son she would not let him go alone to the world of the spirits. If the leader decides the baby may not live, she asks him to curse her." She slipped out of the formal language and pleaded, "I beg you, Brun, I beg you to let my son live. If he has to die, I don't want to live."

Ayla's fervent plea surprised the leader. Some women, he knew, wanted to keep their babies in spite of malformations and disfigurements, but most were relieved to dispose of them as quickly and quietly as possible. A deformed child stigmatized the mother. It advertised a certain inadequacy, an inability to produce a perfect baby. It made her less than desirable. Even if the deformity was small enough not to pose a major handicap, there were considerations of status and future mates. A mother's later years could be difficult if her children or her children's mates could not take care of her. Though she would never starve, her life could be miserable. Ayla's request was unprecedented. Mother love was strong, but strong enough to follow her child to the next world?

"You want to die with a deformed baby? Why?" Brun asked.

"My son is not deformed," Ayla motioned with the barest trace of defiance. "He's just different. I'm different, I don't look like people of the Clan. My son is, too. Any baby I ever have will look like him, if my totem is ever defeated again. I'll never have a baby that will be allowed to live. I don't want to live either, if all my babies have to die."

Brun looked at Mog-ur. "If a woman swallows the spirit of a man's totem, shouldn't the baby look like him?"

"Yes, it should. But don't forget, she has a male totem, too. Perhaps that's why it fought so hard. The Cave Lion may have wanted to be part of the new life. There could be something to what she says. I would have to meditate on it."

"But the child is still deformed?"

"It often happens when a woman's totem refuses to give in completely. It makes her pregnancy difficult and deforms the baby," Mog-ur replied. "I'm more surprised the child was male. If a woman's totem puts up a strong fight, it usually makes the child female. But we haven't seen him, Brun. Perhaps we should examine him."

Should he bother? Brun wondered. Why not just curse her now and dispose of the baby? Ayla's early return and penitent groveling eased Brun's wounded pride, but he was far from mollified. He had come too close to losing face because of her, and it wasn't the first problem she had caused him. She had returned, but what would she do next? And then there was the Clan Gathering, as Broud had reminded him so many times.

It was one thing to let Iza pick up a strange child and take her into his clan. But Brun had cause to reflect often lately on the impression it would make on the other clans to arrive at the meeting with a woman born to the Others. He wondered, looking back, how he had made so many decisions that were so unorthodox. Each one, at the time, didn't seem too unreasonable. Even allowing the woman to hunt was logical then. But, added together, and seeing them from an outsider's point of view, the effect was an overwhelming breach of custom. Ayla had been disobedient, she deserved to be punished, and cursing her would eliminate all his worries.

But a death curse was a serious threat to the clan, and he had already exposed them once to evil spirits because of her. Her voluntary return had prevented his disgrace—Iza was probably right, she had lost her mind temporarily from the shock and the pain. He did tell Iza he would have considered a request to let the baby live, if he had been asked. Well, she did ask. She came back knowing the full extent of her offense, knowing it and willing to face it, begging for the life of her child. He could at least examine the baby. Brun did not like making hasty decisions. He gave Ayla an abrupt signal, motioning toward Creb's hearth, then strode away.

Ayla ran into Iza's waiting arms. If nothing else, at least she would see the woman who was the only mother she knew, one last time.

"You've all had a chance to examine him," Brun said. "Under normal circumstances, I would not bother you; it would be a simple decision. But I want to know your opinions; a death curse is a strong possibility, and I don't like exposing the clan to evil spirits again. If I find the boy is acceptable, I can hardly curse the mother. Without her, another woman would have to take him, he'd have to live with one of you whose mate has a nursing child. If the baby is allowed to live, the punishment for Ayla should be less severe. Tomorrow is the naming day; I need to make the decision soon, and Mog-ur will need some time to prepare for a curse, if that is to be her punishment. It must be done before the sun rises in the morning."

"It's not only his head, Brun," Crug started. Ika was still nursing her youngest and Crug had no desire to have Ayla's infant added to his hearth, farfetched though the possibility was. "That's bad enough, but he can't even hold it up. It has to be supported. What will he be like when he's a man? How will he hunt? He'll never be able to provide for himself; he'd only be a burden on the whole clan."

"Do you think there's any chance his neck will get stronger?" Droog asked. "If Ayla dies, she will take part of Ona's spirit with her. Aga would take her son—she feels she owes Ayla that much—though I don't think she really wants a deformed baby. If she's willing, I suppose I would be, too, but not if he will burden the whole clan."

"His neck is so long and scrawny and his head is so big, I don't think it will ever be strong enough," Crug commented.

"I won't have him at my hearth for any reason; I wouldn't even bother to ask Oga how she feels about it. He's not fit to be a sibling to her sons; it would make him a brother to Brac and Grev—I won't allow that. Brac will survive even if she does take a little piece of his spirit with her. I don't know why you're even considering it, Brun. You were ready to curse her. Just because she came running back a little early, you're ready to take her back, and talking about taking her defective son besides," Broud gestured bitterly.

"She defied you by running away; coming back doesn't make her disobedience any less. What's there to discuss? The baby is deformed, and she should be cursed. That's the end of it. Why do you always waste our time with these meetings about her? If I were leader, she would have been cursed already. She's disobedient, she's insolent, and she's a bad influence on the other women. How else can you explain Iza's misbehavior?" Broud was working himself up to a fury, his gestures becoming more excited. "She deserves to be cursed, Brun, how can you think of anything else? Why can't you see it? Are you blind? She's never been any good. If I were leader, she would never have been accepted in the first place. If I were leader..."

"But you're not leader yet, Broud," Brun returned coldly, "and you're not likely to be if you can't keep yourself under better control. She's only a woman, Broud, why do you feel so threatened by her? What can she possibly do to you? She must obey you, she has no choice. 'If you were leader, if you were leader,' is that all you can say? What kind of leader is so anxious to kill a woman that he's willing to jeopardize the whole clan?" Brun was on the edge of losing control himself. He had put up with all he could take from the son of his mate.

The men were shocked and uneasy. An open battle between the present leader and the future one was distressing. Broud had overstepped his bounds to be sure, but they were accustomed to his outbursts. It was Brun who caused the dismay; they had never seen the leader so close to losing his control. And he had never before openly questioned the qualifications of the son of his mate to follow him as leader.

For a tense moment, the two men locked eyes in a battle of wills. Broud looked down first. No longer jeopardized by loss of face, Brun was firmly in control again. He was leader, and not ready to step down. It put the young man on his guard; his footing wasn't as secure as he thought. Broud fought down the feeling of impotence and bitter frustration that welled up inside. He still favors her, Broud thought. How can he? I'm the son of his mate, she's just an ugly woman. Broud struggled to remain calm, swallowing the bitterness that rankled his soul.

"This man regrets he has caused the leader to misunderstand him," Broud motioned formally. "This man's concern is for the hunters he must lead one day, if the present leader thinks this man is capable of leading hunters. How can a man hunt if his head wobbles?"

Brun stared hard and angrily at the young man. There was an inconsistency in the meaning of the formal gestures and the unconscious signals of expression and posture. Broud's overly polite response was sarcastic, and it irritated the leader far more than direct disagreement. Broud was trying to hide his feelings and Brun knew it. But Brun was feeling shame at his own outburst. He knew it was prompted by Broud's increasingly derogatory remarks that cast doubt on his judgment. They had rubbed a sore spot on his pride. But that was no excuse for losing his own self-control enough to disparage the son of his mate so openly.

"You've made your point, Broud," Brun signaled stiffly. "I realize the baby will grow up to be more a burden to the leader who follows me and the one after, but the decision is still mine. I will do what I think best. I have not said the baby will be accepted, Broud, or that the woman will not be cursed. My concern is for the clan, not her or her child. A death curse can put everyone in danger; lingering evil spirits can bring bad luck, especially since they've been released before. I think the child is too deformed to live, but Ayla is blind to her baby's affliction. She can't see it. It may be that her strong desire to have a child has affected her mind. When she returned, she begged me to curse her if her son was not acceptable. I asked for your opinions because I wanted to know if anyone else saw something about the infant that I didn't. A death curse to punish her or to grant her request, it is still not a decision to make lightly."

Broud's frustration eased. Maybe Brun isn't favoring her after all, he thought. "You're right, Brun," he said contritely, "a leader should think of the dangers to his clan. This young man is grateful for such a wise leader to instruct him."

Brun felt his tension melt. He hadn't seriously considered replacing Broud, not ever. He was still the son of his mate, the child of his heart. Self-control isn't always easy, Brun thought, remembering his own irritation. Broud just has a little more trouble than most, but he is improving.

"I'm glad you understand that, Broud. When you are leader, you will be responsible for the safety and welfare of the clan." Brun's comment not only let Broud know he was still heir apparent, it relieved the rest of the hunters. They wanted the security of knowing that the traditional rightness of the clan hierarchy, and their own place in it, would be maintained. Nothing disturbed them quite so much as uncertainty about the future.

"It is the welfare of the clan I was thinking about," Broud motioned. "I don't want a man in my clan who can't hunt. What good will Ayla's son ever be? Her disobedience does deserve severe punishment, and if she wants to be cursed, it will satisfy her, too. We'd be better off without them. Ayla defied Clan traditions, deliberately. She doesn't deserve to live. Her son is so deformed, he doesn't deserve to live."

There was a general round of agreement. Brun detected a certain element of insincerity in Broud's reasoned argument, but he let it go. The animosity between them had dissipated and he didn't want to stir it up again. Open strife with the son of his mate disturbed Brun as much as it did the others.

The leader felt he should add his agreement, but something made him hesitate. It is the right thing to do, he thought, she's been a problem from the beginning. Of course Iza will be upset, but I didn't promise to spare either of them, I only said I would consider it. I didn't even say I would look at the baby if she returned; who ever expected her to return, anyway? That's just the problem, I never know what to expect from her. If the grief weakens Iza, well, there's still Uba. After all, she was the one born to the line, and she can get more training from the medicine women at the Clan Gathering.

If the part of Brac's spirit she carries dies with Ayla, is it really so much of him to lose? Broud isn't worried about it, why should I worry? He's right, she does deserve the severest punishment, doesn't she? Such strong love for a baby isn't even normal. What do old women's tales prove? She can't even see that her son is deformed; she must be out of her mind. Can there be that much pain in giving birth? Men have suffered worse, haven't they? Some have walked all the way back after a painful hunting injury. Of course, she's only a woman, she can't be expected to bear as much pain. I wonder how far she went? The cave she mentioned can't be that far, can it? She nearly died giving birth, she was too weak to travel very far, but why couldn't we find it?

Besides, if she's allowed to live, I'll have to take her to the Clan Gathering. What would the other clans think? It would be worse if I allow her deformed child to live. It's the right thing to do, everyone thinks so. Maybe there wouldn't be so much of a problem with Broud, maybe he could control himself better if she wasn't around. He's a fearless hunter; he'd make a good leader if only he had a little more sense of responsibility, just a little more self-control. Maybe I should do it for Broud's sake. For the son of my mate, it might be better if she was gone. It is the right thing to do, yes, it really is; it's the right thing to do, isn't it?

"I have reached my decision," Brun signaled. "Tomorrow is the naming day. At first light, before the sun breaks ..."

"Brun!" Mog-ur interrupted. He had kept himself out of the discussion; none of them had seen much of him since the birth of Ayla's child. He had spent most of the time in his small annex searching his soul for an explanation of Ayla's actions. He knew how hard she had struggled to accept the ways of the Clan, and he thought she had succeeded. He was convinced there was something else, something he hadn't realized that had driven her to such an extreme.

"Before you commit yourself, Mog-ur would speak."

Brun stared at the magician. His expression was enigmatic, as usual. Brun had never been able to read Mog-ur's face. *What can he say that I have not considered? I've made up my mind to curse her and he knows it.*

"Mog-ur may speak," he motioned.

"Ayla has no mate, but I have always provided for her, I am responsible for her. If you will allow it, I would speak as her mate."

"Speak if you will, Mog-ur, but what can you add? I have already considered her strong love for the child and the pain and suffering she went through to have him. I understand how difficult it may be for Iza; I know it may weaken her too much. I've thought of every possible reason for excusing her actions, but the facts remain. She defied Clan customs. Her baby is not acceptable to the men. Broud made it clear neither one deserves to live."

Mog-ur pulled himself up to his feet, then threw his staff aside. Wrapped in his heavy bearskin cloak, the magician was an imposing figure. Only the older men, and Brun, ever knew him as anything but Mog-ur. The Mog-ur, the holiest of all the men who interceded with the world of the spirits, the most powerful magician of the Clan. When moved to eloquence during a ceremony, he was a charismatic, awe-inspiring protector. It was he who braved the invisible forces far more fearsome than any charging animal, forces that could turn the bravest hunter into a quaking coward. There was not a man present who did not feel more secure knowing it was he who was the magician of their clan, not a man who hadn't stood in fear of his power and magic at some time in his life, and only one, Goov, who dared to think of trading places with him.

Mog-ur, alone, stood between the men of the clan and the terrible unknown, and he became part of it by association. It imbued him with a subtle aura that carried over into his secular life. Even when he sat within the boundaries of his hearthstones, surrounded by his women, he was not really thought of as a man. He was more than, other than; he was Mog-ur.

As the dread holy man fixed a baleful eye on each man in turn, there wasn't one, including Broud, who didn't squirm in the depths of his soul with the sudden realization that the woman they had condemned to die lived at his hearth. Mog-ur seldom brought the force of his presence to bear outside his function, but he did then. He turned last to Brun.

"A woman's mate has the right to speak for the life of a deformed child. I am asking you to spare the life of Ayla's son, and for his sake, I am asking that her life be spared, too."

All the reasons Brun had so recently considered as rationale for sparing her life seemed to have far more weight now, and the arguments for her death, insignificant. He almost agreed on the force of Mog-ur's request alone, and it attested to the strength of his own character that he did not. But he was leader. He could not capitulate so easily in front of all his men, and despite a strong desire to give in to the force of the powerful man of magic, he held firm.

When Mog-ur saw the look of firm resolution replace the moment of indecision, the magician seemed to change before Brun's eyes. The otherworldly character left him. He became a crippled old man in a bearskin cloak, standing as straight as his one good leg would hold him without his staff for support. When he spoke, it was with the common gestures punctuated with the gruff words of everyday speech. His face held a determined, yet strangely vulnerable look.

"Brun, ever since Ayla was found, she has lived at my hearth. I think everyone will agree that women and children look to the man of their hearth to set the standard for men of the clan. He is their model, their example of what a man should be. I have been Ayla's example, I have set the standard in her eyes.

"I am deformed, Brun. Is it so strange that a woman who grew up with a deformed man as her model would find it difficult to understand a deformity in her child? I lack an eye and an arm, half my body is shriveled and wasted. I am half a man, yet from the beginning, Ayla has seen me as whole. Her son's body is sound. He has two eyes, two good arms, two good legs. How can she be expected to acknowledge any deformity in him?

"She was my responsibility to train. I must take the blame for her faults. It was I who overlooked her minor deviations from Clan ways. I even convinced you to accept them, Brun. I am Mog-ur. You rely on me to interpret the wishes of the spirits, and you have come to rely on my judgment in other ways. I did not think we were so wrong. Sometimes it was difficult for her, but I thought she had become a good Clan woman. I think now I was too lenient with her. I did not make her responsibilities clear. I seldom reprimanded her and I never cuffed her, I often let her go her own way. Now she must pay for my lack. But Brun, I could not be harsher with her.

"I never took a mate. I could have chosen a woman and she would have had to live with me, but I did not. Do you know why? Brun, do you know how women look at me? Do you know how women avoid me? I had the same need to relieve myself as any other man when I was young, but I learned to control it when women turned their back so they would not see me make the signal. I would not force myself, my crippled, deformed body, on a woman who shrunk from me, who turned away with disgust at the sight of me.

"But Ayla never turned from me. From the first, she reached out to touch me. She had no fear of me, no revulsion. She gave me her affection freely, she hugged me. Brun, how could I scold her?

"I have lived with this clan since my birth, but I never learned how to hunt. How can a one-armed cripple hunt? I was a burden, I was taunted, I was called woman. Now I am Mog-ur and no one ridicules, but no manhood ceremony was ever held for me. Brun, I am not half a man, I am no man at all. Only Ayla respected me, loved me—not as a magician, but as a man, as a whole man. And I love her as the child of the mate I never had."

Creb shrugged off the cloak he wore to cover his lopsided, malformed, wasted body and held out the stump of an arm he always hid.

"Brun, this is the man Ayla saw as whole. This is the man who set her standard. This is the man she loves and compares with her son. Look at me, my brother! Did I deserve to live? Does Ayla's son deserve to live less?"

The clan started gathering outside the cave in the dim half-light of predawn. A fine misty drizzle cast a glistening sheen on rocks and trees and collected in tiny droplets in the hair and beards of the people. Thin wispy tendrils snaking down from fog-shrouded mountains clung to hollows, and thicker masses of the ethereal vapor obscured all but the nearest objects. The ridge to the east rose indistinctly from a nebulous sea of mist in the fading darkness, wavering vaguely just on the edge of visibility.

Ayla lay awake on her furs in the darkened cave, watching Iza and Uba moving silently about the hearth stoking coals in the fireplace and putting water on to boil for a morning tea. Her baby was beside her making sucking noises in his sleep. She hadn't slept all night. Her first joy at seeing Iza had quickly given way to a desolate anxiety. Initial attempts at conversation broke down early and the three females of Creb's hearth spent the entire long day after Ayla's return within its boundary stones communicating their despair with anguished looks.

Creb had not set foot inside his domain, but Ayla caught his eye once as he left the small adjoining cave to join the men in the meeting Brun had called. He looked away quickly from her silent appeal, but not before she had seen the look of love and pity in his soft liquid eye. She and Iza exchanged a tremulous, knowing glance when they saw Creb hurry into the place of the spirits after a talk with Brun held in a remote section of the cave in guarded gestures. Brun had made his decision and Creb went to prepare for his part in it. They did not see the magician again.

Iza brought the young mother her tea in the familiar bone cup that had been hers for several years, then sat quietly beside her as she sipped it. Uba joined them, but she could offer no more than her presence for comfort, either.

"Nearly everyone is out. We'd better go," Iza signaled, taking the cup from the young woman. Ayla nodded. She got up and wrapped her son in the carrying cloak, then picked up her fur wrap from the bed and threw it over her shoulders. Eyes glistening with moisture that threatened to overflow, Ayla looked at Iza, then Uba, and with an aching cry, reached out to both of them. All three huddled in a clinging embrace. Then, with a heavy heart and dragging step, Ayla walked out of the cave.

Staring down at the ground, seeing an occasional heelmark, the imprint of toes, the blurred outline of a foot encased in a loose leather covering, Ayla had the uncanny sensation that it was two years before and she was following Creb out of the cave to face her doom. He should have cursed me forever that time, she thought. I must have been born to be cursed; why else must I go through this again? This time I will go to the world of the spirits. I know a plant that will make us both go to sleep and never wake up, not in this world. I will get it over quickly, and we'll walk in the next world together.

She reached Brun, dropped to the ground, and stared at the familiar feet wrapped in muddy foot coverings. It was getting lighter, the sun would soon be up. Brun would have to hurry, she thought, and felt a tap on her shoulder. Slowly, she looked up at Brun's bearded face. He began without preliminaries.

"Woman, you have willfully defied the customs of the Clan and you must be punished," he motioned sternly. Ayla nodded. It was true. "Ayla, woman of the Clan, you are cursed. No one will see you, no one will hear you. You will endure the full isolation of the woman's curse. You may not go beyond the boundaries of your provider's hearth until the next moon is in the same phase as now."

Ayla gazed at the stern-faced leader with astonished disbelief. The woman's curse! Not the death curse! Not utter and complete ostracism, but nominal isolation confined to Creb's hearth. What did it matter that no one else in the clan would acknowledge her existence for an entire moon, she would still have Iza and Uba and Creb. And afterward, she could rejoin the clan just like any other woman. But Brun was not through.

"As further punishment, you are forbidden to hunt, or even mention hunting, until the clan returns from the Clan Gathering. Until the leaves have dropped from the trees, you will have no freedom to go anywhere that is not essential. When you look for plants of healing magic, you will tell me where you are going and you will return promptly. You will always ask my permission before you leave the area of the cave. And you will show me the location of the cave where you hid."

"Yes, yes, of course, anything," Ayla was nodding in agreement. She was floating in a warm cloud of euphoria, but the next words of the leader pierced her mood like an icy shaft of cold lightning, drowning her elation in a deluge of despair.

"There is still the problem of your deformed son who was the cause of your disobedience. You must never again try to force a man, much less a leader, against his will. No woman should ever try to force a man," Brun said, then gave a signal. Ayla clutched her infant desperately and looked in the same direction that Brun was looking. She couldn't let them take him, she couldn't. She saw Mog-ur limping out of the cave. When she saw him throw his bearskin aside, revealing a red-stained wicker bowl held firmly between the stump of his arm and his waist, incredulous joy flushed her face. She turned back to Brun hesitantly, unsure if what she thought could possibly be true.

"But a woman may ask," Brun finished. "Mog-ur is waiting, Ayla. Your son must have a name if he is to be a member of the clan."

Ayla scrambled to her feet and raced to the magician, taking her baby from her cloak as she dropped at his feet and holding the naked infant up to him. His first squall at being taken from his mother's warm breast and exposed to the damp cool air was greeted by the first rays of the sun breaking over the top of the ridge, burning through the misty haze.

A name! She hadn't even thought about a name, she hadn't even wondered what name Creb would choose for her son. In formal gestures, Mog-ur called the spirits of the clan's totems to attend, then reached into the bowl and scooped out a dab of red paste.

"Durc," he said loudly above the lusty cries of the cold and angry baby. "The boy's name is Durc." Then he drew a red line from the junction of the baby's supraorbital ridges to the tip of his smallish nose.

"Durc," Alya repeated, holding her son close to warm him. Durc, she thought, like Durc of the legend. Creb knows that's always been my favorite. It was not a common Clan name and many were surprised. But perhaps the name, dredged from the depths of antiquity and fraught with dubious connotations, was appropriate for a boy whose life had hung in the balance of such uncertain beginnings.

"Durc," Brun said. He was the first to file past. Ayla thought she saw a glimmer of tenderness from the stern, proud leader as she looked at him in gratitude. Most of the faces were a blur seen through tear-filled eyes. As hard as she tried, she could not control them, and kept her head down in an effort to conceal her wet eyes. I can't believe it, I just can't believe it, she thought. Is it really true? You have a name, my baby? Brun accepted you, my son? I'm not dreaming? She remembered the glittering nodules of iron pyrite she had found and put in her amulet. It was a sign. Great Cave Lion, it was truly a sign. Of all the artifacts in her amulet, she treasured that one the most.

"Durc," she heard Iza say and looked up. The joy on the woman's face was no less than Ayla's for all that her eyes were dry.

"Durc," Uba said, and added with a quick gesture, "I'm so glad."

"Durc." It was said with a sneer. Ayla glanced up in time to see Broud turn away. She suddenly remembered the strange idea about the way men started babies she had while she was hiding in the small cave, and shuddered at the thought that somehow Broud was responsible for the conception of her son. She had been too busy to notice the battle of wills between Brun and Broud. The young man was going to refuse to acknowledge the newest member of the clan, and only a direct order from the leader finally forced the issue. Ayla watched him walk away from the group with clenched fists and tense shoulders.

How could he? Broud walked into the woods to get away from the hated scene. How could he? He kicked a log in vain attempt to vent his frustration, sending it rolling down a slope. How could he? He picked up a stout branch and sent it crashing into a tree. How could he? How could he? Broud's mind kept repeating the phrase as he smashed his fist again and again into a moss-covered bank. How could he let her live and accept her baby both? How could he do it?

22

"Iza! Iza! Come quick! It's Durc!" Ayla grabbed the medicine woman's arm and dragged her toward the entrance to the cave.

"What's wrong?" the woman motioned, hurrying to keep up. "Is he choking again? Is he hurt?"

"No, he's not hurt. Look!" Ayla gestured proudly when they reached Creb's hearth. "He's holding his head up!"

The infant was lying on his stomach looking up at the two women with large solemn eyes that were losing the dark, indistinct color of newborns and becoming the deep brown shade of people of the Clan. His head bobbed with the effort, then dropped back down on the fur blanket. He shoved his fist in his mouth and began sucking noisily, oblivious of the stir his efforts had caused.

"If he can do it this young, he'll be able to support it when he grows up, won't he?" Ayla pleaded.

"Don't build your hopes up yet," Iza replied, "but it is a good sign."

Creb shuffled into the cave, staring into space with the unfocused, faraway look characteristic of him when lost in thought.

"Creb!" Ayla called, running up to him. Jolted back to reality, he looked up. "Durc held his head up, didn't he, Iza?" The medicine woman nodded in agreement.

"Hhmmf," he grunted. "If he's getting that strong, I think it's time."

"Time for what?"

"I've been thinking I should have a totem ceremony for him. He's a little young, but I've had some strong impressions. His totem has been making himself known to me. There's no reason to wait. Later, everyone will be busy getting ready to leave, and I should do it before the Clan Gathering. It might be unlucky for him to travel if his totem doesn't have a home." Seeing the medicine woman reminded him of something else. "Iza, do you have enough roots for the ceremony? I don't know how many clans will be there. Last time one of the clans that moved to a cave farther east was thinking of going to a Clan Gathering south of the mountains. It would be a little farther away for them but easier traveling. Their old mog-ur was against it, but his acolyte wanted to go. Make sure you bring plenty."

"I won't be going to the Clan Gathering, Creb." Her disappointment was obvious. "I can't travel that far, I'll have to stay behind."

Of course, what's wrong with me, he thought, looking at the thin, nearly white-haired medicine woman. Iza can't go. Why didn't I think of that before? She's too sick. I thought she was going to leave us last fall; I don't know how Ayla pulled her through. But what about the ceremony? Only the women of Iza's line know the secret of the special drink. Uba's too young; it has to be a woman. Ayla! What about Ayla? Iza could teach her before we leave. It's time she was made a medicine woman anyway.

Creb watched the young woman as she stooped to pick up her son and suddenly saw her more critically than he had for years. But will they accept her? He tried to see her as the people of other clans would see her. Her golden hair hung loose around her flat face, tucked behind her ears and parted haphazardly at the center, exposing her bulging forehead. Her body was definitely a woman's, but slender except for a slightly flaccid stomach. Her legs were long and straight, and when she stood up she towered over him.

She does not look like a Clan woman, he thought. She's going to get a lot of attention, and not much of it favorable, I'm afraid. We just might have to forget that ceremony. The other mog-urs might not accept the drink if Ayla makes it. But it would not hurt to try. If only Uba were a little older. Maybe Iza could train them both, though I don't think they'll be willing to accept a girl any more than a woman born to the Others. I think I'll go talk to Brun. If I'm going to call the spirits for Durc's totem ceremony, we might as well make Ayla a medicine woman at the same time.

"I must see Brun," Creb motioned abruptly, and started toward the leader's hearth. He turned back to Iza. "I think you should teach both Ayla and Uba to make the drink, but I'm not sure it will do any good."

"Iza, I can't find the bowl you gave me for the medicine woman of the host clan," Ayla gestured frantically after pawing through piles of food, furs, and implements stacked on the ground near her sleeping place. "I've looked everywhere."

"You already packed it, Ayla. Settle down, child. There's still time. Brun won't be ready to leave until he's through eating. You'd better sit down and eat, yourself, your mush is getting cold. Uba, you too." Iza shook her head. "I've never seen such carryings-on. We went over everything last night, it's all ready."

Creb was sitting on a mat, Durc in his lap, watching the last-minute commotion with amusement. "They're not any different from you, Iza. Why don't you sit down and eat?"

"I'll have plenty of time after you leave," she replied. Creb propped the baby up against his shoulder. Durc looked around from his new vantage point. "Look how strong that baby's neck is," Iza remarked. "He doesn't have any trouble holding his head up now. It's hard to believe. Ever since his totem cermony, it's been getting stronger all the time. Let me take him, I won't be able to hold him all summer."

"Perhaps that's why the Gray Wolf wanted me to do it so soon," Creb motioned. "He wanted to help the boy."

Creb sat back and watched the small brood over which he was patriarch. Though he kept it to himself, he had often longed for a family like the other men. Now, in his old age, he had two doting women who did everything they could to make him comfortable, a girl who was following in their footsteps, and a healthy baby boy to cuddle the way he had done with the two girls. He had talked to Brun about the boy's training. The leader could not allow a male member of his clan to grow up without the necessary skills. Brun had accepted the child knowing he would be living at Creb's hearth and felt responsible for him. Ayla was grateful when Brun announced at Durc's totem ceremony that he would personally take charge of the baby's training if he became strong enough to hunt. She could think of no better man to train her son.

The Gray Wolf is a good totem for the boy, Creb mused, but it makes me wonder. Some wolves run with the pack and some are loners. Which one is Durc's totem?

When everything was packed and secured in bundles, and loaded on the backs of the young woman and the girl, they all trooped out of the cave together. Iza gave the baby a last hug while he nuzzled her neck, helped Ayla wrap him in the carrying cloak, and then took something from a fold of her wrap.

"This is for you to carry now, Ayla. You are the medicine woman of the clan," Iza said, giving her the red-dyed bag that held the special roots. "Do you remember every step? Nothing must be left out. I wish I could have shown you, but the magic can't be made just for practice. It's too sacred to be thrown away and it can't be used for any ceremony, only very important ones. Remember, it's not just the roots that make the magic; you must prepare yourselves as carefully as you prepare the drink."

Uba and Ayla both nodded as the young woman took the precious relic and put it in her medicine bag. Iza had given her the otter-skin pouch the day she was made medicine woman, and it still reminded her of the one Creb had burned. Ayla reached for her amulet and felt for the fifth object she carried in it now: a piece of black manganese dioxide nestled in the small pouch along with the three nodules of iron pyrite stuck together, a red-stained oval of mammoth ivory, the fossil cast of a gastropod, and a chunk of red ochre.

Ayla's body had been marked with the black ointment, made by crushing and heating the black stone and mixing it with fat, when she became the repository of a part of the spirits of every member of the clan, and, through Ursus, of the entire Clan. Only for the highest and holiest of rituals was a medicine woman's body printed with black marks, and only medicine women were allowed to carry the black stone in their amulets.

Ayla wished Iza was going with them, and she worried about leaving her behind. Deep coughing spasms shook the fragile woman often.

"Iza, are you sure you're going to be all right?" Ayla motioned, after giving her a quick hug. "Your cough is worse."

"It's always worse in winter. You know it gets better in summer. Besides, you and Uba collected so many elecampane roots, I don't think there's a single plant left around here, and we probably won't have many black raspberries this season with all the roots you dug up to mix with wort flowers for my tea. I'll be fine, don't worry about me," Iza assured her. But Ayla noticed the relief from the medication was temporary at best. The old woman had been doctoring herself with the plants for years; her tuberculosis had progressed too far for them to be very effective anymore.

"Make sure you go outside on sunny days, and rest a lot," Ayla urged. "There won't be much work to do around here, there's plenty of food and wood. Zoug and Dorv can keep the fire going to keep animals and evil spirits away, and Aba can do the cooking."

"Yes, yes," Iza agreed. "Hurry now, Brun's ready to start."

Ayla fell into her customary place at the rear, while everyone looked at her and waited.

"Ayla," Iza motioned. "No one can start until you get in your right place."

Sheepishly, Ayla moved to the front of the group of

women. She had forgotten her new status. Her face turned pink with embarrassment as she stepped in line ahead of Ebra. She was uncomfortable; it just didn't seem right for her to be first. She waved an apologetic signal to the mate of the leader, but Ebra was accustomed to her second place. It seemed strange, though, to see Ayla in front of her instead of Iza; it made her wonder if she would be going to the next Clan Gathering.

Iza and the three people too old to make the trip accompanied the clan as far as the ridge and stood watching after them until they were small dots on the plain below. Then they returned to the empty cave. Aba and Dorv had missed the last Clan Gathering and were almost surprised they were alive to miss another, but it was the first time for Zoug and Iza. Though Zoug still went out with his sling occasionally, he returned empty-handed more often now, and Dorv couldn't see well enough to go out at all.

The four of them huddled around the fire at the entrance to the cave even though the day was warm, but they made no attempt at conversation. Suddenly, Iza was overcome by a fit of coughing that brought up a large, bloody mass of phlegm. She went to her hearth to rest and soon the others wandered into the cave and sat idly within their respective hearths. They had not been infected with the excitement of the long journey or the anticipation of seeing friends and relatives from other clans. They knew their summer would be unbearably lonely.

The freshness of early summer in the temperate zone near the cave changed character on the open plains of the continental steppes to the east. Gone was the rich green foliage that filled out brush and deciduous trees, and still betrayed the new season's growth of conifers with needles a shade lighter at the tips of branches and spires. Instead, quick-rooting and sprouting herbs and grasses, already chest high, whose youthful verdancy was lost to the drab hue indeterminate between green and gold, stretched to the horizon. Thick, matted, old-season growth cushioned their steps as the clan wove their way across the illimitable prairie, leaving a temporary ripple behind showing the way they had come. Clouds rarely marred the boundless expanse above except for an occasional thunderstorm, more often seen from a distance. Surface water was scarce. They stopped to fill waterbags at every stream, unsure if they would find any conveniently close when they camped for the night.

Brun set a pace to accommodate the slower-moving members of the traveling party, but one that pushed them. They had a long way to go to reach the cave of the host clan in the high mountains of the mainland to the east. It was difficult going for Creb in particular, but anticipation of the great Gathering and the solemn ceremonies he would lead buoyed his spirits. Though his body was crippled and atrophied, and further degenerated by arthritis, it did not impair the mental power of the great magician. The warm sun and Ayla's painkilling plants eased his aching joints, and after a time the exercise toughened the muscles even in the leg of which he had only limited use.

The travelers settled into a monotonous routine, one day blending into the next with weary regularity. The advancing season changed so gradually, they hardly noticed when the warm sun became a scorching ball of flame searing the steppes, turning the flat plain into a jaundiced monochrome of dun earth, buff grass, and beige rocks against a dust-laden, yellowish drab sky. For three days their eyes smarted with smoke and ashes carried by the prevailing winds from a sweeping prairie fire. They passed massive herds of bison, and giant deer with huge palmate antlers, horses, onagers, and asses; more rarely, saiga antelope with horns growing straight out of the tops of their heads slightly curved back at the tips; tens upon tens of thousands of grazing animals supported by the extensive grassland.

Long before they neared the marshy isthmus, which both connected the peninsula to the main continent and served as the outlet for the shallow salty sea to the northeast, the massive mountain range, second highest on the earth, loomed into view. Even the lowest peaks were capped with glacial ice to halfway down their flanks, coldly unmoved by the searing heat of the plains. When the level prairie merged into low rolling hills, dotted with fescue and feather grass and red with the richness of iron ore—the red ochre making it hallowed ground—Brun knew the salt marsh was not far beyond. It was a secondary and more tenuous link. The primary connection of the peninsula to the mainland was the northern one that formed part of the western boundary of the smaller inland sea.

For two days they struggled through putrid, mosquito-infested swamps of brackish water, broken through by occasional channels, before they reached the mainland. Scrub oak and hornbeam quickly led to the cool, welcome shade of parkland oak woods. They passed through an almost pure stand of beech, relieved by a few chestnut, and into a mixed forest dominated by oak, but including boxwood and yew, draped with clinging ivy and clematis. The lianas thinned out, but still climbed an occasional tree when they reached a belt of fir and spruce intermixed with beech, maple, and hornbeam. The western part was the wettest of the entire range and carried a dense cover of forests, and the lowest snowline.

They caught glimpses of forest bison and the red deer, roe deer, and elk of wooded landscapes; they saw boar, fox, badger, wolf, lynx, leopard, wildcat, and many smaller animals, but not a single squirrel. Ayla sensed something was missing in the fauna of these mountains before she realized the absence of the familiar creature. It was more than made up for by their first sighting of a cave bear.

Brun threw up his hand in a signal to stop, then pointed ahead at the monstrous shaggy bruin rubbing his back against a tree. Even the children sensed the awe with which the clan viewed the massive vegetarian. His physical presence was impressive enough. The brown bears of their own mountains, and of these too, averaged about three hundred and fifty pounds; the weight of a male cave bear, during the summer while he was still fairly lean, was closer to a thousand. In late fall, when he was fattened for winter, his bulk was much greater. He towered above the men of the clan by nearly three times their height, and with his huge head and shaggy coat, seemed even bigger. Lazily scratching his back on the rough bark of the old snag, he appeared unaware of the people frozen in their tracks so close by. But he had little to fear from any creature and was simply ignoring them. The smaller brown bears inhabiting the area near their own cave had been known to break the neck of a stag with one blow of a powerful foreleg; what couldn't this huge bruin do? Only another male during rutting season, or the female of the species protecting her cubs, would dare to stand up to him. She was invariably successful.

But it was more than the tremendous size of the animal that held the clan spellbound. This was Ursus, the personification of the Clan itself. He was their kin, and more, he embodied their very essence. His bones alone were so sacred they could ward off any evil. The kinship they felt was a spiritual tie, far more meaningful than any physical one. It was through his Spirit that all the clans were united into one and meaning was given to the Gathering they had traveled so far to attend. It was his essence that made them Clan, the Clan of the Cave Bear.

The bear tired of his activity—or his itch was satisfied—and he stretched to his full height, walked on hind legs a few paces, then dropped down on all four legs. Muzzle drooping close to the ground, he moved ponderously away with a lumbering gallop. For all his great size, the cave bear was basically a peaceful creature and rarely attacked unless he was annoyed.

"Was that Ursus?" Uba motioned, agog with wonder.

"That was Ursus," Creb affirmed. "And you will see another cave bear when we get there."

"Does the host clan really have a living cave bear in their cave?" Ayla asked. "He's so big." She knew it was the custom for the clan that hosted the Clan Gathering to capture a cave bear cub and raise him in the cave.

"He's probably in a cage outside the cave now, but when he was young, he lived in the cave with them and was raised like a child, with every hearth feeding him whenever he wanted to eat. Most clans claim their cave bears even learn to talk a little, but I was young the time we hosted the Clan Gathering. I don't remember very much about it, so I can't say if that's true. When the bear is about half grown, he is put in a cage so he can't hurt anyone, but everyone still feeds him tidbits and pets him when they walk by so he will know he is loved. He will be honored at the Bear Ceremony and will carry our messages to the world of the spirits," Creb explained.

They'd been told about it before but, after seeing a cave bear, the story took on new meaning to those who were too young to remember or had never been to a Clan Gathering.

"When can we host a Clan Gathering and get a cave bear to live with us?" Uba asked.

"When it's our turn, unless the clan whose turn it is can't. Then we can offer. But clans seldom miss the opportunity to host the Clan Gathering, though hunters may have to travel a long way to find a cave bear cub, and the danger from the mother bear is very great. The clan that is hosting this time is fortunate. Cave bears still live near their cave.

They have helped other clans to get cave bears, but now it's their turn. There are none left around our cave, but there must have been once, since the bones of Ursus were in our cave when we found it," Creb answered.

"What if something happens to the clan that is supposed to host a Gathering? Our clan doesn't even live in the same cave as before," Ayla asked. "If it was our turn, how would anyone know where to find us?"

"We'd send runners to the nearest clan to spread the news, either to tell the clans where the new cave is or to give another clan the chance."

Brun signaled, and the clan got under way again. When they passed the tree used by the cave bear as a back scratcher, Creb examined it closely and retrieved a few tufts of hair still caught in the rough bark. He wrapped them carefully in a leaf held in his teeth, then tucked them away in a fold of his wrap. The hair from a living wild cave bear would make powerful charms.

The giant conifers of the lower foothills were replaced by shorter, sturdier upland varieties as they ascended, opening up to breathtaking views of the glistening mountaintops they had seen from a distance as they crossed the plains. Birch thickets appeared, and low-trailing juniper and rosy pink azalea, whose many-flowered blossoms were just beginning to bloom, splashing the primary green of nature with bright color. A multitude of wild flowers added more shades to the palette of vibrant hues: spotted orange tiger lilies, mauve and pink columbine, blue and purple vetch, light lavender iris, blue gentian, yellow violet, primrose, and whites in a diversity of shapes. The southern mountain range, like the one at the lower tip of the peninsula which was folded during the same orogeny, was a refuge for the flora and fauna of a continent during the Ice Age.

Occasional chamois made an appearance, and heavy-horned mouflon. They were almost into the scrubby dwarf trees of mountainous taiga, bordering the high meadows of low sedges and grass, before they came to a well-worn path that traversed a steep incline. The men of the host clan had much farther to go before they reached the open plains north of the mountains to hunt, but the proximity of cave bears made the place so lucky, they were willing to accept the inconvenience. It also made them more adept at hunting the elusive forest animals.

The people running to greet the newly arriving clan, when they first saw Brun and Grod appear around a bend in the trail, stopped short at the sight of Ayla. The training of a lifetime could not prevent the shocked stares. Her position in front of the women, as the travel-weary clan filed silently to the open space near the cave, caused a flurry of speculation. Creb had warned her, but Ayla wasn't prepared for the sensation she caused; nor was she prepared for the throng of people. Over two hundred stunned individuals crowded around to see the strange woman. Ayla had never seen so many people in her life, much less in one place.

They stopped in front of a huge cage of stout poles sunk deep in the ground, lashed firmly together. Inside was another of the massive bears they had seen on their way, this one even bigger. Hand-fed for three years with a super-abundance that kept him placid and tame, the gigantic cave bear lolled in lazy indolence within the fenced enclosure, almost too fat to stand up. It had been a labor of devotion and reverence for the small clan to maintain the huge bear for so long, and even the many gifts of food, implements, and furs brought by the visiting clans could not make up for the effort it took. But there wasn't a single person who didn't envy the members of the host clan, and every clan eagerly awaited its turn to take on the same task and reap the spiritual benefits and status of the great honor.

The cave bear waddled over to see what was causing the commotion, hoping for more handouts, and Uba crowded in closer to Ayla, as much overwhelmed by the crush of people as by the bear. The leader and the magician of the host clan approached them and made gestures of greeting, quickly followed by an angry question.

"Why have you brought one of the Others to our Clan Gathering, Brun?" the leader of the host clan motioned.

"She is a woman of the Clan, Norg, and a medicine woman of Iza's line," Brun returned, more calmly than he felt. A murmur rose from the watching people and a flash of excited hand signals.

"That's impossible!" the mog-ur gestured. "How can she be a woman of the Clan? She was born to the Others."

"She is a woman of the Clan," The Mog-ur repeated, just as adamantly as Brun. He fixed the host clan leader with a baleful glare. "Do you doubt *me*, Norg?"

Norg looked at his mog-ur uncomfortably, but got no satisfaction from the magician's confused expression.

"Norg, we have traveled far and we are tired," Brun said. "This is hardly the time to discuss it. Do you deny us the hospitality of your cave?"

It was a tense moment. If Norg refused them, they would have no choice but to return the long distance back to their cave. It would be a grave breach of propriety, but to allow Ayla entrance would be tantamount to accepting her as a woman of the Clan; at least it would give Brun a clear edge. Norg looked again at his mog-ur, then at the powerful one-eyed man who was The Mog-ur, then back at the man who was leader of the clan ranked first of all the clans. If The Mog-ur said so, what could he do?

Norg signaled his mate to show Brun's clan to the place reserved for them, but he marched in beside Brun and The Mog-ur. As soon as they were settled, he was going to find out how a woman obviously born to the Others had become a woman of the Clan.

The entrance to the cave of the host clan was smaller than the entrance to the cave of Brun's clan, and the cave itself seemed smaller when they first walked in. But rather than one large room with a small adjunct for ceremonies, this cave was a series of rooms and tunnels that honeycombed their way far into the mountain, most of them unexplored. There was more than enough room to house all the visiting clans, though they might not have the advantage of light from the mouth. Brun's clan was led to the room second from the front and filled one whole side of it. It was a favorable location befitting their top-ranked status. Though several clans were already settled farther back, the place would have been held for them until the beginning of the actual Bear Festival. Only then, when it was certain they weren't coming, would it be given to the next-highest-ranked clan.

The Clan as a whole had no leader, but there was a hierarchy of clans just as there was a hierarchy of members within a clan, and the leader of the highest-ranked clan became, in effect, the leader of the Clan, simply because he was the highest-ranking member. But it was by no means a position of absolute authority. The clans were too autonomous for that. All were led by independent, dictatorial men who were accustomed to being a law unto themselves, meeting only once in seven years. They did not yield easily to greater authority, save tradition and the world of the spirits. The way each clan fit in the hierarchy, and therefore, the one man acknowledged leader of the Clan, was decided at the Clan Gathering.

Many elements contributed to a clan's status; ceremonies were not the only activity, competitions were of equal if not greater importance. The necessity of cooperation within clans for survival, which imposed the stricture of self-control, found an acceptable outlet in contests with other clans. And it was as necessary for survival in a different way. Controlled competition kept them from each other's throats. Nearly everything became a competition when the clans met. The men vied in wrestling, sling-hurling, bola-throwing, arm strength with use of a club, running, more complicated running-and-spear-stabbing races, toolmaking, dancing, storytelling, and the combination of both in dramatic hunt reenactments.

Though theirs were not given as much weight as the men's competitions, the women made their contribution. The great feast was an opportunity to display cooking skills. The gifts brought for the host clan were first arranged in plain view for everyone's inspection, critically examined, and judged by a consensus of the other women. The handiwork included soft pliable skins, luxuriant furs, watertight baskets, open-weave carrying baskets, mats of subtle texture and design, containers of stiff rawhide or bark, strong cords of sinew or fibrous plants or animal hair, long thongs of even width with no weak spots, wooden bowls finished to a uniform smoothness, serving platters of bone or the thinner sections of logs, cups, bowls and ladles, hoods, hats, foot coverings, hand coverings, and other pouches; even babies were compared. The honors were not awarded as obviously among the women. Theirs was a more subtle game of differences in expression or gesture or posture that discriminated with finesse, but it was no less honest in perceptively distinguishing mediocre from good work and awarding approbation to that which was truly fine.

The relative position of each clan's medicine woman and mog-ur was a consideration in determining status. Iza and Creb had both contributed to the first place of Brun's clan, as did the fact that the clan had been first for several generations before him, only, however, giving Brun a slight edge when he first became leader. As important as all the contributing factors were, it was the leadership capability of the head of the clan that was decisive. And if the competition among the women was subtle, the determination of which leader was most capable was infinitely more so.

Partly, the determination depended on how well the men of each clan performed in the competitions, showing how well a leader trained and motivated them; partly on how hard the women worked and how well they conducted themselves, showing a leader's firm guiding hand. Part was based on adherence to Clan tradition, but most of a leader's position, and consequently his clan's, was based on the strength of his own character. Brun knew he would be pushed to the limit this time; he had already lost ground by bringing Ayla.

Clan Gatherings were also a time to reestablish old acquaintances, see relatives from other clans, and exchange gossip and stories that would enliven many a cold winter evening for the next few years. Young people, unable to find mates within their own clan, vied for each other's attention, though matings could only take place if the woman was acceptable to the leader of the young man's clan. It was considered an honor for a young woman to be chosen, especially by a clan of a higher status, although moving away would be traumatic for her and her loved ones left behind. Despite Zoug's recommendation and the status of Iza's line, Iza thought it was doubtful that Ayla would find a mate. Having a child might have helped if her son had been normal, but her deformed baby precluded any hope for her.

Ayla's thoughts were far from finding a mate. She was having enough trouble just getting up courage to face the congregation of curious, suspicious people outside the cave. She and Uba had unpacked and set up the hearth that would be their home for the duration of their visit. Norg's mate had seen to it that stones for fireplaces and definition of boundaries were piled conveniently nearby, and skins of water were available for guest clans. Ayla had taken great care to display her gifts for the host clan the way Iza had explained, and the quality of her work had already attracted notice. She washed off the travel grime, changed to a clean wrap, then nursed her son while Uba waited impatiently. The girl was anxious to explore the area near the cave and see all the people, but reluctant to face them alone.

"Hurry, Ayla," she motioned. "Everyone else is out already. Can't you feed Durc later? I'd rather sit out in the sun than in this dark old cave, wouldn't you?"

"I don't want him to start crying right away. You know how loud he cries. People might think I'm not a good mother," Ayla said. "I don't want to do anything to make them think any worse of me than they do. Creb told me people would be surprised when they saw me, but I didn't think they might not let us stay. And I didn't think they'd stare like that."

"Well, they let us in, and after Creb and Brun get through talking to them, they'll know you're a Clan woman. Come on, Ayla. You can't stay in the cave forever, you've got to face them sooner or later. They'll get used to you after a while, just like we did. I don't notice that you look different hardly at all; I really have to think about it."

"I was there before you were born, Uba. They've never seen me before. Oh, all right, I might as well get it over with. Let's go. Don't forget to bring something for the cave bear to eat."

Ayla got up, leaned Durc against her shoulder, and patted his back as they started out. They made a gesture of respect to Norg's mate as they passed her hearth. The woman returned a greeting gesture and quickly turned back to her task, suddenly conscious that she had been staring. Ayla took a deep breath as she neared the entrance and held her head up a little higher. She was determined to ignore the curiosity about her; she was a woman of the Clan and she belonged here as much as anyone.

Her determination was tested to the fullest when she walked into the bright sunlight. Every person of every clan had found some reason to stay near the cave to wait for the strange Clan woman to come out. Many of them tried not to be obvious about it, but many more forgot, or ignored, common courtesy and stared in open-mouthed wonder. Ayla could feel her face flush. She changed Durc's position as an excuse to look at him rather than the multitude of faces turned in her direction.

It was fortunate she was looking at her son. Her action focused attention on Durc who had been overlooked at the first shock of her appearance. Expressions and gestures, some not so discreet, made it clear what they thought of her son. He would not have had to look like one of their babies; if he resembled her, they could have accepted him better. Regardless of what Brun and The Mog-ur said, Ayla was one of the Others; her baby could have fit into the same mold. But Durc had enough Clan characteristics to make his modifications seem to be distortions. He was a grossly deformed baby that should not have been allowed to live. Not only did Ayla's worth drop, Brun lost more ground, too.

Ayla turned her back on the suspicious stares and gaping mouths, and she and Uba went to look at the cave bear in his cage. When he saw them approach, the huge bruin lumbered over, sat up, and reached through the bars of the cage for the expected treat. They both backed off at the sight of the monstrous paw with its thick, rather stubby claws, more adapted to digging the roots and tubers that made up a large part of his normal diet than to hauling his huge bulk up trees. Unlike brown bears, only the cubs of cave bears were agile and small enough to climb. Ayla and Uba put their apples on the ground just beyond the stout poles that had once been reasonably mature trees.

The creature, raised like a well-loved child and never allowed the least bit of hunger, was entirely tame and comfortable around people. The intelligent animal had learned that certain actions invariably brought additional choice tidbits. He sat up and begged. Ayla would have smiled at his clownish antics if she had not remembered to control it in time.

"Now I know why clans say their cave bears talk," Ayla motioned to Uba. "He's asking for more; do you have another apple?"

Uba gave her one of the small, hard, round fruits, and this time Ayla went to the cage and gave it to him. He put it in his mouth, then moved closer to the bars and rubbed his huge, shaggy head against a projection on one of the tree trunks.

"I think you want to be scratched, you old honey-lover," Ayla gestured. She had been warned never to motion bear or cave bear or Ursus in his presence. If he was called by his real names, he would remember who he was and know he was not just a member of the clan who raised him. It would make him a wild bear again, void the Bear Ceremony, and ruin the whole reason for the festival. She scratched behind his ear.

"You like that, don't you, winter sleeper," Ayla motioned

and reached to scratch behind the other ear he had turned in her direction. "You could scratch your own ears if you wanted to—you're just lazy; or do you want attention? You big furry baby."

Ayla rubbed and scratched the huge head, but when Durc reached for a handful of shaggy hair, she backed away. She had petted and scratched the small wounded animals she had brought to their own cave enough to sense that this was just a bigger, tamer variety of the same thing. Protected by the heavy cage, she quickly lost her fear of the bear, but her baby was another matter. When Durc reached his tiny hands for a fistful of hair, the huge mouth and long claws suddenly looked dangerous.

"How could you get so close to him?" Uba motioned with awe. "I'd be afraid to get that close to his cage."

"He's really just a big baby, but I forgot about Durc. That animal could hurt him with a friendly nudge. He may seem like a baby when he's begging for food or wants attention, but I'd hate to think what he could do if he ever got angry," Ayla said as they walked away from his cage.

Uba wasn't the only one surprised at Ayla's fearlessness, the whole Clan had been watching. Most visitors shied away, especially at first. Young boys made a game of dashing up, reaching in the cage and touching the bear to show off their bravery, and men were too proud to show fear whether they felt it or not. But few women, outside the host clan, ever went very close, and to reach through the bars to scratch him at first look was unexpected from a woman. It didn't exactly change their opinion of Ayla, but it made them wonder.

Now that they had all gotten a good look at Ayla, people were drifting away, but she was still conscious of surreptitious glances. The outright stares from small children didn't bother her nearly as much. Theirs was the natural curiosity of the young for anything unusual and didn't carry connotations of suspicion or disapproval.

Ayla and Uba headed for a shady spot under an overhanging rock on the outer fringes of the large, sloping, cleared area in front of the cave. From that discreet distance, they could watch the activities without discourtesy.

There had always been a closeness of a special quality between Ayla and Uba. Ayla had been sister, mother, and playmate to the younger girl, but since Uba had begun training in earnest, and especially after she followed Ayla to the small cave, their friendship shifted to a more equal relationship. They were close friends. Uba was almost six and had reached an age where she was beginning to show an interest in the opposite sex.

They sat in the cool shade, Durc lying on his stomach on top of the carrying cloak between them, kicking and waving his arms, and lifting his head up to look around. During the trip, he had begun to babble and make cooing noises, which no Clan baby ever did. It worried Ayla, yet in some inexplicable way pleased her. Uba commented on the older boys and young men, and Ayla teased her about it in a friendly way. By unspoken agreement, no mention was made of possible mates for Ayla though she was of a far more matable age. They were both glad the long journey was over and speculated about the Bear Ceremony since neither had been to a Clan Gathering before. While they talked, a young woman approached, and in the formal, silent, universally known language, shyly asked if she could join them.

They welcomed her; it was the first friendly gesture they had received. They could see she had a baby in her carrying cloak, but it was sleeping and the woman made no move to disturb it.

"This woman is called Oda," she motioned formally after she sat down, and made a gesture that indicated she wanted to know their names.

Uba responded. "This girl is called Uba, the woman is Ayla."

"Aay...Aayghha? Name-word not know." Oda's common dialect and gestures were a little different, but they understood the essence of her comment.

"The name is not Clan," the blonde woman said. She understood the difficulty the rest of them had with her name; even some in her own clan could not say it quite right.

Oda nodded, lifted her hands as though she was going to say something, then changed her mind. She seemed nervous and uncomfortable. Finally she motioned toward Durc.

"This woman can see you have an infant," she said, rather hesitantly. "Is the infant a male or a female?"

"The infant is a male. The infant's name is Durc, like Durc of the legend. Is the woman familiar with that legend?"

Oda's eyes had a strange look of relief. "This woman

knows of the legend. The name is not common with this woman's clan."

"The name is not common with this woman's clan, either. But the infant is not common. Durc is special; the name is suitable," Ayla motioned with a hint of proud defiance.

"This woman has an infant. The infant is female. The name is Ura," Oda said. She still seemed nervous and hesitant. A strained silence followed.

"Does the infant sleep? This woman would see Ura if the mother would allow," Ayla finally asked, not knowing what else to say to the woman whose friendliness had such a hesitant quality.

Oda seemed to consider the request for a while, then, as though making a decision, took the baby from her cloak and laid her in Ayla's arms. Ayla's eyes flew open in stunned amazement. Ura was young—she could not have been born much more than a moon before—but it wasn't the newborn look that surprised the tall woman. Ura looked like Durc! She looked enough like Durc to be his sibling. Oda's baby could have been hers!

Ayla's mind reeled with the impact. How could a Clan woman have a baby that resembled hers? She thought Durc looked different because he was part Clan and part her, but Creb and Brun must have been right all along. Durc wasn't different, he was deformed, just like Oda's baby was deformed. Ayla was at a loss; she was so upset, she couldn't think of anything to say. Uba finally broke the long silence.

"Your baby looks like Durc, Oda." Uba forgot to use the formal language, but Oda understood her.

"Yes," the woman nodded. "This woman was surprised when she saw Aayghha's baby. That's why I...this woman wanted to talk to you. I didn't know if yours was a boy or a girl, but I hoped the infant would be male."

"Why?" Ayla signaled.

Oda looked at the baby in Ayla's lap. "My daughter is deformed," she gestured without quite looking at Ayla. "I was afraid she would never find a mate when she grows up. What man would have such a deformed woman?" Oda's eyes pleaded when she looked at Ayla. "When I...when this woman saw your infant, I hoped he was male because ...it will not be easy for your son to find a mate, either, you know."

Ayla hadn't thought about a mate for Durc. Oda was

right, he might have trouble finding a woman to mate. She understood now why Oda had approached them.

"Is your daughter healthy?" she asked. "Strong?"

Oda looked at her hands before she answered. "The infant is thin, but the health is good. The infant has a weak neck," she gestured, "but it's getting stronger," Oda added fervently.

Ayla looked more closely at the baby girl, asking permission with a questioning look before removing her swaddling. The infant was more stocky than Durc, closer to the build of Clan babies, but her bones were thinner. She had the same high forehead and general shape to her head, only the brow ridges were much smaller. Her nose was almost petite, but it was clear she would have the prognathous, chinless jaw of the Clan. The female baby's neck was shorter than Durc's, but definitely longer than normal for Clan babies. Ayla lifted the girl, automatically supporting her head, and saw the familiar early efforts of the baby to support her own head.

"Her neck will get stronger, Oda. Durc's was even weaker when he was born, and look at him now."

"Do you think so?" Oda answered eagerly. "This woman would ask the medicine woman of the first clan to consider this female infant as mate for her male infant," Oda asked formally.

"I think Ura would make a good mate for Durc, Oda."

"Then you'll ask your mate if he will allow it?"

"I have no mate," Ayla replied.

"Oh. Then your son is unlucky," Oda gestured with disappointment. "Who will train him if you are not mated?"

"Durc is not unlucky," Ayla insisted. "Not all babies born to unmated women are unlucky. I live at The Mog-ur's hearth; he does not hunt, but Brun himself has promised to train my son. He will be a good hunter, and a good provider. He has a hunting totem, too. The Mog-ur said it is the Gray Wolf."

"It doesn't matter, an unlucky mate would be better than no mate at all," Oda motioned with resignation. "I hope you're right. Our mog-ur has not revealed Ura's totem yet, but a Gray Wolf is strong enough for any woman's totem."

"Except Ayla's," Uba interjected. "Her totem is the Cave Lion. She was chosen."

"How did you ever have a baby?" Oda asked with astonishment. "Mine is the Hamster, but he really fought hard this time. I didn't have so much trouble with my first daughter."

"My pregnancy was hard, too. Do you have another daughter? Is she normal?"

"She was. She walks in the next world, now," Oda motioned sadly.

"Is that why Ura was allowed to live? I'm surprised you were allowed to keep her," Ayla remarked.

"I didn't want to keep her, but my mate made me. It's my punishment," Oda confessed.

"Your punishment?"

"Yes," Oda nodded. "I wished for a girl when my mate wanted a boy. It's just that I loved my first baby so much. When she was killed, I wanted another girl just like her. My mate says Ura is deformed because I had the wrong thoughts when I was pregnant. He says if I had wished for a boy, my baby would have been normal. He made me keep her so everyone would know I am not a good woman. But he didn't give me away, maybe because no one else would have me."

"I don't think you're such a bad woman, Oda," Ayla gestured with a look of compassion. "Iza wished for a girl when she was carrying Uba. She told me she asked her totem for a girl every day. How did your first daughter die?"

"She was killed by a man." Oda flushed with embarrassment. "A man who looked like you, Aayghha, a man of the Others."

A man of the Others? Ayla thought. A man who looks like me? She felt a chill crawl up her spine and a tingling at the roots of her hair. She noticed Oda's discomfiture.

"Iza says I was born to the Others, Oda, but I don't remember anything about them. I am Clan now," she said encouragingly. "How did it happen?"

"We were on a hunting trip, two other women and me besides the men. Our clan lives north of here, but that time we went farther north than we ever went before. The men left camp early; we stayed to collect wood and dried grass. There were lots of blowflies and we knew we'd have to keep a fire going to get the meat dried. All of a sudden, these men ran into our camp. They wanted to relieve their needs with us, but they didn't make the signal. If they had made the signal, I would have assumed the position, but they didn't give me a chance. They just grabbed us and threw us down. They were so rough. They didn't even let me put my baby down first. The one who grabbed me tore off my wrap and my cloak. My baby fell, but he didn't notice.

"When he was through," Oda continued, "another man was going to take me, but one of the other men saw my baby. He picked her up and gave her to me, but she was dead. She hit her head on a rock when she fell. Then the man who found her made many loud words, and they all left. When the hunters came back, we told them, and they took us back to the cave right away. My mate was good to me then; he grieved for my daughter, too. I was so glad when I found out my totem had been defeated again so soon after losing her. I didn't even have the woman's curse once; I thought my totem was sorry I lost my baby and decided to let me have another to make up for her. That's why I thought I might have another girl, but I shouldn't have wished for a girl."

"I'm sorry," Ayla said. "I don't know what I'd do if I lost Durc; I almost did once. I'll talk to The Mog-ur about Ura; I'm sure he will talk to Brun, he's fond of my son. I think Brun might agree, too. It would be easier than trying to find a woman of our clan to mate with a deformed man."

"This woman would be grateful to the medicine woman, and I promise to train her well, Aayghha. She will be a good woman, not like her mother. Brun's clan has the highest status; I think my mate will agree. If he knows there is a place for Ura with Brun's clan, he might not be so angry with me. He's always telling me my daughter will be nothing but a burden and never have any status. And when Ura gets older I can tell her she doesn't have to worry about finding a mate. It can be difficult for a woman if no man wants her," Oda said.

"I know," the tall blonde woman replied. "I'll talk to The Mog-ur as soon as I can."

After Oda left, Ayla was pensive and preoccupied. Uba sensed her need for quiet and didn't disturb her. Poor Oda, she was happy, had a good mate and a normal baby. Then those men had to come and spoil everything. Why didn't they just make the signal? Couldn't they see Oda had a baby? Those men of the Others, they're as bad as Broud.

Worse. At least Broud would have let her put her baby down first. Men and their needs! Clan men, men of the Others, they're all alike.

As she mused, her mind kept going back to thoughts of the Others. Men of the Others, men who look like me, who are the Others? Iza said I was born to them, why don't I remember anything about Others? I can't even remember what they look like. Where do they live? I wonder, how does a man of the Others look? Ayla remembered the reflection of herself in the still pool near their cave and tried to imagine a man with her face. But when she thought of a man, the image of Broud came to her mind, and with a flash of insight, the confused jumble of ideas spinning around in her head fell into place.

Men of the Others! Of course! Oda said one of them relieved his needs with her and she didn't have the curse even once after that. Then she gave birth to Ura, just like Durc was born after Broud relieved his needs with me. That man was of the Others and I was born to them, but Oda and Broud, they're both Clan. Ura is not deformed any more than Durc is. He's part me and part Clan, and so is Ura. Or rather, she's part Oda and part that man who killed her baby. Then Broud did start Durc—with his organ, not the spirit of his totem.

But the other women with Oda didn't have deformed babies. And as often as men and women do it, if a baby is started every time, there'd be nothing but babies. Maybe Creb is right, too. A woman's totem has to be defeated; but she doesn't swallow the totem's essence, a man puts it inside her with his organ. And then it mixes up with the essence of a woman's totem. It's not just men, it's women, too.

Why did it have to be Broud? I wanted a baby, my Cave Lion knew how much I wanted a baby, but Broud hates me. He hates Durc, too. But who else would have? None of the other men are interested in me, I'm too ugly. Broud only did it because he knew how much I hated it. Did my Cave Lion know Broud's totem would finally win? His essence must be potent; Oga already has two sons. Brac and Grev must have been started by Broud's organ, too, like Durc.

Does that mean they're siblings? Brothers? Like Brun and Creb? Brun must have started Broud inside Ebra, too. Unless it was some other man; it could have been any man. Probably not, though. Men don't usually give the signal to the leader's mate, it's discourteous. And Broud doesn't like to share Oga. On the mammoth hunt, Crug always used Ovra. Everyone could see his need, and Goov was more considerate. Even Droog did once or twice.

If Brun started Broud, and Broud started Durc, does that mean Durc is part of Brun, too? And Brac and Grev? Brun and Creb are siblings; they were born to the same mother and probably started by the same man. He was a leader, too. Does that mean Durc is part of Creb, too? And what about Iza? She's a sibling. Ayla shook her head. It's all too confusing, she thought.

Broud did start Durc, though. I wonder if my totem led Broud to give me the signal that first time? It was awful, but it could have been another test, and maybe there was no other way. My totem must have known, must have planned it. He knew how much I wanted a baby, and he did give me a sign that Durc would live. Wouldn't it infuriate Broud if he knew? He hated me so much, he gave me the one thing I wanted most.

"Ayla," Uba said, interrupting her train of thought, "I just saw Creb and Brun go into the cave. It's getting late, we should start preparing something to eat, Creb will be hungry."

Durc had fallen asleep. He woke when Ayla picked him up, but soon settled back down, snuggled in the cloak next to his mother's breast. I'm sure Brun will let Ura come and be Durc's mate, she thought as they walked back to the cave of the host clan. They are more right for each other than Oda realizes. But what about me? Will I ever find a mate that's right for me?

23

When the last two clans arrived, Ayla went through a similar ordeal, on a smaller scale, as the one that greeted her entrance. The tall blonde woman was an oddity among the nearly two hundred and fifty Clan people from ten clans that had gathered together. She was noticed wherever she went, and her every action scrutinized. As abnormal as she appeared, no one could detect any deviation in her behavior. Ayla was extremely careful to make sure no one would.

She displayed none of the peculiar characteristics that still slipped out in the more relaxed atmosphere of their own cave. She didn't laugh, or even smile. No tears wet her eyes. No long strides or free-swinging arm movements betrayed her unwomanly inclinations. She was a paragon of Clan virtue, an exemplary young matron—and no one noticed. No one, outside her clan, ever knew a woman who acted any other way. But it made her presence acceptable, and, as Uba predicted, they got used to her. There were too many other activities at a meeting of the clans for the novelty of one strange woman to hold their attention for long.

It wasn't easy to maintain such a large aggregation within the close confines of the cave environment for an extended period of time. It took cooperation, coordination, and a large dose of courtesy. The leaders of the ten clans were far busier than they ever were with only their own members to worry about; the numbers of people added together multiplied the problems.

Feeding the horde meant hunting expeditions had to be organized. While established patterns and ranks within any one clan made disposition of the hunters easy, when two or more clans hunted together, problems arose. Clan status determined the leader of the combined group, but which third-ranked man was more competent? They tried different arrangements at first, careful to exchange positions so no one would be offended. After the competitions started, it would become easier, but no hunting party went out without first deciding the relative positions of the men.

The women's plant-gathering forays had their problems, too. Theirs was a case of too many women trying to select the choicest produce. An area could be depleted quickly with no one getting quite enough. Preserved food brought with them supplemented the diet of every clan, but fresh foods were always more desirable. The host clan always foraged far away from their cave before a Gathering, but even that courtesy was inadequate to satisfy the needs of all. Though no long journey limited their time to store food for winter, the clan that hosted the meeting still had to build up an extra reserve. By the time it was over, edible food plants in their vicinity would be exhausted.

There was an adequate supply of water from the glacier-fed stream flowing nearby, but firewood was at a premium.

Cooking was done outside the cave, unless it rained, and clans prepared their food as a unit, rather than at separate hearths. Even so, most of the dried fallen deadwood and many living trees, which would take more than a season or two to replenish themselves, were used up. The environment around the cave after the Clan Gathering would never be the same.

Supply was not the only problem, disposal was an issue of equal importance. Human waste and other refuse had to be accommodated. And space had to be provided. Not only living space within the shelter of the cave, but space to cook, space to assemble, space for competitions and dancing and feasting, and space to move around. Organizing the activities was no small feat in itself. All of it involved interminable discussion and compromise, within an atmosphere charged with intense competition. Custom and tradition played a large role in smoothing out many of the bumps, but it was in this arena that Brun's administrative mind came to the fore.

Creb was not the only one whose enjoyment of the Clan Gathering was largely because of association with his peers. Brun enjoyed the challenge of pitting himself against men whose authority equaled his own. That was his contest: to vie for domination of the other leaders. Interpretation of ancient ways sometimes required fine hair-splitting, the ability to make a decision and the strength of character to hold to it, yet to know when to yield. Brun was not first leader without reason. He knew when to be forceful, when to be conciliatory, when to call for a consensus, and when to stand alone. Whenever the clans gathered, one strong man usually emerged who could forge the authoritarian leaders into a cohesive, workable entity, at least for the duration of the meeting. Brun was that man. He had been since he first became leader of his own clan.

Had he lost face, his own self-doubt would have lost him his advantage. Without the base of surety in his own judgment, his diffidence would have cast doubt over his decisions. He could not face a Gathering, and the other leaders, under those circumstances. But it was just that background of strength and compromise, within the unyielding framework of Clan tradition, that had allowed him to make the concessions he had toward Ayla. And once the threat to himself was past, he began to view her differently.

Ayla had tried to force a decision, but it was within the

structure of Clan custom, as she interpreted it, and it wasn't in a wholly unworthy cause. True, she was a woman and must understand her place, but she had come to her senses and seen the error of her ways in time. When she showed him the location of her small cave, he was privately amazed that she had reached it in her weak condition. He wondered if a man could have done it, and masculinity was measured by stoic endurance. Brun admired courage, determination, endurance; they showed strength of character. In spite of the fact that Ayla was a woman, Brun admired her grit.

"If Zoug were here, we would have won the sling competition," Crug motioned. "No one could have beaten him."

"Except Ayla," Goov commented with guarded gestures. "Too bad she couldn't compete."

"We don't need a woman to win," Broud gestured. "The sling contest doesn't count for that much, anyway. Brun will win the bola-throwing, he always has. And there's still the spear-and-running contest."

"But Voord already won the running competition; he stands a good chance to win in running-and-spear-stabbing, too," Droog said. "And Gorn did well with the club."

"Just wait until we show them our mammoth hunt. Our clan is bound to win," Broud answered. Hunt reenactments were a part of many ceremonies; occasionally they happened spontaneously after an especially exciting hunt. Broud enjoyed acting them out. He knew he was good at evoking the sense of excitement and drama of the hunt and loved being the center of attention.

But hunt reenactments served a purpose greater than showing off. They were instructive. With expressive pantomime, and a few props, they demonstrated hunting techniques and tactics to youngsters and other clans. It was a way of developing and sharing skills. Had they been asked, everyone would have agreed that the prize awarded to the clan that came out best in the complicated competition was status: to be acknowledged first among peers. But there was another prize awarded, though it was not acknowledged. The competitions sharpened skills necessary for survival.

"We'll win if you lead the hunt dance, Broud," Vorn said. The ten-year-old boy, fast approaching manhood, still idolized the future leader. Broud courted his adoration by admitting him into the men's discussions whenever he could.

"Too bad your race doesn't count, Vorn. I was watching; it

wasn't even close. You were way out in front. But it's good practice for next time," Broud said. Vorn glowed under the praise.

"We've still got a good chance," Droog motioned. "But it could go the other way. Gorn is strong, he gave you a good fight in the wrestling match, Broud. I wasn't sure you could take him. Norg's second must be proud of the son of his mate; he's grown since the last Gathering. I think he's the biggest man here."

"He's got the strength, all right," Goov said. "It showed when he won with the club, but Broud is quicker, and almost as strong. Gorn came in a close second."

"And Nouz is good with that sling. I think he must have seen Zoug last time and decided to work on it; he just didn't want to let an older man beat him again," Crug added. "If he's practiced as much with the bola, he may give Brun a good contest. Voord is a fast runner, but I thought you were going to catch him, Broud. That one was close, too, you were just a step behind him."

"Droog makes the best tools," Grod gestured. The laconic man seldom volunteered comment.

"Selecting the best and bringing them here is one thing, Grod, but it will take luck to make them well with everyone watching. That young man from Norg's clan has skill," Droog replied.

"That's one contest where you'll have the advantage just because he is younger, Droog. He'll be more nervous and you have more experience in competing. You'll be able to concentrate better," Goov encouraged.

"But it still takes luck."

"They all take luck," Crug said. "I still think old Dorv tells a better story than anyone."

"You're just used to him, Crug," Goov motioned. "That's a hard competition to judge. Even some of the women tell a good story."

"But not as exciting as the hunt dances. I think I saw Norg's clan talking about how they hunted a rhino, but they stopped when they saw me," Crug said. "They may show that hunt."

Oga approached the men diffidently and signaled that their evening meal was ready. They waved her off. She hoped it wouldn't take them too long to decide to come and eat. The longer they waited, the longer it would delay them from joining the other women who were gathering to tell stories, and she didn't want to miss any of it. Usually it was the older women who acted out the legends and histories of the Clan with dramatic pantomime. Often the stories were intended to educate the young, but they were all entertaining: sad stories that wrung the heart, happy stories that brought joy and inspiration, and humorous stories that made their own embarrassing moments feel less ridiculous.

Oga went back to the fireplace near the cave. "I don't think they're hungry, yet," she motioned.

"It looks like they're coming after all," Ovra said. "I hope they don't linger too long over the meal."

"Brun's coming, too. The leaders' meeting must be over, but I don't know where Mog-ur is," Ebra added.

"He went into the cave with the mog-urs earlier. They must be in this clan's place of spirits. No telling when they'll be out. Do we have to wait for him?" Uka asked.

"I'll set something aside for him," Ayla said. "He always forgets to eat when he's getting ready for ceremonies. He's so used to eating his food cold, sometimes I think he likes it better. I don't think he'll mind if we don't wait for him."

"Look, they're starting already. We're going to miss the first stories," Ona gestured with disappointment.

"It can't be helped, Ona," Aga said. "We can't go until the men are through."

"We won't miss too many, Ona," Ika consoled. "The stories will go on all night. And tomorrow the men will show their best hunts and we'll be allowed to watch. Won't that be exciting?"

"I'd rather watch the women's stories," Ona said.

"Broud says our clan is going to do the mammoth hunt. He thinks we're sure to win; Brun is going to let him lead it," Oga gestured, her eyes glowing with pride.

"That will be exciting, Ona. I remember when Broud became a man and led the hunt dance. I couldn't even talk yet, or understand anyone, but it was still exciting," Ayla motioned.

After the meal was served, the women waited anxiously, casting longing glances at the congregation of women gathered at the far end of the clearing.

"Ebra, go ahead and watch your stories, we have things to discuss anyway," Brun gestured.

The women picked up babies and herded young children toward the group seated around an old woman who had just started a new story.

" . . . and the mother of Great Ice Mountain . . ."

"Hurry," Ayla motioned. "She's telling the legend of Durc. I don't want to miss any of it, it's my favorite."

"Everyone knows that, Ayla," Ebra said.

The women of Brun's clan found places to sit and were soon caught up in the tale.

"She tells it a little differently," Ayla motioned after a while.

"Every clan's version is a little different, and every story-teller has his own way, but it's the same story. You're just used to Dorv. He's a man, he understands men's parts better. A woman tells more about the mothers, not only the mother of Great Ice Mountain, but how sad the mothers of Durc and the other young people were when they left the clan," Uka answered.

Ayla remembered that Uka had lost her son during the earthquake. The woman could understand a mother's sadness at losing her son. The modified version gave the legend a new meaning to Ayla, too. For a moment her brow furrowed with concern. My son's name is Durc; I hope that doesn't mean I'll lose him someday. Ayla hugged her baby. No, it can't be. I almost lost him once, the danger is over now, isn't it?

A stray breeze stirred a few loose tendrils of his hair, cooling for a moment his sweat-beaded brow, as Brun carefully gauged the distance to the stump of a tree near the edge of the cleared space that fronted the cave. The rest of the tree, sheared of branches, formed part of the palisade that surrounded the cave bear. The whiff of air only teased. It brought no respite from the stifling afternoon sun glaring down on the dusty field. But the ethereal zephyr moved more than the tensely watching throng that lined the periphery.

Brun was as still as they, standing with feet apart, his right arm hanging down at his side grasping the handle of his bola. The three heavy stone balls, wrapped in leather shrunk to fit, and attached to braided thongs of unequal length, were splayed out on the ground. Brun wanted to win this contest, not only for the sake of the competition—though that, too, was important—but because he needed to show the other leaders he hadn't lost his competitive edge.

Bringing Ayla to the Clan Gathering had cost him. He realized now that he, and his clan, had become too accustomed to her. She was too great an anomaly for the others to accept in so short a time. Even The Mog-ur was fighting to maintain his place, and he hadn't been able to convince the rest of the mog-urs that she was a medicine woman of Iza's line. They were willing to forgo the special drink made from the roots rather than allow her to make it. The loss of Iza's status was one more support knocked out from under Brun's crumbling position.

If his clan came in less than first in the competitions, he was certain to lose status, and though they were in the running, the outcome was far from assured. But even winning the competition wouldn't guarantee his clan top rank, it would only give him an even chance. There were too many other variables. The clan that hosted the Gathering always had an edge, and it was Norg's clan that was giving his the stiffest competition. If they ran a close enough second, it might give Norg enough backing to come out on top. Norg knew it and was his most relentless opponent. Brun was holding his own by sheer force of will.

Brun squinted as he eyed the stump. The movement, barely discernible, was enough to halt the breath of half the watchers. The next instant the still figure became a blur of motion, and the three stone balls, whirling around their center, flew toward the stump. Brun knew the moment the bola left his hand that his throw was off. The stones hit the target, then bounced away, failing to wrap around it. Brun walked over to pick up his bola while Nouz took over his place. If Nouz missed the target entirely, Brun would win. If he hit the stump, they would each have a second try. But if Nouz wrapped his bola around it, the match would be his.

Brun stood off on the sidelines, face impassive, resisting the urge to clutch his amulet, and only sent a mental plea to his totem. Nouz had no such compunctions. He reached for the small leather pouch around his neck, closed his eyes, then sighted the post. With a sudden burst of rapid motion, he let the bola fly. Only long years of firm self-control kept Brun from letting his disappointment show when the bola wrapped around the stump and held. Nouz had won, and Brun felt his position slip even more.

Brun stayed in his place while three hides were brought onto the field. One was lashed to the rotted stump of an old snag, a huge old tree whose jagged, broken top was a little taller than the men. Another was laid over a moss-covered fallen log of respectable proportions near the edge of the woods and held down with stones, and the third was spread out on the ground and again held in place with stones. The three formed a triangle of more or less equal sides. Each clan chose one man to compete in this contest, and they lined up in order of clan status near the hide spread on the ground. Other men, carrying sharpened spears, mostly made of yew, though birch, aspen, and willow were also used, went to the other targets.

Two young men from among the lower-ranked clans paired up first. Each holding a spear, they waited tensely, side by side, eyes glued on Norg. At his signal, they made a dash for the upright snag and slammed their spears into it through the leather, aiming for the place where the animal's heart would be if the hide still covered him, then grabbed a second spear from their clansmen waiting beside the target. They sprinted to the fallen log and jammed the second spear into it. By the time the third spear was snatched, one man was clearly in the lead. He ran back to the hide on the ground, thrust the spear deep, as close to the middle as he could, then raised his arms triumphantly.

After the first heat, five men were left. Three of them lined up for the second race, this time from the highest-ranked clans. The one who came in last was given another chance against the remaining two. Then the two men who came in second were paired up, leaving a field of three for the final race—the two first-place winners and the winner of the preceding race. The finalists were Broud, Voord, and the man from Norg's clan, Gorn.

Of the three, Gorn had run four races to earn his place in the finals, while the other two were fairly fresh after only two. Gorn had won the first paired heat but came in third when the three highest-ranked clans raced. He ran again with the last two men and came in second, then paired off with the man who had come in second in the race where he ran third, this time beating him. By sheer guts and stamina, Gorn had made it to the finals and had won the admiration of everyone there.

When the three men lined up for the last race, Brun stepped out on the field.

"Norg," he said. "I think it would make the last race more fair if we delayed it to give Gorn a chance to rest. I think the son of the mate of your second-in-command deserves it."

There were nods of approval, and Brun's standing inched up, though Broud scowled. The suggestion put his own clan in a less competitive position, it took away the edge Broud might have in racing against a man already tired, but it showed Brun's fairness, and Norg could hardly refuse. Brun had quickly weighed the alternatives. If Broud lost, his clan stood to lose their position; but if Broud won, Brun's evident fairness would boost his prestige, and it gave the impression of confidence he didn't altogether feel. It would make the win clean—there could be no question that Gorn might have won if he had been fresher—providing Broud won. And it was more fair.

It was late in the afternoon before everyone gathered around the field again. Tensions held in abeyance were revived, and more. The three young men, all rested now, pranced around stretching muscles and hefting spears to find the right balance. Goov moved to the snag with two men from the other clans, and Crug went to the fallen log with two others. Broud, Gorn, and Voord lined up three abreast, fastened their eyes on Norg, and waited for his signal. The leader of the host clan lifted his arm. He dropped it quickly and the men were off.

Voord sprang to the lead with Broud at his heels and Gorn pounding hard behind. Voord was already reaching for his second spear as Broud rammed his into the rotted snag. Gorn put on a fresh burst of speed that urged Broud forward as they raced for the fallen log, but Voord was still ahead. He jabbed his spear into the hide-covered log just as Broud pulled up, but he hit a hidden gnarl and the spear clattered to the ground. By the time he retrieved it and thrust again, both Broud and Gorn had passed him by. He grabbed for his third spear and set out after them, but for Voord, the race was lost.

Broud and Gorn raced for the final target, legs pumping, hearts pounding. Gorn started gaining on Broud, then inched out ahead, but the sight of the broad-shouldered giant of a man making Broud eat his dust enraged him. He thought his lungs would burst as he surged forward, forcing every muscle and sinew. Gorn reached the hide spread on the ground an instant before Broud, but as he raised his arm, Broud darted beneath and planted his spear into the ground through the tough leather as he ran across the hide. Gorn's spear bit through at the next heartbeat. It was a heartbeat too late.

As Broud slowed to a stop, the hunters of Brun's clan crowded around him. Brun watched them, his eyes glowing with pride. His heart was beating almost as fast as Broud's. He had agonized every step of the way with the son of his mate. It was close, for a few tense moments Brun was sure he was going to lose, but he had given his all and come through. It was a crucial race, but with this win, he had more than a chance. I must be getting old, Brun thought, I lost the bola throw, but not Broud. Broud won. Maybe it's time to turn the clan over to him. I could make him leader, announce it right here. I'll fight for the first rank and let him go home with the honor. After that race, he deserves it. I'll do it! I'll tell him right now!

Brun waited until the men were through congratulating him, then approached the young man, looking forward to Broud's joy when he found out the great honor he was about to receive. It would be a fitting reward for the fine race he had run. It was the greatest gift he could give to the son of his mate.

"Brun!" Broud saw the leader and spoke first. "Why did you have to delay the race? I almost lost. I could have beat him easily if you hadn't given him time to rest. Don't you care if our clan is first?" he motioned petulantly. "Or is it that you know you'll be too old to be leader next Gathering? If I'm going to be the leader, the least you could do is let me start as first, like you did."

Brun stepped back, stunned by Broud's vituperative attack. He struggled to control his conflicting emotions. You don't understand, Brun thought, I wonder if you will ever understand? This clan is first; if I can help it, it will stay first. But what will happen when you become leader, Broud? How long will this clan be first then? The pride left his eyes, and a great sorrow overwhelmed him, but Brun controlled that, too. Perhaps he's just too young, he rationalized, maybe he just needs a little more time, a little more experience. Have I ever really explained? Brun tried to forget that no one had to explain to him.

"Broud, if Gorn had been tired, would your win have been as good? What if the other clans doubted that you could beat him if he hadn't been tired? This way they know for sure that you won, and so do you. You did well, son of my mate," Brun motioned gently. "You ran a good race."

In spite of his bitterness, Broud still respected this man more than anyone he ever knew, and he could not help but respond. At that moment Broud felt, as he had on his first manhood hunt, that he would give anything for such praise from Brun.

"I didn't think about that, Brun. You're right, this way everyone knows I won, they know I'm better than Gorn."

"With this race, and Droog winning the toolmaking competition, if our mammoth hunt wins tonight, we're sure to come out first," Crug said enthusiastically. "And you will be one of those chosen for the Bear Ceremony, Broud."

More men crowded around Broud to congratulate him as he walked back to the cave. Brun watched him go and then saw Gorn walking back, too, surrounded by Norg's clan. An older man clapped his shoulder in a gesture of encouragement.

Norg's second has a right to be proud of the son of his mate, Brun thought. Broud may have won the race, but I'm not sure he's the better man. Brun had only controlled his sorrow, not eliminated it, and though he struggled to bury it deeper, the pain would not die. Broud was still the son of his mate, the child of his heart.

"The men of Norg's clan are brave hunters," Droog admitted. "It was a good plan, digging a hole in the path the rhinoceros takes to his drinking place and covering it with brush to hide it. Maybe we could try it sometime. It took courage to drive him back when he bolted; rhinos can be more fierce than mammoths, and much more unpredictable. Norg's hunters told it well, too."

"But it still wasn't as good as our mammoth hunt. Everyone agreed," Crug said. "Gorn deserved to be one of the chosen, though. Almost every contest was between Broud and Gorn. For a while I was afraid we would not win the competitions this year. Norg's clan is a very close second. What do you think of the third choice, Grod?"

"Voord did well, but I would have chosen Nouz," Grod replied. "I think Brun preferred Nouz, too."

"It was a hard choice, but I think Voord deserved it," Droog commented.

"We won't be seeing much of Goov until after the festival," Crug said. "Now that the competitions are over, the acolytes will be spending all their time with the mogurs. I hope the women don't think that just because Broud and Goov won't be eating with us tonight, they don't have to make as much. I'm going to eat well; there won't be anything else until the feast tomorrow."

"I don't think I'd want to eat if I were Broud," Droog said. "It's a great honor to be chosen for the Bear Ceremony, but if he ever needed courage, Broud will need it in the morning."

The first morning light found the cave empty. The women were already up working by firelight, and the rest couldn't sleep. The preliminary preparations for the feast had consumed days, but the work was nothing compared with the task ahead. Full daylight was upon them long before the glowing disc burst over the tops of the mountains, flooding the cave site with burning rays from a sun already high.

Excitement was tangible, tension unbearable. With the competitions over, the men had nothing to do until the ceremonies, and they were restless. Their nervous agitation infected the older boys, and they in turn stirred up the rest of the youngsters, driving the busy women to distraction; milling men and chasing children all got in their way.

The turbulence subsided temporarily when the women served cakes of crushed millet mixed with water and baked on hot stones. The breakfast of bland biscuits was eaten with solemnity. They were reserved for this one day alone out of every seven years, and, except for nursing babies, were the only food anyone would eat until the feast. The millet cakes were a token only and did little more than whet the appetite. By midmorning, hunger, stimulated by delicious smells emanating from various fires, intensified the turmoil, raising excited anticipation to a fever pitch as the time for the Bear Ceremony drew near.

Creb had not approached either Ayla or Uba with instructions to prepare themselves for the ritual that would be held later, and they were sure the mog-urs had found neither of them acceptable. They were not alone in wishing Iza had been well enough to make the journey. Creb had used every power of persuasion at his command to convince the other magicians to let one of them make the drink, but as much as they wanted the ritual and, for them, the rare experience of the drink made from the roots, Ayla was too strange and Uba too young. The mog-urs refused to accept Ayla as a woman of the Clan, much less a medicine woman of Iza's line. The celebration of Ursus affected more than the clans that were in attendance; the consequences, good or bad, of any rituals performed at any Clan Gathering redounded to the entire Clan. The mog-urs would not chance the possibility of invoking bad luck that would cast misfortune on all Clan people everywhere. The stakes were too high.

Eliminating that traditional ritual of the ceremony contributed to the devaluation of Brun and his clan. For all the efforts of his men in the competitions, Brun's acceptance of Ayla posed more threat to the clan's position than anything ever had before. It was too unconventional. Only Brun's adamant stand in the face of increasing opposition kept the issue undecided, and he wasn't at all sure he would win out in the end.

Not long after the millet cakes were served, the leaders arranged themselves near the mouth of the cave. They waited quietly for the attention of the assembled clans. The silence spread out like the ripples of a stone cast in a pond as the presence of the leaders was made known. Men moved quickly into positions defined by clan and personal rank. The women dropped their work, signaled suddenly well-behaved children, and silently followed suit. The Bear Ceremony was about to begin.

The first beat of the smooth hard stick on the hollowed-out wooden bowl-shaped drum resounded like a sharp crack of thunder in the expectant hush. The slow, stately rhythm was picked up by the stamping of wooden spears against the ground, adding a muted depth. A contrapuntal rhythm of sticks beating on a long, hollow, wooden tube wove around the strong steady beat in a seemingly random pattern of sound, apparently independent from it. Yet the staccato rhythms, played at varying tempos, had a stressed beat that coincided with every fifth thrum of the basic rhythm as if by accident. They combined to produce an increasing sense of expectation, almost of anxiety, until the beats came together. Each release began another surge of tension in wave after hypnotic wave of sound and sensation.

All sound came to a sudden halt on a final, satisfying beat. As if they had materialized out of thin air, the bearskin-cloaked mog-urs stood nine abreast in front of the cage of the cave bear, with The Mog-ur alone in front of them. The feel of the strong beat still echoed inside the heads of the people in the overpowering silence. The Mog-ur held a flat, long oval of wood attached at one end to a cord. As he spun it round and round, a barely audible whir increased to a loud roar filling the silence. The deep, haunting resonance of the bullroarer raised gooseflesh as much for its significance as for its sonorous timbre. It was the voice of the Spirit of the Cave Bear warning all other spirits away from this ceremony devoted to Ursus alone. No totemic spirits would come to their aid; they had placed themselves entirely under the protection of the Great Spirit of the Clan.

A high-pitched warble penetrated the deep-throated bass; its thin, wailing ululation sent cold shivers down the spines of the most fearless as the bullroarer wound down. Like nothing so much as a disembodied spirit, the eerie, unearthly trill pierced the bright morning air. Ayla, standing in the front row, could see the sound was coming from something held to the mouth of one of the mog-urs.

The flute, made from the hollow legbone of a large bird, had no finger holes. Its pitch was controlled by stopping and unstopping the open end. In the hands of a skillful player, a full five-note pentatonic scale could be drawn from the simple instrument. To the young woman, no less than the rest, it was magic that created the unfamiliar music; it sounded like nothing ever heard on earth. It had come from the world of the spirits at the command of the holy man, for this ceremony alone. As the bullroarer symbolized and imitated the roar of the cave bear in physical form, the flute was the sound of the spiritual voice of Ursus.

Even the magician who played the instrument felt the sanctity of the sound that issued forth from the primitive pipe, though he himself had made it. Making and playing the magic flute was the esoteric secret of the magicians of his clan, a secret which usually brought those magicians to first rank. Only Creb's unique ability had displaced the mog-ur who played the flute to second, but it was a powerful second. And it was he who most opposed the acceptance of Ayla.

The huge cave bear was pacing his cage. He had not been fed and he wasn't used to going without food; he had never known a hungry day in his life. Water had been withheld from him as well, and he was thirsty. The crowd, smelling of tension and excitement, the unaccustomed sounds of wooden drums, bullroarer, and flute, all combined to make the animal nervous.

When he saw The Mog-ur limping toward his cage, he hauled his massive, overweight bulk up on his hind legs and roared a complaint. Creb jerked in startled reflex, but recovered quickly and masked it with a normal-seeming jerky step. His face, like the rest of the magicians' faces, blackened with a paste of manganese dioxide, showed no sign of his rapidly beating heart as he tilted his head back to look up at the unhappy giant. He carried a small bowl of water, the shape and ivory gray color making it obvious that the bowl had once been a human skull. He put the macabre water container into the cage and stepped back while the shaggy bruin dropped down to drink.

While the animal lapped up the liquid, twenty-one young hunters surrounded his cage, each carrying a newly made spear. The leaders of the seven clans not fortunate enough to have a man selected for special honors had each chosen three of their best hunters for the ceremony. Then, Broud, Gorn, and Voord ran out of the cave and lined up outside the securely lashed door of the cage. They were naked except for small loincloths, and their bodies were daubed with red and black markings.

The small amount of water did little to satisfy the thirst of the great bear, but the men so near his cage made him hopeful that more was coming. He sat up and begged, a gesture that had rarely gone without response before. When his efforts went unrewarded, he lumbered over to the nearest man and poked his nose through the heavy bars.

The music of the flute ended on an uncomfortably unfinished note, heightening the anticipation in the anxious silence. Creb retrieved the skull bowl, then shuffled to his place in front of the magicians lined up across the mouth of the cave. At an unseen signal, the mog-urs began the movements of the formal language in unison.

"Accept your water as a token of our gratitude, O Mighty Protector. Your Clan has not forgotten the lessons learned from you. The cave is our home, protecting us from the snow and cold of winter. We, too, rest quietly, nourished by the food of summer, warmed by furs. You have been one of us, lived with us, and know we keep your ways."

Faces blackened, and dressed in identical cloaks of shaggy bear fur, the magicians resembled a well-rehearsed dance troupe moving as one as they spoke with stately flowing gestures. The Mog-ur's eloquent one-handed symbols that matched yet modified the others, punctuated the elegant movements and added emphasis.

"We venerate you first among all Spirits. We beg you to speak for us in the world of the Spirits, to tell of the bravery of our men, the obedience of our women, to make a place for us when we return to the otherworld. We beseech your protection from the evil ones. We are your People, Great Ursus, we are the Clan of the Cave Bear. Go with honor, Greatest of Spirits."

As the mog-urs made the symbols for the names of the great animal in his presence for the first time, the twenty-one young men thrust their spears between the stout trees of the cage, piercing the tremendous shaggy bulk of the revered creature. Not all drew blood, the cage was too large for all the spears to penetrate deeply, but the pain enraged the nearly full-grown cave bear. His angry roar shattered the silence. The people jumped back with fear.

At the same time, Broud, Gorn, and Voord began to cut away the lashings on the door of the cage, scrambling up the trees until they reached the top of the palisade. Broud reached the top first, but Gorn managed to grab the short thick log put there earlier. The pain-maddened cave bear reared up on his hind legs again, bellowed an angry roar, and lumbered toward the three young men. His massive domed head nearly reached the tallest tree trunks of the enclosure. He reached the opening, pushed at the gate, and sent it crashing to the ground. The cage was open! The monstrous, angry bear was loose!

The hunters with their spears raced to form a protective phalanx between the provoked brute and the anxious audience. Women, fighting an urge to run, held their babies tighter while older children clung to them in wide-eyed terror. Men gripped their spears ready to jump to the defense of vulnerable women and terrified children. But the people of the Clan held their place.

As the wounded cave bear lumbered out of the gaping hole in the fence of logs, Broud, Gorn, and Voord, poised at the top, leaped on the surprised bruin. Broud stood on his shoulders, reached over and seized the fur on his face, and yanked up. Meanwhile, Voord had landed on his back. He grabbed the shaggy hair and pulled down with all his weight, tightening the loose skin around his neck. Their combined efforts forced open the cavernous mouth of the struggling animal, and Gorn, sitting astride his shoulder, quickly shoved the log broadside into his mouth. The bear clamped down as Broud let go, wedging the log fast between his jaws, impeding his breath and disabling one weapon in the cave bear's arsenal.

But the tactic did not disarm the bear entirely. The enraged bruin swiped at the creatures clinging to him. Sharp claws dug into the thigh of the man on his shoulder and dragged the screaming young hunter into his mighty arms. Gorn's agonized cry was cut short as a powerful bear hug snapped his spine. A long wail rose from one of the watching women as the cave bear dropped the limp body of the courageous young man.

The bear waded into the squad of spear-wielding men who closed in on him. A swing of the raging animal's powerful foreleg cleared a swath, knocking down three men and catching a fourth with a ripping gash that tore the muscles of his leg to the bone. The man doubled over in pain, in shock too severe to scream. The others stepped over and around him as they jostled to get in close enough to thrust spears into the belligerent beast.

Ayla clutched Durc in horrified awe, petrified that the bear would reach them. But when the man fell, his life's blood spilling on the ground, she didn't think, she just acted. Shoving her baby at Uba, she dashed into the melee. Forcing her way through the close-packed men, she half-dragged, half-carried the wounded man clear of the milling, stomping feet. Leaning hard on the pressure point in his groin with one hand, she held the end of the thong of her wrap in her teeth and cut off a piece with her other hand.

The tourniquet was in place and she was wiping away blood with her baby's carrying cloak before two other medicine women followed her lead. Fearfully skirting the dangerous struggle, they ran to help her. The three of them carried the wounded man into the cave, and in their frantic efforts to save his life, weren't even aware when the huge bear finally succumbed to the spears of the hunters of the Clan.

The moment the cave bear was down, Gorn's mate broke away from the restraining arms of those who sought to comfort her, and ran to his body sprawled in an unnatural position on the ground. She threw herself on him, burying her face in his hairy chest. Sitting back on her knees, in frantic gestures she pleaded with him to get up. Her mother and Norg's mate tried to pull her away as the mog-urs approached them. The most holy magician leaned close and gently tilted her head up to look at her.

"Do not grieve for him," The Mog-ur signaled with a tender look of compassion in his deep brown eye. "Gorn's was the greatest honor. He was chosen by Ursus to accompany him to the world of the spirits. He will help the Great Spirit intercede for us. The Spirit of the Great Cave Bear selects only the finest, the bravest, to travel with him. The Feast of Ursus will be Gorn's feast, too. His courage, his will to win, will be remembered in legend and told at every Clan Gathering. Just as Ursus returns, so will the spirit of Gorn. He will wait for you so that you may return together and mate again, but you must be as brave as he. Put your grief aside and share your mate's joy in his journey to the next world. Tonight, the mog-urs will give him a special honor so that his bravery will be shared by everyone, so it will pass on to the Clan."

The young woman strove visibly to control her anguish, to be as brave as the awesome holy man said she must. She didn't want to dishonor her mate's spirit. The lopsided, disfigured, one-eyed magician whom everyone feared, somehow didn't seem so fearsome anymore. With a look of gratitude, she got up and walked stiffly back to her place. She must be brave: Hadn't the Mog-ur told her Gorn would wait for her? That someday they would return together and mate again? Her mind clung to that promise, and she tried to forget the desolate emptiness of the rest of this life without him.

When Gorn's mate returned to her position, the mates of the leaders and their seconds deftly began to skin the cave bear. The blood was collected in bowls, and after the mog-urs made symbolic gestures over it, the acolytes passed through the crowd holding the vessels to the mouth of each member of their clan. Men, women, children all had a taste of the warm blood, the life fluid of Ursus. Even the mouths of babies were opened by their mothers and a fingerful of fresh blood placed on their tongues. Ayla and the two medicine women were called from the cave to partake of their share, and the injured man, who had lost so much of his own, had a gulp of bear's blood restored to him. Everyone shared in the communion with the great bear that bound them together as one people.

The women worked rapidly while the Clan watched. The thick, subcutaneous layer of the purposely fattened animal was carefully scraped away from the skin. The rendered fat had magical properties and would be distributed to the mog-urs of each clan. The head was left attached to the hide, and while the meat was lowered into the waiting stone-lined pits, heated by fires, for a full day, the acolytes hung the huge bearskin on poles in front of the cave, where his unseeing eyes could watch the festivities. The Cave Bear would be an honored guest at his own feast. When the bearskin was mounted, the mog-urs picked up Gorn's body and with solemn dignity carried it into the deep recesses of the cave. After they were gone, Brun gave a signal, and the crowd broke up. The Spirit of Ursus had been sent on his way with full and proper ceremony.

24

"Then how did she do it? None of the others dared to get him, but she had no fear." The mog-ur of the clan to which the wounded man belonged was speaking. "It was almost as though she knew Ursus wouldn't hurt her, just like the first day. I think The Mog-ur is right, Ursus has accepted her. She is a woman of the Clan. Our medicine woman said she saved his life, she's not only well-trained, she has a natural skill, like she was born to it. I believe she must be of Iza's line."

The mog-urs were in a small cave deep inside the mountain. Stone lamps, shallow saucers filled with bear grease absorbed by a dried moss wick, formed circles of light that pushed back the absolute black that surrounded them. The feeble flames glinted off hidden facets in the crystal matrix of the rocks, and were reflected in the glistening sheen of damp stalactites hanging in eternal icicles from the roof, longing to reach their inverted counterparts growing from the floor. Some had succeeded in forming a union. Strained through the stone of ages, the calcereous drops had culminated in stately columns that reached from floor to vaulted ceiling, thinning at the center. One straining stalactite missed the satisfying kiss of its stalagmitic mate by barely a hairbreadth—that would take more ages yet to bridge.

"She did surprise everyone when she showed no fear of Ursus that first day," another magician said. "But if it is agreed, is there still time for her to prepare?"

"There is time," The Mog-ur answered, "if we hurry."

"She was born to the Others, how can she be a woman of the Clan?" the flute-playing mog-ur demanded. "Others are not Clan, they never will be. You say she came to you already marked with Clan totem scars, but those are not the marks of a woman's totem. How can you be sure they're Clan marks? Clan women do not have Cave Lion totems."

"I never said she was born with it," The Mog-ur said reasonably. "Are you saying a Cave Lion cannot choose a woman? A Cave Lion can choose whoever he wants. She was nearly dead when she was found; Iza brought her back to life. Do you think a young girl could escape a cave lion if she wasn't under the protection of his Spirit? He marked her with his sign so there could be no doubt. Those are Clan totem marks on her leg, no one can deny that. Why would she be marked with Clan totem scars if she wasn't intended to become a woman of the Clan? I don't know why, I don't claim to understand why spirits do anything. With the help of Ursus, sometimes I can interpret what they do. Can any of you do any better? I will only say she knows the ritual; Iza has given her the secret of the roots in the red bag, and Iza would not have told her if she wasn't her daughter. We don't have to give up the ritual. I've already given you all my arguments before. You must decide, but do it soon."

"You said your clan thinks she's lucky," Norg's mog-ur motioned.

"Not so much that she is lucky, but she seems to bring luck. We have been very lucky since she was found. Droog thinks of her as a sign from one's totem, something unique and unusual. Perhaps she's lucky, too, in her own way."

"Well, it's certainly unusual enough for a woman of the Others to be a woman of the Clan," one of them commented.

"She brought luck to us today, our young hunter is going to live," the wounded man's mog-ur said. "I am agreeable; it would be a shame to miss Iza's drink if we don't have to." There were several nods of agreement.

"What about you?" The Mog-ur signaled to the magician who was second. "Do you still think Ursus will be displeased if Ayla makes the ritual drink?"

All heads turned to look at him. If the powerful magician still objected, he could sway enough of the other mog-urs to prevent it. If he just adamantly refused to participate, even if the rest agreed, it would be enough. Agreement had to be unanimous; there could be no schism in their ranks. He looked down, pondering the question, then at each man in turn.

"It may or it may not displease Ursus. I am not convinced. Something about her bothers me. But it's obvious no one else wants to eliminate the ritual, and it seems she is the only one available. I'd almost prefer to use Iza's true daughter, in spite of her youth. If everyone else agrees, I will withdraw my objection. I don't like it, but I won't prevent it."

The Mog-ur looked at each man and received a nod of approval. With a relieved sigh, covered by his efforts to pull himself up, the crippled man quickly left. He hobbled through several passages that opened into rooms then narrowed again into passages, guided by stone lamps. They gave way to torches placed at closer intervals as he neared the living quarters of the clans.

Ayla was sitting beside the wounded young man in the front cave. Durc was in her arms and Uba on her other side. The man's mate was there, too, watching him sleep, occasionally glancing up at Ayla with gratitude.

"Ayla, quickly, you must prepare yourself. There is little time," Mog-ur gestured. "You will have to hurry, but do not overlook a single step. Come to me when you are ready. Uba, give Durc to Oga to feed; Ayla won't have time."

They both stared at the magician, stunned by the sudden change in plans. It took a moment to comprehend, then Ayla nodded. She ran quickly to the hearth in the second cave to get a clean wrap. Mog-ur turned to the young woman anxiously watching her sleeping mate.

"The Mog-ur would know how the young man fares."

"Arrghha says he will live and may walk again. But his leg will never be the same." The woman spoke with a different dialect and everyday gestures modified so much that Ayla and Uba had had trouble communicating with her except with the formal language. The magician, however, had more practice with the common speech of other clans but used the formal language to make his meaning more precise.

"The Mog-ur would know this man's totem."

"Ibex," she signed.

"This man is as sure-footed as that mountain goat?" he asked.

"It has been said this man is," she began. "This man was not so agile on this day, and now I don't know what he'll do. What if he never walks again? How will he hunt? How will he provide for me? What can a man do if he can't hunt?" The young woman slipped into the common language of her clan as her taut nerves put her on the edge of hysteria.

"The young man lives. Is that not most important?" The Mog-ur said to calm her.

"But he's proud. If he can't hunt, he may wish he hadn't lived. He was a good hunter, he might have been second to the leader one day. Now he may never gain status, he'll lose status. What will he do if he loses status?" she pleaded.

"Woman!" The Mog-ur motioned with mock severity. "No man loses status who is the chosen of Ursus. He has already proved his manhood; he was almost chosen to walk with Ursus to the next world. The Spirit of Ursus does not choose lightly. The Great Cave Bear decided to allow him to remain, but he was still marked. This man is honored to claim Ursus as his totem now; his scars will be the marks of his new totem, he can wear them with pride. He will always be able to provide for you. The Mog-ur will speak with your leader; your mate has the right to claim a share of every hunt. And he may walk again, he may even hunt again. Perhaps he won't be as agile as the Ibex, he may walk more like a bear, but that doesn't mean he won't hunt again. Be proud of him, woman, be proud of your mate who was chosen by Ursus."

"He is the chosen of Ursus?" the woman repeated with a look of awe. "The Cave Bear is his totem?"

"And the Ibex, too. He can claim both," The Mog-ur said. He noticed the beginning of a bulge under her wrap. No wonder she is so distraught, he thought. "Does the woman have children yet?"

"No, but life has started. I am hoping for a son."

"You are a good woman, a good mate. Stay with him. When he wakes, tell him what The Mog-ur has said."

The young woman nodded, then glanced up as Ayla hurried by.

The small river near the cave of the host clan became a torrent of angry water in spring, only slightly less violent in fall, tearing giant trees out by the roots, gouging huge boulders from the rocky face, and hurtling them down the mountain. Even in its quieter moods, the surging stream, foaming down the middle of a rock-strewn floodplain many times wider than itself, had the greenish, cloudy cast of glacial runoff. Ayla and Uba had scouted the region near the cave shortly after they arrived to find the cleansing plants necessary to purify themselves in case one of them was called upon to participate in the ceremony.

Ayla was nervous as she raced to dig up soaproot, horsetail fern, and red-rooted pigweed, and her stomach was a bundle of knots while she waited anxiously for boiling water from one of the cooking fires to extract the insecticidal element from the fern. The news that she would be allowed to perform the ritual spread rapidly through the Clan. The mog-urs' acceptance of her revised everyone's opinion of the Clan woman born to the Others, and her worth increased proportionately. It confirmed that she was indeed Iza's daughter and elevated her to the medicine woman of highest rank. The leader of the clan that had members who were Zoug's kin reconsidered his flat refusal to accept her. Zoug's recommendation just might have some merit after all. Maybe one of the men would take her, if only as second woman. She could be a valuable addition.

But Ayla was too worried to notice the comments fluttering around her. She was more than worried, she was terrified. I can't do it, her mind screamed, even as she ran to the small river. There isn't enough time to get ready. What if I forget something? What if I make a mistake? I'll disgrace Creb. I'll disgrace Brun. I'll disgrace the whole clan.

The glacier-fed river was icy, but the cold water calmed her raw-edged nerves. She felt more relaxed as she sat on a rock pulling tangles out of her long blonde hair drying in a light breeze, and watching the glowing pink mountaintop, reflecting the setting sun, deepen to a rich bluish purple. Her hair was still damp when she put her amulet back over her head and her clean wrap on. Stuffing her tools in the folds, she picked up her other wrap and ran back to the cave. She passed Uba holding Durc on her way, and gave her a quick nod.

The women were working frantically, unhelped by totally unmanageable children. The gory ritual slaying of the cave bear had them keyed up; they were unused to going hungry and the smells of cooking stimulated appetites already sharp and made them irritable; and their mothers' preoccupation gave them a rare opportunity to indulge in misbehavior seldom allowed children of the Clan. Some of the boys had picked up the cut thongs from the bear's cage and wore them wrapped around their arms as badges of honor. Other boys, not as quick, tried to take them away, and all of them were racing around cooking fires. When they tired of the game, they teased the girls, supposed to be tending crying younger siblings, until the girls started chasing them around or running to their mothers to complain. It was a riotous, disorganized madhouse. Even the occasional stern command of some woman's mate did little to quell the unusually rambunctious youngsters.

Children were not the only ones hungry. Food, prepared in enormous quantities, tantalized the tastebuds of everyone, and anticipation of the great feast and evening ceremony added to the frenzied excitement. Heaps of wild yams, white starchy breadroots, and potatolike groundnuts boiled gently in skin pots slung over fires. Wild asparagus, lily roots, wild onions, legumes, small squashes, and mushrooms were cooking in various combinations with subtle seasonings. A mountain of wild lettuce, burdock, pigweed, and dandelion leaves, freshly washed, was waiting to be served raw with a dressing of hot bear grease, seasonings, and salt, added at the last moment.

One clan's specialty was a combination of onions, mushrooms, and the round green legumes of milk vetch, seasoned with a secret combination of herbs and thickened with dried reindeer moss. Another brought a special variety of pinecones, from a tree that was unique to the area of their cave, that yielded large tasty nuts released by the heat of a fire.

Norg's clan toasted chestnuts gathered from the lower slopes and made a nut-flavored porridge sauce from cracked beechnuts, parched grains, and slices of small, hard, tartsweet apples, cooked long and slowly. The area for some distance in the vicinity of the cave was stripped of blueberries, high-bush cranberries, and from the lower elevations, raspberries and wild mountain blackberries.

The women of Brun's clan had spent days cracking and grinding the dried acorns they brought. The pulverized nuts were put in shallow holes in the sand near the river and quantities of water poured over the pulpy mixture to leach out the bitterness. The resultant dough was baked into flat cakes, soaked in maple syrup until they were thoroughly saturated, then dried in the sun. The host clan, who also tapped their maple trees in early spring and boiled the watery sap for long days, were interested as soon as they saw the familiar birchbark containers that were used to store maple sugars and syrup. The sticky, maple-sweet acorn cakes were an unusual treat that the women of Norg's clan decided to try later themselves.

Uba, keeping an eye on Durc while helping the women, looked at the seemingly endless quantity and variety of food and wondered how they would ever be able to eat it all.

Smoke drifting upward disappeared into the still dark night filled with stars so thick a gossamer haze veiled the vault of the heavens. The moon was new and gave no hint of its presence, turning its back to the planet it circled and reflecting its light into the cold depths of space. The glow of cooking fires lighted the area near the cave in contrast to the darkness of the surrounding woods. Food had been moved away from the full force of the heat, but left near enough to keep it hot, and most of the women had retired to the cave. They were changing into new wraps and relaxing for a few moments before the festivities.

But even the tired women were too excited to stay inside the cave for long. The space in front began to fill with a milling crowd eagerly waiting for the feast and the beginning of the ceremony. A still hush descended as the ten magicians and their ten acolytes filed out of the opening, followed by a scramble to find places. It appeared to be a random assemblage that faced the holy men. Positions of the audience were not defined by location so much as relationship to other people. Orderly ranks were not important, only that each individual was ahead or behind, or on the correct side of certain other individuals. There were always last-minute shufflings as people tried to find the best vantage point within their sphere of relationships.

With dignified ceremony, a large fire was lit in front of the dark hole in the mountain. Then the stones were removed from the tops of the cooking pits. The mates of the leaders of the first-ranked and host clans had the signal honor of lifting out the huge haunches of tender meat, and Brun's chest swelled with satisfaction when he saw Ebra step forward.

The mog-urs' acceptance of Ayla had finally decided the issue. Brun and his clan were a stronger first than they had ever been. Unlikely as it had appeared at first, the tall blonde female was a woman of the Clan, and a medicine woman of Iza's prestigious line. Brun's obdurate insistence that it was so had been proved correct, it was the will of Ursus. Had he wavered, for even a moment, his prestige would not have been as great, or his success as sweet.

Clouds of succulent steam caused empty stomachs to growl as the bear meat was removed with forked sticks. That was the signal for the other women to begin heaping platters of wood and bone and filling large bowls with the food they had labored so long to prepare. Broud and Voord stepped forward carrying large flat trays and stood in front of The Mog-ur.

"This Feast of Ursus also honors Gorn, chosen by the Great Cave Bear to accompany him. While he lived with Norg's clan, Ursus learned that his People had not forgotten his lessons. He grew to know Gorn well and found him a worthy companion. Broud and Voord, for your courage, your strength, your endurance, you were selected to show the Great Spirit the bravery of the men of his Clan. He tested you with his great strength and he is pleased. You did well, and you are privileged to bring him the last meal he will share with his Clan until he returns from the Spirit World. May the Spirit of Ursus always walk with us."

The two young men passed by each of the women standing beside dishes heaped with food and selected the choicest morsels of each, with the exception of the meat. The captive cave bear had never been fed meat, though in the wild, he occasionally indulged when it was easily available. The trays were placed in front of the bear hide mounted on the poles.

Then, the Mog-ur continued: "You drank of his blood, now eat of his body and be one with the Spirit of Ursus."

The benediction signaled the beginning of the feast. Broud and Voord received the first portions of the bear meat, then proceeded to fill plates for themselves, followed by the rest of the Clan. Delighted sighs and grunts rose as they settled down to enjoy their repast. The meat from the hand-fed, vegetarian bear was tender and rich with marbled fat. Vegetables, fruits, and grains, prepared with meticulous attention, were savored to the fullest, and the appetizer of hunger made everything taste even better. It was a feast worth waiting for.

"Ayla, you're not eating. You know all the meat must be eaten tonight."

"I know, Ebra, but I'm just not hungry."

"Ayla's nervous," Uba gestured between mouthfuls. "I'm glad I wasn't chosen. This is so good, I wouldn't want to be too nervous to eat it."

"Eat some meat, anyway. You must do that. Do you have some broth for Durc? He should have a little, it will make him one with the Clan."

"I gave him some, but he didn't want much. Oga just fed him. Oga, is Grev still hungry? My breasts are so full, they're getting sore."

"I would have waited, but they were both hungry, Ayla. You can feed them tomorrow."

"I'll have enough milk for them and two more by then. They won't want anything tonight, they'll be sleeping. The datura sedative is all ready. Next time they're hungry, make them drink that first, so they will sleep. Uba will tell you how much, I have to see Creb right after we eat, and I won't be back until after the ceremony."

"Don't be too long, our dance will start after the men go into the cave. Some of the medicine women are really good at making the rhythms. The women's dance at Clan Gatherings is always special," Ebra motioned.

"I haven't learned to play very well, yet. Iza taught me a little, and the medicine woman from Norg's clan was showing me, but I haven't had much practice," Ayla said.

"You haven't been a medicine woman very long, and Iza has spent more time teaching you the healing magic than the rhythms, although they're magic, too," Ovra gestured. "Medicine women have to know so much."

"I wish Iza were here," Ebra motioned. "I'm glad they finally accepted you, Ayla, but I miss Iza. It seems so strange not having her with us."

"I wish she were here, too," Ayla said. "I hated leaving her behind. She's sicker than she likes to let anyone know. I hope she's getting lots of sun and rest."

"When it's her time to walk in the next world, she will

go. When the spirit calls, no one can stop her," Ebra said.

Ayla shivered, though the night was warm, and a sudden sense of foreboding washed over her—a vague, uneasy feeling like a chill wind that hinted of the end of summer warmth. Mog-ur signaled and she quickly got up, but she couldn't shake the feeling as she walked to the cave.

Iza's bowl, white-lined with a patina from generations of use, was on her sleeping fur where Ayla had put it. She took the red-dyed pouch out of her medicine bag and emptied the contents. In the torchlight she began examining the roots. Though Iza had explained many times how to estimate the correct quantity, Ayla still wasn't sure how many to use for the ten mog-urs. The strength of the potion depended not only on number, but on the size of the roots and how long they had aged.

She had never seen Iza make it. The woman had explained many times the drink was too venerable, too sacred to be made for practice. Daughters usually learned by watching their mothers, from repeated explanations, and even more from the innate knowledge they were born with. But Ayla was not born to the Clan. She picked out several roots, then added one more to be sure the magic would be effective. Then she went to the place just inside the entrance, near a supply of fresh water, where Creb had told her to wait, and watched the beginning of the rites.

The sound of wooden drums was followed by the thudding of spear butts, and then the staccato of the long, hollowed-out tube. Acolytes moved among the men with bowls of datura tea, and soon they were moving to the heavy beat. The women stayed in the background; their time would come later. Ayla stood by anxiously, her wrap draped loosely around her, waiting. The men's dance grew more frenzied, and she wondered how much longer she'd have to wait.

Ayla jumped at a tap on her shoulder—she hadn't heard the mog-urs coming out of the back of the cave—but she relaxed when she recognized Creb. The magicians moved silently out of the cave and arranged themselves around the bearskin. The Mog-ur stood in front, and from her vantage point she got a fleeting impression that the cave bear, mounted upright with its mouth open, was about to attack the crippled man. But the monstrous animal towering over The Mog-ur was held in suspended motion, a mere illusion of strength and ferocity.

She saw the great magician signal the acolytes who were playing the wooden instruments. They stopped at the next accented beat and the men looked up, a little stunned to see the mog-urs where just an instant before, or so it seemed, there had been none. But the sudden appearance of the magicians was an illusion, too, and now the young woman knew how it was done.

The Mog-ur waited, letting the suspense build, until he was sure everyone's attention was riveted on the giant figure of the cave bear highlighted by the ceremonial fire and flanked by the holy men. His signal was inconspicuous and he made a point of looking in another direction, but it was the one Ayla was waiting for. She slipped out of her wrap, filled the bowl with water, and clutching the roots in her hand, she took a deep breath and walked toward the one-eyed man.

There was a startled gasp as Ayla walked into the circle of light. Clothed in her wrap, tied with a long cord that hid her shape with loose folds and pockets, and acting like any other female, she had begun to seem one of them. But without the disguising bulges, her true form stood out in sharp contrast to women of the Clan. Rather than the round, almost barrel-shaped body structure characteristic of both men and women, Ayla was lean. From side view she was slender, except for her milk-filled breasts. Her waist dipped in, then filled out to rounded hips, and her legs and arms were long and straight. Not even the red and black circles and lines painted on her naked body could hide it.

Her face lacked the jutting jaw, and with her small nose and high forehead it seemed more flat than they remembered. Her thick blonde hair, framing her face in loose waves and reaching halfway down her back, picked up highlights from the fire and gleamed golden; an oddly beautiful crown for the ugly, obviously alien, young woman.

But more astounding was her height. Somehow, when she was moving in a hurried, hunched-over shuffle or sitting at the feet of some man, they hadn't been so aware of it before. Standing opposite the magicians, it was obvious. When she bowed her head, she looked down at the top of The Mog-ur's. Ayla was taller, by far, than the tallest man of the Clan.

The Mog-ur made a series of formalized gestures invoking the protection of the Spirit that still hovered near them.

Then Ayla put the hard, dried roots in her mouth. It was difficult for her to chew them. She didn't have the large teeth and strong, heavy jaws of the people of the Clan. As much as Iza had cautioned her against swallowing any of the juices that formed in her mouth, she couldn't help it. She didn't really know how long it was supposed to take to soften the roots, but it seemed to her she had to chew and chew and chew. By the time she spat out the last of the masticated pulp, she was feeling light-headed. She stirred it until the fluid in the ancient, sacred bowl turned a watery white, then she passed it to Goov.

The acolytes had waited while she worked at the roots, each holding a bowl of long-steeped datura tea. Goov handed the bowl of white liquid Ayla gave him to Mog-ur, then picked up his bowl and gave it to Ayla as the other apprentice magicians gave theirs to the medicine women of their clans. An exchange in kind and value. The Mog-ur took a sip of the liquid.

"It's strong," the holy man motioned in guarded gestures to Goov. "Give less." Goov nodded and took the bowl, then walked to the mog-ur who was second.

Ayla and the medicine women carried their bowls to the waiting women and gave controlled amounts of the liquid to them and the older girls. Ayla drained the last dregs from her bowl, but she was already feeling a strange sense of distance, as though a part of her was detached and watching from some other place. Several of the older medicine women took up the wooden drums and began to beat out the rhythms of the women's dance. Ayla watched the moving sticks with intense fascination, each beat sounding precise and clear. The medicine woman of Norg's clan offered a bowl drum to her. She listened to the rhythm, tapping lightly, then found herself playing along.

Time lost all meaning. When she looked up, the men were gone and the women gyrating with a wildly free, erotic frenzy. She felt an urge to join them, put the drum down, and watched it fall over and spin a few times before it stopped. Her attention was diverted by the bowl shape of the instrument. It reminded her of Iza's bowl, the precious ancient relic entrusted to her care. She remembered staring into the white, watery liquid, her finger stirring it round and round. Where is Iza's bowl? she thought. What happened to it? She dwelled on the bowl, worried over it, became obsessed with it.

She had an image of Iza and tears came to her eyes. Iza's bowl. I've lost Iza's bowl. Her beautiful ancient bowl. Passed on by her mother, and her mother's mother, and her mother's mother's mother. In her mind she saw Iza, and another Iza behind her, and another and another; medicine woman after medicine woman lined up behind Iza into an ancient misty past, each holding a venerable, white-stained bowl. The women faded, and her mind's eye zoomed in on the bowl. Then, suddenly, the bowl cracked, fell away in two parts, broken down the center. No! No! The scream was inside her mind. She was frantic. Iza's bowl, I've got to find Iza's bowl.

She stumbled away from the women and staggered toward the cave. It took forever. She scrambled through bone platters and wooden bowls holding the remains of the feast congealed in them, searching for the treasured container. The cave entrance drew her, dimly outlined by torches within, and she stumbled toward it. Suddenly her way was blocked. She was trapped, caught in the meshes of some coarse, hairy creature. She looked up and gasped. A monstrous face with a huge, open mouth stared down at her. Ayla backed away, then ran toward the beckoning cave.

As she passed through the entrance, her eye was caught by something white near the place where she had waited for Mog-ur's signal. She fell to her knees and carefully picked up Iza's bowl, cradling it in her arms. Milky fluid still sloshed around the softened root pulp in the bottom. They didn't drink it all, she thought. I made too much. I must have made too much. What will I do with it? I can't throw it away, Iza said it can't be thrown away. That's why she couldn't show me, that's why I made too much, because she couldn't show me. I made it wrong. What if someone finds out? They might think I'm not a real medicine woman. Not a woman of the Clan. They might make us leave. What should I do? What should I do?

I'll drink it! That's what I'll do. If I drink it, no one will know. Ayla held the bowl to her lips and drained it. The mysterious drink was strong to begin with, but the roots soaking in the small amount of liquid made it far more potent. She started into the second cave with the vague idea of putting the bowl in a safe place, but before she reached her hearth, she began to feel the effects.

Ayla was so disoriented, she didn't notice dropping the bowl on the ground just within the hearth's boundary stones. There was a taste in her mouth of ancient, primordial forest: rich damp loam, musty rotted wood, towering large-leafed trees wet with rain, huge fleshy mushrooms. The walls of the cave expanded, receding farther and farther away. She felt like an insect crawling along the ground. Minute details sprang into sharp focus. Her eyes traced the outline of a footprint, saw every small pebble, each grain of dust. She caught a movement out of the corner of her eye and watched a spider climbing a shining cable of silk glistening in the light of a torch.

The flame hypnotized her. She stared at the flickering, dancing light and watched black smoke curling up to the dark ceiling. She moved closer to the torch, then saw another one. She followed its beckoning flame, but when she reached it, another torch beckoned, and then another, drawing her ever deeper into the cave. She didn't notice when the fires of torches became the fires of small stone lamps spaced far apart, and she wasn't noticed when she passed by a large interior room full of men lost in a deep trance or the smaller room that held adolescent boys led by older acolytes in a ceremony that gave them a taste of the adult male experience.

With single-minded purpose, she walked toward each tiny flame, only to be drawn to the next one. The lights led her through narrow passages that opened into larger rooms, then narrowed again. She stumbled on the uneven floor, groping for the damp rocky wall spinning around her. She turned into a passage and at the far end saw a large, rosy glow. It was incredibly long; it went on and on forever. Often, she seemed to see herself from a great distance staggering along the dimly lit tunnel. She felt her mind drawn farther into the distance, into a deep black void, but she quailed before the immensity of nothingness and struggled to retreat from it.

Finally, she neared the light at the end of the tunnel and saw several figures seated in a circle. From some well of caution buried deep in her drug-clouded mind, she stopped short of the last mesmerizing flames and hid behind a stone pillar. In their lighted chamber, the ten mog-urs were deeply involved in a ritual. They had begun the ceremony that included all the men of the Clan, but left their acolytes to conclude it and retreated to the inner sanctum alone to conduct rites too secret even for acolytes.

Each man, cloaked in his bearskin, sat behind the skull of

a cave bear. Other skulls adorned niches in the walls. In the middle of their circle was a hairy object Ayla couldn't identify at first. But when she did, only her drug-induced stupor kept her from crying out. It was the severed head of Gorn.

She watched with fascinated horror as the mog-ur of Norg's clan reached for the head, turned it over, and with a stone enlarged the foramen magnum, the great opening of the spinal column. The pink-gray jellied mass of Gorn's brain lay exposed. The magician made silent gestures over the head, then reached into the opening with his hand and tore out a piece of the soft tissue. He held the quivering mass in his hand while the next mog-ur reached for the head. Even in her stupor, Ayla felt a deep revulsion, but she was held spellbound as each magician dipped into the grisly head and withdrew a portion of the brain of the man who had been killed by the cave bear.

A whirling, spinning vertigo brought Ayla to the brink of the deep emptiness. She swallowed to keep from being sick. Desperately, she clung to the edge of the void, but when she saw the great holy men of the Clan move their hands to their mouths and eat Gorn's brain, she let go. The act of cannibalism drove her into an abyss of black space.

She screamed soundlessly, unable to hear herself. She was unable to see, unable to feel, devoid of any sensations, but she knew it. She hadn't escaped into a mind-blanking sleep. The void had another quality, a terrifying, empty quality. Fear, all-encompassing fear, gripped her. She struggled to return, screamed silently for help, but was only drawn deeper. She sensed movement she could not sense as, faster and faster, she fell into the deep black infinity, into the endless cold void.

Suddenly, her motionless motion slowed. She felt a tickling sensation inside her brain, inside her mind, and a counterpull that slowly drew her back over the edge, out of the infinite hole. She sensed emotions alien to her, emotions not her own. Strongest was love, but mixed in was deep anger and great fear, and then, a hint of curiosity. With a shock, she realized Mog-ur was inside her head. In her mind, she felt his thoughts, with her emotions, his feelings. There was a distinctly physical quality to it, a sense of crowding without its unpleasantness, more like a touching that was closer than physical touching.

The mind-altering roots from Iza's red bag accentuated a

natural tendency of the Clan. Instinct had evolved, in Clan people, into memory. But memory, taken far enough back, became identical, became racial memory. The racial memories of the Clan were the same; and with perceptions sensitized, they could share their identical memories. The trained mog-urs had developed their natural tendency with conscious effort. They were all capable of some control over the shared memories, but The Mog-ur was born with a unique ability.

Not only could he share the memories, and control them, he could keep the link intact as their thoughts moved through time from the past to the present. The men of his clan enjoyed a richer, fuller ceremonial interrelationship than any other clan. But with the trained minds of the mog-urs, he could make the telepathic link from the beginning. Through him, all the mog-urs shared a union far closer and more satisfying than any physical one—it was a touching of spirits. The white liquid from Iza's bowl that had heightened the perceptions and opened the minds of the magicians to The Mog-ur, had allowed his special ability to create a symbiosis with Ayla's mind as well.

The traumatic birth that damaged the brain of the disfigured man had impaired only a portion of his physical abilities, not the sensitive psychic overdevelopment that enabled his great power. But the crippled man was the ultimate end-product of his kind. Only in him had nature taken the course set for the Clan to its fullest extreme. There could be no further development without radical change, and their characteristics were no longer adaptable. Like the huge creature they venerated, and many others that shared their environment, they were incapable of surviving radical change.

The race of men with social conscience enough to care for their weak and wounded, with spiritual awareness enough to bury their dead and venerate their great totem, the race of men with great brains but no frontal lobes, who made no great strides forward, who made almost no progress in nearly a hundred thousand years, was doomed to go the way of the woolly mammoth and the great cave bear. They didn't know it, but their days on earth were numbered, they were doomed to extinction. In Creb, they had reached the end of their line.

Ayla felt a sensation akin to the deep pulsing of a foreign bloodstream superimposed on her own. The powerful mind of the great magician was exploring her alien convolutions, trying to find a way to mesh. The fit was imperfect, but he found channels of similarity, and where none existed, he groped for alternatives and made connections where there were only tendencies. With startling clarity, she suddenly comprehended that it was he who had brought her out of the void; but more, he was keeping the other mog-urs, also linked with him, from knowing she was there. She could just barely sense his connection with them, but she could not sense them at all. They, too, knew he had made a connection with someone—or some*thing*—else, but never dreamed it was Ayla.

And just as she understood Mog-ur had saved her and was still protecting her, she knew the profound sense of reverence with which the magicians had indulged in the cannibalistic act that had so revolted her. She hadn't realized, she had no way of knowing, that it was a communion. The reason for the Gathering of the clans was to bind them together, to make them Clan. But Clan was more than the ten clans here. They all knew of clans that lived too far away to travel to this meeting; they went to Clan Gatherings closer to their own caves. They were still Clan. All Clan people shared a common heritage, and remembered it, and any ritual performed at any one Gathering had the same significance for all. The magicians believed they were making a beneficial contribution to the Clan. They were absorbing the courage of the young man who was journeying with the Spirit of Ursus. And since they were mog-urs, with special abilities within their brains, it was they who were capable of dispersing the courage to all.

That was the reason for Mog-ur's anger, and his fear. By long tradition, only men were allowed to share in the ceremonies of the Clan. The consequences of a woman viewing even an ordinary ceremony held by a single clan meant that the clan was doomed. This was no ordinary ceremony. This was a ceremony of great significance for the whole Clan. Ayla was a woman; her presence could mean only one thing—irreversible, irredeemable misfortune and calamity to them all.

And she was not even a woman of the Clan. Mog-ur knew that now with a surety he could no longer deny. From the moment he became aware of her presence, he knew she was not Clan. He understood, as quickly, the consequences of her presence, but it was already too late. They were implacable and he knew that, too. But her crime was so great, he wasn't sure what to do about her; even a death curse was not enough. Before he decided, he wanted to know more about her, and through her, more about the Others.

He was surprised he felt her cry for help. The Others were different, but there had to be similarities, too. He felt he needed to know for the sake of the Clan, and he had a curiosity greater than normal for his kind. She had always intrigued him; he wanted to know what made her different. He decided to try an experiment.

Forcing his way into deeper recesses, the powerful holy man—controlling the nine brains that matched his and willingly acquiesced and, separately, another that was similar and yet different—took them all back to their beginnings.

Ayla tasted the primordial forest again, then felt it turn to warm salt. Her impressions were not as clear as the rest—it was new to her, this feeling of being and remembering the dawn of life, and her memories of it were subconscious and vague. But her innermost, earliest levels matched. The beginnings were the same, Mog-ur thought. She felt the individuality of her own cells and knew when they split and differentiated in the warm, nurturing waters still carried within her. They grew and split and diverged, and motion had purpose. Again a divergence and soft pulsations of life became hard and gave shape and form.

Another divergence, and she knew the pain of the first explosion of air breathed by creatures in a new element. Diverge, and rich loamy earth and the green of a young verdancy and burrowing to escape crushing monsters. Diverge, and security in reaching a limb across a chasm, and suddenly heat and dryness, and drought driving her back to the edge of the sea. Diverge, and traces of a missing link lost in the sea that enlarged her form and stripped her fur and changed her contours—and left cousins behind to revert to an earlier, more streamlined shape, but still air-breathing and milk-nursing.

And now, she walked upright on two hind legs, leaving forelegs free to manipulate, and eyes to see a farther horizon, and the beginnings of a forebrain. She was veering away from Mog-ur, starting a different path, yet not so far apart that he couldn't track it with his own, almost parallel one. He broke contact with the others, but they were far enough along to continue their own way. It was nearly time to break it anyway.

Just the two of them remained linked, the old man of the Clan and the young woman of the Others. He was no longer guiding, but he still tracked, and not only did he track her course, she tracked his. She saw land change from warmth to ice, even deeper and more bone-chilling than the ice of their own times. It was a land far away in space as well as time, far to the west, she sensed, not far from a great sea many times larger than the sea that surrounded their peninsula.

She saw a cave, the home of some ancestor of the great magician, an ancestor who looked much like him. It was a hazy picture, seen across the chasm that separated their races. The cave was in a steep wall that faced a river and a flat plain. At the top of the cliff, a large boulder stood out distinctly. It was a long, slightly flattened column of rock that tilted over the edge, as though caught in the act of falling and frozen in place. The stone was from a different location, of a different material, an erratic, moved by raging waters and shifting earth until it lodged at the edge of the cliff that housed the cave. The picture wavered, but the memory of it stayed with her.

For a moment she felt an overwhelming sorrow. Then she was alone. Mog-ur could follow no more. She found her own way back to herself, and then a little beyond. She had a fleeting glimpse of the cave again, followed by a confusing kaleidoscope of landscapes, laid out not with the randomness of nature, but in regular patterns. Boxlike structures reared up from the earth and long ribbons of stone spread out, along which strange animals crawled at great speeds; huge birds flew without flapping their wings. Then more scenes, so strange she couldn't comprehend them. It happened in an instant. In her rush to reach the present, there was a slight overshoot, a small spike beyond her time, just to where she might have diverged again. Then her mind was clear, and she looked out from behind a pillar at ten men seated in a circle.

The Mog-ur was looking at her, and she saw in his deep brown eye the sorrow she had felt. He had forged indelible new paths in her brain, paths that let her glimpse ahead, but he could not forge new paths in his own. While she looked beyond, he caught a glimpse, not of the future, but of a sense of future. A future that was hers, but not his. He grasped the concept imperfectly, but he understood the potential of it, and quailed before it.

Creb could make almost no abstractions. He could count, only with great effort, to just beyond twenty. He could make no quantum leaps, no intuitive strokes of genius. His mind, he knew, was more powerful than hers by far; more intelligent perhaps. But his genius was of a different nature. He could identify with his beginnings, and hers. He could remember more and better than any of his own ancient Clan. He could even force her to remember. But in her, he sensed the youth, the vitality of a newer form. She had diverged again, and he had not.

"Get out!" Ayla jumped at his sharp command, surprised he had spoken so loud. Then she realized he hadn't spoken at all. She had felt, not heard him. "Get out of the cave! Hurry! Get out now!"

She sprang from her hiding place and ran down the passage. Some of the stone lamps had burned through the moss wicks, other were sputtering and dying. But there were enough to guide her way. No sound emerged from the inner caves where all the men and boys now slept the dreamless sleep. She came to the torches, some of them guttered, too, and finally dashed out of the cave.

It was still dark, but the faint glimmerings of a new day were beginning. Ayla's mind was clear, no trace of the powerful drug remained, but she was completely spent. She saw the women sprawled out on the ground, purged and drained, and lay down beside Uba. She was still naked, but noticed the morning chill no more than the other naked, sleeping women.

By the time Mog-ur reached the mouth of the cave after following behind her more slowly, she was in a deep, dreamless sleep. He hobbled up to her and looked down at her tousled blonde hair, as distinctly different from the rest of the women's hair as Ayla was herself, and a great heaviness descended on his soul. He should not have let her go. He should have brought her before the men and had her killed outright, then and there, for her crime. But what good would it do? It would not undo the catastrophe her presence had wrought, it would not cancel the calamity the Clan must bear. What good would it do to kill her? Ayla was only one of her kind, and she was the one he loved.

25

Goov walked out of the cave, blinked at the morning sunlight, rubbed his eyes, and stretched. He noticed Mog-ur sitting hunched over on a log, staring at the ground. So many lamps and torches are out, he thought, someone could make a wrong turn and get lost. I'll ask Mog-ur if I should refill the lamps and put up new torches. The acolyte strode purposefully toward the magician, but stopped when he saw the old man's drawn face and the despondent slump of his shoulders. Maybe I won't bother him, I'll just go ahead and do it.

Mog-ūr is getting old, Goov thought, walking back into the cave with a bladder of bear grease, new wicks, and extra torches. I keep forgetting how old he really is. The trip here was hard on him, and the ceremonies take a lot out of him. And there's still the journey back. Strange, the young acolyte mused, I never thought of him as old before.

A few more men wandered out of the cave rubbing sleepy eyes and stared at the naked women scattered on the ground, wondering, as they always did, what made them so exhausted. The first women to wake up ran for their wraps, then began to wake the others before too many more men came out of the cave.

"Ayla," Uba called, shaking the woman, "Ayla, wake up."

"Mmmmfff," Ayla mumbled, and rolled over.

"Ayla! Ayla!" Uba said again, shaking her harder. "Ebra, I can't get her up."

"Ayla!" the woman said louder, shaking her roughly. Ayla opened her eyes and tried to signal an answer, then closed them again and curled up in a tight ball.

"Ayla! Ayla!" Ebra said again. The young woman opened her eyes once more.

"Go into the cave and sleep it off, Ayla. You can't stay out here, the men are getting up," Ebra commanded.

The young woman stumbled toward the cave. A moment later she was back out, wide awake, but drained of color.

"What's wrong?" Uba motioned. "You're white. You look like you've seen a spirit."

"Uba. Oh, Uba. The bowl." Ayla slumped to the ground and buried her face in her hands.

"The bowl? What bowl, Ayla? I don't understand."

"It's broken," Ayla managed to gesture.

"Broken?" Ebra said. "Why should a broken bowl bother you so much? You can make another."

"No, I can't. Not like that one. It's Iza's bowl, the one she got from her mother."

"Mother's bowl? Mother's ceremonial bowl?" Uba asked, her face stricken.

The dry, brittle wood of the ancient relic had lost all its resilience after so many generations of use. A hairline crack had developed but went unnoticed beneath the white coating. The shock of dropping from Ayla's hand to the hard stone floor of the cave was more than it could take. It had split in two.

Ayla didn't notice Creb look up when she ran out of the cave. The knowledge that the venerable bowl was broken put a grim note of finality on his thoughts. It's fitting. Never again will the magic of those roots be used. I will never again hold any ceremony with them, and I will not teach Goov how they were used before. The Clan will forget them. The old cripple leaned heavily on his staff and pulled himself up, feeling twinges of pain in his arthritic joints. I have sat in cold caves long enough; it is time for Goov to take over. He's young for it, but I'm too old. If I push him, he can be ready in a year or two. He may have to be. Who knows how much longer I'll last?

Brun noticed a marked change in the old magician. He thought Mog-ur's depression was caused by a natural letdown after the excitement, especially since this would be his last Clan Gathering. Even so, Brun worried how he would weather the trip back and was sure he would slow them down on the way home. Brun decided to take his hunters on one last foray, and then exchange the fresh meat for some of the host clan's stored provisions to supplement their supply for the return trip.

After the successful hunt, Brun was in a hurry to leave. A few clans had left already. With the festivities over, his thoughts returned to the home cave and the people left behind, but he was in good spirits. The challenge to his position had never been greater; it made the victory all the more satisfactory. He was pleased with himself, pleased with his clan, and pleased with Ayla. She was a good medicine woman; he had seen it before. When someone's life was threatened, she forgot everything else, just like Iza. Brun knew Mog-ur had been instrumental in persuading the other magicians, but it was Ayla herself who proved it when she saved the young hunter's life. He and his mate were going to stay with the host clan until he was well enough to travel, probably wintering with them.

Mog-ur never spoke of Ayla's clandestine visit to the small chamber deep in the mountain—except once. She was packing, getting ready to depart the next morning, when Creb shuffled into the second cave. He had been avoiding her, and it hurt the young woman who loved him. He stopped short when he saw her, and turned to leave, but she cut off his departure by rushing up and sitting at his feet. He looked down at her bowed head, heaved a sigh, and tapped her shoulder.

She looked up, shocked to see how much he had aged in just a few days. The disfiguring scar and flap of skin that covered his empty eye socket were shriveled and sunk deeper into the shadow of his overhanging brow ridges. His gray beard hung limp from his prognathous jaw, and his low, back-slanted forehead was emphasized by a receding hairline; but it was the dark sorrow in his one, liquid, deep brown eye that overwhelmed her. What had she done to him? She wished fervently she could take back her trip into the cave that night. The hurt she felt for Creb when she saw his body racked with pain was nothing to the anguish she felt for the pain in Mog-ur's soul.

"What is it, Ayla?" he motioned.

"Mog-ur, I...I..." she fumbled, then rushed on. "Oh, Creb. I can't stand to see you hurting so. What can I do? I'll go to Brun, if you want, I'll do anything you ask. Just tell me what to do."

What *can* you do, Ayla, he thought. Can you change who you are? Can you take back the damage you did? The Clan will die, only you and your kind will be left. We are an ancient people. We have kept our traditions, honored the spirits and Great Ursus, but it is over for us, finished. Maybe it was meant to be. Maybe it wasn't you, Ayla, but your kind. Is that why you were brought to us? To tell me? The earth we leave is beautiful and rich; it gave us all we needed for all the generations we have lived. How will you leave it when it is your turn? What can you do?

"There is one thing you can do, Ayla," The Mog-ur gestured slowly, emphasizing every movement. His eye turned cold. "You can never mention it again."

He stood as tall as his one good leg would allow, trying not to lean too much on his staff. Then, with all the pride in himself and his People he could gather, he turned with stiff dignity and walked out of the cave.

"Broud!"

The young man strode over to the man who had greeted him. The women of Brun's clan were hurrying to finish the morning meal, they planned to leave as soon as they ate, and the men were taking one last opportunity to talk to people they would not see again for seven years. Some they would never see again. They were lingering over the details of the exciting meeting to make it last just a little longer.

"You did well this time, Broud, and by the next Gathering, you will be leader."

"Next time you may do as well," Broud gestured, puffing up with pride. "We were just lucky."

"You are lucky. Your clan is first, your mog-ur is first, even your medicine woman is first. You know, Broud, you're lucky to have Ayla. Not many medicine women would brave a cave bear to save a hunter."

Broud scowled slightly, then saw Voord and walked over to him.

"Voord!" he hailed, motioning a greeting. "You did well this time. I was glad when they chose you over Nouz. He was all right, but you were definitely better."

"But you deserved to be first choice, Broud. You ran a good race, too. Your whole clan deserves its place; even your medicine woman is best, though I had my doubts at first. She'll be a good medicine woman to have around when you are leader. I only hope she doesn't get any taller. Between you and me, I feel strange having to look up at a woman."

"Yes, the woman is too tall," Broud said with stiff gestures.

"But what does it matter, as long as she's a good medicine woman, right?"

Broud barely nodded, then waved aside further discussion

and walked away. Ayla, Ayla, I'm getting tired of Ayla, he thought, heading across the cleared space.

"Broud, I wanted to see you before you left," a man said, walking over to meet him halfway. "You know there is a woman in my clan with a daughter deformed like the son of your medicine woman. I talked to Brun and he has agreed to accept her, but he wanted me to talk to you. You'll most likely be leader by then. The mother has promised to raise her daughter to be a good woman, worthy of the first clan and the son of the first medicine woman. You don't have any objections, do you, Broud? It's a logical match."

"No," Broud gestured curtly and turned on his heel. If he hadn't been so angry, he might have objected, but he didn't feel like getting into a discussion about Ayla.

"By the way, that was a good race, Broud."

The young man didn't see the comment, his back was already turned. As he stalked toward the cave, he saw two women avidly engrossed in conversation. He knew he should look away to avoid seeing what they were saying, but he just stared straight ahead, affecting not to notice them.

"...I just couldn't believe she was a woman of the Clan, and then, when I saw her baby... But the way she walked right up to Ursus, just like she belonged to the host clan, not afraid of him or anything. I couldn't have done it."

"I talked to her for a while, she's really nice, and she acts perfectly normal. I can't help but wonder, though, do you think she'll ever find a mate? She's so tall, what man wants a woman taller than he is? Even if she is a first-ranked medicine woman."

"Someone told me one clan is considering her, but there just wasn't time to work out the details, and I think they want to talk about it. They said they'd send a runner if they decide to accept her."

"But don't they have a new cave? They say she found it, and that it's very big, and lucky, too."

"It's supposed to be near the sea, and the paths are well used. I think a good runner could find them."

Broud passed the two women and had to restrain an urge to cuff the lazy, gossiping busybodies. But they weren't of his clan, and though it was his prerogative to discipline any woman, it wasn't good policy to cuff one from another clan without permission of mates or leaders, unless the infractions were obvious. It was obvious enough to him, but it might not be to someone else.

"Our medicine woman says she's skilled," Norg was saying as Broud entered the cave.

"She is Iza's daughter," Brun motioned, "and Iza has trained her well."

"It's a shame Iza couldn't make it. She is ill, I understand."

"Yes, that's one reason I want to hurry. We have a long way to go. Your hospitality has been excellent, Norg, but one's own cave is home. This has been one of the best Clan Gatherings. It will be long remembered," Brun said.

Broud turned his back, clenching his fists, before he could see the compliment Norg paid to the son of Brun's mate. Ayla, Ayla, Ayla. Everybody is talking about Ayla. You'd think no one did anything at this Clan Gathering except her. Was she first chosen? Who was on the bear's head while she was safely on the ground? So what if she saved that hunter's life, he'll probably never walk again. She's ugly, and she's too tall, and her son is deformed, and they should know how insolent she is at home.

Just then, Ayla ran past, carrying several bundles. Broud's look of hate was so full of malice it made her flinch. What did I do now? she thought. I've hardly seen Broud the whole time we've been here.

Broud was a full-grown, powerfully built man of the Clan, but the threat he posed was far greater than mere physical harm. He was the son of the leader's mate, and destined to be leader himself one day. He thought about that as he watched Ayla put her bundles down outside the cave.

After they ate, the women quickly packed the few utensils they had used to make the morning meal. Brun was impatient to leave, and so were they. Ayla had a few last gestures with some of the medicine women, Norg's mate, and a few others, then wrapped her son in his carrying cloak and took her place in front of the women of Brun's clan. Brun gave a signal, and they started across the cleared area in front of the cave. Before rounding the bend in the trail, Brun stopped, and they all turned to look back one last time. Norg and his whole clan were standing at the mouth of their cave.

"Walk with Ursus," Norg signaled.

Brun nodded and started out again. It would be seven years before they saw Norg again—or perhaps never. Only the Spirit of the Great Cave Bear knew.

Just as Brun had thought, the return trip was difficult for Creb. No longer buoyed by anticipation, and further depressed by brooding over the knowledge he kept secret, the old man's body betrayed him time and time again. Brun's concern deepened; he had never known the great magician to be so dispirited. He lagged behind. Many times Brun had to send a hunter back to find him while they waited. The leader slowed the pace, hoping it would make it easier for him, but Creb just didn't seem to care. The few evening ceremonies, held at Brun's insistence, lacked force. Mog-ur seemed reluctant, his gestures stiff, as though his heart wasn't in it. Brun noticed that Creb and Ayla kept their distance, and though she had no trouble keeping up, Ayla's step had lost its spring. There's something wrong between those two, he thought.

They had been traveling through tall, sere grass since midmorning. Brun glanced back; Creb was nowhere in sight. He started to signal one of the men, then changed his mind and walked back to Ayla instead.

"Go back and find Mog-ur," he motioned.

She looked surprised, then nodded. Giving Durc to Uba, she hurried back along the trail of bent, stepped-on grass. She found him quite a distance behind, walking slowly and leaning heavily on his staff. He seemed to be in pain. Ayla had been so stunned by his response to her loving remorse she hadn't known what to say to him afterward. She was sure he was suffering from his aching, arthritic joints, but he had refused to let her give him anything for the pain. After the first few rebuffs, she didn't offer again, though her heart ached for him. He stopped when he saw her.

"What are you doing here?" he gestured.

"Brun sent me back for you."

Creb grunted and started walking again. Ayla fell in behind him. She watched his slow, painful movements until she couldn't stand it anymore. She went around him and dropped to the ground at his feet, forcing him to stop. Creb looked down at the young woman for a long time before he tapped her shoulder.

"This woman would know why The Mog-ur is angry."

"I'm not angry, Ayla."

"Then why won't you let me help you?" she pleaded. "You never refused before." Ayla struggled to compose herself. "This woman is a medicine woman. She is trained to help those in pain. It is her place, her function. It hurts this woman to see The Mog-ur suffer, she cannot help it." Ayla couldn't maintain the formal posture. "Oh, Creb, let me help you. Don't you know I love you? To me, you are like the mate of my mother. You have provided for me, spoken for me, I owe my life to you. I don't know why you stopped loving me, but I haven't stopped loving you." Tears streamed down her face in hopeless desperation.

Why does water always come to her eyes when she thinks I don't love her? And why should her weak eyes always make me want to do something for her? Do all the Others have that problem? She is right, I never minded her help before, why should it matter now? She is not a woman of the Clan. No matter what the rest think, she was born to the Others and she will always be one of them. She doesn't even know it. She thinks she's a Clan woman, she thinks she's a medicine woman. She is a medicine woman. She may not be of Iza's line, but she is a medicine woman, and she has tried to become a Clan woman, as hard as it was for her sometimes. I wonder, how hard is it for her? This is not the first time water has come to her eyes, but how many times has she fought to hold it back? It's when she thinks I don't love her that she can't hold it. Can it hurt her so much? How much would it hurt me if I thought she didn't love me? More than I'd like to think. If she loves the same, can she be so different? Creb tried to see her as a stranger, as a woman of the Others. But she was still Ayla, still the child of the mate he never had.

"We'd better hurry, Ayla. Brun is waiting. Wipe your eyes, and when we stop, you can make me some willow-bark tea, medicine woman."

A smile broke through her tears. She scrambled up and fell in behind him again. After a few paces, she moved up to his weak side. He halted a moment, then nodded and leaned on her for support.

Brun noticed an improvement immediately and soon picked up the pace again, though they still weren't traveling as fast as he would have liked. There was an air of melancholy about the old man, but he seemed to be trying harder.

I knew there was a problem with those two, Brun thought, but they seem to have worked it out. He was glad he had the idea to send her back for him.

Creb did let Ayla help him, but there was still a distance between them, a breach too great for him to span. He couldn't forget the difference in their destinies and it created a strain that dampened the easy warmth of earlier days.

Though the days were hot as Brun's clan trekked back to their cave, the nights were growing cool. The first sight of snowcapped mountains far to the west heartened the clan, but as the distance hardly diminished with the passing days, the range at the southern tip of the peninsula became just a part of the scenery. The distance did diminish, though, however imperceptibly. As they continued day after weary day in their westward direction, the blue depths of crevasses gave character to the glaciers and the indistinct purple below the icy crown took on shapes of outcrops and ridges.

They pushed on until dark before they made camp the last night on the steppes, and everyone was awake at first light. The plains merged into a parkland of open meadow and tall trees, and the sight of a grass-eating, temperate-climate rhinoceros brought a feeling of familiarity, after it went on its way without deigning to notice them. The pace quickened when they came to a path that wound up the foothills. Then they rounded a familiar ridge and saw their cave, and every heart beat faster. They were home.

Aba and Zoug were rushing to meet them. Aba welcomed her daughter and Droog joyously, hugged the older children, then took Groob in her arms. Zoug nodded at Ayla as he ran toward Grod and Uka, then Ovra and Goov.

"Where is Dorv?" Ika motioned.

"He walks in the world of the spirits now," Zoug replied. "His eyes got so bad, he couldn't see what anyone was saying. I think he gave up and didn't want to wait for your return. When the spirits called, he left with them. We buried him and marked the place so Mog-ur could find it for the death rites."

Ayla looked around, suddenly anxious. "Where's Iza?"

"She is very ill, Ayla," Aba said. "She hasn't been out of her bed since the last new moon."

"Iza! Not Iza! No! No!" Ayla cried, running toward the

cave. She threw her bundles down when she reached Creb's hearth and rushed toward the woman lying on her furs.

"Iza! Iza!" the young woman cried. The old medicine woman opened her eyes.

"Ayla," she said, her gruff voice barely audible. "The spirits have granted my wish," she motioned feebly. "You're back." Iza held out her arms. Ayla embraced her and felt her thin, frail body, hardly more than bones covered with wrinkled skin. Her hair was snow white; her face, dried parchment stretched over bones with hollow cheeks and sunken eyes. She looked a thousand years old. She was just past twenty-six.

Ayla could hardly see for the tears that streamed down her face. "Why did I go to the Clan Gathering? I should have stayed here and taken care of you. I knew you were sick; why did I go away and leave you?"

"No, no, Ayla," Iza motioned. "Don't blame yourself. You can't change what is meant to be. I knew I was dying when you left. You couldn't have helped me, no one could. I just wanted to see you one more time before I went to join the spirits."

"You can't die! I won't let you die! I'll take care of you. I'll make you get well," Ayla gestured wildly.

"Ayla, Ayla. There are some things even the best medicine woman cannot do."

The exertion brought on a coughing spell. Ayla held her propped up until the cough quieted. She shoved her fur behind the woman to raise her up and make her breathing easier, then began rummaging through the medicines stored near Iza's bed.

"Where's the elecampane? I can't find any elecampane."

"I don't think there's any left," Iza motioned weakly. The fit of coughing had exhausted her. "I used a lot of it and couldn't go out to get more. Aba tried to find some, but she brought back sunflowers."

"I shouldn't have gone," Ayla said, then raced out of the cave. She met Uba, carrying Durc, and Creb at the entrance.

"Iza's sick," Ayla waved frantically, "and she doesn't even have any elecampane. I'm going to get some. There's no fire at the hearth, Uba. Why did I go to the Clan Gathering? I should have stayed here with her. Why did I leave?" Ayla's bleak face, grimy with travel, was streaked with tears, but she neither noticed nor cared. She ran down the slope as Creb and Uba hurried into the cave.

Ayla splashed across the stream, raced to the meadow where the plants grew, and dug up the roots with her bare hands, tearing them out of the ground. Stopping at the stream just long enough to wash them, she sped back to the cave.

Uba had a fire going, but the water she had started heating was just barely warm. Creb was standing over Iza making formal motions with more fervor than he had felt for many days, calling on every spirit he knew to strengthen her life essence, and pleading with them not to take her, yet. Uba had put Durc on a mat. He was just starting to crawl and pulled himself up on his hands and knees. He scooted toward his mother busy cutting up the root into small pieces, but she pushed him away when he tried to nurse. Ayla had no time for her son. He started to howl while she dumped the root into the water and added more rocks, impatient for it to boil.

"Let me see Durc," Iza motioned. "He's grown so much."

Uba picked him up and brought him to her mother. She put the baby on Iza's lap, but he was in no mood to cuddle with an old woman he didn't remember, and struggled to get down again.

"He's strong and healthy," Iza said, "and he doesn't have any problems holding his head up."

"He even has a mate already," Uba said, "or at least a baby girl that has been promised for him."

"A mate? What clan would promise a girl to him? So young, and with his deformity."

"There was a woman at the Clan Gathering with a deformed daughter. She came and talked to us the first day," Uba explained. "The baby even looks like Durc, at least her head does. Her features are a little different. The mother asked if they could be mated; Oda was so worried that her daughter would never find a mate. Brun and the leader of her clan arranged it. I think she will be coming here to live after the next Gathering, even if she's not a woman. Ebra said she could live with her until they were both old enough to mate. Oda was so happy, especially after Ayla made the drink for the ceremony."

"So they did accept Ayla as a medicine woman of my line. I wondered if they would," Iza gestured, then she stopped. Talking made her tired, but just seeing her loved ones around her again rejuvenated her spirit, if not her body. She rested for a while, then asked, "What is the girl's name?"

"Ura," Iza's daughter answered.

"I like the name, it has a good sound." Iza rested again, then asked another question. "What about Ayla? Did she find a mate at the Clan Gathering?"

"The clan of Zoug's kin is considering her. They refused at first, but after she was accepted as a medicine woman, they decided to think it over. There wasn't time to settle anything before we left. They might take Ayla, but I don't think they want Durc."

Iza just nodded, then closed her eyes.

Ayla was grinding meat to make into a broth for Iza. She kept checking the boiling water with the root for the right color and flavor, impatient for it to be done. Durc crawled up to her, whining, but she brushed him off again.

"Give him to me, Uba," Creb motioned. It quieted the boy for a while, sitting in Creb's lap, intrigued with the man's beard. But he soon grew tired of that, too. He rubbed his eyes and struggled to get loose of the restraining arm, and when freed crawled straight for his mother again. He was tired, and he was hungry. Ayla was standing over the fire and hardly seemed to notice when the cranky baby tried to pull up on her leg. Creb heaved himself up, then dropped his staff and signaled Uba to put the boy into his arm. Limping heavily without his support, he shuffled to Broud's hearth and laid Durc in Oga's lap.

"Durc is hungry and Ayla is busy making medicine for Iza. Will you feed him, Oga?"

Oga nodded, took the baby from him, and gave Durc her breast. Broud glowered, but one dark glance from Mog-ur made him cover his anger quickly. His hatred of Ayla did not extend to the man who protected and provided for her. Broud feared Mog-ur too much to hate him. He had discovered at an early age, however, that the great holy man seldom interfered in the secular life of the clan, confining his activities to the spirit world. Mog-ur had never tried to prevent Broud from exercising control over the young female who shared his hearth, but Broud had no wish to lock horns with the magician directly.

The man shuffled back to his hearth and began to search through the bundles that had been dumped for the bladder of cave bear grease that was his share of the rendered fat from the ceremonial animal. Uba saw him and hurried over to help. Creb took it with him into his place of the spirits. Though he was sure it was hopeless, he was going to use every bit of magic at his command to help Ayla try to keep Iza alive.

The roots had finally boiled long enough and Ayla scooped out a cup of the liquid, impatient now for it to cool. The warm broth fed to her earlier, in small sips with Ayla propping her head up just as Iza had done for her when she was a five-year-old and near death, had revived the old medicine woman somewhat. She had eaten little since she had taken to her bed, and not much before. Food brought to her often went untouched. It had been a desolate, lonely summer for Iza. With no one around to watch her and make sure she ate, she often forgot, or just didn't bother. The other three had all tried to help when they saw she was failing, but they didn't know how.

Iza had roused herself when Dorv's end was near, but the oldest member of the clan went quickly and there was little she could do except try to make him more comfortable. His death had cast a pall on the others. The cave seemed far emptier with him gone and it made them all realize how close they were to the next world. His was the first death since the earthquake.

Ayla was sitting beside Iza, blowing on the liquid in the bone cup and tasting now and then to see if it was cool enough. Her concentration on Iza was so complete, she didn't notice Creb leaving with Durc or see him go into his small cave, and she wasn't aware that Brun was watching her. She heard the soft bubbling sounds of Iza's breath and knew she was dying, but wouldn't let herself believe it. She searched her memory for treatments.

A poultice of the inner bark of balsam, she thought. Yes, and a yarrow tea. Breathing the steam will help, too. Blackberries and wort, and maidenhair. No, that's just for a minor cold. Burdock roots? Maybe. Starchwort? Of course, and the fresh root is best in fall. Ayla was determined to fill Iza with teas, cover her with poultices, and drown her in steam, if necessary. Anything, everything, to prolong the life of her mother, the only mother she knew. She could not bear the thought of Iza's death.

Though Uba was acutely conscious of the seriousness of her mother's illness, she was not unaware of Brun's presence. It was not common for men to pay a visit to another man's hearth when he wasn't there, and Brun made Uba nervous. She scurried to pick up the bundles strewn around the hearth to tidy it up, glancing from Brun to Ayla to her mother. With no one to guide her and give her direction, she didn't know how to handle Brun's visit. No one acknowledged him, no one welcomed him, what was she supposed to do?

Brun observed the trio of females—the old medicine woman, the intense young medicine woman who bore no resemblance to the Clan, yet was their highest-ranked woman of healing, and Uba, destined to be a medicine woman, too. He had always been fond of his sibling. She was the baby girl who was petted and coddled, and welcomed, once a healthy boy had been born to take over the leadership. He had always felt protective toward her. He would never have chosen the man who had been her mate for her; Brun never had liked him, a braggart who ridiculed his crippled brother. Iza had no choice, but she handled it well. Yet she had been happier since her mate died than she ever had before. She was a good woman, a good medicine woman. The clan would miss her.

Iza's daughter is growing up, he thought, watching her. Uba will be a woman soon. I should start thinking about a mate for her. It should be a good mate, one who will be compatible. It's better for a hunter, too, if his mate is devoted to him. But who is there except Vorn? There's Ona to consider, too, and she can't mate Vorn, they're siblings. She'll have to wait until Borg is a man. If she becomes a woman early, she could have a child before Borg is ready to mate. Perhaps I should push him a little, he's older than Ona. Once he's old enough to relieve his needs, he's old enough to become a man. Will Vorn be a good mate for Uba? Droog has been a good influence on him, and he likes to show off around her. Perhaps there is an attraction there. Brun filed his thoughts away in his orderly mind for future reference.

The elecampane-root tea was cooled and Ayla wakened the old woman who had dozed off, tenderly cradling her head while she fed her the medicine. I don't think you will pull her through this time, Ayla, Brun said to himself, watching the frail woman. How did she age so fast? She was the youngest; now she looks older than Creb. I remember the time she set my broken arm. She wasn't much older than Ayla was when she set Brac's, but a woman and mated. She did a good job, too. It's never given me any trouble, except a few twinges lately. I'm getting old, too. My hunting days will soon be over, and I'll have to pass the leadership to Broud.

Is he ready for it? He did so well at the Clan Gathering, I almost gave it to him then. He's brave; everyone told me how lucky I am. I am lucky, I was afraid he might be chosen to go with Ursus. It would have been an honor, but that's one honor I was glad to forgo. Gorn was a good man, it was hard on Norg's clan. It always is when Ursus chooses. Sometimes it's lucky not to be honored; the son of my mate still walks this world. And he is fearless. Maybe too fearless. A bit of daring and recklessness is fine for a young man, but a leader must be more sober. He must consider his men. He must think and plan so the hunt will be successful, yet not endanger his men needlessly. Maybe I should start to let him lead a few hunts, to give him the experience. He's got to learn there's more to leadership than daring. There's responsibility and self-control.

What is it about Ayla that brings out the worst in him? Why does he demean himself by competing with her? She may look a little different, but she's still a woman. Brave for a woman, though, determined. I wonder if Zoug's kin will take her? It would seem strange without her, now that I've gotten used to her. And she is a good medicine woman, an asset to any clan. I'll do what I can to make sure they appreciate her value. Look at her—not even her son, the son she was ready to follow to the next world, can take her mind off Iza. Not many would brave a cave bear to save a man's life. She can be fearless, too, and she's learned to control herself. She behaved well at the Gathering, in every way a proper woman, not like when she was younger. No one had anything but praise for her by the time it was over.

"Brun," Iza called out in a weak voice. "Uba, bring the leader some tea," she motioned, trying to sit up straighter. She was still the proper mistress of Creb's hearth. "Ayla, bring a fur for Brun to sit on. This woman regrets she is unable to serve the leader herself."

"Iza, don't trouble yourself. I didn't come for tea, I came to see you," Brun gestured, sitting down beside her bed.

"How long have you been standing there?" Iza asked.

"Not long. Ayla was busy; I chose not to disturb her, or you, until she was through. You were missed at the Clan Gathering."

"Was it successful?"

"This clan is still first. The hunters did well; Broud was chosen first for the Bear Ceremony. Ayla did well, too. She received many compliments."

"Compliments! Who needs compliments? Too many make the spirits jealous. If she did well, if she brought honor to the clan, that is enough."

"She did well. She was accepted, she behaved as a proper woman. She is your daughter, Iza. How can anyone expect less?"

"Yes, she is my daughter, as much as Uba is my daughter. I was fortunate, the spirits chose to favor me with two daughters and both of them will be good medicine women. Ayla can finish training Uba."

"No!" Ayla interrupted. "You will finish Uba's training. You're going to get well. We're back now, we'll take care of you. You'll get well, just wait and see," she motioned with earnest desperation. "You have to get well, mother."

"Ayla. Child. The spirits are ready for me, I must go with them soon. They gave me my last wish, to see my loved ones before I go, but I can't make them wait much longer."

The broth and medicine had stimulated the last of the sick woman's reserves. Her temperature was rising in her body's valiant effort to fight off the disease that had sapped her. The sparkle in her fever-glazed eyes and the color it lent to her cheeks gave her a false look of health. But there was a translucent glow to Iza's face as though lit from within. It was not the flush of life. The eerie quality was called the spirit glow, and Brun had seen it before. It was the rising of the life force as it prepared to leave.

Oga kept Durc at Broud's hearth until late, returning the sleeping child long after the sun had set. Uba laid him on Ayla's furs that she had spread out. The girl was frightened and lost. She had no one to turn to. She was afraid to interrupt Ayla in her efforts to save Iza, and afraid to disturb her mother. Creb had returned only long enough to paint symbols on Iza's body with a paste of red ochre and bear fat, while he made his gestures over her. He returned to the small cave immediately afterward and didn't return.

Uba had unpacked everything and set the hearth in order, made an evening meal that no one ate, and cleared it away. Then she sat quietly beside the sleeping baby, wishing she could think of something to do, anything to keep busy. Though it didn't still the terror in her heart, activity at least kept her occupied. It was better than just sitting there watching her mother die. Finally she lay down on Ayla's bed, curling herself around the baby, cuddling close to him in a forlorn attempt to draw warmth and security from someone.

Ayla worked constantly over Iza, trying every medicine and treatment she could think of. She hovered over her, afraid to leave her side, afraid the woman would slip away while she was gone. She was not the only one who maintained a vigil that night. Only the young children slept. At every hearth in the darkened cave, men and women stared at the red coals of banked fires, or lay on furs with open eyes.

The sky outside was overcast, blotting out the stars. The darkness inside the cave faded into a deeper black at the wide entrance, shrouding any hint of life beyond the dying embers of the cave fire. In the still of early morning, when the night was full into its somber depths, Ayla jerked her head up from a momentary doze.

"Ayla," Iza said again in a hoarse whisper.

"What is it, Iza?" she motioned. The medicine woman's eyes reflected the dim light of the ruddy charcoal in the fireplace.

"I want to say something before I go," Iza gestured, then dropped her hands. It was an effort for her to move them.

"Don't try to talk, mother. Just rest. You'll be stronger in the morning."

"No, child, I must say it now. I won't last until morning."

"Yes, you will. You have to. You can't go," Ayla signaled.

"Ayla, I'm going, you have to accept it. Let me finish, I don't have much longer." Iza rested again, while Ayla waited in mute hopelessness.

"Ayla, I always loved you best. I don't know why, but it's true. I wanted to keep you with me, wanted you to stay with the clan. But soon I'll be gone. Creb will find his way to the spirit world before long, and Brun is getting old, too. Then Broud will be leader. Ayla, you cannot stay here when Broud is the leader. He will find a way to hurt you." Iza rested again, closing her eyes and fighting for breath and strength to continue.

"Ayla, my daughter, my strange willful child who always tried so hard, I trained you to be a medicine woman so you would have enough status to stay with the clan, even if you never found a mate. But you are a woman, you need a mate, a man of your own. You are not Clan, Ayla. You were born to the Others, you belong with them. You must leave, child, find your own kind."

"Leave?" she motioned, confused. "Where would I go, Iza? I don't know any Others, I wouldn't even know where to look for them."

"There are many to the north of here, Ayla, on the mainland beyond the peninsula. My mother told me the man her mother healed came from the north." Iza stopped again, then forced herself to go on. "You cannot stay here, Ayla. Go and find them, my child. Find your own people, find your own mate."

Iza's hands dropped suddenly and her eyes closed. Her breathing was shallow. She strained to take a deep breath and opened her eyes again.

"Tell Uba I love her, Ayla. But you were my first child, the daughter of my heart. Always loved you ... loved you best ..." Iza's breath expired with a bubbling sigh. She did not take another.

"Iza! Iza!" Ayla screamed. "Mother, don't go, don't leave me! Oh, mother, don't go."

Uba woke at Ayla's wail and ran to them. "Mother! Oh, no! My mother is gone! My mother is gone."

The girl and the young woman stared at each other.

"She told me to tell you she loved you, Uba," Ayla said. Her eyes were dry, the shock still hadn't fully registered in her brain. Creb shuffled toward them. He was already out of his cave before Ayla screamed. With a heaving sob, Ayla groped for them both, and they all found themselves clasped in a grieving embrace of mutual despair. Ayla's tears wet them all. Uba and Creb had no tears, but their pain was not less.

26

"Oga, will you feed Durc again?"

The one-armed man's gesture was plain to the young woman despite the squirming baby he held. Ayla should feed him, she thought. It's not good for her to go so long without nursing him. The tragedy of Iza's death and his confusion over Ayla's reaction were both apparent in Mogur's expression. She could not refuse the pleading magician.

"Of course I will," Oga said, and took Durc in her arms.

Creb hobbled back to his hearth. He saw Ayla still had not moved, though Ebra and Uka had taken Iza's body away to prepare it for burial. Her hair was disheveled and her face still smudged with travel grime and tears. She wore the same stained and dirty wrap she had worn during their long trek back from the Clan Gathering. Creb had put her son in her lap when he cried to be fed, but she was blind and deaf to his needs. Another woman would have understood that even deep grief could, eventually, be penetrated by a baby's cries. But Creb had little experience with mothers and babies. He knew women often fed each other's children, and he couldn't let the baby go hungry as long as there were other women who could nurse him. He had taken Durc to Aga and Ika, but their youngest were close to being weaned and they had only a limited supply of milk. Grev was only a little more than a year old and Oga always seemed to have plenty, so Creb had brought Durc to her several times. Ayla didn't feel the ache of her hard and caking unsuckled breasts; the ache in her heart was greater.

Mog-ur picked up his staff and limped toward the back of the cave. Rocks had been brought in and piled in a heap in an unused corner of the large cavern, and a shallow trench scooped out of the dirt floor. Iza had been a first-ranked medicine woman. Not only her position in the clan hierarchy, but her intimacy with the spirits dictated a burial place within the cave. It guaranteed that the protective spirits that watched over her would linger near her clan, and she herself could look in on them from her home in the next world. And it assured that no scavenger would scatter her bones.

The magician sprinkled red ochre dust inside the oval of the trench, then made his one-handed gestures. After he consecrated the ground where Iza would be buried, he hobbled over to a lumpy shape draped loosely with a soft leather hide. He pulled the cover back to reveal the gray naked body of the medicine woman. Her arms and legs had been flexed and tied into a fetal position with red-dyed sinew. The magician made a protective gesture, then lowered himself down and began to rub the cold flesh with a salve of red ochre and cave bear fat. Bent into a fetal position and covered with the red that resembled the blood of birth, Iza would be delivered into the next world the same way she had arrived in this one.

Never had it been more difficult for him to perform this task. Iza had been more than sibling to Creb. She knew him better than anyone. She knew the pain he had endured without complaint, the shame he had suffered because of his affliction. She understood his gentleness, his sensitivity, and she rejoiced for his greatness, his power, and his will to overcome. She had cooked for him, cared for him, soothed his aches. With her he had known the joys of family life almost like an ordinary man. Though he had never touched her as intimately as he did then, rubbing her cold body with salve, she had been more "mate" to him than many men had. Her death devastated him.

When he returned to his hearth, Creb's face was as gray as the body had been. Ayla still sat next to Iza's bed staring blankly into space, but she stirred when Creb began to rummage through Iza's belongings.

"What are you doing?" she motioned, protective of anything that was Iza's.

"I'm looking for Iza's bowls and things. The tools she used in this life should be buried with her so she has the spirit of them in the next world," Creb explained.

"I'll get them," Ayla said, pushing Creb aside. She gathered together the wooden bowls and bone cups Iza had used to make her medicines and measure dosage, the round hand stone and flat stone base used for crushing and grinding, her personal eating dishes, a few implements, and her medicine bag, and put them on Iza's bed. Then she stared at the meager pile that represented Iza's life and work.

"Those are not Iza's tools!" Ayla gestured angrily, then jumped up and ran out of the cave. Creb watched her go, then shook his head and began to gather up Iza's tools.

Ayla crossed the stream and ran to a meadow where she and Iza had gone before. She stopped at a stand of colorful hollyhocks on long graceful stems and gathered an armful of different hues. Then she picked the many-petaled, daisy-like yarrow used for poultices and pain. She ran through the meadows and woods collecting more plants Iza had used in making her healing magic: white-leafed thistle with round, pale yellow flowers and yellow spikes; large, brilliant yellow groundsels; grape hyacinths, so blue they were almost black.

Every one of the plants she picked had found their way into Iza's pharmacopoeia at some time, but she selected only those that were also beautiful, with colorful, sweet-smelling flowers. Ayla was crying again as she stopped on the edge of a meadow with her flowers, remembering the times she and Iza had walked together gathering plants. Her arms were so full, she had trouble carrying them without her collecting basket. Several blossoms dropped and she knelt down to pick them up again and saw the tangled branches of a woody horsetail with its small flowers, and almost smiled at the idea that occurred to her.

She searched in a fold, pulled out a knife, and cut a branch of the plant. In the warm sun of early fall, Ayla sat at the edge of the meadow twining the stems of the beautiful blossoms in between and around the supporting network until the entire branch was a riot of color.

The whole clan was astonished when Ayla marched into the cave with her floral wreath. She went straight to the back of the cave and laid it beside the body of the medicine woman resting on its side in the shallow trench within an oval of stones.

"These were Iza's tools!" Ayla gestured defiantly, daring anyone to dispute her.

The old magician nodded. She's right, he thought. Those were Iza's tools, those were what she knew, what she worked with all her life. She might be happy to have them in the world of the spirits. I wonder, do flowers grow there?

Iza's tools, the implements and the flowers, were put in the grave with the woman, and the clan began to pile the stones around and on top of her body while Mog-ur made motions that asked the Spirit of Great Ursus and her Saiga Antelope totem to guide Iza's spirit safely to the next world.

"Wait!" Ayla suddenly interrupted. "I forgot something." She ran back to the hearth and searched for her medicine bag, and carefully withdrew the two halves of the ancient medicine bowl. She rushed back, then laid the pieces in the grave beside Iza's body.

"I thought she might want to take it with her, now that it can't be used anymore."

Mog-ur nodded approval. It was fitting, more fitting than anyone knew; then he resumed his formal gestures. After the last stone had been piled on, the women of the clan began to lay wood around and on top of the stone cairn. An ember from the cave fire was used to start the cooking fire for Iza's burial feast. The food was cooked on top of her grave, and the fire would be kept burning for seven days. The heat from the bonfire would drive all the moisture from the body, desiccating it, mummifying it, and rendering it odorless.

As the flames took hold, Mog-ur began a last, eloquent lament in motions that stirred the soul of every member of the clan. He spoke to the world of the spirits of their love for the medicine woman who had cared for them, watched over them, helped them through sickness and pain as mysterious to them as death. They were ritual gestures, repeated in essentially the same form for every funeral, and some of the motions were used primarily during the men's ceremonies and were unfamiliar to the women, yet the meaning was conveyed. Though the outward form was conventional, the fervor and conviction and ineffable sorrow of the great holy man imbued the formalized gestures with significance far beyond mere form.

Dry-eyed, Ayla gazed over the dancing fire at the flowing graceful movements of the crippled, one-armed man, feeling the intensity of his emotions as if they were her own. Mog-ur was expressing her pain and she identified with him entirely, as though he had reached inside her and spoke with her brain, felt with her heart. She was not the only one who felt his sorrow as her own. Ebra began to keen her grief, then the other women. Uba, holding Durc in her arms, felt a high-pitched, wordless wail rise in her throat and with a burst of relief joined in the sympathetic lament. Ayla stared vacantly ahead, sunk too far into the depths of her misery to express it. She couldn't even find the release of tears.

She didn't know how long she stared into the mesmerizing flames with unseeing eyes. Ebra had to shake her before Ayla responded, then she turned blank eyes toward the leader's mate.

"Ayla, have something to eat. This is the last feast we will ever share with Iza."

Ayla took the wooden plate of food, automatically put a piece of meat in her mouth, and almost gagged when she tried to swallow it. Suddenly she jumped up and ran from the cave. Blindly, she stumbled through brush and over rocks. At first her feet started to take her along a familiar route to a high mountain meadow and a small cave that had offered shelter and security before. But she veered away. Ever since she had shown the place to Brun, it didn't seem to be hers anymore, and her last stay held too many painful memories. She climbed instead to the top of the bluff that protected their cave from the north winds screaming down the mountain in winter, and deflected the strong winds of fall.

Buffeted by gusts, Ayla fell to her knees at the top, and there, alone with her unbearable grief, she yielded to her anguish in a plaintive chanting wail as she rocked and rocked to the rhythm of her aching heart. Creb hobbled out of the cave after her, saw her silhouetted against the sunset-painted clouds, and heard the thin, distant moan. As deep as his own grief was, he couldn't understand her rejection of the solace of company in her misery, her withdrawal into herself. His usual perceptiveness was dulled by his own sorrow; he didn't realize she was suffering from more than grief.

Guilt racked her soul. She blamed herself for Iza's death. She had left a sick woman to go to a Clan Gathering; she was a medicine woman who had deserted someone in time of need, someone she loved. She blamed herself for Iza's trek up the mountain to find a root to help her keep the baby she wanted so desperately, resulting in the near-fatal illness that weakened the woman. She felt guilty about the pain she had caused Creb when she unwittingly followed the lights to the small chamber deep in the cave of the mountains far to the east. More than grief and guilt, she was weak from lack of food and suffering from milk fever from her swollen, aching, unsuckled breasts. But even more than that, she was suffering from a depression Iza could have helped her with, if she had been there. For Ayla was a medicine woman, dedicated to easing pain and saving life, and Iza was her first patient who had died.

What Ayla needed most was her baby. She not only needed to nurse him, she needed the demands of caring for him to bring her back to reality, to make her understand that life goes on. But when she returned to the cave, Durc was asleep beside Uba. Creb had taken him to Oga to feed again. Ayla tossed and turned, unable to sleep, not even realizing that it was fever and pain that kept her awake. Her mind was turned too deeply inward, dwelling on her sorrow and guilt.

She was gone when Creb woke up. She had wandered out of the cave and climbed the bluff again. Creb could see her from a distance and watched her anxiously, but he couldn't see her weakness, or her fever.

"Should I go after her?" Brun asked, as baffled as Creb by Ayla's reaction.

"She seems to want to be alone. Maybe we should let her," Creb answered.

He worried about her when he could no longer see her, and when she still hadn't returned by evening, he asked Brun to look for her. Creb was sorry he hadn't let Brun go after her sooner when he saw the leader carrying her back to the cave. Grief and depression had taken their toll, weakness and fever had done the rest. Uba and Ebra cared for the clan's medicine woman. She was delirious, alternately shaking with chills and burning with fever. She cried out if her breasts were barely touched.

"She's going to lose her milk," Ebra said to the girl. "It's too late for Durc to do any good now. The milk is caked, he can't draw it out."

"But Durc is too young to be weaned. What will happen to him? What will happen to her?"

It might not have been too late if Iza had been alive or if Ayla had been coherent. Even Uba knew there were poultices that might have helped, medicines that might have worked, but she was young and unsure of herself, and Ebra seemed so positive. By the time the fever passed, Ayla's milk had dried up. She could no longer feed her own son.

"I will not have that deformed brat at my hearth, Oga! I will not have him brother to your sons!"

Broud was furious, shaking his fists, and Oga was cowering at his feet.

"But Broud, he's just a baby. He's got to nurse. Aga and Ika don't have enough milk, it wouldn't do any good for them to keep him. I have enough, I've always had too much milk. If he doesn't eat, he'll starve, Broud, he'll die."

"I don't care if he dies. He should never have been allowed to live in the first place. He will not live at this hearth."

Oga stopped shaking and stared at the man who was her mate. She didn't really believe he would refuse to let her keep Ayla's baby. She knew he would rant and rave and storm about it, but in the end, she was sure he would allow it. He couldn't be that cruel, he couldn't let a baby starve to death, no matter how much he hated Durc's mother.

"Broud, Ayla saved Brac's life, how can you let her son die?"

"Hasn't she gotten enough for saving his life? She was allowed to live, she was even allowed to hunt. I don't owe her anything."

"She wasn't allowed to live, she was cursed with death. She returned from the world of the spirits because her totem wanted her to, he protected her," Oga protested.

"If she had been cursed properly, she wouldn't have returned, and she would never have given birth to that brat. If her totem is so strong, why did she lose her milk? Everyone said her baby would be unlucky. What could be more unlucky than losing his mother's milk? Now you want to bring his bad luck to this hearth. I will not allow it, Oga. That's final!"

Oga sat back and looked up at Broud with calm deliberation.

"No, Broud," she motioned. "It's not final." She was no longer timorous. Broud's expression turned to shocked surprise. "You can keep Durc from living at your hearth; that is your right and I can't do anything about it. But you can't keep me from nursing him. That is a woman's right. A woman may nurse any baby she wants, and no man can keep her from it. Ayla saved my son's life, and I will not let hers die. Durc will be brother to my sons whether you like it or not."

Broud was stunned. His mate's refusal to abide by his wishes was totally unexpected. Oga had never been insolent, never been disrespectful, never shown the least sign of disobedience. He could hardly believe it. Shock turned to fury.

"How dare you defy your mate, woman. I'll make you leave this hearth!" he stormed.

"Then I will take my sons and leave, Broud. I will beg another man to take me. Maybe Mog-ur will allow me to live with him if no other man will have me. But I *will* nurse Ayla's baby."

His only answer was a sharp blow with a hard fist that knocked her flat. He was too filled with rage for any other reply. He started after her again, then turned on his heel. I will see about such blatant disrespect, he thought, as he stalked to Brun's hearth.

"First she contaminates Iza, now her willfullness has spread to my mate!" Broud gesticulated the moment he stepped beyond the boundary stones. "I told Oga I would not have Ayla's son, I told her I did not want that deformed boy as brother to her sons. Do you know what she said? She said she would nurse him anyway! She said I couldn't stop her. She said he would be brother to her sons whether I liked it or not! Can you believe it? From Oga? From my mate?"

"She's right, Broud," Brun said with controlled calm. "You can't stop her from nursing him. What baby a woman suckles is not a man's concern, it has never been a man's concern. He has more important things to worry about."

Brun was not at all pleased at Broud's violent objection. It was degrading for Broud to be so emotionally concerned in matters that were in a woman's domain. And who else could do it? Durc was Clan, especially after the Bear Festival. And Clan always took care of their own. Even the woman who had come from another clan and never produced a single child was not left to starve after her mate died. She may have had no value, she may have been a burden, but as long as the clan had food, she was given enough to eat.

Broud could refuse to take Durc into his hearth. That imposed the responsibility of providing for him and training him along with Oga's sons. Brun wasn't happy about it, but it wasn't unexpected. Everyone knew how he felt about Ayla and her son. But why should he object if his mate nursed the boy, they were all the same clan?

"Do you mean to tell me that Oga can be willfully disobedient and get away with it?" Broud raged.

"Why should you care, Broud? Do you want the child to die?" Brun asked. Broud flushed at the pointed question. "He is Clan, Broud. For all that his head is misshapen, he does not appear to be retarded. He will grow up to be a hunter. This is his clan. A mate has even been arranged for him, and you agreed. Why are you so emotional about your mate feeding someone else's baby? Is it still Ayla that you're emotional about? You are a man, Broud, whatever you command of her, she must obey. And she does obey you. Why do you compete with a woman? You belittle yourself.

Or am I wrong? Are you a man, Broud? Are you man enough to lead this clan?"

"It's just that I don't want a deformed child to be brother to the sons of my mate," Broud gestured lamely. It was a weak excuse, but he hadn't missed the threat.

"Broud, what hunter has not saved the life of another? What man does not carry a piece of every other man's spirit? What man is not brother to the rest? Does it matter if Durc is brother to your mate's sons now, or after they all grow up? Why do you object?"

Broud had no answer, none that would be acceptable to the leader. He could not admit to his all-consuming hatred of Ayla. That would be admitting he wasn't in control of his emotions, admitting he wasn't man enough to be leader. He was sorry he had come to Brun. I should have remembered, he thought. He always takes her side. He was so proud of me at the Clan Gathering. Now, all because of her, he's doubting me again.

"Well, I don't care if Oga nurses him," Broud motioned, "but I don't want him at my hearth." On that point he knew he was within his rights and would not give. "You may think he's not retarded, but I'm not so sure. I don't want to be responsible for his training. I still doubt that he'll ever be a hunter."

"That's your choice, Broud. I assumed the responsibility for training him; I made that decision before I ever accepted him. But I did accept him. Durc is a member of this clan and he will be a hunter. I'll make sure of it."

Broud turned back toward his own hearth but saw Creb bringing Durc to Oga again and walked out of the cave instead. He did not give vent to his fury until he was sure he was well out of Brun's sight. It's all that old cripple's fault, he said to himself, then tried to erase the thought from his mind, afraid that somehow the magician would know what he was thinking.

Broud was fearful of the spirits, perhaps more than any man in the clan, and his fear extended to the one who dwelt so intimately with them. After all, what could one hunter do against a whole array of incorporeal beings who could cause bad luck or sickness or death, and what could he do against the man who had the power to call them at will? Broud had recently returned from a Clan Gathering where many a night was spent with young men of other clans who tried to scare each other with tales of misfortune caused by mog-urs who had been crossed. Spears turned at the last moment preventing a kill, terrible illnesses that caused pain and suffering, gorings, maulings, all kinds of terrifying calamities were blamed on angry magicians. The horror stories were not so prevalent in his own clan, but still, The Mog-ur was the most powerful magician of all.

Though there had been times when the young man thought him more worthy of ridicule than respect, Mog-ur's malformed body and horribly scarred, one-eyed face added to his stature. To those who did not know him, he seemed inhuman, perhaps part demon. Broud had capitalized on the fear of the other young men, enjoying their look of incredulous awe when he bragged that he did not fear The Great Mog-ur. But for all his swaggering, the stories had left their impression. The reverence of the Clan for the stumbling old man who couldn't hunt made Broud more wary of his power.

Whenever he daydreamed of the time when he would be leader, he always thought of Goov as his mog-ur. Goov was too close in age, and too close a hunting companion, for Broud to view the future magician in the same light. He was sure he could cajole or coerce the acolyte into going along with his decisions, but he didn't dream of taking on The Mog-ur.

As Broud walked through the woods near the cave, he made one firm decision. Never again would he give the leader cause to doubt him; never again would he put the destiny he was so close to realizing in jeopardy. But when I'm leader, I'll make the decisions, he thought. She turned Brun against me, she even turned Oga against me, my own mate. When I'm leader, it won't matter if Brun takes her side, he won't be able to protect her anymore. Broud remembered every wrong she had done to him, every time she had stolen his glory, every imagined slight to his ego. He dwelt on them, relishing the thought of paying her back. He could wait. Someday, he said to himself, someday soon she will be sorry she ever came to live with this clan.

Broud wasn't the only one who blamed the old cripple; Creb blamed himself for Ayla's loss of mother's milk. It made little difference—now—that it was his concern that had brought such disastrous results. He just hadn't understood the way of a woman's body, he had had too little experience with women. It wasn't until his old age that he had ever come in close contact with a mother and baby. He didn't realize that when a woman nursed another's child, the favor was reciprocated more for her sake than to relieve any obligation. No one had ever told him; no one had to after it was too late.

He wondered why such a terrible calamity had happened to her. Was it just that her child was unlucky? Creb looked for reasons, and in his guilty introspection he began to doubt his own motives. Was it really concern, or did he want to hurt her as she had unknowingly hurt him. Was he worthy of his great totem? Had The Mog-ur stooped to such petty revenge? If he was an example of their highest holy man, perhaps his people deserved to die. Creb's conviction that his race was doomed, the death of Iza, and his guilt over the sorrow he had caused Ayla plunged him into a melancholy despondency. The most difficult test of Mog-ur's life came near its end.

Ayla didn't blame Creb, she blamed herself, but watching another woman nurse her son when she couldn't was more than she could bear. Oga, Aga, and Ika had each come to her and told her they would nurse Durc for her, and she was grateful, but most often it was Uba who brought Durc to one of them and stayed to visit until he was through. With the loss of her milk, Ayla lost an important part of her son's life. She still grieved for Iza and blamed herself for the woman's death, and Creb had withdrawn so far into himself that she couldn't reach him and was afraid to try. But every night when she took Durc to bed with her, she was grateful to Broud. His refusal to accept him meant her son wasn't lost to her completely.

In the waning days of fall, Ayla took up her sling again as an excuse to go off alone. She had hunted so little the past year, her skill was rusty, but with practice, her accuracy and speed returned. Most days she left early and returned late, leaving Uba to care for Durc, and only regretted that winter was closing in on them so quickly. The exercise was good for her, but she had a problem to overcome. She hadn't hunted much after she became a fully developed woman, and heavy breasts bobbing at every step annoyed her when she ran or jumped. She noticed that men wore a leather loincloth to protect their exposed and delicate organs, and she fashioned a band to hold her bosom in place, tied around her back. It made her more comfortable, and she ignored the curious sidewise glances cast at her when she put it on.

Though hunting strengthened her body and occupied her mind while she was out, she still carried her load of grief and sorrow. To Uba, it seemed that the joy had left Creb's hearth. She missed her mother, and both Creb and Ayla had an aura of perpetual sadness. Only Durc, with his unknowing baby ways, brought a hint of the happiness she had once taken for granted. He could even rouse Creb out of his lethargy on occasion.

Ayla had left early and Uba was away from the hearth looking for something in the back of the cave. Oga had just brought Durc back and Creb was keeping his eye on the boy. He was full and contented, but not very sleepy. He crawled toward the old man and pulled himself up on wobbly, unsure legs, clutching at Creb for support.

"So you're going to start walking soon," Creb motioned. "Before this winter is over, you'll be running all over this cave, young man."

Creb poked him in his little pot belly to emphasize his gestures. The corners of Durc's mouth turned up and he made a sound Creb had heard from only one other person in the clan. He laughed. Creb poked him again and the boy doubled over in a babyish giggle, lost his balance, and sat down on his firm little rump. Creb helped him up again and looked at the child as he had never looked at him before.

Durc's baby legs were bowed, but not nearly as much as other babies of the clan; and though they were chubby, Creb could see his bones were longer and thinner. I think Durc's legs are going to be straight when he gets older, like Ayla's, and he's going to be tall, too. And his neck, it was so thin and scrawny when he was born, he couldn't hold his head up; it's just like Ayla's neck. His head isn't like hers, though, or is it? That high forehead, that's Ayla's. Creb turned Durc's head to look at his profile. Yes, definitely her forehead, but the brows and the eyes, they're Clan, and the back of his head, that's more like Clan, too.

Ayla was right. He's not deformed, he's a mixture, a mixture of her and Clan. I wonder, is that the way it always is? Do the spirits mix? Maybe that's what makes girls, not a weak male totem. Does life start with a mixing of male and female totem spirits? Creb shook his head, he didn't know, but it set the old magician to thinking. He thought often of Durc that cold lonely winter. He had a feeling Durc was important, but just why eluded him.

27

"But Ayla, I'm not like you. I can't hunt. Where will I go when it gets dark?" Uba implored. "Ayla, I'm afraid."

The frightened face of the young woman made Ayla wish she could go with her. Uba was not quite eight years old and the thought of spending the days alone away from the security of the cave terrified her, but her totem's spirit had battled for the first time and it was required. She had no choice.

"Do you remember that small cave where I hid when Durc was born? Go there, Uba. It will be safer than staying out in the open. I'll come up to see you every evening and bring you some food. It's only for a few days, Uba. Make sure you take a fur to sleep on and a coal to start a fire. There's water nearby. It will be lonely, especially at night, but you'll be all right. And just think, you're a woman now. You'll be mated soon and maybe have a baby of your own before long," Ayla consoled.

"Who do you think Brun will choose for me?"

"Who do you want Brun to choose for you, Uba?"

"Vorn is the only unmated man, though I'm sure Borg will be one soon. Of course, he might decide to make me the second woman of one of the others. I think I'd really like Borg. We used to play we were mated, until the time he really tried to relieve his needs with me. It didn't work very well, and now he's shy and so close to being a man, he doesn't like to play with girls anymore. But Ona is a woman, too, and she can't mate with Vorn. Unless Brun decides to give her to a man who already has one mate, there's no one else but Borg for her. I guess that means Vorn will be my mate."

"Vorn has been a man for a while, he's probably eager to mate by now," Ayla said. She had come to the same conclusion herself. "Do you think you'd like Vorn for a mate?"

"He tried to act like he doesn't notice me, but he looks at me sometimes. He might not be so bad."

"Broud likes him, he'll probably be second-in-command someday. You don't need to worry about the status, but it would be good for your sons. I didn't like Vorn much when he was younger, but I think you're right. He's not so bad. He's even nice to Durc, when Broud isn't around."

"Everyone's nice to Durc, except Broud," Uba said. "Everyone loves him."

"Well, he certainly makes himself at home at every hearth. He's so used to being handed around to nurse, he even calls every woman mother," Ayla motioned with a fleeting frown. A quick smile replaced her unhappy look. "Remember that time he walked into Grod's hearth, just like he lived there?"

"I remember; I tried not to look, but I just couldn't help it," Uba recalled. "He walked right past Uka, just greeted her and called her mother and went straight to Grod and crawled up on his lap."

"I know," Ayla said. "I never saw Grod look so surprised in my life. Then he climbed down and went straight for Grod's spears. I was sure Grod was going to get mad, but he just couldn't resist that brazen child when he started to drag his biggest spear away. When Grod took it away from him, he said, 'Durc hunt like Grod.'"

"I think Durc would have dragged that heavy spear right out of the cave if Grod had let him."

"He takes the little spear Grod made for him to bed," Ayla gestured, still smiling. "You know, Grod never says much. I was surprised when he came over that day. He barely greeted me, just went straight to Durc and put that spear in his hands, even showed him how to hold it. When he walked out, all he said was, 'If the boy wants to hunt so much, he should have his own spear.'"

"It's a shame Ovra never had any children. I think Grod would like it if the daughter of his mate had a baby," Uba said. "Maybe that's why Grod likes Durc, he's not really attached to any man. Brun likes him, too, I can tell; and Zoug is already showing him how to use a sling. I don't think he's going to have any problem learning to hunt even though there isn't a man at his hearth to train him. The way the men act, you'd think every man in the clan is his mother's mate, except Broud." She paused. "Maybe they are, Ayla. Dorv always said every man's totem combined to defeat your Cave Lion."

"I think you'd better go now, Uba," Ayla said, changing the

subject. "I'll walk with you part of the way. It's stopped raining, and I think the strawberries are ripe. There's a big patch of them partway up the path. I'll come up to see you later."

Goov painted the symbol of Vorn's totem over the symbol of Uba's totem with yellow ochre paste, blurring her mark and showing his dominance.

"Do you accept this woman as your mate?" Creb gestured.

Vorn tapped Uba's shoulder and she followed him into the cave. Then Creb and Goov performed the same ritual for Borg and Ona and they went to their new hearth to begin the period of isolation. The summer-dressed trees, still a shade lighter than they would be later, stirred in the light breeze as the congregation broke up. Ayla picked up Durc to carry him into the cave, but he squirmed to get down.

"All right, Durc," she motioned. "You can walk, but come in and have some broth and mush."

While she was preparing breakfast, Durc wandered out of the hearth and headed toward the new hearth now occupied by Uba and Vorn. Ayla ran after him and carried him back.

"Durc want see Uba," the child gestured.

"You can't, Durc. No one can visit her for a while. But if you're good and eat your mush, I'll take you hunting with me."

"Durc be good. Why can't see Uba?" the boy asked, mollified by the promise to go along with his mother. "Why Uba not come eat with us?"

"She doesn't live here anymore, Durc. She's mated to Vorn now," Ayla explained.

Durc wasn't the only one who noticed Uba's absence. They all missed her. The hearth seemed empty with only Creb, Ayla, and the child, and the strain between the old man and the young woman was more noticeable. They had never found a way to overcome their mutual remorse over the hurt they had caused each other. Many times when Ayla saw the old magician lost in the depths of melancholy, she wanted to go to him, put her arms around his shaggy white head, and hug him as she had when she was a little girl. But she restrained herself, reluctant to force herself upon him.

Creb missed the affection, though he didn't realize its absence added to his depression. And many times when Creb saw Ayla's pain as she watched another woman nurse her son, he wanted to go to her. If Iza had been alive, she would have found a way to bring them back together, but without such a catalyst, they drifted farther apart, each longing to show their love for the other, and neither knowing how to bridge the gap that separated them. They were both ill at ease during the first morning meal without Uba.

"Do you want more, Creb?" Ayla asked.

"No. No. Don't bother, I've had enough," he motioned.

He watched her cleaning up while Durc dived into a second helping with both hands and a clamshell spoon. Though just a little more than two years old, he was essentially weaned. He still sought out Oga—and Ika now that she had a new baby again—to nurse for comfort and closeness, and because they let him get away with it. Usually, when a new baby was born, any older children still nursing were cut off, but Ika made an exception in Durc's case. The child seemed to sense not to push his privilege too far. He never drained her, never deprived her new infant of milk, just cuddled up for a few moments as if to prove he had the right.

Oga was lenient toward him, too, and though Grev was technically past his nursing year, he took advantage of his mother's indulgence. Both were often found together on her lap, each suckling a breast until their interest in each other overcame their desire for mothering, and they let go to tussle with each other. Durc was as tall as Grev, though not nearly as stocky; and though Grev usually won over Durc when they wrestled playfully, Durc easily outdistanced the older boy when they raced. The two were inseparable; they sought each other out at every opportunity.

"You're going to take the boy with you?" Creb gestured after an uncomfortable silence.

"Yes," she nodded, wiping the child's hands and face. "I promised to take him hunting with me. I doubt that I'll be able to hunt much with him along, but I need to gather some herbs, too, and it's a nice day."

Creb grunted.

"You should go out, too, Creb," she added. "The sun would be good for you."

"Yes, yes, I will, Ayla. Later."

For a moment, she thought she ought to coax him out of the cave with the offer of a walk beside the stream as they used to do, but he already seemed turned inward. She left him sitting where he was, picked up Durc, and hurried out.

Creb didn't look up until he was sure she was gone. He reached for his staff, then decided it was too much effort to get up, and put it down again.

Ayla worried about him as she started out with Durc on her hip and her collecting basket strapped to her back. She sensed his mental power was diminishing. He was more absentminded than ever, and he repeated questions she had already answered. He hardly stirred himself to go out of the cave, even when the weather was warm and sunny. And when he sat for long hours in what he called meditation, he often fell asleep sitting up.

Ayla's strides lengthened once she was out of sight of the cave. The freedom of movement and the beautiful summer day eased her concern into a more remote part of her mind. She let Durc walk when they came to a clearing and stopped to collect some plants. He watched her, then grabbed a handful of grass and purple-flowered alfalfa and pulled it out by the roots. He brought it to her clutched in his little fist.

"You're a big help, Durc," she motioned, taking it from him and putting it into the basket beside her.

"Durc get more," he gestured, running off.

She sat back on her heels watching her son tugging at a larger handful. It gave suddenly, and he sat down hard. He screwed up his face to cry, more in surprise than in pain, but Ayla ran to him, picked him up, and tossed him into the air, catching him again in her arms. Durc giggled with delight. She put him down and pretended she was going to chase him.

"I'm going to get you," Ayla motioned.

Durc ran away on his baby legs, laughing. She let him get ahead of her, then chased after him on hands and knees, grabbing him and pulling him over on top of her, both of them laughing at the game. She tickled him just to hear him laugh again.

Ayla never laughed with her son unless they were alone, and Durc learned early that no one else either appreciated or approved of his smiles and giggles. Though Durc made the gesture for mother to all the women in the clan, in his baby heart, he knew Ayla was special. He always felt happier with her than with anyone else, and he loved it when she took him with her alone, without the other women. And he loved the other game only he and his mother played.

"Ba-ba-na-nee-nee," Durc sounded.

"Ba-ba-na-nee-nee," Ayla mimicked the nonsense syllables.

"No-na-nee-ga-goo-la," Durc voiced another set of sounds.

Ayla copied him again, then tickled him. She loved to hear him laugh. It always brought laughter to her own lips. Then she made a set of sounds, sounds she liked to hear him make more than any others. She didn't know why, except it stirred in her a feeling of such tenderness it came close to bringing tears.

"Ma-ma-ma-ma," she said.

"Ma-ma-ma-ma," Durc repeated. Ayla wrapped her arms around her son and held him close. "Ma-ma," Durc said again.

He wriggled to get free. The only time he liked to cuddle for long was when he went to sleep snuggled beside her. She wiped a tear away from the corner of her eye. Watering eyes were one peculiarity he did not share with her. Durc's large brown eyes, deep set below heavy brow ridges, were Clan.

"Ma-ma," Durc said. He often called her by the syllables when they were alone, especially after he was reminded. "You hunt now?" he gestured.

The last few times she had taken Durc with her, she spent some time showing him how to hold a sling. She was going to make one for him, but Zoug beat her to it. The old man didn't go out anymore, but his pleasure in trying to train the boy also pleased Ayla. Though Durc was young, Ayla could see he would have her aptitude with the weapon, and he was as proud of his miniature sling as he was of his small spear.

He liked the attention he got as he strutted with a sling draped through the cord around his waist—all he wore in summer besides his amulet—and a spear in his hand. Grev had to have small weapons, too. The pair of them brought glimmers of amusement to the eyes of the clan, and comments about what fine little men they were. Their future role was already being defined. When Durc discovered that imperious bossiness to little girls was approved, and even benignly condoned toward grown women, he never hesitated to push to the limits allowed—except with his mother.

Durc knew his mother was different. Only she laughed with him, only she played the game of sounds with him, only she had the soft golden hair he loved to touch. He could never remember her nursing him, but he would sleep with no one else. He knew she was a woman because she answered to the same motion as the other women. But she was much taller than any man, and she hunted. He wasn't exactly sure what hunting was, except men did it—and his mother. She fit into no category; she was woman and not woman, man and not man. She was unique. The name he had begun to call her, the name made with sounds, seemed to suit her best. She was Mama; and Mama, the golden-haired goddess he adored, did not nod approvingly when he attempted to boss her.

Ayla put Durc's little sling in his hands, and holding hers over his, tried to show him how to use it. Zoug had done the same thing, and he was beginning to get the idea. Then she took her sling from her waist thong, found some pebbles, and hurled them at nearby objects. When she set small stones on larger boulders and proceeded to knock them off again, Durc thought it was funny. He toddled over with more stones to see her do it again. After a while he lost interest, and she went back to gathering plants while Durc followed after her. They found some raspberries and stopped to eat them.

"You are a mess, my sticky son," Ayla motioned, laughing at him with red juice on his face, hands, and round belly. She picked him up, tucked him under one arm, and carried him to a creek to wash him. Then she found a large leaf, folded it into a cone, and filled it with water for Durc and her to drink. Durc yawned and rubbed his eyes. She spread her carrying cloak out on the ground in the shade of a large oak, and lay down beside him until he fell asleep.

In the quiet of the summer afternoon, Ayla sat with her back against the tree watching butterflies flitting then coming to rest with folded-back wings and insects buzzing in perpetual motion, and listened to a twittering symphony of chirping birds. Her mind wandered back to the events of the morning. I hope Uba will be happy with Vorn, she thought. I hope he's good to her. It's so empty with her gone, even if she isn't far away. It's just not the same. She'll be cooking for her mate now, and sleeping with him after the isolation. I hope she has a baby soon, that would make her happy.

But what about me? No one has ever come from that clan to ask about me. Maybe they just can't find our cave. I don't think they were all that interested, anyway. I'm glad. I don't want to mate a man I don't know. I don't even want any of the ones I do know, and none of them want me. I'm too tall; even Droog barely reaches my chin. Iza used to wonder if I would ever stop growing. I'm beginning to wonder myself. Broud hates it. He can't stand having a woman around taller than he is. But he hasn't bothered me at all since we got back from the Clan Gathering. Why does it make me shudder every time he looks at me?

Brun's getting old. Ebra's been getting medicine for his sore muscles and stiff joints lately. He's going to make Broud leader soon. I know it. And Goov is going to be mog-ur. He's doing more of the ceremonies all the time. I don't think Creb wants to be mog-ur anymore, not since that time I watched them. Why did I go into the cave that night? I don't even remember how I got there. I wish I had never gone to the Clan Gathering. If I hadn't gone, I might have kept Iza alive for a few more years. I miss her so much, and I never did find a mate. Durc did, though.

It's strange that Ura was allowed to live, almost as if she was meant to be Durc's mate. Men of the Others, Oda said. Who are they? Iza said I was born to them; why don't I remember? What happened to my real mother? To her mate? Did I have any siblings? Ayla felt a faint queasiness in the pit of her stomach—not nausea, exactly, just a sense of unease. Then suddenly her scalp crawled when she remembered something Iza had told her the night she died. Ayla had pushed it out of her mind; it was too painful to think about Iza's death.

Iza told me to leave! She said I wasn't Clan, she said I was born to the Others. She told me to find my own people, find my own mate. She said Broud would find a way to hurt me if I stayed. North, she said they live north, beyond the peninsula on the mainland.

How can I leave? This is my home. I can't leave Creb, and Durc needs me. What if I couldn't find any Others? And if I did, they might not want me anyway. No one wants an ugly woman. How do I know I'd find a mate even if I did find some Others?

Creb is getting old, though. What's going to happen to me when he's gone? Who will provide for me then? I can't just live with Durc, some man will have to take me. But who? Broud! He's going to be leader; if no one else wants me, he'll have to. What if I have to live with Broud? He wouldn't want me either, but he knows I'd hate it. He'd do it just because I'd hate it. I couldn't stand living with Broud, I'd rather live with some man I don't know from another clan, but they don't want me either.

Maybe I should leave. I could take Durc and we could both go. But what if I didn't find any Others? And what if something happened to me? Who would take care of him? He'd be all alone, just like I was. I was lucky that Iza found me; Durc might not be so lucky. I can't take him away, he was born here, he is Clan, even if he is part me, too. He has a mate arranged for him. What would Ura do if I took Durc away? Oda is training her to be Durc's mate. She's telling her there is a man for her even if she is deformed and ugly. Durc will need Ura, too. He will need a mate when he grows up, and Ura is just right for him.

But I couldn't leave without Durc. I'd rather live with Broud than leave Durc. I have to stay, there's no other way. I'll stay and live with Broud, if I have to. Ayla looked at her sleeping child and tried to compose her mind, tried to be a good Clan woman and accept her fate. A fly landed on Durc's nose. He twitched, rubbed his nose in his sleep, then settled down again.

I wouldn't know where to go anyway. North? What does that tell me? Everything is north of here, only the sea is south. I could wander around for the rest of my life and not find anyone. And they can be as bad as Broud. Oda said those men forced her, didn't even let her put her baby down. It would be better to stay here with a Broud I know, than some man who might be worse.

It's late, I'd better get back. Ayla woke her son, and as she walked back to the cave, tried to push thoughts of Others out of her mind, but stray wisps of wondering kept insinuating themselves. Once recalled, she couldn't quite forget the Others.

"Are you busy, Ayla?" Uba asked. She had an expression that was both shy and pleased, and Ayla guessed why. She decided to let Uba tell her anyway.

"No, I'm not really busy. I've just been mixing some mint and alfalfa and wanted to taste it. Why don't I put some water on for tea."

"Where's Durc?" Uba asked while Ayla stirred up the fire and added more wood and a few cooking stones.

"He's outside with Grev. Oga's watching them. Those two, they're always together," Ayla motioned.

"That's probably because they nursed together. They're closer than brothers. They're almost like two born together."

"But two born together often look alike, and they certainly don't. Do you remember that woman at the Clan Gathering with two born together? I couldn't tell them apart."

"Sometimes it's unlucky to have two born together, and three born together are never allowed to live. How could a woman feed three at one time—she only has two breasts?" Uba questioned.

"With a lot of help. It's enough strain on a woman to have two. I'm grateful Oga has always had plenty of milk, for Durc's sake."

"I hope I have plenty of milk," Uba gestured. "I think I'm going to have a baby, Ayla."

"I thought so, Uba. You haven't had your woman's curse since you were mated, have you?"

"No. I think Vorn's totem has been waiting a long time. It must have been very strong."

"Have you told him yet?"

"I was going to wait until I was sure, but he guessed. He must have noticed that I didn't go into isolation. He's very happy about it," Uba motioned proudly.

"Is he a good mate, Uba? Are you happy?"

"Oh, yes. He's a good mate, Ayla. When he found out I was going to have a baby, he told me he waited for me for a long time, and he was glad I didn't waste any time getting one started. He said he asked for me even before I became a woman."

"That's wonderful, Uba," Ayla said.

She didn't add that there wasn't anyone else in the clan he could have mated, except herself. But why would he want me? Why would he want a big, ugly woman when he could have someone as attractive as Uba, and she was born to Iza's line. What's the matter with me? I never wanted to mate Vorn. I guess I must still be thinking about what will happen to me when Creb is gone. I'm going to have to take good care of him so he lives a long time. It just seems that he doesn't want to live. He hardly ever goes out of the cave anymore. If he doesn't exercise, he won't be *able* to leave the cave.

"What are you thinking about, Ayla? You've been so quiet lately."

"I was thinking about Creb. I'm worried about him."

"He's getting old. He's much older than mother, and she's gone. I still miss her, Ayla. I'm going to hate it when Creb walks in the next world."

"So will I, Uba," Ayla gestured with feeling.

Ayla was restless. She hunted often, and when she wasn't hunting, she worked with tireless energy. She couldn't stand not having something to do. She sorted through the stores of medicinal plants and rearranged them, then scoured the countryside to replenish old or used-up medicines, then reorganized the whole hearth. She wove new baskets and mats, made wooden bowls and platters, containers of stiff rawhide or birchbark, made new wraps, cured and dressed new furs, then made leggings, hats, hand and foot coverings for the next winter. She waterproofed bladders and stomachs for water and other liquids, constructed a new frame firmly tied with thong and sinew to support skins for boiling over the fire. She nicked out flat stones to make a deeper well for fat for lamps, and she dried new moss wicks, knapped a new set of knives, scrapers, saws, borers, and axes, searched the seashore for shells to make spoons, ladles, and small dishes. She took her turn traveling with the hunters to dry the meat, gathered fruits, seeds, nuts, and vegetables with the women, winnowed and parched and ground grains to a superfine texture to make it easier for Creb and Durc to chew. And still she couldn't find enough to do.

Creb became the object of her intense interest. Ayla pampered him, cared for him as she never had before. She cooked special foods to encourage his appetite, made medicinal brews and poultices, made him rest in the sunshine, and coaxed him into long walks for exercise. He seemed to enjoy her attention and company and to regain some of his strength and verve. But there was something lacking. The special closeness, the easy warmth, the long rambling talks of earlier years were gone. They usually walked in silence. The conversation they did have was strained, and there were no spontaneous demonstrations of affection.

Creb was not the only one growing old. The day that Brun watched the departing hunters from the ridge until they were tiny dots on the steppes below jolted Ayla into a sudden awareness of how much he had changed. His beard was not grizzled, it was gray, and it matched his hair. Deep wrinkles lined his face, cutting chasms into the skin at the corners of his eyes. His hard, muscular body had lost tone, his skin was more flaccid, though he was still powerful. He walked back to the cave slowly and spent the remainder of the day within the boundaries of his hearth. He went with the hunters the next time; but the second time Brun stayed behind, Grod did too, still the loyal lieutenant.

One day near the end of summer, Durc came running into the cave.

"Mama! Mama! A man! A man is coming!"

Ayla rushed to the mouth of the cave, along with everyone else, to watch the stranger walking up the path from the seacoast.

"Ayla, do you think he might be coming for you?" Uba gestured excitedly.

"I don't know. I don't know any more than you, Uba."

Ayla's nerves were taut, and her emotions mixed. She hoped the visitor was from the clan of Zoug's kin, and afraid he would be. He stopped to talk to Brun, then walked with the leader to his hearth. Not long afterward, Ayla saw Ebra leave and head straight for her.

"Brun wants you, Ayla," she motioned.

Ayla's heart beat wildly. Her knees felt like water, she was sure they would never hold her up as she walked to Brun's hearth. Gratefully she collapsed at Brun's feet. He tapped her shoulder.

"This is Vond, Ayla," the leader said, motioning toward the visitor. "He has traveled far to see you, all the way from Norg's clan. His mother is sick, and their medicine woman has not been able to help her. She thought you might know of magic that could help."

Ayla had established a reputation as a medicine woman of great skill and knowledge at the Clan Gathering. The man had come for her magic, not for her. Ayla's relief overpowered her regret. Vond stayed only a few days, but he brought news of his clan. The young man who had been wounded by the cave bear had wintered with them. He left early the following spring, walking on his own legs, his limp hardly noticeable. His mate had given birth to a healthy son who was named Creb. Ayla questioned the man and prepared a packet for Vond to take back with him, along with instructions for their medicine woman. She didn't know if her remedy would be any more effective, but he had come so far, at least she could try.

Brun thought about Ayla after Vond left. He had put off

making any decision about her while there was hope that some other clan might find her acceptable. But if one runner could find their cave, others could too, if they wished. After so long, he could no longer sustain any hope. Some arrangement would have to be made for her in his clan.

But Broud would be leader soon, and he was the one who should take her. It would be best if that decision came from Broud himself, and as long as Mog-ur lived, there was no need to rush it. Brun decided to leave the problem for the son of his mate. He seems to have overcome his violent emotions toward her, Brun thought. He never bothers her anymore. Perhaps he's ready, perhaps he's finally ready. But a seed of doubt still remained.

The summer drew to its polychrome close and the clan settled down to the slower pace of the cold season. Uba's pregnancy progressed normally until well beyond her second trimester. Then the stirrings of life stopped. She tried to ignore the growing ache in her back and the discomforting cramps, but when she began spotting blood, she hurried to Ayla.

"How long has it been since you felt movement, Uba?" Ayla asked, concern etched on her face.

"Not for many days, Ayla. What am I going to do? Vorn was so happy with me when life started so soon after we mated. I don't want to lose my baby. What could have gone wrong? It's so close. Spring will be here soon."

"I don't know, Uba. Do you remember falling? Did you strain to lift something heavy?"

"I don't think so, Ayla."

"Go back to your hearth, Uba, and go to bed. I'll boil some black birchbark and bring the tea to you. I wish it were fall—I'd get that rattlesnake root Iza got for me. But the snow is too deep to go very far now. I'll try to think of something. You think about it, too, Uba. You know almost everything Iza knew."

"I have been thinking, Ayla, but I can't remember anything that will start a baby kicking again once it's stopped."

Ayla couldn't answer. In her heart she knew as well as Uba that it was hopeless, and shared the young woman's anguish.

For the next several days, Uba lay in bed hoping against hope that something would help, and knowing there was nothing she could hope for. The pain in her back became almost unbearable, and the only medicines that stopped it were those that put her to sleep, a drugged unrestful sleep. But the cramps would not grow into contractions, labor would not start.

Ovra almost lived at Vorn's hearth, offering her empathetic support. She had been through the same ordeal herself so many times that she, more than anyone, could understand Uba's pain and sorrow. Goov's mate had never been able to bring a baby to full term and had become even more quiet and withdrawn as the years passed and she remained childless. Ayla was glad Goov was gentle with her. Many men would have turned her out, or taken a second woman. But Goov felt a deep attachment for his mate. He would not add to her grief by taking in another woman to have children for him. Ayla had begun to give Ovra the secret medicine Iza told her about that prevented her totem from being defeated. It was too hard on the woman to continue having pregnancies that produced no babies for her. Ayla didn't tell her what the medicine was for, but after a time, when Ovra stopped conceiving, she guessed. It was better that way.

On a cold, dismal morning in late winter, Ayla examined Iza's daughter and made a decision.

"Uba," she called softly. The young woman opened eyes ringed with dark circles that made them seem even more deep-set below her brow ridges. "It's time for the ergot. We've got to get the contractions started. There's nothing that can save your baby, Uba. If it doesn't come out, you'll die, too. You're young, you can have another baby," Ayla motioned.

Uba looked at Ayla, then Ovra, then back to Ayla again.

"All right," she nodded. "You're right, there's no hope. My baby is dead."

Uba's labor was difficult. It was hard to get the contractions started and it made Ayla reluctant to give her anything too strong for pain for fear they would stop. Though the other women of the clan stopped by for short visits to offer their encouragement and support, none wanted to stay for long. They all knew her pain and effort would be in vain. Only Ovra stayed to help Ayla.

When the stillborn was delivered, Ayla quickly wrapped it with the placental tissue in the leather birthing blanket.

"It was a boy," she told Uba.

"Can I see it?" the exhausted young woman asked.

"I think it's best that you don't, Uba. It will only make

you feel worse. You rest, I'll dispose of it for you. You're too weak to get up."

Ayla told Brun that Uba was too weak, she would dispose of the baby, but she refrained from mentioning anything else. It wasn't a son that Uba had delivered, it was two sons that had never separated properly. Only Ovra had seen the pitiful, sickening thing barely recognizable as human with too many arms and legs and grotesque features on a head too large. Ovra had to fight to keep from regurgitating the contents of her stomach, and Ayla swallowed hard herself.

This was not Durc's modification of Clan characteristics with hers, this was a deformity. Ayla was glad the grossly malformed thing had not survived long enough for Uba to have had to deliver it live. She knew Ovra would never tell anyone. It was best to let the clan believe Uba had given birth to a normal stillborn son, for Uba's sake.

Ayla put on her outdoor clothes and plowed through deep snow until she was far from the cave. She opened the wrappings and left them exposed. It's better to make sure all evidence is destroyed, Ayla thought. Even as she turned to go back, she caught a slinking movement out of the corner of her eye. The smell of blood had already brought the means.

28

"Would you like to sleep with Uba tonight, Durc?" Ayla asked.

"No!" the boy shook his head emphatically. "Durc sleep with Mama."

"That's all right, Ayla. I didn't think he would. He's been with me all day, anyway," Uba said. "Where did he get that name he calls you, Ayla?"

"It's just a name he uses for me," Ayla answered, turning her head aside. The Clan stricture against unnecessary words or sounds has been so firmly ingrained in Ayla from the time she first arrived, she felt guilty about the word game she played with her son. Uba didn't press, though she knew there was something Ayla was withholding.

"Sometimes when I go out with Durc alone, we make sounds together," Ayla admitted. "He just picked those sounds for me. He can make a lot of sounds."

"You can make sounds, too. Mother said you used to make all kinds of sounds and words when you were little, especially before you learned to talk," she gestured. "I still remember when I was a baby, I used to love that sound you made when you rocked me."

"I guess I did when I was little, I don't really remember too well," Ayla motioned. "Durc and I just have a game we play."

"I don't think there's anything so wrong with that," Uba said. "It's not like he can't talk. I wish these roots weren't so rotten," Uba added, throwing a large one away. "It's not going to be much of a feast tomorrow with only dried meat and fish and half-rotten vegetables. If Brun would only wait a little longer, there would at least be some greens and shoots."

"It's not just Brun," Ayla said. "Creb says the best time is the first full moon after the beginning of spring."

"How does he know the beginning of spring, I wonder?" Uba remarked. "One rainy day looks like another to me."

"I think it has something to do with watching the sun set. He's been watching it go down for days. Even when it rains, you can often see where the sun goes to sleep, and there've been enough clear nights to see the moon. Creb knows."

"I wish Creb wasn't going to make Goov the mog-ūr, too," Uba said.

"So do I," Ayla motioned. "He sits around too much doing nothing these days as it is. What will he do with himself when he doesn't even have ceremonies to perform? I knew it had to happen sometime, but this is one feast I'm not going to enjoy."

"It will seem strange. I'm used to Brun as the leader and Creb as Mog-ur, but Vorn says it's time for the younger men to lead. He says Broud has waited long enough."

"I suppose he's right," Ayla motioned. "Vorn has always admired Broud."

"He's good to me, Ayla. He didn't even get angry when I lost the baby. He just said he would ask Mog-ur for a charm to make his totem strong again so it could start another one. He must like you, too, Ayla. He even told me to ask you to let Durc sleep with us. I think he knows how much I like having him around," Uba confided. "Even Broud hasn't been so bad to you lately."

"No, he hasn't bothered me much," Ayla motioned. She didn't know how to explain the fear she felt every time he looked at her. She could even feel the hair rising on the back of her neck if he stared at her when she wasn't looking.

Creb stayed late with Goov in the place of the spirits that evening. Ayla fixed a light meal for Durc and herself and put something aside for Creb to eat when he returned, though she doubted if he'd bother to eat it. She had awakened that morning with a feeling of anxiety that grew worse as the day wore on. The cave seemed to close in on her and her mouth felt dry as dust. She only managed to choke down a few bites, then suddenly jumped up and ran to the mouth of the cave and stared out at the leaden sky and the heavy, soaking rain making small craters in the saturated mud. Durc crawled into her bed and was already asleep when she returned to the hearth. As soon as he felt her crawl in beside him, he snuggled closer and made a half-conscious gesture that ended with the word, "Mama."

Ayla wrapped her arm around him, feeling his beating heart as she held him, but sleep was long in coming for her. She lay awake looking at the shadowed contours of the rough rock wall in the dim light of the dying fire. She was awake when Creb finally returned, but she lay still, listening to him shuffling around, and finally drifted off to sleep after he had crawled into his bed.

She woke up screaming!

"Ayla! Ayla!" Creb called, shaking her to bring her fully awake. "What's wrong, child?" he motioned, his eye full of concern.

"Oh, Creb," she sobbed, and threw her arms around his neck. "I had that dream. I haven't had that dream for years." Creb put his arm around her and felt her trembling.

"What's wrong with Mama?" Durc motioned, sitting up wide-eyed with fear. He had never heard his mother scream before. Ayla put her arm around him.

"What dream, Ayla? The one about the cave lion?" Creb asked.

"No, the other one, the one I can never exactly remember." She started shaking again. "Creb, why should I have that dream now? I thought I was all over having bad dreams."

Creb put his arm around her to comfort her again. Ayla hugged him back. They both suddenly realized how long it had been, and held each other with Durc between them.

"Oh, Creb, I can't tell you how often I've wanted to hug you. I thought you didn't want me; I was afraid you'd push me away like you did when I was an insolent little girl. There's something else I've wanted to tell you. I love you, Creb."

"Ayla, I had to make myself push you away even then; but I had to do something, or Brun would have. I never could be angry with you, I loved you too much. I still love you too much. I thought you were upset because you lost your milk and it was my fault."

"It wasn't your fault, Creb. It was mine. I never blamed you."

"I blamed myself. I should have realized a baby has to keep nursing or the milk will stop, but you seemed to want to be alone with your grief."

"How could you know? None of the men know much about babies. They like to hold them and play with them when they're full and happy, but let them start fussing and all the men are quick to give them back to their mothers. Besides, it didn't hurt him. He's just starting his weaning year, and he's big and healthy even though he's been weaned for a long time."

"But it hurt you, Ayla."

"Mama, you hurt?" Durc interrupted, still worried about her scream.

"No, Durc, Mama's not hurt, not anymore."

"Where did he learn to call you that word, Ayla?"

She flushed slightly. "Durc and I play a game of making sounds sometimes. He just decided to call me by that one."

Creb nodded. "He calls all the women mother; I guess he needed to find something to call you. It probably means mother to him."

"It does to me, too."

"You made a lot of sounds and words when you first came. I think your people must talk with sounds."

"My people are Clan people. I am a woman of the Clan."

"No, Ayla," Creb gestured slowly. "You are not Clan, you are a woman of the Others."

"That's what Iza told me the night she died. She said I wasn't Clan; she said I was a woman of the Others."

Creb looked surprised. "I didn't think she knew. Iza was a wise woman, Ayla. I only found out that night you followed us into the cave."

"I didn't mean to go into that cave, Creb. I don't even know how I got there. I don't know what hurt you so much, but I thought you stopped loving me because I went into that cave."

"No, Ayla, I didn't stop loving you, I loved you too much."

"Durc hungry," the child interrupted. He was still disturbed by his mother's scream, and the intense conversation between her and Creb bothered him.

"You're hungry? I'll see if I can find something for you."

Creb watched her as she got up and went to the fireplace. I wonder why she was brought to live with us, Creb thought. She was born to the Others, and the Cave Lion has always protected her; why would he bring her here? Why not back to them? And why would he let himself be defeated, let her have a baby, then allow her to lose her milk? Everyone thinks it's because he's unlucky, but look at him. He's healthy, he's happy, everyone loves him. Maybe Dorv was right, maybe the spirit of every man's totem mixed with her Cave Lion. She was right about that, he's not deformed, he's a mixture. He can even make sounds like she can. He's part Ayla and part Clan.

Suddenly, Creb felt the blood drain from his face and gooseflesh rise. Part Ayla and part Clan! Is that why she was brought to us? For Durc? For her son? The Clan is doomed, it will be no more, only her kind will go on. I know it, I felt it. But what about Durc? He's part of the Others, he will go on, but he's Clan, too. And Ura, she looks like Durc, and she was born not long after that incident with the men of the Others. Are their totems so strong they can overcome a woman's in so short a time? It may be; if their women can have Cave Lion totems, they may have to be. Is Ura a mixture, too? And if there is a Durc and a Ura, there must be others, too. Children of mixed spirits, children that will go on, children that will carry the Clan on. Not many, perhaps, but enough.

Perhaps the Clan was doomed before Ayla saw the sacred ceremony, and she was led there only to show me. We will be no more, but as long as there are Durcs and Uras, we will not die. I wonder if Durc has the memories? If only he were older, old enough for a ceremony. It doesn't matter; Durc has more than the memories, he has the Clan. Ayla, my child, the child of my heart, you do carry luck and you brought it to us. Now I know why you came—not to bring us our death, but to give us our one chance for life. It will never be the same, but it is something.

Ayla brought her son a piece of cold meat. Creb seemed lost in thought but looked at her when she sat down.

"You know, Creb," she said thoughtfully. "Sometimes I think Durc isn't just my son. Ever since I lost my milk, and he got used to going from hearth to hearth to nurse, he eats at every hearth. Everyone feeds him. He reminds me of a cave bear cub, it's like he's the son of the whole clan."

Ayla felt a great outpouring of sadness from Creb's one dark, liquid eye. "Durc is the son of the whole clan, Ayla. He's the only son of the Clan."

The first light of predawn glowed through the opening of the cave, filling in the triangular space. Ayla lay awake looking at her son sleeping beside her in the glowing light. She could see Creb in his bed beneath his fur and from his regular breathing knew he was asleep, too. I'm glad Creb and I finally talked, she thought, feeling as though a terrible load had been lifted from her shoulders, but the queasiness in the pit of her stomach that she had been feeling the whole day and night grew worse. She had a dry lump in her throat and thought if she stayed in the cave another instant, she'd suffocate. She slipped quietly out of bed, quickly threw on a wrap and some foot coverings, and moved silently toward the entrance.

She took a deep breath as soon as she stepped beyond the cave's mouth. Her relief was so great, she didn't care that icy rain soaked through her leather wrap. She slogged through the mucky quagmire in front of the cave toward the stream, shivering from a sudden chill. Patches of snow, blackened by soot sifting out from the many fires, sent muddy runnels of water down the slope adding their small measure to the drenching downpour that swelled the ice-locked channel.

Her leather foot coverings gave small purchase on the reddish brown ooze, and she slipped and fell halfway down to the stream. Her limp hair, plastered against her head, hung in thick ropes extending into rivulets that cut through the mud clinging to her wrap before the rain washed it away. She stood for a long time on the bank of the watercourse struggling to break free of its frozen keep, and watched the dark water swirl around chunks of ice, finally break them loose, and send them careening to some unseen destination.

Her teeth were chattering when she struggled back up the slippery slope, watching the overcast sky grow imperceptibly lighter beyond the ridge to the east. She had to force herself through an invisible barrier that blocked the mouth of the cave, and felt the sense of uneasiness again the moment she entered.

"Ayla, you're soaked. Why did you go outside in this rain?" Creb gestured. He picked up a piece of wood and put it on the fire. "Get out of that wet wrap and come here by the fire. You'll catch a cold."

She changed, then sat beside Creb at the fire, grateful that the silence between them was no longer strained.

"Creb, I'm so glad we talked last night. I went down to the stream; the ice is breaking loose. Summer's coming, we'll be able to take some long walks again."

"Yes, Ayla, summer's coming. If you want, we'll take long walks again. In summer."

Ayla felt a chill. She had a horrible feeling she would never take a long walk with him again, and she had the feeling Creb knew it, too. She reached for him, and they held each other as though for the last time.

By midmorning the rain eased to a dreary drizzle and by afternoon stopped altogether. A wan, tired sun broke through the solid cloud cover but did little to warm or dry the drenched earth. Despite the dismal weather and sparse fare, the clan was excited by so notable an occasion for a feast. A change in leadership was rare enough, but a new mog-ur at the same time made it exceptional. Oga and Ebra would have a part to play in the ceremony, and Brac as well. The seven-year-old would be the next heir apparent.

Oga was a tight bundle of stretched nerves. She jumped up every other moment to check every fireplace where food was cooking. Ebra tried to calm her, but Ebra wasn't so settled herself. Trying to seem more grown-up, Brac was issuing commands to the small children and busy women. Brun finally stepped in and called him off to the side to practice his part once more. Uba took the children to Vorn's hearth to get them out of the way, and after most of the preparations were completed, Ayla joined her. Aside from helping to cook, Ayla's only role would be to make datura for the men since Creb had told her not to make the drink from the roots.

By evening, only a few wisps of clouds remained to dart fitfully before the full moon that lit the bare, lifeless landscape. Inside the cave, a large fire burned in a space behind the last hearth, defined by a circle of torches.

Ayla sat alone on her fur staring at the small hearth fire that snapped and crackled nearby. She still hadn't been able to shake her uneasiness. She decided to walk to the cave's entrance to look at the moon until the festivities began, but just as she stood up, she saw Brun's signal and turned heavy steps the other way. When everyone was in their correct places, Mog-ur came out of the place of the spirits followed by Goov, both cloaked in bearskins.

As the great holy man called forth the spirits for the last time, the years seemed to fall from him. He made the eloquent, familiar gestures with more power and force than the clan had seen for years. It was a masterful performance. He played his audience with the skill of a virtuoso, drawing forth their response with perfect timing in peak after suspenseful peak of evocative emotion, to a climax that wrung out their last drop and left them drained. Beside him, Goov was a faded copy. The young man was an adequate mog-ur, even a good one, but he couldn't match The Mog-ur. The most powerful magician the Clan had ever known had conducted his last and finest ceremony. When he turned it over to Goov, Ayla wasn't the only one who cried. The dry-eyed clan wept with their hearts.

Ayla's mind wandered as Goov went through the motions that retired Brun and raised Broud to the rank of leader. She was watching Creb and remembered the first time she saw his one-eyed, scarred face and reached out to touch him. She recalled his patience when he was trying to teach her to communicate, and her sudden burst of understanding. She reached for her amulet and felt a tiny scar on her throat where he had expertly nicked her to draw her blood as a sacrifice to the ancient spirits that allowed her to hunt. And she cringed with the memory of her clandestine visit to a small cave deep in a mountain. Then she remembered his look of loving sadness and his cryptic, enigmatic statement of the night before.

She only picked at her food at the feast celebrating the

succession of the next generation to the realms of authority. The men filed into the small sacred cave to complete their ceremony in seclusion, and Ayla passed out the datura received from Goov, now a mog-ur. But she had no heart for the women's dance, her rhythms lacked verve, and she drank so little of the ceremonial tea, the effects wore off quickly. She returned to Creb's hearth as soon as she appropriately could and was asleep before Creb returned, but she slept fitfully. He stood over her bed watching her and her son before he hobbled to his own sleeping place.

"Mama go hunting? Durc go hunting with Mama?" the boy asked, jumping out of bed and heading for the mouth of the cave. Only a few people were stirring, but Durc was wide awake.

"Not until after breakfast, anyway, Durc. Come back here," Ayla motioned and got up to get him. "Probably not at all today. Spring is here, but it's not that warm yet."

After he ate, Durc spied Grev and forgot about hunting as he raced to Broud's hearth. Ayla watched him go, with a feeling of tenderness turning up the corners of her mouth. The smile faded when she saw the way Broud looked at him. It made her scalp crawl. Both boys ran out together. Suddenly a feeling of claustrophobia overwhelmed her with such force, she thought she would vomit if she didn't get outside the cave. She bolted for the opening, feeling her heart beating rapidly, and took several deep breaths.

"Ayla!"

She jumped at the sound of her name spoken by Broud, then turned around, bowed her head, and looked down at the new leader.

"This woman would greet the leader," she gestured formally. Broud seldom stood face to face with her. She was much taller than the tallest man in the clan, and Broud was not among the tallest. He barely reached her shoulder. She knew he didn't like looking up at her.

"Don't go running off anywhere. I'm going to have a meeting out here soon."

Ayla nodded obediently.

The clan slowly congregated. The sun was shining, and they were glad Broud had decided to have his meeting outdoors in spite of the soggy ground. They waited for a while, then Broud strutted to the place formerly taken by Brun, supremely conscious of his new status.

"As you know, I am your new leader," Broud started. His nervousness at speaking to the entire clan in his new capacity was betrayed by an opening statement that was patently obvious.

"Since the clan has a new leader and a new mog-ur, this is a good time to announce some other changes," he continued. "I want to make it known that Vorn is now my second-in-command."

There were nods; it was expected. Brun thought Broud should have waited until Vorn was older before raising his position above more experienced hunters, but everyone knew it was coming. It's probably just as well to do it now, he said to himself.

"There are some other changes," Broud motioned. "A woman in this clan is not mated." Ayla felt herself flush. "Someone must provide for her, and I do not want to burden my hunters with her. I am leader now and I must be responsible for her. I will take Ayla as second woman to my hearth."

Ayla had expected it, but it didn't make her any happier to know she was right. She may not like it, Brun thought, but Broud is doing the right thing. Brun looked proudly at the son of his mate. Broud is ready for leadership.

"She has one deformed child," Broud went on. "I want it known now, no more deformed children will be accepted into this clan. I don't want anyone to think it has anything to do with my personal feelings, when the next one is refused. If she has a normal child, I will accept it."

Creb was standing near the entrance to the cave and shook his head as he watched Ayla blanch and bow her head lower to hide her face. Well, you can be sure I won't have any more children, Broud, not if Iza's magic works for me, she thought. I don't care if babies are started by men's totems or their organs, you won't start any more in me. I'm not going to give birth to babies that have to die because you think they're deformed.

"I've made it plain before," Broud went on, "so this shouldn't come as any surprise. I will not have any deformed children living at my hearth."

Ayla's head jerked up. What does he mean? If I have to move to his hearth, my son comes with me.

"Vorn has agreed to take Durc to his hearth. His mate is fond of the boy, in spite of his deformity. He will be well cared for."

There was a disturbed murmur and a flurry of hand

signals from the clan. Children belonged with their mothers until they were grown. Why would Broud take Ayla but refuse her son? Ayla broke out of her place and threw herself at Broud's feet. Broud tapped her shoulder.

"I am not through yet, woman. It is disrespectful to interrupt the leader, but I will overlook it this time. You may speak."

"Broud, you can't take Durc away from me. He's my son. Wherever a woman goes, her children go with her," she motioned, forgetting to use any form of polite greeting or to phrase her statement as a request in her anxiety. Brun was glowering, his pride in the new leader gone.

"Are you, woman, telling this leader what he can or cannot do?" Broud motioned with a sneer on his face. He was pleased with himself. He had planned this for a long time, and he had gotten just the reaction he had hoped for.

"You are no mother. Oga is more mother to Durc than you are. Who nursed him? Not you. He doesn't even know who his mother is. Every woman in the clan is mother to him. What difference does it make where he lives? He obviously doesn't care, he eats at everyone's hearth," Broud said.

"I know I haven't been able to nurse him, but you know he is my son, Broud. He sleeps with me every night."

"Well, he won't sleep with me every night. Can you deny that Vorn's mate is 'mother' to him? I have already told Goov . . . I mean the mog-ur, that the mating ceremony will be held after this meeting. There is no point in waiting. You will move to my hearth tonight, and Durc will move to Vorn's. Now go back to your place," he commanded. Broud glanced around the clan and noticed Creb leaning on his staff near the cave. The old man looked angry.

But not nearly as angry as Brun. His face was a black rage as he watched Ayla return to her place. He struggled to control himself, to keep from interfering. There was more than anger in his eyes, the pain in his heart showed, too. The son of my mate, he thought, who I raised and trained and just made leader of this clan. He is using his position for revenge. Revenge against a woman, for wrongs he has imagined. Why didn't I see it before? Why was I so blind to him? Now I know why he raised Vorn's status so soon. Broud arranged the whole thing with him; he planned to do this to Ayla all along. Broud, Broud, is that the first thing a new leader does? Puts his hunters in jeopardy with a young and inexperienced second to avenge himself against a woman? What pleasure can it bring you to separate a mother and her child when she has suffered so much pain already? Have you no heart, son of my mate? All she has of her son is to share her bed with him at night.

"I am not finished, I am not through," Broud gestured, trying to get the attention of the shocked and uneasy clan. They finally settled down.

"This man was not the only one raised to a new position. We have a new mog-ur. There are certain privileges that go with increased status. I have decided that Goov...the mog-ur, will move to the rightful hearth of the magician of the clan. Creb will move to the back of the cave."

Brun shot a glance at Goov. Was he in on the arrangement, too? Goov was shaking his head with a puzzled look on his face.

"I don't want to move to The Mog-ur's hearth," he said. "That has been his home ever since we moved into this cave."

The clan was becoming more than uneasy about their new leader.

"I have decided you will move!" Broud gestured imperiously, angry at Goov's refusal. When he had noticed the crippled old man leaning on his staff glaring at him angrily, he suddenly realized the great Mog-ur was magician no more. What did he have to fear from a deformed old cripple? On impulse, he had made the offer, expecting Goov to jump at the choice spot in the cave as Vorn had jumped at the chance for increased status. He thought it would cement the new mog-ur's loyalty to him, make Goov obligated to him. Broud hadn't counted on Goov's loyalty, and love, for his mentor. Brun was unable to hold back any longer and was just about to speak out, but Ayla beat him to it.

"Broud!" Ayla shouted from her place. His head shot up. "You can't do that! You can't make Creb move from his hearth!" She was stomping toward him full of righteous wrath. "He needs a protected place. The wind blows too hard into the back. You know how he suffers in the winter." Ayla had forgotten herself as a Clan woman; she was now the medicine woman protective of her patient. "You're doing it to hurt me. You're trying to get back at Creb because he took care of me. I don't care what you do to me,

Broud, but leave Creb alone!" She was standing in front of him, towering over him, gesticulating angrily in his face.

"Who gave you permission to speak, woman!" Broud stormed. He swung at her with a clenched fist, but she saw it coming and ducked. Broud was startled at reaching nothing but air. Rage replaced his surprise as he started after her.

"Broud!" Brun's shout brought him to a standstill. He was too accustomed to obeying that voice, especially when it was raised in anger.

"That is Mog-ur's hearth, Broud, and will be his hearth until he dies. That will happen soon enough without your bringing it on sooner by moving him. He has served this clan long and well; he deserves that place. What kind of leader are you? What kind of a man are you? Using your position to get revenge on a woman? A woman who has never done anything to you, Broud, who couldn't if she tried. You are no leader!"

"No, you are the one who is no leader, Brun, not anymore." Broud had regained the realization of his position, and Brun's, after his initial impulse to obey. "I am leader now! I make the decisions now! You have always taken her side against me, always protected her. Well, you can't protect her anymore!" Broud was losing control, gesticulating wildly, his face purple with rage. "She will do what I say, or I will curse her! And it won't be temporary! You just saw her insolence, and you still stick up for her. I won't stand for it! Not anymore. She deserves to be cursed for it. And I will! How do you like that, Brun? Goov! Curse her! Curse her! Now, right now! I want her cursed now. No one will tell this leader what to do, least of all that ugly woman. Did you understand me? Curse her, Goov!"

Creb had been trying to get Ayla's attention from the moment she lashed out at Broud, trying to warn her. It didn't matter to him where he lived, front or back of the cave, it was all the same to him. His suspicions had been aroused from the moment Broud said he would take Ayla as second woman. It was too responsible a move for Broud to make without some reason. But his suspicions hadn't prepared him for the ugly scene that followed. When he saw Broud order Goov to curse her, the last bit of fight went out of him. He didn't want to see any more, and turned his back to shuffle slowly into the cave. Ayla glanced up just as he disappeared into the hole in the mountain.

Creb wasn't the only one upset by the confrontation.

The whole clan was in an uproar, gesturing, shouting, milling around in confusion. Some couldn't bear to watch, while others gazed in rapt disbelief at the spectacle not one of them ever expected to witness in their entire lives. Their lives were too ordered, too secure, too bound by traditions and customs and habits.

They were surprised at Broud's irregular and unreasonable announcements separating Ayla and her son; they were shocked at Ayla's confrontation with the new leader no more than Broud's decision to move Creb; they were stunned as much by Brun's angry denunciation of the man he had just made leader as by Broud's uncontrolled temper tantrum demanding that Ayla be cursed. They were yet to be traumatized.

Ayla was shaking so hard she didn't feel the trembling beneath her feet until she saw people toppling over, unable to keep their balance. Her own face mirrored the stunned expressions of the rest as they changed to fear, and then stark terror. It was then she heard the deep, terrifying rumble from the bowels of the earth.

"Duurrrc!" she screamed, and saw Uba grab for him then fall on top of him as though trying to protect his small body with her own. Ayla started toward them, then suddenly remembered something that filled her with horror.

"Creb! He's inside the cave!"

She scrambled up the swaying slope trying to reach the large triangular entrance. A huge rock rolled down the steep wall that held the opening and, deflected by a tree that splintered under the impact, crashed to the ground beside her. Ayla didn't notice. She was numb, in shock. The memories locked in her old nightmare were released, but jumbled and confused by sheer panic. In the roar of the earthquake, not even she heard the word in a long forgotten language torn from her lips.

"Motherrr!"

The ground beneath her dropped several feet, then heaved up again. She fell over and struggled to get up, and then saw the vaulted ceiling of the cave collapse. Jagged chunks, torn from the high roof, crashed down and split on impact. Then more fell. All around her, boulders bounced and tumbled down the rocky face, rolled down the gentler slope, and splashed into the icy stream. The ridge to the east cracked and half of it toppled.

Inside the cave it was raining rocks and pebbles and dirt,

mixed with the intermittent thunder of large sections of the walls and vaulted dome. Outside, tall conifers danced like clumsy giants and naked deciduous trees shook bare limbs in an ungraceful jitter, moving in speeded time to the thunderous dirge. A crack in the wall, near the east side of the opening, opposite the spring-fed pool, widened with an explosive gush that flushed out loose rock and gravel. It opened another underground channel that deposited its load of debris on the broad front porch of the cave before making its maiden voyage to the stream. The roar from the earth and the smashing rocks overpowered the screams of the terror-stricken people. The sound was deafening.

Finally the quaking subsided. A last few stones tumbled off the mountain, bounced, rolled, then came to rest. Dazed and frightened people started to pick themselves up and wandered around with blank stares trying to collect their shaken wits. They began to gather around Brun. He had always been their rock, their stability. They gravitated toward the security he had always represented.

But Brun did nothing. He believed, in all his years as leader, the worst judgment he had ever shown was making Broud leader. He realized, now, how blind he had been to the faults of the son of his mate. Even his virtues, his fearless bravado and reckless courage, Brun now saw as manifestations of the same uncaring ego and impulsive temper. But that wasn't the reason Brun refused to act. Broud was leader now, for better or worse. It was too late for Brun to step back in and train another man, though he knew the clan would have let him. The only way Broud could ever hope to lead, the only hope for the clan, was to make him lead now. Broud said he was the leader—defiantly, totally out of control, Broud said he was leader. Well, *lead*, Broud, Brun thought. Do something. Whatever decisions Broud made from now on, or lack of them, Brun would not interfere.

When the clan was convinced that Brun was not going to take back the leadership, they finally turned to Broud. They were used to their traditions, accustomed to their hierarchy, and Brun had been too good a leader, too strong, too responsible. They were used to his taking command in times of crisis, used to depending on his calm and reasoned judgment. They didn't know how to act on their own, to make decisions for themselves without a leader. Even Broud expected Brun to take over; he needed someone to lean on, too. When Broud finally came to the realization that the burden was now on him, he tried to assume it. He did try.

"Who is missing? Who is hurt?" Broud motioned. There was a small collective sigh of relief. Someone was finally doing something. Family groups started to gather together, and as the clan assembled amid gasps of surprise at seeing a loved one they were afraid was gone, miraculously, no one seemed to be missing. With all the falling rocks and shaking earth, no one was even badly hurt. Bruises, cuts, scrapes, but no broken bones. That wasn't entirely true.

"Where's Ayla?" Uba cried with an edge of panic.

"Here," Ayla answered, walking back down the slope, forgetting for the moment why she was there.

"Mama!" Durc cried, breaking loose of Uba's protective grip and running to her. Ayla broke into a run, swooped him up, hugged him tightly, and carried him back.

"Uba, are you all right?" she asked.

"Yes, nothing serious."

"Where's Creb?" Then Ayla remembered. She shoved Durc at Uba and ran back up the slope.

"Ayla! Where are you going? Don't go into the cave! There may be aftershocks."

Ayla didn't see the warning, nor would she have heeded it. She ran into the cave and straight for Creb's hearth. Stones and gravel cascaded spasmodically, making small piles on the ground. Except for a few rocks and a layer of dust, their place in the cave was undamaged, but Creb was not there. Ayla checked every hearth. Some were totally demolished, but most had some salvageable items. Creb was not at any of the hearths. She hesitated at the small opening that led to the place of the spirits, then started in, but it was too dark to see. She'd need a torch. She decided to check the rest of the cave first.

A spattering of gravel fell on her and she jumped to the side. A jagged boulder crashed to the ground, grazing her arm. She searched the walls, then crisscrossed the room, poking into deep shadows behind storage containers and large boulders in the unlit cave. She was ready to get a torch, then decided to try one last place.

She found Creb beside Iza's burial cairn. He was lying on his deformed side with his legs pulled up, almost as if they had been tied into a fetal position. The large, magnificent skull that had protected his powerful brain, protected it no longer. The heavy rock that crushed it had rolled a few feet away. He had died instantly. She knelt down beside his body and her tears began to flow.

"Creb, oh, Creb. Why did you go into the cave?" she motioned. She rocked back and forth on her knees, crying out his name. Then, for some inexplicable reason, she stood up and began to make the motions she had seen him make over Iza, the burial rite. Silent tears clouded her vision as the tall blonde woman, alone in a rock-littered cave, flowed through the ancient, symbolic movements with a grace and subtlety as accomplished as those of the great holy man himself. Many of the motions she did not understand. She never would. It was her final offering to the only father she knew.

"He's dead," Ayla gestured to the faces staring at her as she emerged from the cave.

Broud stared at her along with the rest, then a great fear gripped him. It was she who had found the cave, she whom the spirits favored. And after he cursed her, they shook the earth and destroyed the cave she found. Were they angry at him for wanting her cursed? Did they destroy the cave she had found because they were angry at him? What if the rest of the clan thought he had brought this calamity down on them? In the deepest recesses of his superstitious soul, he quavered before the ill omen and feared the anger of the spirits he was sure he had unleashed. Then, in an impulsive flash of twisted reasoning, he thought if he blamed her before anyone could blame him, no one could say it was his fault, and the spirits would turn on her.

"She did it! It's her fault!" Broud gestured suddenly. "She's the one who made the spirits angry. She's the one who flouted the traditions. You all saw her. She was insolent, she was disrespectful to the leader. She should be cursed. Then the spirits will be happy again. Then they will know how we honor them. Then they will lead us to a new cave, even better, even luckier. They will. I know they will. Curse her, Goov! Now, do it now! Curse her! Curse her!"

Every head turned to Brun. He stared straight ahead, jaws clenched, fists doubled up, the muscles of his back shaking with tension. He refused to move, refused to interfere, though it took every bit of willpower he had. The clan looked uneasily at each other, then Goov, then Broud.

Goov stared at Broud in absolute disbelief. How could he blame Ayla. If anyone, it was Broud's fault. Then Goov understood.

"I am the leader, Goov! You are the mog-ur. I order you to curse her. Curse her with death!"

Goov turned abruptly, picked up a burning, pitchy pine branch from the fire that had been started while Ayla was in the cave, walked up the slope, and disappeared into the dark triangular mouth. He picked his way carefully around fallen rubble, watching the occasional fall of rocks and gravel, knowing an aftershock could bring tons down on his head, and wishing it would before he did the thing he had been ordered to do. He went into the place of the spirits and lined up the sacred bones of the cave bear in parallel rows, making formal gestures with each one. The last bone was put into the base and out the left eye socket of a cave bear skull. Then he said aloud the words known only to mog-urs, the terrible names of the evil spirits. The recognition that gave them power.

Ayla was still standing in front of the cave as he walked past her with unseeing eyes.

"I am the mog-ur. You are the leader. You have ordered Ayla cursed with death. It is done," Goov motioned, then turned his back on the leader of the clan.

No one could believe it at first. It was too fast. That wasn't the way it should be done. Brun would have discussed it, reasoned it out, prepared the clan for it. But he wouldn't have cursed her in the first place. What had she done? She was insolent to the leader and it was wrong, but was it cause for death? She had just been defending Creb. And what had Broud done to her? Taken her child from her and turned the old magician out of his hearth to get even with her. Now, no one had a hearth. Why did Broud do it? Why did he curse her? The spirits had always favored her, she brought good luck, until Broud said he wanted to curse her, until he told the mog-ur to curse her. Broud brought the bad luck on them. Now what would happen to them? Broud had made the protective spirits angry and then unleashed the evil ones. And the old magician was dead, The Mog-ur couldn't help them now.

Ayla was so lost in her grief, she wasn't aware of the rapid currents swirling around her. She saw Broud order her cursed, and saw Goov tell him it was done, but her grief-filled mind didn't comprehend. Slowly, the meaning impinged on her consciousness. When it penetrated, with all its ramifications, the impact was devastating.

Cursed? Death cursed? Why? What did I do that was so bad? How did it happen so fast? The clan was as slow to comprehend as she. They hadn't fully recovered from the earthquake. Ayla watched them with a curious detachment as, one after the other, eyes became glazed and unseeing. There goes Crug. Who's going to be next. Uka. Now Droog, but not Aga yet. There she goes, she must have seen me look at her.

Ayla wasn't moved into action until Uba's eyes went blank and she began to keen for the mother of the boy she held in her arms. Durc! My baby, my son! I'm cursed, I'll never see him again. What will happen to him? There's only Uba left. She'll take care of him, but what can she do against Broud? Broud hates him because he's my son. Ayla looked wildly around, and saw Brun. Brun! Brun can protect Durc. No one else but Brun can protect him.

Ayla ran to the stoic, strong, sensitive man who, until the day before, had led the clan. She dropped to the ground at his feet and bowed her head. It took a moment before she realized he would never tap her shoulder. When she looked up, he was looking over her head at the fire behind her. If he wanted, his eyes could see her. He can see me, Ayla thought. I know he can. Creb remembered everything I said to him, so did Iza.

"Brun, I know you think I'm dead, a spirit. Don't look away! I beg you, don't look away! It happened too fast! I'll go, I promise I'll go, but I'm afraid for Durc. Broud hates him, you know he does. What will happen to him with Broud as leader? Durc is Clan, Brun. You accepted him. I beg you, Brun, protect Durc. Only you can do it. Don't let Broud hurt him!"

Brun slowly turned his back on the pleading woman, turning his gaze away as though he was shifting position, not as if he was trying to avoid looking at her. But she saw the barest glimmer of recognition in his eyes, a hint of a nod. It was enough. He would protect Durc, he had promised the spirit of the boy's mother. It was true it was too fast, she hadn't had time to ask him before. He would bend his decision not to interfere with Broud that much. He would not let the son of his mate harm Ayla's son.

Ayla got up and walked purposefully toward the cave. She hadn't decided to leave until she told Brun she would, but once she did, it made up her mind. Her grief over Creb's death was pushed into a corner of her mind, to be brought out later when her survival was not at stake. She would go, perhaps to the world of the spirits, perhaps not, but she would not go unprepared.

She hadn't been as aware of the destruction inside the cave the first time she went in. She stared at the unfamiliar place, grateful that the clan had been outside. Taking a deep breath, she hurried to Creb's hearth, ignoring the treacherous condition of the cave. If she didn't get what she needed to survive, she'd be dead for sure.

She moved a rock from her bed, shook out her fur wrap, and began to pile things on it. Her medicine bag, her sling, two pairs of foot coverings, leggings, hand coverings, a fur-lined wrap, a hood. Her cup and bowl, waterbags, tools. She went to the back of the cave and found the supply of concentrated, high-energy traveling cakes of dried meat, fruit, and fat. She searched through the rubble and found birchbark packets of maple sugar, nuts, dried fruit, ground parched grain, strips of dried meat and fish, and a few vegetables. It was not too great a variety so late in the season, but adequate. She dumped dust and rocks out of her collecting basket and began to pack it.

She picked up Durc's carrying cloak and held it to her face, feeling the tears well up. She'd have no need for it, she wasn't taking Durc. She packed it. At least she could take something that had been close to him. She dressed herself warmly. It was still early in the season; it would be cold on the steppes. North, it might still be winter. She hadn't made any conscious decision about her direction; she knew she was going to the mainland north of the peninsula.

At the last moment, she decided to take the hide shelter she used when she went with the men on hunting trips, though technically it wasn't hers. She could take anything that belonged to her; whatever was left behind would be burned. And she felt a share of the food was rightfully hers, too, but the shelter was Creb's for the use of the people of his hearth. Creb was gone and he never did have a use for it; she didn't think he would mind.

She packed it on top of her collecting basket, then hoisted the heavy load on her back and tied the thongs that held it securely in place. Tears threatened again as she stood in the middle of the hearth that had been her home since a few days after Iza found her. She would never see it again. A kaleidoscope of memories tumbled through her mind, stopping for an instant at significant scenes. She thought last of Creb. *I wish I knew what caused you such pain, Creb. Maybe someday I'll understand, but I'm so glad we talked the other night, before you left for the spirit world. I'll never forget you, or Iza, or the clan.* Then Ayla walked out of the cave.

No one looked at her, but everyone knew when she reappeared. She stopped at the still pool just outside the cave to fill her waterbags, and had another memory. Before dipping in and disturbing the mirrored surface, she leaned over and looked at herself. She studied her features carefully; she didn't seem so ugly this time, but it wasn't herself she was interested in. She wanted to see the face of the Others.

When she stood up, Durc was struggling to get free of Uba's restraining arms. Something was going on that concerned his mother. He wasn't sure what, but he didn't like it. With a jerk, he broke loose and ran to Ayla.

"You're going away," he accused, beginning to understand and indignant that he hadn't been told. "You're all dressed and going away."

Ayla hesitated only a fraction of an instant, then held out her arms as he flew into them. She picked him up and hugged him tight, fighting back tears. She put him down and hunkered down to his level, looking directly into his large brown eyes.

"Yes, Durc, I'm going away. I have to go away."

"Take me with you, Mama. Take me with you! Don't leave me!"

"I can't take you with me, Durc. You have to stay here with Uba. She will take care of you. Brun will, too."

"I don't want to stay here!" Durc gestured fiercely. "I want to go with you. Don't go away and leave me!"

Uba was coming toward them. She had to, she had to take Durc away from the spirit. Ayla hugged her son again.

"I love you, Durc. Never forget that, I love you." She picked him up and put him in Uba's arms. "Take care of my son for me, Uba," she motioned, looking into her sad eyes that looked back and saw her. "Take care of him...my sister."

Broud watched them, getting more furious. The woman was dead, she was a spirit. Why wasn't she acting like one? And some of his clan weren't treating her like one.

"That's a spirit," he gestured angrily. "She's dead. Don't you know she's dead?"

Ayla marched straight to Broud and stood tall before him. He was having trouble not seeing her, too. He tried to ignore her, but she was looking down at him, not sitting at his feet as a woman should.

"I'm not dead, Broud," she gestured defiantly. "I won't die. You can't make me die. You can make me go away, you can take my son from me, but you can't make me die!"

Two emotions vied within Broud, fury and fear. He raised his fist in an overwhelming urge to strike her, then held it there, afraid to touch her. It's a trick, he told himself, it's a spirit's trick. She's dead, she was cursed.

"Hit me, Broud! Go ahead, acknowledge this spirit. Hit me and you'll know I'm not dead."

Broud turned to Brun, to look away from the spirit. He lowered his arm, uncomfortable that he could not make it look natural. He hadn't touched her, but he was afraid just raising his clenched fist had acknowledged her, and he tried to pass the bad luck on to Brun.

"Don't think I didn't see you, Brun. You answered her when she was talking to you, before she went into the cave. She's a spirit, you'll bring bad luck," he denounced.

"Only on myself, Broud, and what more could I have? But when did you see her talk to me? When did you see her go into the cave? Why did you threaten to strike a spirit? You still don't understand, do you? You acknowledged her, Broud, she has beaten you. You did everything you could to her, you even cursed her. She's dead, and still she won. She was a woman, and she had more courage than you, Broud, more determination, more self-control. She was more man than you are. Ayla should have been the son of my mate."

Ayla was surprised at Brun's unexpected eulogy. Durc was squirming to get away again, calling out to her. She couldn't bear it and hurried to leave. As she passed Brun, she bowed her head and made a gesture of gratitude. When she reached the ridge, she turned and looked back one more time. She saw Brun raise his hand as if to scratch his nose, but it looked as if he made a gesture, the same gesture Norg had made when they left the Clan Gathering. It looked as if Brun had said, "Walk with Ursus."

The last thing Ayla heard as she disappeared behind the broken ridge was Durc's plaintive wail—

"Maama, Maaama, Maamaaa!"

ABOUT THE AUTHOR

JEAN M. AUEL began researching *The Clan of the Cave Bear* in 1977. In addition to spending many hours in the library studying the Ice Age, she joined a survival class to learn how to construct an ice cave and how it feels to live in one. She learned how to make arrowheads from a man in La Grande, Oregon. Before that, she had worked at temporary and part-time clerical jobs, been a circuit board designer and a technical writer, and earned her M.B.A. Born and raised in Chicago, Mrs. Auel met her husband, Ray, at the age of eighteen and was the mother of five children before she was twenty-five. She now lives with her family in Portland, Oregon, where she is at work on the second novel in the Earth's Children series.